# THE SWORD OF MOSES

## DOMINIC SELWOOD

CORAX

Published in Great Britain by
CORAX
London

Visit our author's blog
www.dominicselwood.com/blog

British Library Cataloguing in Publication Data.
A catalogue record for this book is available from the British Library.

ISBN 978-0-9926332-0-2

Typeset in Monotype Dante 11/14
by Corax and Odyssey Books

FOR
DELIA, INIGO, ARMINEL, ANDREAS

## Acknowledgements

My very real thanks and immense gratitude to:

Rachel Thorn, my peerless editor, for her consummate skill and sure-footed guidance.

For expertise on a range of subjects: Tony Ayres, Dr Lindsay G H Hall, Charles Pierre MacDonald, Mrs Claire Powell, Mike Morton, Saif Sakhran, the Rev. Dr Simon Thorn, and Tom Ward.

For graphics, artwork and design: Louisa Fitch, Michelle Lovi, Delia Selwood, and Andrew Smith,

The staff of so many wonderful libraries.

My parents, for everything.

My brother, Andreas, for his ceaseless insistence on receiving the next chapter, and for his indefatigable championing of the book.

Inigo and Arminel, for their constant encouragement.

And finally to Delia, who has supported the book at every turn, inspired me, advised and guided me with an unfailing sure touch, and contributed to it in so many millions of ways.

D.K.S.
London
1st December 2013

'The LORD is a man of war: the LORD is his name'

EXODUS 15:3
(From a short passage widely believed to be
the oldest in the Bible)

# DAY ONE

 ◆ 

## I

*Church of Our Lady Mary of Zion*
*Aksum*
*Tigray Region*
*The Federal Democratic Republic of Ethiopia*
*Africa*

THEY CAME BEFORE dawn, from the East, out of the Danakil desert.

The two white air-conditioned Land Cruisers sped through old Aksum, ancient city of warrior emperors, now a forgotten curiosity—a relic.

Only a few hundred miles to the east lay the vast Afar Depression—the Horn of Africa's arid and scorching cradle of humanity. But the town of Aksum itself was fertile and lush, rich with grass and spreading trees.

As first light began to bleed over the horizon, they raced past Queen Sheba's grandiose bathing pool—its once petal-strewn waters now murky and stagnant, long neglected.

Then on to the eerie Field of Stones, with its monumental rows of obelisks stretching higher than the tallest in Egypt.

And finally to their destination, the sacred historical church complex of Our Lady Mary of Zion—the holiest place in all Ethiopia, coronation site of the *Neguse Negast*, the King of Kings.

He had given them good directions.

In the leather passenger seat of the lead Land Cruiser, Aristide Kimbaba pulled a black balaclava over his face and flicked the safety catch on his 7.62 millimetre AK-47 into the semi-automatic position. He fingered the cold steel weapon appreciatively. It was an authentic Russian model, not a cheap Far-Eastern copy. It even had a military-grade POSP telescopic sight mounted onto it.

He had given Kimbaba and his men good equipment.

The militiaman smiled to himself. He had come a long way for this, and knew it was a good plan from the moment he had been told of it.

Looking around, he was pleased to observe there was no one about in the hot sleepy town. The narrow dusty streets of the church complex were entirely deserted.

He glanced down at the plastic-sleeved map resting on his knee.

"Stop here," he ordered the driver in a low growl, directing him to pull up outside an ornate building nestling in a glade of trees between a large modern church to the north and a small ancient one to the south.

Its alternating green and rose-tinted stone was barely visible in the morning glow.

If Kimbaba had cared about such things, he would have noted that the multicoloured building was numerologically perfect—a square, with one door and three windows per wall. One, three, four, and twelve—all sacred numbers. But these subtleties were lost on him. His untutored eye noticed only its discreet onion dome and slim metal cross hinting at a religious purpose.

The militiaman stepped briskly out of the vehicle.

At six foot three inches tall, he was an intimidating figure—his inherent physical menace heightened by an unbuttoned camouflaged jacket revealing a well-muscled torso, olive trousers tucked into black para boots, and a khaki canvas waistcoat bulging with spare magazine clips.

Striding swiftly up to the iron fence surrounding the chapel, he looked at it keenly, assessing the thickness of its bars and the depth of the concrete into which they had been set.

Roused by the noise of the Land Cruisers' engines at this early hour, the chapel's groggy guardian monk appeared at its age-worn oak doors.

His tired yellow robes and green pillbox hat were the only splashes of colour in the grey morning half-light.

Catching sight of the militiaman's gun and balaclavad head, the guardian stopped dead at the top of the steps, paralyzed.

Kimbaba had heard the church doors open, and reacted instantly.

Raising his gun, he tucked its heavy stock into the padding over his right shoulder and looked directly down its sights at the frozen monk.

"*Ouvrez la grille!*" he growled, advancing quickly to the gate. His Congolese French was heavily accented. "*Ouvrez.*"

The elderly monk looked blank.

Kimbaba stopped at the gate. He tried the handle, but was met with decades of rust welding it tightly shut. He was not surprised. He knew only one guardian monk lived inside the compound, and the gate was only opened when he died and a successor replaced him.

Kimbaba was less than ten yards from the stunned guardian. He pointed the gun directly at him, switching to English. "Open it!" His voice was menacing.

The elderly monk continued to stare blankly at the armed man shouting at him.

Kimbaba turned to Simplice Masolo, his wiry deputy, who had moved in swiftly behind him, also training his gun on the elderly figure.

"Get the c-4," Kimbaba grunted.

Masolo strode back to the Land Cruiser and took two lumps of off-white explosive from a steel box on the back seat. He had gutted a pair of Claymore anti-personnel mines for exactly this purpose, and quickly moulded two charges onto the fence—one just above ground level, the other at shoulder height. Attaching long wires, he ran them back to a small handheld metal detonator.

He motioned all the balaclavad men to take cover behind a nearby crumbling stone wall. When they were out of blast range, he pressed the detonator's worn button.

The charges exploded with a deep staccato boom, sending twisted shards of metal hurtling through the air at a lethal speed.

As the smoke cleared, Kimbaba strode through the jagged gap in the fence where moments earlier the gate had hung. He walked straight up to the guardian monk, who was still standing on the steps, miraculously unhurt.

Without pausing, Kimbaba smashed the buff tape-covered butt of his rifle straight into the guardian's surprised face, tearing the corner of his mouth, felling him instantly with the force of the blow.

Satisfied, he stood astride the prone monk and looked at the blood seeping from his mouth onto the dusty ground. Bending down, he rolled the guardian onto his front, grabbed his arms, and tied his wrists roughly behind his back with a quick-action plasticuff.

The whole manoeuvre was swift and violent. It had taken less than five seconds.

Without pausing, he dragged the guardian to his feet, jamming the cold muzzle of his gun into his prisoner's left kidney, and pushed him up the smooth steps towards the open wooden doors of the chapel.

The stunned guardian made no attempt to resist. He stumbled forward, dazed.

Four of Kimbaba's men followed quickly at his heels. The other two stayed by the twisted gap in the fence, rifles at face height, scanning the approach through their sights.

As the heavily armed men entered the darkened building, they fanned out to avoid presenting a solid target. But they need not have worried.

It was empty.

They were alone.

As Kimbaba's eyes adapted to the gloom, he could see the windows were draped in thick dusky curtains to exclude all natural light. The chapel's roughly plastered stone walls were covered in ancient embroidered hangings of saints and religious scenes. There was a crudely carved reddish-brown eucalyptus altar at the far end of the room, and a dirty mattress with a crumpled blanket in a corner where the monk slept.

Otherwise, the room was empty.

The thing they had come for was not there.

Kimbaba turned to the monk. "Is this a joke?" His voice was deep— the Congolese accent unmistakable.

The guardian stared blankly back at him, unfocused, blood still dripping from his mouth.

The militiaman took a step further towards him. "I'm not going to ask again." His tone was ugly. "Where is it?"

The monk seemed not to be aware what was happening.

Without warning, Kimbaba struck him viciously across the face with the back of his hand, drawing a spurt of crimson blood from the jagged tear to the corner of his mouth.

The fresh flash of pain seemed to jerk the yellow-robed monk out of his reverie. His eyes settled on Kimbaba, soft and distant. When he spoke, his voice was calm. "What do you want here?"

"Where is it?" The militiaman glowered at him, sweat beginning to appear on his bull-like neck. "The *tabot*?"

The guardian eyed him closely before answering slowly and gently. "The *tabot* is not for you."

Without warning, Kimbaba slammed his fist into the guardian's solar plexus. The monk doubled up, crumpling to the floor.

Kimbaba leaned over him, his expression unchanged. "Now."

There was a pause while the monk looked up at the hulking man looming over him. Despite the pain contorting his face, there was no anger in his eyes.

His voice, when it came, was a resolute whisper. "No."

Kimbaba unclicked his Patriot combat knife from its Kydex belt sheath. He held it out for a moment, the black blade glinting dully in front of the monk's face, before jamming its sharpened steel point into the stubbly dark flesh under the old man's chin. His eyes gleamed, leaving the monk in no doubt of his intentions.

The elderly guardian looked calmly at Kimbaba. "I have been ready all my life." His voice was mild and measured. "You cannot kill my soul."

Kimbaba kicked him hard in the ribs, sending him sprawling. "You will not meet your God today, *tabot*-man, however much you will soon beg for it."

The monk's face twisted in pain as he eyed his tormentor, but his voice remained slow and deliberate. "Your threats are worthless—my life is a holy living sacrifice."

Kimbaba returned his prisoner's gaze for a moment, rocking his large head from side to side, sucking his teeth. Turning to Masolo, he flicked his eyes towards the entrance. "Get it."

Masolo nodded to the balaclavad man nearest him, and together they disappeared through the ancient oak doors.

Returning a few minutes later, they placed a black anodized roof-rack, a jerrycan, and a coil of slim rope onto the floor beside him.

Kimbaba rolled the prisoner over with his boot, then bent down and sliced through the plasticuffs binding his slender wrists.

Grasping the monk by the shoulders, he forced his frail body face-up onto the cold metal bars of the rack, spreadeagling him. "As a religious man, you'll appreciate this. It was invented by the Spanish Inquisition." He grunted, cutting short lengths of the grimy rope and tying the monk's bony wrists and ankles to the rack's rigid frame.

The guardian eyed Kimbaba closely. "I fear Hell and damnation. Not you, or pain."

Kimbaba nodded. "There will be no pain." His eyes glinted with anticipation. "Just terror."

He held the knife's razor-sharp point to the flesh under the monk's chin again, pushing harder this time. "Last chance."

The monk shook his head fractionally as the knife broke the skin, drawing fresh blood. "I chose my path long ago," he murmured quietly, unflinching.

The militiaman pulled the knife down hard, tearing open the guardian's flimsy old yellow robes. He hacked off a large section of the material, then ripped it in two. Folding the smaller piece into a strip, he bound it tightly around the monk's shaved head, blindfolding him.

The monk began chanting softly, finding the quiet place inside himself that allowed him to separate his mind from his body. *"Abune zebesemayat, yitkedes simike, timsa mengistike weyikun ... ."*

Kimbaba did not understand the language. If he had, he would have recognized it as Ge'ez, the ritual language of the Ethiopian Orthodox Church—a Semitic tongue closely linked to the Aramaic spoken by the monk's God in Galilee two thousand years ago.

Kimbaba motioned Masolo to help drag the monk over to the altar. As they hooked the rack's bottom end over the wooden lip of the altar top, the veins on the guardian's lined forehead began to bulge from the blood rushing rapidly to his brain.

The militiaman looked down at the helpless body. "Your soul may be ready to die, priest—but there's a part of your mind that is not."

The monk seemed not to hear him, but continued his litany. *"... fekadeke, bekeme besemay kemahu bemedir ... ."*

"You will tell me what I need to know," Kimbaba's voice was low and certain.

The monk was not listening. *"... keme nihneni nihidig leze'abese lene ... ."*

Surprised at the resolve in the guardian's voice, Kimbaba grabbed the ten-inch-high silver cross from the altar, and tore it free of its wooden base, revealing a sharpened end where the metal had been driven into the wood. He placed the cross in the monk's hand, folding the thin wizened fingers around it.

"Drop it when you are ready to talk," he instructed, piling the remainder of the torn yellow robes over the monk's face.

Satisfied, he nodded to Masolo, who opened the cap of the green metal jerrycan and handed it to him.

With no further warning, Kimbaba held the jerrycan over the monk's rag-covered face, and sloshed a cupful of water onto his smothered mouth and nose. After a brief pause, he repeated the process, pouring in short one-second bursts.

The warm rusty liquid soaked through the rags instantly, drenching them and running freely over the monk's face.

The guardian clamped his mouth shut, but could not stop his nostrils from quickly filling. As the water collected at the back of his throat, he opened his mouth to spit, but it only served to fill it with the flowing liquid. Struggling for air and beginning to panic, he could no longer stifle the reflex to breathe. As he opened his throat to suck down the air he craved, his lungs took in the water.

Kimbaba knew the old man would not last long. Nobody did. That is why the CIA preferred it to all other 'enhanced interrogation' techniques.

The fact it left no visible bruises was an added bonus.

Kimbaba also knew that one session was usually enough. He had seen the desperate panic in victims' eyes as their brains' most ancient and primitive instinct centres took over, fighting for animal survival.

But if the monk proved to be strong, Kimbaba was ready to do it again and again for as long as it took. There would be lung damage, but the process could be repeated almost indefinitely. He had heard that some inmates at Guantanamo Bay had been waterboarded nearly two hundred times.

With water pouring off his face, the monk began to writhe violently, trying to tear his slender body free of the rack.

Kimbaba smiled to himself.

It was so simple.

He had watched with amusement as a fresh-faced CIA man on television had explained in neutral tones that waterboarding was not torture, or even dangerous. It was merely psychological, the agent said—a simulation of drowning.

Kimbaba knew different. Waterboarding did not simulate anything. It was real drowning—controlled, agonizing, and terrifying.

The monk's writhing and choking became more frantic. Kimbaba looked at the old man's scraggy hand, waiting for him to drop the cross in submission. But he was gripping it more firmly than ever, his fingers clenched white around it.

The large militiaman paused for a moment, allowing the monk a moment to retch up the putrid water.

Wiping the sweat from his brow with the back of his hand, Kimbaba bent low over the guardian's blindfolded face. "We can end this," he growled. "Where is it?"

With a firmness that surprised the militiaman, the monk shook his head.

Without waiting, Kimbaba seized hold of the sodden yellow rag lying over the guardian's face and rolled it into a wet ball, stuffing it deep into the monk's mouth, blocking his ability to breathe.

With no further warning, the militiaman started pouring the warm water onto the monk's face again, still in short bursts, but faster this time.

After a few seconds, the guardian began thrashing. Kimbaba noted with satisfaction that this time there was a real panic, a frenzy that had not been there before.

The monk tried with all his force to wrench himself free—the sound of the rack slapping against the floor now reverberating around the stone room. As his struggling grew more wild, Kimbaba finally saw the wizened old hand open a split second before the monk used all his remaining strength to hurl the heavy silver cross down onto the floor's dark red tiles beside him. The noise cannoned around the room, as the monk started smacking his hand on the metal rack in desperation.

Nodding, Kimbaba stopped pouring and put the jerrycan down. He pulled the sodden yellow rag clear of the monk's mouth, before ripping off the blindfold to reveal his bulging eyes, darting wildly, filled with terror.

The old man turned his head and vomited more water, before looking up at his torturer, gasping and choking for air.

Kimbaba put a paw-like hand on the monk's trembling shoulder. "You're ready." It was a statement not a question.

Slowly, almost imperceptibly, the guardian nodded.

Stepping backwards, Kimbaba and Masolo unhooked the bottom end of the rack from the altar and laid the monk flat on the floor again. Kimbaba put a heavy boot on the old man's sweat-sodden stomach, pinning him to the tiles. He glared down at him expectantly.

The guardian coughed in an effort to clear his lungs. Rolling his head to one side, he spat out a mix of phlegm and water. Kimbaba thought he heard the words, "Forgive me," but too late registered that the monk's bony hand was no longer tied to the rack. It had slipped free from the wet ropes, and in a movement quicker than Kimbaba thought possible, the guardian had grabbed the heavy silver cross from the floor beside him.

The metal glinted as the cross arced through the air.

Grunting with surprise, Kimbaba tried to kick it out of his hand. But the old man was too fast. Kimbaba's foot failed to connect, and before he could aim another kick, the monk had punched himself hard in his dripping emaciated chest.

The bony body arched and went rigid as the cross's sharpened metal point slammed through the weak thoracic muscles and embedded itself deep into his heart. Before Kimbaba could react, the old man had slumped back onto the floor, his eyes still and lifeless, a pool of crimson blood flowing over his punctured chest and down onto the warm tiles.

Kimbaba cursed loudly, kicking the rack with the dead monk still lashed to it, sending it skidding across the wet floor.

Aged six, he had seen his first murdered body in the nameless slum where he grew up. Aged eight, he had gunned down his first man in the foetid backstreets of Kinshasa. Since then, he had killed so many and so often he did not even dream about their faces any more.

He cared nothing for the monk's early death—but the old man's inability to talk any more was a complication he had not planned on.

"Find it!" he bellowed with rage at the sweat-sheened men standing around staring at the grimacing corpse.

They spread out immediately, and began expertly ransacking the room.

Masolo stripped the altar. Another turned over the monk's mattress and blankets, scattering his few simple effects.

It was soon clear there was nothing there.

The room was largely empty.

"Rip it down," Kimbaba shouted, indicating the heavily embroidered curtains and gilded hangings adorning the walls, his frustration boiling over. "It's here."

As the men began tearing the heavy dusty materials off the walls, Masolo grabbed a silk hanging behind the altar. The fabric's once-glistening colours had faded long ago, leaving it dulled with dust and grime, but it was still an impressive cloth, depicting rows of stylized figures in lavish Ethiopian Church clothing.

As the heavy silk crumpled to the floor, it revealed a large niche in the wall behind it. Eyeing the recess carefully, Masolo spotted a small latch in the shadows. Reaching forward and pressing it, an almost invisible narrow door clicked open.

"Here!" he shouted, pushing the door wide to reveal a small staircase lit by the glow of candles.

Kimbaba elbowed impatiently past him, leaving Masolo and the others to follow down the age-smoothed stone steps.

At the bottom, Kimbaba finally saw what they had come for.

It stood in the centre of the windowless stone crypt.

Around it, the guardian had banked up hundreds of guttering white candles and dozens of varied antique oil lamps. Their flickering lights danced in thousands of reflections on its uneven gold surface, throwing eerie patterns onto the gold-threaded hangings covering every inch of the walls.

As Kimbaba took in the sight, his eyes began to sting. The air was cloudy, thick with the bitter-sweet fumes of burning frankincense and oud from four ornate braziers, one on each side of the object.

Kimbaba turned and nodded to his men.

They knew what to do.

Working clumsily, they quickly set about clearing a path to it. With no method, they haphazardly shunted the candles and lamps out of the way, spilling hot wax and warm oil onto the patchwork of threadbare carpets. Almost immediately, the air became thicker and more pungent as the acrid wisps of smoke from the greasy snuffed candles mixed with the heady incense.

Once the object was exposed, Kimbaba could see it had carrying poles at the base on both sides.

He gestured for the four men to take a pole each and follow him.

Striding for the stairs, he had no idea who may have been alerted by the c-4 explosions. Now he had what he came for, he wanted to get out as quickly as possible.

The strain showed on the men's faces as they lifted the object. It was made of thick wood, with hammered gold covering every inch of its surface. Two gold statues on the lid only added to the dead weight.

With a supreme effort, they carried it up the stairs and out into the breaking daylight, their bodies gleaming with fresh sweat.

Kimbaba bolted the building's heavy wooden doors shut, as the men carefully loaded their prize into the lead Land Cruiser, covering it with a grimy tarpaulin to shield it from view.

Kimbaba slammed the tailgate shut, and the men climbed quickly into the two vehicles. Their mission completed, they sped out of town to the rendezvous at the airfield.

Inside the crypt, a knocked-over candle connected with a gathering slick of oil from an upturned lamp. The flames rapidly took hold, dancing their way across the floor, licking up a cocktail of oil and dry carpet.

———— · ◆ · ————

## 2

*U.S. Central Command* (USCENTCOM)
*Camp as-Sayliyah*
*The State of Qatar*
*The Arabian Gulf*

"Do you know what my biggest problem is, Dr Curzon?" General Hunter turned to Ava solemnly. He spoke slowly but authoritatively, a marked Alabama drawl complementing his oversized frame.

Ava really had no idea. The adrenaline coursing through her system was not helping her concentrate either.

She shook her head. She did not even know why she was there.

She was still heavily disorientated.

She had started the day in the quiet hush of Baghdad's National Museum, where her overfilled office was one of the few areas of constant activity among the closed and dust-sheeted galleries.

She had been looking out of her large window at the museum's massive entranceway—a replica of ancient Babylon's famed Ishtar Gate—when two uniformed and armed soldiers of the U.S. Marine Corps had appeared unannounced in her doorway.

Without giving her a choice, they had taken her down to their armoured Humvee, and driven her through the perimeter concrete blast-walls and razor-wire of the international Green Zone, then on to what had been Forward Operating Base Prosperity—the ultra-high-security U.S. military camp at its heart.

Everyone in Baghdad knew Prosperity by reputation. It had been one of Saddam Hussein's gilded marble palaces before the U.S. military commandeered it as their Baghdad command and control centre. When the army pulled out, the site had become home to the U.S. State Department, and remained a formidable outpost.

Ava had never been through its staggered checkpoints and multiple security screens before—still less under armed escort and without an explanation.

Arriving at the barriers into the ultra-secure zone, her escorts had produced a pass emblazoned with a white letter A on a blue background rimmed by a red circle and the word 'ARCENT'. Despite the long queue of vehicles waiting to enter, the soldiers on guard took one look and waved them straight through.

Once inside the heavily fortified base, the escort took her directly to its busy helipad, and ushered her onto a desert-camouflaged US-101 headed south.

In response to her repeated questions, they said little other than her presence was required immediately by U.S. Central Command in Qatar, seven hundred miles to the south in the turquoise Arabian Gulf.

After an uncomfortable four-and-a-half-hour flight, the pilot had eventually dropped low over Qatar, skimming Doha's skyline of concrete mosques and minarets before landing to the south-west of the city at the desert moonscape of Camp as-Sayliyah, the U.S. Forward Command Centre in the Arabian Gulf.

Stepping out of the helicopter, she was instantly enveloped by the suffocating furnace-like heat of the desert air. It was much hotter than Baghdad—one hundred and twenty degrees in the shade, according to the ground crew. Not that she could see any shade. There was nothing living for miles around.

She was instantly hurried indoors.

Passing through the full-body x-ray at security had been quick. She was clearly being fast-tracked by the soldiers on duty, who gave her appreciative looks as they issued her identity pass. She guessed they did not see many women in anything other than the local flowing black *abaya*, usually with the whole face except the eyes covered by a *niqab* veil.

With her gold-flecked brown eyes and long dark hair, she could have passed for local, but the open-necked soft casual shirt, combats, and loose ponytail immediately gave her away as a westerner.

Now, less than ten minutes after landing, she was sitting at a stripped oak table in the heavily air-conditioned strategic nerve-centre of U.S. combat operations in the Middle East.

She had never been in a U.S. military control room before.

A guard from the front desk had shown her onto the floor of a hanger filled with groups of soldiers in khaki and sand-coloured uniforms clustered about workstations and banks of wall-mounted screens. He had led her directly to a soundproofed glass box 'briefing zone' in the centre, from where she was now looking out at the activity on the floor all around her.

It was a far cry from the warm wooden shelving and tables piled with books, catalogues, and artefacts in her quiet lo-tech office back in Baghdad.

Opposite her at the table, flanking General Hunter, were a man and a woman in civilian clothes. All three of them had slim brown files on the desk in front of them, each stamped with the blue flaming torch and atom-ringed globe of the U.S. Defense Intelligence Agency.

Ava was feeling at a distinct disadvantage. There had been no time for a coffee or to freshen up after getting off the chopper. And she had been given no opportunity to prepare for whatever they wanted to talk to her about.

General Hunter looked keenly at her, a solemn expression in his pale grey eyes. "You see that, Dr Curzon," he pointed through the glass wall to a screen in the main room showing a sequence of numbers flashing blue and green as they increased and decreased in value by the second. "That's the cost on the NYMEX of WTI Light Sweet Crude delivered to Cushing, Oklahoma." He paused. "To you and me, that's the price the world pays for gas."

Ava peered more closely at the screen. The number was flickering around one hundred and five dollars a barrel.

Looking back into the room, she noted that General Hunter's desert-pattern combat uniform was sun-bleached and worn, as were the two faded stars on each shoulder. She was not surprised—he was clearly no armchair soldier. He had the air of a man who led from the front.

He continued, evidently wanting her to understand. "Before we started Operation Iraqi Freedom in 2003, it was around twenty a barrel. By mid-2008, it was one hundred and forty-six. Early last year it was one hundred and ten. Now it's a shade lower. But who knows where it's headed. It's got a mind of its own, not connected to anything real any more. With the ongoing instability in the region, the number could break loose any time and punch through the two hundred mark." He looked at her solemnly. "Every industrialist and motorist in the world is feeling the effect of what we do here."

Ava was not at all sure where the conversation was going. She was not an expert in petrochemical economics.

"And," he grimaced, gesturing to a white board visible through the glass in the control room, "that's the reality no one wants to see. I make sure it's updated and on display here at all times."

She read the handwritten script:

**Insurgent Forces**

| | | |
|---|---|---|
| Iraqi Sunnis | 65,000 | 50% |
| Iraqi Islamists | 32,500 | 25% |
| Iraqi Shi'a | 29,900 | 23% |
| al-Qae'da & Jihaadis | 2,600 | 2% |
| Total | 130,000 | |

She was beginning to feel extremely uncomfortable. She knew a huge amount about Iraq. But this was not her area at all—she was not a military analyst.

A soldier entered the glass box quietly without knocking. He had the regulation high-and-tight shaved head and the same desert-pattern combat uniform as Hunter. His sleeve showed the three chevrons and rockers of a master sergeant.

He stooped to whisper something in Hunter's ear, then left without waiting for a reply.

Hunter pursed his lips before turning to the woman sitting to his right. She was neatly dressed in a light grey suit, with long slightly wavy auburn hair pulled back into an austere bun.

"Seven Revolutionary Guard boghammars have been spotted on the wrong side of the Shatt al-Arab, intention unknown." He spoke softly but decisively. "When we finish here, I want an incident response unit set up immediately."

"Washington's going to want to know," she replied, typing something rapidly into her Blackberry.

He nodded curtly.

Ava was rapidly getting the feeling she was being involved in something of major strategic importance—she doubted General Hunter had time for purely social meetings. But looking around the room, she had no idea how her skills fitted in.

The general leaned his ox-like frame towards her. She could see why he had risen to the top. He oozed authority. "Dr Curzon, none of these are in themselves my biggest problem. The real headache is that embedded into each of them—oil, insurgents, and border-disputes to name a few—is one unknowable factor." He paused and looked at her grimly, before answering his own question with five words—"The Islamic Republic of Iran."

Ava decided it was time to say something before the situation developed further. It was obvious there had been some kind of serious mistake.

She looked at him apologetically "General, if I can speak directly, I think you may have the wrong person. I don't—"

He silenced her with a dismissive wave of his massive hand. "Dr Curzon, we know this isn't your field of expertise. You're an archaeologist. That's why you're here."

Ava heard the words, but it still felt like there had been a fundamental mistake. "General, I'm not engaged in any field work at present. I just—"

Hunter cut her off. "Okay. So let's get on. Starting with your experience. We'd be grateful for an overview of your résumé."

Although still lost as to how she fitted into General Hunter's hi-tech military world, she breathed a little more easily.

It was not a difficult question.

"I'm a specialist in the ancient Middle East," she began. "I studied archaeology and ancient Middle-Eastern languages at Oxford, Cairo, and Harvard. In 2005, I joined the British Museum's Department of the Middle East. In mid-2007, I was seconded to the National Archaeological Museum in Amman, Jordan. In 2009, given my regional experience in the field, I was invited to head up the Iraqi UNESCO taskforce to trace the tens of thousands of artefacts looted from the National Museum of Iraq during the war."

She paused, looking across at Hunter to see if he wanted more detail.

"Baghdad's a dangerous place for a civilian working outside the Green Zone."

The unexpected comment came from the athletic man to Hunter's left. His accent was British. Although not in uniform, he looked wind-swept and tanned from an active outdoor lifestyle. She guessed he was in his mid-thirties.

She glanced at the identity tag hanging round his neck. It simply read, 'DAVID FERGUSON'. There were no other details.

Ferguson's interruption had been a statement not a question. He was now looking at her closely with none of Hunter's affability. She met his gaze, wondering what he meant. But his expression told her nothing.

She ignored the comment and turned back to Hunter. "My task is to spearhead reassembling the museum's decimated collections. It's going to take decades. We're finding looted artefacts as far away as Peru."

Hunter's expression changed. For a split second she thought she saw a flash of remorse, then it was gone. "We dropped the ball on that one, Dr Curzon. We know that now. The chain of command just didn't appreci-ate how important the museum was."

"Yes, you did," she replied, anger flaring briefly. "You just had other priorities." Her eyes flicked to the screen showing the real-time oil price.

She knew that for weeks before the hostilities began, the coalition's assault armies had been begged by diplomatic channels to protect the museum and its unique holdings. She knew because she had been tasked with coordinating a briefing paper for the military high command. In it, she had painstakingly explained that the collection was priceless, unique, and irreplaceable—as important to cataloguing human history as the holdings of the British Museum, the Vatican, or the Louvre.

But in April 2003, as the street-by-street artillery battle raged furiously in Baghdad's al-Karkh district around the museum complex and the neighbouring Special Republican Guard base, the pleas for the museum's security were ignored. Unguarded and vulnerable, tens of thousands of its priceless artefacts disappeared into the dark Iraqi night. Some went into pockets and underneath flapping *dishdashas*, while others were strapped onto borrowed and stolen flatbed trucks.

International newspapers quickly began to talk of the unprecedented rape of the world's heritage. They reported that over one hundred and seventy thousand of humanity's earliest records of writing, literature, maths, science, sculpture, and art were all gone—stolen, destroyed, or lost.

Ten years on, it still made her furious. It had been a completely preventable catastrophe. But for whatever reason, the coalition military staff had taken the operational decision to sacrifice the museum.

She had no words to describe how angry it made her.

Ferguson interrupted her thoughts. "You were telling us about your experience?"

She nodded, pulling herself back to the present. "My published work deals mainly with the countries of this region's fertile crescent. My specialism is the Bronze Age." She smiled. "To most people that means I do the archaeology of the Old Testament period of the Bible."

Ferguson looked up from the file, making direct eye contact with her this time. "It says here you had trouble fitting in at school."

Ava wondered if she had heard correctly.

*What sort of a question was that?*

She had assumed she was there to help, not to be insulted.

She looked at the files the three of them were leafing through.

*Were they personnel files?*

*On her?*

She stared back at him.

*Was this some kind of test?*

He continued. "And that aged sixteen, you broke out of your boarding school in England. You found an African tourist company on the Earls Court Road in London, and impressed them so much with your knowledge of east African languages that you talked your way into a job as a tour guide on a Blue Nile Sudan cruise from Sannar. Once they'd flown you there and you'd completed the job, you made your own way cross-country into Ethiopia, back to your family home in Addis Ababa, where your father had been on the British embassy's staff for many years." He glanced up at her. "That's very impressive. Are you sure you're not wasted as an academic?"

Ava could feel her blood rising.

*Was he purposefully trying to provoke her?*

Hunter intervened with a slight smile. "Dr Curzon, let me assure you, you're among friends here." He tapped the DIA file. "We know you followed in your father's footsteps, and that after graduating you worked for a number of years with the British Secret Intelligence Service, MI6."

Ava could feel the tension in the room mounting.

*Was that what this was about?*

"I'm not allowed to talk about it," she replied. Despite the unwanted memories, her voice stayed calm. "And I don't particularly want to, either."

There was an uneasy silence.

"You were top of your intake." It was Ferguson again. "I see you were the first ever female MI6 officer to work in theatre on an operation with the Increment. That's also very impressive." There was a look of genuine curiosity on his face. "Why did you leave?"

She shook her head. "I said I can't talk about it. Let's just say I'd had enough." It was more than she wanted to say, but it was the truth.

"So you returned to your first love," he continued. "Archaeology?"

She nodded.

The woman to Hunter's left cleared her throat. Looking over at her, Ava realized for the first time how tall she was, even sitting down.

"Dr Curzon, my name is Anna Prince," the woman began. "I'm with the U.S. Defense Intelligence Agency in DC. We'd like you to have a look at this." Her accent was east coast—calm and precise.

The lighting above them dimmed, and the squat projector in the middle of the table hummed into life, throwing a dusty tunnel of light onto the far wall.

The projected image was of a golden box, about the size of a packing trunk.

Ava looked at it with professional interest, but it only took her a few milliseconds to recognize it.

"It's a model of the Ark of the Covenant," she said, feeling a bit absurd. She had not been flown to the largest American military base in the world outside the U.S. just to tell them that. Most of the GIs within its razor-wired perimeter could have said as much.

"What can you tell us about it?" Prince asked.

Ava looked at the picture more closely. "It's a photograph of a model—an artist's impression of what the Ark of the Covenant might have looked like."

"Why just an impression?" Hunter asked, frowning. "What does the real one look like?"

Ava shook her head. "No one knows. There are no carvings, sculptures, or paintings. All recreations are just informed guesswork based on a brief description in the Bible."

"What can you tell us about this particular model?" Prince asked. "Is there anything that jumps out?"

Ava looked back at the image glowing on the wall. "It's hard to judge the scale, but it looks perhaps a bit larger than normal. More unusual, too. Most of today's models are broadly similar, but I haven't seen one quite like this before." She picked up the laser pointer on the table. "May I?"

Hunter nodded.

Ava aimed the pinprick of light at the two winged statues dominating the Ark's golden lid.

"From an artistic point of view, this model has some unique features. For instance, the angels on the lid, called cherubim, are atypical. It's a poor quality photograph, and I can't see them clearly because their wings are in the way, but it looks like there's a hint of something Egyptian there."

"Egyptian?" Prince asked, frowning. "What does that mean?"

"It means," Ava replied, "the artist is a clear thinker, and not someone who sheepishly follows the crowd. Most people depict the cherubim as Christian angels—like on greetings cards and in church windows. But, of course, according to the legend, the Hebrews built the Ark in the desert on their return from a hundred years of slavery in Egypt. So it would be logical for the Ark to have Egyptian influences—especially because, many experts believe, the ancient Hebrews didn't have their own artistic style."

Ava put the laser pointer down, not really sure what they wanted her to say.

"Legend?" Prince asked. Unless Ava was misreading it, there was a note of surprise in her voice. "You said the Exodus, when the Hebrews wandered in the desert and built the Ark, was a legend?"

Ava nodded. She knew this was a sensitive topic for many people. "The truth is," she answered, "no one knows for sure. The vast majority of events in the Bible are uncorroborated by independent texts or archaeological evidence. Scholars are divided on whether the adventures of the ancient Hebrews chronicled in the Bible ever really happened—whether figures like Abraham, Moses, David, or Solomon ever existed in the way they're described, or at all. Even King Solomon's Temple isn't universally accepted, as no evidence of it has ever been found."

"The Bible stories never happened?" Hunter asked, unable to mask his curiosity.

"Not necessarily," Ava replied. "For instance, each story may contain an embedded trace element of an ancient historical event, but over time it has been so interwoven and embroidered with the heroic and the supernatural that it's no longer recognizable. It's not an uncommon process. You see the same with the Norse myths, the adventures of Greek and Roman heroes and demigods, the Indian *Mahabharata*, and even folk stories like the tales of King Arthur and his knights of the round table."

Hunter raised an eyebrow. "Well, Dr Curzon, you don't disappoint. You clearly call it as you see it." He eyed her carefully. "I like that."

"But surely the Ark of the Covenant existed?" Prince pressed her.

Ava hesitated. There was a knack to finding the right balance with every audience. In her experience, discussing the Bible in the context of scholarship and science often proved a flammable mix.

"For those who believe in the Bible—" she began, but was cut short by Hunter.

"It's okay," he interrupted, "just give it to us straight."

Ava nodded. "The Ark is attested many times in the Bible. In my view it, or something very like it, almost certainly existed. But we cannot be confident how, when, or where it was created, or what its purpose was."

All of the people around the table were listening intently. Prince was making detailed notes.

"What did it do?" Hunter asked, tapping his fingers thoughtfully on the table. "I mean, what was it for?"

"Again, we only have the Bible for guidance," Ava answered. "The Book of Exodus says the Hebrews used the Ark as a strongbox to carry the stones engraved with the Ten Commandments. They also put in it a pot of manna, the miraculous food that fell from the heavens as they crossed the desert. Another part of the Bible says that it also contained the ceremonial staff of Moses's brother, Aaron, the first high priest." Ava paused. "It was essentially their tribal treasure chest, a coffer containing key symbols of their cultural identity."

"That's it?" Ferguson asked. "Then why was it was so sacred, if it was just a decorated carrying case?"

Ava nodded. "There's more. The lid was called the Mercy Seat. Yahweh, the Hebrews' God, told them he would meet with them there, above the lid, between the wings of the cherubim, in order to give them instructions. That's why it was thought to possess divine power, and why the Hebrews carried it into battle with them," Ava paused. "As a divine object, access to it was strictly controlled. According to the Bible, on one occasion Yahweh killed fifty thousand and seventy people just for looking at it."

Prince shifted in her seat.

"And it was kept in King Solomon's Temple, right?" Hunter asked after a pause.

"Later," Ava nodded. "If the Bible is correct, it was built around 1290 BC. At first, the wandering Hebrews kept it in a tent called the Tabernacle, which they pitched whenever they stayed anywhere for a period. But once King David had conquered Jerusalem and the Hebrews ceased to be a nomadic tribe, his son Solomon completed the first solid Temple around 957 BC, and placed the Ark in it as its most sacred treasure."

"What happened?" Prince asked. "What became of it?"

Ava took a sip of the water Hunter passed her. "The Ark disappeared from history's pages in 597 BC, when the armies of King Nebuchadnezzar of Babylon razed Jerusalem to the ground in one of the most cataclysmic events ever to befall the Hebrews."

"Babylon?" Prince frowned. "Wasn't that in Mesopotamia or somewhere near there?"

"Mesopotamia is modern Iraq," Ava confirmed. "Babylon is about fifty miles south of Baghdad."

A silence fell across the table.

Ava had no idea what she had just said, or why the three of them were staring at her.

Hunter spoke next, this time slowly and deliberately, wrinkling his brow as he directed the question at her carefully.

"So, Dr Curzon, you're telling us that a long time ago an Iraqi warlord sacked Jerusalem and took away the Hebrews' most sacred religious object—their God's throne?"

Ava was beginning to feel the strain of not knowing what this was about. "The Bible says Nebuchadnezzar razed Jerusalem and carried off all but the poorest people from the southern kingdom of Judah. He took them to Babylon, where they lived undisturbed, but in exile. Before leaving, he torched the Jerusalem Temple and melted down its great pillars and other bronze objects, and carried off all the booty to Babylon. There's no specific record of what happened to the Ark, but Nebuchadnezzar looted everything of monetary or propaganda value—and the Ark must have been top of his list."

She took another sip of the water. "But there are other legends, too. Contradictory ones. Like the Ark being kept in the Jerusalem Temple on a mechanical apparatus for lowering to safety into a subterranean tunnel system if ever danger loomed."

There was another long pause.

*Too long.*

Ava was keenly aware the atmosphere in the room was becoming increasingly charged by the moment.

"If you don't mind me asking," she turned to Hunter. "Why are you so interested in the Ark's history and this model?"

Hunter pursed his lips, interlacing his fingers. Fixing her with his grey eyes, he took a deep breath and sat forward in his chair. "Let's just say this is now a military priority, and something we all need to learn about real quick."

Ava could feel her palms growing moist.

*Had she heard right?*

She bunched her hands into fists under the table, and dug her nails into the flesh of her palms. She was barely aware of asking the next question.

She heard her voice, as if from a distance. "Where did this model come from?"

Hunter looked over at Prince. After a pause, the tall woman nodded slowly.

He turned back to Ava, placing his huge hands flat onto the table in front of him. "Dr Curzon, this is not a model in a museum. It's a photograph, taken this morning by a hostile party in a warehouse in Kazakhstan. It comes to us with an assurance that it's the real Ark of the Covenant, and with certain very serious political demands."

Ava heard his words, but had trouble processing them. It was as if he was talking in slow motion.

Her mind whirred.

*Was this some kind of elaborate hoax?*

When she spoke, her voice was hoarse and cracked. She addressed the question to the whole table. "Are you telling me you believe this might really be the genuine Ark of the Covenant?"

Hunter fixed her with a hard stare and exhaled deeply. When he spoke, it was in a low and quiet voice. "That, Dr Curzon, is precisely what you're going to tell us. The hostile party has said we can send an independent expert to verify the artefact. You just got the job. Major Ferguson here will go with you as your technical assistant."

Ava's head spun.

"Your plane leaves for Kazakhstan in forty minutes." Hunter got up to leave. "Ms Prince will see you are provided with everything you need for your trip."

A thousand questions flooded Ava's mind.

"General, I'll need lab conditions to examine the artefact—special lighting, tools and chemicals, photographic equipment—"

Hunter waved his hand dismissively as he opened the door for her. "I'm afraid none of that will be possible. You'll be fully briefed on arrival in Astana. I believe you already know Peter DeVere. He'll be joining you there, and he'll fill you in."

Despite the reassuring tone in Hunter's voice, the effect the name had on Ava was anything but comforting. As she heard the words, she felt as if she had just been punched hard in the stomach.

$$\cdot\ \blacklozenge\ \cdot$$

# 3

*U.S. Central Command* (USCENTCOM)
*Camp as-Sayliyah*
*The State of Qatar*
*The Arabian Gulf*

PRINCE HAD SHOWN Ava to the visitors' facilities so she could freshen up and take a hot shower.

Once the tall American had left, Ava headed for the ablutions area. It was basic—a heavily air-conditioned section of the large prefabricated hangar, indistinguishable from the rest of Camp as-Sayliyah.

Her head was buzzing as she stepped under the steaming jets of water.

Despite the outside temperature, she could feel her shoulders dropping as the hot water began to work out the tension that had been building ever since the escort of marines had arrived at her Baghdad office that morning.

With the steam rising around her, she tried to make sense of the bombshells General Hunter had dropped on her in the briefing room, and to calm the maelstrom they had set swirling inside her head.

She had been completely unprepared for the news that the American and British governments believed the historical Ark of the Covenant might be sitting at that moment in a Kazakh warehouse.

And she had been knocked sideways to learn that she had been chosen by them to go and evaluate it. The Ark was one of those objects that all archaeologists dreamed of, but none ever expected to see. She was still having difficulty digesting the information fully.

But the Ark aside, she had been equally overwhelmed to find out that an organization she had wanted nothing to do with for the last eight years now seemed to be back in her life. General Hunter had mentioned Peter DeVere, and if DeVere really was waiting for her in Kazakhstan, then it could only mean that MI6 was closely involved.

Her stomach tightened.

She had known DeVere for as long as she could remember. Throughout her childhood, he had been her father's most trusted friend in the Firm. He had become a frequent visitor to their home, and practically an adopted member of the family.

She tried to brush the memories away, but images kept flooding back from mid-December 2002. She and her father had left the house for work together as usual, both heading through the biting cold to the Firm's colourful and iconic Babylonian-ziggurat headquarters at Vauxhall Cross. At the end of the day, as usual, she had returned home.

He never did.

The next time she saw him was at his snowy funeral a few days before Christmas, when she, her mother, and her brother buried the man they had all loved so much.

Dozens of his work colleagues had packed the intimate service at the triangular-windowed and white-blanketed Saxon church in the small Somerset village, but a wall of official silence had already descended around the exact circumstances of his death. 'On her Majesty's service' was all the family was ever told.

And DeVere reminded her too painfully of that time. She had left the Firm not long after, severing all ties, disenchanted with its covert world for a growing number of reasons. DeVere had stayed on, and in the following years she had not been able to bring herself to see him.

The emotions were all still too raw.

As she shifted under the hot water, the sound of a jet coming in to land on the strip outside pulled her back to the present.

Aware her flight to Kazakhstan would take off soon, she quickly towelled herself dry and dressed. Before leaving, she gratefully drained the cup of black coffee Prince had left out for her, and polished off the two *Hooah!* energy bars lying beside it on the tray.

When she was done, she headed out onto the hot tarmac, still lost in thought.

Scanning the darkened desertscape that greeted her, she could see the outline of a jeep waiting to ferry her to the sleek military Learjet C-21A parked further out on the apron. In the gloom, she could just make out a shadowy ground crew finishing the refuelling and last minute checks.

Glancing at the rugged field watch she always wore, its illuminated hands told her it was just gone 8:00 p.m. The sun had set an hour and a half earlier, and she was surprised to feel the air temperature had barely changed.

She gazed up at the desert night sky, losing herself for a moment in its enormity. Unlike Baghdad, there was almost no light pollution, and the stars shone with spectacular brightness and clarity in the blue-black sky.

"So, what are the chances this Ark is real?"

She had not noticed Ferguson walk up beside her. He had changed for the trip, and was in a pair of blue jeans and a light jacket.

The same question had been gnawing away at her ever since Hunter told her why he had brought her to Qatar.

Like many starry-eyed and indomitable archaeology students, she had spent her first years at university dreaming of finding the Ark.

In the rare spare moments she had to herself between learning everything from ancient Egyptian human embalming techniques to the similarities between Genesis and the Babylonian *Epic of Gilgamesh*, she had fantasized about the Ark.

In her mind it had always topped the list of biblical archaeology's greatest prizes—Noah's Ark, the Tower of Babel, King Solomon's Temple, the Holy Grail dish used at the Last Supper, and the True Cross of the crucifixion. They were the greatest icons of western archaeology— elusive, quasi-mythical quests.

But as her student days had faded into memory and the professional archaeologist's world of museums, libraries, private collections, and digs had increasingly consumed her, thoughts of these larger-than-life artefacts had receded to the realms of her youthful fantasies. For years now, like all experienced archaeologists, she had accepted they were not going to surface any time soon—still less on her watch.

So General Hunter's revelation that a hostile group claimed to be holding the real Ark of the Covenant in Kazakhstan had reignited a spark in her that had lain dormant for many years. It was as if a childhood dream, long ago abandoned as make-believe, had suddenly come to life again—but this time for real.

She had never doubted the Ark had once existed. But she now felt herself being torn between two worlds. The seasoned professional in her was aware the Kazakh Ark was guaranteed to be a hoax—a waste of everyone's time and effort, and quite possibly a highly dangerous venture. But the optimistic and exuberant young archaeologist in her had never quite died, and she was finding herself irresistibly drawn towards the thrill of being on a once-in-a-lifetime hunt for the genuine Ark of the Covenant.

"Well is it?" he asked. "Real?"

She dug her hands deeper into her pockets, enjoying the desert's night-time breeze across her face. "Honestly?" She paused. "I don't know. But if there's the slightest chance it's genuine, then we have to do whatever we can to prove it one way or the other."

She was watching him, noticing his quick intelligent expressions as she was talking, as if he was taking in everything—not just what she was saying, but how she was saying it.

Intrigued by his curiosity, she turned the question back on him. "Why, what's your interest in it?"

He shrugged. "It doesn't really matter to me if it's real or not. More important is who has it. In the wrong hands, a fake is just as dangerous if people believe it's real."

Ava raised her eyebrows. "Dangerous?" It was not a word she would have used to describe it. She very much doubted the tales of Yahweh striking down those who touched it.

Ferguson stopped walking, and turned to her. His tone was sombre. "We believe the group holding the Ark stole it to order. But we think they reneged on the deal and have now gone freelance, using the Ark for their own political ends."

Ava returned his gaze. This was new information. "What sort of ends?"

He looked grim. "They're threatening that unless we meet their demands, they'll sell it to the Iranians, who will unquestionably use it in their propaganda war to humiliate the Israelis. Maybe the mullahs in Tehran will parade it in front of the international cameras as booty. Or perhaps they'll destroy it on prime time global television. Either way, it'll be received as an outrage to Israel and its allies."

Ava did not need Ferguson to explain the implications any further. After all her years in the Middle East, she was acutely aware of the knife-edge relationships that kept the many delicate diplomatic balances from tipping over into chaos and carnage. She knew the Jerusalem-Tehran faultline was one of the most sensitive, and could instantly see how Iranian possession of the Ark, Israel's former symbol of glory and might, would be cataclysmic.

She took a deep breath of hot night air. That explained the high-level military interest. This was not about archaeology. It was a political question of Israel and Iran, of the stability of the brittle region—and potentially the world.

As she and Ferguson neared the dark green jeep waiting to take them out to the Learjet, a desert-camouflaged open-backed Humvee coming the other way pulled up sharply beside them.

As the six-and-a-half-litre turbodiesel engine cut out, four uniformed and heavily armed U.S. soldiers jumped down from the back of its modified flatbed. A fifth stood on the vehicle's back platform, beside a man shackled to the beige roll-bar fitted along the rear of the cab.

The man was Middle Eastern, Ava could immediately see, wearing crumpled black jeans, faded beige baseball boots, and a tired-looking ragged blue shirt, out of which was sticking an unusually long neck and a thin unshaved face. Even by the runway's distant lights, he looked gaunt and haggard.

Squinting to see clearly, the soldier on the flatbed unlocked the man's handcuffs from the roll-bar.

Suddenly, in a blur of confusion, she saw the man in the blue shirt snatch at the soldier's chest, pulling a pistol from a holster set into the complex webbing of pouches and equipment bound around his torso.

With a speed that could only come from a massive surge of adrenaline, the man grabbed the startled soldier by the shoulder and spun him round, pinning the front of his chest against the roll-bar, jamming the pistol's muzzle into the back of the infantryman's shaved head just under the line of his desert-brown helmet.

Instantly, the scene around her erupted into pandemonium, and before she could react, she was pushed hard, face down onto the tarmac.

Winded, she looked up from her sprawling position to see the soldiers had all brought their black M-4 assault rifles up to the firing position, and were pointing their short but lethal barrels directly at the gunman.

Ferguson still had his left hand on Ava, but was rapidly rising from his crouch with a small steel-blue automatic pistol in his other, also trained on the gunman.

Everyone was yelling at once.

The gunman was shouting in Arabic, grinding the pistol hard into the back of his prisoner's skull. The other soldiers were frantically ordering him to drop the weapon and release the hostage.

Despite the chaos, she could make out that the gunman was repeating the same phrase again and again, a look of desperation on his face. *"Rajj'ouni a'ala beiti! Rajj'ouni a'ala beiti!"*

As she watched, the soldiers continued to bellow over him, the strain audible in their voices as the tension mounted by the second.

Looking around quickly, she could instantly see that no one appeared to be in charge, and everyone was panicking. She knew from experience this was the type of situation that could rapidly go fatally wrong.

Pushing the hair back from her face, she looked up at the soldier nearest her. He was short, with close-cropped brown hair visible under his helmet at the temples. "Do you know what he's saying?" she yelled, pointing to the gunman.

The soldier's eyes swivelled to her. He tapped the side of his helmet with the first two fingers of a gloved hand, as if trying to get the earpiece to work properly. "No ma'am," he answered crisply, "no interpreter."

Ava rose to her knees.

"Down!" Ferguson pushed her back onto the tarmac again.

Surprised by the sudden movement, the gunman's eyes flitted to her, unsure of her intentions.

Ava brushed Ferguson's hand off her shoulder. "Stay here. I'll be right back," she countered, standing up and striding over to the brown-haired soldier, focusing in on his rank insignia and the sand-coloured name-strip fixed onto his combat jacket. "Sergeant Kozinski?" she asked, shouting over the noise.

He nodded.

She put her mouth up to his helmet, speaking slowly and clearly to be heard over the mounting noise. "The man is saying 'Take me home'."

Kozinski took a moment to process the information. He leant close to Ava's ear to reply. "We are, ma'am. He's going on a flight back to Fallujah. Mistaken identity. Negative intel value."

Ava had seen enough.

She turned and shouted something in Arabic up to the gunman.

Immediately, a large soldier with a corporal's stripes a dozen feet to her right swivelled his gun, training it directly onto her. Through the confused yelling, she could hear another voice now barking, "Do not communicate with the enemy."

It took her a few moments to realize the order was coming from the large corporal pointing his carbine at her.

She looked back at his young face peering at her from behind the weapon. He was anything but calm. There were beads of sweat running down his mud-caked face, and the deep rings around his eyes suggested he had not slept in days.

She knew every second was critical. There was no time for lengthy explanations.

She turned away from the soldier threatening her and yelled something else in Arabic to the gunman, who was still repeating the same phrase over and over, more frantically now, his hand shaking as he ground the pistol into the back of his captive's head.

The large corporal advanced on her, covering the distance between them in quick strides. He was pointing the assault rifle straight at her head, screeching now. "Do not communicate with the enemy!"

"Get him off me!" Ava bellowed across at Kozinski, motioning to the corporal. But Kozinski was not listening. He was glued to the scene unfolding on the truck, focusing through his Aimpoint sights, oblivious to what was going on around him.

From the corner of her eye she saw Ferguson switching his aim from the gunman to the soldier threatening her. She shook her head at him urgently. She did not need that kind of complication. The situation was already fractious enough.

She took a deep breath and concentrated on shutting the threat out of her mind. She shouted something else to the gunman. It was unintelligible to the others, just a string of guttural and aspirated noises.

On the flatbed, the man looked at Ava hesitantly, seemingly unsure how she fitted into the emerging picture, and clearly confused by the fact that an American was advancing on her with a weapon aimed directly at her head.

After what felt to Ava like an eternity in which the gunman was visibly assessing his options, he finally seemed to make up his mind. Hesitantly at first, he answered her, speaking in rapid panicky bursts.

Ava turned to Kozinski and began translating. "He doesn't want to hurt anyone. He just wants to be released."

Kozinski was not listening. All his attention was locked onto aiming at the gunman.

With her frustration mounting, Ava called something else out to the gunman, more urgently this time. He answered immediately, the words tumbling out in a stream of Arabic.

The large corporal with his gun on Ava continued to screech at her, but what had been a warning was now an unambiguous threat. "You have three seconds to disengage or you will be treated as hostile!"

Ava continued talking in Arabic to the man on the flat back of the Humvee.

A conversation of sorts was developing.

The corporal was now so close he was obscuring her view, and she could clearly hear the strain in his voice as he continued to shout at her. "I'm now treating you as hostile!" His trigger finger was no more than a metre and a half from her, and the gun's muzzle was so close it felt as if it were burning a hole in her head. She concentrated on blocking the image out of her mind completely, and looked back at the man on the flatbed, conscious she was now on borrowed time—the soldier could open fire on her any moment.

"Yalla! Qarrir bsor'aa!" she urged the gunman, aware it was probably her last chance. At pointblank range, if the soldier next to her pulled the trigger and shot her in the head, she would be dead before she hit the floor.

Ava looked expectantly at the gunman, hoping she had done enough.

From his wild-eyed look, she was not at all sure.

Agonizingly slowly, he began to pull the muzzle of the pistol away from the back of his hostage's skull.

With a look of resignation mixed with terror, he held both his hands in the air as a sign of surrender, before bending down and placing the gun on the floor of the flatbed.

The immediate danger averted, Kozinski seemed to snap out of his trance and burst into action, issuing authoritative commands. "Tell him to step off the truck and lie on the ground."

Ava translated the command, and the gunman slowly climbed down from the back of the vehicle and lay face down, prostrate on the tarmac.

One of the soldiers roughly handcuffed him, before placing a boot hard in the middle of his back.

Ava saw the pain register on the man's lean face as she turned to Kozinski. "What's going to happen to him?"

"Like I said, ma'am," he answered, sweat dripping from his grimy face, "we're taking him home."

Ava looked Kozinski directly in the eye. "I've just given him your personal assurance no harm will come to him now."

Kozinski blinked slowly at her. "Were you not looking?" There was a new aggression in his tone. "He just seriously assaulted a U.S. soldier."

The other men exchanged uneasy glances.

Ava continued, undeterred. "He thinks he's about to disappear into your network of undisclosed prisons and never get out. I've given him your word that will not happen, and he will be taken directly home."

"On what authority?" Kozinski looked unsure.

"You told me he was going home?" she continued, ignoring the question.

He nodded.

"I assume 'negative intel value' means you have nothing on him?"

Kozinski did not respond. She could see his jaw tightening.

She lowered her voice so that only Kozinski could hear her. "I'm sure you're aware that for the last decade western forces haven't had a great reputation for due process around here?"

Kozinski stared blankly back at her.

Ava changed tack. "Are you seriously telling me that if one of your men was in his shoes, he wouldn't do anything to avoid detention and interrogation at a foreign army's black site?"

Kozinski pursed his lips.

"I hope you'll do the right thing." She gave him one long last hard stare before turning and walking back over to where Ferguson was still standing.

"I can see I'm going to have to watch you," Ferguson nodded towards her, his body visibly relaxing. "What *did* you say to Mr Blue Shirt?" He sounded mystified.

Ava shrugged. "I gave him my guarantee he would see his family soon if he put his weapon down."

"I thought you just said you gave him Kozinski's word?" Ferguson asked, opening the jeep's low side door for Ava to get in.

"Why would he trust that?" Ava shot the question back at him. "He's been lifted off the streets, held in military custody, no doubt subjected to torture, and all apparently for no good reason. He's never going to trust another soldier again for as long as he lives."

Ferguson looked bewildered. "So he put his gun down? Just like that? Because you gave him your word?"

Ava shook her head. "I also told him the soldiers aiming at him couldn't hit a barn door with a cannon, so they weren't going to risk shooting their colleague. But I said you were a British spy who would kill him cleanly with one shot between the eyes, and you wouldn't even have to file a report about it."

Ferguson raised an eyebrow. "You really said that?"

"It's true isn't it?" She pulled the jeep's door closed. "You field guys don't do paperwork, do you?"

Ferguson slipped the small Sig Sauer P230 neatly back into its leather ankle holster and dropped his jeans down over it, covering it completely. It was so expertly concealed she had not even noticed it earlier.

He nodded at Ava. "I can see this is going to be quite a trip."

Ava gazed at the pencil-like Learjet against the horizon. "It's not just museum artefacts this war has carried far from home," she spoke quietly to herself.

While they had been talking, Prince had arrived at the jeep. She climbed in, folding her long frame into the cramped space.

"What was all that about?" she asked Ava, having caught the end of the standoff. "Did I see you being threatened by one of our soldiers?"

"Just a misunderstanding," Ava replied as the jeep pulled away, looking over her shoulder to see the man in the blue shirt being transferred into another vehicle.

"It's a bit different here to running a museum, I suppose," Prince noted sympathetically.

"Not as much as you'd think," Ava answered with a shrug. "The museum in Baghdad was founded by a woman—a good friend of Lawrence of Arabia. She had guns pointed at her more times than you can imagine. Times haven't changed much. It goes with the territory." She paused, turning to Ferguson. "Even for an academic."

"I can see why the Firm was sorry to lose you." Ferguson was shaking his head with incredulity.

As the jeep pulled up alongside the Learjet, Ava jumped out and walked ahead quickly, arriving at the aircraft's small forward loading ramp ahead of Ferguson and Prince.

As she started to climb it, she stopped and turned back to look at them both square in the face, her dark brown eyes flashing. "Before we do this, just so we're clear. I'm here as an independent expert. I don't work for any of you anymore."

---  ◆  ---

# 4

*Institute for Intelligence and Special Operations (Mossad)*
*West Glilot Junction*
*Tel Aviv*
*The State of Israel*

"SIT DOWN, URI." Moshe motioned him to a modern-looking brown leather chair in front of the large wooden desk.

The lean young Mossad officer took the seat and looked across at the older man. It had been a few years since he had last seen him, but he never seemed to age.

Moshe Stahl was a legend—a decorated veteran of the Six Day and Yom Kippur Wars, and one of the masterminds behind the Raid on Entebbe. He had been involved in training and selecting Mossad's *katsa* agents for as long as anyone could remember. In particular, as a quasi-royal prerogative, he had the final say on all new recruits into the *Metsada* department. His instincts, honed by long years of experience, were the final word on whether or not a *katsa* had the aptitude for its black ops.

Uri looked around the room. It was large, but simply furnished. Moshe's desk was bare. Everything was locked away. There were no photographs, diplomas, or memorabilia.

Moshe kept his private life at home.

He was Old School.

Moshe stood up and padded over to the single grey steel filing cabinet, returning with a brown manila folder. He laid it on the desk and opened it, thumbing through its pinned contents.

"Still no computer, sir?" Uri asked. It was a longstanding joke in the Institute.

Moshe looked up at him coldly, killing any humour in the air. "To read my papers, someone has to get into this building, onto this floor, and then into my office," he replied. "Until the IT wizards can guarantee me that level of security on computer files, I don't want one. And besides," the corners of his mouth twitched almost imperceptibly, "if I leave a paper file on the Tel Aviv to Jerusalem train by mistake, I probably don't have to tell anyone. But if it was a whole laptop ... ."

Uri smiled to himself. Moshe might be the same age as his grandfather, but his brain had not slowed with the years.

"You've been in Europe for four-and-a-half years, Uri." Moshe leaned back in his chair, staring at the younger man.

*Had it been that long?* Uri wondered.

In any event, he had been pleased to get the call from Moshe that morning calling him back to Tel Aviv. A summons to HQ usually meant something important was about to happen.

"You're clearly talented, Uri." Moshe's tone was now more genial. But everyone in the Institute quickly learned this did not mean he tolerated anything less than excellence.

Uri thought back to his first European operation. His first job for the Institute. No one had ever suspected anything untoward about another heart attack at a nondescript nursing home in a poor suburb of Amsterdam. But then no one in the nursing home had ever suspected that the tetchy private old man on the third floor had once signed papers sending trainloads of Dutch Jews to their chemical deaths at Auschwitz II-Birkenau. Planning and carrying out the job had given Uri a lot of satisfaction.

Moshe continued. "But you're also unorthodox." He looked at Uri over the file, glaring at him through his thick-rimmed glasses.

For a moment Uri wondered if something had gone wrong, if there had been some fallout from his last job. He was sure he had covered his tracks well. Trapping the fugitive Algerian in Marseille had required him to break a few rules. But it had then been plain sailing to take him over the Spanish border in the boot of his car and hand him to the Americans in the small sleepy Pyrenean village. He was not aware there had been any problems. At the time he had been pleased with how well it had worked.

The older man continued. "Fortunately for you, I don't have any use for a yes-man who can recite the Geneva Convention. I need someone who doesn't mind doing what it takes, and who has a record for getting the job done."

Uri had been recruited from a dead-end job in advertising. He had assumed the Institute would use his skill for twisting language in a succession of 'diplomatic' postings to far-flung embassies where he would sit in the basement writing cables and filing reports. But instead, to his surprise as much as anyone else's, it gradually became clear he had a very real talent for the dark work of the *Metsada* section.

He had been shocked at first. But he soon realized it made a strange kind of sense. He had always been drawn to extremes. He enjoyed anything that pitted him against the odds. He found the most satisfaction in solo physical activities—cross-country running, skiing, diving. Ultimately, anything where he only had to rely on himself. The work of the *Metsada* section allowed him a lot of leeway to be his own man. He liked that. They gave him jobs. He had to deliver. How he did it was up to him.

Of course, he did not agree with everything. And he had no appetite for the politics, which he was happy to leave to men like Moshe. But the cold act of killing did not bother him. He had long found that people were hypocritical on the subject. Hundreds of thousands of men and women had killed in wartime, including many world leaders. As he saw it, Israel was at war, and he was a soldier. What he did was always sanctioned by the president. What more justification could there be?

Now, after a string of successful operations, he could not think of anything else he was better qualified to do.

"I'm putting you on a flight to Astana in Kazakhstan." Moshe interrupted his thoughts. "There's an African militia holed up there, playing a dangerous game with the Americans and British. I need you to go and make an assessment of how to gain possession of an asset they're holding, then physically take it from them. You're required to bring the asset back here."

Moshe looked at him sternly. "Usual rules apply. If you're caught, you're on your own. If you're not, you will inflict on anything or anyone whatever level of damage you feel is necessary to get the job done. Clear?"

Uri nodded.

Moshe paused. "Exactly how religious are you, Uri?" The old man looked at him sharply over the top of the folder.

Uri was unprepared for the question. He dealt with those sorts of inquiries every year in his annual performance appraisal, when the Institute tried to gain an insight into whether he was still a reliable member of the silent army. But he had not been expecting this sort of question today. It took him a second to get his thoughts together.

"Never mind," the older man continued. "Religion is for the young and the old. Not you."

"Sir?" Uri raised an eyebrow.

"Shut up and listen." Moshe closed the folder on his desk and leaned back in his chair. "How well do you know the old stories? Moses, the Exodus, wandering in the desert? Do they still teach it all properly in school?" Moshe peered at him closely. "What do you know of the Ark of the Covenant?"

"*The* Ark of the Covenant?" Uri asked quietly. "That's what we're talking about here?" He was sitting still and paying attention now. This just got interesting.

"The old rabbis say it went missing when the First Temple was destroyed." Moshe paused, drumming his fingers on the table. "But they also say that back in the dawn of time, Solomon and the Queen of Sheba were lovers."

Uri had not heard that before. "King Solomon, as in David's son, the builder of the Temple?"

"Read the prophets, Uri. The book of Kings says King Solomon had seven hundred wives and three hundred concubines. We can safely conclude that the pleasures of the bed were not unknown to him."

Moshe took his glasses off and rubbed the bridge of his nose with his large hands. "The story goes that the illegitimate son of Solomon and Sheba took the Ark with him to Ethiopia."

Uri was listening carefully now.

"The Ethiopians have always maintained they have the real Ark," he paused. "And maybe they're right. Have you ever wondered about Beta Israel?"

Uri nodded. "The Jews from Africa."

"Ethiopia, Uri," Moshe scowled. "Details matter." He flicked the corner of the brown folder with his thumb. "They have full rights of *aliyah* under the Right of Return. They're as Jewish as you or me. We even sent the military in to airlift them here in '84, '85, and '91."

"Aren't they supposed to be the lost tribe of Dan?" Uri asked.

The veteran gazed into the middle distance before turning back to Uri. "It's a mess. Maybe they're from the tribe of Dan. Or perhaps they're truly descended from the Jews who went to Ethiopia at the time of Solomon and Sheba. The State of Israel has no official view either way, except they're true Jews, unquestionably entitled to full Israeli citizenship."

Moshe leaned back in his chair. "To make it more complicated, centuries ago, a group of them converted to Ethiopian Christianity, and they inherited the Ark. But they're the most Jewish Christians you ever met. They're more Jewish than most people in this building."

Uri leaned forward in his chair. "Why haven't we ever tried to take the Ark back then?"

Moshe nodded slowly. "We asked a few times, but the Ethiopians weren't interested. It seems it's very sacred to them. A sole monk has guarded it in a monastery for as long as anyone can remember now. Its presence in Ethiopia has been a core part of their Christian belief for centuries, and we have no political appetite for a major diplomatic rift with Christians over it. We rely on their goodwill for too many other things."

"But now an armed militia has taken it." Uri could see where this was going.

"Congolese." The old man answered gravely. "And that changes everything. Now we have a chance to get it back without upsetting anyone important."

Moshe stood up, indicating the meeting was over.

Uri followed him to the door. As the veteran neared it, he grabbed Uri's upper arm. He leaned in close, and Uri could see the steel in the old man's eyes.

"Do you appreciate the implications of this, Uri, for us, if the Ark falls into the hands of the enemies of Israel? Do you understand how weak we will look, and the damage it will do? They'll say our God has abandoned us." The grip on Uri's arm was vice-like.

"Yes, sir, I do," Uri answered, keenly aware that religion and politics were inseparable in this country, where the people's right to be there rested on a promise made to them by God.

Moshe released Uri's arm, and ushered him out of the door. "You'd better. That's why I'm giving this job to *Metsada*. Don't screw it up."

———— · ◆ · ————

# 5

*Grand Lodge of Ethiopia*
*Addis Ababa*
*The Federal Democratic Republic of Ethiopia*
*Africa*

GRAND MASTER SAMSON Kelile looked around his historic office in Addis Ababa's old colonial Grand Lodge building.

Behind him, in pride of place on the main wall, hung a large embossed warrant covered in ornate calligraphy and an array of imposing seals. It was dated 1941, when the British had been in Ethiopia helping patriot forces expel the Italian fascist occupiers. It was signed at the bottom by the Grand Master of the United Grand Lodge of England himself, chartering the practice of Free and Accepted Masonry in Ethiopia under the authority of the newly created Grand Lodge in Addis Ababa.

Kelile swivelled his chair round and looked at the elaborate document with pride, as he always did. Not only did it prove that everything was in order, that Ethiopian freemasonry was bound by an umbilical cord to the world's premier Grand Lodge in London—but just as important to him, it had been presented to his grandfather, Ethiopia's first Grand Master.

Growing up, Kelile had been in awe of the 'gentle Craft', and the day his grandfather had initiated him into freemasonry in that very building had been the proudest of his life.

In his turn, he had been thrilled to rise through the mysterious ranks of Entered Apprentice, Fellow Craft, and Master Mason. The ceremonies had been baffling and intriguing, but not nearly as bizarre and arcane as those he was to experience afterwards.

When he became a Master Mason, he thought he had seen everything freemasonry had to offer. But after a few years he had been invited to join other freemasonic orders, where he mixed in increasingly exclusive and elite circles that most freemasons had no idea even existed.

Six years ago, in recognition of his loyal service, his freemasonic brothers had bestowed the ultimate honour on him, appointing him Grand Master of Ethiopia, just like his grandfather. It was the achievement of a lifetime.

Although at the time he thought he had seen it all, a few months later he had been invited into the ultra-exclusive Strict Rite Knights Templar of the Holy City. To his rising excitement, as he worked his way ever deeper into the order, he had gradually become aware of an inner circle at its centre—an order within the order. At first he sensed it only hazily, in glimpses, but it seemed to be somehow connected with the whole organization of freemasonry, from the top to the bottom. No one ever spoke to him about the inner order, yet he knew with increasing certainty it was there and it was real.

Then one day he had been tapped lightly on the shoulder at a select gathering of the Strict Rite, and a discrete request was made. He was passed a telephone number, and asked to call it if ever a certain event occurred.

He never thought it would, and he had thought less and less about it as the years went by. No one ever mentioned it to him again, and over time he had come to wonder if maybe someone in the order had been playing a practical joke on him.

But he was not laughing as he heard the news on the radio about the blaze in the chapel of the *Tabot*, at the monastery of Our Lady Mary of Zion in Aksum. There were no further details. But it was enough.

He knew what he had to do.

He gazed up at the solemn portraits of the Grand Masters who had gone before him. They were wearing their full ceremonial regalia, bristling with medals—or jewels, as they were called. He wondered if any of them had known when they joined the 'Craft' just how deep the waters of freemasonry ran. He certainly had not. But he was not complaining.

Far from it. To belong to one of the most powerful organizations in the world was a privilege and an honour. Still more to be called upon as one of its trusted sentinels.

He turned the radio off and walked quickly over to the safe in the far wall. Spinning the tumblers, he removed an envelope and opened it, taking out a small card before sitting back at his desk again.

He placed the stiff white card on the shiny mahogany surface in front of him and stared at it for a moment before picking up the smoky black telephone receiver and dialling a +968 number in Oman.

"*As-salaamu aleikum*, how can I help you?" The voice spoke perfect English.

Even though years of making freemasonic speeches had cured Kelile of almost all nerves, he found himself needing to steady his voice. "I bring news from the East." He knew that Addis Ababa was about one-and-a-half thousand miles south-west of Oman—but this was not a statement of geography.

"What day is it?" the voice asked.

"The 13th of October 1307," Kelile answered without hesitation.

"And who are you?" The voice spoke crisply.

"A knight of vengeance." Kelile knew the sequence of questions and answers by heart.

"Do you bring anything?" There was a hint of urgency in the voice.

"Fidelity and honour." Kelile answered quickly.

There was a pause. Kelile heard the phone clicking through to a different extension.

Another voice—older this time. The English was again perfect. "Speak, Brother Kelile. Tell us your news from the East."

———————— • ◆ • ————————

# 6

*Yesil District*
*Astana*
*The Republic of Kazakhstan*

PETER DEVERE OF MI6 was not waiting for Ava when she arrived in Astana. He was tied up on official business all day, but had left instructions to be picked up outside the *Zaraysk* restaurant after dinner.

As Ava's car pulled up, she instantly recognized the figure standing just inside the restaurant, which was decorated as a kitsch Russian village house. She could even see a hay-cart near the door.

DeVere was as slim as ever, despite being in his early sixties. He still sported the same distinctive dark-rimmed glasses he had worn for as long as she could remember, although she was surprised to see he was nearly completely bald, save for a horseshoe of white hair skirting the back of his head.

"Let's not hang about," he announced jovially, climbing into the large four-wheel drive. "And it's always a good idea to keep things locked down around here," he added, pushing the button to close the window beside him.

As the car pulled away, he turned to Ava with a warm grin. Reaching for her shoulders, he gave her a strong hug. "I can't tell you how good it is to see you!"

Ava had spent the flight wondering how she would react when she saw him. Now she was looking at him sitting in the car next to her, she could feel the emotional conflict intensifying. He had once been a good friend, and she felt instantly warm towards him as the memories rushed back. Yet at the same time he represented a world she had fallen whole-heartedly out of love with—one she no longer saw the same way he did, and she knew it would be a gulf between them.

"I should've known you'd be mixed up in this," she answered, returning the hug quickly.

"Well, you know, I'm not one to shy away from the interesting stuff." He beamed at her before settling back into his seat. "Are you joining us again, then?" There was a sparkle in his eyes. "We'd be thrilled to have you back, you know. We don't get your calibre very often."

She smiled briefly. "So who are the people holding the Ark?" she asked, deflecting the question, not yet ready to discuss her personal life with him, and not wanting to ruin the moment.

DeVere glanced over at Prince, who appeared cramped and uncomfortable despite the size of the SUV.

The tall American nodded.

"They belong to the RMF," he explained, his voice now serious, "a Marxist guerilla faction from Congo. As you know, Congo is a dramatically failed state, like Yemen or the Sudan. The war of 1998–2003, the 'African World War', was the deadliest conflict since the Second World War, and the aftershocks are still being felt. It may seem a long way away, but Congo is no sideshow. After Algeria, it's Africa's largest country— eighteen times the size of England."

He sat back in the SUV's large upholstered seat. "Yesterday, a militia of the RMF, led by a minor warlord named Aristide Kimbaba, broke into the sacred compound of the monastery of Our Lady Mary of Zion in Aksum and stole the Ark from the solitary guardian monk. There's evidence they tortured the monk to death, although the picture is a little unclear as the body was incinerated beyond recognition when the building went up in flames."

Ava shuddered. Since leaving the Firm, she had not missed the violence that seemed to be an obligatory part of the background to every operation.

DeVere continued. "The demands received from the RMF require the American and British governments to ensure the United Nations recognizes the RMF *junta* as the new military government of Congo. If we don't, they'll sell the Ark to the Iranians—which they rightly predict will set all Hell loose."

He paused. "At this stage, we have no option other than to take their claims and threats seriously. But before we make any irreversible decisions, we obviously need to verify if the Ark is genuine or not. Therefore, they've agreed to let in an inspector and a technical assistant."

Prince looked across at Ava. "Dr Curzon, you're in charge of physically examining and verifying the Ark. We've put together a bag of equipment you might find useful—magnifiers, a microscope, regular and UV lighting, and a few tools. It won't be the same as having the Ark in a lab, but I hope it's adequate."

Ava nodded. She would clearly have to make do with whatever was available.

"Major Ferguson, you're Dr Curzon's bag carrier. You're also responsible for her security," she added.

"When's the rendezvous?" he asked, glancing at his watch.

"In thirty minutes, at the Republika Fountain," DeVere confirmed. "The contacts will be driving a red Mercedes with a white stripe on the bonnet. They'll take you directly to the Ark."

Ava stared out of the smoked-glass window. Beyond the city, the vast landscape was bleak and uninspiring. She had never been to the steppes before, and knew little of the region other than it had been a wilderness throughout history—infamous for its brutal Gulag camps, where millions of Soviet political prisoners were 'processed' from the 1920s to 1950s.

A tourist poster at the airport had proudly proclaimed that Astana had been the capital of Kazakhstan since 1997, when the government had relocated its historical powerbase from ancient Almaty on the borders with Kyrgyzstan and China to Astana in the north, where the population was more resolutely Russian.

Gazing out into the Kazakh night, Astana appeared to Ava just like she imagined a former Soviet city would—dull and monochrome, with a smattering of hi-tech buildings that had shot up since the fall of the Union.

As they passed a spectacularly tall tower of twisted white latticework supporting an immense golden egg, she realized Prince was talking to her. "Dr Curzon, you and Major Ferguson need to get out here. Good luck."

It had been agreed that DeVere would stay in the car with the driver. He would note down the red Mercedes's number plate, then tail it once Ava and Ferguson were inside.

At the same time, Prince would be on foot in the area around the Republika fountain. Once she had seen Ava and Ferguson get into the Mercedes, she would jump into a waiting car and join DeVere in tailing them. At the same time, a vanload of Kazakh National Security Committee commandos would be in the vicinity on standby, in permanent radio communication with DeVere and Prince in case anything went wrong.

Ava stepped out of the SUV and breathed in the cold night air, pulling her coat closer around her shoulders.

The fountain was dead ahead. Through gaps in the traffic, she caught glimpses of its four monumental grey stone fish spraying jets of icy shimmering water high into the night air.

She watched DeVere's car move to the other side of the fountain. To her right, she spotted Prince stop by an all-night refreshment kiosk about twenty-five yards off. The man sitting in it looked cold and bored.

Ava checked her watch.

*11:45 p.m. Still time to kill.*

Standing on the pavement side by side, she and Ferguson looked for all the world like a carefree tourist couple admiring the fountain. All that was missing were the guidebooks and cameras.

The bag of equipment Prince had given her was on the pavement between them. It was a large white canvas holdall, doubling as the identifying signal for the militiamen to recognize them.

"So you know all about me?" she asked, looking straight ahead and not at Ferguson. "The DIA file you had in Qatar seemed pretty detailed."

His expression remained fixed.

"What about you?" she asked, aware she knew nothing about him. "What's your role in this?"

"I enjoy exotic travel," he answered non-committally, as he continued to scan the traffic.

Ava stamped her feet to warm them up. "You can do better than that," she pressed him. "I know an ex-soldier when I see one."

He turned to look at the roads leading to the roundabout. "What do you remember of your hostage training?"

Ava was in no mood for a lecture. "I always assumed I'd have a fulfilling relationship with my captors and develop Stockholm syndrome."

"I'm being serious," he cut in, watching a group of drunken men approaching. "There are rules that could save your life."

"I can look after myself," she answered bluntly, turning to look him full in the face. "I appreciate you coming along, but I didn't ask for a babysitter, and I don't need one—"

He grabbed her arm firmly, nodding towards the far side of the fountain.

Now visible through the shimmering silvery spray, she could see a red Mercedes with a white stripe on its bonnet swinging around towards them through the traffic.

She looked over to where DeVere was parked on the other side of the fountain.

*Good. He was watching.*

She had spent years of her life growing up in Africa avoiding putting herself or anyone else in unnecessary danger from warlords and militiamen. It was not a habit she was keen to break now, and she was reassured to know there was backup.

As the Mercedes drew closer, she could feel her breath quickening.

The men in the Mercedes spotted her, and she subtly glanced towards DeVere again to make sure he had seen them.

*Bad timing.*

A double-length articulated blue passenger bus was snaking around the fountain—completely blocking DeVere's view of the rendezvous.

Her heart began to beat faster.

The bus appeared to be stationary as the Mercedes's doors opened, and four men got out. They were wearing thick outer clothing and heavy woollen hats.

Ava looked again in DeVere's direction.

*His view was still blocked.*

She breathed deeply.

She could see Prince over by the kiosk, furiously punching numbers into her mobile phone.

Ferguson had also spotted the problem. He glanced across at Ava.

"We continue," she confirmed, anticipating his question. The blue bus would clear the roundabout in a moment.

Ferguson signalled to the approaching militiamen. They covered the ground rapidly, closing in on her and Ferguson. As they did so, the Mercedes pulled away and rejoined the traffic.

Ava felt a rough spike of adrenaline course through her.

*What was happening?*

*This was not the plan.*

She looked across at Prince, who was speaking hurriedly into the microphone on her phone's hands-free cord.

As Ava glanced across at the Mercedes, she saw it exit the roundabout and drive off into the night.

On the pavement, the militiamen were now no more than three yards away.

Her senses were all firing as she looked back to where DeVere was parked.

*This was not good.*

DeVere had pulled out, and was now swinging around the round-about, following the Mercedes.

She took a deep breath. DeVere had obviously assumed she and Ferguson were in the Mercedes. But by now Prince must have explained to him what had happened, so he would just go around the roundabout and return to where he had previously been parked up.

But she had no time to think about it any further. The four militiamen had moved around her and Ferguson, surrounding them. They had their hands deep in their coat pockets, and from the telltale bulges, it was clear they were holding concealed handguns.

The plan had evidently changed.

"Walk," one of them ordered gruffly in a thick Congolese accent. "Quickly."

The group moved off, with Ava and Ferguson being steered by the armed men behind them.

Ava scanned the road ahead for the replacement vehicle they were switching to. It seemed logical. The militiamen were being methodical, cleaning off any unwanted tails. In the old days, she would probably have done the same. Still, it was good to know that Prince, and by now hopefully DeVere, were close by and would simply follow the new vehicle.

As they headed away from the roundabout, Ava could periodically feel the padded barrel of a handgun jabbing into her lower back. Around her on the pavement, pedestrians and evening revellers walked past, oblivious.

With mounting concern, Ava realized she could not see any vehicles with open doors. She strained to look about in all directions, but could identify no one obviously waiting for them.

*What were they doing?*

Before she had time to think, the man behind her spoke again. "In here," He indicated an open steel door, behind which Ava could hear the deep thump of heavy pulsating music.

It looked like some sort of nightclub.

As the men pushed her though the metal-reinforced entranceway, she felt a blast of warm air from the overdoor heaters as the earsplitting sub-bass thuds of the techno trance music hit her.

Scanning the room quickly, she could just make out a long dark bar bathed in a neon blue-black glow. Disorientated by the light and noise, she had no time to register anything else before she felt a gun in her back again, propelling her forwards, more roughly this time.

The militiaman steered her towards the grey steel door of an industrial elevator being held open by another member of the team, clearly waiting for them.

As she was shoved into the elevator, Ferguson glanced towards her, and his expression told her everything she needed to know.

*These guys were professionals.*

---
· ◆ · ───────

# 7

*Bar Akmola*
*Saryarka District*
*Astana*
*The Republic of Kazakhstan*

IT WAS LATE when Uri's taxi dropped him off at the *Bar Akmola* in Astana's north-east Saryarka district. It was the industrial part of town, rough and dilapidated—cluttered with rundown Soviet-era buildings.

After paying the driver, he pushed through the bar's battered door to reveal its shabby interior—a tawdry world where regulars blotted out the cold and the grinding monotony of life with cheap vodka.

Uri immediately saw the liaison officer across the long smoky room. His white logo-plastered *Lokomotiv Astana* football shirt was distinctive without drawing unwanted attention.

"Do you have the correct time?" Uri asked, approaching the table. "My watch has stopped." He tapped it. "Freebie from a catalogue."

The man looked up at Uri. "Sorry." His tone was sarcastic. "I guess that's why I missed my supper. Again."

Uri glared at him. He didn't have time for this.

Clearly sensing Uri's irritation, the man adopted a more professional tone. "All right—yes, I set my watch from the television news every day."

Uri pulled out a greasy chair from under the low wooden table and sat down facing him.

"So this is a fun country," Uri smiled mechanically.

"I love it here," the man replied, his voice heavy with irony. "I was bored of the sunshine and bikinis of Haifa anyway. I prefer the coldest capital on earth. The standard of living is great, too. I'm having a ball. My wife can't understand why we didn't come here before on holiday."

Uri felt sorry for him. He looked genuinely fed up.

The man held out his hand. "Zvi. Zvi Ehrenwald. Diplomatic liaison."

Uri shook the offered hand. "So, what can you tell me?"

Zvi did not seem surprised Uri had not reciprocated with his own name.

He took a swig of his beer. "When I heard you were coming, we got our friends in the *Militsiya*, the local police, to pull some guys off the street—middle-ranking hoods from the local crime families who are always happy to cooperate in return for certain accommodations."

Uri was watching him closely.

"You're looking for a group of Africans, right? Heavily armed?" Zvi looked at him expectantly.

Uri nodded.

"Try Omsk Street. You can't miss it—a dark green warehouse, smaller than the others. Seems a bunch of Africans have been seen coming and going there recently. Word is they flew in on a private plane with some kind of merchandise."

"Thanks." Uri made a mental note not to have anything to do with the local families. "What about practicalities?"

Zvi reached down to his feet and passed Uri a tatty dark blue rucksack under the table. "There's a .22 Beretta, twenty clips of ammunition, keys to a brown saloon car with a full tank parked across the street, and keys to a safe flat nearby. There's a map with directions to the flat in there, as well as a number you can call twenty-four hours a day."

Uri took the bag. "Thanks, *achi*." He stood up to go. "Have a nice night."

"Count on it," Zvi answered. "I bet that redhead in the black lace miniskirt over there's dying to party with an overweight married Jewish guy in a borrowed football shirt."

Uri shook his head. "And I thought you diplomatic boys all led such dull lives."

Zvi walked up to the bar and ordered another beer. "Maybe not the redhead," he smiled at Uri, "but seeing as I'm working late tonight, a few more beers on the Institute won't hurt."

Uri slapped him on the shoulder before slinging the rucksack over his shoulder and making for the door.

Outside, he took a deep lungful of the cold night air.

He had work to do.

# DAY TWO

———————— ◆ ————————

# 8

*Diamonds Nightclub*
*Yesil District*
*Astana*
*The Republic of Kazakhstan*

PRINCE HAD SEEN it all unfold from her vantage point at the all-night refreshment kiosk.

When she realized DeVere's view of Ava and Ferguson was blocked by the bus, she punched his number furiously into her mobile phone, angry with herself for not having it on speed-dial. But too late. When DeVere answered, she could hear the engine noise of his car revving as his driver swung into the traffic to follow the Mercedes.

"Stop!" she yelled into the microphone, breaking into a run as she pursued Ava, Ferguson, and the militiamen along the pavement. "The red Mercedes is a decoy. They're on foot. I'm following."

Through the crowds, she saw them turn and enter a metal door under a flashing sign reading: *Diamonds Nightclub*.

Once inside the hot windowless box, the noise of the throbbing music drowned out whatever DeVere was saying into her ear in reply.

Looking around, she instantly saw the bank of industrial elevators to her right. There were three of them. According to the colourful graffiti on the wall, each floor of the building offered a dance-floor playing a different style of techno music.

The dull doors of the middle elevator were already closing, and she just had time to see the militiamen, Ava, and Ferguson crammed inside its shabby metal interior before the doors clicked shut and the red LED number above the control console starting to increase.

*"Diamonds Nightclub.* They're in the elevator," she shouted into the microphone as she watched the number rise, then stop at four.

"They're on the fourth floor," she yelled, hoping DeVere could hear her over the thudding dance tracks.

Looking around, she figured the most likely way out of the building was the way they had all come in—through the front door. She assumed they had taken the elevator hoping anyone following them would be busy searching the ground floor, or knowing that if they had been seen getting into the elevator, anyone following would have taken the next one. Either way, after bouncing between a few floors, they would make straight for the ground floor again, and leave. It was a crude but effective way to throw off any tails.

Prince's eyes remained locked on the middle elevator's LED display. It was staying motionless at four.

*Why wasn't it moving down again?*

She could feel the sweat breaking out on her lower back.

*What were they doing?*

For the first time, she noticed that the other two elevators were now descending.

*Had they switched elevator?*

She kicked herself for not having seen which floors the other two had come from.

*Not smart.*

She could feel her heart starting to hammer.

*Could they actually have got off at four? Was there a fire escape up there?*

The left elevator stopped one floor above her.

She held her breath.

The right one came back down to the ground floor. She ran towards it, sweat beads now beginning to cluster on her forehead. The elevator doors opened, and a gang of drunk locals piled out.

*This was not happening.*

She ran over to the left elevator, which had moved slowly down to the ground floor and was now opening.

*Please let them be in this one.*

Its doors slid open, revealing an empty cabin.

She cursed as DeVere's voice came over the phone. "I'm in the nightclub now. I'll cover downstairs. You head on up."

Without pausing, Prince ran for the door to the fire-stairs next to the elevator shaft.

Sprinting up the bare stone steps as fast as she could, she emerged onto the fourth floor, where she could hear thudding trance beats coming from a dance-floor beyond a bar off to her left. The middle elevator was still there, motionless. She headed towards it, and saw it was wedged open with a fire-extinguisher.

*They had this planned. Right down to the last detail.*

She began to feel panicky.

*They could be anywhere.*

DeVere was shouting in her ear for an update.

"I don't know," she yelled, sprinting into the bar. "I'm checking the fourth floor." She ripped the earpiece from her ear—the music was so loud it was useless. She would not have been able to hear DeVere even if he had been standing next to her.

She ran to the end of the bar area again, and saw that it dropped down onto a dance-floor where groups of people were dancing in a firestorm of coloured lights and strobes. There was a DJ booth at the far end of the floor, but no other doors.

They were not here.

She looked around frantically before running back through the bar again, jamming the earpiece back into her ear. As she reached the elevator hall, DeVere came through loud and clear. "They've gone." She could hear the anger and frustration in his voice.

"What do you mean, gone?" Prince yelled back into the microphone, fighting to keep the desperation from her voice.

"The basement. Come down to the basement," He sounded dejected.

She punched open the door to the emergency fire-stairs and flung herself down the narrow grey steps, her long legs carrying her quickly down the five double flights.

At the bottom was a large set of metal fire-doors. She banged through them, and saw DeVere at the end of the corridor, standing beside an open external loading door.

She reached him quickly, pulling the mobile phone earpiece from her ear again. She could see through the door into a loading bay, but the area was deserted.

"An unmarked white van," he said, looking through the doors. "It was just screeching out onto the road when I got here."

"They must've gone up to the fourth floor, wedged the elevator open, then run down the stairs to the waiting van," she panted, punching the wall behind her. "Damn!"

She wiped the sweat from her face and leaned up against the cool wall to catch her breath.

General Hunter was not going to be pleased.

———————— · ◆ · ————————

# 9

*The Grand Assembly Hall*
*Castrum Lucis*
*Musandam Peninsula*
*The Sultanate of Oman*
*The Arabian Gulf*

OLIVIER DE MOLAY, one hundred and fourth Grand Master of the Poor Knights of Christ and of the Temple of Solomon, sat on the wide gothic marble throne that dominated the centre of the ancient assembly chamber's east wall.

The atmosphere in the castle was electric.

The meeting had been called at short notice, and the knights had been flying in all day.

Although the Order of the Temple had been officially abolished, outlawed and destroyed by the pope in AD 1312, the knights who had been arriving at the castle's private helipad knew better.

De Molay placed his hands on the medieval seat's cold arms.

It was the same throne his ancestors had governed from in an unbroken line for seven centuries—first in Jerusalem, then Acre, Cyprus, and finally Oman. When King Philip the Fair of France had arrested all Templars in his kingdom on Friday the 13th October 1307 for heresy and blasphemy, a select group of Templars in Cyprus had reacted rapidly. On the secret orders of their Grand Master, they had quickly and covertly moved the throne from the Order's headquarters in Limassol to Oman.

De Molay valued the link the seat gave him to the past. It was a tangible connection to nine centuries of the Order's uninterrupted existence.

Like all the knights in the room, he wore a white monk's habit. His hooded cowl was raised, shrouding his head so observers could see only glimpses of his quick dark eyes, aquiline nose, and neatly trimmed black goatee beard.

Emblazoned on the crisp white wool of his left breast was a blood-red cross patty—its arms flaring at the ends in the universally recognized symbol of the Knights Templar. Over the habit, he wore a simple white cloak, with another large red cross patty embroidered prominently onto the left side, running from his upper arm to his knee.

He looked for all the world like the old European nobleman he was.

His instinct had been to consider the options for longer before calling the knights together in a Grand Chapter. He liked to mull things over thoroughly, examining all the angles. He had learned long ago that rashness was for younger men.

But his magisterial court had been rightly concerned that time was critical. Even the ageing Edmund Saxby, his usually reticent Seneschal and right-hand man, had spoken eloquently on the need to act swiftly in this particular case.

As the noise in the chamber died, Saxby turned slowly to him. "Grand Master," he prompted in a quiet sonorous voice that advancing years had only made deeper and richer.

De Molay nodded.

Saxby had been by his side ever since he had first entered the Order aged twenty-one, when his father had been Grand Master. In those early years, as he prepared to inherit the throne, he had relied heavily on Saxby's encyclopaedic knowledge of the Order's rules and customs. But now, having been Grand Master for over thirty years, he knew the Order's ways as intimately as anyone ever had, and Saxby fulfilled a different role for him—faithful confidant and adviser.

De Molay rose to his feet, clapping once.

The staccato sound reverberated around the stone chamber, bouncing off its midnight-blue vault, a replica of the night sky, brightly spangled with iridescent gold stars. Around him, hundreds of pairs of black and white candles flickered in niches cut into the honey-coloured walls. And above it all, a vast red enamel cross hung in the air, suspended from the ceiling on gold chains, its edges studded in precious stones, shimmering and glinting in the reflected candle light.

"Brothers," he spoke with accustomed authority. "Assist me to open this Grand Chapter." His voice was clear and strong, with a pronounced French accent.

The white-robed knights lining the north and south walls either side of him rose to their feet as one, their faces also hidden by raised cowls.

At the same time, two knights seated on smaller thrones along the empty west wall also rose. They were spaced widely apart, facing De Molay—their three thrones together forming an isosceles triangle.

The Grand Master turned to the knight standing by the chamber's thick studded oak doors. He was white-robed and hooded like the others—but in addition he carried a loaded sleek black FAMAS assault rifle.

The Grand Master used the words set out in the ancient Rule. "Brother Sentinel, has the moon reached its meridian?" His voice echoed clearly around the silent room.

The Sentinel stepped forward and raised his weapon to the present-arms salute. "It has, Grand Master." He spoke with the hint of a Spanish accent.

Still looking directly at him, De Molay continued. "Brother Sentinel, are any strangers present in the Chapter?"

The Sentinel remained at attention. "None, Grand Master."

He continued with the age-old questions. "Brother Sentinel, as only professed brethren may attend this Grand Chapter, do you vouch that each of the brothers present has proved to you on entry that he is of the House of the Temple?"

The Sentinel nodded curtly. "I do, Grand Master."

De Molay asked a final question. "Brother Sentinel, is a trusted Watcher posted on the roof, ever vigilant for intruders, according to ancient custom?"

"He is, Grand Master." The Sentinel replied crisply, before stepping back towards the door, cradling the weapon in his arms again.

De Molay sat down, and Saxby rose to his feet, turning to the knight seated on the throne in the north-west corner of the grand chamber.

"Brother Marshal, what is our Order?"

The knight gave the traditional reply. "We are the *Ordo Antiquus*."

Saxby then addressed the other, in the south-west corner. "Brother Standard-Bearer, what is our banner."

"The unerring *Bauçeant*," he responded.

Saxby turned again to the knight in the north-west corner. "Brother Marshal, what does the *Bauçeant* symbolize?"

"The mystical duality of life," he replied automatically.

It was hypnotic—an ancient ritual antiphon performed at the opening of all Grand Chapters.

Everyone present knew the words by heart.

As Saxby went through the time-honoured formulas, De Molay's mind returned to the pressing issue.

He was in no doubt recent events constituted a crisis. The knights were the keepers of a unique and powerful tradition—a secret so closely guarded that no one outside the Order had ever suspected it.

The Order alone had the global resources necessary to deal with the unexpected turn of events, even down to the secluded headquarters from where they could control operations. They were sitting in it—the fourteenth-century *Castrum Lucis,* the Castle of Light.

It was a formidable fortress, tucked away in north-eastern Oman's Musandam peninsula, invisible to all except the black and white hawks, vultures, eagles, and falcons circling in the white-hot sky.

The castle's dark outer stones were weather-beaten and smooth, rising out of the sheer cliffs that fell away into the sea. Except to those who knew the narrow tortuous paths, access was all but impossible by land. That was why his ancestor had chosen it all those centuries ago.

It was nevertheless in a globally strategic spot. From its ancient battlements, he could look out over the turquoise waters of the Straits of Hormuz. With high-powered binoculars, he could see across the thirty-five miles of narrow ocean channel to ancient Persia, now the Islamic Republic of Iran.

The introductory ritual concluded, and Saxby sat down.

Only a few of the knights knew why the Grand Chapter had been called so suddenly.

The sense of taut anticipation in the ancient hall was tangible.

All eyes were on the Grand Master.

He leant forward.

His voice was deep and rich, needing no microphone to cut into the expectant silence. "Dear brother knights, we are grateful to you for answering our summons so promptly. This convocation has not been assembled lightly."

The tension in the room rose palpably.

He continued. "We have news of the most grave kind, and we will need all our resources for what has to be done."

For the next hour and a half, he explained to the stunned assembly what had happened, and what plan would be put into place.

When the closing ritual was over, De Molay rose from the ancient marble throne to leave.

As he passed out of the hall, he contemplated the diamond chequerboard pattern of the medieval black and white floor tiles. The slabs bore the patina of age, smoothed from centuries of use. Gazing down at them, he was reminded of their traditional meaning—light and dark, good and evil.

Experience and years had taught him that there was a fundamental truth in their design.

Good and evil were rarely far apart.

———————————— ◆ ————————————

## IO

*Omsk Street*
*Saryarka District*
*Astana*
*The Republic of Kazakhstan*

AFTER DROPPING THE rucksack off at the safe flat, Uri headed for the warehouse.

The four-door Lada which Zvi had sourced for him was perfect. He was grateful the local bureau followed standard operating procedures properly. Attention to the small details made all the difference between a smooth operation and a string of headaches.

He looked around the car's monochrome cabin, noticing the tired fabric and the brown towel on the back seat. He could not have asked for better. The car would go unnoticed anywhere in the city, but its unseen retrofitted top-of-the-range engine was capable of getting him away from any trouble quickly.

It was late as he headed deeper into the north-east part of the warehouse district. The streets were shabby and deserted, populated only by the occasional drunk and roadside prostitute.

Zvi's map was old but adequate, and Uri found Omsk Street without trouble.

It was a long road, lined with derelict buildings—many with smashed windows and open doorways.

He found the warehouse he was looking for quickly. It was exactly as Zvi had described it—set back from the road, clearly identifiable by its narrower width and lower roof. A small security light on the front confirmed its peeling paint was dull green.

He drove a few hundred yards past it, then did a U-turn, coming back to look again from the other direction. There was no one outside it, so he pulled the car over onto a piece of wasteland fifty yards further down the street.

Walking swiftly but quietly back to the warehouse, he could see it was cheaply built and hastily assembled—prefabricated from compressed steel sheets.

He walked around the building to get a feel for the surroundings. But there was nothing to see on the industrial wasteland except bits of broken crates, rusty metal, and a few empty bottles.

It had plainly been a while since any major commercial activity had happened in the area.

The warehouse itself had three large skylights, a row of small high windows down either side, a single set of hangar doors, and no other obvious entry or exit points.

*It would have to be the front doors then.*

Pulling out the Beretta which Zvi had given him, he inserted a clip, chambered a round, then bent down and picked up a small lump of broken brick.

He retired to fifty feet from the warehouse. Checking again there was no one around, he threw the brick hard at the large steel doors, then moved swiftly to take cover behind a mound of shipping crates.

He looked at his watch, and waited.

After a pause, a low access-port in the warehouse's large hangar doors swung open.

He checked his watch again.

Forty-two seconds.

*They weren't camped out near the main doors, then.*

Ten seconds later, a man emerged. He looked about thoroughly, scanning the area immediately in front of the warehouse and to the sides.

Uri did not have photographs of his targets, but the man was not wearing a security guard's uniform, was African, and was armed with an AK-47.

There could not be many answering that description in the warehouse district that evening.

The man continued looking about. He carefully walked the length of the warehouse in both directions again, staring intently into the night. Eventually seeming satisfied, he stopped again by the access door, lit a cigarette, smoked it quickly, then went back inside.

Uri had what he needed. There was one man on guard. No external security systems. No men on the outside.

*This was going to be easy.*

He waited ten more minutes to make sure all was quiet, then stepped out from behind the packing crates.

After inspecting the warehouse one more time to burn the building's details into his mind, he headed to the car and drove back.

Once at the flat, he pulled the cap off a bottle of cold beer from the fridge, and opened the file he had hidden behind the radiator. Reading it again, he made sure he had memorized all its details.

When he was done, he walked over to the gas cooker, turned on a ring, and lit a corner of the file. Dropping the burning papers into the kitchen's metal bin, he watched the leaves buckle and curl inside the tongues of flame, before crumbling to ash.

As the fire died, he finished his beer, lay down on the sofa, and took out his phone.

Logging onto a secure network, he texted Moshe an encrypted message for immediate action.

His work finished for now, he placed the phone onto the table beside him and flicked the television on. It was showing a documentary about Kazakhstan's uranium mining industry—which the colourful charts seemed to claim was the world's largest. He could not understand a word of the commentary, but was too wired to sleep.

In less than a minute, his phone buzzed with a reply.

---------------- ◆ ----------------

## I I

*Western Suburbs*
*Astana*
*The Republic of Kazakhstan*

IT WAS HOT in the back of the van.

From the warm acrid smell filling Ava's nostrils, it was evident the militiamen had been living rough for a while.

She was lying on her side next to Ferguson on the grimy floor, her wrists bound behind her back. Two militiamen were sitting up front, the other four were lolling on wooden benches along the sides of the van's interior, staring grimly at their prisoners.

No one spoke.

Ava's heart was pounding. They had not hurt her or Ferguson so far. She kept telling herself that was a good sign.

Despite her joke earlier, she was in no danger of developing Stockholm syndrome. The last things she felt towards her captors were warmth, trust, or gratitude.

One of the men near her lit a match. With all her senses on overdrive, its hot sulphurous smell was overpowering, filling her nostrils, before being replaced by the cloying fumes of cheap tobacco.

Opposite her, another of the militiamen leant across and unzipped one of the grubby holdalls on the van's floor, removing what looked like a black T-shirt.

He stared at her provocatively—the slow movement of his dilated pupils and yellowed eyes suggesting long-term drug use. Without taking his gaze off her, he separated the black material into two pieces, and laid them out on his knees.

As Ava took in the shapes, she realized with a start what they were.

Her body released a jolt of adrenaline and she fought to stave off a rising wave of nausea.

*Hoods.*

She glanced at Ferguson, who had also seen what the man was doing.

Looking on with dread, she watched as the man leant towards Ferguson and pulled the black bag over his head, before sealing the opening around his neck with strips from a roll of shiny black duct tape.

Ava clamped her jaw tightly shut as the man turned to her, bending forward, angling the second hood towards her.

As she smelled the gun oil and tobacco on his fingers, every fibre of her being screamed at her to resist.

But she knew it would be futile, and would only result in her getting unnecessarily hurt. She had no idea what lay in store when they reached their destination, and needed to avoid any injuries that could compromise her ability to react.

Sucking in deep breaths, she offered no resistance while the man hooded her.

As the darkness descended, she could feel strips of sticky duct tape being wound round the base of her neck, sealing the hood onto her head, shutting out the last slivers of light.

Enveloped in blackness, defenseless and vulnerable, she closed her eyes to try and fight the panic that was welling up inside her.

It was frightening enough being tied up, a prisoner, hurtling through the Kazakh night in the back of a vehicle with armed militiamen and no backup.

Being deprived of her primary senses only intensified the mounting fear.

————————— ◆ —————————

# 12

*The Knights' Refectory*
*Castrum Lucis*
*Musandam Peninsula*
*The Sultanate of Oman*
*The Arabian Gulf*

THE GRAND CHAPTER meeting was over. A plan had been devised, and was already being implemented.

The Templars were now in the Knights' Refectory—a low stone-vaulted room set with three long wooden tables, each weighed down by an imposing array of silver candelabra, plates, goblets, and other vessels. The metalware glowed a pale orange colour, reflecting the warm stone lit softly by the guttering candles.

The knights ate in silence on benches, their white cowls hooding their heads and faces. In the timeless monastic tradition, they communicated only by occasional hand-signals, while one brother stood in a stone pulpit in the corner, reading extracts aloud from the Order's medieval rule.

Two of the long tables ran the length of the room, the other joined them to form a U-shape. Each was dominated by a large ornamental jewelled metal centrepiece.

The imposing sculpture in the middle of the right-hand table was a silver ring, a foot high, off which radiated seven flames, seemingly frozen in time, wrought in silver and multicoloured precious stones. As the glow from the room's candles bounced off its gems, the metal flames appeared to dance in the mellow light.

On the left-hand table, the centrepiece was an ornate silver triangle enclosing a large all-seeing Eye of Horus, gleaming in gold and blue lapis lazuli.

Grand Master Olivier De Molay sat on the high table, raised on a stone dais at right angles to the others. He was flanked by seven knights either side of him. The centrepiece on his table was a gold and ruby sculpture with the letters 'xv' enclosed in a fifteen-pointed star.

As the last of the food was cleared away, De Molay rose to his feet.

"Brothers." His voice filled the low stone room, as his predecessors' had for generations.

"This year is the eight hundred and ninety-third anniversary of the foundation of our Order by Master Hugh de Payns—a poor knight of Jerusalem with a humble vision for the defence of the Holy Land. Yet from these small beginnings, the mightiest of Orders grew."

The knights were all listening carefully. The Grand Master rarely spoke unless he had to.

"This year is also the seven hundred and sixth anniversary of the relocation of the *Ordo Antiquus*, the Order within the Order, to our new headquarters here at *Castrum Lucis*—ordered by Grand Master Jacques de Molay himself in 1307 when he foresaw the imminent destruction of the wider Order."

De Molay looked around solemnly. "Since then, the world around us has changed beyond recognition. But our loyalty to the cause and to each other has never faltered. We stand together now, stronger than we have ever been."

There were nods of agreement from the knights.

"Lest we forget, we are still a fighting Order—and we have a mission, which has been our purpose for centuries."

He surveyed the room.

Every eye was on him.

"Our founding of the elite French Foreign Legion in 1831 has enabled us to recruit the toughest and most disciplined special forces in the world—with full land, sea, and air capabilities."

He looked at those on the right-hand table seated around the seven-flamed ring. "Brother Knights of the East and West, you are the world's finest military forces. You have risen through the *Légion*'s elite Sword and Axe fraternity. You travel the globe. You live in inhospitable climes. You are the true inheritors of our desert fathers' warrior legacy."

He raised his heavy gold goblet in their direction. Each of them had been hand-picked by their superiors in the Foreign Legion as suitable for initiation into the Templars. "*Vos salutamus,*"[1] he toasted them earnestly, honouring them with the Grand Master's ancient salute.

"And yet our strength goes wider and deeper," he continued. "For we live in a world where civil society wields many powers. Through our founding of freemasonry in the early fourteenth-century, we have long drawn on the finest of the civilian world."

He looked at the men on the left-hand table grouped around the Eye of Horus. "Freemasonry has ever brought us exceptional men from all walks of life—public and private, from every field of human endeavour. Any freemason selected for elevation into this Order has shown his deep commitment to our arts and mysteries, and has proved his skill in maintaining the utmost fidelity and secrecy." He raised his goblet to them. "Brother Knights Kadosh, *vos salutamus.*"

He paused, replacing the goblet on the table.

"And finally, my brothers of The Elect of Fifteen." He turned to survey those on the dais alongside him. "You are the family descendants of the fifteen knights who first escaped and journeyed here in 1307 at the command of my ancestor, Grand Master Jacques de Molay. You are the blood link to our forebears, who carried their heavy secrets here that we may preserve them. Your families belong to our Order as of right, in perpetuity. You are our beating heart." He raised his goblet a third time. "To you also my brothers, *vos salutamus.*"

De Molay lowered the heavy goblet once more and surveyed the room slowly. "My brothers, these are dark times. And they may yet get darker. But we have always prevailed. And we shall again. It is our privilege, and our duty."

He paused, and in a ritual gesture made a fist of his right hand, before thumping it hard onto the left side of his chest, where he held it. "Brothers of the House of the Temple of Solomon of Jerusalem," he called in a raised voice. "*Si vis pacem ... .*"[2]

---

1 "We salute you."
2 "If you wish for peace ... . "

The hall filled with the sound of scraping as the benches were pushed back and every man in the room stood, likewise thumping their fists to their chests, and bellowing the ritual reply, the sound ringing around the stone walls of the room, as it had done for seven centuries, " ... *para bellum!*"[3]

---

3 " ... prepare for war!"

———————— • ◆ • ————————

# 13

*Western Suburbs*
*Astana*
*The Republic of Kazakhstan*

EVENTUALLY, AVA FELT the van slowing down.

She had no idea how long she had been lying on its floor in the dark. They had stopped for a while at one stage, and she had a feeling the van had taken one particular road a number of times, judging by its uniquely noisy surface and the number of distinctive sharp bends. But she had no visual clues to where they had driven her.

It felt like they had been travelling for half a day. But realistically she suspected it had been no more than several hours.

The driver cut the engine, and in the welcome silence she could hear the sound of men outside.

Before she could work out what they were doing, the doors were wrenched open.

As the fresh air flooded in, she gulped it down hungrily, grateful for relief from the foetid smoky atmosphere in the back of the van.

But she was immediately conscious of the new danger, and with no warning she felt hands grab her, pulling her roughly into a crouching position.

A spasm of pain shot through her cramped shoulders, which had been forced into an unnatural position on the floor for too long. As she was dragged forward, she discovered the rope binding her wrists behind her back had dug in, and she could not feel her hands at all.

"*Allez, bougez!*" She recognized the heavy Congolese-French accent immediately.

Hands guided her out of the van, shoving her forwards.

The sweat was pouring down her face inside the hot hood.

There was gravel under her feet, but it suddenly gave way to a harder surface, then a step.

As she concentrated on finding her footing, with no warning the floor began to move impossibly, rolling towards her.

A wave of panic flooded through her as she sensed her balance failing. She tried to reach out and grab something to steady herself, but her wrists were still tied tightly behind her back.

With a sickening jolt, she realized she had no way of protecting herself from the fall.

Unable to stop herself tumbling face forward, she braced for the impact, twisting her body sideways in the hope her shoulder would hit the floor before her head.

But someone caught her, and she was shoved forward again, arms guiding her from behind.

Her heart hammering, she staggered and stumbled, before the floor suddenly disappeared from under her feet entirely.

Her brain spun uncontrollably, and she felt a hot surge of primal terror flush through every muscle of her body.

*What had she fallen off?*

Her mind filled with images, flashing through at breakneck speed— cliffs, tall buildings, and even the high ledges people were cast off in the ancient biblical execution of stoning, condemning them to a gory death on the stone-flagged floor far below.

But then she realized there were arms holding her from behind, and now there were more, grasping her from the front.

She could make no sense of what was happening. She was gulping in breaths. Trying not to shout or struggle.

She kicked out with her legs, but they sliced ineffectually through empty air.

Completely disorientated, and struggling to visualize where she was, the arms suddenly released her, and she was shoved down into what felt like a hard chair.

Gasping for breath, she tried to steady herself. But immediately, hands began groping at her neck.

For a moment, another spike of adrenaline coursed through her strung-out system, filling her with a fresh panic that she was about to be strangled.

But a moment later, there was a searing pain at the base of her neck, and the hood was gone.

---------------- • ◆ • ----------------

# 14

*Omsk Street*
*Saryarka District*
*Astana*
*The Republic of Kazakhstan*

ON TOP OF the warehouse, Uri narrowed his eyes against the cold morning wind.

He looked at his ops watch. Its tritium hands and markers showed 3:30 a.m.

He had specifically chosen this early hour so that if the militiamen in the warehouse were asleep, they would likely be in the deepest part of the cycle, and disorientated on waking. Their grogginess could prove invaluable, buying him a few precious extra seconds before they realized what was happening.

He looked around the crumbling district carefully. Everything was quiet, aside from the occasional purr of a car on the main road a hundred yards behind him.

Nobody was about.

He nodded to the three men on the roof with him. Moshe had delivered quickly, and the small team from the elite *Sayeret Mat'kal* division had arrived fast. They could not have come from Tel Aviv in that time, but Uri knew better than to ask.

He peered into the warehouse through the large middle skylight. The building was dark inside—he could see nothing.

Working quickly, the team silently forced the skylight's rotting frame and lifted off the glass. Without speaking, they expertly anchored hooks and single kernmantel ropes to the roof, before running the ends into their quick-release harnesses.

They were dressed in full black tactical ops kit and vests over kevlar body armour. It was generic clothing that would not identify their country of origin. They carried no objects or papers. Even their weapons were non-traceable—standard NATO Heckler and Koch G3 assault rifles. If anything went wrong, they were on their own. They would be disowned by Israel. It was part of the deal.

On Uri's silent signal, they pulled on their helmets and flicked the selector switches on their weapons to auto-fire. Each checked their night-vision was turned off, then waited.

With everyone ready, Uri held a pair of M-84 flash-bang stun grenades over the open skylight. He pulled the pins a second apart, before dropping them into the gloomy space below.

As the grenades tumbled through the darkness, he looked away, holding his hands over his ears. The men with him did likewise, as two searing bursts of blinding magnesium-white light split the darkness, and a pair of thunderously deep bangs ripped through the warehouse.

Uri did not need to give any additional signal. With a precision borne from years of intense repetitive training, the team flicked on their night vision and hurled themselves into the void, rappelling down the single ropes at breakneck speed.

They all knew they had only five seconds before the militiamen below would be able to see again, and perhaps a little longer until the sensory disorientation and sleepiness wore off.

All four of them hit the cracked concrete ground hard.

In one orchestrated motion, they brought their weapons up to the fire position and spread out, covering all corners of the hangar, ready to return any hostile fire.

There was none.

Uri quickly scanned the warehouse, but could immediately see it was completely empty.

There were no adjoining rooms—just a large bare space.

As the men fanned out, Uri studied the floor. It was littered with cigarette ends and take-away food wrappers, and fresh ash covered an area of burnt concrete where a fire had been lit for cooking and heating. He held his hand over the ashes—they were still warm.

The building had clearly been occupied until very recently.

But the militiamen were now gone. And so was the object they had brought with them.

Uri cursed quietly under his breath.

After swiftly checking the front door for booby-traps, he waved the men out into the morning air. Even though it would be a while before anyone turned up to investigate the explosions, they ran to the car—another habit instilled by years of disciplined training.

Speeding off into the Astana night, Uri pulled out his mobile to text Moshe the bad news.

————————— · ◆ · —————————

# 15

*Western Suburbs*
*Astana*
*The Republic of Kazakhstan*

AVA WINCED WITH pain.

As the hood was pulled off, the light tore directly into her dilated pupils, which began contracting immediately, but not fast enough to prevent a searing pain ripping through her head.

She looked around, blinking, and instantly understood why the floor had moved as she had been led there, and why it had then suddenly disappeared completely.

She was in the rusty hold of a grimy stripped-down tug boat. To get her there, the men must have walked her along the yawing deck, then lifted her through the open hatchway she could see off to her left.

It was bare and functional—just reddish-brown rusty bulkheads enclosing an empty section of the hold. Two naked bulbs lit the space— not well, but enough to force her to squint as her eyes adjusted to the unaccustomed light.

Through the portholes she could see it was still pitch black outside. A cracked clock on the wall showed the time as just gone 3:30 a.m.

Ferguson was sitting next to her, also on a cheap hard wooden chair. He was still hooded, with his hands bound behind his back.

The white holdall lay at his feet.

Directly ahead of her, a large African man was standing in front of a pallet. He was unusually tall, heavily muscled, and wore the regulation beret of the paramilitary. He had not been part of the snatch-squad in the Mercedes.

She assumed he was the leader, Kimbaba.

She took in all this information in a few seconds, before her eyes were magnetically drawn to what was behind Kimbaba, on the pallet.

It was an object the size of a large packing trunk, shrouded under a beige tarpaulin.

A cocktail of emotions flooded through her. She had been so preoccupied with what was happening around her that she had temporarily forgotten why she was there.

But now, looking at the object veiled under the thick material, she was completely focused—finding it hard to believe she was not dreaming, and that a few yards from her sat potentially the greatest archaeological find of all time.

Never in her wildest dreams had she imagined she might one day come face to face with the genuine Ark of the Covenant. Even though the voice of experience told her it was almost certainly a fake, she could not suppress her excitement at the thought it might be real.

It was almost too much for her to take in.

As she traced the outline of the object under the grimy canvas, she realized Kimbaba was speaking to her. "Let me apologize for the manner in which you have been brought here." His English was good, although strongly accented.

"You must also forgive the change in plan." Despite the apologetic words, his expression was as hard as flint. "Someone was taking an unhealthy interest in us." His eyes were flicking around, restlessly. "But my country is rich. We have friends, and have been able to find this quiet place for you to examine the … merchandise."

Ava winced at hearing the Ark described as 'merchandise'—as if it was just another crate of whatever Kimbaba usually bought and sold. Contraband tin ore, she imagined, if he was plugged into the usual government-run black market circles in Kinshasa.

He continued, nodding at Ferguson's hooded and bound figure. "Your friend will stay where he is while you carry out the inspection."

Ava was barely listening to him. Her eyes were fixed on the tarpaulin.

"We will have to check you first," he announced. "Stand up."

Ava did as he asked, not taking her eyes off the object she had come to see.

Kimbaba nodded to his wiry deputy in the doorway.

Ava had not noticed the three militiamen standing off by the hatch. There had been more of them in the van. She assumed the others were guarding the rest of the boat.

Masolo stepped forward. Reaching Ava, he began patting her down. She remained motionless—her hands still tied behind her back.

He started with her upper body, then squatted down to rub her thighs, shins, and ankles. When he had finished, he stood again, and began patting her ribs once more—his hands lingering on her, his smug smile openly betraying his enjoyment at touching her.

As his eyes connected with hers, he gripped her hips firmly and fixed her with a suggestive leer.

Something inside Ava snapped.

An anger had been building since the kidnapping back at the nightclub. She felt misled, mistreated, and bruised. And the last thing she was in the mood for was being touched up by one of Kimbaba's men.

Without warning, she kicked him viciously in the kneecap, and pulled away defiantly, her eyes blazing.

Masolo crumpled to the floor, his face a mask of pain. He spat out a word she did not understand, but the sense was unambiguous in any language.

Kimbaba seemed amused. He stepped towards her, and sliced through the rope binding her wrists,

She rubbed her hands, grateful to get the circulation flowing again.

Kimbaba smiled, took her by the arm, and walked her toward the tarpaulin. "This is a big day. One we will all remember for a long time." He paused for effect. "Because you are going to tell the world what this is."

As they approached the pallet, something vibrated quietly on Kimbaba's belt.

He pulled the small rubberized phone off his beltclip, and answered it.

After listening briefly, he hung up, his features expressionless.

Walking across to Masolo, he said something to him in a low voice, before striding over to Ferguson, who was still tied to the chair.

Kimbaba ripped the duct tape from around Ferguson's neck and pulled the hood away roughly. "I'm very disappointed," he hissed, his eyes narrowing.

He stepped back, and made way as Masolo stalked over to Ferguson. In one swift movement, Masolo hooked his foot under one of the chair's front legs, at the same time shoving Ferguson hard in the chest.

Ferguson and the chair toppled over sideways. Without pausing, Masolo aimed a savage kick at his midriff.

Ferguson grunted with the pain, bringing his knees up to his chest as Masolo kicked him again, this time in his kidney.

Without pausing to think, Ava launched herself at Masolo. She caught him off guard, ramming her shoulder hard into his solar plexus, winding him, and sending them both crashing to the hard rusty floor.

She had been quick and had the element of surprise, but he was stronger. He grabbed her right wrist with one of his large hands, and roughly spun her over onto her front. Ramming her face hard into the floor, he twisted her arm up behind her back with an animal brutality.

A bolt of white-hot pain seared through her shoulder. She tried to push him away, but felt her strength ebbing as she was overcome by an overpowering urge to vomit.

Masolo knelt on her to restrain her struggles. She was semi-paralyzed by the sheer agony of her shoulder, and could feel his breath on her neck and his knee grinding into the middle of her back. Twisting her head, she stared up at him defiantly, fuelled with adrenaline and rage, but unable to resist.

Masolo looked quizzically at his boss, who nodded for him to keep her pinned down.

Kimbaba stepped over to Ferguson and hunched over him. "Did you really think you could steal it from me?"

Ava fought to keep her expression neutral.

"You've made a serious error of judgement." The militiaman's voice was rising.

Ferguson said nothing.

Ava had no idea what Kimbaba was talking about.

"Who do you think you're dealing with?" He was working himself up into a fury, but still speaking slowly and menacingly. His tone was chilling. "We left a lookout at the warehouse, who saw your whole operation."

Ava still had no idea what he was talking about.

*What operation?*

She struggled to understand. Prince and DeVere had been with them until they were separated. They had not mentioned any attack on the warehouse. And there was nobody else involved as far as she knew.

*Was General Hunter playing some other game?*

Kimbaba was breathing heavily now. He moved round to the pallet and laid his hand on the rough canvas, stroking it thoughtfully.

Turning, he looked back directly at Ferguson. "Do you expect me to believe it's a coincidence that four armed men just hit my warehouse?" His tone was coldly aggressive.

When Ferguson answered, his voice was clear and measured. "A lot of people are interested in your 'merchandise'. It could've been anyone."

Kimbaba's eyes scanned the room rapidly. He pursed his lips, then looked at Ava—still on the floor with Masolo pinning her down.

He seemed to have made a decision.

Striding towards the three men by the door, he waved in the direction of the pallet. "Pack it away," he ordered them

He stopped at the door and spun to face Ava and Ferguson. "You've just made a tactical error of great magnitude. Your governments will come to regret their decision." He paused. "And so will you." Despite the cold night air, his lined face was shining with sweat.

Twisting her head, Ava watched in horror as Masolo pulled a syringe out of his dirty combat jacket pocket.

Her eyes widening in fear, her body took over, kicking and writhing to get as far away from the needle as she could.

But Masolo was too strong.

As if in slow motion, she saw the needle puncture the skin of her exposed hip as he pushed it in hard.

Before she could struggle any more, she was filled with a sudden rush of warm nausea, then everything went black.

---

## 16

*River Ishim*
*Western Suburbs*
*Astana*
*The Republic of Kazakhstan*

AVA AWOKE SLOWLY.

She struggled to rise through the mental fog of sleep, but a thick bitter haze hung over her, pushing her down.

She was hot, and unbelievably thirsty. Her head was pounding, and the inside of her throat was dry.

Forcing her eyelids open slowly, she was rewarded with bursts of shimmering black, purple, and white stars exploding across the back of her retinas.

As her surroundings came half into focus, she saw she was lying on her back on the rusty floor of an old boat. It was an empty shell of dull brown metalwork, covered in layers of grease and dirt.

There was something lying on the floor beside her.

It took her a few moments to recognize Ferguson, slumped a few feet away.

The effort of moving her eyeballs to take in the scene caused a fresh series of explosions in her head.

She felt sick.

Somewhere in the distance she could hear a faint buzzing sound. It was low and smooth—almost rhythmical. She struggled to work out what it was, but it eluded her.

Out of the nearest smeary porthole, she could see the boat was moored in an old abandoned wharf next to a rundown railway bridge. The red-brown bricks were dirty and water-damaged—covered in stains and graffiti. The surrounding area was littered with old refuse—bottles, tins, and twisted plastic. A large scorched oil drum looked like it had last been used as a brazier. She guessed the area was home only to those who had nowhere better to go.

She tried to remember why she was on the boat, but her thoughts were disjointed, confused.

Struggling to piece her thoughts together, she suddenly remembered Masolo's face, the needle, a swelling sense of warmth, then nothing.

*She had been drugged.*

That explained everything.

That was why she felt so sick.

As her memory of events began trickling back, she was suddenly aware of the stiffness in her shoulder where the wiry militiaman had twisted her arm, and the pain in her lower back where he had knelt on her.

Looking about, she wondered how long she had been there, then realized from the light filtering into the cabin that it must be the following day.

But despite the calm scene, she sensed something was wrong.

Something did not fit.

She coughed, her head still pounding, and glanced across at Ferguson.

He looked fine. He was breathing regularly—his face was red-cheeked and healthy.

She fought off the urge to sleep.

The buzzing was still bothering her.

It sounded familiar. But somehow out of place. Incongruous.

*What was it?*

Suddenly, her jumbled brain made the connection.

*The engine.*

The boat's engine was on, ticking over slowly and quietly. It was purring smoothly—softly, but distinctly audible.

She frowned, struggling to understand.

*Why was the engine running?*

She looked out of the porthole again. It was as she thought. The boat was not moving.

Waves of lightheadedness rocked her.

The taste in the back of her mouth was foul and metallic.

Then, from nowhere, the memory of why she was on the tug boat came flooding back.

*The Ark!*

She looked across to where the shrouded object had been resting the night before. The pallet was still there, but whatever had been on it was gone.

Her mind drifted back to the buzzing.

*What was the engine doing on?*

Why was it running if Kimbaba, Masolo, and the Ark had gone? And if it was on, why was the boat not moving?

She looked up at the porthole again, but the scene outside it remained unchanged.

The boat was definitely stationary.

She swivelled her eyes to glance again at Ferguson.

He was insensible to it all.

Through the mental fog, a disturbing idea suddenly occurred to her.

She looked around the cabin more carefully, peering intently at the portholes and hatch.

Then she saw it.

*There!*

There it was, in the corner of the hatchway, jammed into place by the lid—an ugly black rubber hose poking into the cabin, with a dark haze around its tip evidencing all too clearly the lethal sooty fumes pumping out of it.

As her brain tried to take control of the situation, the adrenaline kicked into her system.

She had no idea how long she had been breathing the poison, but knew that if she did not get out fast, she would drift back into unconsciousness.

*Possibly for ever.*

Perhaps Ferguson already had?

He was closer to the hose.

She tried to lift her arm to push herself up, but found to her horror that it would not move.

The renewed effort triggered another bout of nausea.

With no warning, a fuzziness began to descend, and she felt herself being pulled down by an immense fatigue. She was overwhelmed by the overpowering urge to sleep, suddenly more tired than she could ever remember. She began to wonder why she was even bothering with the effort of thinking about it all. If she was honest, it was easier just to be drifting. It was like being drunk. Perhaps she should simply enjoy it. She smiled to herself. It was not so bad.

She could feel herself slipping uncontrollably into unconsciousness, like sliding into a warm bath.

*No!*

A voice thundered deep inside her.

*Move!*

The urgency of the voice triggered a memory. For a moment she was back outside Thal in Southern Waziristan. She was lying in a mud hut, delirious with a raging fever, while her fellow MI6 officer left her so he could push deeper into the north-western frontier, to make contact with a potential asset.

She had lain hallucinating on the sodden straw until it was too dangerous for everyone if she stayed any longer. Wracked with fever, she had stumbled south for two days to Bannu, where she had found a UN rep and been put on a plane out of the country.

On her febrile forty-eight-hour trek, she had been conscious that she was alone in one of the most dangerous regions on earth for a foreigner—especially a woman, and a western spy. But a deep animal survival instinct had pushed her relentlessly on.

She had moved only at night, staying off roads and tracks, avoiding all human contact, holing up by day in whatever derelict shelter she could find.

Although she had learned from being abandoned that the mission always came before any individual, the experience had also taught her how strong the mind could be, even when the body was badly damaged.

But she was not sitting safely on the plane out of Bannu now.

She was suffering from advanced carbon monoxide poisoning, along with the effects of whatever she had been injected with.

Her vision was blurring.

She knew she had get out of the cabin.

She did not have the strength to stand, so would have to move onto her front and push herself up.

Summoning what little energy she had, she tried to raise her right shoulder off the floor.

For what seemed like an age, she feared she did not have the strength.

With increasing desperation, she blocked out all other thoughts except forcing her shoulder over. On the verge of passing out, she finally felt her body roll, and she flopped over onto her front.

Her face was suddenly crushed painfully against the metal floor, but she barely noticed.

She willed her arms to extend, and a kaleidoscope of flashes exploded in her head, but she kept pushing until she was on her knees.

With a strength she did not know she possessed, she began to crawl.

It was painfully slow at first, inching her way across the rusty metal floor towards the blistered wooden hatch cover. Her movements were drunken and uncoordinated, and she cut her hands on the sharp twists of metal sticking up from the floor. But she was oblivious to it.

Her lungs were starting to burn from sucking down increasingly rapid breaths. Her body was crying out for oxygen. She knew she was inhaling poison, but gulped it down hungrily, unable to stop herself.

As she got closer to the black cracked hose belching out its toxic gas, her head felt like someone was hammering red hot nails into it, and her mouth was on fire, as if she was drinking scalding water.

She was teetering on the threshold of unconsciousness, half-hallucinating a nightmare in which she was being hounded by a clock counting inexorably down to nothingness.

As she somehow reached the short flight of black steps, the darkness finally descended, and she blacked out.

But she was only unconscious for a few seconds, before the sensation of retching brought her round for long enough to take a swipe at the hose nestling in the corner of the broken hatchway.

She missed.

Her vision was fading fast, and she realized she only had seconds before passing out again. Perhaps this time for good.

With a resolve that came from some primal cortex of her brain, she powered herself up the decrepit stairs in one last burst of effort, hammering the warped wooden hatch lid off with her shoulder, sending the hose flying harmlessly out onto the rusty deck.

As her legs gave way, she crashed through the hatchway, collapsing onto the surrounding wooden housing.

With her head finally away from the toxic smog below, she began gulping in huge mouthfuls of fresh cool air.

As her lungs saturated her blood with oxygen and her heart pumped it quickly round her body, she could feel the nausea and dizziness starting to recede.

She lay there for a few minutes, breathing deeply, staring blankly at the cold sky until her hammering heart started to calm.

But she could not relax. She needed to move quickly.

When she felt sufficient strength, she forced herself to stand up and head haltingly back to the stairs.

Steadying herself on the handrail, she descended into the cabin again, and over to where Ferguson was lying.

He was too big for her to lift, so she grabbed him by the wrists and, with more willpower than bodily strength, dragged him towards the hatch.

As she reached the base of the steps, the hose now gone, she left him there to breathe in the chill morning air.

After a few minutes, she could see the telltale rosy colour of the poisoning leaving his face as he started to breath more regularly. When at last his eyes opened and he awoke, she put his left arm around her neck, and hauled him up the stairs.

The July morning was crisp and bright. There was no other traffic on the river, and the dilapidated wharf was still.

There was not a soul in sight.

Ferguson hung over the boat's railings, coughing hard and sucking in air. Ava leaned against the wheelhouse, her eyes closed, breathing deeply.

When she felt strong enough, she walked over to Ferguson.

He looked awful. His eyes were bloodshot, and the rosiness in his cheeks had been replaced by an ashen pallor.

She realized she must look similar.

"Come on," she croaked, her voice a hoarse whisper. "Let's get the blood flowing."

They stumbled off the boat and onto dry land.

"I told you I didn't need a babysitter," she rasped, as they found their feet and began trudging along the quay. There was no triumph in her voice. It was a statement of fact.

Looking around for any recognizable landmark, she saw in the far distance the large latticework white tower topped with the golden egg.

She pointed to it. Ferguson nodded, too tired to speak.

With resignation, they turned towards it, and began the long walk back into Astana.

---

## 17

*Quedlinburg*
*Saxony-Anhalt*
*The Federal Republic of Germany*

MALCHUS HEADED FOR the picturesque old quarter, the *Altstadt*.

Ever since the pretty German town of Quedlinburg emerged from behind the Iron Curtain in 1990, it was permanently busy with sightseers.

But now it was early in the morning—and the normally bustling central *Marktplatz* was empty. Later in the day, tourists would be sitting at the cafés' immaculately laundered tablecloths sipping bitter German *Kaffee* and eating sweet cakes with lashings of whipped cream. But at this hour, all was quiet.

Malchus glanced up at the aged and imposing St Benedikti church, with its small house halfway up the spire—a bizarre medieval sentry box for the town's watchmen of old.

*If only they knew.*

He was keenly aware that, like so many ancient churches, it lay on the site of a much older tradition.

At the corner of the picture-postcard *Marktplatz* he turned off abruptly into a maze of narrow medieval streets.

He was oblivious to the blasts of wind rolling down off the rugged

Harz mountains, and he ignored the clusters of antique houses expertly maintained by the Communists for so many years.

He was not here for the tourist sites.

Quedlinburg held other attractions for a man of his interests.

He gazed up at the Brocken, twenty miles to the west—the highest peak in northern Germany. When the weather was good, tourists enjoyed its botanical gardens and narrow-gauge railway. But, as Malchus knew well, the mountain had a far more sinister side.

For centuries, traditionalists had congregated there on its isolated and desolate slopes to mark *Walpurgisnacht*—the eve of Mayday: the cross-quarter day between the spring equinox and the summer solstice. Local girls kept up the age-old spring fertility ceremonies by weaving ribbons around a maypole. Neo-pagans lit bonfires and celebrated their spring rituals. Malchus had been there many times, to the Devil's Pulpit and the Witches' Altar, where he had witnessed other darker and still more ancient rites that continued to take place there on that sacred night. Just as they always had.

*Walpurgisnacht* was a hallowed time for those who followed the path. That is why the *Führer* chose it in 1945 as the evening on which to commit suicide a hundred miles to the north-east, in the doomed and febrile atmosphere of the Berlin bunker.

As Malchus strode deeper into the *Altstadt*, his hard-soled leather shoes rang out on the smoothed cobblestones. Leaving the modern world ever further behind him, the medieval houses were now uniformly half-timbered *Fachwerk*, punctuated with low doors and small windows.

Arriving at his destination, he stopped sharply. It looked at first like a residential house, although a small sign to the left of the door indicated it was a discrete shop: '*Okkultismus*'.

He pushed the wooden door open. As he stepped down onto its cold stone-flagged floor, a small brass bell mounted on the doorjamb rang once.

It was gloomy inside, and the air smelled faintly of bitter herbs, incense, and wax.

Looking up, he saw a familiar phrase burned in gothic letters into a gnarled low black beam:

HE THAT WALKETH FRAUDULENTLY REVEALETH SECRETS
BUT HE THAT IS OF A FAITHFUL SPIRIT CONCEALETH THE MATTER

Malchus noted approvingly that, unlike the gaudy tourist bazaars around the *Marktplatz*, this shop had no chrome and glass displays, no canned music. Instead, it was piled high with arcane books and objects.

He looked appreciatively at the titles on the dusty shelves—*De Philosophia Occulta*, *The Book of Abramelin the Mage*, *Arbatel of Magick*, *The Black Pullett*, *Corpus Hermeticum*, *Kybalion*, *The Lesser Key of Solomon*, *Necronomicon*, *Hermetic Arcanum*, and others familiar to him for many years.

He brushed past a table of ceremonial tools—knives, censers, lamps, and braziers. He smiled to himself, enjoying the fact this was not a place for teenage girls wanting glittery candlesticks or love spells. No. This place was for those who trod a different path. An ancient, more sinister one. And he savoured it.

As he stepped to the back of the dimly lit shop, he breathed in the pungent smell of the incense packets bristling in a rack on the side wall.

Reaching the oversized dark wooden counter, he noted there were no knick-knacks on it, no leaflets or posters. There was not even a cash register.

Almost immediately, a short man came out from a doorway in the grimy back wall. His thinning grey hair was long, tied in a ponytail with a small black ribbon.

The man took in Malchus's hairless fleshy features, heavy eyelids, and bulky dark overcoat. He recognized his peculiar customer immediately. "*Guten Morgen,*" he nodded. "Please, a moment. I have your order."

Malchus did not acknowledge the greeting.

The shopkeeper disappeared into the back of the shop again, returning a few moments later with a silver flight case, which he carefully laid onto the counter.

"My sincerest apologies for the delay," he muttered to Malchus. "But I think you'll be pleased."

He flipped open the metal catches on the case, carefully lifted the lid, and turned the box around so Malchus could see its contents.

Inside, on a bed of thick dark blue velvet, lay two round bronze discs, each three inches deep and ten inches wide. Countersunk depressions filled all but a small rim of their top faces.

"Are the sizes exact?" Malchus asked, examining the discs closely. "Precisely?" His German still carried a slight eastern accent from his native Dresden.

"Of course," the shopkeeper nodded gravely.

"Exactly faithful to the drawings I provided?" Malchus stretched out a hand and picked the discs up. They were cold and heavy. "I must insist upon this."

The shopkeeper suppressed a look of irritation. "Yes, *mein Herr*. I know my trade. You are not the only one who has requested such things."

Malchus's eyes shot to his. "You have made these for someone else?" His tone was sharp.

"Of course not." The shopkeeper gave him a placatory smile. "Not these. Different designs."

The shopkeeper looked down at the discs which Malchus had placed back in the flight case. "I guarantee you, this work is unique."

Malchus touched the discs again. All that mattered was that they were flawlessly accurate.

The details were vital.

The shopkeeper looked earnestly at Malchus, clearly sensing his unease. "I assure you, *mein Herr*, there's nothing to worry about. The objects are completely faithful to your instructions. The delay was only because I wished to verify your drawings against the originals. I therefore had to obtain a high quality image of Dr Dee's designs. Such a task is not easy in the case of a four-hundred-year-old drawing, as I'm sure you'll appreciate. You should not trust modern reproductions." He nodded towards the inscription on the beam. Malchus read it again:

HE THAT WALKETH FRAUDULENTLY REVEALETH SECRETS
BUT HE THAT IS OF A FAITHFUL SPIRIT CONCEALETH THE MATTER

Malchus was annoyed now. "What I gave you was precisely what I wanted." He glared at the shopkeeper.

The man looked back at him with respect. "And I changed nothing. Your drawings were flawless."

Malchus snapped the flight case's catches shut. "I do not make mistakes." He reached into his breast pocket for a small crisp envelope, and handed it to the shopkeeper. "As agreed, the second payment of one thousand euro."

The shopkeeper counted the ten notes, then slipped the envelope into his trouser pocket. "Thank you." He reached for a ledger. "Would you like a receipt, *Herr* ... ." He looked apologetic as his voice trailed off. "I'm sorry, what did you say your name was?"

"I didn't," Malchus replied, picking up the flight case brusquely and heading for the door.

————— ◆ —————

# 18

*U.S. Central Command* (USCENTCOM)
*Camp as-Sayliyah*
*The State of Qatar*
*The Arabian Gulf*

THE MILITARY FLIGHT back to Qatar was uneventful.

Ava's experiences in Kazakhstan had left her exhausted, and she had been grateful for the opportunity to collapse into the hard seat and recharge.

Her clothes still reeked of exhaust fumes, and she was a long way off full strength. But having devoured the steaming foil pack of chilli and rice the loadie had passed her, and then had some sleep, she awoke feeling more refreshed.

When the plane nosed down onto the scorching tarmac at Camp as-Sayliyah, she was ready to face General Hunter.

Prince had no doubt reported back to him, so he would at least be aware all had not gone according to plan in Astana. Ferguson had headed straight back to London, and would by now have debriefed with DeVere, who may have passed some of it on to Hunter.

So what she had to say to him would not come as a total surprise.

The plane door popped open with a click and hiss. Dazzlingly bright desert morning sunlight filtered into the bare cabin, followed by a rush of hot air which hit her hard in the face and throat as if someone had opened a large oven door. But after the dampness of Astana, she was pleased to feel the warmth.

As she stepped to the door and looked out across the bleak desert-scape of eastern Qatar, she could see a camouflaged figure striding towards the plane.

It was General Hunter.

Even at a distance, he towered over his surroundings.

His expression suggested all was not well. "What the hell happened out there?" he bellowed over the deafening noise of the two tail-mounted jets powering down.

Ava was taken aback by the tone of his question. "You're asking *me*?" she yelled back. "It should be me asking *you*!"

As she got to the bottom of the ramp, he ushered her into a green open-topped jeep heading back to the main building.

After hours in a stuffy plane, she was grateful for the fresh air. The breeze was refreshing, and she was enjoying the wind on her face.

"This wasn't a complicated operation," Hunter began, tapping his knee impatiently with his hand. "You'd better tell me what happened."

Ava felt the tension of the last twelve hours bubbling over. "Let's get one thing straight," she turned to him indignantly. "You came to me with a problem. I was very happy to help —"

"Of course you were," he interrupted. "It's the chance of a lifetime for you—"

She cut him off. "But I expected at the very least some professional assistance. So far, I'm pretty underwhelmed, General. Your team lost us at the outset. Someone thought it was a smart idea to double-cross the Congolese, which they didn't take well. We were drugged, gassed, and left for dead." She glared at him. "I may have been out of the loop for a few years, but even in my day that wouldn't have been considered a model operation."

Hunter looked blank. "Double-crossed?"

Ava nodded. "Something about a recce then an assault on the warehouse where the militia had been holding the Ark. So they changed the plan and took us to a boat."

Hunter looked surprised. "An assault? That's news to me. I can assure you the order didn't come from my office."

He looked at the airstrip speeding by for a moment before running a large hand over his close-cropped grey hair. "So did you get to examine the Ark, before it all came unstuck?"

Ava shook her head. "The meeting turned nasty too soon. I never even saw it."

Hunter grimaced. "Well, so be it." His tone was businesslike once more. "The RMF militia has now broken off all communication. You were the last person to hear from them."

He paused, changing tack. "If they were going to sell it, how would they do it?"

Ava considered the question for a moment. "The world of antiquities attracts a lot of crooks. Objects are regularly stolen—often to order. Export permits are forged. Officials are bribed to turn a blind eye. It's all done privately through brokers, away from the taxman. The sums changing hands can be immense, running into the tens, sometimes even hundreds of millions of dollars."

"But if you were them," Hunter interrupted, "who would you go to if you wanted to sell something like the Ark?"

"Not so much who, as where," Ava answered. "Black market antiquities obey a simple rule—they follow the money. If I was offloading an artifact as unique as this to a broker, it would have to be into Russia, the Gulf, or China. As it's a Judeo-Christian object, I'd say one of the Russian brokers. They operate mostly out of St Petersburg, in the area around the Hermitage and the Nevsky Prospekt."

She narrowed her eyes. "But the RMF have a political agenda. They're not looking for a straightforward cash sale."

"True," Hunter nodded.

"Then that's the market for power and politics, not the art market. For that, they'd probably use a go-between to get access into Tehran's government circles. I'd guess that Beirut, Dubai and London are all home to the right kind of fixers."

Hunter exhaled slowly, before pulling a card out of his top pocket. "Well, we've hit a brick wall for now. The militia has disappeared with the Ark, and there's no guarantee we'll see them again." He gave the card to Ava. "These are my numbers. Call me if you hear anything—anything at all."

Ava stared at him in disbelief.

*That was it?*

*The end?*

"You're just walking away?" she asked, failing to keep the incredulity out of her voice.

Hunter raised his eyebrows. "Dr Curzon, we have many military commitments in this region. Unless we get credible intelligence the Ark is real and the militia is on the verge of engaging with the Iranians, then I can no longer allocate resources to this. I'm handing the file over to the Defense Intelligence people." He buttoned up the pocket he had taken the card from. "They'll call you if they need anything, I'm sure."

Ava could hardly believe what she was hearing.

Hunter massaged the bridge of his nose with his chunky fingers. "So you really think they have the original Ark from King Solomon's Temple?"

"I don't know," Ava replied quietly.

The driver pulled the jeep up outside the large main building where she had first been briefed. Hunter nodded for him to kill the engine.

He stared off into the distance, visibly troubled, before turning back to Ava. "There's something else you should know. I've been in two minds whether to tell you."

Ava raised an eyebrow. Nothing Hunter had said from the moment she first met him had been dull.

"We're getting reports that the man behind the operation is a German, named Malchus. He was recently released early from serving a prison sentence in Turkey."

The name meant nothing to Ava.

"He used to be a high-flying officer in the East German Stasi," Hunter continued. "I know I don't have to tell you what that means. When the wall came down in '89, he went freelance, embracing the underworld of the new capitalism. By all accounts he's an extremely nasty piece of work."

"If he's the average eastern-bloc gangster-capitalist, what's his interest in biblical artefacts?" Ava could not see the connection. "Surely weapons and drugs are more his line?"

"Well, here's the thing." Hunter exhaled deeply. "The information we have says he's into black magic and all that kind of stuff," he grimaced. "And I don't mean playing heavy metal records backwards and lighting joss sticks. He's a highly dangerous man with heavy connections, and he's deeply involved in some very twisted things."

Ava smiled sadly. "You're talking to the wrong Curzon, General. It's my father who specialized in people like him. He set up a unit within MI6 focused on observing and penetrating occult-political movements. He worked hard to demonstrate that there are networks of them on every continent. It was his life's work. He was convinced a modern intelligence service should know what these occultists are up to, and understand that they pose a permanent risk of going political. He only needed to cite Rasputin and Himmler to get people's attention. He broke up a number of significant politico-occult circles, and foiled a handful of religious ritual killings ... ." Her voice trailed off. "But, as I say, that was his line, not mine. I do straight archaeology."

"I know about your father," Hunter answered. "That's why I'm going to give you this information—because your world just collided with his." He pulled a photo out of his breast pocket and gave it to her. "That's Malchus."

She looked at the picture.

The image was of a stocky man with a full hairless face and fleshy lips. A pair of cold sea-green eyes stared out from heavy eyelids. Ava felt a shiver. It was a chilling face.

"I still don't understand." She looked at Hunter. "What's this got to do with me?"

"I don't know what the British authorities told you about your father's death. But our files say he was investigating Malchus when he was killed."

Ava went rigid.

She had never been told anything.

Even though she was employed by MI6 at the time, the details were never passed to her, despite her many requests. She had merely been told it was classified information, like all deaths in service.

There had been nothing else.

Hunter continued. "Our files show your father did Malchus's group quite some damage, and that he was getting close to Malchus himself." He paused. "Here's the thing—our files also suggest there's a strong chance it was Malchus himself who killed your father."

With no warning Ava felt a bolt of white-hot anger well up and shoot through her as a cocktail of hormones and emotions ripped around her system. This was not the frustrated anger she had felt when he had died. It was different. And she knew instantly what it was.

It was rage.

She could not believe that now, after eleven years, she was hearing this for the first time. She had put her life on the line for the Firm more times than she could remember, yet they had never even given her this simple but life-changing piece of information.

Almost as quickly as it had begun, the heat passed, leaving her feeling drained. She breathed in slowly and deeply, and with it her mind settled into a sense of cold purpose.

"Why was this information never given to the police?" she asked, startled at how steady her voice sounded.

Hunter shrugged. "Maybe it was? Who knows."

She thought angrily of DeVere. He had been her father's partner. He had worked alongside him. He had been to their home innumerable times. And yet he had been satisfied with the explanation that her father had died on active service. But then she had always known that he was at heart a career man. He did things by the book. He was a safe pair of hands, and never ruffled feathers unnecessarily.

That was another reason why she had left.

The Firm made people less human.

She looked down at the photograph of Malchus again, her sense of focus now cold and crystal clear.

Regardless of her involvement with the Ark, she was going to see to it that Malchus was made to answer for his role in her father's death—whatever part he may have played.

She had long ago given up all hope of finding out exactly how her father had died. Now, when she least expected it, she felt the deep drive of a sense of purpose to track down his killer.

She was staring so intently at the photograph that she barely heard Hunter. "Dr Curzon, I'm telling you this for your own safety. If there's any possibility that Malchus still bears a grudge and might now turn his attention onto you—"

"I'll recognize him," Ava finished his thought in a low voice. "You can be sure of that."

"Okay. We've done all we can for now." From the tone of his voice she could tell the discussion was over.

He opened his door and got out of the jeep, then walked round to Ava's side. "If I didn't say so before, I'm sorry for what happened last night. Do you want our medics to check you over?"

Ava shook her head. "A paramedic cleared me before we took off."

Hunter held out his hand to shake hers. "Then thank you for your time and courage, Dr Curzon. Needless to say, you've never been here, and yesterday and today didn't happen. Please feel free to make use of the facilities on camp before we get you home."

Ava shook his hand. "You know where to find me if the Ark surfaces again." She nearly added "or Malchus", but that was now her own personal issue. No need to confuse the two.

Hunter thumped the driver on the shoulder. "Make sure Dr Curzon gets home safely, door-to-door."

She watched as Hunter headed through the large dusty doors into a sea of desert-pattern camouflage uniforms.

As the driver started the engine and they headed over to the visitors' block, she had a deep feeling that, far from being over, her involvement with the Ark—and now with Malchus—was only just beginning.

————————— • ◆ • —————————

# 19

*Quedlinburg*
*Saxony-Anhalt*
*The Federal Republic of Germany*

MALCHUS RETRACED HIS steps back to Quedlinburg's touristy *Marktplatz*.

It was still deserted.

He passed the statue of Roland, Charlemagne's famous paladin. The heroic knight was a common sight in Germany's market-squares, but he did not find this one particularly impressive—not nearly as mighty as the ancient one in Bremen.

As he walked past the medieval *Rathaus*, the townhall, he stopped briefly to look at the strange carving of a dog over the doorway. But he soon carried on, turning west, leaving the old city behind.

The day was turning nasty, and angry clouds had descended, hiding the mountains and heralding rain.

But he was oblivious to the elements.

He clutched the silver flight case to his chest, and walked as quickly as he could. He only stopped once to visit the ancient Roman Catholic church of St Kastor, before arriving at his destination in under twenty minutes.

It was a nondescript nineteenth-century house. The cream paint had faded, the garden was a little overgrown, and it all had a general air of genteel neglect.

It was perfect for him. Hotels were busy, and asked for too many details. He wanted anonymity and privacy on this trip, and the unobtrusive *pension* fitted the bill exactly.

Entering the house, he closed the glass-panelled front door quietly behind him, and looked down the corridor past the ornate hall mirror and framed prints and maps. He could hear the television on in the back parlour, along with Frau Hahn's muffled laughs at the jokes of the breakfast show host.

Without taking off his coat, he slipped swiftly and softly up the once elegant stairs.

His room was basic—not at all what he was used to. Nevertheless, he could see that Frau Hahn had done her best—furnishing it with featureless heavy wooden furniture that had obviously been in her family for generations. She had tried to make it welcoming with some cheap pictures and fabric curtains, but they could not mask the fact it was a tired room for rent.

Closing the door gently behind him, he took off his heavy coat and hung it in the naphtha-scented wardrobe.

Lying on the bed, he picked up a book from the bedside table—a 1611 version of the *Missa Niger*, bound in the original tooled black calfskin.

Opening the slim volume, he began to read the spiky gothic writing, mouthing and repeating the words aloud as he perfected his memorization of the text he had first learned so many years ago.

Lunchtime came and went, but he did not move from the bed.

At around 4:00 p.m., he padded through to the adjoining kitchenette and boiled a white enamel pan of water, from which he brewed himself a cup of thick bitter coffee.

Returning to his bed, he continued to read the ancient ritual until it got dark.

As the sun finally disappeared over the horizon to the west, he got off his bed and locked the door firmly, before picking up a thick leather bag from the bottom of the wardrobe and carrying it over to the small table by the window.

There was not much space in the room, but it was enough.

He pulled the curtains closed, and extinguished the lights.

After stripping off his clothes, he took four waxy black candles from the leather bag, and laid them on the floor to mark out the four cardinal points. As he lit them, a pungent musky odour began to permeate the room.

Taking a rune-engraved silver knife from the bag, he sliced a neat incision across the flesh of his left palm, then moved slowly around the room anticlockwise, dribbling blood to create the circumference of an imaginary circle around the points marked out by the candles.

Tracing an inverted five-pointed star in blood on his forehead, he sat down in the middle of the circle, and began, *"Gloria deo, domino inferorum ..."*[4]

---

4 "Glory be to God, Lord of Hell."

———————— ◆ ————————

# 20

*Quedlinburg*
*Saxony-Anhalt*
*The Federal Republic of Germany*

THE RESERVED LANDLADY of the house, Frau Hahn, had been delighted to have a guest in this low season, even if it was only for two nights.

The quiet man was her first lodger since the three walkers in January, and she had needed to clean the house specially for him. But she did not mind. It was nice to have company again, and the money was very welcome.

Since arriving, her guest had kept to himself and not been any bother. She liked customers like him. Much better than the ones who wanted to talk endlessly, or who expected to be waited on hand and foot. She was quite happy to see her guests for breakfast, and otherwise only in passing on the stairs. It was enough for her to know they were there. It made the house feel less empty.

She nearly made an exception in his case. She was intrigued by the way he talked, unable to place quite where he came from. His German was native, but it was not an accent she recognized.

She looked at her small gold-plated watch. It was getting on for 9:30 p.m.

She had eaten her main meal at lunchtime, so had no great appetite for supper. She would probably just have a little something before bed—a small roll with some cold cuts of *Schinken* and a spoonful of the leftover potato salad would be perfect.

Meanwhile, she opened the drinks cabinet and poured herself another generous measure of *Jägermeister*.

Life had been quiet—too quiet—since her husband died four years ago, and she doubted anyone would begrudge her the occasional glass of the warming liquid to see her through the lonely evenings.

As she flicked channels on the television set, she drained the glass and poured another. A third was naughty, she knew, but then she had a lodger for the first time this season, and that was cause for celebration.

She found an interesting documentary on the mysteries of marine life in the deep seas, and watched it through to the end, before getting up to make her bedtime snack.

As she moved into the hallway and looked up the stairs, she thought she should probably first go and check on her guest.

She did not usually bother the lodgers, but he had been so quiet all day, and had not come down for any food even though she had it ready prepared. She wondered if perhaps he was ill in his bed? If he was, she would be happy to make him a hot drink, or even heat him some soup.

She put her glass down on the wooden hall table, and softly climbed the carpeted stairs to the first floor.

Arriving outside Malchus's door, she momentarily caught the whiff of a strange odour. She inhaled deeply a few times, and smelled it again. Frowning, she turned her head and sniffed the air in the rest of the corridor.

Nothing.

The smell definitely seemed to be coming from the guest's room.

She raised her hand to knock on the door, but then thought better of it. She did not want to disturb him if he was asleep.

The smell was odd, though. She hoped nothing was burning in his room.

She put her ear against the door and listened.

She could hear nothing at first. But straining for even the slightest sound, she thought she could hear a voice, speaking slowly and quietly.

As her ear tuned in to the sound, she began to make out individual words.

"Turn again and quicken us. *Veni Satana, imperator mundi.*"[5]

---

5 "Come Satan, Lord of the world."

She strained to make sense of what she was hearing, but her mind was feeling a little fuzzy from the alcohol.

*Was it Latin?*

It sounded a bit like things the priests at her school used to say during mass, before everything was switched to German.

Struggling to hear more clearly, she bent lower and pushed her ear against the keyhole.

"Make them like a wheel, and as stubble before the face of the wind. Stir up thy might, lord Satan and come. Avenge the blood of thy servants which has been shed. Brothers and sisters, we are debtors to the flesh, to live according to the flesh."

Perhaps he had bought himself a television, and was watching one of those films? she wondered. Or maybe it was a play on the radio?

As she continued to listen, the voice became slightly louder. Was it now closer to the door, she wondered, pondering how that could be.

"May this incense rise before thee, infernal lord, and may thy blessing descend upon us."

With a shudder of realization, she suddenly knew it was not the television or a radio. That was her lodger's voice. She recognized the distinctive accent. She clapped a hand over her mouth to muffle her involuntary gasp.

But not quickly enough.

The door flew open, and her eyes widened in horror at the hellish scene in front of her.

Malchus stood before her, naked, a bloody star daubed on his forehead.

A wave of nausea washed over her as she saw the floor behind him, where there was a circle marked out around four black candles, in the centre of which she could make out what looked like a pair of brass discs, smeared and glistening with something dark and wet.

As her eyes swept the room, the sickness turned to terror at the sight of what lay beside the wet brass discs.

A simple Roman Catholic all her life, she immediately recognized the holy round wafer of Christ's most precious body, unmistakably stamped with the sacred IHS monogram. But whereas she was used to seeing the wafers nestling in the silver cup in the priest's hand, the one she was looking at on the floor was dripping with a dark liquid, and raggedly speared through by a dark-stained silver knife.

Putting a hand onto the door post to steady herself, her eyes fell on a shape she could not make out at first.

And then with a sickening lurch, she knew.

It was the gutted body of her cat, lying torn and eviscerated outside the circle. Its blood was seeping out onto the floor, and through her tipsy haze she realized he had used its gore to douse the brass discs and the holy wafer.

She tried to scream, but only a dry hoarse rasp came out. Stumbling backwards to distance herself from the horrific sight, blackness descended as she fainted in terror.

---

$\cdot \blacklozenge \cdot$

---

## 21

*Quedlinburg*
*Saxony-Anhalt*
*The Federal Republic of Germany*

A FEW MOMENTS earlier, Malchus thought he heard a noise outside the door.

He did not stop the ritual, but listened acutely. When he heard the stifled gasp, he knew for certain someone was there.

It was an unwelcome development. The gasp could only indicate his nosy landlady had been listening at the door and had heard him.

He cursed. It meant he would have to interrupt the all-important ritual at a crucial stage.

He knew instinctively that there was only one thing to do now.

He could not let anything or anyone compromise the project.

Not now he had come this far.

Nothing could be allowed to jeopardize the work.

His mind clear, he pulled the door open in time to see her expression of horror as she peered into the room, stumbled, then fainted.

He looked down at her coldly. At least if she was unconscious it would save him the bother of trying to keep her quiet.

Bending low over the still body, he caught a whiff of the spicy spirits on her breath.

Dominic Selwood

Perfect.

This was going to be easy.

He threw on his dressing gown, and pulled on a pair of black gloves from his bag.

Padding down the stairs, he almost immediately saw what he wanted—the half-empty glass on the hall table.

He sniffed it carefully, recognizing the distinctive botanical aroma of the spirit she had been drinking.

Heading into the curtained back parlour, he quickly found the large antique drinks cabinet. Inside was a pathetic selection—an earthenware bottle of garishly labelled German gin, a cheap cherry Schnapps, and an open bottle of the *Jägermeister* she had been enjoying.

Picking up the bottle, he headed back to the upstairs hallway, where he knelt beside the limp body, lifting her lolling head onto his knee.

Unscrewing the metal cap with his gloved fingers, he held the bottle to her lips, and began to pour the neat alcohol into her mouth.

As the liquid hit the back of her throat, she took a large reflex gulp before choking, spraying the spirit over her chin.

The large dose of fiery liquid was sufficient to bring her round from the faint, and Malchus saw her pale watery eyes widen first with surprise then terror as she looked up at his cold bloodless face.

"Drink," he ordered, jamming the neck of the bottle hard into her mouth.

He could feel her struggle, but her elderly muscles were no match for him. He held her firm, and angled the bottle so the spirits ran down her throat.

When she again choked in a fit of racking coughs, he placed his thumb over the bottle's open neck and drizzled a few splashes over her collar and dress front—enough to leave the impression she was sufficiently tipsy to have missed her mouth a few times.

He sloshed a little of the drink onto her right sleeve, then took her head between his hands.

Looking into her terrified wide eyes, he offered a quiet prayer, *"Ecce mitto angelum meum ante faciem tuam, qui praeparabit viam meam."*[6]

It was the last thing Frau Hahn ever heard, as with a quick brutal twist, he snapped her neck cleanly.

6 "Behold, I send my angel before thy face, who shall prepare my way."

Hoisting the frail body onto his shoulder, he carried her down the stairs, putting the nearly-empty bottle of spirits on the hall table next to her glass.

He carried her through to the simple neat kitchen, where the food he had not eaten that day was laid out in a bowl covered with a tea-towel.

Spying the narrow white cellar door, he flipped its small latch and pushed it open with his foot, before pulling the cord to turn on the naked bulb that lit the narrow stairs.

Seeing a red plastic basket of washing nearby, he kicked it hard down the cellar steps, watching with satisfaction as the clothing sprayed out over the steps and floor at the bottom. The basket rolled for a moment, then came to a halt a few yards from the foot of the stairs.

Taking the lifeless body of Frau Hahn off his shoulder and standing her upright at the top of the stairs, he leaned her slightly forward, then let go.

He watched with fascination as the still-warm body crumpled, then gravity pulled it tumbling down the cellar steps with a series of sickening cracks and wet thumps, bringing it to rest on the cold cellar floor, the head twisted at an unnatural angle.

Malchus looked critically over the scene. Satisfied it looked like a tragic drunken accident, he took the bowl of food and scraped its contents into the bin, before placing the bowl carefully in the sink.

Back in the hall, he picked up the nearly empty bottle of *Jägermeister* and the half-full glass and moved them into the parlour, setting them on the faded lace cloth covering the wooden side-table next to Frau Hahn's saggy television armchair.

Returning upstairs, he swiftly washed the bloody star off his forehead and dressed, before packing his things away and meticulously tidying the room.

He took the sheets he had lain on and stuffed them into his bag, before finding a cloth in the adjoining kitchenette and dusting down the room's hard surfaces to remove any finger prints. He had not left any elsewhere in the house. It was a habit of his to be cautious.

Once he was satisfied he had removed all traces of his visit, he picked up his bag and the silver flight case, and padded down the stairs and along the main hall.

Clicking the front door quietly closed behind him, he slipped out of the house, and into the night.

# DAY THREE

———————— • ◆ • ————————

## 22

*National Museum of Iraq*
*Baghdad*
*The Republic of Iraq*

FIFTY MILES NORTH of Babylon, Ava walked through the Ishtar Gate.

Even though it was not the real one from ancient Babylon, it still made her smile. She pictured in her mind's eye the spectacular original with its glazed blue tiles studded with rows of golden animals—a design so beautiful it had drawn ancient travellers from the ends of the earth, lured by its renown as one of the wonders of the world.

Emerging from the shade of the arched gateway, she squinted at the heavy artillery damage to the museum compound's walls. The jagged pockmarks had weathered in the intervening ten years, but remained a clear reminder of the ferocity of the urban battle that had raged around the area.

She nodded to the sleepy security guard as she sauntered into the main building. Its long polished corridors were eerily empty—closed to the public since the war had decimated the museum's priceless holdings.

She opened her office door, and glanced around the familiar sight of her home-from-home.

It was a large high-ceilinged airy room—its polished floorboards strewn with faded oriental rugs. She had furnished it comfortably with a desk, a pair of map tables and filing cabinets, and a sofa area around a low wide coffee table inlaid with pearl and exotic woods.

The shelves running around its walls were lined with books, catalogues, pamphlets, folders, and piles of papers in English, French, Arabic, Hebrew, and a range of current and ancient regional languages and dialects. Arranged among them on the shelves were artefacts she had collected over the years—busts, figurines, carvings, terracotta oil lamps, and a variety of other small pieces.

Behind the desk was a small photograph of a woman in early 1900s clothing. She was one of Ava's inspirations: Gertrude Bell—archaeologist, explorer, diplomat, spy, architect of modern Iraq, and founder of the museum.

On the long wall, a large map of the world bristled with a rainbow of pins, photographs, and strands of coloured cotton showing where many of the museum's thousands of stolen artefacts were believed to be.

Ava had been very happy in the office for the last five years. It was as big as her entire apartment in Baghdad, and in many ways more comfortable.

After leaving MI6, she had first spent three years working for the British Museum—much of it conducting fieldwork in the Middle East. Then, with only the briefest period of notice, she had been seconded to the National Archaeological Museum in Amman for two years.

Altogether, it had been an adrenaline-filled transition from MI6 back into the real world.

She had revelled in again being part of the colourful chaos of the Middle East—bumping across the hot and dusty country to map, catalogue, photograph, and dig archaeological sites. And she had been delighted to be free of the issues that had led to her resignation from the Firm.

She had handed in her notice at MI6 three months after her father died. It was not just that she had been appalled at how badly the service had managed his death, although that was part of it—the whole experience had left her with a bad taste in her mouth.

But she had begun to have serious doubts, and started seeing things from a different perspective, feeling increasingly alienated from the government community she had been told many times would always be there for her.

She had tried to focus on her work, yet it started to throw up more problems than solutions.

She saw the growing number of reports over the winter of 2002 detailing the selective targeting of Iraqi military installations, along with the other combat activities of western covert forces already on the ground in Iraq since the summer.

She listened with increasing disbelief as the politicians talked publicly of peace, while she knew the ground war was already fully under way.

She helped write numerous reports setting out assessments of the potentially disastrous regional consequences of war. But somehow the Joint Intelligence Committee, which funnelled all such concerns to the Prime Minister, did not speak up loudly enough.

When, in March 2003, the world's media finally showed the futuristic sleek black F-117 Nighthawk stealth bombers dropping two-thousand-pound laser-guided bunker busters on Baghdad, she resigned, disillusioned—unable to recognize the organization she had once been so excited to join.

Shaking off the memories, she stepped into her office and walked over to the desk, collapsing onto the worn Turkish cushion strapped to the creaky wooden swivel chair beside it.

Powering up the laptop on her desk, she turned to the small pile of envelopes in front of her.

There was a letter from a laboratory with analysis results on a medieval textile, a request for cooperation in mapping some ancient mud brick foundations the coalition forces had uncovered while building a helipad, and the usual museum industry literature.

Only when she had finished going through the letters and looked up did she see the small brown package no bigger than a cigarette packet.

Picking it up, she was surprised by how heavy it was. It was also strange that it was addressed to her personally, but with no postmark, stamp, or any indication where it had come from.

Security was a constant priority, and she was not expecting a package. Putting it down, she punched the mailroom's extension into her desk phone.

The man who answered confirmed that an elderly gentleman had dropped the packet off earlier by hand. The mailroom security team had scanned it for explosives and other harmful agents, but finding nothing, had delivered it to her desk.

Ava turned the package over in her hands. It was not unusual for people to return looted artefacts to the museum anonymously—it saved embarrassing questions about how they came to have them.

But she was curious that the packet was addressed to her personally, as her name was not widely known outside the museum.

She slit open the brown paper carefully and peeled it off to reveal a blue-grey round-cornered ribbed steel box. It looked like a case for photographic equipment, only on a miniature scale.

Snapping the box open, she saw it was lined with plump deep red velvet.

But what caught her eyes immediately was the object the box and velvet were protecting.

As she realized what it was, her eyes widened and she gasped in surprise, instantly sure that what she was looking at had never belonged to the museum. If it had, it would have been one of its most outstanding exhibits.

She gazed at it, spellbound.

It was an oval of green jasper, about two inches long. On the front was the unmistakable portrait of Alexander the Great. On the back was the bizarre image of a man with a cockerel's head and feet made of curling snakes. He was holding a whip in an upraised hand, and defending himself with a shield. Around him were seven stars, and a scorpion nestled by his feet above the inscribed words:

Ιησουσ Χριστοσ

The writing was easy to identify—*koine* Greek, the language of the Church in the first few centuries.

The words were also not difficult to translate. But she could feel her heart beginning to race as she considered the implications of what they were doing on the object.

She read the words aloud: "Iesous Christos."

Jesus Christ.

Without consulting any books, she knew exactly what the object was, and when it dated from.

Her excitement mounting, she pulled a magnifying loupe out of the desk drawer and examined the amulet more closely.

The jasper was the right size and colour for the region. The writing was higgledy-piggledy, as she would have expected, and the individual letters were the correct shapes for the period.

She held it under her desk lamp, peering at it closely. Turning it carefully, there were no marks indicating it had been made with the help of machines, and it was appropriately worn for something of its age.

She sat back, her mind whirring.

If the amulet was what she thought it was—and she would stake her career on the fact it was—then she was holding one of only a few such objects ever found. She had only heard of them in the Vatican collections.

She turned the ancient green stone over in her hands again.

Despite the fact she touched ancient objects every day, the more extraordinary ones still sent a shiver of electricity jolting through her.

She did not need a second opinion on this one.

What she was holding was a direct connection back to the complex beliefs of the second and third centuries AD, when Middle-Eastern Christians still clung onto their old gods as well as their new one, and their evolving ideas of Christianity swirled in a cocktail of older magical beliefs.

The portrait of Alexander the Great was not an unusual image. He regularly featured on religious artefacts—widely worshipped for centuries as a sun god, the new Apollo.

But it was what was on the other side that made it so rare. Turning it over, she could not for the moment remember the name of the magical cockerel god with the snakes and scorpion. But he had been popular among Gnostic Christians, and to see him along with the words Jesus Christ made the amulet a piece with undoubted global historical significance.

She turned to the laptop beside her, and pulled up an internet search page to look up the strange god's name—but was distracted by a winking envelope at the bottom right of her screen indicating she had e-mail.

She clicked on the little yellow rectangle, and a message instantly popped up.

> I HOPE YOU LIKE THE AMULET? IT'S THIRD CENTURY,
> PROBABLY SYRIAN. THINK OF IT AS A FIRST GIFT TO THE
> MUSEUM. I TRUST YOU CAN FIND A PLACE FOR IT.
>     YOURS, E.S.

Stunned, she checked the time the e-mail had been sent.

One minute ago.

For the second time that morning she felt the wind knocked out of her sails.

*How on earth … ?*

She looked towards the window.

*Was she being watched?*

On her guard now, she wondered how the sender had got hold of her personal e-mail address. Old habits died hard, and she always kept her internet identity closely protected.

The sender's initials, E.S., meant nothing to her. Nor did his e-mail address, es@trample.net.

She quickly typed 'www.trample.net' into the address line on her browser.

It returned nothing—a cyber void. The e-mail address was a meaningless placeholder.

She still had friends who would do her a favour and trace the servers E.S. was bouncing through, but she instinctively knew it would be a pointless exercise. If E.S. was any good—and he or she did seem to be—the entire trail would have been thoroughly anonymized.

Her curiosity piqued, she quickly typed a reply.

DO I KNOW YOU?

In less than a minute, the envelope icon winked again.

She opened the e-mail.

> I HAVE OTHER ARTEFACTS I MAY LIKE TO DONATE FOR DISPLAY
> IN YOUR MUSEUM. I'LL BE AT THE ABBASID PALACE FOR THE
> NEXT HOUR ONLY.
>     YOURS, E.S.

E.S. was not lacking in confidence, she had to give him or her that. Baghdad was not a city in which people met up with strangers. Kidnappings were a daily reality. She was required to brief her staff regularly on the risks.

Thinking quickly, she typed a reply:

WHY WOULD I TRUST YOU?

An answer came back in under a minute.

I HAVE TRUSTED YOU WITH AN IMMENSELY VALUABLE
ARTEFACT. NOBODY KNOWS YOU HAVE IT. IF IT NEVER
APPEARED IN THE MUSEUM, NO ONE WOULD EVER KNOW. IF
I WANTED TO DO YOU HARM, THERE WOULD BE EASIER WAYS.
IF YOU'RE WORRIED ABOUT SAFETY, BRING SECURITY. I'LL BE
WEARING A LIGHT GREY SUII AND IVORY TIE.

YOURS, E.S.

Ava sat back.

*So, it was a man.*

They were not young men's clothes or colours, so it was quite possibly the old man who had dropped the package off.

It was not much to go on. But it was a start.

She looked down at the amulet again. It was exquisite. The museum had nothing like it.

As she felt its smooth surface, her mind buzzed with questions. Lost in thought, she turned her chair and stared at the photograph of Gertrude Bell.

Reaching a decision, she flicked off the computer and stood up. She put the amulet back in its steel case, and locked it in the safe behind her desk. Slipping her phone into a pocket, she left the office, pulling the door shut behind her.

On her way out, she stopped at the large desk in the echoing front hall and called round one of the pool cars.

She had already decided she would not take security. She knew how to look after herself, and could not afford to lose the time it would take to book a minder. She had no idea how heavy the traffic would be, and she did not want to miss the window to meet E.S.

She had a hunch the meeting was going to be very worth attending.

_____ ◆ _____

# 23

_Undisclosed location_

IDENTITY THEFT.

Malchus loved the whole idea. It was so easy.

He wondered why, in this day and age, anyone still did it the old-fashioned way—spending weeks setting up a fake identity with forged passports and complex alibis.

These days it was so much simpler—there were thousands of lives on the internet just there for the taking.

He had quickly found out that the old adage was correct—truth was indeed much stranger than fiction.

People's desire for publicity meant the internet warehoused all sorts of quirky and unexpected details about their otherwise anonymous lives. The result was a treasure-chest of off-the-peg identities—infinitely more colourful, textured, and credible than anything he could have invented.

He looked out of the window at the vast expanse of deep blue water stretching ahead of him in the valley below, ringed by the blues and greens of the spectacular low mountains all around.

It was the perfect spot. But then he always knew it would be, all those years ago when he had first come here. Since then, it had never disappointed.

_It was His. He had been here. The rooms were still filled with His presence._

Malchus walked through into the clean white Bauhaus-style study, and sat down at the taut white leather and metal desk.

After a few hours hunched over his laptop, he was done.

It was child's play.

It had not taken him long trawling the backwaters of cyberspace to find his man—Professor Erik Schottmüller of the University of Vienna.

Professor Schottmüller was ideal—a German-speaking specialist in the early-modern history of central Europe. He was exactly who Malchus needed to be. And there was more information on him than Malchus would ever need.

The professor's biography page on the university's website gave his full curriculum vitae, research interests, the courses he taught, the location of his office, a full list of all his published books and articles, and even the hours he was available to students.

His career had been impressive. He was evidently a busy and devoted scholar, whose published works demonstrated that he had sifted through many of the world's greatest libraries. Over the course of a solid career he had risen from junior teaching posts to the prestigious appointment six years ago as a professor at the oldest university in the German-speaking world.

As Malchus combed through the hundreds of hits on Professor Schottmüller, he slowly put together a picture of the distinguished academic's life—professional and personal.

A newspaper interview revealed he was not married and enjoyed spending time hiking in Austria's natural parks. Court papers relating to a class action against a failed holiday travel company provided his home address and an indication he liked classical Aegean holidays. And a prickly e-mail he once sent a colleague had been archived as part of a chain posted to a public newsgroup, showing he was tetchy and irascible.

Malchus assiduously collected all these small gobbets of information. They were gold dust.

Best of all, he noted with satisfaction that there were no photographs of the professor anywhere on the internet, and the university website wisely did not give his direct dial phone number or e-mail address.

Malchus printed out the professor's bio page, along with his full curriculum vitae and list of publications. He put them onto his scanner, and quickly turned them into .pdf files.

Next, he found a sharp good quality image of the University of Vienna's impressive medieval logo and dropped it into a new document which he swiftly built into a formal-looking piece of university stationery.

He added Professor Schottmüller's name and list of degrees, before printing it out on heavy white paper.

Examining it critically, he was pleased with the result. It looked grand and self-important—the way he knew continental academics liked it.

Finally, he registered the domain name www.univienna.ac.at. It was close enough to the real one, www.univie.ac.at, and would fool most people. He took a screenshot of the university's real homepage, and uploaded it to his fake site with a small banner across it announcing the site was undergoing temporary maintenance.

He then created a mailbox for the e-mail address e.schottmuller@univienna.ac.at, before adding it to the letterhead. It was not Schottmüller's real e-mail address, of course, but no one would compare it to the genuine one. Who had time for that?

Next, he set up a remote +431 Viennese telephone number and routed it to his virtual internet telephone, before adding the number to the letterhead as Schottmüller's private office number at the university.

Happy with his morning's work, he addressed a letter on Professor Schottmüller's new official stationery to the curator of the Prehistory and Europe Collection at the British Museum.

He wrote quickly, the words coming easily.

> Dear Sir,
>
> As part of my current research trip, I shall be in London tomorrow afternoon, and would very much like to be given private access to examine your unique collection of artefacts formerly belonging to Dr John Dee (1527–1608), chief mathematician and astrologer to Queen Elizabeth I. My ongoing research into sixteenth-century intellectual life in Prague has caused me to spend an increasing amount of time focusing on Dr Dee, who, as you know, was prominent in the city and at Emperor Rudolph II's court in the 1580s.
>
> I fervently hope you will be able to extend me this accommodation, as I shall only be in London for the day, before returning to my duties in Vienna.
>
> I attach my credentials.

Yours faithfully,
Professor Erik Schottmüller, DrPhil

Malchus printed the letter off, signed it with a fine-nibbed fountain pen, scanned it, and attached it along with the other .pdf files to an e-mail from the professor's new e-mail address.

Finally he addressed the e-mail to the curator of the Prehistory and Europe Collection at the British Museum, and pressed SEND.

He watched with satisfaction as a little bar on the screen quickly zipped from zero to a hundred per cent, showing the e-mail was now seconds away from hitting an inbox at the British Museum.

Malchus was at his desk several hours later when the call came through.

It was a polite lady from the British Museum. She confirmed to him that he was most welcome to visit, and she would put a study room at his disposal for the afternoon. She carefully explained the opening and closing times, and said she would e-mail him a map and a formal letter to show to security when he came to the Enlightenment Gallery in the East Wing. On arrival, he was to ask for her by name, Mrs Pamela Richards, and she would look after all his requirements during his visit.

He thanked her profusely and rather formally for her help, and apologized courteously for the short notice.

When the letter from the curator arrived in his inbox, he printed it off and slipped it into his soft brown leather satchel.

He was already packed, and within ten minutes he had left the house and was on his way to London.

---  ◆  ---

# 24

*Abbasid Palace*
*Baghdad*
*The Republic of Iraq*

As SHE STEPPED from the air-conditioned SUV outside the ancient palace, Ava asked the driver to come and find her if she was not back within the hour.

Passing through the grand main entrance, the honey-stoned twelfth-century building spread out geometrically around her. She headed for its large central courtyard, where two floors of intricately carved and high-arcaded passageways wrapped themselves around a central fountain.

She could see E.S. immediately, standing in the shade of the colonnade to her left.

He need not have said he would be wearing a grey suit and ivory tie. He was one of only a handful of people milling about the building—and he was noticeably the sole westerner.

She headed through the nearest archway into the gallery, and moved up the cool elaborately decorated stone corridor towards him. The arabesque detailing of the niches, walls, and ceiling was exquisite, but she had no time to stop and look.

She had not given E.S. a description of herself, yet he moved forward to greet her immediately.

"Dr Curzon, how good of you to come." He smiled affably, extending his hand. "No security? Then I have not underestimated you."

She shook his hand, looking at him closely.

He was probably in his late sixties, yet he still had a full head of silver hair, and a surprisingly firm handshake. She guessed he was around six foot two, and he carried the height with poise—there was no sign of even the slightest stoop.

He released her hand, and set off gently along the shady corridor. "Let's walk," he suggested. "I think more freely when I'm moving." His accent was old-fashioned and precise, Ava noticed—a relic of a fast-dying English aristocracy.

"How did you know to address the package to me?" Ava asked. It had been bothering her.

He shot her a friendly smile. "Come, come, Dr Curzon, we're both professionals." His tone was playful. Yet Ava noticed something else there, too—a reserve, protecting his privacy. It was not uncommon, in Ava's experience, among the wealthy.

"You haven't told me yours," Ava replied.

"Forgive me. How rude." He paused. "Edmund Saxby."

Old English name, Ava thought. It suited him.

"So you have an interest in early Christian magical artefacts?" Ava decided to keep her first questions general.

"Among other things," he replied nonchalantly. "But to be perfectly honest, the Abraxas amulet is not mine."

*Abraxas.*

She remembered it now. That was the name of the cockerel-headed god on the back of the amulet. She had been about to look it up when Saxby's e-mail had distracted her. Now it all came back. Abraxas was a strange magical man-animal figure much loved by the early Gnostic Christians. But as the pope and his army of bishops gained in power, they stamped out lingering pagan practices, and Abraxas and other magical deities like him were sidelined and forgotten.

"Not yours?" Ava asked, her curiosity piqued.

"I represent a collector," he explained. "A very private man. I conduct some of his more sensitive business affairs—on his behalf."

They paused to turn a corner of the gallery, which enclosed all four sides of the courtyard, allowing them to stroll around in a circuit under its elaborate coffered ceiling.

"How much does he want for it?" Ava asked, although even before he answered she knew she would have to give it back. There was no way the museum could afford it. "Nobody simply gives rare objects like that away."

"You're right that he's an unusual man." Saxby affirmed. "But I can assure you it's a gift—a humble one, with no strings attached. He genuinely wants to see it on public display. Most museums have so many artefacts they can only show a fraction of them. But your museum is low on exhibits, so he would like you to have it."

"I'm sorry to have to ask," Ava replied, "does he have the papers to prove its legal provenance?"

Saxby shook his head slightly. "I'm afraid not." Seeing Ava's raised eyebrows, he continued. "But I can assure you the amulet doesn't appear on any police or other list of stolen artefacts. It's been in the same private collection for many centuries. It belongs to him as surely as anything ever belongs to anyone."

"Which collection are we talking about?" She was intrigued. The world of private collections was a shadowy one, and all manner of treasures still lay in darkened vaults, as unknown to scholars as to the taxman.

"It's a type of private foundation," Saxby answered, "linked to my client's family."

Ava waited for him to continue, but it seemed he had said as much as he intended.

"We will, of course, have to research the amulet's ownership history," she explained, wanting to be clear about the museum's procedures. "But meanwhile please tell your principal it's a most generous and appreciated gift. Can the museum at least thank him in person? I'd very much like to."

Saxby shook his head. "I'm afraid that won't be possible either." He looked apologetic. "But I'll certainly convey your gratitude."

They carried on in silence for a few moments, walking around the shaded ambulatory. "Anyway," he continued, "as I mentioned, he has another artefact he wishes to donate."

Ava stopped. "You'll forgive me. But in my experience, if anything looks too good to be true, it usually is. So I can't help asking myself why someone wants to give my museum free antiquities."

Saxby smiled. "How very astute you are. As you rightly suspect, the next artefact will not be for free."

Ava nodded. That made more sense. "You must understand," she replied, "the museum is not a wealthy institution. If all the objects in your principal's collection are of a comparable quality to the amulet, then I doubt we can afford to purchase any of them."

"Have no concern for the cost," he shook his head dismissively. "He doesn't want money for it."

Ava inhaled deeply, not sure she quite liked the direction the conversation was taking. "Then I don't quite understand."

Saxby stopped walking, and turned to face her directly. "The additional artefact would be payment for a private service he is inviting you to render for him—personally, and discretely."

Ava was on her guard now. It would not be the first time someone had asked her to get involved in shady antiquities dealings. If that was what this was about, then it was going to be a very short conversation. "Go on. I'm listening," she replied.

Saxby set off walking down the corridor again, moving between the dappled shadows from the traceried architecture. He waited for a few moments before beginning. "He's very interested in a significant biblical artefact that was last seen in Kazakhstan." He paused, shooting a glance at her. "I believe you're familiar with it."

Ava stopped dead in her tracks, poleaxed—her mind whirring.

*How could he possibly know?*

She exhaled deeply.

*And he had known exactly the moment when she was opening the amulet in her office.*

She stared at him, her defences on full alert.

*What was going on?*

Her mind cycled through the possibilities.

*Who was he?*

Had Hunter sent him? If so, why the subterfuge? Was U.S. Central Command setting this up as a deniable operation? Or, more worryingly, was he connected to the militia? If so, she had made a bad decision in coming with no security.

"Listen." The friendliness in her voice was gone. "If our transatlantic colleagues in Qatar sent you, tell them to call me themselves—I'm not available for cloak-and-dagger work. And if you represent our Congolese friends, then I'm not remotely interested—I like some excitement now and then, but their way of doing business doesn't agree with me."

Saxby nodded distractedly, evidently weighing something up in his mind.

Reaching a decision, he put his hand into the inside pocket of his jacket, and took out a small stiff white envelope. He gave it to her. "Open it."

Ava hesitated, before eventually taking it.

Tearing the envelope open, she could see inside it a rectangle of shiny black metal about the size of a credit card. She pulled it out, mystified.

The metal card had a round hole in its centre, and she could see it had a wide circular band of slightly lighter-toned surface on one side. Embossed on both faces was a large golden symbol of the looped astrological sign for Leo.

"It's a CD." Saxby explained.

Ava turned it over. He was right. It was smaller than usual, and rectangular instead of round, but the lighter shading was clearly data, engraved into the metal.

He continued. "It's a key. Or should I say—an invitation."

"To what?" Ava asked hesitantly. "And who's doing the inviting?"

Having made his decision to share the disc with Ava, Saxby now seemed keen to talk. "The RMF militia from Congo no longer have the object we're talking about. It's passed into other hands—a Russian fixer by the name of Arkady Sergeyevich Yevchenko, and it's now the subject of an auction. Only twelve invitations have been sent—all to connoisseurs. You're holding one of them." He looked at her gravely. "Be careful. There are people who would kill for it."

Ava looked down at the metal card, dozens of questions spinning in her head. "Why doesn't your principal go himself, or send you?"

Saxby smiled apologetically. "I know nothing about ancient artefacts, Dr Curzon. I could easily be duped into buying a fake. My client, on the other hand, is very discerning, but also highly reclusive. He'd much rather send a real expert—like you."

"What makes him think I'd be interested?" Ava replied. "I work for the Baghdad Museum Project. I'm not freelance."

Saxby gave her another smile. "He was rather hoping you'd find it an irresistible opportunity."

They walked on in silence, turning the corners and completing a whole circuit before they spoke again. "So, Dr Curzon," he said quietly as they approached the central double-height arch where they had started, "I need an answer."

Ava's mind was a maelstrom.

Of course she wanted to get back on the trail of the Ark. She had barely thought of anything else since regaining consciousness on the boat in Astana.

But she did not want it on any terms, or at any cost.

She was not prepared to work for the wrong people.

At the same time, since General Hunter had told her what was in the file on her father, she had not been able to stop thinking about Malchus either. And from everything she had heard, if the Ark was in the market and up for grabs, then Malchus would not be far away.

"So, will you do it?" Saxby pressed her.

Ava breathed in deeply, trying to order her conflicting thoughts. "I'm not saying yes or no, but what's the budget for bidding?" she asked.

Saxby face remained impassive. "Exceptionally for this item—it's unlimited."

Ava could barely hear herself think over the sound of the blood pounding in her ears.

Saxby pursed his lips. "So what'll it be Dr Curzon? Will you go to the auction for us?"

Ava paused, then slowly nodded her head. "I wouldn't miss it for the world."

Saxby smiled. "Then we have an agreement. I've already made the necessary travel arrangements, just in case. The auction is tomorrow, at the Burj al-Arab hotel in Dubai. A suite has been booked in your name. The tickets and reservations will be e-mailed to you within the hour, along with a number you can call to report in afterwards."

He shook her firmly by the hand. "The invitation disc contains all the details you'll need. Good luck, Dr Curzon."

Ava leaned up against the cool ancient stone wall and watched Saxby cross the courtyard and leave through the main gateway.

She could feel her heart still hammering and perspiration breaking out down her back. She was not at all sure what she was letting herself in for. But she knew she would never have forgiven herself if she had said no.

Tucking the mini-disc into the back pocket of her jeans, she headed for the exit.

## 25

*National Museum of Iraq*
*Baghdad*
*The Republic of Iraq*

AVA NEEDED TO clear her head—to think about what she was getting herself into.

She headed from the Abbasid Palace down to the nearby banks of the river. She always found it helpful to look at the ancient slow-flowing waters of the mighty Tigris. There was something timeless about its permanence—connecting her directly to the ancient world she spent her days thinking about.

Even its name evoked exotic images in her mind.

She took a mental boat ride, from its source in the snowy peaks of eastern Turkey, down past Baghdad, and on for another three hundred and fifty miles south, until it joined with the equally powerful Euphrates, where the two rivers together pushed through the Shatt al-Arab waterway and out into the Arabian Gulf.

She had been down in the fertile marches around the Shatt al-Arab earlier in the year. It was a vitally important area for her ongoing research work.

Along with most other modern archaeologists, she believed it was the most likely site of the biblical Garden of Eden. She had even written an audio-guide for the British Museum on the reason why—explaining that key elements of the Genesis story all came from older Iraqi tales. The creation of the world from a formless void with darkness over the waters, six phases of creation, making man in God's image, a plant of immortality, a serpent that caused man to lose eternal life, a temptress, a loss of innocent nakedness, and even the Flood with its ark and rescued animals, were not originally written by the Hebrews in the Bible, but were borrowed directly from Iraqi creation traditions that were thousands of years older.

Ava found that many people were at first shocked by this, but it made more sense to them when she pointed out the Bible specifically stated that Abraham originally came from Ur—a city in southern Iraq by the lush fertile marches of the Shatt al-Arab, where it also explained that his ancestors 'worshipped other gods'.

Her musings on the Bible brought her back to the Ark of the Covenant—another ancient Hebrew story with modern resonances. One, she was now aware, that was taking centre stage again in the Middle East.

Once the driver had dropped her back at the museum, she flicked on the laptop in her office and slipped in the sleek black disc.

As she watched, the screen went inky black, and a fiery scrollwork border of iridescent lions and sphinxes appeared, marching around to form an edge. Once it was complete, neat silvery text started appearing inside the animal border—each sentence materializing then dissolving into the next with a shimmering liquid effect.

It read:

WELCOME, LEO.

TWELVE IS THE FIRST SUBLIME NUMBER.

TWELVE IS THE NUMBER OF GODS OF OLYMPUS,

LABOURS OF HERCULES, TRIBES OF ISRAEL,

SONS OF ODIN, SIGNS OF THE ZODIAC, DISCIPLES,

IMAMS, BATTLES OF ARTHUR, DAYS OF CHRISTMAS,

MONTHS OF THE YEAR,

AND HOURS OF THE DAY AND NIGHT.

NOW TWELVE WILL PARTICIPATE.

AN ARTEFACT OF INCOMPARABLE MYTH

AND MYSTIQUE.

VIEWING AT TWELVE NOON.

AUCTION AT TWELVE MIDNIGHT.

ENTRANCE BY THIS TICKET ONLY.

That was it. Nothing further.

There was no date or venue, but Saxby had given her all the details she needed.

She popped the disc out of the computer and put it safely in her pocket.

After printing out the travel documentation and the phone number for her to call afterwards, she gathered her things, grabbed the emergency overnight bag she always kept in her office, checked she had her passport, and left for the airport.

# DAY FOUR

— ♦ —

# 26

*British Museum*
*Bloomsbury*
*London WC1*
*England*
*The United Kingdom*

IT WAS DRIZZLING lightly as the paunchy academic made his way up the grey stone steps of the British Museum's south entrance.

High above the Ionic columns, monumental Grecian statues looked down on him and the other insignificant people beetling across the grand esplanade.

The academic nodded approvingly at the pagan Greek style of the building, thinking of all the adepts down the ages who had handled the powerful objects within. It was a fitting tribute to the great *Mouseion*, the Temple of the Muses in ancient Alexandria, after which all museums were named.

Carrying a clear collapsible umbrella and brown leather satchel, and dressed in a dark grey mac flapping around a green suit and light brown shoes, he looked every inch the continental intellectual. The impression was completed by a pair of round horn-rimmed glasses.

Arriving at the top of the stairs, he pushed through the portico's heavy wood and glass doors and into the neo-classical Weston Great Hall. It was teeming with visitors criss-crossing the floor, flitting between the galleries, concierge services, and shops.

Heading out of the hall, he moved into the iconic Great Court—the largest covered square in Europe, spanned by a breath-taking airy vault of triangular glass panels funnelling into a central point above the old reading room.

Turning right through the East Wing's grand doorway, he entered his destination—the Enlightenment Gallery.

His usually sea-green eyes were now brown, thanks to the cheap cosmetic contact lenses he had picked up at a chemist that morning, and the towel taped around his waist changed his normally athletic figure into the flabbier form of a man who sat in libraries all day.

On entering the gallery, he was immediately confronted by the vast Roman Piranesi vase. At nearly nine feet tall, its ancient Bacchic scenes dwarfed the visitors milling about it.

He looked around, noting that the book-lined walls and first-floor gallery had clearly changed little since they were built to house King George III's library in the early 1820s. It was, he knew, one of the oldest rooms in the museum.

But he was not here to mingle with the tourists and museum goers gawping at the exhibits from the Age of Enlightenment. He was in the gallery for a specific purpose—Case 20.

He could have found it in his sleep. Turning left, he headed towards the gently lit north end. Case 20 was on his right. It was a tall antique glazed wooden display cabinet labelled 'Religion and Ritual Magic—Mystery and Rites'.

He was aware most people thought of the Enlightenment as a rational age. But he knew better. For all its empiricism, it had remained heavily influenced by magic and alchemy—the forerunners of modern experimental science. There was a reason, he liked to remind himself, that Sir Isaac Newton, the greatest scientist of the time, had been described as not the first of the age of reason, but the last of the magicians.

Peering through the cabinet's glass, he could see small white labels explaining that the case housed, among other things, artefacts formerly belonging to Dr John Dee.

Malchus shivered with anticipation as he noted that Dee's possessions had been removed, leaving visible gaps filled only with small handwritten notices simply stating 'temporarily unavailable'.

Two greasy looking young men with rucksacks and cameras were complaining loudly to each other, annoyed by the removal of Dee's collection. Malchus looked at the gory T-shirt one of them was wearing advertising a death metal band. He snorted quietly to himself in derision—the name of the band, 'Legio Lucifero', was a basic schoolboy error of Latin grammar.

*Idiots.*

He made his way to the guard standing at the end of the ornate gallery, and handed him the letter from the curator, explaining that Mrs Pamela Richards was expecting him.

The guard asked him to wait, before returning a few minutes later accompanied by an attractive dark-haired lady in her early forties.

"Professor Schottmüller?" Pamela Richards greeted him, extending her hand and shaking his warmly. "Please follow me."

She cheerily led him through a labyrinth of corridors, before showing him into a small room with a chair, a simple Formica desk and black Anglepoise lamp, and a window covered by a thin beige roman blind.

On the desk were a number of objects, each nestling on plump grey cushions in a pair of large padded trays.

"Do you know much about our Dee Collection, Professor?" she asked, walking over to the table.

*A lot more than you do.* Malchus kept the thought to himself—he had a role to play.

"A little," he answered. "But it's all somewhat new to me. My work has mainly been on Renaissance humanism. I've known about Dr Dee for a long time, of course, but I have only recently had cause to concentrate on him."

"Well, handling objects a historical person used is always the best way to connect with that individual," she smiled, "to help get into their mind. We have over eight million artefacts here. I just wish more people could handle the collections. It makes history so much more immediate."

He nodded, feigning interest. *If only you knew.*

She handed him a folder. "I thought you might be interested in these. It's just a small collection of articles on Dr Dee, covering his time as astrologer and mathematician to Queen Mary then Queen Elizabeth I, his work on maps and the Gregorian calendar reform and, of course, his obsession with using shiny objects to communicate with angels."

*Scrying,* Malchus mentally rebuked her. *It's called scrying.*

She pointed to the objects on the desk. "Two of them are what he called his 'shew stones', as they showed him messages from angels."

She picked up a polished round flat black stone. "This is the most famous one. We just call it Dr Dee's mirror. It's actually volcanic obsidian glass from Mexico, and was brought back to Europe by conquistadores under Cortés, becoming one of Dr Dee's most treasured possessions. Apparently it was originally used by Aztec sorcerers in their sacrificial cults."

*Not sorcerers.* He was getting impatient. *Sacrificial priests of the great god Tezcatlipoca, or Smoking Mirror. And not just any sacrifices—human sacrifices. The mirror was a sacred channel.*

He gritted his teeth to stop himself saying anything. He just wanted her to leave so he could be alone with the objects.

He had waited so long for this moment.

"Aside from the shew stones, the collection also includes his seals." She indicated the three large wax discs on the trays.

Malchus nodded. "Are these all the ones you have?" He knew the answer perfectly well, but did not want to appear too knowledgeable.

"Yes, just the three I'm afraid," she shot him an apologetic glance. "But they're very good examples, in excellent condition considering their age. We're particularly proud of the biggest one, the *Sigillum Dei*, or Seal of God. It's Dee's version of an ancient magical device known from at least the 1200s." She pointed to a grey wax seal the size of a dinner plate, three fingers thick. It was covered in magical symbols, with a large pentagram in the centre.

"The seals all worked together," she explained to him. "Dr Dee put a small one under each leg of a special table." She pointed to the two smaller ageing grey seals. "We only have two of the four, unfortunately. Then he put the *Sigillum Dei* onto the surface of the table, and a shew stone on top of that. He called it his 'Table of Practice'—it helped him talk to angels, he believed."

*Not talk to angels.* Malchus was finding it increasingly hard to bite his tongue at her inane prattling. *Dee was not an idiot. It helped him summon the angelic energies.*

"Anyway," she concluded. "The details are all in here." She handed him the folder.

"Thank you," Malchus took the folder, nodding his appreciation.

"Well, you know what you're doing," she smiled at him as he set down his satchel and took out a notebook and pencil. "We do, of course, ask that you use the gloves we provide." She indicated a pair of white cotton gloves on the desk. "How long will you need?"

"Two-and-a-half, maybe three hours," he replied, anxious for her to leave so he could get started.

She made a quick call on the wall-mounted telephone by the door, and a few moments later a guard appeared. He wore the universal security guard's uniform—black trousers, white shirt, and black tie, but in addition the shirt had black epaulettes with a crown and the designation 'BM SECURITY'.

"Peter will sit in with you," she explained to Malchus, nodding towards the guard. "I do apologize for the intrusion, but it's museum policy, I'm afraid."

Malchus smiled absent-mindedly back at Mrs Richards. "Of course. I quite understand."

He had assumed he would be watched. He had chosen the afternoon specifically for this reason. The guard would no doubt be getting dozy soon.

"It's just that we have to be particularly careful with the Dee Collection. You probably heard that one of Dr Dee's shew stones was stolen from the Science Museum a few years ago."

"Yes—terrible." Malchus looked down at the floor.

"Fortunately they got it back, thank heavens. And we still have ours."

"Some people," Malchus muttered, shaking his head.

"Well, I'll leave you to it then," she concluded. "If you need anything at all, just call me on extension 43." She pointed to the wall-phone, and left the room.

The security guard nodded at Malchus, sat down on a chair just inside the door, and pulled out a book.

Alone with his thoughts at last, Malchus moved over to the desk, and turned his full attention to the trays.

―――――――――― ◆ ――――――――――

## 27

*British Museum*
*Bloomsbury*
*London WC1*
*England*
*The United Kingdom*

MALCHUS GAZED COVETOUSLY at the ancient objects resting in their cushioned trays in front of him—a gold disc, a small crystal ball, the three seals, and the Aztec mirror of Tezcatlipoca.

Making a selection, he tentatively stretched out a hand and picked up the golden disc.

It was about three inches in diameter, with a small hole punched through it, as if it had once been attached to a cord.

Etched onto its shiny surface was an image Malchus knew intimately—the diagram of the four castles from the Cracow vision of 1684. The design was formed of two concentric circles—one near the edge, and a smaller one just inside it. Within the band they created were four castles, one at each point of the compass. Inside the smaller circle, filling the disc, a wide equilateral cross radiated off a central motif, creating four quadrants, each filled with minute theurgic writing.

He wrapped his hand tightly around the occult talisman and closed his eyes. Breathing in deeply, he willed the cold metal to yield up some of the energies left by Dee and his séances.

*Yes.*

It felt good. There was still power in it. Dee's magic had been strong.

Placing it onto the velvet again, he turned to the seals.

His eyes fell first on the large *Sigillum Dei*.

Dee had left precise descriptions and exact drawings of the enormous seal, so Malchus had been able to give detailed specifications to the owner of the *Okkultismus* shop in Quedlinburg.

*Soon. Very soon.* He told himself.

Turning to the smaller seals, he examined them closely.

They were the second most important reason he was at the museum.

He placed them side by side, and exhaled with pleasure, drinking in the sight.

They were the same waxy grey colour as the *Sigillum Dei*, each the size of a saucer.

Unlike the *Sigillum Dei*, he had not found any drawings or descriptions of them, so it was crucial that he did not miss anything in what he was about to do.

Turning them over, he noted that one had extensive damage to the front face where a section had been smashed off, taking a portion of the image with it. But he was relieved to note the other was identical and fully intact, with only minimal chipping to one of its grimy edges.

He gazed at the occult stars and symbols on each of them, revelling in their power.

*Exquisite.*

Putting aside the broken seal, he concentrated on the undamaged one.

He took out a ruler and callipers and began measuring it exactly, making detailed notes in his book.

Then he pulled a slim silver digital camera from his pocket. It was a specialist model, with advanced macro options for detailed close up work.

Attaching the camera to a lightweight mini desktop tripod, he plugged in the shutter release cable, set a small aperture, disabled the flash, and began to take long exposure photographs, turning the seal carefully to ensure he got it from all angles with maximum depth of field.

He sensed the guard looking up at him occasionally, but he seemed unconcerned by Malchus photographing the objects.

He was careful not to miss anything.

Finishing the macro shots, he flicked the lens to a more normal image ratio and took a series of photos at regular magnification.

When he was done, he cycled through the pictures on the camera's display screen to make sure they had come out sharply. They all looked crystal clear—exactly what he needed. He would e-mail them directly to Quedlinburg when he got home.

Putting the camera, tripod, and cable back into his satchel, he knew that photographic images alone would not be enough. He would also need precise physical information about the depth and contours of the complex ridges and whorls of the image ornamenting the seal.

Keeping his back between the desk and the security guard behind him, he pulled a miniature perfume atomizer from his pocket, and sprayed a fine mist of fluid over the seal's grey surface.

Next, he took out of his satchel a shallow flat round tin a shade larger than the seal and half an inch deep. He gently eased off the lid to reveal a clear-coloured plastic putty.

Throwing a quick glance over his shoulder to check the guard was still engrossed in his book, he pulled the seal closer towards him, ensuring his back blocked the guard's view of what he was doing.

Taking the seal, he carefully placed it face down into the putty, pressing hard enough to register a clean impression.

As he lifted it gently, he was pleased to see it came away cleanly and that the silicone spray had prevented any of the putty from sticking to its ancient wax.

Placing the lid carefully back onto the tin, he slipped it unobtrusively back into his leather satchel.

*So far so good.*

With another surreptitious glance over his shoulder to the security guard, he pushed the tray with the seals aside, and turned his attention to the mirror of Tezcatlipoca.

*This was it.*

His heart beat faster.

*This is what he had been yearning for.*

It looked an unassuming object—a flat piece of shiny black glass cut into a circle no bigger than the span of his hand and no thicker than a finger. It had a small bulge the size of a large coin on one side with a hole bored through it to enable the mirror to be hung on a rope or chain. It was an odd object, he mused—most people would probably have thought it was a kitchen stand for a hot pan.

He sneered. People were so unobservant. They wandered blindly around their pointless lives, never seeing what lay right in front of their faces.

He stretched out a slightly trembling hand, and shuddered at the small electrical charge he felt as his fingers closed around the cold black glass.

He closed his eyes to savour its power.

*At last.*

He had waited so long, and now he could finally feel its energies coursing through him.

He saw before him the terrible and wondrous annual Aztec ceremony. A young man was dressed as the fearsome god Tezcatlipoca for a full year, honoured in the court, and ritually seduced again and again by four nubile ceremonial wives. At the year's end, he climbed the pyramid and was offered to the god of the smoking mirror—his chest cracked open and his steaming beating heart held aloft as a bloody living sacrifice before his flesh was eaten and his head hacked off, cleaned out, and displayed on the skull rack.

Malchus let the image fade, and moved forward in time, still gripping the mirror tightly.

Now he was in sixteenth-century Mortlake—a town just west of London. It was night-time, and he was inside an Elizabethan room—the smoky candles illuminating a low-ceilinged study with leaded casement windows. Sitting at the Table of Practice, he could see Dr Dee, with his high white ruff and black skull cap, his lined elderly face shining with perspiration as he pored over the mirror, reading in its smoky black surface the mysteries of the universe revealed by the angelic hosts.

Malchus pulled himself slowly out of the scene.

*Not yet.*

He opened his eyes and put the mirror down, careful to check his back was still blocking the security guard's view.

*Patience.*

He breathed deeply and counted to ten.

*Now.*

Reaching into his leather satchel, he pulled out a replica of the mirror and a small sealable watertight bag.

He looked at the two mirrors side by side, and felt an icy chill run through him.

They were identical.

No one would be able to tell them apart.

It had been simplicity itself to obtain the duplicate. He had given the elderly glass-cutter photographs of the original mirror—which were easy to find in books on Dee, and the old man had visited Case 20 in the Enlightenment Gallery numerous times to ensure he had exactly the right colour of volcanic obsidian and that he cut and polished it accurately. For a craftsman of his experience, it was child's play.

Checking that the guard was still reading his book, Malchus smoothly placed the reproduction mirror onto the padded tray in front of him, and slipped the real one into the sealable plastic bag.

*Simple.*

Standing up, he lifted his grey mac off the back of the chair where he had draped it. As he unfolded the material to put it on, he dropped the watertight bag into a large poacher's pocket he had specially ordered to be sewn into the mac's lining.

The guard looked up. "Finished, sir?"

Malchus shook his head, grimacing. "My back gives me pain. I need to stretch. I'll have a coffee in the excellent café across the road. I'll be back in twenty minutes."

"No problem, sir," the guard eyed the table, checking all five objects were still there. "Just knock on the door when you want to come in again."

Malchus nodded, and headed out into the corridor, the mirror nestled safely inside the folds of his mac.

He retraced his steps along the route Pamela Richards had brought him earlier. He had memorized it carefully, noting all the doors leading off it.

Slipping into the washroom he had spotted without needing to ask her, he made for one of the old shiny wooden-doored cubicles, pushing its brass handle, and locking himself in.

Once inside, he was relieved to see his research had been accurate. The plumbing in the non-public parts of the building had not been modernized, and the Victorian cubicle was like thousands of others in old English institutions up and down the country, exactly as he had expected it to be.

Above the large rectangular porcelain bowl and smooth mahogany seat, a short shiny brass pipe led up to a white porcelain cistern tank bolted to the wall with curled wrought-iron brackets.

He gently lifted the cistern's lid, wincing at the grating sound as it came free. Inside, the cistern was full of clear water, and a large red limestone-stained ball bobbed on a brass rod, operating the water flow system for refilling the tank.

As he had anticipated, there was plenty of room, and he slipped the sealed bag containing the mirror into the water, carefully wedging it into the side behind the refill pipe so it did not obstruct the ball and rod. When it was done, he replaced the lid.

Back in the public part of the museum, he made his way out of the building, across the esplanade filled with tourists taking photographs, and into the café. He chose a seat by the window, where he sat sipping the hot liquid, impatient to be done here and to start work back home.

When he had drained the last of the bitter coffee, he headed back into the museum, and up to the private study room.

The guard let him in without fuss. He hung his mac over the chair once more, and sat back at the table.

He had nothing more to do for the afternoon, so leafed through the folder of articles on Dr Dee that Pamela Richards had given to him.

There was nothing in them he did not know. It was the usual pointless academic dross—obsessively focusing on trivial biographical details, completely missing the importance of the ancient traditions Dee followed.

He despised people like Professor Schottmüller. What pathetic lives they led. What was the point of knowledge without power?

He checked his watch repeatedly and waited patiently until its hands showed it was half past five. He wanted to be sure the building would be emptying of back-room staff keen to get home for the day.

Feigning a stretch and a yawn, he stood up and turned to the security guard. "That's everything, thank you, Peter."

The guard stood up, and put his book on the seat before heading to Malchus's table. "You're welcome. I'll just have to check the objects, sir."

Malchus stiffened.

The guard walked over to the table and picked up a clipboard. He read off the items and checked they were in the trays. "Well, that all seems to be in order, sir."

Malchus put his coat on and turned to leave. He could not believe the museum's idiocy. How could they trust priceless objects to a security guard who probably would not have realized if he had swapped the mirror for one made of sugar pink plastic?

The guard held out his hand. "I'll just need to check your bag, sir."

Malchus froze. "Yes, of course," he answered robotically.

The guard took the leather satchel off the table, unzipped it, and peered inside. Malchus knew what he would find. A notepad and pencil. Ruler and callipers. Camera equipment. And the impression pad.

*Damn.*

He should have put the impression pad into the cistern too.

He felt in his pocket for the knife. He could not allow the guard to find the impression pad and create a scene. That would cause delays and questions. Doubtless they would soon find out he was not Professor Schottmüller.

He could not let that happen.

Inside his pocket, he flicked open the knife's blade and locked it, preparing to do what was necessary.

The guard zipped the bag up again and handed it to Malchus. "That's fine, sir."

Malchus breathed a sigh of relief. He would have no problem ending the guard's worthless life. But it would be messy, and the last thing he needed was unnecessary police involvement.

"Thank you again," Malchus replied with a formal nod, taking his hand out of his pocket, picking up the bag, and heading for the door.

Once in the corridor, he made straight for the washrooms, and the cubicle he had visited earlier.

There was no one in it, and he locked the solid wooden door, before again removing the cistern's heavy white porcelain lid.

His heart beat harder as he felt around in the water—but his fingers quickly found the bag and fished it out of the tank.

Pulling his prize from the wet bag, he slid it into his pocket, and flushed the plastic bag down the bowl.

After washing his hands, he stepped out into the hallway, and headed briskly for the door leading back into the public part of the museum.

Reaching it, he heard a familiar voice. "Professor Schottmüller?"

He turned.

It was Pamela Richards. She was running towards him.

With alarm flaring, he forced himself to breathe—slowly.

She reached him in seconds.

"I was just in the room checking the objects," she began breathlessly.

Malchus felt a rush of anger washing over him.

*Stupid interfering woman.*

He looked about quickly. There was no one else in the corridor, and he could see no security cameras.

He felt for the knife again. The blade was still locked open.

*No one was going to disrupt the work.*

"I went back to collect this," she continued. "And saw that … ."

Malchus looked down at the folder of academic articles on Dee she was carrying. As he did so, he scanned again for any other movement in the corridor.

There was none.

They were alone.

He tightened his grip on the knife.

"… you had been reading them." She paused. "I just wondered if you wanted to keep the folder? I had the articles copied from the master file for you—so you're welcome to take them with you."

She handed him the folder, smiling. "I know how much bother it can be to get copies of articles from some of the more obscure academic journals."

He exhaled deeply, and forced a smile. "Thank you, Mrs Richards. You've been most kind." He took the folder she was holding out. "You've helped me very much today. In fact, you've no idea how much."

"Our pleasure," she answered. "Thank you for visiting. Do, please, come again." With that, she turned and headed back down the corridor.

Malchus tucked the folder under his arm and left the museum quickly, joining the massed crowds of tourists spilling out onto the narrow streets of Bloomsbury.

In no time he was gone, lost in the London evening, along with one of the most famous black magic objects in history.

# DAY FIVE

———— · ◆ · ————

## 28

*Burj al-Arab Hotel*
*Dubai*
*The United Arab Emirates*
*The Arabian Gulf*

IT HAD BEEN late the previous night when Ava had arrived in Dubai. A car had been waiting for her at the airport, but she had been too exhausted to take up the driver's offer of a tour of the nocturnal city. Instead, he had merely whisked her speedily through the streets of skyscrapers and onto the hotel's private causeway, from where she had got her first close-up look at the iconic building shaped like a dhow's billowing sail.

On being ushered inside, she had been startled to find herself standing on a luxurious blue, cream, cerise, and apricot carpet in the unmistakable shape of the mystical *vesica piscis*. Looking up, she saw the same shape was echoed on the ceiling, where a vast curvaceous sculpture of a three-dimensional mandorla hung in amber and gold. She had never seen the ancient magical symbol in Arabia before, where anything redolent of the occult had long been banished.

Looking around, she had been equally amazed to find the hotel had no check-in desk.

Instead, a personal butler in white tie and tails had materialized, as if from nowhere. He had shown her to a seventeenth-floor suite, checked her in, and quietly made the necessary arrangements for her comfort. Before finishing, he had laid out a pile of complimentary brochures and vouchers for her.

Glancing briefly at them, she had immediately spotted a thick black envelope embossed with the same astrological symbol for Leo as on the mini-disc Saxby had given her.

When the butler had finally disappeared, she had torn open the envelope to find a stiff black card informing her in gold lettering that the midday previewing of the Ark would take place in the hotel's library.

Still tired from the ordeal in Kazakhstan, and now with more jetlag, she had crawled upstairs. Ignoring the thirteen different pillow options and the interchangeable mattress cassettes for optimum comfort, she had simply collapsed into the gargantuan bed, and fallen asleep immediately.

But now the bright Gulf light was streaming in from around the curtains, and she awoke feeling rested and refreshed.

Dressing quickly, she decided to explore.

Looking around her suite, it was quickly evident that she was not in a typical hotel—more a sheikh's palace. When Saxby had said a suite had been reserved for her, she had pictured a pleasant but ordinary hotel room with a small adjoining sitting area.

She could not have been more wrong.

Her 'room' was split over two floors. There was a chandeliered double-height hallway, sweeping marble staircase with gold and silver banisters, panoramic bedroom, sitting room, living-dining room, bar, kitchen, dressing room, and an intricately mosaicked bathroom that alone was bigger than most hotel rooms she had ever stayed in.

The whole suite was decked out in a riot of gold leaf, deep plush fabrics, exotic woods, and Carrara marble. Everything oozed opulence that even the most lavish spenders had probably only dreamt of. The butler had proudly informed her that the building was decorated in over fifteen thousand square feet of twenty-four carat gold leaf. As she flipped through the brochures on the table, she was amazed to learn there were seven suite options. More opulent ones came with their own private elevators, cinemas, and other refinements for the truly discerning visitor.

Leaving her room to stroll around the building, she had never imagined that places like this existed. It was as if she had stepped into an Arabian palace from a Walt Disney set of *The Thousand and One Nights*.

Every corner she turned opened onto a fountain strewn with rose petals or orange blossoms, or a set of doors in hammered gold leading to an incensed *majlis*.

Exploring further, she found the famous helipad-tennis-court jutting precariously off the twenty-eighth floor, and even discovered a basement seafood restaurant that she could only reach via a submarine simulator.

The assault on her senses was so sustained she soon started to feel numb.

It occurred to her that people had not built or lived so decadently since the Roman Empire hit its dizzy heights of excess.

The contrast with battle-scarred and rubble-filled Baghdad could not have been greater. They were both world-famous Middle-Eastern cities only eight hundred and fifty miles apart, but it may as well have been a light year.

Eventually, dazed by the extravagant and at times surreal surroundings, she headed back to her room, where she opened her bag and pulled out the books she had brought with her.

If she was going to identify and assess the Ark, then she needed to remind herself of a few things.

She padded over to the kitchen, poured herself a glass of juice, then settled down on the cushion-strewn sofa to reacquaint herself with some of the finer details of gold working in the late Bronze Age.

After a few moments, a thought occurred to her, and she got up to hunt through the suite's various drawers for the usual Bible left by the Gideons.

Then she remembered she was in Arabia.

Glancing up at the ceiling, she soon found the little *qiblah* arrow pointing the way to Mecca.

She telephoned the concierge instead, and within a few minutes her butler appeared with a pristine-looking Bible wrapped in a luxuriously thick embroidered cloth.

She flipped it open at the book of Exodus, turned to chapter twenty-five, and started reading:

> Have them make an ark of acacia wood … . Overlay it
> with pure gold, both inside and out, and make a gold
> moulding around it. Cast four gold rings for it and fas-
> ten them to its four feet, with two rings on one side

and two rings on the other. Then make poles of acacia wood and overlay them with gold. Insert the poles into the rings on the sides of the ark to carry it. The poles are to remain in the rings of this ark; they are not to be removed. … Make an atonement cover of pure gold … . And make two cherubim out of hammered gold at the ends of the cover. Make one cherub on one end and the second cherub on the other; make the cherubim of one piece with the cover, at the two ends. The cherubim are to have their wings spread upward, overshadowing the cover with them. The cherubim are to face each other, looking toward the cover. Place the cover on top of the ark and put in the ark the tablets of the covenant law that I will give you. There, above the cover between the two cherubim that are over the ark of the covenant law, I will meet with you and give you all my commands for the Israelites.

Further on, there was a description of more gold working, when the Hebrews had become bored waiting for Moses to come back down the mountain with instructions from their new God. So they made an idol to an old one on the orders of Aaron, Moses's brother. He commanded them:

"Take off the gold earrings that your wives, your sons and your daughters are wearing, and bring them to me." So all the people took off their earrings and brought them to Aaron. He took what they handed him and made it into an idol cast in the shape of a calf, fashioning it with a tool. Then they said, "These are your gods, Israel, who brought you up out of Egypt."

It was clear to Ava that what was being described in both cases was advanced metallurgy.

If the wooden core of the Ark was covered in gold, its makers would have required detailed knowledge of building and firing a crucible to melt the gold, and experience in beating the hot metal into even sheets.

Whichever way she looked at it, these were highly skilled tasks.

Moreover, casting the cherubs and the calf would have been even more technical—requiring additional knowledge of moulds, clay, wax, casting techniques, and firing temperatures.

Whoever had been engaged to undertake the work with such precious materials would have been highly experienced goldsmiths—or indeed whole workshops under master craftsmen.

But according to the book of Exodus, the Ark and other sacred golden objects for the Tabernacle tent were made in the desert by Bezalel of Judah and Aholiab of Dan, two men randomly chosen on the spot and 'filled with wisdom' to work the metal and wood and to cut and set the precious stones.

Was it possible, she wondered, that amateurs, living rough in the desert, could have gained the knowledge and equipment to create metal sculptures of that complexity?

She lived these problems every day.

Biblical archaeology was always controversial.

Some people accepted the early books of the Bible as unerring literal fact. Others saw them as an intricate collection of fireside tribal tales which the centuries had interwoven with myth and symbol until only trace elements of any real historical events remained.

She picked up a book on biblical archaeology she had taken from her bag, and re-read the now famous passage by the highly respected director of the Institute of Archaeology at Tel Aviv University. He had published it in 1999, and it was still causing waves today:

> This is what archaeologists have learned from their excavations in the Land of Israel: the Israelites were never in Egypt, did not wander in the desert, did not conquer the land in a military campaign and did not pass it on to the 12 tribes of Israel. Perhaps even harder to swallow is the fact that the united monarchy of David and Solomon, which is described by the Bible as a regional power, was at most a small tribal kingdom. And it will come as an unpleasant shock to many that the God of Israel, Jehovah, had a female consort and that the early Israelite religion adopted monotheism only in the waning period of the monarchy and not at Mount Sinai.

Ava knew only too well that he was by no means the only Israeli scholar to share that view. On the next page, another archaeology professor from the University of Tel Aviv was quoted describing Jerusalem in the period as 'a hill-country village'. And he had likened King David to a 'raggedy upstart akin to Pancho Villa', whose fighting men were 'five hundred people with sticks in their hands shouting and cursing and spitting'—not the great royal army of chariots described in the Bible.

The question of Yahweh's wife was even more controversial. She had spent a lot of time in Amman looking into it—and had found to her surprise there were a number of them.

There was the terrible Anat, a brutal war goddess. Ava's research had found there was solid evidence of Yahweh and Anat being worshipped together by biblical Hebrews as a warrior couple, even as far afield as Elephantine in southern Egypt.

Another of Yahweh's wives was Asherah, who was widely worshiped alongside Yahweh as Queen of Heaven from before the time of Moses, during the reign of Solomon, and right up to the Babylonian captivity. Ava had counted up the number of times Asherah was mentioned in the Bible, and it came to over seventy. The book of Exodus explicitly referred to the male prostitutes' quarters in Solomon's Temple where women wove the robes used for Asherah worship. And for a while there was even a sacred statue of Asherah in the Temple itself. Ava had taken part in archaeological digs in Israel whose finds of pottery inscribed 'to Yahweh and his Asherah' had confirmed Asherah's status beyond doubt.

Although this shocked many people, Ava regularly had to explain to them that modern historians and archaeologists had found a great deal of evidence that the Hebrews worshipped many gods up until the mid-500s BC, when they gave them up during their forced exile in Babylon. This was the true start of their monotheism, seven to eight hundred years after Moses and Mount Sinai.

The Bible confirmed this original polytheism in many places, with repeated commands for the Hebrews to stop worshiping gods such as Baal, Moloch, Tammuz, the sun god, and the moon god in the shape of a calf.

And worship of these other deities was not a fringe activity. Ava was well aware of the section in the book of Kings which stated explicitly that King Solomon worshipped many other gods besides Yahweh, and built them temples, too.

These differences between people's long-held beliefs and modern scholarship intruded into Ava's life every day. She had to make fine judgements, based on all the evidence.

Putting the books down, she looked out of the window at the azure water around her.

Would the Ark be a crude desert-made object consistent with the Bible account, or would it be something more sophisticated from an established workshop, as modern scholarship suggested?

If she was going to evaluate the physical Ark now, in the hotel's library, she would have to be ready to make some assumptions about what was possible, plausible, or probable in the period. And she would have to think laterally, focussing on the Bible descriptions and all available modern scholarship.

She looked at her watch. It was coming up to midday.

She got up off the sofa and grabbed the mini-disc. Shutting the suite's door firmly behind her, she headed up to the library where she hoped, with mounting excitement, a great many things would very soon become much clearer.

---

## 29

*Burj al-Arab Hotel*
*Dubai*
*The United Arab Emirates*
*The Arabian Gulf*

AVV HEADED STRAIGHT for the eighteenth floor.

Turning left out of the elaborately etched gold lift doors, she passed through a small antechamber with four Greek-inspired columns, entered the circular spa area, and headed up a deep red back staircase to its upper level.

Ahead of her, across a short hallway, she immediately spotted what she was looking for.

The two men standing outside a pair of heavy dark wooden double doors were the only clue she needed. As were the two restless chained Doberman Pinschers beside them—not a common sight in a culture where dogs were not welcomed.

The men were wearing the regulation dark suits with coiled-wire ear-pieces disappearing under their crisp white collars, and handguns tucked obtrusively into under-arm holsters. She knew firearms were illegal in Dubai—but like everywhere in the Middle East, as she had learnt over the years, influential people were afforded a certain leeway.

Arriving in front of them, she held up the mini-disc. Without a word of acknowledgement, they opened the doors wide enough for her to slip through.

She was in the library—a long snug rectangular room, stretching away from her. It gleamed with marble and polished wood—the sides broken up by glistening black columns. The whole effect was unmistakably ancient Egyptian, with blues and golds adorning the columns, walls, alcoves, and bright carpets, and delicate golden metal screens separating the sections with pharaonic lotus motifs.

At the far end she could see an adjoining billiards room, lifted straight from a London gentlemen's club, filled with deep armchairs and a full-size blue baize billiards table.

The library had obviously been chosen with security in mind. There were no windows in either room, and the only illumination came from carefully recessed lighting and tall sculptured lamps resting on wooden tables in the painted alcoves.

It would have been a tranquil enough scene, except for the pairs of security guards lining the walls every few yards. All were armed with Heckler & Koch MP5 submachine guns. Ava counted sixteen of them, forming a cordon around both rooms.

As she surveyed the scene, her eyes were pulled to the centre, where a space had been cleared, and a large shiny black plinth was set up.

But to her disappointment, there was nothing on it yet.

As the door closed behind her, she looked down at the heavy desk blocking her entry. On it, a sleek electronic disc reader was plugged into a large monitor whose flat-screen display was entirely black, aside from the outlines of the twelve signs of the zodiac arranged in a large circle.

The stocky guard standing behind the desk motioned for her to place her mini-disc in the reader. As she did, it whirred for a moment, then the sign for Leo on the screen changed from glowing dark red to bright green.

She noticed that nine of the other signs were also green, and looking around the room she counted the same number of men sitting reading books from the shelves lining the walls.

There was no conversation.

Taking her cue from the others, she headed over to one of the bookcases, and selected a large illustrated volume of Wilfred Thesiger's 1940s photographs of the people and landscapes of Arabia's Empty Quarter. Folding herself into an oversize upholstered chair, she opened the book, and waited.

--- • ◆ • ---

# 30

*Burj al-Arab Hotel*
*Dubai*
*The United Arab Emirates*
*The Arabian Gulf*

USTAIRS ON THE twentieth floor, in his larger-than-average suite, Arkady Sergeyevich Yevchenko was particularly pleased with life.

He had been furious when he heard Kimbaba and his men had been hit by a jack-knifing lorry. They had been on a flyover crossing the infamous Sheikh Zayed Road—the lethal ten-lane highway that ran like a treacherous artery through the city. The incident report, which Yevchenko had seen, noted that the vast decorated Indian lorry, despite being covered in protective bells, tassels, and multicoloured images of gods, cows, and elephants, had flipped, crushing Kimbaba's car like plywood, before spitting it out and sending it hurtling over the side of the flyover.

Kimbaba and his entourage had been killed instantly.

Until that moment, Yevchenko had been working on putting together a unique business deal for the militiaman.

A lucrative Iranian opportunity.

Yevchenko was perfectly suited to such work. According to his business card, he was a lawyer. But anyone who engaged his services soon found he was not an ordinary one. He did not do wills and divorces and neighbour disputes. He was specialized—brokering and bringing people together for deals that required unique contacts and maximum discretion. As a result, his clients were not ordinary either.

Iranian work was not his only expertise—but years flying in and out of Dubai meant it was definitely one of his major strengths.

When Kimbaba told him he had the Ark of the Covenant, had shown it to him, and intimated he wanted to sell it to Tehran in a game of cat-and-mouse with the United Nations, Yevchenko had dropped everything to focus on the deal. Normally he would take two-and-a-half per cent for brokering. But this was special. He could smell the money from the first meeting, and Kimbaba had not batted an eyelid when he told him he wanted ten.

However, when no one came forward to claim the Ark after Kimbaba's sudden and unexpected death, Yevchenko's anger and frustration turned to excitement as he suddenly saw the chance to convert ten per cent into a hundred. He had provided Kimbaba with the house and guards to look after the Ark while it was in Dubai. So now, with Kimbaba gone, the Ark was his. And no one was any the wiser.

If he had thought about it earlier, he might even have engineered Kimbaba's accident himself. But he had not. It had been sheer luck.

Now, as the Ark's undisputed owner, he was not interested in continuing with the Iranian plan. That had been personal and political. With Kimbaba gone, he was free to turn it into a straight cash deal to the highest bidder. Clean. The way he liked it. He did not even need to bother getting the Iranians interested. That was difficult business at the best of times. Lucrative, yes, but only because it attracted a premium for keeping under the radar of the U.S. federal agencies. As there was no need for all that any more, he could just monetize the Ark the good old-fashioned way.

After a day spent on conference calls and in meetings, he had a list of twelve people who would offer him serious money for the Ark. The rest was easy. He just needed to get them to Dubai, have them bid against each other in an auction, then fly out a day later with a lot of new zeros in his main offshore account in the Turks and Caicos Islands.

So far, it had gone perfectly. All that now remained was to pick up some of the security guards from the library, go to the hotel's strong room, collect the Ark, take it up to the library, and let the previewing begin.

He took a final sip of his coffee. Picking up his Audemars Piguet watch from the table, he slipped it over his wrist and under the cuff of his black silk shirt, and headed for the door.

He never got to it.

The door flew open, and seven men in black jumpsuits charged in.

Their stocky green-eyed leader was the first to reach Yevchenko. He caught him completely off guard, swinging his elbow viciously into the Russian's surprised face, simultaneously driving his kneecap hard into his groin. Yevchenko dropped to the floor, yelling in pain as the blood spurted from his splintered nose.

But he recovered fast, burying the toecap of his right shoe hard into his attacker's ankle. The green-eyed man was thrown off balance, stumbling backwards into a glass side-table, which cracked and smashed to the floor, along with the red crystal vase of orchids sitting on it.

Yevchenko tried to stand up, but the rest of the men were on him immediately, raining fists and boots down into the soft flesh of his face, abdomen, and groin.

Through the blows, Yevchenko became aware of a pair of hands holding him by his shirtfront, lifting his head and shoulders off the ground. He opened his swollen eyes to find himself staring into the cold expression of the man who had first attacked him.

"You know what I've come for." He had a German accent. Although he was speaking calmly, Yevchenko could see from his glistening eyes that he was high on a rush of endorphins from the violence.

"I don't know what you're talking about," Yevchenko growled. "You've got the wrong guy."

Still holding the Russian by the shirt, the stocky man dragged him upright. As he did so, other pairs of hands grabbed Yevchenko from behind, pinning his arms behind his back.

The leader let go and walked to the large polished wooden dining table covered with the lawyer's papers and mobile computing equipment. With one deft swipe, he sent it all crashing to the floor. Looking back over to his men, he nodded for them to lay Yevchenko on the table, then motioned for them to drag the table into the kitchen.

With so many pairs of hands holding him down, there was nothing Yevchenko could do to resist as the table was manoeuvred into his suite's large kitchen, angled so his feet were by the stove.

He watched, wide eyed, as his glossy leather shoes and cashmere socks were pulled off, and one of the men began sloshing cooking oil over his exposed feet. Meanwhile, the green-eyed man walked to the stove and turned on the gas rings.

"Wait—you've got the wrong guy ... ," Yevchenko whispered, terror rising in his voice.

———————— • ◆ • ————————

# 31

*Burj al-Arab Hotel*
*Dubai*
*The United Arab Emirates*
*The Arabian Gulf*

SOMETHING WAS CLEARLY wrong.

The two remaining buyers had arrived, and the flat screen zodiac display on the security desk now showed all twelve astrological signs glowing bright green.

Ava had lost count of the number of times she had checked her watch. It was 12:45 p.m., three-quarters of an hour after the preview was due to start, and there was still no sign of the Ark.

The other buyers were showing signs of impatience, with a number speaking anxiously into their mobile telephones.

Ava slipped the book she was reading back into the row of volumes behind her, and walked over to the security desk. "Is there a problem?" she asked the guard standing behind it, who was drumming his fingers quietly on the polished wooden surface.

He shook his head.

Sensing he had no more information than she did, Ava opened the heavy library doors. The two security guards and their Dobermans made no effort to stop her. Their orders clearly only covered who could enter the room.

Needing time to think, she headed back to the seventeenth floor, past the butler at his desk guarding access to the suites.

She walked down the left-hand aisle wrapping around the hotel's great atrium—the tallest in the world, she had read in one of the brochures—before stopping to look down over the balcony's wavy edge. The light was soft and almost dreamlike, and she felt much higher than seventeen floors up, until she realized, from looking at the honeycombed rainbow of differently coloured balconies beneath her, that every suite in the hotel was a duplex. She was therefore thirty-four floors up.

An idea forming, she headed for the bank of elevators. On arrival at the lower lobby and main entrance, she spotted a gold desk on either side of the atrium, each housed inside a giant gold shell. She knew from her arrival the previous night that they were not check-in desks. But even if they had been, she was aware that the staff behind them, like hotel staff the world over, would be under strict orders not to give out the type of information she wanted.

It had been one of the tests the Firm had set her class while going through MI6's intelligence officers' new entry course. She and her fellow trainees on the IONEC had been tasked to enter a hotel and find out the room number of a specified guest. On that occasion it had been a small hotel in Portsmouth, near the Firm's training centre, and Ava had succeeded by jamming the revolving front doors so the lone receptionist left the counter long enough for Ava to check the hotel's computer.

But this was a much more complicated proposition.

Thinking fast, she headed out of the main doors, and made straight for the unobtrusive white desk offering bellboy and valet parking services.

The midday sun was already hot, but a fine cooling spray was drifting off a large round fountain at the centre of the drop-off bay.

As she approached the desk, she caught the eye of an attendant in a long embroidered robe. Pulling out her wallet, she flashed her Baghdad museum identity card at him. It had an imposing looking crest, her photograph, and a few lines of Arabic writing. She was taking a gamble, praying the Filipino man could not read Arabic.

"UAE Federal Customs Authority," she said, holding the card up so the man could see it.

He straightened up instantly with a small glint of fear in his eyes, reminding Ava of the power of government officials in the Middle East.

Without pausing, she continued. "A Russian guest recently arrived with a very large and heavy flight case. It would have taken at least four people to carry it."

The attendant nodded. She could see from the vast number of suitcases being unloaded out of a recently arrived gas-guzzler that the hotel was used to dealing with travellers bringing back-breaking quantities of luggage. But she suspected the size and weight of the Ark must have been unusual—even for the kind of patron who visited the Burj al-Arab.

"Yes, ma'am," he nodded, speaking hurriedly, running his eye expertly down the list on his desk, flipping several pages backwards. "Mr Arkady Yevchenko, room 2004."

Ava passed him a twenty dirham note. She doubted officials from the Federal Customs Authority tipped hotel staff when on duty, but she figured he could probably use the money.

Heading back into the hotel, she made straight for the upper lobby and elevators, slipping into one just as it was closing.

Emerging on the twentieth floor, she could see straight ahead of her the butler at his circular desk guarding access to the floor's suites. She waved her room key at the smartly dressed duty butler, and strode past him along the balcony of even-numbered rooms.

She had learned long ago that confidence was everything.

Arriving at the heavy door, she realized she need not have bothered thinking up an excuse for ringing Yevchenko's bell.

The door was slightly ajar.

Taking a deep breath, she pushed it open, slipping quietly into the room.

It was chaos inside.

Furniture, lamps, and glassware lay smashed and scattered. There had evidently been a struggle—but the room had also been professionally ransacked. The fabric of the furniture had been slashed, the insides ripped out, and the contents of drawers and cupboards strewn all over the floor.

It was a war zone.

On high alert now, she listened intently, straining to hear if there was anyone still in the room.

She did not want any surprises—especially as she was unarmed.

She could hear nothing, and no one seemed to be around. From the faint lingering odour of cooking coming from the kitchen, she assumed

Yevchenko's butler had recently prepared him an early lunch before he left.

She looked through a sheaf of papers lying scattered on the floor, but it did not seem to contain anything of value—just travel arrangements and bills.

As she put them back, her eye was caught by a laptop which was hidden underneath the mess. She pressed the power button to boot it up, but froze instantly on hearing a faint sound coming from the kitchen.

Her heart beating faster, she stood up silently, and slowly edged closer to the kitchen doorway, stooping to pick up the heavy wooden leg of a smashed chair.

She held her breath, her back flat against the wall next to the open kitchen doorway.

She waited for several minutes, but there was no further sound.

As she began to relax, she heard it again, barely audible this time.

It was a low moan—little more than a sigh.

Steeling herself for a confrontation, she swung into the kitchen, the chair leg raised high.

Of all the things she was expecting to see, she was completely unprepared for the scene in front of her, and overwhelmed by the sudden urge to retch.

Putting a hand out to steady herself, she looked away, but the image was already burned into her mind.

The dining table had been dragged into the kitchen, and was pushed up close against the cooker. A man was lying on the table, with his feet and ankles stripped bare of shoes and socks, his lower legs resting on the cooker. The gas fire rings were now off, but they had clearly been on very recently.

She felt momentarily lightheaded as she looked at where his feet had once been. All that remained were blistered charred stumps.

Looking at the rest of the body, the man's black silk shirt had been ripped open, and she could clearly make out the telltale ragged puncture marks and bruises to his chest from repeated injections directly into his heart.

The injuries were among the worst she had ever seen.

Bending down, she picked up a handful of the discarded medical phials littering the floor, and saw what they were—ephedrine and epinephrine.

She knew exactly what that meant.

Both substances were used by combatants the world over as stimulants to keep their bodies functioning when they had pushed themselves too far. The combination was, in effect, a cocktail of amphetamines and adrenaline. Whoever had done this to Yevchenko had been pumping him full of the alkaloid and hormone to revive him repeatedly for interrogation each time he passed out from the agony of the torture.

Steeling herself, she stepped towards Yevchenko and put her ear directly over his mouth.

His breathing was feeble and shallow, only just audible.

Putting the chair leg down on the floor, she took his wrist and felt for a pulse—it was weak and erratic. She doubted he would last much longer.

"Who did this to you?" she asked him gently.

She could see the effort on his face as he tried to reply. But the only sound that came out was a low wet rasping noise.

Holding her ear over his mouth to make out any words, she heard the unmistakeable sound of the front door clicking shut.

Looking about rapidly, she reached down and silently picked up the heavy chair leg again, before tucking herself in behind the far side of the tallboy fridge, where she would be invisible to anyone entering the room.

As she held her breath, a man stalked into the kitchen and made straight for Yevchenko. He was average height, slim, with close-cropped dark hair, dressed in a black jumpsuit and combat boots.

Pulling a Walther PPK from a hip pocket, he advanced towards the table, and held the end of the small steel barrel to the bridge of Yevchenko's nose, directly between his eyes.

"Hello again, Arkady." He spoke with an east London accent. "I hope you've had some time to think about your priorities. We need to go now, so it's *do svidaniya, tovarishch.*"

Ava watched as the intruder slowly began to squeeze the trigger.

Moving with lightning speed, she leapt from behind the fridge and brought the finely turned but heavy column of wood down on the back of his head with all her force.

The intruder barely had time to register the blur of movement before the sickening crunching noise of wood on bone indicated it was all over. His finger relaxed on the trigger, and he sagged to the floor.

Bending down quickly, she went through his pockets. But they were empty apart from a spare clip of ammunition and a slim metal walkie-talkie.

There was nothing to identify him or the group he was with.

She looked back at the dying lawyer on the table. He was waxy and pale—his breathing now coming in shallow bursts.

She repeated her question. "Arkady, tell me—who did this to you?"

He did not respond. His bruised eyes were swollen and closed, and there was now a pale sheen of greenish sweat covering his face and chest.

She was running out of ideas, and time. She could see he would not last much longer.

Quickly filling a cup from the water cooler, she poured a few soothing dribbles onto his lips and put her ear close to his mouth again. "Arkady, tell me."

Visibly summoning all his remaining strength, she distinctly heard the word "insurance"—but it was otherwise lost in his rattling breathing.

"What insurance?" she asked, more urgently. "What do you mean, Arkady?"

But she knew from the long slow wheeze escaping from his blue lips that there was no point.

He was dead.

She looked down at the motionless body—anger rising.

The Ark was proving to be a dangerous companion.

First the murder of the monk at Aksum. Then Kimbaba's attempt on her and Ferguson's lives. And now the brutal murder of Yevchenko.

The usual dangers in archaeology were exposure to the elements, unclean water and, occasionally, mould or bacteria in long-sealed rooms, caves, or tombs. But so far the injuries surrounding the Ark were all very manmade, and the body count was mounting.

She turned with a start as the intruder's walkie-talkie on the floor crackled into life. Against a whine of background engine noise, she could hear the command, "Exfil in two minutes."

*So the rest of the team were still around.*

She did not have much time.

Thinking quickly, she knew they could not have gone far.

Just as importantly, she had to assume that if they were leaving, it was because they already had the Ark.

She forced herself to focus.

The noise on the walkie-talkie had been engine noise. She was sure of that. Very loud engine noise. But not a car—it was bigger. More like an aeroplane.

She struggled to think.

There was no airport nearby.

Then it hit her.

*Of course,*

She spurred herself into action.

Grabbing the walkie-talkie, she sprinted for the door, then out onto the twentieth floor.

The route she had taken earlier that morning to the helipad was complex, via the ballroom on the twenty-seventh floor.

She had no time for that now. She would have to go directly. And she could not afford to lose valuable seconds waiting for an elevator.

Throwing herself up the back stairs, she sprinted up to the twenty-eighth floor.

Her lungs were burning as she burst through the sliding doors at the top.

Exiting into the harsh sunlight, she found herself on a platform built out six hundred feet above the sea. There was a strong wind, and the view down to the blue water below caused her to sway for a moment, unnerved by the height of the sheer drop.

Squinting against the wind, she could see a set of white-painted metal steps leading up to the helipad about twenty yards away.

Resting on it was the source of the noise—the unmistakable shape of a Bell Huey helicopter, its rotors whining deafeningly. It was painted a dull green with no identifying markings, but was unambiguously military.

She counted two men in the chopper and four loading a large matt silver flight case into its cabin. All were dressed in black jumpsuits and boots identical to those worn by the man who had come back to execute Yevchenko.

As the men climbed aboard and the helicopter's side door slid shut, she sprinted for the steps.

Flinging herself up the stairs, she arrived on the circular platform just as the helicopter was lifting into the air.

Shielding herself from the rotor wash as the blades angrily sliced the air, she peered into the helicopter's windows, trying to catch a glimpse of the men's faces inside, hoping it would give a clue to their identity.

But the glass was heavily tinted, and she could see nothing except reflections of the iconic hotel.

She pressed the walkie-talkie to her ear and squeezed the transmit button.

"This is not over." she yelled into the metal microphone over the deafening roar. "I will find you."

There was a pause before the answer came. It was a slow mocking laugh.

"Who are you?" Ava shouted into the receiver.

When the reply came, it was in a cold precise voice. *"Legio mihi nomen est, quia multi sumus."* [7]

Despite the burning midday sun, Ava felt a chill, immediately recognizing the demonic biblical quotation, as well as the unmistakable tones of an east-German accent.

From everything she had learned, it could only be one person.

*Malchus.*

The handset went silent.

Boiling over with frustration, she flung the walkie-talkie to the floor, only just resisting the urge to kick it hard off the edge of the helipad.

Seething, she knew there was nothing she could do except watch as the anonymous chopper finished its vertical ascent and turned, heading out over the azure waters of the Gulf—with the Ark stowed safely on board.

---

7 "My name is Legion, for we are many."

—————— · ◆ · ——————

# 32

*Burj al-Arab Hotel*
*Dubai*
*The United Arab Emirates*
*The Arabian Gulf*


AVA HURRIED BACK to her suite.

She ignored the sculpture of tropical fruit wedges set with dramatic shards of white, dark, and milk chocolate on her dining table, and dialled the number Saxby had given her at their meeting in the Abbasid Palace.

He answered before the first ring had finished.

Adrenaline was still coursing through her system.

She took several deep breaths to slow herself down. "I'm afraid things didn't go to plan," she reported.

"They rarely do." His voice was calm.

"It was stolen," she continued, "by an assault team—almost certainly military or paramilitary. They killed Yevchenko, and lifted it off by helicopter." She paused, struggling to keep her frustration in check. "It's gone."

She could hear him exhale. "I see." There was disappointment in his voice. "Was it the genuine object?"

"I can't say," she admitted, barely able to suppress her anger. "It all happened before the preview."

There was a moment's silence. "Who knows about this?"

"Just me, I think," she answered. "I got closer to them than I really wanted to."

"You're okay though?" There was immediate concern in his voice.

"I'm fine," she replied truthfully. "But there's one fewer of them on the flight home."

"Dear God." Saxby was clearly horrified. "I can only apologize if I put you in danger."

"I can look after myself," she reassured him.

He breathed out audibly. "You realize this changes things?"

"Does it?" She was not quite sure what he meant.

"With regret," he replied, "I must cancel our arrangement. If I'd known I was placing you in danger, I'd never have got you involved. Please—accept my sincerest apologies. We'll conclude the matter with a donation to your museum that'll hopefully make this unpleasant incident worthwhile for you. And let's leave it at that."

"No, wait a minute," Ava interrupted. "This is no time to pull out."

Saxby's answer had not been at all what she wanted to hear.

She could hear Saxby sigh with resignation. "Dr Curzon, from what you've told me, this is no longer the relatively simple exercise I'd hoped it would be. I cannot have any harm to you on my conscience, so we'll end it here."

"Look," she was thinking quickly. "You could've engaged anyone for this. But you chose me. And you made the right decision. I'm more than qualified to see this through and recover the artefact for you."

"It's out of the question," he replied firmly. "The man I represent would be mortified if you were placed in any danger on his account."

Ava could feel the discussion slipping away from her. "There's another way to look at this," she countered, needing to turn the conversation around quickly. "The Ark now in transit somewhere over the Arabian Gulf may be genuine. And the men who took it are exactly the kind of people who should never have it. So whether it's real or fake, whatever one believes about its historical importance, someone has to get it back from them—for everyone's sake. And right now, I don't see anyone better placed than us."

There was a long pause at the other end of the line. "Do you know what you're asking?"

"I do." She was taking a gamble—but right now Saxby was her best option if she wanted to stay in the game.

"Would you truly be willing to see this through?" His tone was sombre.

"You'd be making the right decision," she replied, deadly serious. She was not at all sure who Saxby was, or what lay behind the Foundation he represented. She could follow the Ark on her own if she had to. But she had a strong feeling she would stand a better chance with the Foundation backing her. Along the way, she would make sure she found out who they really were. She could always cut her losses later if she did not like what she discovered.

"Very well," Saxby paused. "Leave it with me. Meanwhile, I suggest you head to London and wait there. I'll be in touch."

With that, the phone went dead.

Ava breathed out heavily. She was not good at waiting, but she had done as much as she could for now. She had to trust Saxby—and hope he came back with the answer she wanted.

Walking up to the bedroom, she looked out of the panoramic window, and for the first time took in the extraordinary sight of the brand new city—miraculously transformed in only a few decades from a washed-up pearl-diving hamlet in a forgotten corner of the Gulf, to the hi-tech business capital of the Middle East.

She could see the world's tallest building spiking up into the blue, dominating the ultra-modern skyline—a one-and-a-half-billion-dollar shimmering needle of triumphant engineering. If the original tower of Babel was the ziggurat temple in Babylon to Marduk, patron-god of the city, then the tower she was looking at was in the same tradition—a temple to Dubai's gods of ambition and conquest.

As much as she had always wanted to explore the desert metropolis, her number one priority now was to get out of the hotel before an unfortunate chambermaid discovered the carnage in Yevchenko's room.

Quickly throwing her belongings into her bag, she picked a wedge of dragon-fruit off the arrangement on the table. Taking a bite of the nutty seed-studded flesh, she closed the door of the suite behind her, and headed for the rank of air-conditioned taxis lined up outside the hotel.

---

$\cdot \blacklozenge \cdot$

---

## 33

*Undisclosed location*

THE OLD HOUSE lay isolated and screened off by dense trees.

It nestled on the side of the windswept hill, far from the other rural buildings scattered around the edge of the great freshwater lake.

The locals shunned the place.

For generations, they had taken the longer road around the hill to avoid passing close by it. Their rural Christianity was strong, and had sustained them for over a thousand years. They knew when something unhallowed was in their midst.

They rarely spoke of the house, save to whisper to their children that it was cursed—a place beyond God's law where unholy forces still walked.

All of them knew the rumours that were passed down from parent to child.

The old priest told it best.

A wealthy Englishman had come before the first war. He had shut himself away in its secluded rooms for month after month, poring over magical texts. He had no visitors, and lived as a recluse.

It was said he built a diabolical oratory lined with mirrors, in which he invoked infernal powers at dawn and dusk. After many months of vigils, abstinence, and study, it is said he succeeded in conjuring up the twelve kings and dukes of Hell.

Occasional visitors came to the village having heard of the house and its history. But the locals did not encourage their kind of tourism, and most were sent on their way, never having found the house.

A succession of non-locals had owned the house since the Englishman left. Mainly the owners kept to themselves, and the villagers could only speculate what went on there.

Tonight, there were lights on inside the house.

---

# 34

*Undisclosed location*

MALCHUS WAITED UNTIL it was almost totally dark before leaving the secluded house.

In the valley below, the great lake was still—a vast sheet of smoky black glass.

Its shores were dotted with trees, and a sizeable wood began just behind the house—dense with birch, fir, larch, and pine.

Despite the inky darkness, he headed straight for it.

He had been looking forward to this. But he had forced himself to wait until tonight. Until the time was right. He needed the moon to be waning—in its most destructive phase.

He liked working unobserved in the isolated woods, just as the Englishman had done nearly a hundred years earlier. It gave him a visceral sense of continuity.

Even back in Dresden, when he had first come across the life and work of the English adept, he knew that their destinies were somehow indissolubly connected.

They were both travellers on the same ancient path.

Ever since, he had sensed the magus's long-dead hand in things—as if he was somehow guiding him from afar.

He knew coincidences did not exist. So he did not believe it was an accident when the Englishman's isolated house came onto the market at a time when he had the means to acquire it.

He was certain it was part of the Plan

To his joy, he found the house not only brought him closer to his guide: it also turned out to be perfect for his work—large, spacious, and well away from prying eyes. He thought of it as his spiritual monastery, in the true meaning of the word—a place where he could be *monos*, alone.

He headed deeper into the woods. Although they were on his private land, there was no need for high fences or barriers to stop trespassers. He knew how the locals felt about the old house.

He was never disturbed.

As he strode along the dark path, the weak moonlight only filtered through occasionally, when a sufficient break in the canopy let a pale glow penetrate the foliage. But he did not need any light. He knew his way by heart. He had been there many times.

He was looking forward to his work tonight. He had prepared everything that afternoon. All he needed now was inside the leather bag slung over his shoulder.

As he penetrated further into the heart of the forest, he was aware of the deep silence. There were no animal sounds—just his firm footfalls on the path and the occasional dry snapping twig under his boots. He blended into the darkness and silence—a natural part of the wood's nocturnal malevolence.

Approaching the clearing, he could just make out the freshly cut logs he had carefully built into a pyramid, and the makeshift iron frame he had rigged over them, on which he had hung a large cooking pot. He could also see the grey box standing off to the side, almost black in the moonlight.

Everything was as he had left it.

Approaching the centre of the clearing, he put the leather bag down on the mossy ground, and bent low under the pot. Striking a match, he lit the layer of kindling beneath the log pyre.

Fanned by the night breeze, the fire took quickly. In no time, yellow tongues of flame were excitedly licking the bottom of the blackened pot.

He unbuckled the leather bag, and took out a bundle of soft cloth. Unwrapping it, he revealed the two large brass discs he had collected from the *Okkultismus* shop in Quedlinburg.

As he lay them in the cloth spread on the ground, the orangey-gold metal glinted in the flickering light from the fire. He had polished them meticulously, even swabbing them with neat alcohol. They had to be surgically clean—totally free of the cat's blood and gore he had drenched them in when blessing and dedicating them back in Quedlinburg.

Now the discs were properly prepared, he could finally use them for their intended purpose.

Shivering with anticipation, he ran his fingers over the large counter-sunk depression in each one, feeling the ridges and whorls.

Ready, he pressed the discs together, hollowed out sides facing inwards, and aligned the teeth and slots so they locked, fusing together to form a shallow sealed cylinder.

He placed it on its edge, and rotated it like a wheel, stopping when he saw the aperture in the join. It was the thickness of a child's finger, and opened into a small tunnel bored through to the hollow centre of the discs.

Returning to his bag, he took out a number of large grey blocks.

He knew he had surprised the owner of the candle factory when he arrived unannounced and demanded several kilos of pure grey wax. But the factory owner seemed happy for the cash. He had paid a good price, and from the man's pleased expression, he figured he could do with more customers like him. It must have been easier money than making and selling candles.

Malchus dropped the wax blocks into the cooking pot. They were unperfumed—he had insisted on that. As they began to melt, the lumpy viscous soup gave off its natural greasy odour.

Taking two small glass jars from his bag, he poured the thick dark liquid in each into the wax. As he did so, he intoned in a low voice. "*Benedicas haec dona, haec munera, haec sancta sacrificia illibata.*"[8]

For a moment the air filled with a strong sharp metallic smell, then it was gone.

Malchus stared at the pot until the blocks were melted and the hot wax was liquid. Then he knelt down by the discs and placed a small black ceramic funnel into the aperture.

Slipping on a heat-resistant glove, he began scooping the molten wax out of the steaming pot with a ceremonial silver cup, before pouring the hot liquid into the funnel.

---

8 "Bless these gifts, these offerings, these holy and unblemished sacrifices."

When the mould was full and the wax was running freely over the top of the funnel, he removed it, and wiped the waxy residue from around the aperture. Picking it up, he carried it over to the grey box, which was emitting a faint hum. As he lifted the lid, an icy blast of air escaped.

Placing the discs carefully inside the camping freezer, he checked the time. He figured an hour should do it—enough to harden the wax.

After stoking the fire under the pot, he bent down and opened his bag to retrieve another bundle of cloth—smaller this time.

Inside was a second set of brass discs, about half the size of the ones now in the freezer. They had also been made by the shop in Quedlinburg, but this time from the impression and photos he had taken of Dr Dee's undamaged smaller seal at the British Museum.

He had checked the accuracy of the discs the moment they had arrived from Quedlinburg.

Once again, the artisan had done a flawless job.

As with the larger mould, he had blessed and dedicated it with the blood and entrails of a sacrificial life. This time it had been a small dog he had caught sniffing around in the woods. Even if somebody missed it, he doubted they would come looking anywhere near his house.

*People were such hypocrites,* he mused, remembering the dog's last frantic convulsions as he sliced open its small throat.

He especially despised the sanctimonious followers of the ancient biblical texts, who cherry-picked from their own sacred writings—taking what suited them, and ignoring what they did not like.

Didn't their God specifically and repeatedly demand animal sacrifices in the Bible? Didn't he give explicit instructions on how to build the altars and slaughter the animals, which parts to eat and which to burn, and how to splash the animal's blood over the altars? Didn't he repeatedly say how pleasing he found the aroma of a living sacrifice's charring flesh?

Malchus's lip curled with derision. And how they fulminated at human sacrifices.

*Hypocrites again!*

It was all in their sacred book—that treasure-house of ancient wisdom. How Jephthah sacrificed his young daughter to Yahweh as a burnt offering, and how Josiah immolated the pagan priests on their own altars as a burnt offering to renew the covenant. And there was more—lots more, in that holy book of theirs that even their priests rarely read with honesty.

But he had.

And he had understood it all.

*People were weak. They had turned from the path that had been clearly shown to them.*

Malchus felt an overwhelming contempt for them—all those who failed to see, or chose to ignore, what was clear to anyone who read the texts.

When the hour was up, he opened the lid of the freezer, and took out the cold brass discs. Prizing them carefully apart with the blade of a wide knife, he lifted the top disc off to reveal a large wax seal nestling inside the mould.

He gazed down at the perfect recreation of Dr Dee's Elizabethan *Sigillum Dei*—his heart beating faster as he sensed the progress he was making in the Work.

He pulled the seal free and turned it over again and again in his hands, soaking up every intricate detail of the glyphs and symbols enciphered in the oldest language of all—the sacred script known only to initiates.

His eyes glowed with pleasure as he saw in the moonlight that the grey wax was shot through with pink streaks, stained by the blood he had added—taken from the dying cat and dog as their lives slowly bled out for him. He smiled to himself. That had not been part of Dr Dee's instructions, but then he had a few other improvements on Dr Dee's work in mind, too.

He looked carefully at the intricate designs on the waxy surface, all rendered faithfully on the new seal—the first *Sigillum Dei* to be cast in four hundred years.

*It was sublime.*

He would trim off the sprue tomorrow, and it would be indistinguishable from Dr Dee's all-powerful original.

Turning back to the smaller mould, he aligned the two halves and pressed them together. He needed to make four identical seals with it.

It would be a long night.

———— · ◆ · ————

# 35

*Gatwick Airport*
*Crawley*
*West Sussex RH6*
*England*
*The United Kingdom*

AVA LOOKED AROUND at London Gatwick airport's depressing immigration hall.

After Dubai airport's acres of gleaming marble, touching down at Gatwick felt like arriving in the third world. The Gulf emirate's terminal had offered a surplus of smiling staff, a forest of sparkly white columns, walls of flowing silver water, indoor palm trees stretching up to the impossibly high roofs, and gentle hints of incense and perfume.

By contrast, Gatwick featured a stretched skeleton staff, an overheated gloomy immigration hall, a stained dank threadbare carpet held together in places with black masking tape, polystyrene ceiling panels hanging off at angles or missing, and stale air smelling of unwashed bodies.

Ava was regularly amazed that first time visitors to the UK did not turn back within fifteen minutes of getting off the plane.

When she eventually reached the front of the queue, the bleary-eyed immigration official surveyed the assortment of Middle-Eastern stamps in her passport with suspicion, before slipping the photo page under the

176

winking red eye of the electronic scanner.

Glancing at his small screen, he paused, then looked up slowly. When he spoke, his tone was apologetic. "I'm sorry, Dr Curzon. I'm going to have to ask you to step to one side."

Before Ava had a chance to register her surprise, two uniformed Border Agency guards arrived at the booth and escorted her away.

As she walked between them, she could sense hundreds of judging eyes watching her from the snaking lines of tired passengers waiting their turn, and could feel her cheeks burning.

*What did Immigration want with her?*

Thoughts were tumbling around her mind as they marched her through a door marked 'PRIVATE' and into the non-public part of the building.

It opened into a shabby lino-floored corridor. As they reached the end, one of the men opened a door to reveal a grotty windowless room.

Two jaded-looking uniformed policemen were sitting at a bare table drinking tea from beige vending cups. They looked up as the door opened.

"Dr Curzon?" the one nearest the door asked, rising.

She nodded.

He was in his mid-forties, with a physique that suggested he had spent more time in recent years behind a desk than on the beat. "We've orders to take you to London, madam."

"Whose orders?" Ava asked, not at all happy at the turn of events.

"We're just the delivery men," he answered, pushing his chair out of the way. "Please follow us." He stepped out into the corridor and indicated for her to follow.

"Am I under arrest?" Ava asked. After all that had happened, she just wanted to get back home and collect her thoughts in peace.

"Not by us," he answered. "Our orders are to escort you into London." He pressed the button for a lift.

"Where?" she asked. It had been a long few days, and she was not in the mood to be given the run around.

He shook his head. "Just follow us, please. Someone wants to talk to you."

It was clear she was not going to get any more information. And there was little alternative to accompanying them. She would not get far if she made a run for it. The two Border Agency guards were still behind her.

Down in the neon-lit car park, she slid into the battered backseat of the fluorescent-striped police car.

She was pleased to see the two policemen climb into the front, leaving her space to be alone with her thoughts in the rear.

If she was honest, she was not surprised that someone in the UK was taking an interest in her. Even back at the first meeting at Camp as-Sayliyah in Qatar, she had known there was more going on than Hunter and Prince were telling her. Not because they were obviously concealing anything—but just in her experience, there always was. People rarely revealed the whole picture.

She knew her priority now was to find out what Malchus was up to. She had no proof, but assumed he had been behind the heist at the Burj al-Arab. At this stage she had no idea why he wanted the Ark, or what was so important he had to kill Yevchenko over it. But instinctively she knew that the voice she had heard over the walkie-talkie quoting the demon from the Bible could only have been Malchus.

Just as pressing, she needed to get to the bottom of who Saxby was fronting for. It was obviously someone wealthy and discrete, but it was not clear why he was staying in the shadows. Or why he was so interested in the Ark.

The journey to London passed in silence.

Turning it all over in her mind, she gazed out of the rain-spattered window at the night around her—watching as the pale moonlit fields and hedgerows gave way to the beginnings of London's sprawling suburbs, uniformly studded with colourful all-night kebab and chicken shops.

As the car drove towards the south bank of the Thames, she eventually saw the MI6 building ahead at Vauxhall Cross.

*So that was it.*

She felt her stomach turn.

She had not been back since she left nine years ago, and she was surprised to find the sight of the building immediately brought back the same feelings of uneasiness she had worked so hard in the intervening years to forget.

She looked up as it loomed over them out of the London night.

Affectionately known as 'Legoland', the Vauxhall Cross building was a bold statement by the British government that it possessed a world-class foreign spy service. Gone were the days of men in raincoats slipping in and out of Piccadilly offices rented in false names, or the bland and nondescript Century House in London's down-at-heel borough of Lambeth, where her father had spent much of his career.

Legoland was one of London's most easily identifiable buildings, dominating all around it.

With its bizarre multi-level design of bold ziggurats and turrets, all set off in a striking sand and turquoise colour scheme, it looked as if it had been clicked together using a giant child's set of vast plastic building blocks.

As the car pulled up outside the fortified building, the policeman in the front passenger seat got out and opened Ava's rear door.

The rain was tipping down now, leaving her a dreary view of the quasi-deserted bleak Victorian railway arches the other side of the road. She turned away from the depressing sight, which always reminded her of the seedy railway arch lockups in London gangster films.

As she walked around the car towards the bright modern lights of Legoland, right on cue DeVere appeared at the top of the steps, spotlit in the driving rain. He beamed at Ava, and headed down towards her.

"Ava! Good to see you again!" he yelled over the noise of the hammering water, ushering her under the protection of a large blue golf umbrella.

"This is a bit dramatic, isn't it?" Ava smiled, relieved it was DeVere. "You could've just phoned."

"Well," he answered, directing her up the stairs and towards security. "I thought we'd get you through customs and into town as quickly as possible. Police car is always faster than taxi, I find."

"I'm being serious, Peter," she answered. "Just call me if you want to talk next time. All this effort is really not necessary."

"Actually, it wasn't really my decision." He sounded apologetic as the security guard passed her a visitor's ID card with a four-digit number on it. "I'm afraid Uncle Sam is running this one. I just do what I'm told."

Ava glanced around the large designer atrium. Gentle lighting washed over it from overhead, making it feel more like the foyer of a boutique hotel than a government building.

As she approached the row of six Perspex security bubbles, she swiped the card and typed in the number. A small green light went on beside the bubble in front of her, and the clear door slid open. She stepped inside onto its pressure mat, and the door closed behind her with a hiss, allowing the machine to test the air around her for traces of firearms and explosives, and to record her weight on entering and exiting the building.

After a few seconds, the Perspex door in front slid open, allowing her into the main body of the building.

DeVere emerged from the bubble next to her, and steered her into one of the two massive elevator columns. He punched a number into the control panel, and the elevator began to ascend quietly.

Once on the fourth floor, DeVere led her down the corridor to the video suites.

"She's in here," he said in a confidential tone, swiping his ID pass into an unobtrusive metal security scanner outside one of the doors. "I think she's a bit upset about Dubai." He rolled his eyes in mock exasperation as the lock clicked, then pushed open the heavy wooden door to reveal a neat well-ordered room.

It was lit only by the soft green glow of a brass and glass banker's lamp on a low side table next to a deep chocolate-brown leather sofa and a pair of matching armchairs.

There was a two-yard-wide glass screen suspended from the ceiling by the far wall, and a very tall woman on the sofa was cycling through images on it with a slim silver remote control.

Ava recognized Anna Prince immediately.

"Did you find anything?" DeVere asked Prince, dropping down into one of the armchairs and glancing up at the sequence of photographs.

Prince looked up. She flicked off the screen and stared hard at Ava for a few moments, gauging her, then indicated for Ava to sit down opposite her.

When Ava was seated, Prince exhaled audibly. "Dr Curzon, I thought we had an understanding?" Her tone was not friendly.

Ava raised an eyebrow, indicating she did not follow.

Prince continued, unfazed. "You were *meant* to tell us if you heard anything further about the Ark."

Ava shot a glance at DeVere. He shrugged discretely, making it clear this was Prince's show.

"Yes. About that—" Ava began, before she was cut off by Prince, who was clearly in no mood for polite chat.

"This is a serious matter," Prince looked none too pleased. "We need to know we can trust you."

"Why? So you can support me, like you did in Kazakhstan?" Ava had no intention of being patronized by Prince. "I didn't feel a lot of transatlantic trust when you nearly got me killed in Astana."

Prince seemed not to have heard. "Well you should be thanking me now." She slapped a cardboard folder onto the coffee table between them, and opened it to reveal a pile of photos Ava quickly recognized as her entering Yevchenko's room in the Burj al-Arab hotel.

"You're in a *lot* of trouble, Dr Curzon," Prince continued. "Our friends in the UAE wanted to pull you at Dubai airport. It took a great deal of effort to keep you out of an Emirati police station."

"What on earth do they want me for?" Ava did her best to sound surprised and outraged.

Prince spread the photos out, revealing one of Yevchenko's corpse on the table, and another of his executioner sprawled on the kitchen floor.

"Hotel CCTV shows you were the second last person to enter the room of a Mr Arkady Sergeyevich Yevchenko, room 2004. He's the dead one on the table. The last person to enter the room—he's the one on the floor—obviously never left it either." Prince glared at Ava. "Although he would've found it hard, as you can see—the back of his skull has been pulped." Prince paused. "The curious thing is that the hotel's CCTV record shows you were in the room with the pair of them. Yet you're the only one who left it alive."

Ava could feel Prince eyeing her carefully for any reaction. "So understandably," she continued. "The Dubai authorities are keen to speak with you."

Ava was unimpressed. "And presumably the CCTV also shows a group of men in black jumpsuits going into Yevchenko's hotel room some time earlier? Did it occur to anyone they may have something to do with it?"

Prince made no comment.

"Why are they so concerned about the death of one of Yevchenko's murderers?" Ava countered. "I would've thought they ought to be much more worried how a fee-paying guest was tortured and executed under their noses in one of the hotel's suites, before the hit-team made a getaway from the hotel's helipad? I'm no travel agent, but that has to be bad publicity for a seven-star hotel welcoming a string of wealthy people, many of whom have made a few enemies on their road to riches."

Prince nodded. "But they still want to talk to you."

"Of course they do!" Ava exploded, exasperated. "An armed hit-squad doesn't just land on the Burj al-Arab's helipad, torture a guest to death in broad daylight, then lift off into the blue." She stared at Prince. "Do you know how much organization and collaboration that stunt will have taken? They'll have had to file flight plans in and out of Dubai airspace, a range of permissions and approvals to use the hotel's helipad, and a host of other bureaucratic forms. They are, without doubt, being helped by people on the ground, including officials. So it's a lot easier for everyone concerned to avoid the awkward questions by moving the focus onto me—even though some would say I did them a favour."

Prince drummed her fingers on the table. When she spoke her voice was quieter, although barely concealing her anger. "You don't get it, do you? We all understand you have many talents, but you told us you would let us know if you heard any more about the Ark. Yet now we find you've been busy in Dubai on the trail of the Ark behind our backs."

"Who said anything about the Ark?" Ava ventured.

Prince looked incandescent. "This all works on give and take. We've just pulled you out of pretty hot water. And it took a lot of doing. I don't mind saying there were a number of senior people on our side who wanted to know why we should make the effort to help you, given your disregard for our agreement." She stared at Ava. "I've gone out on a limb for you here. There are people on my team a lot angrier than I am. I hope you can appreciate that."

Ava did not respond.

"Good. So we understand each other?" Prince looked expectantly at Ava.

"Well, I understand you want something more from me," Ava returned her gaze. "Or you wouldn't have gone to all this trouble."

Prince pursed her lips. For a moment she looked as if she was going to lose control, but then she held back.

Smiling briefly, she got up and walked over to the sideboard. She poured a cup of hot coffee from a heavy black thermos, and put it down beside Ava.

Flicking the large glass screen back on, she began to scroll through a number of images. "Look at these."

Ava watched as pictures flashed across the glass panel. They were all of men, dressed in what looked like pale grey Nazi uniforms.

Looking more closely, she could see their dark green collar flashes had the three lions *passant* of England, and a small ribbon wrapped around the tunic's second button was the red, white, and blue of the British flag.

As her eye moved down the pictures, she noted the cuffs of the left sleeves were encircled with a white-bordered black tape embroidered in bold white Gothic lettering with the words: 'BRITISCHES FREIKORPS'.

She did a double take. But she was not mistaken.

More extraordinary still, above the cuff-tape was a black-bordered shield of the British Union Jack—or Union Flag, as some of the more pedantic people in the Firm used to remind unwary newcomers.

She frowned.

Just as oddly, on the right sleeve she could see a band with an upside down silver-edged black pentagram. Underneath it, she read the single embroidered word: 'THELEMA'.

Ava was momentarily lost. These were Second World War German military uniforms, but it was quite obvious the photos were not sixty-eight years old. In one, a man pressed a slim black mobile phone to his ear. In another, a group of them were huddled around a sleek flat-screen computer monitor.

"Who are they?" Ava asked DeVere, baffled.

"I hate Nazis," DeVere muttered. "Especially ones like these."

"Nazis?" Ava repeated. "Does anyone still take all that seriously?"

"Very much so," Prince cut in.

"So who are they?" Ava asked.

"In the Second World War, the ss didn't just take the cream of German society, those with ancestry going back to 1750 on both sides of the family. They also had the clever idea of recruiting abroad, from among non-German populations." Prince pointed to the lettering on their left sleeves. "They called these foreign units the *Freikorps*, or Free Corps. What you are looking at is the uniform of the ss British Free Corps."

Ava was having trouble taking this in. "Excuse me?"

"You heard," Prince answered. "British units of the Nazi *Waffen-ss*."

Ava was stunned. "Did British men actually fight, for the enemy?"

Prince nodded. "But not against the British. That was part of the deal. Most of them belonged to the British Union of Fascists, and joined the ss *Freikorps* to fight the common enemy—the communists on the eastern front."

DeVere shook his head in bewilderment. "But wasn't the ss supposed to be the cream of Germany's Aryan supermen? *Blut und Boden*—Blood and Soil, and all that? Why did they let foreigners in?"

"For propaganda," Prince replied. "For instance, the British *Freikorps* soldiers were regularly sent around the prisoner-of-war camps, telling British prisoners how wonderful life was in the ss. Some of them even tried to convert the hardened British escapees of Oflag IV-C Colditz—but they didn't get far with that particular audience."

"These photos are recent." Ava observed, still reeling from the idea there had been British soldiers in the SS. "Are you telling me the *Freikorps* still exist?"

Prince stood and poured herself a coffee. "Yes and no. Many of the British *Freikorps* men were hanged for treason at the end of the war, and the SS was officially disbanded, although there have always been strong indications of continued activity in South America and elsewhere via the ODESSA. As far as we know, any stragglers of the original *Freikorps* were never organized enough to be dangerous. But these men today," she paused, staring at the screen, "these men are quite different."

"Look at the right sleeve, Dr Curzon," Prince zoomed in on the photo as she spoke. "The pentagram, and word 'THELEMA' are new. It indicates their creative spin on the SS ideal—their own special brand of nastiness."

Prince stopped cycling through the photographs, and left the screen displaying a close-up image of a bald fleshy-faced stocky man wearing the same British *Freikorps* uniform as the others.

Ava recognized the cold sea-green eyes and hairless face immediately. *Malchus.*

"I hadn't noticed that before." It was DeVere. He sounded intrigued. "He's wearing the Knight's Cross with oak leaves, swords, and diamonds."

"What's does that signify?" Ava asked. "And how on earth do you know about it?" She grinned at him.

"Oh—you pick these things up at school in England," he answered lazily, "while gluing together models of tanks and aeroplanes. It's a grand version of the Iron Cross—for very distinguished soldiers."

"Can you zoom in on it?" Ava asked.

As Prince homed in on the medal and blew up the resolution, they could all see what Ava had spotted. In place of the usual silver embossed swastika at the centre of the medal, there was an upside down pentagram.

"His name is Malchus," DeVere said. "He's a former officer of the East German Stasi."

DeVere clearly did not know that Hunter had told her about Malchus. She let him continue.

"He runs the Thelema order of British neo-Nazis. He's not British, but he claims some Scottish blood, and that's good enough for them. They value him mainly because he's a nasty piece of work, is intensely into the occult, and has well-honed organizational skills from his long years with the Stasi. He's the perfect leader for this organization."

"So what are the pentagrams all about?" Ava asked, aware the five-pointed star was a universal symbol of the occult, but not quite seeing its relevance for a modern-day group of neo-Nazis.

"It's hard to believe," DeVere answered, "but Himmler and his senior ss officers were fascinated by the occult. Their interest is extremely well documented. Himmler even had a medieval castle in Germany remodelled so his 'knights' of the ss could re-enact twisted tales mixing Arthurian legends with blood-and-iron Nazi *völkisch* racism. Himmler was apparently obsessed by it all—the darker the better."

"Which just leaves the reference to 'Thelema' on their sleeves," Ava replied. "I know the Greek word means 'the will', but what's the significance here?"

There was a long pause.

"To be honest, we don't know." Prince answered quietly. "This organization stays firmly off the radar. There are still a lot of blanks." She put down the remote control. "Frankly, we're lucky to have these images."

There was an even longer pause. Ava could feel the tension in the room mounting.

She decided to break it. "Let me guess," she ventured. "It's something you want me to help with?"

The tall American nodded slowly. "We believe Malchus is after the Ark. In fact, we suspect he was the one who arranged for the RMF militia to steal it in the first place, before they double-crossed him and tried to use it for themselves."

"And you figure I'll help you because … ." Ava left the sentence hanging.

"We know you're also after the Ark, Dr Curzon," Prince replied curtly. "And we frankly have no reason to believe you're about to stop any time soon. So why don't we just help each other?"

"The Ark is not my main concern," Ava replied truthfully.

*I want Malchus*, she nearly added, but bit her tongue.

"Dr Curzon." Prince was losing her patience, and making no attempt to hide it now. "We know you went to Dubai to bid on the Ark. And we know you walked into a messy scene out there. You're fortunate to be alive. And frankly you're damned lucky not to be cooking in a tin-roofed prison in the Dubai desert right now. It seems to me you could do with some help."

Ava exhaled, thinking quickly. "Okay. Just tell me this. Was it … ," she pointed to the image of the man on the screen "Malchus, who stole the Ark from Dubai? Was it his men who killed Yevchenko?"

Prince's eyes narrowed, examining Ava minutely. After a pause, she answered slowly. "Again we don't know. We were hoping you could help us with—"

DeVere cut in. "It would be a big help, Ava. We need to stop this man. But we stand no chance of doing that unless we understand what he wants. You know more about the Ark than anyone, and it seems you're one of the few people to have taken on one of the Thelema and won." He spread his hands in a gesture of openness. "There's no one we can turn to with a better curriculum vitae for this job than you."

Ava finished the coffee and put the cup down, lost in thought.

"Don't decide now," DeVere concluded. "Sleep on it. We'll be in touch tomorrow."

Prince got up. Ava was struck again by how tall she was, although there was nothing clumsy about her. Prince nodded to DeVere. "We're done here for tonight."

Needing no further prompting, DeVere headed for the door. "I'll show you out, Ava—follow me."

"Goodnight Dr Curzon," Prince called over her shoulder, turning back to the folder of photographs on the coffee table. "Think about it. I hope you'll see it as a good opportunity for us all to get what we want."

*What I want is personal*, Ava thought. *And I don't need your or anyone else's help.*

Ava nodded goodnight to Prince, and slipped out of the door with DeVere.

"Get security to call you a cab," he advised her as they headed down in the elevator. "See you tomorrow. Oh, and Ava—do try and keep out of trouble."

As he walked out of the elevator, she waved goodbye, and he was gone.

She picked up her luggage from security, and ordered a cab.

When it arrived, she climbed in, pulled the heavy black door shut, and looked out of the window at the rainy London evening.

*I really don't miss all this*, she thought, watching the drenched figures scurrying under their umbrellas.

As the driver turned on the meter, she began to run back over the meeting in her head. She was pleased by the way it had gone—she had learnt a great deal.

Startled by a sudden knocking at the window on the far side of the car, she spun round to see a wet face peering in at her.

It took a second before she recognized it.

*Prince.*

"Mind if I get in?" the American asked, opening the door and climbing into the taxi without waiting for Ava's reply.

Ava's heart sank. This was unlikely to be a good development.

"Be my guest," Ava answered with resignation. The jetlag was kicking in, and she had no desire to go another round with Prince right now.

"Look, we got off on the wrong foot," Prince began. "I thought maybe we could have a less formal chat."

Ava saw little point in protesting. They were stuck in a taxi together, although she was not in the mood for small talk.

"You're a long way from home," Prince began. "What's really going on?"

"I could ask you exactly the same question." Ava countered.

"London's my second home," Prince answered. "But you're right. This business of the Ark has got everyone back in Washington and Virginia really running around. We're very concerned about the military implications for Middle-Eastern security. I've been sent here to look after the European side of the operation."

"How do DeVere and the Firm fit in?" Ava asked carefully.

"Oh, you know, the special relationship, and all that," Prince answered. "But how come you left the Firm? Your file suggests you were a high flyer."

"I don't know about that." Ava shrugged. "I suppose I stopped seeing the world the way they did. I no longer felt at home."

"You developed a conscience?" Prince asked.

"Yes, but not the way you think," Ava replied. "I didn't suddenly start worrying about watching people, or listening to their calls, or putting agents into dangerous situations. I long ago realized that someone has to do all those things if the world is going to be kept safe."

"Then what?" Prince asked.

"After 9/11, I thought people like me, who knew the Middle East well, could help our governments distinguish friend from foe." She paused, biting her thumbnail absentmindedly. "But I underestimated people's desire for simple solutions."

She looked out of the window as the black taxi swept past the illuminated Houses of Parliament. Once upon a time she had believed the grand gothic gables and arches housed one of the most enviable institutions in the world—a bastion of experience and principled thinking, relatively free from corruption or self-interest.

But not any longer.

"No one really listened," she continued. "When we invaded Iraq in 2003, hundreds of people in government, intelligence, the military, and think-tanks, knew definitively there was no link with al-Qa'eda and there were no weapons of mass destruction. Many of us made our views plain." She paused, staring into the black night. "After a while, I realized I was not helping the government to see the problems. I *was* the problem. As long as people like me worked for the government, we gave the politicians a veneer of respectability in their Middle-Eastern affairs. We were being used as a smokescreen. As long as we were on the payroll, the government could claim to be working closely with experts."

Prince was watching Ava closely.

"So you might say I looked around me, and no longer liked what I saw."

Prince did not answer.

"But I'm learning people don't just walk away from the Firm." Ava ran a hand through her hair. "They wind up being sent to meet terrorists in Kazakhstan, and dragged into offices late at night to look at photos of neo-Nazis."

Prince smiled ruefully.

"So what are you and DeVere doing about getting the Ark back?" Ava asked, changing the subject to something of more immediate concern to her.

Prince sighed. "We're under orders to leave it at large for now, watch it, and see who surfaces."

"But you think you should go in and get it?" Ava prompted.

"Sure, I do." Prince looked unapologetic. "Better safe than sorry. Although what I think doesn't officially count."

Ava could not resist a creeping smile of satisfaction. *Here it comes.* "Which is why, I suppose, we're having this little off-the-record chat?"

Prince bit her lip, then nodded slowly.

"You want me to keep actively looking for it, so I can be an early warning system if I find anything out?" Ava voiced the American's thought for her. "Unofficially, of course."

"Something like that," Prince conceded. "DeVere thinks you're just helping to find out more about Malchus. But I always like to think ahead a little, so I'm asking you to go further. Dr Curzon, we need the Ark."

Ava thought she had been clear about this back in Qatar. "I don't work for the Firm any more. Those are no longer my loyalties. I'm working for a private collector at present. If I discover anything, I report to him. Why do you think I'd tell you anything?"

Prince put her hand into her long blue coat, and pulled out a flash drive. "Because I'm going to help you." She slid the stick across the seat to Ava. "I'm hoping you'll feel a little indebted to me for this. And then, if your collector pulls out or is out-priced, you might think it worth a tip off back to me." Prince smiled at Ava. "A favour for a favour—the old fashioned way in our business."

Ava picked up the flash drive. It was a metallic grey plastic tube the size and length of half a cigarette. On one side, she recognized the unmistakable thirty-pin connector for an iPhone. "What's on here?"

"You'll like it." Prince replied confidently. "It's information about where to find Malchus. This weekend."

Ava glanced sharply at Prince.

*How did she know?*

"Don't worry," Prince replied reassuringly. "General Hunter told me about your little conversation in Qatar. He also told me that when he left you afterwards, you looked murderous. So I put two and two together. And I can already see I've not misjudged you."

"DeVere doesn't need to know about this," Ava replied quietly. "This remains between us."

"Fine by me." Prince nodded. "So we have an understanding." It was a statement not a question.

Prince handed Ava a card with her numbers. "Call me if you need anything." She paused. "There's just one more thing."

*There always is with these people*, Ava thought, but kept it to herself.

"We're supposed to be watching you. And we're responsible for your safety, however you might feel about that. So we have orders for you to take a chaperone from now on."

"You?" Ava fought to keep the alarm out of her voice. Having Prince tagging along would be a disaster.

Prince shook her head. "Ferguson. And you don't have a choice, I'm afraid."

"I really don't need a minder," Ava replied, tucking the flash drive and Prince's card into her coat pocket. "I can look after myself. I don't know if you heard about Kazakhstan, but let's just say Ferguson and I did some role reversal."

Prince raised an eyebrow.

"I don't need his help," Ava insisted.

"Sorry," Prince replied. "Nothing I can do about it."

The taxi hummed down Victoria Street and stopped at the traffic lights by the station.

Prince hammered on the glass partition separating the driver from the passenger cabin.

As the car pulled in by the curbside, she popped open the door, and unfolded herself from the car. "Well, good night, Dr Curzon" she said, straightening up. "I'm sure we'll meet again soon."

With that she was gone into the rain.

## 36

*10b St James's Gardens*
*Piccadilly*
*London SW1*
*England*
*The United Kingdom*

AVA SPENT THE rest of the journey in silence, lost in thought, staring out of the window at the glistening pavements and bright windows of the empty shops, all long since closed for the night.

The cab eventually stopped outside her flat—the ground floor of a large building tucked away in the quiet streets of eighteenth-century houses behind London's historic Green Park.

It was not a flat she would, or could, ever have bought. It had belonged to her mother's grandparents, and different members of the family had made use of it over the years.

Ava had lived there while working at the Firm, and then afterwards when at the British Museum. Her father had spent the working weeks there with her, but had gone back to the family home in Somerset for weekends.

After he died, no members of her family spent time in London any-more, so when she moved to the Middle East, she decided not to rent it out, but leave it free for when she was in town. She came back a couple of times a year, and relished having a space furnished with her own things, instead of the empty cupboards of a bland hotel. It was a luxury, but always open to family and friends when she was away.

She turned the key and pushed open the dark blue door. It was set back from the road under a white pillared portico, and looked just like any of the other wooden front doors on the street. What passers-by did not know was that it had been custom-made in Sweden out of rolled steel, and could withstand an attack with power-tools for twenty minutes. The police had installed it for her father when he had started receiving threats during a particularly nasty operation.

Inside, the flat was warm and welcoming. The ceilings were low, and the rooms small—but it had the perfect proportions of housing built in Hanoverian London, and previous owners had looked after its original ornamental features well. As a result, it was cosy and elegant.

An upstairs neighbour and family-friend came in every day to arrange the curtains and set the light timers, and Ava had telephoned ahead to let her know she was coming. The old lady had thoughtfully fired up the boiler and flicked on a selection of welcoming table lamps. Ava was delighted to see she had also stocked the fridge.

Slipping off her coat, she poured herself a glass of chilled white wine and loaded a plate with some food.

Carrying it through to the book-lined study, she settled into the single armchair. It was an old-fashioned room, largely as her great-grandfather had left it. No one had seen any reason to redecorate, and it was Ava's favourite place in the house.

She pulled Prince's flash drive from her pocket and examined it for a moment, turning it over in her fingers before clicking it smoothly into the bottom of her iPhone. She had never seen a flash drive for an iPhone before—it was clear the techies at the Pentagon still enjoyed a world-class research-and-development budget.

As she gazed at the phone's screen, wondering what would happen next, a new icon appeared, simply entitled 'MM'. It was greyed out, but when the little bar inside it had rapidly filled, the small square glowed a deep blue.

Tapping the new icon, her camera roll opened, revealing a number of images that had not been there before.

Swiping through them, she instantly recognized the photographs of Malchus and the Thelema which Prince had shown her and DeVere earlier.

They told her nothing new.

As she came to the end of the photographs, she was beginning to wonder if Prince had made a mistake, when the screen suddenly filled with the image of a typed document.

As she read the opening lines, her heart skipped a beat:

FM: LONDON STATION

TO: MOD

TO: CABINET OFFICE

TO: JIC

TO: SECURITY SERVICE

IMMEDIATE

CX 08 / 6378468 / 03 JULY 2013

SUBJECT: HOSTILE INFILTRATION OF M.O.D. CIVILIAN STAFF

SOURCE: A RELIABLE ASSET CLOSE TO THE COLUMBIAN TRADE

DELEGATION

Ava recognized the layout immediately.

It was a CX report. She had written and read many in her time.

She knew the style intimately.

She also knew that by possessing it without official MI6 authorization, she was committing an imprisonable offence.

CX reports dated back to the earliest days of the service, and were the information lifeblood that flowed through the corridors of MI6.

The service's indefatigable founder, Captain Mansfield Cumming, had required all material to be passed solely to him—so the reports were marked 'cx', short for 'Cumming exclusively'. When the new C took over after Cumming's sudden death, he saw no reason to change the system. And the tradition had stuck.

Almost as quickly as she realized it was a CX report, she noted it was copied to both the Cabinet Office and its all-powerful Joint Intelligence Committee.

Most CX reports never made their way out of Legoland. Only the most important were flagged up to other government departments.

The distribution list she was looking at meant this particular report was deemed to contain nationally important intelligence.

Prince had clearly run a very real risk in passing it to her.

Taking a sip of the cool wine, Ava enlarged the image to full screen size, and settled down to read it thoroughly.

Scanning through its pages, she was disappointed to find it turned out not to be about Malchus. Instead, it dealt with civilian staff working for the Ministry of Defence on Wiltshire's ancient isolated and mysterious Salisbury Plain.

The report briefly alluded to the one hundred and fifty square miles of military installations on the Plain, then went on to catalogue the findings of a seven-month undercover operation which had unearthed evidence of Columbian infiltration of the civilian game wardens. It explained that the wardens regularly ranged across the more remote reaches of the Plain, and consequently had intimate knowledge of the location of sensitive and secluded installations that did not feature on any map.

The report highlighted the Firm's real concern that the Columbians could gain front-row seats to covert trials of new military vehicles, weapons, equipment, and tactics. While of little practical use to the Columbians, the information would readily attract buyers on the open market.

Ava read on. Although disappointed, she was not surprised that the main subject of the report seemed irrelevant.

It was frequently the way.

Nuggets of intelligence rarely came pre-packaged and labelled. Useful information lurked in the strangest places. If the report contained information about Malchus, it was quite likely to be an incidental reference—not significant to the report writer, but gold dust to the right reader.

She swiped quickly through the main body of the report, and found Prince had highlighted a section in the appendix.

It dealt with forthcoming events on the Plain.

Ava read on, discovering there was to be a rally one-and-a-half miles south of the garrison town of Larkhill, at the mysterious prehistoric temple of Stonehenge.

From what she could gather, it was some sort of pan-pagan festival, scheduled to last for three days.

There were groups listed from Wiccans and druids to far-out Odinist heathens and Irminist Aryans. The report writer was evidently concerned one or more of them may not be quite what they seemed.

Ava could not see any obvious Columbian connections among the participants. Instead, the names were redolent of pre-Christian paganism, with groups promoting everything from nature and woodland worship to cultic gods and goddesses of love, sex, night, discord, war, and countless other time-honoured human preoccupations.

She stopped scanning the list and slowly read the section Prince had highlighted.

It was a schedule of events, and stated that a 'Meister Marius Malchus' would address the rally on the subject of 'The Underground Tradition and the Will'.

Ava's pulse quickened as she saw the date of his appearance.

*Tomorrow.*

There was no additional detail. But it was enough.

Reaching the end of the document, she started at the beginning again, reading over the whole text once more, memorizing anything that seemed relevant.

When she had finished, she turned to the internet, pulling up page after page on the pagan groups listed, trying to piece together a coherent picture of what they each stood for, and how they related to each other.

This was Malchus's world, and if she was going to find him, she needed to become familiar with it.

As her eyelids became heavier, she wished her father was there. He would have unwrapped it all for her in a moment.

But he was not.

She had to do this by herself.

When fatigue finally overtook her, she unplugged the flash drive and slipped it into her pocket. As she did so, the 'MM' icon disappeared from the screen.

Impressed, she opened the phone's camera roll to be sure, and saw the photos from the flash drive had also gone. Knowing from hard experience that once photos were deleted from the phone they were gone for good, she gave a mental nod of appreciation to the white coats at the Pentagon. They thought of everything—even sparing her the need to run a separate sanitization app.

After checking the following day's train times to Salisbury, she crawled into bed to sleep off the jetlag.

As her brainwaves slowed and her mind started to switch off for the day, jumbled images began to flash before her eyes, along with a certainty that she had now gone beyond the point of no return with Malchus and the Ark.

The last thought she was aware of was that she would have her role to play in Malchus's story, whether he liked it or not.

# DAY SIX

————— • ◆ • —————

# 37

*The Pride of Normandy*
*The English Channel*
*50°41'09.73" N 1°02'49.55" W*

No PASSENGERS WERE interested in the windy rain-lashed deck of *The Pride of Normandy*.

Instead, as the bulbous ferry nosed through the wet black night, they filled the boat's duty-free bars—making the most of the untaxed alcohol.

The few passengers who had chosen the unsociable sailing time from Cherbourg to Portsmouth and were not in the stale-smelling bars were dozing or sleeping on the saggy plastic-covered chairs lining the ship's interminable corridors.

None were outside on deck.

Except one.

Moving quickly along the lowest deck on the port side, Uri tucked himself behind a large lifeboat crane, and quickly opened his dry sack. It was largely empty aside from a long coil of ten-millimetre rope, a pair of lightweight trousers, a shirt, and fifty thousand pounds sterling in cash.

It all weighed next to nothing.

He took out the rope and, as a final act of preparation, breathed in deeply, clearing his head and relaxing himself, savouring the salty tang in the air.

From here on in, he was on his own. Moshe had been very clear about that.

There was to be no contact with anyone in England. No one was to know about this operation—not even his Institute colleagues lurking in the Israeli embassy in Kensington.

There would be no assistance or backup if he got into trouble or needed any favours. The mission was a hundred per cent deniable, and he was going in sterile, with nothing to link him back to his country.

If he was caught, the State of Israel would deny all knowledge of him. As far as Tel Aviv was concerned, he did not exist.

It was fine with him.

He had never been a team player anyway.

There was one contact channel only, and it was strictly one way—for Moshe to inform him if there were any critical developments, or if he was to stand down.

That was it.

He breathed the salty air in deeply, grateful for the rain. It reduced visibility, and meant he would not be disturbed.

Both were added bonuses.

For speed, he had changed in the washrooms below—donning a three-millimetre full-length wetsuit and a lightweight harness under the thin overcoat.

He checked again that there was no one about.

But he need not have bothered.

He was quite alone.

No one wanted to be on deck in the English Channel in the small hours of the night.

It was too early even for the seagulls.

Slipping off the overcoat and canvas shoes, he dropped them into the dry sack, slid it onto his back, and tightened the straps so it was clamped close to his body.

Then he looped the rope around one of the thick stanchions supporting the handrail, and carefully threaded a munter-hitch through the wide carabiner on his harness.

With one final glance around, he swung himself over the rail and took a firm hold of the rope—one hand in front, the other behind. Without pausing, he hurled himself out into the darkness, quickly rappelling down the side of the ship.

As he approached the numbing water, he braced himself, aware the low water temperature and the even colder night air were a lethal combination. The wetsuit would keep his body core warm, but his hands, head, and feet would soon seize up in the inky coldness of the night swim.

There had been no time for acclimatization training against hypothermia. He would simply have to make the best of it by keeping moving.

Treading the chilly water, he tugged on the rope, which slithered round the stanchion and slid down into the sea.

He let it sink. He would not need it again.

He also did not need the extra weight of the harness, but he could get rid of it later. Right now, speed was the only priority—to get as far away as possible from the ship and its giant propellers.

As he began to swim, he could just about make out the lights of the Isle of Wight glinting a mile off in the distance. But he did not need them for orientation—the high strength magnet in his luminescent wrist compass would guide him directly to the rock, pebble, and sand beach at Bembridge, the easternmost village on the island.

He had calculated he could make it in around thirty to forty minutes. The sun would not rise for another hour after that, giving him plenty of time to change, find a café for a steaming hot breakfast, then catch the hovercraft to Southampton and the train on to London.

He smiled to himself.

*Who needed a passport anyway?*

---

## 38

*Piccadilly*
*London SW1*
*England*
*The United Kingdom*

AVA CHECKED HER watch as she clicked the flat's heavy front door shut.

She was relieved to see it was just before 7:00 a.m.

She paused on the doorstep and breathed in the cool morning air. After the heat and dust of the Middle East, the smell of an English summer morning was a sensual treat of earth and plants. She had not particularly noticed it when she lived in London before. But now, when she visited England, it seemed as exotic as the perfumes of the Middle East once had.

Even though the sun had been fully up for several hours, the air still felt damp, and there were pockets of dew on the rainbow of flowers nestling in the rows of window boxes lining the quiet street.

She looked around carefully, scanning the street in both directions, before heading to the popular French café and bakery on the corner.

The aroma of hot coffee and fresh buttery pastries had already drawn a buzzing crowd of people grabbing breakfast on their way to work.

Service was quick. But as she picked up her steaming foam cup of scalding black coffee, she felt a strong hand on her arm.

"What a surprise!" It was a man's voice—sounding unusually cheerful for the time of the morning.

She recognized it immediately.

She turned, and found herself face to face with Ferguson—looking significantly healthier than when she had last seen him in Kazakhstan.

He beamed at her, hooking his sunglasses into the neck of his T-shirt. "Dr Curzon, I didn't know you lived round here."

"An amazing coincidence." She wondered how long he had been outside her house waiting for her to emerge, and kicked herself for not having seen him.

She needed to be more vigilant.

Pressing the plastic lid down hard onto the hot cup, she turned towards the door. "Well, it was great seeing you again," she added, anxious to get away. Prince had clearly been hard at work—passing her address to Ferguson and sending him to stake it out.

"Actually," he looked expectantly at her, "as we're neighbours, maybe we could have breakfast together? Get to know each other a little better? It all ended so quickly last time. Unless," he paused, "there's anywhere you need to be going right now?"

Ava had no desire to take Ferguson to Stonehenge with her, whatever Prince expected.

"That's a kind offer," she answered, buttoning up her black velvet jacket and opening the door of the café. "But if it's all the same to you, I have to be going. I've got a busy day ahead of me."

"Why don't I give you a lift," he suggested breezily, following her onto the pavement and opening the door of a large steel-grey four-by-four parked directly in front of the café. "It'd be a shame for you to spend such a lovely summer's day alone."

Ava needed to be at the railway station in thirty minutes, and had no desire to waste time pointlessly fencing with Ferguson.

She moved closer to the café's outside wall and stood under the navy blue awning overhanging the metal tables and chairs, indicating for him to follow.

She waited until he was close enough for her to speak without being overheard. "Look, I'm sure you've got better things to do today than follow me around," she began. "So why don't you just tell Prince that I gave you the slip? I won't say anything. You can have a day off, doing whatever you do." She smiled at him encouragingly.

Ferguson dug his hands into his jeans pockets and nodded several times, making a show of weighing up the options. "Well, I could. It's actually pretty tempting. But then you'd miss my important update on Malchus, which I'd be free to tell you about at length in the comfort and privacy of the car on our drive to wherever you need to go."

Ava could feel her jaw tightening.

*Prince had this all worked out.*

She hesitated for a moment, chewing the inside of her lip as she digested this new piece of information.

Making her decision, she stepped over to the passenger door and threw him a threatening look. "For your sake, it'd better be good."

Ferguson nodded, and headed around to the driver's side.

While he was out of sight, Ava quickly bent down and wedged Prince's flash drive under the car's front wheel, before climbing into the oversized cabin and firmly closing the door.

She put her coffee into the holder by her armrest. "Strange that you were queuing in the café, though," she said to him, "when you didn't want any coffee."

Ferguson looked for a moment like a rabbit caught in the headlamps. "Not really." He shook his head, recovering quickly. "Caffeine interferes with my spider senses."

Ava groaned inwardly. It was going to be a very long day.

As Ferguson edged out of the parking space, she opened her window in time to hear the satisfying sound of two tonnes of vehicle splintering Prince's flimsy flash drive into a thousand pieces.

———————— • ◆ • ————————

# 39

*Maze Hill*
*London SE10*
*England*
*The United Kingdom*

THE TRIP TO London had been easy. It had gone like clockwork.

After swimming ashore onto the Isle of Wight at Bembridge, a combination of hovercraft and trains had brought Uri to London's Maze Hill station within four hours.

*So far so good.*

He had never been to Maze Hill before, but his research suggested it had everything he required—good transport, cheap temporary accommodation, anonymity, and a strong history of support for extreme far-right groups.

As he headed away from the railway station and towards the centre of Maze Hill, he nodded to himself. It was pretty much as he had expected.

The streets were scruffy and dirty. Tattered posters advertising 'OLD SKOOL' club nights and upcoming TV dramas fluttered from hoardings and boarded-up shop fronts. Sandwiched between them, discount stores and fast-food takeaways hid behind chicken wire screens and graffiti-daubed metal security shutters.

The overwhelming feeling of decades-old neglect and economic deprivation was palpable. Whatever boom had built the chrome and glass skyscrapers of London's financial district, visible in the distance, it had passed Maze Hill by.

*This would do just fine.*

Heading into a shabby newsagent's, he bought a copy of the local paper from the shopkeeper, who merely nodded at him before returning to watch a small television under the counter showing a foreign-language film.

Next door was a tired-looking *Money Converters* pawn shop. He slipped inside, and picked up a battered pay-as-you-go mobile phone that still had a few pounds of credit on it.

He could get top-up cards for it anywhere.

*Perfect. Untraceable.*

He knew all too well how mobile phone data was used by law enforcement and the intelligence community. Every registered user's movements could be exactly tracked by triangulation from masts, or directly by GPS. He could not risk either. He did not want to appear on any system.

Spotting a workers' café, *The Lite Bite*, across the road, he pushed open the door, took a seat at a small plastic table, and ordered a mug of tea.

There was a group of labourers on the other side of the room tucking into an early lunch of thick greasy bacon sandwiches and crisps.

Uri shook his head in bewilderment.

*How did people live on that?*

Turning away, he spread the newspaper out on the table and flicked to the property classifieds, where he scanned the columns for one-bedroom flats to rent. He did not want anything out of the ordinary—just something any average working man in the area might live in.

He would start ringing around once he had finished his tea. Not that he liked milky English tea. He would have preferred strong black mint tea, like they served back home. But his task now was to fit in, not stand out.

He had never felt particularly warmly towards the English. They had not done his country any favours over the years. But this assignment was the chance of a lifetime, in whichever country it unfolded.

And there were aspects of it he was already looking forward to very much.

———— · ◆ · ————

## 40

*Wiltshire*
*England*
*The United Kingdom*

"So, PRINCE IS serious about you tailing me around then?" Ava asked. She hoped from her tone of voice that Ferguson would get the message she was not enthusiastic about the idea.

"She's worried about the company you're keeping," he replied, keeping his eyes on the road.

She could not tell if he was being serious, but dropped it. The traffic was already heavy, and he was concentrating on navigating the oversize MI6 car through the grandiose but often narrow streets of west London.

She waited until they had slipped out of the built-up area and onto the leafy road down to Wiltshire before opening the main subject on her mind. "What have you got?" she asked. "On Malchus."

Ferguson turned down the radio. "I've been doing some digging. If I'm going to be tasked to you on this, I want to know who we're dealing with. And I figure you do, too. DeVere and the Firm don't seem to have a file on him, but Prince was able to pass me a good chunk of the American one."

"Not all of it?" If there was a file, she wanted to know what it said.

He shook his head. "Apparently it's not a thin file, so she just gave me the highlights. But it's enough."

Ava looked dubious. "I don't like partial information. Especially when I feel people are hiding things from me."

"I don't think there's much missing," he reassured her.

"Okay," she replied, taking a sip of her coffee. "I'm listening."

Ferguson overtook a car pulling a horse-trailer, and settled back in the seat. "His real name is Oskar Boehme. He was born in Dresden in 1960. Back then, of course, it was part of communist East Germany."

Ava looked unimpressed. "You can skip the geography lesson—I know where Dresden is."

Ferguson carried on unabashed. "Do you know much about the East German Stasi?"

Ava nodded. "Enough to know I'm glad I was never their guest."

"Highly unpleasant bunch," Ferguson grimaced. "And it seems Malchus was one of their finest."

"I can believe that," Ava replied, keen for him to get onto the details.

"His career started off in his home town of Dresden, where school held little interest for him. He preferred the education he got from the city's black-marketeers. He began with the usual—smuggling and hawking contraband goods, but quickly graduated to hardcore criminality. By the time he was fifteen, the school barely knew what he looked like. Unsurprisingly, he was expelled. And that was when the Stasi started to see his potential."

"Any family connections to the Stasi?" Ava asked.

Ferguson shook his head. "His father was a successful industrialist with the usual communist party connections, so they lived in a big house in a nice part of town. But he was also an alcoholic sadist, who regularly battered his wife and son."

"At around the time Malchus was expelled from school, his father beat his mother so badly she was hospitalized with a fractured eye socket, ripped ear, and broken hip. When his father died the next day, the official report recorded he had accidentally electrocuted himself in the kitchen with a faulty kettle."

"I think I can see where this is going," Ava murmured.

"The Stasi files give another story," Ferguson confirmed. "Malchus had grown to violently resent his father, and saw his opportunity. He stripped the wiring in the kettle's power lead, electrifying the metal. When his father came to turn it on the next morning, he plugged himself directly into the Free State of Saxony's main grid."

"So that's how the Stasi roped him in?" Ava asked. "Blackmail?"

Ferguson nodded. "They kept his little secret for him, and in return he began to inform on the area's black-marketeers. It turned out to be a marriage made in heaven. Malchus was able to earn two lots of wages, and at the same time clear his competition off the streets into the Stasi's prisons and torture basements."

"So when did he move to Berlin?" Ava was unsurprised by what she was hearing. Someone like Malchus clearly had a violent past.

"After several years, the local Stasi bosses had come to appreciate his quick mind, brutality, and naked ambition. And it wasn't long before he attracted the attention of a talent-spotter from head office. He was soon transferred to Berlin's Ministerium on Ruschestrasse, and given more sensitive assignments."

"I can imagine." Ava knew the Ministerium's reputation only too well. Along with the Lubyanka in Soviet Moscow and Berlin's Prinz-Albrecht-Strasse under Nazi Germany, it ranked among the twentieth century's most brutal fortresses of state torture and terror.

"He was tasked to stay involved in the black-market side of things given he had an excellent network by this stage. The arrangement suited him, as he could continue to enjoy the bribes and favours that went with the role. But he also started working on political dissidents, which was a much darker trade altogether, and he soon developed quite a reputation for his innovative methods."

Ava raised an eyebrow. She wondered what it would take to stand out among the Stasi's torturers.

"It seems the incident with his father gave him a long-lasting love of electricity and water. In the basements of the Ministerium, he was able to fine-tune his techniques with car batteries and buckets."

Ava shuddered. She had met men like him before. They were never the ones to be found 'just following orders'—they were a different breed, enjoying the power and brutality. "What about the occult side?" she asked, changing the subject. "How does that fit in?"

"It doesn't really," Ferguson replied. "He kept business and pleasure separate. Magic was his personal obsession. According to the Stasi file, when he was a young teenager, he was rummaging around an abandoned convent to find a hiding place for a consignment of smuggled cigarettes when he stumbled across a book called the *Grimoire of Turiel*. The file doesn't say what it's about, but he was deeply influenced by it. After that, he began his own odyssey into the occult. As he became increasingly obsessed, he bribed and burgled his way into assembling his own dark library."

Ferguson paused to overtake a lorry. "But getting hold of books—especially occult ones—was not easy behind the Iron Curtain. So when the wall came down in '89, Malchus seized the opportunity. As the crowds partied and hacked off wall souvenirs, he slipped into the throngs of revellers, and that was the last the Stasi ever saw of him."

"Where did he go?" Ava asked.

"Wherever he could get what he wanted. He moved around Europe: Paris, Rome, Madrid, but ended up in London. He was occasionally spotted hanging around counterculture bookshops in Covent Garden, and he dabbled with what was left of the Order of the Golden Dawn. But his tastes were much darker. He quickly disappeared, sucked into the spider's web of occult groups that make up Britain's black magic subculture."

"And what about his extremist politics?" Ava asked. "When did that start?"

"The file's not clear," Ferguson admitted. "It seems he fell off the radar. No one was very interested in him at that time. The world was busier with other things, and he was by no means the only ex-Iron Curtain security officer on the loose in Europe. There were thousands of them, and he wasn't on anyone's priority list. So not much is known of his politics in this period, but he seems to have drifted strongly to the right, falling in with fringe and extremist groups. The Thelema is only the latest in a long line of them—although it's by far and away the most serious. Which is why he's now getting the attention he managed to avoid for so long."

No wonder her father had been so interested in him, she mused. Malchus's mixture of occultism and extreme politics was exactly the combination he had been trying to warn people about.

And yet again, it seemed he had been right.

Ferguson turned towards her. "So that's what we know."

Ava lapsed into silence. The information was valuable—what Ferguson had said, and what he had not said. It gave her a lot to mull over.

Lost in thought, she gazed out of the window as the vast empty expanse of green downland sped by, taking them closer to Salisbury Plain's mysterious centre.

—— • ◆ • ——

# 41

*Quai Henri IV*
*4ᵉ arrondissement*
*Paris*
*The Republic of France*

OLIVIER DE MOLAY shielded his eyes from the sun as he looked out over the glistening water of the river Seine.

To his right, he could see the hulking gothic mass of the great cathedral of Notre-Dame—its massive flying buttresses straddling the Île de la Cité like some gigantic medieval stone insect.

He wondered how long it would be until it was taken down, and a shrine to the next great religion was put up in its place—just as it had itself been jubilantly built on the ruins of an earlier pagan temple.

He leant on the low river wall in the shadow of the ubiquitous plane trees and turned to Saxby, who was standing beside him. "So, Edmund, tell me the news."

Saxby's expression was grim. "Grand Master, I'm afraid to report it has disappeared again."

De Molay's expression fell. "I thought I had been clear?" His tone was troubled. "I was explicit: we should pay whatever it takes."

Saxby shook his head. "Our representative was at the auction. We had prepared everything. She had the invitation and instructions to bid

208

freely. But before the auction took place, before even the preview, a para-military team murdered the seller and seized it." He paused. "I'm afraid we just don't know where it is. It's disappeared."

De Molay scowled. "This is not acceptable, Edmund."

"Grand Master, rest assured, I'm taking personal responsibility. Our partner is an expert. The very best." Saxby went over the details of Ava's experience, his discussions with her, what had happened in Dubai, and her desire to keep working on the project.

De Molay lapsed into silence, looking thoughtful, before he spoke again. "You know, Edmund, this spot where we are standing is very sacred to my family. And it has a particular resonance in the current situation."

Saxby looked about. He had wondered why De Molay had wished to meet him here, rather than in one of the city's more comfortable venues. The bohemian Marais district was just behind them. And across the water was the lively *Quartier Latin*, with its students and quintessentially Parisian atmosphere. Both had many comfortable cafés and bistros in which to sit and chat.

De Molay was speaking softly. "In 1314, my ancestor, the last official Grand Master of the Templars, was burned at the stake on this very spot."

Saxby looked confused. "Surely it was in the Square du Vert Galant on the Île de la Cité, over there." He pointed west. "In the shadow of Notre-Dame, where there's even a plaque to mark the spot?"

De Molay sighed. "Even these simple things elude people. And the authorities don't remember or care where they executed him." He bent down and picked up some earth, letting it run slowly through his fingers. "It was here that his hot old blood spilled into the ground—right where we are standing."

He pointed to the river. "In his day, there were four islands in the Seine. Now you only see two."

Saxby nodded. "The Île de la Cité over there, with the cathedral of Notre-Dame on it. And the Île Saint-Louis next to it."

De Molay continued. "The Île de la Cité has always been there, home to the great cathedral and the medieval royal palace. But the sleepy and exclusive Île Saint-Louis used to be two islands—the Île aux Vaches. What wrong-foots historians and tourists alike is that there used to be a fourth island, called the Île aux Javiaux, which belonged to the monks of the Abbey of Saint-Germain-des-Prés. It was little more than a garden.

But it is where the pyre was lit, and where he and his deputy died in the flames." De Molay turned to Saxby. "And, my dear Edmund, we are standing on it."

"But this isn't an island, "Saxby objected.

De Molay stared out at the water. "Rivers are always moving, my friend. And sometimes we move them, too. A hundred and fifty years ago, Louis-Philippe, the last king of France, filled in the river channel to the north of here, permanently annexing the Île aux Javiaux to the mainland and, in a way, wiping the island off the map." He paused. "Where we are standing was not on the mainland in Jacques' day. It was the Île aux Javiaux." He pointed behind them at the Marais district. "Ironically, if you looked that way on the day Jacques was executed, as he may have done from his pyre, you would have seen the great towers and fluttering banners of the Paris Temple, his stronghold. But they have dismantled that, too—and few now know where it stood."

"So the plaque to your ancestor on the Pont Neuf, at the tip of the Île de la Cité … ?" Saxby's voice trailed off.

"For tourists," De Molay shook his head. "It's in a pretty square, in a dramatic position. It makes a nice photograph. But nothing more."

De Molay faced Saxby. "On the 18th of March 1314, as the canons of Notre-Dame cathedral lit the lamps and started burning incense for the evening *lucernare* ceremony, the king's men kindled the wooden pyres here for Jacques and his deputy. The two died in the flames, just as nearly sixty other tortured Templars had done over the previous few years, taking their secrets with them to the grave rather than confessing them."

"And we protect them still," Saxby replied sombrely, "by the oath we all take."

De Molay looked out over the water again. His voice was soft. "We cannot fail, Edmund. Too many of our brethren have died over the centuries for us to yield now. The sacred chain may not be broken."

Saxby look resolute. "We have the freemasons calling in all their contacts—dealers, collectors, governments, everyone. And the Foreign Legion are tracking down the paramilitaries. We're doing everything we can. We'll know soon enough where it is—and who has it."

De Molay began walking back to his car. "Thank you, Edmund. Keep your archaeologist on the case. We don't know who we're up against yet, and in such circumstances we should stay low. We don't want to alert anyone to our involvement. Until we know who we're dealing with, or until we have no choice, we must let hers be our only face."

De Molay opened the heavy door of his sleek black vintage Citroën DS, and climbed in.

Unwinding the window as he started the engine, he looked over to Saxby. "We must stay out of sight, Edmund. But make sure Dr Curzon is given all the assistance she needs. There's no second place in this battle."

---

·◆·

## 42

AVA GAZED OUT of the car window at the lines of ancient hedgerows breaking up the rolling hills—the endless green dotted with clusters of black-faced sheep grazing contentedly in the bright morning sunshine.

After Ferguson had given her the background on Malchus, they had lapsed into silence—each lost in their own thoughts.

The motion of the car gently nosing its way down the motorway was making Ava feel dozy. It had been a punishing few days, and she had a significant amount of sleep to catch up on.

Without warning, a loud electronic ringing shook her back to the present.

She glanced at the caller-ID display on the dashboard, but it read simply 'NUMBER WITHHELD'.

Ferguson pressed a grey button with the image of a green telephone on the steering wheel. The ringing stopped immediately, and was replaced with the sound of an open phone line.

"I'm hoping there are two of you there." The American accent boomed out from the car's powerful speakers, filling the cabin, injecting a heavy bass register into Prince's voice that was not normally present.

"How can we help?" Ferguson asked, his tone businesslike. Ava guessed Prince was not his favourite person to work for.

"It was actually Dr Curzon I wanted to speak to," Prince sounded anxious.

Ava sat up in her seat, alert now, wondering what could have cropped up since Prince had got out of the cab the previous evening. She had not been expecting to hear from her for quite some while.

"Dr Curzon. A strange thing has happened, and we're all scratching our heads over here. Seeing as you grew up in Ethiopia, I was wondering if maybe you could help."

"Of course." As far as Ava was concerned, anything related to Ethiopia was instantly interesting.

"Great." Prince sounded pleased. "Late last night, an Ethiopian man walked into our embassy on the Avenue Gabriel in Paris. He claimed to represent the crown prince of the Solomonic house of Ethiopia. He said the prince was deeply troubled about the loss of his Ark, and demanded to know what we are doing about it."

Ava felt a tingle of excitement.

*News travelled fast.*

Prince continued. "Dr Curzon, does any of this mean anything to you?"

*It certainly did.*

Ava had been wondering if something like this might happen. "It makes total sense," she confirmed.

"Please, fill us in." Prince sounded relieved.

Ava paused for a second, wondering where to start. "The last reigning emperor of Ethiopia, Haile Selassie was head of the Royal House of Solomon—the oldest royal line in the world. He was deposed by a communist *junta* in '74, and his heir is now the non-reigning crown prince. If the Aksum Ark can be said to belong to anyone, it's to that family."

"Hold on," interrupted Prince. "Haile Selassie? The man worshipped by Rastafarians as the living reincarnation of Jesus Christ? You're saying he's linked to King Solomon?"

"More than linked," Ava affirmed. "He's widely believed to be Solomon's genetic descendant."

Ferguson glanced across at Ava incredulously. "There's a Hebrew royal bloodline in Africa?"

Ava pushed up the sleeves of her jumper, as if settling down to work. "According to the Bible, one day King Solomon received an exotic and glamorous visitor—the fabulously wealthy Queen Makeda of Aksum, better known by her biblical title: the Queen of Sheba."

"I didn't realize she was a real person," Ferguson interjected.

"Very real," Ava nodded. "She was the powerful and influential queen of Ethiopia and probably Yemen, too—where the frankincense trees filled her coffers with gold. There are lots of historical records of her reign, quite independently from the Bible."

"Anyway, according to a sacred Ethiopian text called the *Kebra Negast*, the Queen of Sheba was so impressed by Solomon that she converted to the Hebrew religion and bore him a son, Menelik, thereby uniting the royal houses of Israel and Ethiopia. Menelik's direct descendants today still claim the same lineage—the Royal House of Solomon."

"King Solomon had an affair?" Prince sounded incredulous.

Ava smiled. "Middle-Eastern society was a bit different back then. The Bible says quite openly that Solomon had seven hundred wives, including the Pharaoh of Egypt's daughter, and three hundred foreign concubines. It says he loved them all and worshipped their gods and goddesses, like Astarte, Chemosh and even Moloch, infamous for his cult of child sacrifices."

Ferguson turned to stare at Ava in disbelief. "King Solomon? The builder of the temple, known for his wisdom?"

Ava nodded.

"This is all news to me," Prince sounded unconvinced. "So in this tale, did Solomon officially recognize his illegitimate son?"

Ava was surprised by Prince's combative tone. She had not put her down as a religious conservative.

"According to the text," Ava continued, "once Menelik was emperor, he visited his father in Jerusalem. Solomon asked him to stay permanently and inherit, but Menelik insisted he must return to his mother. Solomon therefore brought together the firstborn sons of Israel's leading nobles and priests, and sent them back with Menelik to Ethiopia—to create a Hebrew client-kingdom there."

Prince cut in again. "Is there any evidence for this?" There was a marked scepticism in her voice.

"Look," Ava countered, "you hired me as an expert in this area. I'm just telling you what any archaeologist or historian knows. The Solomonic line is a widespread belief in Ethiopia. And yes, there is some evidence, although no consensus."

"Go on then." Prince's tone was bordering on hostile.

"According to the story, as Menelik's party was assembling to leave Jerusalem, Azariah, the son of Zadok the high priest, made a decision that was to echo down the ages. Distraught at being sent away, he banded together with a group of conspirators and broke into the Jerusalem Temple, where he stole the Ark and hid it in Menelik's baggage train. This is the crucial bit. To disguise the crime, he left an exact replica of the Ark in its place in the Jerusalem Temple."

"The son of the high priest stole the Ark?" Prince interjected with disbelief.

Ava continued. "Apparently Menelik did not discover what had happened until the caravan of young Hebrews had left Jerusalem with him and was halfway to Ethiopia. But when he did, he was delighted, and skipped about 'like a young sheep', it is said, recognizing it was all part of Yahweh's plan."

"A born politician," muttered Ferguson.

"And so," Ava concluded. "For as long as anyone in Ethiopia can remember, the Ark has been in Ethiopia—most recently in a special chapel in the church complex of Our Lady Mary of Zion at Aksum, where it is guarded by a single virgin monk, who never leaves the compound until he dies and the next guardian is appointed."

"Stop." There was a distinct frostiness in Prince's voice now. "When you told us back in Qatar that King Nebuchadnezzar sacked the Jerusalem Temple centuries after King Solomon's day and carried the Ark off to Babylon, I was assuming there was only ever one Ark, which somehow was later moved from Babylon to Aksum. But what you are now telling us is there are quite possibly two Arks, and we have no way of telling which is which."

"That's correct." Ava nodded. "In fact, there's even a hint in the Bible that Solomon may have made another Ark himself—so perhaps there were three."

There was a tense silence, finally broken by Prince. "Dr Curzon, are you trying to be funny?" She did not sound like she was finding things remotely amusing.

"Look," Ava replied, feeling her patience running out. "If this was straightforward, people would have unravelled it all years ago. The fact is that biblical archaeology is at times highly complex, with only a few scraps of information, frequently contradictory, from which we can try to reconstruct events that occurred many thousands of years ago. Biblical archaeology is not a hard-wired science—it's a world of veils and mirrors. That's just how it is."

"So what do you think happened?" Ferguson glanced across at her. "Is this Queen of Sheba story likely? Is there any proof of a Hebrew connection in Ethiopia?"

Ava recalled the first time she had entered an Orthodox church in Ethiopia—it had been quite an education. "Archaeologically speaking, there's rarely smoke without fire, and there's undoubtedly a lot of smoke here."

"Can you substantiate that?" Prince challenged her.

"Sure." Ava was beginning to enjoy this. "Early Ethiopian emperors observed Hebrew religious rites for centuries until they converted to Orthodox Christianity—so you have to ask yourself: where did they learn them? Second, even today, Ethiopian Orthodox Church rituals are shot through with Hebrew practices—for instance, they keep kosher, circumcise all boys, celebrate the holy day on Saturday, and have a model of the Ark, which they call the *tabot*, in every church, just like in Jewish synagogues. And finally, the State of Israel has recognized over a hundred thousand Ethiopians as genuine Jews, fully entitled to settle in Israel with identical rights to all other Jews. Needless to say, these African Jews trace their origins in Ethiopia to Solomon and the Queen of Sheba. "

Prince interrupted abruptly. "So, going back to this messenger who came into our Paris embassy last night. Let me be clear. You're saying he represents the lineal genetic African descendants of King Solomon?"

Ava could feel Prince bristling at the idea. "Correct. He's not emperor any more, of course, but he's still crown prince of Ethiopia, head of the Imperial House of Ethiopia, and the head of the House of Solomon. The Ark at Aksum is therefore a critical part of his family's history."

"I can see why he wants answers," Ferguson noted, raising his eyebrows. "I would."

"So that's the story." Ava concluded. "It looks like the Ark's owner has now formally registered his family's interest in what's happening."

Ferguson looked across at her. "Well, I'm not going to remember all those details, but at least I've learned that we definitely have the right person for the job."

"I'm very far from convinced," Prince interrupted brusquely. "There seem to be a lot of ifs and buts, Dr Curzon. And the Bible doesn't say anything about a relationship between Solomon and the Queen of Sheba. Until anyone can prove it to me, I'm not going to assume these

Ethiopian ex-royals have any legitimate claim on the Ark."

"But if the Queen of Sheba story isn't true, how do you explain the Ark's presence in Ethiopia and all the Hebrew links?" Ferguson asked.

"I don't have to." Prince snapped. It was clear from her voice that her mind was made up. "It's not a priority. From what I hear, there's a fifty per cent chance the Ark being held by Malchus is the real Ark. Therefore, until it's safe again and well away from the likes of Malchus or the Iranians, my only priority is to ensure its well-being. We can worry about who owns it later."

"Of course," Ava interrupted, "to complicate things further, much of all this depends on whether you believe many of the biblical characters ever even existed. There's no consensus on that either."

"Fair enough." Ferguson concluded, pointing ahead at the large circle of exposed prehistoric standing stones appearing on the horizon.

"Okay. We're done here." Prince's voice had more than a touch of ice in it. "Thank you, Dr Curzon. You've made your position perfectly clear." With that, the phone went dead.

"She's a bit touchy," Ferguson observed, swinging off the main road and heading towards the ancient monument.

Ava shrugged. "A lot of this is quite personal. Many people find it hard to challenge beliefs they learned in childhood."

Ferguson nodded.

"It's difficult even for non-religious people." Ava looked across at him. "For example, how would you react if I told you that there are at least three creation stories in the Bible, one of them involving God battling a giant sea monster called Leviathan. Or that of the three sets of Ten Commandments in the Bible, only one is actually called the Ten Commandments and is explicitly said to have been written on stone tablets. However, it doesn't contain the famous 'Thou shalt not kill', but instead absolutely forbids cooking young goats in their mothers' milk. Or that God specifically forbids tattoos, or wearing polyester—well, mixed fibres. Or that God says he will turn unbelievers into cannibals and force them to eat their children. Or that the Bible specifically says Jesus had brothers and sisters." She looked at Ferguson. "Do you want me to continue?"

Ferguson looked across at her with incredulity. "You're making this up, aren't you?"

"Just don't tell Prince," Ava smiled enigmatically, gazing out at the intense green of the rolling plain. "I don't think she'd like it."

$$\cdot \blacklozenge \cdot$$

# 43

*Stonehenge*
*Wiltshire*
*England*
*The United Kingdom*

FOR MOST OF the last four thousand years, no one had paid any attention to the extraordinary and inscrutable stones sitting like a crown on the vast green expanse of Salisbury Plain.

But from the moment seventeenth-century antiquarians became interested in the enigmatic monoliths and began romanticizing the druids they believed once worshipped there, the visitors had started to flock. The local tourist industry encouraged them, ensuring they were titillated by tales of pagan orgies and sensationalist drawings of thirty-foot-high 'wicker men' cages, in which druids imprisoned their victims and burned them alive.

As Ferguson killed the four-by-four's engine, he and Ava looked about the car park. It was teeming with hundreds of visitors. Not the usual tourists—but people the cx report had termed 'neo-pagans'.

Ava had last been there as a student, joining the several thousand who were bussed to the visitor centre every day. In its little huts, they paid their entrance fees and picked up multilingual headsets to learn of the mysteries surrounding the prehistoric temple. With the guide talking to each of them personally, they were funnelled anticlockwise around the mystical menhirs, and buffeted by the biting winds that whipped across the Plain.

When Ava had been there, the reassuring voice in her headphones had explained that the area had been used as a 'city of the dead' burial site since the dawn of time. Then, in 3000 BC, before the pyramids were built in Egypt, the colossal stones had been set up in a standing circle.

The audio-guide confessed that history provided no explanation what prehistoric people used the cryptic circle for. Or why the builders had shipped in the vast fifty-ton blue stones from the misty Preseli Mountains in West Wales.

The most tantalizing clue was that the archway formed by the largest trilithon perfectly framed the sun rising over the enigmatic Hele Stone at the midsummer solstice.

But despite awareness of this unique calendrical feature, the mystery of the stones endured. And after four hundred years of study and research, the twenty-first century's finest minds still had no real idea why the arcane monument had been built.

It was just the sort of puzzle Ava loved.

When she visited as a student, she had watched the visitors soak up the scanty facts and snap their photos, before heading to the gift shop to buy the obligatory post cards and Stonehenge-branded tea towels and fudge.

But not today.

She stepped out of the four-by-four onto the tarmac, and was momentarily stunned by the vibrant colours all around—splashed across robes, scarves, flags, and stalls.

It was a riot of the unconventional.

She and Ferguson headed for the makeshift gate, decorated for the occasion with garlands of summer flowers. A teenage girl with heavy blue eye shadow stood guard, requesting a donation. Ava handed over a few pounds, and the girl stamped their wrists with a smudgy image of an oak tree, then let them in.

There was nothing as organized as a programme or map of the festival, so Ava and Ferguson began to wander among the stalls.

It was immediately obvious that it was a massive gathering.

The stalls spread anarchically from the car park over the neighbouring fields, road, and up to the low rope barriers strung loosely around the stones themselves.

It was plainly the kind of place where people could easily get lost.

Or be hidden.

Close to the car park, Ava could see several groups displaying weather-beaten placards and banners. Their signs announced that the stones were everyone's birthright, should be freely open to all, and urged people to sign petitions calling for the many exhumed bodies, now in museums and laboratories, to be returned to their ancestral resting place. From the well-worn tents and drying washing outside them, it was clear the protestors were a permanent feature of the site, not just there for the festival. But the atmosphere was good-natured, leaving the hulking vans of police in body armour looking out of place and out of touch.

Ava moved further into the labyrinth of stalls. "If we're going to cover the area and find Malchus, we'll need to split up," she suggested to Ferguson, manoeuvring herself into another aisle of tables hawking jewellery, books, CDs, crystals, incense, tarot cards, and countless other new-age accessories. "Otherwise we could miss him altogether."

Ferguson looked uncertain.

"Unless you have a better idea?" she added, raising her eyebrows.

Ferguson eventually nodded. "Rendezvous back here in forty-five minutes. If you go left and take the upper field. I'll head round towards the stones."

With no map and no officials to ask, Ava had no option except to sweep up and down each aisle between the tables, hoping she might see something that pointed towards Malchus and his talk.

As she passed the endless vendors, she wondered how any of them could be making any money, sandwiched between so many other stalls all selling similar wares. Yet many of them were doing a busy trade, serving the hardcore pagans and curious members of the public who jostled side-by-side to try on quartz bangles and sample organic preserves.

Finding nothing in the lower field that seemed linked to Malchus, she headed through the open three-bar gate into the upper field at the back.

There were fewer people here, and as she took in the stalls and their wares, she noted the themes were noticeably darker.

One grimy man by the entrance was displaying tribal wooden carvings with macabre expressions on the crudely chiselled faces.

The stall next to it was offering sinister-looking metal knives and bowls. Ava could only assume they were intended for rituals of some sort.

On her other side, there was a grubby table manned by the Danish chapter of a motorbike gang, whose only connection to neo-paganism seemed to be a taste for gory Nordic images on their back patches. And the battle colours displayed across the front of their stall suggested close-quarter street fighting was more their pleasure than the freedom of the open road.

The atmosphere in the upper field struck Ava as one Malchus would feel at home in. She could not see him having any time for the crystals and fairy magic in the field she had just come from. But as she walked up and down, she could not find anything to suggest an area had been set aside or roped off for any kind of talk.

Turning towards the trilithons where Ferguson was searching, she suddenly saw it, nestled between a battered black caravan offering piercings and tattoos and a greasy couple selling a pungent acrid incense.

Her eyes were drawn to its simplicity.

There were no swastikas or Nazi paraphernalia. But the table was draped in a red flag with the word 'THELEMA' embroidered in black and gold lettering inside a large white circle. The Nazi colours were unmistakable, as was the name.

A pockmarked middle-aged man with spiky white hair sat behind the table on an olive green camping chair, fiddling with a chewed biro and clipboard on which he was gathering names.

There was a pile of leaflets at one end of the flag-draped table. Apart from that, the stall was bare.

Ava approached the man, who was watching her suspiciously.

"I understand there'll be a talk later?" she asked, keeping her voice casual.

A pair of young men approached. One was wearing a loose checked shirt under a denim jacket, the other was in casual sports clothing. The spiky-haired man nodded to them, and they slipped through the narrow gap between the table and the next stall into a collection of cars and vans. After a moment, they disappeared behind a battered old Citroën police bus that had clearly seen better days and now looked as if half a dozen people regularly slept in it.

The spiky-haired man looked back at her suspiciously, eyeing her up and down with an air of distrust, before shaking his head dismissively. "No. Nothing like that here."

It was not the answer Ava wanted to hear. "I've travelled a long way," she shot him a knowing glance, "for the talk."

"I just told you," he replied, not hiding his growing irritation. "There's nothing for you here."

She looked at his granite expression and could see she was getting nowhere. If she carried on, he would just dig his heels in further, closing off all avenues.

She needed to try another tactic.

"I've been a student of the *Meister* for many years," she confided. "He's a very *powerful* man." She emphasized the word powerful, aware it was used in occult circles for someone with strong abilities. It was an inside word—the sign of an initiate.

She was pleased to see she had hit her mark. The man was looking at her with interest now.

She carried on, keen to press home her advantage. "It'd mean a great deal to me to be able to hear the *Meister*." She looked at him earnestly.

"And why is that?" The words came from directly behind her—more an accusation than a question. The voice was deep and resonant. The accent was distinctly German.

Ava spun round to find herself staring into the fleshy face and sea-green eyes from the photograph General Hunter had given her in Qatar.

It took her less than a millisecond to recognize him.

*Malchus.*

He was standing between two thuggish men—although in terms of build and appearance there was little to distinguish the three of them.

Seeing him close up for the first time, she realized how misleading the photograph had been.

His heavy-lidded eyes were more piercing than she had expected—a deep glassy green. But now they were turned to look directly at her, she could feel only their inner hardness. They shone with an icy edge as they coldly took her in. She felt as if she was being scanned by a reptile.

And it was not just his eyes that were unnerving. From this close, she could see that what she had assumed was an affectation—shaving his head and eyebrows—was no such thing. It was his natural condition. Where his eyebrows and hairline should have been, there was just skin. No hair grew there.

"Do I know you?" he asked, eyeing her closely.

Taken off guard, she took a silent deep breath and returned his gaze. Steeling herself, she smiled and extended her hand to greet him. "*Meister*, such an honour finally to meet you."

He did not offer his hand in return, but kept looking at her.

She pulled her arm back, brushing off the rejection. "I heard you'll be speaking," she continued, kicking herself mentally. She had merely intended to snatch a glimpse of Malchus today, to begin putting together a picture of who he was. She had not thought she would meet him face-to-face.

"What exactly is your special interest in my talk?" he asked pointedly, continuing to look penetratingly at her.

She gazed back at him, returning the stare with a confidence she was not feeling.

At the same time, her mind was filling with thoughts about her father. Something in Malthus's manner was kindling a feeling—nothing rational, more of an intuition. It was a quiet voice deep inside telling her that the man standing in front of her had undoubtedly been involved in his death.

His cold gaze never left her.

"My special interest?" She repeated the question, buying a few seconds of thinking time. "To learn from the *Meister* and make progress," she replied, hoping the answer would flatter his ego sufficiently.

As she spoke, she was aware of a new feeling settling over her. Where MI6 had failed to give her any answers surrounding the circumstances of her father's death, she now knew with a visceral certainty that this man could.

She took another quiet deep breath. There was no hurry. She had to do this properly.

First she would have to get close to him.

He continued to eye her intensely, inclining his head toward her. "If that is your interest," he spoke dismissively, "may I recommend you find a good bookshop." He turned away from her. "Now, please leave us." He spoke with the easy authority of someone used to having his orders unquestioningly obeyed.

As if to reinforce the point, one of Malchus's companions threw her a nasty look.

The implied threat was clear.

Malchus headed between the stalls into the area the man at the table was evidently guarding. His two minders followed.

Ava stared after them.

*Was that it?*

She gazed in disbelief as the retreating figures disappeared out of sight.

*He was just walking away?*

Quickly running through her options, she was suddenly all too aware she had no Plan B.

She could force her way through the gap in the stalls and follow them to wherever they were going—but not without creating a scene, which was the last thing she wanted to do.

Furious with herself, she turned and headed back down towards the field's entrance.

One thought was going round and round in her mind.

*That had been a spectacularly amateur performance.*

She was livid with herself. She may have been out of the game for a while, but she still knew a bungled operation when she saw one. Thinking of all the things she should have said, she strode angrily down into the lower field.

*So much for getting close to him.*

She had been presented with a golden opportunity to make real progress, and she had thrown it away.

To make it worse, it was entirely her fault. She had been completely unprepared, and the result was a foregone conclusion.

She remembered her tutor at Fort Monckton, the eighteenth-century castle at Portsmouth, on England's blustery south coast, that MI6 used as a training centre. She had been a regular visitor there for the six months of the Intelligence Officer's New Entry Course. On the first day, he had written on a board in the classroom a quotation from Count von Moltke, the nineteenth-century Prussian general and strategist of modern warfare. It was burned into her mind because he had left it there for the entire six months:

NO BATTLE PLAN EVER SURVIVES CONTACT WITH THE ENEMY

He had gone on to demonstrate that it applied to all undercover and intelligence field work just as much as to military encounters.

And just as importantly, he had explained that von Moltke's solution was as valid today as it was then. Combatants had to plan for every eventuality and scenario that could flow from the initial contact. They must never be without a plan for all outcomes.

And that crucial planning was precisely what she had failed to do.

In her days with the Firm, she would never have gone into the field so unprepared.

She kicked herself again.

She would not make that mistake a second time with Malchus.

But for the moment there was only one priority—to find out what he was doing at the rally.

And if the guard was not going to let her in to his talk through the front, then she was going to have to find a way in from the back.

———— · ◆ · ————

# 44

*Stonehenge*
*Wiltshire*
*England*
*The United Kingdom*

IT WAS IMMEDIATELY clear to Ava that beyond the rows of cars and vans was an area Malchus and his people wanted to keep shielded from the public eye.

And that made it her priority. Something would be happening there.

She was sure of it.

As she walked away from the upper field and into the more vibrant lower one, she skirted along the edge of the jumbled multicoloured stalls until she saw a gap. It lay sandwiched neatly between a long grey refreshment tent and a St John's Ambulance post staffed by a bored looking crew.

Striding purposefully as if she had every right to be there, she slipped into the tunnel between the two large tents.

Once beyond the public area, she found herself in the belt of parking reserved for exhibitors only.

The cars here were not as densely grouped as behind the Thelema stand in the upper field, and she was soon beyond them—moving freely.

As she tracked her way back to the parking area beyond the upper field, she eventually spotted the battered grey Citroën police bus marking out the clump of vehicles into which Malchus and his henchmen had disappeared.

Approaching, she could see that a number of high-sided vans had been carefully parked in such a way as to block any view of what lay beyond them.

Getting closer, she was increasingly sure that whatever was due to happen today was going to take place in the private space behind them.

But she could already see that getting through the belt of parked vehicles unobserved was going to be a problem. She would quickly be spotted if she simply wandered through the cordon of vehicles to where Malchus had gone.

Dropping to the ground, she rolled under the nearest van.

It was cramped, but squeezing herself as thin as she could, she managed to move along its length, and closer to where she strongly suspected Malchus and the others were gathering.

Grateful that the ground was firm and a little springy, she kept as low and flat as she could, using the protection of the vehicle to cover her. She barely had room to move, and the strong smell of petrol, oil, and metal only heightened the sense of claustrophobia.

She lay still for a few moments and prayed no one was about to start the van's engine.

Straining to catch any sounds that would give her clues as to what was happening, she could hear voices up ahead, but they were too muffled and indistinct for her to pick out any individual words.

She checked her watch, aware that Ferguson would soon discover she had failed to show up at the rendezvous. He would most likely come looking for her, but there was very little chance he would find her—which was exactly how she wanted it. Prince was already too close for comfort, and she had no desire for Ferguson to file progress reports on her.

Her priority now was to find out exactly what Malchus was up to.

There seemed nothing for it except to make use of the protection offered by the vehicles in order to crawl closer to where the action was happening.

She was grateful they had been parked so close together. It would allow her to crawl forward and edge under the neighbouring vans without too much difficulty.

Inching ahead slowly, she moved forward until she was under the next vehicle.

She could see a cluster of ankles and feet up ahead.

Moving more cautiously now, she edged her way under the vehicle in front of her. It was a large off-road four-by-four and offered more space under it than the vans, although it was still a tight fit.

But what it lacked in comfort it made up for in the view.

It was a perfect observation post.

As Ava took in the scene, it was immediately obvious the vehicles had been carefully laagered in concentric circles—like wagons around an encampment.

The multiple high-sided vans had obscured what she could now see was a central circle, a dozen yards wide, in which there was a low podium with a small table in front of it, draped in another red and white Thelema flag.

Thirty or forty people were milling around, some talking in small groups.

She did not have to lie there long before there was activity. With a flurry of movement behind the table, Malchus appeared on the podium.

He looked around at the crowd purposefully, and held up a hand. The onlookers who had been watching him advance towards the podium fell silent in anticipation. They stopped shuffling, and the noise died down.

Ava could sense the electricity in the air.

She lay as still as she could, her head angled so she could get a full view of Malchus.

"Brothers," he began in a deep confident voice.

Ava glanced at the faces in the crowd and the pairs of feet she could see, and realized he was right.

There were no women present. The crowd was an undiluted display of brawn.

Malchus continued. "I want to talk to you today about an important but often overlooked aspect of our tradition."

Even from under the four-by-four, she could hear his voice—clear and authoritative.

She kept her eyes on the crowd. They were transfixed.

"Alchemy." He announced with a flourish.

Ava sighed inwardly, preparing herself for the usual mishmash of garbled inaccuracies people endlessly recycled on the subject.

Although alchemy was often scorned as a feeble-minded medieval obsession, it in fact went back much further, to the eastern Mediterranean world. She was intimately familiar with its oldest core texts—the *Corpus Hermeticum* and the infamous *Emerald Tablet*, both from ancient Egypt.

She steeled herself for the usual nonsense about crackpot magicians fixated on turning lumps of lead into mounds of gleaming gold.

"Our quest for knowledge is a long and arduous one," Malchus began in earnest, "beset with difficulties and wrong turns. Today I want to share with you some keys and guides to help you on your journey. And where better to start than with the alchemists of old—the masters of the enciphered path. Gifted men, yes, but much underestimated." He looked about searchingly with a sense of the dramatic. "And much misunderstood."

The crowd murmured its approval, captivated by the proximity to their spiritual leader.

Malchus continued to cast his eyes around the circle of eager onlookers, keen to draw them in. "Contrary to popular belief, the ancient alchemists had no intention of turning lead into gold. They had no interest in material riches. That was the propaganda of the blinkered tyrants, bigots, and inquisitors of the Church, who sought to weaken the alchemists by ridiculing their work." His face began to flush. The venom he felt towards the Church was palpable. Ava could feel it, even from a distance.

"The Church cowered because the alchemists understood the same thing that true adepts throughout the ages have always known. Their goal was change. Not to change metal to gold, but to change *themselves*—from ignorant to enlightened, from weak to powerful."

Ava nodded grudgingly. So far what he said was correct.

"As Nietzsche demonstrated," Malchus continued, "we can see clearly there is man and there is superman. And like Nietzsche's superman, those of us called to the magickal way are set on a journey of change. We train like athletes, but not our physical bodies. We develop our inner strength, honing our skills to harness our innate power for what needs to be done."

Looking at Malchus's bull-like frame, Ava could see he clearly did not neglect his physical training either.

"The ancient Greeks knew about the importance of change. Heraclitus remarked that no person could step into the same river twice, because all existence and movement is change. Yet people misunderstood him."

"And more recently the great Charles Darwin, who knew the importance of racial breeding better than anyone, said it even more clearly. Yet even he was misunderstood. He did *not* talk about the survival of the fittest. That is a common error. He said the planet's true survivors and champions were those most able to *change*. They are the ones who will inherit the earth. And just like the alchemists of old, he fought the Church for the truth of our beliefs."

Malchus had the crowd gripped now. They had clearly all heard of Darwin. But from their surprised faces, they had never thought of him as one of them before.

*Clever*, Ava had to acknowledge.

He was building a rich history for his followers, pinning his personal racist beliefs onto highly regarded historical characters—sewing fiction onto fact to create the world the way he wanted it seen. It was subtle: pretending it had always been understood this way by those possessing the secret knowledge of the initiate—drops of which he was sprinkling onto his mesmerized audience.

"Of course, like all of us in the tradition, like all true seekers, the alchemists of old were ever watchful. To hide their quest from prying eyes, they spoke guardedly, in metaphors. And they were right to. The Church never truly understood their hidden meanings. The ultimate irony, don't you think, as the Church's fictionalized hero, Jesus, also taught in hidden messages that he called parables. Yet the hypocrites who guard his tradition have suppressed and marginalized his hidden teachings, like the *Gospel of Thomas*, in which, along with the masters down the ages, Jesus says, 'He who will drink from my mouth will become like me. I myself shall become he, and the things that are hidden will be revealed to him.' But the deceivers in the Church scorn what they do not understand, destroying anything beyond their 'crapulous creed' as the enlightened magus Aleister Crowley described it."

Ava shifted on her elbow. She would not have put it quite like that, but fundamentally he was right about Jesus' teachings. Not many people realized just how many times in the biblical gospels, and in the less well-known gospels not included in the Bible, Jesus spoke about his outer and inner messages—some aspects of which were for the public, others only for his close circle of initiates.

She could see why the Thelema had accepted Malchus as their leader.

He had all the gifts of a cult guru—including the ability to blend just the right amount of verifiable fact into his twisted world-view to reassure those who wanted easy answers that he was speaking the truth.

"The alchemists had a clear goal," he continued. "And they hid it in symbols. Base metal represented their unawakened state. Gold was the pure magickal being they wished to become. They called their journey 'transmutation', from the Latin *muto*, to change."

He stared around at the crowd. "And how did the alchemists make this change?" He was pausing dramatically, pulling the audience in. "More importantly, how do *we* make this change?" He looked expectantly at the crowd. "What is the ingredient that empowers this mutation?" He had warmed to his theme, and was now in full flow, his voice rising rhetorically.

"The Will." he emphasized the word. "It is no accident that the *Führer* picked up on this theme when he entitled his rise to power *The Triumph of the Will*. And we, too, need to harness that same force in order to change our world."

He put his hand dramatically onto the flag draped over the table in front of him. "That is why the concept is sown into the very fabric of our movement—into our flag and into our hearts. Our very name, the Thelema, means 'the Will' in Greek. And that is what we must do. We must triumph by our Will."

Ava was beginning to feel stiff under the vehicle. She breathed out and relaxed for a few moments, before propping herself on her shoulder again and focusing afresh on Malchus's speech.

She was surprised at its content. She had expected a clumsy neo-Nazi paean of white supremacy and anti-Semitism, with some crude black magic mixed in.

But what she was hearing suggested Malchus was more intellectually agile than she had thought. The politics were vile. But he clearly knew his history, and he twisted and distorted the facts expertly to suit his case. He had plainly studied it all in depth, and was far from the ignorant thug she had imagined he would be.

It did not for a moment change the fact he was an extremely dangerous and sadistic extremist. But it strongly suggested there was nothing random about what he did. He was highly intelligent, fixated, and no doubt did nothing without carefully calculating the consequences.

Whatever his interest in the Ark, she was feeling increasingly sure he was planning something.

If he wanted the Ark, it was for a reason.

He did not strike her as an opportunist.

She pulled herself back to the present and tuned in again to what he was saying.

It was more personal and purposeful now. "We will become who we need to be. We will be just like the great adepts who came before us. Like the Samaritan Simon Magus, who used his dark magic to successfully challenge the hypocritical disciples. Like the necromancer Dr John Dee, who ripped open the veil into the dark world of spirits and brought their voices to us. Like Countess Erzsébet Báthory, who understood it all, but was walled up in her chamber by bigots and intriguers. Like the *strannik* Grigory Rasputin, whose mystical dark woodland skills shone so brightly and entranced a nation until cut short by powerful enemies. Like the magus Fulcanelli, who taunted the world with his alchemical successes, before disappearing never to return. Like Aleister Crowley, who understood more than anyone the power of the Will and its ability to affect destiny. And most of all, like the noble men of the glorious ss, who brought all this together into a sublime distillation of will, blood, and iron. All of these great ancestors were themselves no less than living incarnations of the triumph of the Will."

Ava watched his eyes as he spoke. They were alive and searching, but calculating and callous. She could see why he had risen fast in the Stasi. She pitied those people over whom he had wielded the power of life and death.

"The lesson we learn from these ancients is to stay constant in our fight for knowledge and the ultimate gifts—for the tradition will give illumination to all earnest seekers."

He was lost in his own rhetoric, drunk on what he was saying. "And we will triumph, my brothers in arms. By our will. We *will* succeed." His voice was rising in a crescendo. "We shall see further than our predecessors. We will travel a greater distance down the path than anyone before us."

Ava's concentration was interrupted by a small movement in the corner of her eye.

She snapped her head towards the far end of the vehicle where it had come from.

It took her a moment to recognize what it was, before she was filled with a sudden sense of dread.

*Christ—not now.*

She fought to stay calm.

But there was no mistaking the two-tone black and golden-brown nose of an Alsatian dog, sniffing along the ground by the four-by-four.

She held her breath, hoping that if she did not move, it would not notice her. But she knew Alsatians did not sense by movement alone. They also relied heavily on smell. And there was nothing she could do about that.

It already knew she was there.

Malchus was still in full flow. "To harness the greatest powers of the universe, we need only look within ourselves, and cultivate what we find there. For we are a microcosm of the universe. The ancients summed it up in their mantra: as above, so below."

The powerful dog was drawing level with her. She could see it was on a thick black leather leash. A pair of boots was walking a few feet behind it.

"We all have whatever power we may ever need within us. All we must do is recognize and develop what we have. It can be a journey of many long steps. But the legends of old are there to guide and inspire us—especially in the Norse and heathen tales, which contain a universe of hidden teachings."

Ava was no longer listening. She was focused exclusively on the dog approaching her hiding place.

What happened next was brutally swift.

The dog suddenly began to snarl and bark—in loud staccato bursts, throwing its head back and baring its large teeth.

No sooner had it started than Ava realized with horror it was coming for her—scrambling under the vehicle and hurling itself towards her, the noise of its snarls filling the entire space under the vehicle's chassis.

Her body released a massive surge of adrenaline, filling her muscles with blood and hormones, launching her away from the animal's powerful square head and open jaws as fast as she could.

But in the cramped space under the four-by-four, she was not fast enough, and had barely moved half a foot before she knew what was going to happen.

Her body instinctively braced itself for the impact.

The large dog crashed onto her, its heavy paws cutting into her side and shoulder—its saliva-covered teeth only an inch from her face.

She felt its hot angry breath on her skin as her ears filled with the throaty sound of its attacking snarl. Before she had time to think, another massive dose of adrenaline prepared her body for the imminent crushing bite to her neck or face.

But it never came.

With a series of guttural strangled noises, the dog was yanked out from under the vehicle.

As Ava stared after its retreating form, her heart hammering hard enough to burst her ribcage, the dog was replaced by the dull grey metal of an old Colt handgun pointing directly at her, followed by a man's livid face.

Still in full fight-or-flight mode, her eyes darted about as she tried to assess escape options. At the same time, the man motioned with the handgun for her to come out from under the vehicle.

Without pausing, she lunged for the other side of the four-by-four, propelling herself as fast as she could away from the threat.

As she rolled out from under the vehicle and into the sunlight, she realized her mistake too late.

A group of men was gathered there. They were looking down at her, grim faced—angered by the unwelcome intrusion and interruption.

Before she had time to react, something cold and heavy connected hard with the back of her head, and the world went dark.

––––––––––– ◆ –––––––––––

# 45

*Stockbridge House*
*Nr Newton Tony*
*Wiltshire SP4*
*England*
*The United Kingdom*

AVA AWOKE TO the sound of tyres crunching on gravel.

Opening her eyes slowly, she gradually became aware of being in a moving car.

She winced as the engine slowed to manoeuvre over a speed-bump, feeling a bolt of pain flash across the back of her skull. As the rear wheels rolled down off the hump, she heard a sharp cracking noise inside her head, accompanied by a flash of bright white light.

It felt as if her brain was being sheared in two.

Swivelling her eyes to look through the heavily tinted black windows, she saw the car was turning off an isolated country road and nosing its way gently between a set of monumental ivy-clad grey stone pillars set into a tall dark green hedge.

She blinked, trying to focus on what was happening. But the throbbing pain coming from the back of her head was interrupting her ability to think.

The car was now purring along a private ornamental driveway that snaked down the side of a gently rolling hill and opened onto a breath-taking view of sheep and a village in the lush green valley below. As the narrow road bent away to the other side of the hill and rounded a corner, she caught sight of an imposing country house at the end of the driveway.

It was an idyllic scene of English rural gentility.

The house was built of the same grey stone as the gate pillars on the road. Its small windows were criss-crossed with strips of leading, turning each one into dozens of small glass diamonds. A long range made up the main body of the building, off which three smaller wings protruded at right angles. The resulting E-shape and period windows instantly gave the house away as a classic Elizabethan manor.

Struggling to remember what she was doing tightly strapped into the seat, she turned to look around the car's plush walnut and beige-leather cabin.

With a jolt of horror, she instantly recognized the hairless head of the thickset man squeezed into the front passenger seat.

It was Malchus.

*What on earth … ?*

Her pulse suddenly accelerated as she tried to remember what she was doing in a car with him.

She winced as she remembered the bungled conversation with him by the Thelema stall.

Looking around for an answer, she quickly recognized the other two men. They were his brawny bodyguards from the upper field.

One of the bodyguards was driving, but the larger of the two, the one who had threatened her, was sitting beside her in the back. He still wore the same unpleasant expression, but this time it was backed by a matt black Glock handgun pointing directly at her.

"Glad you could join us," he rasped. The sarcasm dripped from his voice, and the expression of menace in his eyes was anything but wel-coming.

South African, she thought, from the accent. Probably Johannesburg. If he shared Malchus's racist politics, then he had probably come up through the extremist neo-Nazi scene there.

*Nasty.*

As she felt her focus returning, memories of the morning's events came crashing back—shaking off Ferguson, hiding under the car, eavesdropping on Malchus's impassioned speech, and evading the guard dog only to be clubbed into unconsciousness by Malchus's followers.

At least that explained the sickening pain at the back of her skull.

As her head cleared further, she began to register the seriousness of the situation.

After the fiasco by the Thelema stall, she had meant to ensure her next meeting with Malchus was on her terms, so she could begin getting to the bottom of the questions to which she was increasingly sure he held the answers.

But once again she had been caught unaware.

Looking at the ugly muzzle of the semiautomatic gun pointing at her, it was painfully clear the odds were now heavily stacked against her.

She would have a lot of explaining to do, and it would need to be convincing.

Her chances did not look good. She was Malchus's prisoner, in his car, in the middle of nowhere, and no one knew she was there.

As they slowly drew up outside the house's grand frontage, the body-guard gestured with the pistol for her to open the door.

She thought for a moment of tackling him as he got out of the car after her. He would be unstable for a second or two, and she was pretty sure she could separate him from his gun in that time. But she instinctively knew it would be suicide—Malchus and the driver would both be armed.

She clicked open the car's heavy door and stepped out onto the crunchy gravel, scanning the surrounding area, taking in the house's grand doorway, the open expanse of well-manicured lawn, the carefully tended flowerbeds to its right, and the densely wooded area behind and to the left.

She weighed up the options, but none of them were good. If she tried making a run for it in any direction she would be dead on the driveway with half a dozen rounds in her back before she got ten yards.

There was no realistic choice except to go along with whatever Malchus had planned. Her only hope was that he kept her alive long enough for her to devise a way out.

Looking round, she caught a glimpse of Malchus, who was scowling as he got out of the car. Their eyes met briefly, but she could read nothing from their cold hard expression.

The bodyguard grabbed her arm roughly, bent it at the elbow, and twisted it up behind her back. A flash of pain tore up to her shoulder blade, but she suppressed the urge to make any sound.

She was watching all her captors keenly. She needed to stay alert, to be ready for any opportunity that presented itself.

With her arm pinned firmly behind her and the gun rammed into the small of her back, the bodyguard propelled her towards the house.

As they approached the brass-ornamented door, the driver stepped forward, turned a key in its lock, and pushed it open, ushering her into the old building.

The hallway was high, and thick shafts of sunshine streamed in from the diamond-leaded windows, piercing flared tunnels of light deep into the building.

The entrance space was painted a gentle off-white, and bright geometric op art paintings hung on the walls, framing a hallway sparsely filled with simple yet elegant furniture.

Whoever owned the house, Ava noted, was someone with a degree of sensitivity—which ruled out Malchus, who she suspected would have installed stags' heads and suits of armour holding chunky weaponry.

The driver had meanwhile opened a small cupboard just to the right of the doorway, and was entering a security code.

*So they were alone.*

They passed through the hall into a reception room. It was comfortably furnished with three deep brown leather sofas at one end and a large shiny mahogany desk at the other. Halfway down the far wall was a set of French windows leading onto a patio with an attractive bubbling fountain. Along the remainder of the room's walls were a series of carved dark wooden bookcases holding antique leather-bound volumes and modern hardbacks. Between them, she could see delicately lit oil paintings—mostly landscapes.

It was a tasteful room, without pretensions—further proof it was not Malchus's house.

Malchus nodded towards the middle of the room. The bodyguard marched her over to a carpet in the centre, and pushed her down onto her knees, roughly placing her hands behind her head.

Interlacing her fingers, she glared up at him defiantly.

*He was not going to have this all his own way.*

She knew her prospects looked bleak, but for the time being was reassured by the knowledge he was not going to kill her just yet. He of all people knew what a messy business executions were, and she doubted very much he would have brought her into the main room to shoot her.

But the danger was still very real. The bodyguard had not moved. He remained beside her, pressing the cool nylon polymer muzzle of the handgun against her head.

Malchus sat down in the leather sofa facing her. He looked over at her, withdrawing an object from his pocket.

She was surprised to see it was a set of black rosary beads, like those used by traditional Christians the world over. She did a double take, unable to reconcile the devotional object with what she knew of Malchus.

But as she focused on it more closely, she noticed the beads were made of matt black metal. And where the rope of beads usually ended in a crucifix, the one he was holding had a sleek and sharp-pointed black steel star about the size of a dollar coin.

At first glance she thought the pendant was a pentagram. But as it turned in the light she saw it had six points not five—although it looked nothing like the usual six-pointed star on Christmas trees and the flag of Israel.

There was something infinitely more malevolent about it.

He settled himself into the sofa, and began to run the metal beads between his fingers, as if in some silent meditative prayer.

Ava slowed her breathing, telling herself to take longer deeper breaths. Dropping her shoulders, she willed her muscles to untense. She knew she had to relax if she was going to pull this off.

Looking across at Malchus, she could see he was still eyeing her coldly. When at last he spoke, his voice had changed from when she had heard it at the rally.

He was no longer the passionate bold-gestured orator. Now he was angry—speaking slowly and deliberately, every inch the ruthless and mechanical operator she knew he really was.

"Let's get this over with." He looked expectantly at her, as if challenging her to defy him. "Who are you?"

The question was cold. Clinical.

She breathed an inner sigh of relief.

*Good.*

If he wanted her to answer questions, then it gave her a chance to talk her way out of it.

But she would need a cover story. Quickly. And it would have to be good. One thing she knew for sure—there would not be another opportunity.

An idea had begun forming while she had been kneeling, and she was still running through the angles in her head as he began talking. More than anything now, she needed to stall, to give herself the time to put the final pieces of the story together—to get it right in her mind.

Trying to sound as unfazed as possible, she glowered back at him. "Tell your monkey to put his gun away."

Malchus did not rise to the bait. "I'll ask you again—who are you?"

Ava glared at him. She was still thinking through the details of her cover story and needed to play for time. "Call him off."

Malchus kept his eyes fixed on her. There was no flicker of reaction. She stared back at him, refusing to be intimidated. "Go on. Call him off." She nodded in the direction of the bodyguard holding the gun to her head. "Call him off, and I'll talk to you."

Despite the danger, a part of her was enjoying the defiance. If he was going to kill her, she had no intention of begging.

Malchus eyed her carefully, giving her valuable seconds before at length answering. "You're in no position to negotiate anything."

She nodded. "If you kill me, you'll never know why I'm here." She was pleased to hear that her voice sounded strong. Combative.

She waited keenly for his answer. There was a serious point to her demands. The way he responded would tell her how she needed to handle him. If he acquiesced even slightly, then she knew she had the ability, however small, to influence him. But if he did not, then she had her work cut out if she was going to talk her way free.

Without warning, he stood up and strode over to her. The blow came so fast she had no time to protect herself.

The intensity of the pain surprised her, but she stifled the urge to shout out.

It had been an open-handed slap, but hard enough to knock her sideways. As she righted herself, she felt him grab a handful of her hair. He yanked it hard, and bent low over her so their faces were only inches apart.

"Believe me when I tell you I'm in no mood for your games." He tightened his grip on her hair. The pain was excruciating. Her heart was hammering, and there was a rushing noise in her ears. "In a very short time you have become a considerable nuisance to me."

With his free hand he put something cold on her face. It felt sharp, and he was pressing it into the flesh at the bottom of her eye socket. As she tried to work out what it was, she could see the black metal beads of his rosary flowing out of his clenched hand. With a wave of revulsion, she realized he was pushing one of the sharpened tapering points of the hexagram pendant into the flesh just under her eye.

His voice was menacingly quiet. "You need to start thinking about cooperating with me. Because I'm fast losing patience with you, and I'm very close to ending your ability to bother me." He pushed the lethal point of the evil-looking star a little harder into the soft skin, all the while staring into her eyes.

What she saw in his expression was not reassuring. There was nothing living—just an icy determination.

He let go of her hair and took the vicious star from beneath her eye. Returning to his seat, he stared at her again. "Now, one more time. Who are you?"

She did not have to feign anger or indignation any longer. The blood was coursing through her veins, and she wanted nothing more than to let herself loose on him. But she restrained herself—she had to think of the longer game.

*When the time came, he was going to pay for that*, she promised herself.

Well?" Malchus prompted.

Ava was thinking rapidly. The incident had given her the answer she wanted—Malchus was not open for negotiation.

It had also bought her more time. She had initially wanted to say she was a journalist—it used to be one of the best covers around. But the internet had ruined that. With a few clicks of a mouse anyone could discover she had never been anywhere near a newspaper or written any magazine articles.

But she was now out of time. Ready or not, she had to give him an explanation.

She breathed deeply, forcing back the intense hatred she was feeling towards him, pushing it out of her voice. "There's no need for all this," she began. "I have a proposition for you."

He stared at her, his face granite.

She continued, concentrating for all she was worth on giving the performance of her lifetime. "You have certain unusual needs. And the organization I represent has a range of highly successful solutions to the many challenges you face."

She scanned his face for any reaction—even the smallest indication of interest.

Nothing.

His fingers continued moving over the metal beads.

"We don't offer these services to everyone, I'm sure you understand. My responsibility and speciality is to identify potential partners, and inform them of our services."

Ava was breathing more easily now. It felt good to be talking. The cover was not guaranteed to work, but it was comforting to be slipping into a role. She did not want to be herself in front of Malchus any longer than she had to.

"I came to the rally because I wanted to meet you. As you can imagine, I don't carry a business card, and we don't take out advertisements in the phone book. My organization is not well known, and we keep our business private. That's why we have presidents and prime ministers among our many satisfied customers."

"I don't believe I have any needs you or your organization can fulfil," Malchus stated flatly.

"Yes, you do," Ava countered confidently. "I pick our partners very carefully. And I'm good at what I do. My approach to you is not random."

"You've got two minutes," Malchus replied, looking at his watch.

*Round one.* She smiled to herself. He was interested enough to give her time. Now she just had to keep him engaged.

*But two minutes?*

She felt like she was doing an elevator pitch at some business school. At that moment, there were probably hundreds of students from Texas to Taipei practising it right now: honing how to sell an idea to someone in the time it takes for an elevator to go from the ground floor to the top executive suite.

But none of them had a gun to their head.

Ava launched straight in, trying to make it sound like it was a speech she had given many times before.

"When our partners have cash that comes from sources they want to keep private, we offer assistance. We place their funds into the international money system on their behalf. And then later we return it to them, through accredited routes. Our partners get legitimate money they can spend freely."

"So you're in the laundry business," Malchus sounded bored. "How disappointing. There are many people who can do that."

Ava shook her head. "Not like this. We offer our partners something truly unique." She looked at him conspiratorially. "Our partners are demanding and, as a result, you'll see we're far more sophisticated than most."

Malchus was fingering the black rosary beads slowly. "Laundering is a basic service. It doesn't call for much sophistication."

*Excellent.*

He was slowly engaging in the discussion. It was exactly what she wanted.

"Our methods are proprietary and highly confidential," Ava answered.

"Then this conversation is over," Malchus looked up at her sharply.

She bit her lip.

*Take it slowly.*

"We've been operating for over forty years," Ava countered, unfazed. "And have never had an unsatisfied partner. I can't disclose to you the details of how we do it, but what makes us stand apart from the crowd is that we don't cost you or lose your money. In fact, we make more money for you."

Keen to ensure he had got the point, she pressed on. "Traditional laundering wastes a lot of the money. When the client hands over a million dollars, he's happy to see half a million back in clean funds. He could never spend the dirty million anyway, so it's half a million more than he'd have without the laundering. The lost half a million goes on people who want their cut, officials who need to be paid off, and good old-fashioned losses from haphazardly trading stocks, shares, and assets just to muddy the audit trail, because that's everyone's priority. Covering tracks is much more important than making good investments."

Ava was warming to her theme, enjoying making it all up, "We bring a different sort of expertise. We're investment managers. Good ones. We'll provide the most robust and sophisticated cleaning service currently available, but we'll also make good investments. If a partner gives us a million, we'll give the whole million back with interest. Our partners are unanimous—this is a truly unique and bespoke service."

As she had been mentioning the details, she had seen his eyes widen just a touch.

He was interested.

*No doubt about that.*

She pressed on. "We have many strategies. Let me give you one example."

She remembered a misty Virginia morning in Langley, listening to a humourless CIA anti-money-laundering agent explaining how it all worked. At the time, she had wondered how anyone could do his job, staring at columns of numbers all day. But she had paid enough attention to get a grip of the basics, which she had to admit had a whiff of the exotic, with exclusive banks on tropical islands and go-betweens jetting in and out with steel suitcases.

"We introduce our partners' cash into the banking system in a country with water-tight bank secrecy laws. Forget Switzerland. It's a Hollywood myth. The Swiss were compromised by the U.S. and gave up their independence a while ago. We prefer jurisdictions that still take bank secrecy seriously—like Singapore or Panama."

His eyes widened fractionally for a millisecond. But Ava saw it.

*Bullseye.*

It never ceased to amaze her how getting a few facts right led listeners to assume that speakers had real expertise, and that everything else they said was therefore also accurate.

"It would be rash to assume any jurisdiction is watertight," Malchus observed coldly.

Ava had to resist the urge to nod enthusiastically. "Which is why," she continued, "if ever the accounts are compromised, they all lead back to genuine individuals: highly respectable philanthropists and industrialists—exactly the sort of people who regularly move large sums of money around the world and are beyond suspicion. They work with us, generously allowing us to blend our funds into their accounts in return for certain considerations we can offer them."

Malchus was still watching her. Although the intensity of his gaze was unnerving, Ava was delighted to have his attention. It meant she might be getting somewhere.

She needed this to work.

"Then we go about mixing the money up. As we aim to deliver a profit, we actively invest the cash. We transfer it from the safe accounts to some of the world's biggest banks and fund managers. We keep the amounts relatively small, as small sums attract lighter controls, and we spread the money about as much as possible—to make it virtually untraceable. We invest it in shares, bonds, hedge funds, real estate, commodities—anything that will turn a profit. Then, once the trail is a baffling ball of knitting, the cash is paid on to legitimate businesses. We arrange for our partners to have directorships of these companies, or to provide invoiceable services. So our partners get paid back their money, but to the governmental agencies it just looks like legitimate business payments."

"How real are these end companies?" Malchus asked, frowning.

"It varies—according to price, naturally."

"Naturally," echoed Malchus, nodding. There was no hint of humour.

"They cover all sectors—energy, technology, transport, hospitality, construction, you name it. Our simpler service involves dummy companies with offices in relatively quiet places that rarely get any attention from the authorities—like Copenhagen, Salzburg, Toledo, and other nine-to-five business towns. If anyone investigates, they'll find these businesses are ultimately owned by a network of holding companies and nominee trusts in privacy-friendly countries like Hong Kong or the Cayman Islands. Law enforcement would waste years trying to unravel it."

"And your enhanced service?" Malchus was watching her carefully.

"If our partners have marketable skills or relevant profiles, we can place them directly onto advisory boards and panels of real companies, often household name companies which are entirely unaware of the true nature of the arrangement. On the other hand, if our partners prefer absolute anonymity, we can create services and paperwork through shell-companies for them. So in all cases, our partners are being legitimately paid for their work. We offer many variations on the theme. As I say, this is just one of our services. We have others."

Malchus's eyes were darting about as he evaluated the proposition from all the angles. "And what credentials can your organization provide?"

*Slowly.*

Ava forced herself not to look too keen.

*Reel him in slowly.*

She knew she had him. But he was volatile, and needed careful handling.

"I have to earn my money somehow," Ava said with a smile. "So the security is … ," she paused, "… me."

She had thought that might finally get a response from Malchus.

His face remained unresponsive.

She carried on. "I'll offer you a one-day trade, so you can see how it works. You give me the money in the morning. I'll arrange for it to be placed in a friendly bank. By that evening, you'll have your money back again, fully invoiced and legitimately paid to you for consultancy services you will have provided to a hotel chain. You won't earn much interest for such a short deposit, but you'll have me, as collateral, with you all day."

Ava looked at him hard. "You'll understand that if I did not have absolute confidence in my organization, I wouldn't place myself in this position. We know who you are, and we know what you would do to me if your money was not returned intact. That is how strongly I guarantee our service."

Malchus nodded again.

His robot-like coldness sent a shiver down her spine. She knew he would think nothing of disposing of her.

"After the first trade, of course, we cannot extend you the same security. You'll never see me again—but then I'm sure that's the way you'll want it, too. We won't communicate, although I'll give you ways to contact me in an emergency."

Ava held her breath.

*Had it been enough?*

She had played her cards. Now she could only wait.

Malchus stood up. He was still smoothing his dark rosary. "An unusual proposition." His sea-green eyes seemed to be looking right through her. "I'll need to make some enquiries."

*You mean check-up on me.*

"Let's discuss this again in a few days," he concluded. "I'm sure we both have practicalities to attend to."

"Of course," Ava nodded.

*It had worked.*

She had to force herself to keep the relief and jubilation off her face. She could not quite believe he had bought it.

He turned as the door opened.

His driver entered, carrying a sheet of paper.

As he handed it to Malchus, Ava thought she saw a photograph of herself on it.

Her heart skipped a beat.

*What on earth … ?*

As Malchus took it, she saw the paper more clearly. This time there was no doubt. There was definitely a picture of her on it, kneeling on the floor in the room. It could only have been taken in the last few minutes, while she had been talking. Her eyes scanned the walls, and then she saw it—a small white box mounted above the picture rail, high on the wall in front of her.

A tiny circle of glass in the middle announced it was a security camera.

Malchus sat back down in the dark brown sofa, and stared at the sheet of paper, tapping it with his finger.

At length he spoke, his voice betraying nothing except a cold efficiency. "So, it's all lies."

Ava frowned at him. "What?"

"I'll grant you this—you're good. But," he paused, "not good enough, it seems."

"I don't understand," Ava countered, unsure what was happening, feeling the situation slipping away from her.

"Apparently you have no name and no history." He turned the paper round so she could read it.

It was some kind of identity search. She did not recognize the system or database. Her photograph was matched to an old identity photo, but the boxes for name, height, weight, colour of eyes, nationality, employment, and all the other usual fields were blank.

Ava felt a wave of panic wash over her.

*This was not good.*

Malchus breathed out decisively. "A blank report could be owing to a number of things. Either you never existed—which is plainly not the case. Or maybe you've had an identity change, perhaps with extensive reconstructive surgery?"

He stalked over to her and grabbed her face by the chin. He turned her head roughly from one side to the other, inspecting the skin under her eyes, round her nose, by her ears, and around her hairline.

His grip was vice-like. She twisted her head in defiance, trying to free herself. But he was too strong.

"Or," he continued, still gripping her chin tightly so she could not move her neck, and lowering his face to hers until she could feel his breath, "the international authorities have purposefully erased your profile. And, in my considerable experience of such things, they would only do that if you were in some way connected with them." He released her head, pushing it away from him as if it were something distasteful.

Ava's heart was hammering hard. She had to force herself to keep her breathing under control.

*How could this have happened?*

When she left the Firm, her resettlement programme included resetting her ever-changing profiles in the UK government central intelligence and other databases to her new one. The form Malchus was holding should be showing information on her career in academia and museums, with up-to-date information about her role in Baghdad. It should never, then or now, have been blank. She should have checked out as a legitimate civilian—leaving her free to lead a double life as an unknown money-launderer, or anything else she chose.

*What had happened?*

Her mind was whirring.

"So, who are you?" He stared down at her. "The truth, this time."

Ava allowed herself to show her anger. "I've told you who I am, and why I'm here. My line of business requires a certain amount of discretion, trust, and goodwill—and I'm not feeling any of it from you at the moment."

Malchus screwed the piece of paper up and dropped it by his feet. He turned to the guard standing by Ava's side, who still had the Glock trained on her.

"Take her away. Don't bring her back until she wants to tell the truth."

From the overly precise way in which he had said 'wants', she was in no doubt he had just given the bodyguard a free licence to do whatever he wanted with her.

Malchus turned and left the room, closing the door firmly behind him.

Ava could not stop herself from looking up at the man looming over her. And she was horrified to see that his thuggish expression had been replaced with a leer of expectant sadism and lust.

---  ✦  ---

# 46

*Stockbridge House*
*Nr Newton Tony*
*Wiltshire SP4*
*England*
*The United Kingdom*

THE BODYGUARD WASTED no time in complying with Malchus's instructions.

"I'm going to enjoy messing you up," he leered. His South African accent was thick and precise. "Such a pretty thing, too. But you're going to look even better by the time I've finished with you." He smiled unpleasantly. From the way he was looking up and down her body appreciatively, she was in no doubt he had a particular range of pleasures in mind.

"Why don't we start with some water sports," he smirked, nodding to the large stone fountain in the courtyard outside the French windows. "I want to see you all wet for me."

He motioned with the pistol for her to walk towards the French windows. "Hands above your head." He prodded her with the gun. "If you play any games with me, I'll know you're having fun and want me to take longer." He grunted with pleasure. "I'm going to really enjoy this."

Ava shuddered at the thought of what constituted pleasure for him.

She wanted nothing more than to wipe the unpleasant grin off his face permanently. But she would have to be careful. He was big, and clearly dangerous. No doubt he had earned his position as Malchus's bodyguard the hard way. She had to assume he could handle himself.

She turned to the French windows and began to walk towards them, aware he was keeping the gun trained on her.

She could see the fountain more clearly now. It was made of grey stone, with an ornamental bowl at knee height out of which a spray of water rose gently several feet in the air. It wasn't especially wide, but easily deep enough for him to hold her head under and drown her.

She knew she had to do something before they got to it. If not, she would lose any element of surprise, and he would start hurting her severely.

She could feel her heart racing as her body primed itself, preparing to fight, moving into attack mode.

One way or the other, things were about to get physical. And it was not going to be in the way the guard was planning.

Looking about, she could see only one option.

It was not perfect, but would have to do. She would have to make it work.

Placing herself at the guard's mercy was not an option

Aware she was walking too quickly, she forced herself to slow down, allowing the guard to make up the ground between them and fall into step right behind her.

*Slowly.*

She kept repeating the word inside her head.

*Take it slowly.*

As she drew level with the French windows, she could feel him right behind her.

All her training had taught her that speed, surprise, and maximum aggression were everything.

*Now!*

With a lightning quick twist, she grabbed the pale blue damask curtaining gathered above and around the glass doorway, and yanked it off its runners with all her strength.

To her relief, the fabric was heavy and came away easily. As she had expected, it unfolded itself from the neat gathered pleats and spread out, revealing more than enough material for her purposes.

It fell fast and hard, and she hurdled it onto the guard directly behind her.

Without pausing, she lunged toward him at full speed, smashing her knee hard up into his groin. At the same time, she punched out both hands with all her force, using them as rams. One of her hands connected with his shoulder, the other with his chin. Pushing him, she powered forward, snapping his head back, driving his upper body until he toppled, disorientated by the curtains and destabilized by her unexpected onslaught.

As he keeled over, she took aim, stamping hard on the central area just below the intersection of his bottom two ribs. The heel of her boot found its mark, crushing the massive bundles of sensitive nerves that routed into the soft flesh of his solar plexus.

His body instantly doubled up into a foetal position, and his diaphragm went into spasm. He choked, writhing in agony. As he twisted, the curtain slipped off his right side, revealing his hand still clamped around the grip of the Glock.

Aware she only had a few seconds to finish the job before his strength returned, she quickly leant over him, jamming her index finger inside the pistol's trigger guard so it covered his.

Nauseous from the pain, his reaction was delayed. But as he realized what she was doing, he bellowed, swinging his arm away from his body.

Not quickly enough.

With two rapid squeezes, she pushed his finger against the trigger twice. The noise of the Glock was deafening as it discharged a pair of rounds at over a thousand feet per second straight into the soft flesh of his inner thigh.

When the noise of the explosions faded, she could hear him screaming in agony as he dropped the gun and grabbed his mangled leg, where a dark crimson patch was already bubbling out onto his jeans.

She looked at him lying on the ground, and realized it was a long time since she had been in a hand-to-hand fight. She was breathing hard, but grateful to note that lack of practice had not dulled her reactions or instincts.

Gazing down at the crippled thug, whimpering as he pressed his slippery red hands onto his thigh to staunch the blood loss, she felt no sympathy. He had chosen a life of violence, and this was the price.

Bending over him, she spoke in a low voice. "If you ever try anything like that on me again, next time I'll really hurt you."

He stared up at her—his eyes gleaming with hatred behind the mask of pain.

As she spoke the words, she became aware of the full extent of her pent-up tension. It had been building ever since she had regained consciousness in the car, reaching a peak when Malchus had handed her over to this animal. Now she was out of immediate danger, she felt the tension begin to subside, giving way to a sense of sheer outrage at Malchus's arrogance.

She grabbed the gun and tucked it into the back of her jeans' waistband. She was not clear of the danger yet, and had no idea who may have heard the shots.

Taking a final look at the crippled guard to reassure herself he posed no further threat, she ran quickly out of the French windows and into the garden, heading straight for the woods.

# 47

*The British Library*
*96 Euston Road*
*London NW1*
*England*
*The United Kingdom*

THE ANCIENT MANUSCRIPT was vital.

Without it, the plan would fail.

Malchus knew he needed to choose his target with care.

There was no scope for error. If it went wrong, if his target alerted the authorities—the manuscript would be put under lock and key, and all would be lost.

He had delayed going after the manuscript for some months. But now he was ready.

The time was right.

All he needed was a collaborator.

In his previous life, sitting in his clinical office at the Ministerium in Berlin, it would have taken a team of underlings weeks of trawling through confidential personal files and conducting covert interviews to find a suitable target.

But these days the internet did away with all that. People were stupid. They voluntarily published their most personal information to the world.

He wanted someone who worked in the hushed underworld of the book stacks deep below the library. Not a trained librarian or archivist—someone who pushed the trolleys around would be just perfect.

He had combed social and work networking sites to draw up a short-list of potential targets, before following up on each of them in more detail. He had then built a picture of their personal profiles from entries on user groups, online forums, hobby sites, and the general flotsam and jetsam they left in cyberspace.

It took him a morning, but when he was done, he was extremely pleased with the result.

Alex Hibbit would do nicely.

Once he had chosen Alex, a few hours of invasive hacking into Alex and his friends' online profiles and uploads yielded a crop of photographs showing a dull-faced lanky twenty-something man with a mop of blond hair.

The pictures were easily good enough to identify Alex.

Now, waiting at closing time again on the large chequered piazza outside the British Library, he scanned the stream of readers and employees exiting the brutalist red brick building.

He breathed in deeply, feeling the power, aware that under his feet, in the vast subterranean store rooms, lay the world's greatest collection of black magic manuscripts—the writings of the occult masters going back to ancient Babylonia. He had collected and read most of them over the years. But now, so close to the originals, he could sense their dark energy.

It filled him with renewed purpose.

He looked with disdain at the intellectuals scuttling in and out of the building. He despised them—squandering their efforts on barren studies in that great temple of knowledge. They were mental eunuchs—knowing much but understanding nothing.

He did not have to wait long until he saw Alex sauntering out of the large metal and glass entrance doors.

He followed the younger man at a discreet distance.

*He had better have it with him.*

He was not in the mood for disappointment.

Malchus had been waiting in the library's vast foyer two days earlier. When he had spotted Alex then, for the first time, he had immediately headed for the exit, engineering it so they both arrived at the same time. As they passed through the doors side-by-side, Malchus had purposefully mistimed his step, bumping into Alex, intentionally dropping the notebook and pen he had been carrying.

Alex had looked startled at Malchus's unnerving appearance, but Malchus left him no opportunity to get away—forcing him instead into a conversation, explaining it was his first trip to the library, where he was researching computer simulations.

As Malchus continued and mentioned war-gaming strategy, he was gratified to see interest flicker behind Alex's eyes. He had assumed it would—Alex's cyber footprint had quickly shown he was a keen gamer.

They had headed down the Euston Road, deep in conversation. At King's Cross station, Malchus had suggested he might buy him a pint in a pub they were passing. Sensing the younger man's apprehension, he had reassured him he was not making a pass. Rather, he had been working on developing a new game, and he would welcome the thoughts of a player as expert as he plainly was.

It turned Malchus's stomach to curry favour with someone as insignificant as Alex. But he kept himself focused, thinking about the manuscript.

The pub was typical for a railway station bar. It was cavernous, gloomy, smelled of stale beer, and was fitted out with tatty dark wooden furniture. Fruit machines beeped and flashed in the far corner, while an array of televisions bolted into the ceiling showed a range of soundless sporting fixtures.

Malchus looked contemptuously at its occupants—flabby men with nothing better to do than spend their evenings swilling beer around emptying glasses while staring at screens.

He picked a quiet area of the back bar, and indicated for Alex to sit.

As one drink turned into another, he revealed confidentially that he was developing a totally new type of computer role-playing game—one that would be very special. Inside it, he was going to hide an extra game, a very exceptional one, accessible only to players who proved themselves worthy, on and off the computer. The whole architecture was revolutionary—gamers would not only play in cyberspace, they would need to accomplish certain tasks in the real world, too. It would be like nothing anyone had ever experienced or played before. It would re-write the history of gaming—blurring the online world with the real one

He refilled Alex's pint glass again as he elaborated on the groundbreaking concept, before confiding in him that he was looking for a business partner: one who could add some value to the venture, and help it become a reality that would make them both rich.

Dropping his voice, he asked if Alex could keep a secret. When the younger man affirmed he could, Malchus shared his view that it must be fate they had met that night, as what Malchus needed to finalize the game was inside the library.

Malchus explained that he had discovered there was an old manuscript that was crucial to the game's architecture. It was a unique document, containing details of an ancient tradition. It alone could provide the details needed to finish the adventure at the heart of the revolutionary game, and allow players to plug into a quest that had been spinning down the centuries. Malchus had leaned in conspiratorially, explaining that once the game was launched, the world would never be the same again.

He watched as the alcohol and the tall story began to work on his new friend. His pupils were constricting, and his eyes beginning to gleam. Not just with the alcohol, Malchus noted with satisfaction—but with greed, too.

Sensing the moment, Malchus went for the kill. He pronounced that destiny had surely brought them together, as the answer lay right in front of them—Alex could be his business partner: all he needed to do was get the manuscript.

To prove his good faith, Malchus placed an envelope holding ten crisp fifty pound notes onto the bar counter between them, and told Alex there was another five hundred if he earned his place in the partnership by getting the manuscript. Alex should consider it a sign-on bonus into the business.

Eyeing the money hungrily, the younger man nodded—just as Malchus suspected he would when he had planned the sting.

Alex reassured Malchus he could do it—no problem. Books regularly went missing. Thousands were currently unaccounted for. He explained that security was minimal in the four hundred and something miles of shelving under the building. There was no budget for anything thorough—his access card was about as hi-tech as it got.

Malchus reassured him he would return the manuscript once he had finished with it. It would only be a temporary loan—just long enough for him to study it.

Alex nodded, but had clearly not been so befuddled by the beer to miss an opportunity. He suggested the second payment should be one thousand pounds, not five hundred. After all, he reminded Malchus, he could lose his job if he was caught.

After making a show of indecision, Malchus accepted. This was not the moment to have an argument with his new business partner.

Alex was perfect for the job. Removing the manuscript from the library required no skill or knowledge, so it made little sense for Malchus to do it and put himself at risk. And for a man of Alex's age and prospects, the lure of immediate money and a new life as a computer game mogul was an undreamed-of change in fortune.

Malchus had learned a lot about human nature over the years. Not simply that everyone eventually gave in to unrelenting or extreme pain, but also how easy it was to pull the strings and have people dance to whatever tune he wished.

It was simple with young men—they liked money and grand dreams. The prospect of either of those would give them all the motivation they needed. As they hit middle age, they would still do things for the prospect of money, but were less wide-eyed and more sceptical. Paying an attractive young prostitute to get them drunk and seduce them into a night of long-forgotten pleasures of the flesh was usually easiest—as was the ensuing blackmail.

Malchus had known that hooking Alex would be straightforward. Working in a government library did not pay much, and doubtless Alex had a host of dreams he could indulge if he suddenly came into money.

Finishing up their drinks, Alex assured Malchus he would have the manuscript in two days. Malchus could wait for him outside, at closing time.

So now Malchus stood on the library's great piazza, watching Alex emerge from the library with a rucksack on his back.

He followed the younger man across the esplanade, his excitement mounting.

As Alex turned right onto the Euston Road, Malchus drew alongside him.

"Do you have it?" He had to work to keep his voice calm.

Alex nodded, sending a shiver of anticipation down Malchus's spine. He began to slip his rucksack off.

"Not here," hissed Malchus, gesturing for them to turn up a side street to their right.

Malchus pointed to a blue Mercedes parked a little further up. It had dark tinted windows and a fold-out sunshade covering the front window from the inside.

"Is that yours?" Alex looked impressed. "You must be doing alright for yourself."

"It is," Malchus replied brusquely. At least, it had been for a few hours, since he had stolen it from outside a residential house in south London.

As they drew alongside, Malchus indicated for Alex to open the rear passenger door and climb in. Malchus followed, sliding in after him.

"Show it to me," he ordered the younger man, taking out a pair of silicone medical gloves from his jacket's inner pocket.

"What are those for?" Alex asked, a hint of uncertainty in his voice.

"Manuscripts are fragile." Malchus pulled on the gloves. "Finger grease damages them."

"Where's the money then?" Alex's tone was belligerent.

"All in good time." Malchus replied slowly, fitting the gloves onto each finger carefully.

"It's not that I don't trust you," Alex replied. "I want to see it before we go any further."

"Of course," Malchus answered, taking an envelope from his pocket and handing it to him. "Count it."

Alex tore it open. His eyes lit up as he counted out the twenty fifty pound notes, before pulling out of his jeans pocket the cash Malchus had given him the previous day and putting it into the envelope with his new earnings. "It's not funny money or anything, is it?" he asked, a trace of suspicion in his voice.

Malchus ignored the question. "Show me the manuscript."

Alex unzipped the rucksack resting on his knees, and took out a shallow grey cardboard archive box sealed on top with a string-tie fastener.

Malchus gazed at the box.

*Finally.*

*He had waited for so long.*

He could almost hear the voices from the past speaking to him down the centuries—the ancient words passed on through time so he could accomplish the Work.

The wisdom was over two thousand years old.

And soon it would be his.

He would complete what no one else ever had.

It all lay before him, in that nondescript-looking archive box.

He reached out his hand and took hold of the cardboard, sensing a surge of energy pass through him.

*This was it. This was the key.*

He could feel it.

Unlooping the string tie holding the lid closed, he slowly opened the flaps of the box, his heart beating hard.

He felt an overwhelming sense of excitement that the knowledge was within his grasp.

Inside the box was a folder of stiff white acid-free card. He flipped it open, revealing a sheaf of vellum manuscript pages. The ancient animal skin was light brown, thin and brittle, with clear signs of water damage in places. But the bold writing—Hebrew and Aramaic characters—all stood out as clearly as the day they were written.

He knew in an instant that it had been waiting for *him*—all those years, in the cold basement of the library.

He alone knew what to do.

The time was right.

He sensed that it was all coming together, like a propitious planetary alignment known only to the select.

He turned the quarto-sized folios over carefully, checking they were all legible.

As he reached the last one, he looked up at Alex, an expression of cold rage on his face.

"Where is the twelfth folio?"

Alex shook his head slowly. "That's my insurance," he replied. "When you're done, you give me back the eleven, and I'll give you the twelfth."

With a lightning-fast movement, Malchus pulled a thin black cylinder from his pocket. There was a menacing click as a long narrow steel blade shot out of it. Before Alex had taken in what was happening, the razor-sharp metal was at his throat.

"You disappoint me," Malchus hissed.

Alex's eyes widened in terror as Malchus pushed the evil-looking blade hard against his carotid artery. A small trickle of blood appeared.

With his spare hand, Malchus unzipped the rucksack on Alex's knee, and began to rifle through the contents. It was empty, apart from a fleece and a folder. Malchus pulled out the folder and flipped it open, revealing the missing folio.

"Don't hurt me," whispered Alex, as Malchus opened up the cut on his neck a little wider.

Malchus put his face close to Alex's, so their noses were almost touching. He could feel Alex's breath coming in hard short bursts, and see the terror in the younger man's eyes. "It won't hurt," Malchus answered softly. "Not for long."

Alex tried to push Malchus away, but he was no match for the bigger man's bulk.

"Be calm, now," Malchus murmured, his face only an inch from Alex's. "He is your shield and helper."

"What?" Alex whimpered, pressing his body as far back into the seat as he could to get away from the blade. "What are you on about?"

"And your glorious sword." Malchus continued in a soft tone, leaning closer to Alex, lowering the knife so it was level with his chest.

"I made a mistake," stammered Alex his eyes wide with terror. "I'm sorry. I won't do it again."

"Your enemies will cower before you," Malchus continued, feeling a rush of gratification at the mounting horror he could see in Alex's eyes, and the expanding damp patch staining the crotch of the young man's jeans.

Placing the razor-sharp tip of the blade between the third and fourth ribs to the right of Alex's sternum, he held it there, pushing it so it pricked him.

"What are you doing?" stammered Alex. "Please, God—don't." His breaths were coming in anguished rasps.

"And you will trample down their high places," Malchus concluded quietly, slamming the blade in forcefully, leaning against it with all his weight, pushing it hard through the thick intercostal muscles and deep into Alex's hammering heart.

If Alex had ever read the Bible, he might have recognized Malchus's words as Moses's dying speech from the book of Deuteronomy.

But he had not. So the last words he heard as his life slipped away were meaningless gibberish—spoken quietly by a man he had realized, too late, was quite insane.

Picking up the twelfth sheet of vellum from the folder and placing it into the archive box with the others, Malchus did up the string fastener and put it all into Alex's rucksack along with the envelope of money.

Closing the car door carefully behind him with his gloved hand, he slipped on the rucksack and tightened the straps.

Without turning to look back, he pulled off the silicone gloves and stuffed them into his pocket, before heading down the street to join the anonymous crowds jostling around King's Cross railway station.

———— · ◆ · ————

# 48

*The Malet Arms*
*Newton Tony*
*Nr Salisbury*
*Wiltshire SP4*
*England*
*The United Kingdom*

AVA SAT DOWN by the large inglenook fireplace.

There were no chairs—just a pair of worn oak benches. They had probably been church pews once, she thought. Still, they fitted effortlessly into the small five-hundred-year-old pub, among its gnarled black wooden roof beams, low plaster ceilings, and irregular dark corners.

There were no television screens, arcade games, or speakers chirping out canned music. It was a traditional cosy country inn on the Plain, hung with old horse brasses, prints of rural scenes, and occasional items of hunting memorabilia.

She spotted Ferguson the moment he came through the low door. He ducked to avoid banging his head on the ceiling, and made his way straight over to her.

She had tried to call him from her mobile, but it had been out of battery, so she had used the payphone in the pub.

She had been wondering what she was going to say to him when he arrived. She knew she would have landed him in hot water with Prince by ditching him at Stonehenge. She would not like to be in his shoes when he made his report.

Even though it was summer and there was no fire lit in the grate, a large fawn-coloured English mastiff padded over to the space in front of the fire and flopped down on the tiles.

She scratched its ears absent-mindedly as Ferguson approached.

"I see you're ahead of me again." He nodded at her half-finished drink. "You're making a bit of a habit of that."

"Cider?" She was not quite sure what he meant.

"Being ahead of me. Where did you get to today? You missed the rendezvous." He looked like it had been a long day.

She was not sure how much to tell him. Instinctively, she wanted as little leakage back to Prince as possible. But she was not going to lie to him.

"I had an opportunity to get close to Malchus, and I took it," she answered truthfully.

"That's it?" he asked, when it was clear she was not going to elaborate any further.

She nodded. "Probably best to spare you the details."

"That's a nasty looking cut you've got there." He pointed to her left eye.

She put a finger up to it, and felt a scab where Malchus had jabbed his rosary's sharpened hexagram pendant into her face. She had not noticed it before, but found it was tender to the touch. "It's nothing," she answered dismissively. "I got a tree branch in my face."

From his expression, she could tell he did not believe her for a moment.

"Look, I understand you don't want me around," he admitted, dropping down onto the bench opposite her. "But why call and get me over here if you're not going to tell me what's going on? Why not just slip away into the night?"

Ava felt a little sheepish. "I understand if you want to say 'no', but right now I could do with a bit of help with something that's come up."

Ferguson looked nonplussed. He dug his hands into his jeans pockets and looked pensive, weighing up his response. "I'm not sure that's going to be the best way," he answered. "We need to think a bit more about this." With that, he got up and headed over to the bar.

She watched him wander across the room and start a light-hearted exchange with the landlord as he ordered his drink.

He returned with a pint of beer, and sipped it thoughtfully as he sat down opposite her again, looking appreciatively at the mahogany-coloured liquid before turning his gaze back to her. "Anyway, you want a favour?" He left the rest of the sentence unspoken, but she got his meaning immediately—*even though you don't want me around.* "I've got things to do, too, you know," he continued. "And running around a hippie-trippie festival for six hours trying to find you isn't one of them."

She did not blame him for feeling resentful.

"But," he continued. "I do owe you a favour."

She raised her eyebrows. "You do?"

He took a sip of his beer before continuing. "To pay you back for pulling me off the boat in Kazakhstan."

She would not have thought of it that way. What was the alternative? Leave him there to be gassed? Still, if he wanted to see it as a favour, that was fine by her. "So we have a deal?"

Ferguson shook his head. "Not so fast. Because you owe me a favour, too."

"I do?" It was news to Ava.

Ferguson continued unabashed. "For the file on Malchus I pulled for you. I didn't have to do that."

"Yes, you did," she countered. "You guessed, correctly, that it was your best shot at getting me into your car this morning. You were just doing your job."

"Well, yes and no." He paused. "But I didn't have to share it all with you. And I didn't have to get you this." He reached into his jacket and pulled out a sheet of paper, which he handed to her.

She scanned it quickly.

It was a photocopy of a short typed letter on Foreign and Commonwealth Office notepaper, but bearing MI6's Vauxhall Cross address and signed with a single initial—'C'.

As she read it, her curiosity turned to increasing disbelief.

By the time she had reached the last line, her face had drained of all colour.

"Was this in the file, too?" she asked, her voice hoarse.

Ferguson nodded. "I figured as it was a duplicate file copy, no one would miss it."

Ava stared hard at the piece of paper, trying to make sense of what she had just read.

It was a copy of an official letter from the Chief of MI6 to the Director of Public Prosecutions—the head of the government agency in charge of bringing criminal prosecutions in the UK.

FOREIGN AND COMMONWEALTH OFFICE
85, ALBERT EMBANKMENT
LONDON S.W.8

12th December 2002

Dear Sir,

Under the 1951 guidelines issued by Sir Hartley Shaw-cross and successive Attorneys-General, and as stated in the current *Code for Crown Prosecutors*, prosecutions for criminal offences are to be brought if they are in the public interest.

I hereby inform you that it is not considered in the public interest to contemplate any further investigation into, or prosecution against, the German national Oskar Boehme (also known as Marius Malchus) in connection with the death of Her Majesty's servant Simon Curzon.

Yours, etc.

C

Ava's insides knotted.

She read the letter again, just in case she had misunderstood it. But she had not.

It was clear.

*General Hunter had been telling the truth.*

But he had clearly not told her everything. He had said there was a *suspicion* Malchus was involved in her father's death. Yet if the Chief was ordering a halt to all criminal investigations, it went way beyond a suspicion. This letter was an official whitewash—an unambiguous order not to ask any more questions.

And it came right from the top.

Ava was breathing rapidly, as the years of suppressed frustration turned into palpable resentment.

"Does it seem right to you?" She held out the paper. "Does it? I'm not naïve. I know the Chief signs orders like these to protect agents and operations. But I'm a relative. I was in the service. We were all family. Why on earth wasn't I told? How could they keep this from me?"

She looked up at Ferguson, her eyes dark with anger. "Is this how they show their appreciation, after all he did for them?"

She knew she was speaking more freely than she had intended. She was angry with them. And angry with herself. She could not believe she had allowed herself to be fobbed off so easily. She should have put up more of a fight, and not just accepted that it was policy not to give family members details of deaths on operational duty.

She looked back at the letter.

*This changed everything.*

It was now clear there was a bigger picture behind it all. And the way she saw it, she should have been told. If there had been an ongoing operation, they could have involved her. It would have helped give her closure—helped her to feel she was doing something. But instead they had done what they did best—keep secrets.

When she turned to face him again, her voice was quieter. "Anyway, why are you giving me this? Did Prince tell you to pass it to me? Is this one of her games? To make me grateful so I let you further into my confidence?" Her voice was steady, masking the maelstrom she was feeling inside.

Ferguson shook his head slowly. "No. I'm on my own with this one."

She stared hard at him, defying him to lie to her.

He shrugged. "I figured if it was me, I'd want to know."

She examined his face closely for the first time, searching out signs of tension or conflict. But there were none. She wondered if he was an accomplished deceiver, like so many others who worked for the Firm. But she knew instinctively he was not. He was a soldier—more practised at bravado and banter than deception.

"In which case—thank you," she replied simply. "It's important to me." She paused, aware her reaction had left no doubt of the fact. "But I guess you already knew that."

"So what's the favour?" he asked, changing the subject.

Ava took a sip of her cider and pushed the hair out of her face, as if to brush away what she had just learned.

"I need the details on a big Elizabethan country house about two miles west of here—who owns it, who visits it, anything known about it. The usual. Malchus seems to have an open invitation to treat it as his own."

"No problem. I can get that for you. I've got the gear in the car."

"Good. Let's find out then," she answered decisively, swilling what was left of her cider around the glass before draining it and putting the empty glass down on the low side table.

"Not quite yet," he said, holding up a hand. "There's still the favour you owe me."

She had forgotten, but nodded.

Fair was fair.

"You think I'm in the way, and you don't want me dragging around behind you. But I'll be open with you—I'm not having much fun, either. So I'm going to stop trailing you."

That sounded good. "But that's not exactly me doing you a favour," Ava replied.

"No," he continued, "so here's my request. Give me three days. That's all I ask. Just three days, and then I'm gone if you say so. But in that time, tell me what you're up to. Let me try and help. If, after three days, you still think I'm wasting your time, I'll report back to Prince, tell her you're going nowhere fast, and recommend she should forget about you and explore other avenues."

He looked solemnly at her. "That's it. Three days and we're quits. But you never know, in that time you might find we make a good team."

"Why would you do that?" she asked. "Why would you go back to Prince and get her off my trail?"

"I've got to give you some incentive to keep me around," he smiled. "Because what you're getting into looks way more interesting than anything else I'm likely to be asked to do."

Ava weighed it up. "If you're saying we're quits in three days, and I can move forward without Prince and you on my case, that's a no-brainer."

"We'll see," he answered confidently.

"You're pretty sure of yourself, aren't you?" she shot him a curious look.

"The mind is like a parachute," he replied earnestly.

She raised an eyebrow at him, inviting an explanation

"Useless," he smiled, "unless it's open."

"A bar-room philosopher, too," she shook her head in mock bewilderment. "Then we have a deal. Let's go."

Ferguson leant towards her. "That cut really does look nasty," he peered closely at it with a concerned expression. "You should clean it. I'll see if the landlord has any antiseptic."

Ava pulled back, and stood up. "Let's get one thing straight." She was speaking slowly and deliberately, her friendliness gone. "We may have an understanding. But that's all it is. Leave the personal touch out of it."

The look of concern melted from Ferguson's face, to be replaced with a businesslike expression. "Whatever you say. You're the boss."

"Let's go then," Ava stepped past the dog. "We've got work to do."

Ferguson stared for a moment at his pint of ale, barely touched. With a sigh he put it down and made for the door.

She headed to the bar and had a quick conversation with the landlord before joining Ferguson by the door.

"What was that about?" he asked.

"I just wanted some antiseptic for the cut," she replied.

"But I thought—" he began, before Ava interrupted him.

"I'm not an idiot," she smiled. "Last thing I need is a septic cut on my face. Now let's go."

Ferguson stared after her in disbelief as she stepped out of the door into the dusk.

─────────── • ◆ • ───────────

# 49

*The Lord Nelson*
*Barking*
*London IG11*
*England*
*The United Kingdom*

URI—OR DANNY Motson, as he now called himself—closed the chipped and dented door behind him. It had at one time been painted a cheery blue, but its battered state, together with the general smell of urine and damp in the concrete corridor, comprehensively cancelled any uplifting effect it may once have had.

He had found the small flat pretty easily.

The landlord had met him in a café over a cup of tea and a plate of sausages and eggs. There was no paperwork involved—just a requirement for him to hand over a deposit and a week's rent upfront, along with a threat that if he failed to pay any future sums owing, he would find his belongings in the street. He was also warned that if he caused any trouble at all, he would receive a visit from "associates" he was assured he would rather not meet.

The arrangement was pretty much what he had been expecting, and so was the property—a nondescript flat in one of London's run-down concrete estates.

As he headed down the graffiti-covered stairwell, the smell of urine intensified. It was dingy, and there were no working bulbs behind the caged light-shades bolted into the walls, leaving the steps lit only by the fading daylight.

He had spent the afternoon on an uncomfortable plastic chair in a nearby internet café. Its narrow booths were separated by grimy chip-board partitions, and he barely had enough room to operate the small flimsy mouse. But it had given him the cyber-anonymity he needed, allowing him to immerse himself in the surprisingly complicated world of England's extreme right-wing scene.

As he had expected, there was a wealth of racist material just a click away. None of it struck him as particularly new, insightful, or even shocking—just the usual monologues blaming race, colour, religion, or any combination for all society's evils.

But he was not after the propaganda.

After a few hours of burrowing into usergroups, he finally found something that might serve his purpose.

*Dogs of War*, a band that had previously been arrested for its extremist race-hate lyrics, was playing at a pub in Barking that evening. From the way some of the chat-boards were lit up with the news, it seemed likely to be a popular event.

*It would do nicely.*

Uri took down the details, then caught the train into central London, where he spent the remainder of the afternoon buying the designer label clothes preferred by his target crowd, who had long ago abandoned the black shirts, bomber jackets, and Dr Martens that once singled them out so easily. Now they wore select international designer labels—less visible to the police and public, but just as identifiable to each other.

When he finally made it to *The Lord Nelson*, it was exactly as he had imagined it—a run-down building on a scruffy street corner. It was a typical suburban pub—an Arts and Crafts mock-Tudor building dating from the turn of the twentieth century.

There were no welcoming plants or flower baskets arranged outside, or awards displayed on the door announcing its success in various good pub guides and competitions. Instead, there were rusty grilles over the gloomy windows, and a raised metal roller-shutter above the sturdy front door. A large grey satellite TV dish covered in peeling stickers dom-inated the sloping roof, and a tatty painted blackboard outside featured a bulldog in a Union Jack T-shirt proclaiming that visitors could watch all England's matches on a big screen.

The pub was quite clearly not aimed at the family lunch crowd.

Its political allegiances were also unmistakeable. While one side of the swinging sign-board displayed a portrait of Admiral Lord Nelson, telescope in hand, Uri recognized the other side as England's most infamous fascist, Oswald Mosley, in the same pose as Nelson, but clutching a rolled up map of the British Isles in place of the telescope.

In case that was not enough to warn off any non-English drinkers, the curb of the pavement in front of the pub had been hurriedly painted in faded red, white, and blue stripes.

There was already a rowdy crowd outside. By the puddles of beer and empty glasses on the pavement, it was clear they had been drinking for several hours. That was fine by Uri—their reflexes would be slower if there was any trouble.

Walking confidently, he made his way through the revellers and into the pub.

Despite the tens of thousands of non-white people thronging London's pubs that evening, the faces at *The Lord Nelson* were exclusively white.

Most of the drinkers were in their twenties to mid-thirties—and dressed in the designer label clothes Uri had spent the afternoon browsing. As he passed through the crowd, he noticed that although the clothes and haircuts were smarter and more expensive than those that would have been seen in the pub two decades earlier, beneath it all, the atmosphere was still unmistakably one of fists, boots, and bricks.

Uri was confident. At school in Haifa he had learned British English not American English, so his accent sounded as good as anyone else's in the pub.

He was just another dirty-blond white guy.

Heading for the stripped wooden bar, he ordered a beer. He would drink it slowly. He needed to stay clear and focused.

There was a set of double-doors at the back of the room, pasted with advertising posters for the performance by *Dogs of War* that evening. Uri headed for it, keen to scope out the layout of the pub.

He pushed open the doors to find the back room was a medium-sized space, already filling with drinkers. A third of the floor was taken up with a wooden stage set against the far wall, overhung with stage-lights cycling through a calm pre-programmed display of cool red, white, and blue tunnels of light. Occasionally, a hiss of smoke from a metal box at the back of the stage replenished the theatrical fog hanging over the guitars, amplifiers, and drum kit, whose chromed fittings gleamed brightly whenever caught by the stage-lights.

Behind it all, a large black flag had been tacked to the back wall, featuring the name 'Dogs of War' over a manga-style painting of a medieval battlefield dominated by the heads of three snarling mastiffs, saliva dripping onto their studded collars, all three advancing under a Union Jack pennant.

Uri leaned up against the wall. He had plenty of time. For now he just needed to observe.

The crowd were becoming progressively more drunk, and the atmosphere was increasingly charged with the arrival of ever more people into the backroom.

As the crowd thickened around the stage, the periodic shouts and jeers for the band to start got louder.

Eventually, the house lights dimmed, and the audience began to bay and howl in anticipation, heckling the band to appear.

They did not have to wait long.

The PA soon came to life with the strident opening notes of *Land of Hope and Glory*. The crowd immediately launched into a bellowing accompaniment, before the four musicians appeared on the stage, and the audience began cheering themselves hoarse.

As the drummer shouted the count off for the first song, the speaker stacks on the sides of the stage ripped into life, sending huge pressure waves of sound straight into the audience.

The volume level was ear-splitting—a howl of overdriven guitars chopping across the remorseless thump of the bass and a furious machine-gun drumbeat that Uri could feel drill right through him.

He watched with interest as a large section of audience at the front of the stage started swirling like a whirlpool, dissolving into a seething mass of limbs—fists alternately punching the air and connecting with other members of the audience in a circular maelstrom of rhythmic male violence.

He could barely understand a word of the singer's breakneck delivery. Whatever the sweating shaved-headed front-man was shouting was distorted beyond recognition by the sheer decibel level. But the crowd seemed not to care. They were lost in a vortex of brutal noise and aggression.

Uri looked on as the heady mixture of alcohol and the thudding drumbeats catalyzed the concert room into a free-for-all fight pen. If anyone ever doubted that Viking blood still flowed in English veins, he reflected, they only needed to watch this. All that was missing were the forked beards.

He stood against the back wall and listened to a few songs, until it was clear that all those who wanted to watch the band were there.

Heading back through the double doors into the main bar, he looked around at the dozens of men filling the room.

Standing by the counter, he reflected that he had been given some challenging assignments before, but this was the most stretching yet. It was strange enough being asked to recover the biblical Ark of the Covenant—the most potent legacy of his forebears, but now he found himself in a room full of drunk and violent extremist anti-Semites.

He smiled to himself.

*This is what life in the Institute was all about.*

He loved the danger. Nothing made him feel so alive as knowing it was all hanging by a thread. One that he controlled. Mostly.

This mission was entirely new territory for him, and he was getting a heavy endorphin thrill from it. He knew his colleagues in the political division regularly infiltrated hostile groups. But in the *Metsada*, he usually did quick surgical in-and-out operations, largely relying on his own planning and resources to carry out liquidations.

This was going to be very different. This would require going properly undercover for a sustained period.

And with dangerous people.

He had never known a high like it.

He looked around closely for anyone who might fit the profile of what he was after.

Assessing the crowd, he realized most of them were simply there for the chance to bond with their tribe in the ageless rituals of intoxication and aggression.

But there was a group in the far corner that looked more promising.

A powerfully built dark-haired man dominated a large table. He seemed a few years older that the gang around him—perhaps in his mid-forties. The sleeves of his leather jacket were pushed up, showing muscular forearms wrapped in geometric tattoos. He had a strong physical presence, intensified by his size. Uri ran an expert eye over his seated frame, and estimated he must have been around six foot four, and built like an ox.

Scanning the pub, his eyes kept returning to the large man. It was increasingly clear he was the focal point of the group, surrounded by a deferential audience that nodded and smirked on cue.

"You're very interested in our friend?" The voice next to Uri was strong and confident, with a heavy south London accent.

Uri turned to see a thin angular-faced man in a checked shirt, also a little older, nodding in the direction of the table in the far corner. Uri recognized him—he had been sitting with the big man a little earlier.

Taken by surprise but keeping his cool, Uri answered nonchalantly, "I'm wondering if it's all talk in here, or if you're good for anything real?"

The man bit his lip thoughtfully, looking Uri up and down critically. "That's pretty strong talk, my friend."

"It's a simple question." Uri returned the gaze directly. His challenge was unmistakable.

The man let out a short laugh. "You've got some balls, son. I've been watching you."

"Then so have you," Uri replied. He was not going to let the man assume authority over him.

The man's sociable expression faded. Underneath it, he had a hard face. "Look, my friend" he began slowly, in a tone that was anything but friendly. "Let me tell you something." He was gazing hard at Uri. "You don't fit in here. You stand out. And that's not good. For you. You're on your own, and you're not drinking. That's a load of warning bells, you know? Whoever you are, you're out of your depth. You should go."

"Thanks," Uri ignored the threat. "If you can't help me, then don't waste my time. I'll find someone who can." His tone was purposefully dismissive. It was a fine line. He did not want a fight in the main room. He would soon be outnumbered.

The man stared coolly at Uri, clearly sizing up whether or not to make an issue out of it.

Uri returned the stare, unflinching. He knew this was just as much a ritual as the circle mosh pit in the next room.

At length the man put his glass down on the countertop beside Uri, and turned around with his back to the bar so he was side by side with

Uri. "Alright, son. Let's do it your way. At least for now. So what's your thing?"

"As I said," Uri replied. "Some action."

The man paused. "Like what?"

"Anything heavy." Uri watched the man closely for a reaction.

The man's expression did not change. "You like a bit of contact, do you?"

Uri sighed. "It's going to be a long night if I have to repeat myself." He made no effort to hide his irritation.

"Can you handle yourself?" The man was looking him up and down critically.

Uri had no idea if the discussion was going anywhere. But it was the first contact he had made all evening. And the man he was talking to seemed connected to the big man in the corner. It was worth seeing where the conversation would lead.

"Can you?" Uri was keen to move the conversation on.

The man blinked slowly before changing tack. "Where are you from, son?"

"I move around," Uri answered vaguely. "Family's from Liverpool. I spent the last few years in Australia." It was far enough away to be uncheckable.

"You don't sound like you're from round here," the man pressed.

"As I say, I move around." Uri's tone was non-committal.

The man took a sip of his beer. "So which firms have you been with? Who can vouch for you?"

"No one round here," Uri answered truthfully. "Look, can you get me a meeting with the don over there, or not? He's the only serious guy in here. And I want to know if he's got anything going down."

The man laughed. "Well you've got an eye, son, but what do you think this is? The Salvation Army?" He shook his head. "You don't just walk in here, you know. There are rules. Procedures."

"I'm listening," Uri had no idea what the Salvation Army was, but he got the gist. "But if you mess me around, I'm off, and that would be a shame. For you."

"You don't lack front, do you?" The man chewed his lip. "But you've got to be, how can I put it ... ?" he paused, " ... vetted—and then we'll see who's all talk."

Uri took a swig of his drink. "What did you have in mind?"

"First things first," the man answered. "What's your name?"

"Danny," Uri lied.

"Well, Danny, let's say, for now, my name is Otto." He did not extend a hand. "If you're serious about wanting to meet the Skipper, then I've got a little job for you—to see what you're made of."

Uri looked back at him unblinking, while Otto explained what he wanted him to do.

# 50

*10b St James's Gardens*
*Piccadilly*
*London SW1*
*England*
*The United Kingdom*

IT WAS DARK by the time Ferguson dropped Ava back home.

She washed out the cut under her eye where Malchus had punctured the skin with the metal star, and poured herself a glass of cold white wine from the fridge. Sipping it, she dropped into one of the comfortable armchairs in the sitting room.

Since Ferguson had shown her C's letter from Prince's file earlier, she had not been able to get it out of her mind.

She had been going over and over its implications for the whole of the long journey back to London.

She had never in her wildest dreams imagined that C could have ordered a whitewash of her father's death, ensuring there would be no investigation, and nobody would ever be held to account. It was a big step, and not one he would have taken lightly.

In her experience, both C and the Director General of MI5 used the whitewash power as a last resort—for matters of national security. But she was having difficulty seeing what that national security concern could have been in her father's case.

She could only conclude that her father had been involved in something particularly sensitive. He must have been. Or he would not have got the attention from C.

She wracked her mind for any clue about what it could have been.

*What had he got himself into?*

*Had he made some kind of mistake? Strayed where he should not have gone?*

She dismissed the idea. He was an experienced officer, who had survived a long time in the game. He did not make elementary errors.

*So what had he been doing?*

*And why did C want it hushed up?*

She took a sip of the cold wine, and dialled DeVere's number.

She needed answers.

$$\cdot \blacklozenge \cdot$$

# 51

*Southbank Centre*
*London SE1*
*England*
*The United Kingdom*

DeVere had told Ava to meet him at 9:45 p.m. outside the entrance to the Queen Elizabeth II Hall at London's Southbank Centre.

As she approached it, the largest arts complex in Europe, she could see the hulking collection of concert halls and galleries hugging the bend in the river, dominating a long stretch of the south bank.

It was a bizarre 1950s and 1960s concrete vision of ultra-modernism—a mass of split-level walkways and windswept staircases. But even through the tired materials and omnipresent weather stains, she could still feel something of the radical futurism it had once offered.

She did not have to wait long outside the concert-hall entrance before she saw DeVere.

Wearing his distinctive chalk-striped suit and black-rimmed glasses, he emerged from the doorway with the interval crowd, spotted her immediately, and headed over to where she was standing.

"What a pleasure," he beamed, bending to give her a kiss on the cheek.

"I never had you down as a romantic." She pointed at the concert poster of a Roman general and an Egyptian queen locked in a dramatic stage embrace. The baroque lettering announced the performance was Handel's *Julius Caesar in Egypt*.

"It makes me look sophisticated," he smiled.

Ava knew that was not true. He was being self-effacing. His opera collection at home was the work of a lifetime.

He set off along the riverside walk, before turning into an open concrete stairwell leading up to Waterloo Bridge.

As they emerged onto the top, the two-lane bridge was still humming with traffic in both directions despite the lateness of the hour. DeVere headed onto the pedestrian walkway running down its side, striding out across the river to the north bank.

"This is my favourite bridge in London," he confided as they walked. "You get a wonderful view from here."

She fell into step beside him, peering down over the low white railings. The light was gone, and the river's deep water looked cold and black, conjuring up its old Celtic name, *Tamesas*—dark.

Nearing the centre of the bridge, DeVere stopped and put his hands on the railing, inhaling the night air deeply. Ava halted beside him, taking in the view looking west.

To her left, the elongated capsules of London's four-hundred-and-fifty-foot-high big wheel inched round imperceptibly. She imagined for a moment being on it, but could not remember the last time she had seen life pass by at such a slow pace.

As she looked out straight ahead over the water she could see the two Golden Jubilee Bridges, each spraying down their spot-lit suspension cables like vast water jets from a shower-head, frozen in time in gleaming metal.

But dominating it all, the mellow yellowy floodlit stones of the Houses of Parliament lit up the night in front of her. It was a bizarre sight—its mock gothic high walls, spiky pinnacles, and three great towers making it more of a fortress than a royal palace—although no king or queen had chosen to live on the site for over five hundred years.

DeVere's horseshoe of white hair was being buffeted by the wind, and his usually jovial expression was now one of concern. "No one can hear us here. I've got about ten minutes until I need to get back. So what's bothering you, Ava?"

She had been wondering how she was going to ask him. She had no desire to offend an old family friend. But nevertheless, she needed answers, and she wanted them from him.

"Why didn't you tell me C stopped all investigations into my father's death?" She kept her tone neutral.

He looked out over the water. "Ah. So that's it." He paused. "Would it have helped if I had?" There was a note of fatalism in his voice.

"It wasn't your decision to make, Peter. You should've told me," she answered quietly.

"Why?" he replied. It was not an aggressive question. "What could you have done? It wouldn't have brought him back, and I didn't want you and your family to experience any further pain."

"Well," she paused. "I know now. And I don't understand it. Why did he make the order?"

DeVere shook his head. "Who knows anything for sure in this business? All I knew was that our two-man department was shut down. I was taken off all files, and reassigned. I didn't blame them. I'd have made the same decision. Our desk was nothing without your father. He was the expert."

"But that doesn't explain why C whitewashed his death." Ava persisted. "It just doesn't make sense to me."

"I kept asking, but nobody ever told me why," he answered softly. "Eventually I just stopped asking. I think they wanted to forget the work we were doing. Without the credibility your father brought to the department, I suspect they found it all too difficult to explain. They didn't want publicity around a desk specializing in the politico-occult."

Ava felt a wave of sadness to think that everything he had worked for had been shut down so quickly. Just like that. No questions asked.

DeVere continued. "I also think they were worried any publicity surrounding the department would alarm the public. It was always a fine line. Our work would show people we were taking a real threat seriously. But it would also alert them to a new danger they had probably never thought of. And it would become one more thing for the bureaucrats to be accountable for to the politicians."

He shifted the weight on his feet. "I know it's hard to swallow, after he gave his life for them—but I think his death gave the Firm the excuse they wanted to get back to business as usual. It made life easier for the paper-pushers."

Ava took a deep lungful of the salty air, digesting the information.

As much as it angered her, it made a twisted sort of sense. Underneath everything, the Firm was just another government department—albeit a highly unusual one—run by bureaucrats.

Ultimately, it all came down to paperwork.

She stared out into the evening lights on both sides of the river.

There was something else she needed to clarify. "Peter—I've been told he was investigating Malchus at the time he was killed."

"Christ." DeVere's face drained of colour.

He turned to stare at her. "Seriously? They never told me that. We were each wrapped up in our own projects. I knew he was having some success with a new group and had actively penetrated them—but I never had any details."

He shook his head. "Jesus. So it was these Thelema bastards, even back then?"

Ava clenched her jaw. From what she had experienced with Malchus and his cronies earlier, she was now certain there was a connection. "Malchus was involved. I don't know how, yet—but I'm going to find out."

"Prince?" he asked. "This is from the American files?"

Ava nodded.

"Do you trust her?" he asked quietly.

"Not very much," she answered truthfully.

"Neither do I," he smiled sadly. "But then I don't trust many people."

She looked at him with concern. "You've been doing this too long, Peter."

"It's a survival skill," he grimaced. "It's kept me alive a long time."

It was another reason Ava had become disenchanted with the job. For all the excitement of covert work, she could see the endless secrets and uncertainties about who to trust were ultimately corrosive. It was hard to stay normal.

He turned to her. "Ava, can I give you some advice?" His expression was suddenly serious. "As an old friend?" He did not wait for an answer before continuing. "I don't know how deep this thing goes—but I don't like it. There are too many unknowns. My instinct tells me people are going to get hurt, and I don't want you to be one of them. Maybe you should go back to Baghdad—leave this one alone."

She remembered Malchus's cold sadism that afternoon—the dead expression in his eyes as he had interrogated her. "Let Malchus get away? Give up the Ark?"

She shook her head slowly.

He sighed. "You're on the outside these days, Ava. You left. There is no salvation outside the Church, remember? I can't protect you if it gets serious." He looked at her pleadingly. "You won't help your father by getting yourself killed."

"I appreciate the concern." She shot him a sideways glance. "But I don't need protection—from you or anyone."

"You Curzons are all the same." He looked resigned. "Please, as a personal favour?"

She knew what he was going to ask. "I can't drop it, Peter—not now."

"At least think about it." He looked at her hopefully. "It's not your job anymore. There'll be others who can handle it. And none of it's going to bring him back."

She wanted to be honest with him. "You're not going to change my mind."

He put a hand on her arm. "Well, just think about it. And meanwhile, for God's sake be careful who you trust. I don't know what you're getting into, but I don't like what I've seen so far. As I say, if I've learnt anything in too many years at this job, it's not to trust anyone."

That was fine. She did not trust Prince, and had no intention of involving others. She preferred working alone anyway. In her experience, additional hands may help, but they invariably brought unwelcome complications.

She glanced over to the south bank, where the second half of DeVere's evening was about to start. "Come on, then." She took one last look at the dark still water. "Let's get back. We don't want you to miss Caesar and Cleopatra's big moment."

# DAY SEVEN

———— ◆ ————

## 52

*Undisclosed location*

NOBODY EVER CAME to the secluded house by the lake.

Ever since the infamous Englishman had made it his home all those years ago, no locals had visited. They avoided it like the plague, even shying away from the nearby roads.

It suited Malchus fine.

He relished the isolation.

Glancing out of the large window overlooking the smoky-black water, he saw that the first glow of morning was just beginning to purple the sky.

He had timed it perfectly. Dawn—the moment between two worlds.

He finished bathing, before drying off and anointing himself with the sacred oil he had blended according to the recipe in the thirtieth chapter of the book of Exodus. It was a powerful formula, and he had followed the biblical instructions to the letter—slowly steeping the myrrh, cinnamon, calamus, and cassia into the olive oil.

Now ritually clean, he put on a dark robe and perfumed sandals, before padding through the hallway to the room at the north-western corner of the house—to the small doorway inside it.

He turned the large iron key and pulled the cellar door open, revealing a three-inch-thick steel door immediately behind it.

Taking the thin gold chain from around his neck, he inserted its slim magnetized hexagonal rod into the anodized key plate.

Next he turned to focus on the door's two main features—a combination tumbler lock and a large wheel.

He spun the tumbler the requisite number of times to the left and right—a simple exercise in gematria. When the mechanism clicked quietly, he took hold of the steel wheel and turned it to the left. As the metal ran through his fingers, he could hear the sound of the three locking bars withdrawing from the mortises buried deep in the reinforced doorframe.

It was his only concession to security.

What was below was private.

The heavy door swung open easily, revealing a black stone staircase—unlit save for a dull glow rising from the cavernous cellar below.

Striding confidently down the bare stairs, he descended lower, increasingly aware of the thick bitter-sweet *qetoreth* incense rising from the underground chamber.

Like the sacred anointing oil, the historic incense's recipe was also preserved in the book of Exodus, from the instructions to the Temple priests. It called for equal measures of stacte, onchya, galbanum, and frankincense. While the last two were easy to source, many seekers down the centuries had struggled to identify stacte and onchya. But Malchus had been entrusted with the knowledge by one of the *Kohanim* of Prague—although yielding it up to his violent visitor had been the very last thing the elderly priest ever did.

Malchus inhaled deeply. It was a good smell—a sign things were finally progressing, as he had planned for so long.

Stepping off the last stair, he gazed with intense satisfaction at the sight that greeted him.

The room was a concrete cube.

There were no windows or skylights, and the walls, floor, and ceiling were painted a uniform matt black.

Inlaid into the floor was a large five-pointed star, its tip pointing to the far wall and the whole bordered by a circle. He had built it himself, trusting no one else with the precision required.

Its six lines were scored into the cement, each channel as wide and deep as a fist. They were painted the same black as the floor—clearly visible in the flickering light thrown by the ten wide black candles, one at each of the star's angles.

His eyes moved up to the walls, flicking rapidly across the riot of intricate blood-red glyphs.

He knew that to uninitiated observers the malevolent shapes looked like the insane ravings of a demonically possessed mind.

But the arcane alphabet made complete sense to him.

The symbols were the angelic sigils—seals used by adepts down the ages to name and summon the Guardians: a code passed down each generation from master to disciple.

Even though he had spent weeks painting the sigils onto the walls, he never tired of looking at their powerful jagged lines and the energizing forces they exuded—like electrical symbols or lightning bolts.

He smiled with satisfaction as he surveyed them one by one: "Danel, Turel, Satarel, Ananel, Batarel, Tamiel, Ramiel, Kokabiel, Zaqiel, Sariel, Jomjael, Rameel, Ezeqeel, Samsapeel, Baraqijal, Semyaza, Arakiba, Asael, Armaros ... ."

He read them slowly, mouthing them to himself as if in a prayer, savouring the sounds as he breathed air into them.

Their names were raw power. Assembled together in the same place in this way, they oozed dominion.

His usually lifeless green eyes were shining more brightly now, illuminated by the sigils' dark potency.

Of the thousands of angels he could have selected, he had chosen the two hundred Watchers—those immortals who fell to earth from heaven in the Great War, fuelled by their uncontrollable lust to pleasure themselves with mortal women.

He smiled knowingly.

He liked to imagine what the battle between the angels had been like.

Carnage, destruction, and agony, he was sure—on a celestial scale.

He sneered at the thought of the chubby winged toddlers who passed for angels on a million church ceilings, chocolate boxes, and Christmas cards.

Did no one read any more? The Bible gave detailed physical descriptions. It was all there if anyone cared to look.

And there was nothing serene or innocent about them.

He closed his eyes and pictured the cherubs—Yahweh's terrifying guardians.

They had the bodies of men, the cloven hooves of calves, and could see simultaneously in all directions from their four faces: man, lion, ox, and eagle. They protected Yahweh, speeding alongside his chariot on their four great wings.

Malchus savoured the image. He felt especially connected to cherubs, because according to the book of Ezekiel, one of them was the seal of perfection, full of wisdom, and perfect in beauty.

*Lucifer.*

But despite their famous fallen leader, the cherubs were not the mightiest of the angels.

More powerful still were the seraphs, or burning ones. Malchus saw them in his mind, flying above Yahweh's chariot—the ultimate guardians: all-seeing from the hundreds of eyes covering every inch of their bodies, even the area under their six great wings.

"They lie in ignorance," Malchus snorted with contempt. *"Audiunt sed non auscultant."*[9]

As he looked around the room, he felt gripped by the feeling he always had when he was down here.

It was an oratory of power.

Stepping into the middle of the pentagram, he picked up a thick glass amphora with rams-head handles, and began pouring scented oil from it into the floor's star-shaped grooves.

He had made the oil himself, but it was not the anointing oil from the book of Exodus. This particular mixture was altogether darker and muskier.

Once the star was glistening wet and the viscous liquid had run freely around the never-ending channels, he knelt down and dipped his left hand into the small pool of oil left in the amphora, blessing himself with it—drawing four upside-down crosses from his head to his navel. Counting aloud as he touched himself, each time he reached six he restarted at one. When he had completed the fourth cross, he stopped and traced a large upside cross in the air in front of him with two bold strokes.

His ritual gestures totalled three sixes—the most perfect number.

To finish the opening ceremony, he picked up one of the candles and knelt, touching it to the oil in the floor.

With a gratifying speed, the fire leapt along the length of the deep grooves, instantly transforming the oiled channels into a flaming circled pentagram.

---

9 "They hear but they do not listen."

Now he had prepared both himself and the sacred space, he finally allowed himself to look up towards the east end of the room, where the fifth point of the blazing star pointed to the high altar.

Lifting his eyes, they came to rest on the focal point of the oratory— the object he had been lusting after for all these years.

It stood on a black velvet podium behind the granite altar that usually took pride of place in the dark chapel.

He gazed raptly at the ancient chest, savouring how its hammered and cast-gold decoration flickered and glinted in the low candlelight. By a trick of the shimmering rays, it looked as if its dozens of bas-relief figures were moving jerkily across its beaten panels. Even the wings of the vast cherubs on the lid, whose tips touched to form the Mercy Seat, seemed to be undulating gently.

He stared long and hard at the ancient artefact, feeling his heart rate rising as it always did when he came down to gaze upon it.

He could barely believe it was finally his, after so many years of preparation.

Few people had any concept of the ancient chest's true significance. He felt nothing but contempt for them. At some stage in their pathetic meaningless existences they had decided it was long lost, or a misty legend, or a benign cultural relic with no relevance to their lives.

He despised their ignorance.

They would soon be forced to reassess that view—along with any simplistic Sunday-school idea it was merely an ornamental chest for carrying around the golden pot of manna, Aaron's rod, the stone tablets of the commandments, and the first Torah scroll.

Its true purpose was infinitely more powerful.

Yahweh, the ultimate warrior God, had chosen it as his earthly throne—making it a unique and sacred gateway: a mystical place where the earthly and heavenly realms met, a portal of unique power and potential.

What would happen was inevitable. It would not be his responsibility. It should come as no surprise to anyone. It was all there, in the Bible.

He looked about with a deep contentment.

The flames from the pentagram were low—no more than four inches high, but they threw off enough heat for him to have started gently sweating.

*Good.*

It was time for it all to begin.

The ceremony would be an important turning point.

He walked to the north-west corner of the room, where he found the small wicker basket exactly as he had left it.

Inside, motionless apart from the rhythmic bobbing of its head, was a young cockerel—its sleek dark feathers gleaming in the candlelight with a purplish-black sheen, contrasting strikingly with the deep red of its comb.

Unbuckling the basket's leather strap, he flipped open the lid and grasped the cockerel by its thin neck, lifting it clear.

Carrying it to the other end of the room, he approached the altar, and laid it onto the hard black granite surface.

Sensing imminent danger, or perhaps seeing the wide-bladed knife Malchus had picked up, the cockerel began to struggle—writhing to escape his steel grip.

As Malchus leant on it harder, pinning its small body onto the cold stone, the bird thrashed more wildly, flapping its wings—struggling to be free of the weight bearing remorselessly down on it.

Holding the ritual knife to his lips, Malchus softly kissed both sides of the wide blade. *"Suscipiat dominus sacrificium de manibus meis,"*[10] he murmured, raising it high above his shoulder.

The burnished silver glinted as he brought it down in a great arc—its sharp heavy blade easily slicing into the flesh of the young bird's neck. Its razor-sharp edge passed straight through the carotid, jugular, cartilage, and windpipe, before finally shattering the bone of its spinal column.

As the bird's head rolled away from its body, blood sprayed out in jets from the ragged stump of its neck.

He raised the knife again, and touched its bloodied blade to his lips and tongue. *"Dominus, sum dignus,"*[11] he whispered, relishing the taste of the hot metallic fluid.

Leafing through a copy of the Old Testament propped against an ornate stand on the dark stone altar, he turned to the twenty-ninth chapter of the book of Exodus.

*"Take some of its blood and put it on the lobes of the right ear,"* he intoned, at the same time smearing his right ear with the cockerel's lifeblood.

---

10 "May the Lord receive this sacrifice from my hands."
11 "Lord, I am worthy."

Reading on further, he did as the Bible commanded, daubing blood onto the thumb of his right hand, then the big toe of his right foot.

It was an ordination ceremony, and he knew that for what was to come, he had to follow the instructions precisely.

*"Splash blood against the sides of the altar,"* he recited, grasping the cockerel's warm twitching body and pointing the ragged neck stump at the altar, spraying it with the still-pumping blood like some obscene modernist mural.

Moving to the middle of the room, he picked up the oil amphora and returned to the altar.

Wedging the shredded stump on the cockerel's shoulders into the amphora's neck, he watched as the blood dribbled down, creating deep red blobs floating in suspension on the oil.

Reading further into the ancient book of Exodus, he dipped a small silver asperges rod into the amphora, and flicked the bloody oil onto his robes in a gesture of sanctification.

The blessings complete, he picked up the cockerel's warm but now still body, and placed it in the centre of the altar's granite top.

Still reading aloud, he took up the bloodied knife again, and slit open the bird's abdomen in accordance with the ancient instructions.

As the entrails slithered out, he separated off the internal organs, slicing them out one by one, meticulously observing the details stipulated in the ritual—taking especial care to collect the fat from the viscera, the long lobe of the liver, both kidneys, and the right thigh.

Satisfied, he lifted off a metal grill in the top of the altar and lit the kindling nestling in the recess under it, before replacing the plate into position.

When the flames had died down, he placed the fat, liver, kidneys, and thigh onto the grill.

They hissed quietly as the fat dripped down onto the ashes below.

*"Burn them on the altar,"* he recited, closing the book of Exodus, *"for a pleasing aroma to the Lord."*

The acrid scent of the charring fat and bloody offal filled the room, mixing with the incense.

He inhaled deeply, relishing the spicy bloody meaty aroma.

He knew Yahweh was pleased by animal sacrifices.

Human ones, too.

He sneered at the sanctimonious hypocrites. Had Yahweh not been pleased when Jephthah sacrificed his daughter, or when Josiah conse-crated and sacrificed the pagan priests to him on their own blasphemous altars?

He frowned, not understanding why people could not see it. The Bible was as clear as could be. The book of Deuteronomy explicitly commanded the faithful to put all non-believers to death and torch their towns as a burnt offering to the Lord.

He felt nothing but contempt for them.

Did they really believe Yahweh shied away from bloodshed? The same Yahweh who killed and commanded the death of hundreds of thousands of people, all painstakingly recorded in the Bible. Who according to the book of Samuel had slain fifty thousand and seventy men just for daring to gaze upon the Ark?

And there was more.

Much more.

Had he not sent his angel to execute every first-born in the whole of Egypt so there was not a house in which someone had not been killed?

And in the book of Ezekiel, had he not given the order to the men entering Jerusalem to slaughter all inhabitants—men, women, nursing mothers, even small children?

He could think of countless examples.

He had studied them all.

Yahweh was, then and now, a god of war and conquest, mayhem and destruction, pride and conquest, jealously and revenge.

And his currency was blood.

He felt a mounting excitement as he gazed up with anticipation at the Ark.

They would know soon enough.

—— • ◆ • ——

# 53

*All Hallows College*
*University of Oxford*
*Oxford OX1*
*England*
*The United Kingdom*

As AVA CLIMBED into Ferguson's four-by-four outside the pub the previous evening, he had flicked on his work laptop and hooked it up to the internet via mobile phone.

After quickly entering a sequence of paired passwords, each part-generated by a biometric fingerswipe, the laptop's webcam had verified the unique pattern of blood vessels on both his retinas.

Once past the security, he had navigated to the relevant databases and quickly found the information she was looking for.

The house where Malchus had taken Ava was owned by Lord Drewitt, seventh baron Stockbridge. It had been in his family for generations, and the family coffers had been sufficiently healthy to cope with the death duties and inheritance taxes that had brought many similar aristocratic families to their knees and the bankruptcy courts.

The present Baron Stockbridge, Anselm Drewitt, had inherited the house and title from his late father. Now aged fifty-six, Lord Drewitt had pursued a successful career as an economist, before being appointed

Warden of All Hallows College, Oxford, where he now spent most of his time.

The database contained a wealth of further biographical and confidential information, which Ava had read with increasing interest.

When she had finished, she got hold of Lord Drewitt's secretary's mobile phone number, and made an apologetic but urgent appointment to see him on the pretext she was compiling a biography of the country's hundred most influential people. She doubted he qualified, but it had got her into his diary.

Now, the next morning, walking swiftly under the ancient university city's iconic Bridge of Sighs, she passed the house of Edmund Halley the astronomer, and headed into the medieval high-sided lane leading to All Hallows College.

The passageway's ancient windowless walls were studded with a riot of comical gargoyles, and ended abruptly in a tall square medieval tower, from which a large stone statue of the Virgin Mary gazed serenely down, as she had for the last seven hundred years.

Ava stepped through the wicket in the immense gnarled old wooden gate, and entered an airy quadrangle filled with an immaculately trimmed green oval lawn. It was bordered on all sides by the usual Oxbridge college arrangement—a chapel, a grand hall, and a set of monastic-looking buildings housing the fellows and students.

It was a world of medieval neatness and precision, frozen in time away from the progress of the centuries.

Turning right into the first doorway, as the secretary had directed, she began climbing the narrow wooden stairs up to the Warden's Lodgings.

At the top, she found a deep doorframe fitted with two painted wooden doors—the touching faces upholstered in green baize. The outer one was open, while the inner was closed. It was the traditional arrangement to indicate the Warden was in, and would receive visitors.

She knocked and waited.

After a few moments, the door was opened by a tall bald man in a cream shirt and pale blue bowtie. He had thin lips and a lean face, set off with a pair of large metal glasses.

He ushered her into a plush drawing room—elegant and traditional without being grand. The summer sunlight filtered in from a pair of mullioned windows overlooking the quadrangle and formal gardens, spectacularly edged with a wide herbaceous border of bold-coloured flowers.

"I never tire of the view," he said, noticing her looking out of the window nearest her. "It's the oldest university quad in England, you know— quite revolutionary in the late 1300s. All others are copies of this one."

He ushered her towards an upholstered armchair. "Can I get you some coffee?" he asked genially, "or perhaps a small sherry?" He was clearly comfortable playing the role of the Oxford don.

Ava took a seat in the comfortable chair and shook her head. "Sorry to cut to the chase, but for such an eminent public figure, you keep some unpleasant company."

Drewitt looked bewildered.

She continued before he could answer. "Take Malchus and his national socialist enthusiasts' club for example." She was watching him closely for any signs of reaction, and was pleased to see the skin around his eyes tighten.

"I don't know any such person," he responded coldly, his bonhomie instantly gone. "Now I don't know who you are, or why you're here. But I shall now kindly ask you to leave." Despite the calm words, Ava could hear the strain in his voice.

"Strange that you don't know Malchus," she continued. "He seems most at home in your house down in Wiltshire. He treats it like his own."

Drewitt was already by the door, which he was holding open for her. "This interview is over. Good day."

His voice was icy.

Ava remained firmly in the chair, showing no signs of moving. She glanced down at the side table next to her, at a large glass paperweight with an engraved family crest of three bezants on a plain shield. "*Dexter et sinister!*" she read the motto aloud, lifting it up to examine it more closely. "'To the right and to the left!' An old battle cry, and a very old coat of arms."

"I don't see it's any of your business," he replied curtly. "Now I've asked you to leave."

Ava put the paperweight down again. "I wouldn't want to leave it like this," she replied. "Otherwise I might accidentally tell the wrong people, and perhaps even get some of the facts muddled. I could be mistaken," she paused, "but I don't suppose that would be helpful for a man in your position?"

She could see anger flashing in his eyes. And something else, too.

*Fear.*

"Now look here," he was staring at her with undisguised hostility. "I don't appreciate your insinuations. And I'm too old to care about your threats. Please leave as I have requested, or I'll have you removed."

Ava looked out of the window. "I mean, it all gets so confusing—especially that nasty business in the *Palasthotel* in East Berlin. People could so easily get it all wrong."

She saw his eyes widen in shock, before his face visibly crumpled.

Reaching out a hand to steady himself, he leant on the back of a chair, gaping at her. He was breathing heavily, as if someone had physically winded him.

She had him off guard, and knew she had to press her advantage home now, before he recovered himself. "You see, a lot of government people who watch and listen quietly from the shadows on both sides of the Atlantic are currently very interested in your friend Malchus. And right now that means they're also interested in you."

He sank into the nearest chair, crushed, his bravado gone. "Who are you?" he asked hoarsely.

"Someone you need to talk to," she answered quietly. "Because I'm willing to bet you've got more reason to hate Malchus than most."

He looked visibly older than when she had entered. "I've no love for Malchus, or his politics," he answered bitterly.

"Then we have that in common," she reassured him. "But there are many who won't believe you."

He spoke slowly, emphasizing each word. "I've lived under threat of exposure by that … , that … ." He was clearly struggling for words, overwhelmed by emotion.

Ava got up and walked over to the sideboard between the two windows. It was stocked with several single malt whiskies. She poured a large measure into a heavy cut crystal tumbler and handed it to Drewitt, before returning to her chair.

He took the glass mechanically and began again, speaking quietly. "Not a day goes by when I haven't wondered it if will be the day my world disintegrates. And all this … ," he indicated the room around him, "… everything I have worked for—will all go."

Ava let silence descend for a moment, before changing down a gear. "If you want to tell me about it, I think we may be able to help each other."

Drewitt looked up at her, beaten and weary, his fight visibly gone. "Is there any point? You seem to know it all anyway." He held the glass of honey-coloured liquor in his hand, but did not drink it. He seemed lost in some reverie.

"Start at the beginning," Ava encouraged him.

There was a long pause before he began speaking, his voice low. "In 1988, I was a successful senior economist with a large energy company in London. I was also, I still am, maybe, although a little rusty, a keen competition chess player." He indicated a handsome chess board with porcelain pieces set on a table on the other side of the room.

"I was offered the chance to compete in a friendly amateur tournament against a team from behind the Iron Curtain. Of course, there was nothing amateur about the Communist players—it was a typical Soviet stunt to showcase their intellectual superiority. The competition was to last a week, at the *Palasthotel* in East Berlin—a city the Communists were always proud of showing to Westerners."

Ava nodded. She did not need to say anything. He was talking freely now, seemingly relieved on some level to be sharing the burdens he had carried for so many years.

"There were a dozen of us on our team—from Europe and the U.S. When we landed at Berlin Schönefeld, we were met by our escorts—a group of guides, translators, and a government minder or two."

He hesitated for a moment before continuing. "I should say that I'm not married. And I'm sure, if you've read my file, you've drawn your own conclusions."

Ava nodded her assent.

"Among the group attached to us was a translator—a very striking young man. I was considerably less old then, and flattered by his attentions. He made no attempt to hide his interest in me, and it led to ... an understanding." Drewitt's voice caught in his throat.

He took a gulp of the whisky. "It all happened so fast. I learned later that he had some sort of latent weakness in a blood vessel in his brain. One minute he was very much alive and vigorous, and the next he was not."

Drewitt seemed in a daze as he was speaking. His eyes were unfocused, staring into the middle distance as he relived the traumatic memories. "To my shame, I panicked, fled his room, and hid back in mine until the morning. I was terrified of being implicated in some kind of *crime passionnel*. Additionally, as you note, my family is an old one, and the headlines and scandal would have finished our reputation."

He paused, staring blankly at the golden liquid in the heavy glass. "The next morning, it was obvious to the poor maid who discovered him what had been going on. I had fled without touching anything ... and, well, you get the picture." Drewitt's voice was breaking with emotion. "The maid ran screaming from the room—and the hotel, of course, called the police."

"That's when Malchus entered the scene?" Ava asked.

Drewitt nodded bleakly. "It was only a matter of time before he found me. He calmly explained that the young man and I had been seen together on a number of occasions, and that the hotel's rooms were comprehensively bugged and monitored by a permanent Stasi team resident in the hotel. Malchus got hold of photographs of it all, you see? The animals were watching and listening to everything." Drewitt's voice faltered. "I confessed all, and begged him not to release details. You can imagine the sheer relief I felt when he agreed it was in no one's interest to attract publicity. He duly hushed up the affair in the way only totalitarian states can."

Ava nodded.

Drewitt took another large gulp of the fiery liquor. "At the time I thought my troubles were over. It was only later I came to realize they had only just begun. Men like Malchus don't do anything for nothing. He came to England the following year, after the Berlin Wall came down, and wasted no time in getting in touch with me. Since then, he has extorted increasing amounts of money and favours from me under the threat of releasing the photographs, which he still has, and stoking speculation I was responsible for the young man's death."

Ava could only imagine how terrifying he must have found being blackmailed by Malchus.

"And so I have lived under this threat for almost twenty-five years." He took another large mouthful of the whisky, emptying the glass. "In which time I have come to hate him as I have never hated anyone or anything in my entire life."

Ava sat quietly for a moment, allowing the emotion of the moment to pass.

"What do you know of his neo-Nazi activities with the Thelema?" she asked, changing the subject.

Drewitt walked shakily over to the sideboard and refilled his glass. "I'd say they're a highly dangerous bunch. They seem fully committed to an aggressive ss ideology, and are almost all violent extremists. Malchus has been assembling them for a long time. They're professionals, not weekend warriors—so it's no great surprise to me that the authorities have finally woken up to them as a threat."

"What about his occult activities? Do you know about those?"

Drewitt shook his head. "Afraid not. I largely see what he's up to from the outside. But from what I can tell, he and his cronies have recycled a number of the darker occult strands within Nazism and made them a central feature of their creed. It's pretty toxic as far as I can see."

"What about right now," Ava pressed him, now he was speaking freely. "Is he up to anything in particular?"

Drewitt nodded. "I think so. He made me borrow a medieval Hebrew manuscript from the *Bibliothèque Nationale* in Paris a while ago. I had to pretend we wanted it for display in the college archives. And I know he's become increasingly obsessed with King Solomon's Temple. I'm not sure why. He seems to be recreating bits of it. I'm afraid I don't have much insight into what his perverse mind is devising."

Ava stood up and walked over to the window. She had heard enough to be able to make a decision.

There was no doubt Drewitt was closer to Malchus's activities than anyone else she knew, or was likely to meet.

She turned back to the pale don. "We both have the same objective here. We can help each other."

Drewitt returned her gaze with more animation than he had shown since she had begun talking. "If you think there's a chance you can get him out of my life, I'll do whatever I can."

Ava paused. "I have to be honest. I don't yet know where this will lead. But the more information we can get about what he's up to, the easier it'll be to make the right decision."

Drewitt nodded slowly. "What exactly do you need to know?"

"Anything," Ava replied. "Anything at all. What he's up to. Who he's dealing with. Where he's travelling. What he's focused on. Is he doing anything out of the ordinary? Has he changed his routines? What's his fixation with King Solomon's Temple? Has he acquired anything recently? We need to piece together a full picture of exactly what he's doing."

Drewitt stood up. "How do I get in touch with you?"

"Just call, the old ways are sometimes the best." She walked over to a small antique desk with a pile of college crested notepaper on it and wrote out her mobile number on the top sheet.

Drewitt steered her to the door, and held out his hand to shake hers. "Have I just been recruited?" he asked, managing a weak smile as he shook her hand.

"Something like that," she smiled back, as she slipped out of the doors and onto the ancient creaky wooden stairs.

---  · ◆ ·  ---

# 54

*Stockbridge House*
*Nr Newton Tony*
*Wiltshire SP4*
*England*
*The United Kingdom*

LORD DREWITT GENTLY pushed open the door of his family's country house—the home in which he had grown up.

As a younger man, it had always held fond memories for him.

But ever since Malchus had effectively moved in, he had avoided returning there—preferring to stay at his comfortable rooms up in Oxford.

However, the visit that morning from the young woman, who he later realized had not given her name, had changed everything.

Although it had been a terrible shock to learn that the incident at Berlin's *Palasthotel* all those years ago was in files people were now reading, by the end of the meeting he had been overwhelmingly pleased she had tricked her way in to see him.

If there really was a chance that the net was closing in on Malchus, then he was ready to do everything he could to be helpful.

He had carried the burden of Malchus's demands for so long, like some chronic disease he had come to accept with a black fatalism.

But now he had the chance to do something about Malchus, and it filled him with a newfound optimism and energy.

Once she had left, he had finished up his work for the day, then got on the road down to Wiltshire, eager to begin.

As he drove though the countryside, he had started looking at the situation from all angles, and had begun wondering if maybe it was a trap—if it was some twisted new game Malchus was playing with him.

Perhaps that was how the woman knew about East Berlin?

But after turning it over in his mind for most of the journey, he had concluded it was unlikely to be a trick. He could see no reason why Malchus would go to such lengths to find out he hated him. It was hardly a secret between them.

No. It was far more likely that Malchus had upset the wrong people, and a long-overdue payback was finally coming.

Now, standing on the doorstep, smelling the freshly cut grass from the lawns, he pushed open the heavy front door, and felt an excitement he had not known in years.

Something was finally happening, and he wanted to be a part of it.

Closing the door firmly behind him, he quietly crossed the hallway, and peered into the main drawing room.

It was empty.

Looking about, he could see that everything was in order. There was no sign Malchus had been there recently.

He stepped back out into the hallway and checked all the other rooms on the ground floor, one by one.

They were all likewise empty.

The only other place Malchus was likely to be was on the first floor, where he had taken a suite of private rooms for himself.

Climbing the wide sweeping stairs as stealthily as he could, he turned into the corridor that led to the north wing.

The thick old Afghan rugs muffled the sound of his feet on the polished parquet floors as he strode quietly down the vase- and painting-filled corridor.

Dropping down a shallow step into an older part of the house, he arrived at a set of pillars dividing off an elegant lobby.

Stepping quietly across it, he approached the door leading to the suite of rooms Malchus used.

The doorway to Malchus's study was partly open.

He listened attentively outside it, but could hear nothing.

Nudging the door wider, it swung open, giving him a clear view of the whole room.

There was no one in it.

Even though Stockbridge House had been the Drewitt family's ancestral home for over four hundred years, Malchus had been categorically clear that these rooms were his personal sanctuary. He forbade Drewitt or anyone else from entering.

So as Drewitt stepped quietly into Malchus's study, he knew he was crossing a line.

It was an act of open defiance.

He looked around and could feel his pulse quickening.

Even though his parasitic guest was not at home, he knew enough about Malchus's violent rages to be aware what would happen if he was caught there. But after all the years of fear, it felt good to be one step ahead. And if it helped get Malchus out of his life, it was a risk he was more than willing to take.

He looked round the once-familiar room with distaste.

He had never imagined there being a shrine to such darkness in his home.

Malchus had truly made it his own.

Despite the fact it was afternoon, the curtains were drawn, and no natural light entered.

One wall was hung with a pair of large framed photographs.

To the left was a young Heinrich Himmler in interwar Munich, posing in front of a paramilitary truck alongside the henchmen of his fledgling ss. Drewitt could not see how the scrawny bespectacled bureaucrat, the second most powerful Nazi after Hitler, could have been any use in the orchestrated street violence at which his thugs were by then becoming proficient—but his watery eyes already had that distant mechanical gaze.

Beside it was a signed portrait photograph of ss-*Brigadeführer* Karl Maria Weisthor, who Malchus had explained was 'Himmler's Rasputin'. Weisthor had been drafted into the ss as high priest in charge of spiritual matters, research into runes and the prehistoric Germanic super race, and developing rituals honouring Got, the ancient Germanic deity at the centre of ss worship. It was Weisthor, Malchus had confided, who designed the infamous *Totenkopf* skull-and-rune ring presented to all ss officers—returned on death to a great chest in the crypt of the castle at

Wewelsburg, the ss Valhalla where the fallen were honoured.

It all made Drewitt feel ill.

Above the repulsive photographs hung a parade banner. The large words emblazoned across it read 'THULE GESELLSCHAFT 1919', which Malchus had explained with relish was a group of occult ariosophists that had given birth to the Nazi party—providing the bedrock of magical mystical beliefs that were to underpin the party.

Malchus had stroked the banner reverentially, pointing out that it was embroidered with the early date of 1919, and already prominently featured a swastika swathed in oak leaves.

Drewitt turned away in disgust.

On the opposite wall, as if representing the other half of Malchus's dark longings, was a large brooding image of Baphomet—the demonic deity supposedly worshipped by the heretical and blasphemous medieval Knights Templar.

Malchus had told him the picture was by the renowned French occultist, Eliphas Lévi, who had represented Baphomet as a breasted man with a horned goat's head and hoofs. The beast was sitting cross-legged with one hand pointing to Heaven and the other to Hell, a large pentagram branded into his broad forehead.

Repulsed, Drewitt looked away, towards the far side of the room, where he knew Malchus's prize possession lay—inside the shallow safe sunk into the floor.

He had already decided it would be the best place to start his search.

Stepping over to the room's far corner, he lifted the silk rug to expose the polished floorboards underneath. Pulling up two that were loose, he uncovered the safe and quickly dialled in the combination. He knew the code by heart—his father had put the strong box in many years ago.

When he heard the mechanism click, he turned the heavy handle, lifted the thick steel lid, and peered inside.

He could immediately see that apart from Malchus's prize object, it was empty.

He breathed out deeply with disappointment. He was not sure what he had been expecting to find—but he had hoped there would be something.

Anything.

Instead, he gazed down at the familiar large bundle Malchus had once ecstatically unwrapped for him.

He pulled it out and gingerly took off the small outer rope, curious to see the object again—this time without Malchus insisting that human hands may not touch it.

As he unwrapped the cloth, the material fell away to reveal a narrow leaf-shaped piece of metal about a foot long, tapering to a vicious point. It had clearly been ravaged by time and was a mere shadow of what it had been the day it emerged, white-hot, from the smith's fire. Nevertheless, it was still instantly recognizable—an antique spearhead.

Running his fingers gently over it, he could see it had been mended many times over the years. There was a gold sleeve over the middle section, and the rest was held together by six bands of tightly bound silver wire, which also acted to secure an old nail laid into its blade.

Malchus had told him it was the Lance of Longinus, the Spear of Destiny—the weapon that a Roman soldier had used to slice open Christ's dead flank on the cross. The nail, he had explained, was from the crucifixion itself.

The claim sounded deluded and insane to Drewitt, but Malchus had seemed transported by the object, explaining it had long been believed to give its owner celestial powers over enemies, which is why it had been sought and owned by all history's great warriors, including Alaric, Charlemagne, Barbarossa, and the Hapsburgs.

Malchus told him that Hitler had wasted no time in seizing it from conquered Vienna in 1938, fired up by its role in Wagner's opera, *Parsifal*, and convinced it was a talisman of power he had wielded in a former life.

Hitler had brought it triumphantly back to Nuremberg in an armoured SS train, and put it in the former monastery church of Saint Katharina. Later, in 1944, as the end of the war approached and he became concerned for its safety, he had it moved by his agents to a secret location, from where the liberating American army recovered it in 1945.

But, Malchus had gloated, in the late 1980s, while still a Stasi officer, he had learned that the end of the story was not all it seemed.

Towards the end of the war, a fraternity of Catholic priests of Nuremberg, still secretly devoted to Saint Katharina, had switched the spear, ensuring a fake was handed over to Hitler's agents. So the 'holy spear' discovered by General Patton's victorious army and returned to its glass case in Vienna's Hofburg palace was a useless replica.

Malchus had become obsessed with the priests' treachery, and had tracked down the three elderly celibates, who still guarded the true

spear. He had them seized and brought to the basement of the Ministerium, where he was able to work on them undisturbed. Although they
put up more resistance than he thought possible from elderly men, the
combination of prolonged major trauma and strong drugs proved too
much—as it always did. In their screaming delirium, they confessed the
spear's hiding place, and signed their own death warrants.

So Malchus had taken possession of the spear, and it now lay safely in
Drewitt's house.

He was not concerned about elaborate security, because as far as the
world knew, the spear was safely under permanent guard in the Hofburg
palace in Vienna.

Drewitt shuddered.

Everything in the room reeked of violence, pain, and darkness.

He wrapped up the spearhead again and locked it away in the safe,
dropping the carpet back into place before walking over to the antique
desk against the far wall.

It had once been a favourite room and desk of his—before Malchus
had come. Its top surface was inlaid with old brown leather and edged
with a gold patterned border. Tall bronze lamps sat firmly at either end,
casting their gentle light down over the desk. If the curtains had been
open, the windows would have given an attractive view out over the
gardens.

It had been a restful place to work.

But the thick dark curtains Malchus had installed were firmly closed,
and the lamps cast a pale glow down over his strange books and papers.

Drewitt flicked idly through the top book. It was a leather-bound copy
of something called the *Monas Hieroglyphicas* by Dr John Dee. He had
never heard of it. As he turned the pages, he could see they were all in
Latin, covered with strange geometrical and astrological symbols.

It was like those older books in the college library that ever fewer
people were able to read. He had always wanted to be able to understand Latin properly—not just the occasional word here and there. He
had never needed it for his work as an economist, but it would be a fun
project for his retirement.

Moving the book aside, he could see underneath it several more
ancient leather tomes, all filled with similarly incomprehensible writing
and symbols. The titles were equally strange to him—*Ars Almadel, Ars
Theurgia Goetia, Grimorium Verum, Liber Iuratus Honorii.*

He had no idea what they were all about, but the dark collection of texts left him feeling disturbed.

Before meeting Malchus, he had assumed all these occult materials were mumbo-jumbo. But now he knew very differently. The things men like Malchus were prepared to do in order to find such books, and what they did once they had become intoxicated by them, were very far from harmless.

It was pure evil.

As he moved the books aside to uncover a piece of paper on which Malchus had been writing, he caught sight of a purple leather case hidden under the pile.

It was about the size of a cigar box. The leather was heavily worn, and the silver clasp that once held it together at the front now hung loosely, long broken.

He put a fingernail under the catch, and carefully lifted the lid.

It rose with no resistance, and he exhaled audibly at the sight of what lay nestled on its pearl-coloured silk lining.

It was a seal or a medal—he could not tell the difference, a little larger than the width of his hand.

He knew a thing or two about paintings, but was out of his depth with solid objects.

His first impression was that it was old—but he was worldly enough to know that modern forgers were highly skilled, and regularly duped all but the most experienced specialists. Nevertheless, he could see it had a certain irregularity and smoothness that suggested it had not come out of a Chinese factory or off a counterfeiter's workbench. It had an undefinable inconsistency and mellowness hinting at authentic age.

He touched its surface, tracing the images and writing covering the front face. He could read some of the words, but they made no sense to him.

Prising it gingerly out of the box, he flipped it over, revealing more carvings on the other side. They were in a completely different style— rougher and cruder. Again, he could not make any sense of them.

He turned the object over in his hands again.

It was quite one of the oddest things he had ever seen.

Startled by a noise behind him, he froze, before a second noise triggered a burst of adrenaline that spun him round to face the door.

His heart was hammering as his eyes scoured the room and the hallway outside for even the smallest clue to what may have made the noise.

But there was nothing there.

He took several deep breaths, continuing to stare at the empty doorway.

Forcing himself to remain calm, he listened acutely. But there was only silence.

Relaxing, he lowered his tense shoulders and reminded himself it was an old house. It made noises. It always had. As a child in bed, he had constantly fought the urge to panic when the floorboards creaked, expanding and contracting as the house settled down each night.

He steeled himself to stop imagining things, and turned back to the desk.

Thinking quickly, he pulled the phone from his jacket pocket, and flipped on the camera.

Holding it a foot above the strange seal, he snapped a photograph of the front, then flipped it over and took one of the reverse.

Peering at the phone's screen to make sure the pictures had come out, he noted with satisfaction that they had. All the details were clear and crisp.

Laying the seal back on the box's silk lining, he opened the photographs into an MMS message, and added the telephone number the young woman had given him at his college that morning.

Typing quickly, he wrote her a brief explanation:

ON HIS DESK. MAYBE OF INTEREST TO YOU?
A.D.

He hit the SEND button, and as he did so another noise from the doorway made his heart skip a beat.

This time there was no mistaking it. He was not imagining things.

There was someone there.

Slipping the phone quickly into his pocket, he turned around slowly to see a figure emerge into the doorway.

A hot flush of sweat broke out over his body as he saw it was Malchus, standing quietly, watching him.

As his tormentor stood there, fixing him with an icy expression, he began to feel a knot of cold fear tightening in the pit of his stomach.

"I was just … . I thought perhaps … ," Drewitt blustered, struggling to think up any excuse to explain what he was doing in Malchus's rooms.

He prayed Malchus had not seen him taking the photographs.

"There's no need to explain," Malchus replied coldly. "It's quite clear."

"No, no … you see," Drewitt stammered, "I was looking for today's newspaper. I thought … I thought perhaps you had brought it upstairs." He trailed off, aware Malchus had begun walking over towards him.

He winced as he saw Malchus glancing at the disturbed carpet, where it had folded back onto the floor with a visible wrinkle.

As Malchus drew level with the desk, Drewitt noticed with a sickening lurch that the leather case containing the medal was still open, and Malchus was looking directly at it.

Drewitt struggled desperately for something to say.

At first he thought perhaps he should make light of it, but he listened with growing despair as the rushed words came tumbling out of his mouth. "I'm afraid I couldn't help myself. Academic curiosity, you know. Sorry." He was rambling. Even as he heard the words, he knew they were hopelessly inadequate.

Malchus carried on staring at the medal.

"As I said, no need to explain," Malchus answered robotically. "I can see exactly what's been happening here."

To Drewitt's surprise, Malchus put an arm round his shoulder and began steering him towards the door.

"Well, I honestly—" Drewitt began, unsure what to read into Malchus's reaction. But his thoughts were interrupted by Malchus jabbing his hand into Drewitt's jacket pocket with lightning speed, and pulling out the phone.

Impulsively, Drewitt lunged to grab it back, but Malchus was too quick, and had already stepped away.

At that moment, the phone emitted two short low chimes.

Drewitt felt sick.

"Your correspondent has replied," Malchus opened the incoming message.

"Look, I can explain—" Drewitt began, but Malchus again cut him off.

"MANY THANKS FOR THE PHOTOS"

he read out aloud.

"THEY LOOK FASCINATING. I'LL BE IN TOUCH. KEEP IT UP!"

As Malchus scrolled up to read Drewitt's original message, Drewitt could see the embedded images of the seal's two faces filling the entire screen.

Malchus clicked the phone off, and slipped it into his pocket.

With no more excuses and nothing to hide or lose any longer, Drewitt gazed defiantly at Malchus.

"This is very ... disappointing," Malchus stared at him. "You've violated our arrangement."

Drewitt glared back, finally making no show of hiding his loathing for him.

"I'm afraid this changes things," Malchus said quietly, nodding towards the doorway.

As Drewitt's eyes followed him, he saw one of Malchus's thugs standing in the hallway outside the room.

"Goodbye, Anselm Drewitt," Malchus murmured, with no hint of emotion, walking past the bodyguard into the hallway. "We shall not meet again."

Whatever ambiguity Drewitt felt there may have been in Malchus's parting words quickly evaporated as the bodyguard pulled a long cut-throat razor from his pocket, and advanced into the room.

———————— • ◆ • ————————

# 55

*10b St James's Gardens*
*Piccadilly*
*London SW1*
*England*
*The United Kingdom*

IN HER LONDON house, neatly tucked away behind the rush of Piccadilly, Ava's mobile phone vibrated.

Since arriving back in London from visiting Drewitt in Oxford, she had called Ferguson, and told him to meet her at the house so she could bring him up to speed.

She felt it was the right thing to do.

In the pub the previous evening, he had asked for three days in which to show he could be useful. If he failed, he would go, and take Prince with him.

Ava knew a good deal when she saw one.

So she had decided to enter into the spirit of it properly.

When he arrived, she had briefed him on everything she knew. Fair was fair. She needed to give him the information, otherwise he stood no chance of being useful to her. And she was not risking a lot in telling him what she knew. After all, he was aware of much of it already, or could get it from Prince and DeVere, so she was not giving anything away.

He had listened attentively in silence, and afterwards asked incisive questions, keen to put the pieces of the jigsaw together.

What had she thought General Hunter's motives were in telling her about Malchus and her father? What had she made of Saxby and his sudden appearance? Who did she think Saxby worked for, and why had he passed her the ticket to the Burj al-Arab auction? Did she have any proof the snatch-squad at the Burj al-Arab had been Malchus's men? Why did she think Prince had helped her with the flash drive? What did she realistically expect from Drewitt? And a host of other detailed questions, many of which she had been asking herself incessantly over the last few days.

They had finished going over it all, and Ferguson was now sitting at the table in the main room, configuring his laptop for her wi-fi.

Ava was looking at her phone. "It's from Drewitt," she called out, dropping down onto the sofa as a snippet of preview text appeared on her screen.

She clicked the message open.

"He hasn't wasted any time," Ferguson looked up. "Do you think he's going to be trustworthy?"

"We'll soon find out." Ava had been wondering the same thing herself. "There are some photos coming through. He says they're of something on Malchus's desk."

She scrolled down, as two images appeared on her phone's screen, one after the other.

Looking at the first photograph, she immediately recognized the central image.

It was the Jewish Menorah—the sacred seven-branched gold candelabrum cast by the Hebrews in the desert along with the Ark, the Altar of Incense, and the Table of Showbread. Together, they made up the sacred objects they kept first in the holy Tabernacle tent, then inside King Solomon's Temple.

Although it was now famous as a worldwide symbol of Judaism, she knew that replicas of the Menorah were also widely used by Christians—especially in Orthodox and Catholic churches. Yet another reminder, she thought, that Christianity was originally a heretical sect of Judaism.

But as she took in the rest of the photograph, she realized the writing around the Menorah was like nothing she had ever come across before.

She gazed at it with incredulity.

It was quite one of the most extraordinary inscriptions she had ever seen.

She exhaled a long slow breath, and watched as Ferguson walked over and sat down on the sofa beside her. He looked over her shoulder at the phone's screen, staring at the images for a few moments. "What do you make of it?" he asked.

"I'm really not sure." She frowned, feeling at something of a loss. "There are a lot of odd contradictions."

"But you know what it is?" he sounded hopeful.

She did not answer, but peered more closely at the screen, trying to make sense of what she was seeing. "There are two images," she explained. "The front and back of an object. One side is easy—we don't have to waste much time on it. But the other is truly bizarre. And together, as two sides of the same piece, they are ... well ... I've never seen anything like it."

Intrigued, she sent the photographs to her printer, then stood up and headed across the hall into the study, where she printed them out onto photo paper.

"Fortunately, Drewitt has a decent camera on his phone," she said, re-entering the sitting room and dropping the large colour photographs down onto the coffee table. "They enlarge pretty well."

She sat back on the sofa beside Ferguson, poring over the full-size images, trying to reconcile the striking anomalies she was seeing.

"The second one is easy," she pointed to the picture of the two bearded heads. "It's unquestionably from an old seal, and its meaning is very straightforward."

"It is?" Ferguson sounded surprised. "I can't make head or tail of it."

She smiled, reminding herself this was not second nature to everyone. "Well, there's no mystery about what it is. Although what it's doing here is not at all clear."

"Go on," Ferguson was looking at the image closely. "We're not all ninja archaeologists."

She smiled. He had been particularly impressed at her description of how she had got away from Malchus's bodyguard at Drewitt's country house, wincing as she gave a detailed account of putting two rounds into the thug's inner thigh.

She pulled the photo of the two faces closer to the front of the table. "This image was traditionally used by popes."

Ferguson looked surprised. "You can tell that just from the picture?"

Ava nodded. "It's unmistakeable."

"To you maybe," Ferguson murmured.

"It's the obverse, or front, of a papal bull," Ava explained—but could instantly see from Ferguson's expression that she would have to explain further.

"In the olden days," she continued, "the Vatican sent riders all over Christendom with written orders and letters from the pope. The most important documents were called 'bulls'."

"Like the animal?" he asked, surprised.

She nodded. "Except the word comes from the name of the seal attached to the document—the *bulla*, from the Latin word meaning to boil."

Without pausing, she took a large envelope from the coffee table in front of her and scribbled on one side of it. "Imagine this is the pope's letter." She folded the bottom inch of paper forward and over to make a flap.

"Now," she picked up a pen and poked two holes through the flap and the paper behind it. "They threaded multicoloured silk cords through small slits in the bottom of the document." She pulled a piece of soft twine off the plant that was sitting in a bowl in the middle of the table and threaded it carefully backwards through the holes so that two equal lengths of twine hung down a few inches below the back of the paper.

"Then they cast the seal around the ends of the cords, so it dangled off the document." She took a small book of matches from the table and wrapped it around the twine ends so that only half an inch or so of the twine protruded from the bottom of the packet of matches. "That's how it worked."

Ferguson looked down at her improvised papal bull, then back up at her. "You're a bit obsessive about this stuff, aren't you?"

She felt the colour rise to her cheeks. "No ... I just ... ." But she knew he was right. She always had been.

"The point is," she continued, "bulls made papal letters instantly recognizable all over Christendom. So when one arrived at its destination, perhaps thousands of miles from Rome, the recipient immediately knew who had sent it, and just how important it was."

"So that's the front of an official papal seal?" Ferguson sounded disappointed. "It doesn't look very ... well ... impressive, does it?"

It was true. It was nothing like the grand and elaborate seals used by medieval kings. "Bulls have always been very simple," she explained. "Something to do with looking humble."

"And what does that mean?" Ferguson asked, pointing to the writing above the faces.

Ava dismantled the bull she had made. "In medieval times, people almost never wrote things out in full," she explained. "Like the word 'Xmas', for example, derives from a medieval abbreviation for Christmas. The word 'SPASPE' here," she pointed to the writing above the two heads, "is actually two names. 'SPA' is short for *Sanctus Paulus*, or Saint Paul—and 'SPE' is short for *Sanctus Petrus*, or Saint Peter. You can see the relevant letters directly above each of the faces. On the left, Paul has the straight beard, and on the right Peter has the tight curly beard, which is how they were always shown in early art."

Ferguson looked at the grey colour of the metal in the photos. "What's it made of? Lead?"

Ava had come to the same conclusion. "Most were simple. Gold was saved for very special occasions."

He nodded at the other photo. "What about the other image." He pointed to the first photograph "Why is it baffling if you know this seal is a papal bull?"

It was a good question.

"Four things," she replied, picking up the first picture and putting it in front of them.

"Just the four?" he asked. She could hear a note of good-natured mockery in his voice.

"I can probably come up with more if you don't mind waiting." In fact, the longer she looked at it, the more anomalies she was beginning to see.

"Four's just fine," he answered quickly with a smile.

She decided to keep it brief.

"First. If it was a normal bull, the reverse would be totally plain—with just the pope's name. But this one has text and multiple images—the Menorah, crosses, and stars."

"Second. There are no silk threads running through the seal. Even if they had been trimmed off, we should still see some remains of them."

"Third. It's much too big for a bull. Do you see the pen on Malchus's desk in the corner of the shot? Its size suggests this seal is about four inches across. That's over twice the size of a normal bull."

"So it's not a bull?" Ferguson sounded deflated.

Ava shook her head. "Not like any I've ever seen." She sat back in the sofa, deep in thought, genuinely mystified by the object. It simply did not fit into any category of artefact she knew. "You see, the fourth problem is the biggest of all. Not only does the first image have a lot of text where it should just be the pope's name—but it's in a muddled variety of languages, when it should just be in one: Latin."

"Seriously?" he asked, picking up the photo and staring at it. "What does it say?"

"That's just the point," she answered. "The words are clear enough. But they don't really mean anything."

She continued to stare at the strange object, unable to make sense of it.

It had been a long time since an artefact had stumped her quite as completely as this one.

*What on earth was it?*

She stared at the image of the Menorah and the strange wording around it.

*It made no sense.*

It was a complete mongrel. Normally the problem she faced with the writing on an ancient artefact was that sections of it were broken off or missing, and she had to reconstruct what the original may have said.

But this was completely intact. There was nothing missing that she could see. Yet it still did not make any sense.

It was a total mystery.

She started running through the options in her mind, trying to find reference points—other artefacts she had seen that had any similar characteristics.

But she was drawing a blank.

There was simply nothing like it. Everything about the design seemed odd. There was nothing ordinary or straightforward … .

Then suddenly an idea hit her.

As she let the thought develop, she shook her head in disbelief.

*Could it really be that?*

She stared at it, increasingly convinced she was onto something, seeing it in a whole new light.

*Was that what this was about?*

She could not prevent a broad smile from breaking out across her face.

"What's the matter?" Ferguson asked. "Is it a trick of some sort? A meaningless modern joke?"

"Quite the opposite," her face was deadly earnest again.

He stared across at her, baffled. "What then? What is it?"

She looked at him with rising excitement. "I can't tell you what it means, yet. But I'm willing to bet you any money that it's very old, and was cast by an extremely powerful and secretive organization with something highly important to say."

"You've lost me completely," Ferguson shook his head.

Ava could feel her eyes shining. "It's not a bull or a seal. It was never attached to a document." She paused breathlessly. "Don't you see? The message *is on the object* itself. The words on the front. They're a puzzle.

A clue. A code. A centuries-old riddle. And whatever the hidden message is, it comes straight from the heart of one of the world's most secretive and shadowy organizations—the medieval Vatican."

—————— • ◆ • ——————

# 56

*10b St James's Gardens*
*Piccadilly*
*London SW1*
*England*
*The United Kingdom*

AVA WAS LEANING forward in the sofa, poring over the images Drewitt had sent.

"If it's not a seal," Ferguson asked, "then what is it?"

Ava was still unclear in her own mind "At a guess, it's a religious medal."

Ferguson looked quizzically at her. "The Vatican gave out medals?"

Ava nodded. "But not like military ones for gallantry or service. The Roman world was obsessed with magical talismans, amulets, and charms. When the early Church was born among the bazaars of pagan Rome, the first Christians still wanted all the comforting trinkets they were used to. So the Church tolerated and even encouraged them. They soon created Christian talismans and medals for every need—to ward off the devil, to protect from disease, to mark pilgrimages, and everything else you can think of. People wearing crosses around their necks today is a direct continuation of that ancient pagan tradition."

"But if it's a medal," he countered, "why would it have a puzzle on it and not a clear open meaning?"

318

She had been asking herself the same question, but needed pen and paper to think clearly.

She got up and went to her study, where she picked up a pad of clean paper and a packet of felt tip pens.

Returning to the sitting room, she sat down on the sofa and began carefully copying out the words from the medal, writing them on a sheet of white paper in big capital letters, leaving a large space beneath each line.

✠ EL ✠ SAIN ✠ MUSTIER ✠ DE ✠ ROME ✠

CLEMENS III

HAM OF ÞE HOOLY BLODIG BULLE

SUB TUTELA STELLARUM

"Can you translate it?" Ferguson asked.

"See the first sentence?" She took a red felt tip pen. "It's basic medieval French." She pointed at the line:

✠ EL ✠ SAIN ✠ MUSTIER ✠ DE ✠ ROME ✠

and underneath it quickly wrote out the translation:

✠ THE ✠ HOLY ✠ CHURCH ✠ OF ✠ ROME ✠

"Which fits with the Vatican theory," Ferguson noted, squinting at the photo more closely. "But what are the little crosses between every word?"

"They're common on medieval seals," she answered without looking up, "usually just stylistic, for decoration."

She turned back to the photograph. "The next line is even easier. 'CLEMENS III' is a pope's name, in Latin." She wrote it out in English underneath:

CLEMENT THE THIRD

"Could we date the medal?" Ferguson asked. "By knowing when Clement was pope?"

Ava had never been good at remembering the order of popes. She recalled once looking through a list of them and realizing that, including the disputed popes, there had been around three hundred of them—or one every six-and-a-half years for the last twenty centuries.

She had better things to do with her time than memorize them all.

She pointed to the far side of the room, to a set of thick white wooden bookshelves running the length of the wall. They were filled with books of every colour, shape, and size. "That large blue book on the left of the bottom shelf will tell you."

Ferguson walked over to the bookshelf and pulled out the volume she had indicated, and returned with it.

"This next line is also straightforward." She pointed to it:

HAM OF ÞE HOOLY BLODIG BULLE

"It looks like very old English," Ferguson said, "like something out of *The Lord of the Rings*. But what's that?" He pointed at the sixth letter.

"Ah," Ava nodded. "Ye olde monke's habite."

Ferguson frowned. "Sorry?"

"It's a thorn," she explained. "An old Nordic rune that survived in written English until several hundred years ago. It's a 'th' sound. When printing started, early typesetters often used a 'y' instead because it was all they had in their box of largely Roman letters. So whenever you see a teashop called *Ye Olde Creame Bunne* or a pub called *Ye Olde Cuppe and Mitre*, it's just an old-fashioned way of writing 'the'."

"You mean all those people earnestly saying 'yee oldee' are off the mark?" Ferguson looked amused.

Ava nodded. "Way off."

"How disappointing." He began flicking through the book.

Ava started writing again. "Anyway, it's straightforward medieval English." She wrote out the translation:

HOME OF THE HOLY BLOODY BULL

"A bloody bull?" Ferguson paused. "Like a papal bull, soaked in blood?"

Ava shrugged. She was not at all clear what it meant. She turned back to the photo. "And the last line, 'SUB TUTELA STELLARUM', is Latin."

She added the translation underneath it:

UNDER THE PROTECTION OF THE STARS

Ferguson put his finger on a line in the book. "Clement the third was pope from 1187 to 1191. Apparently there was also an anti-pope called Clement the third, but he was a hundred years earlier, 1080 to 1100." He frowned. "What's an anti-pope? A cure for the first one?"

"Something like that," she smiled, holding up the sheet and standing back. "So if we put it all together, we get: 'THE HOLY CHURCH OF ROME. CLEMENT THE THIRD. HOME OF THE HOLY BLOODY BULL. UNDER THE PROTECTION OF THE STARS'."

"I see what you mean," Ferguson frowned, slipping the book of popes back onto the shelf. "The meaning's no clearer in plain English."

She looked at the sheet.

He was right.

*But why?*

She read the lines again.

*Why was it so mysterious?*

*What was it trying to hide?*

She stared at it, letting it wash over her.

But it still made no sense.

*What was she missing?*

Her phone buzzed to life again, interrupting her thoughts. "It's another message from Drewitt," she said, glancing down at it. "He's been busy."

As she clicked the image open and peered at it, a wave of nausea passed over her.

*Oh God.*

The blood drained completely from her face and ran cold.

Although it had taken her a moment to recognize, it was unmistakeably a photograph of Drewitt.

The image only showed his top half. But it was enough.

His head was lolling impossibly to one side, leaving no doubt his neck had been violently snapped. His mouth was gaping open, and his jaw was dangling at an ugly angle. With a rush of horror, she could see from the amount of blood inside his mouth and from the jagged stump visible in his throat that his tongue had been hacked out.

Feeling the bile rising, she looked down to where his shirt had been removed, and what had at first appeared to be random frenzied lacerations on his chest in fact spelled out letters, carved into his flesh with long deep cuts.

She turned away, her insides churning.

Ferguson had seen her reaction, and leant over to get a look at the screen.

"Christ," he mumbled. "They've done a job on him."

Ava was feeling physically ill.

She got up quickly and hurried to the bathroom. She was not normally squeamish—but this was different.

*Drewitt had been helping her.*

She could not escape the inevitable conclusion, which burst into her mind with another wave of nausea, stronger this time.

*It was her fault.*

Before she could stop herself, she vomited into the lavatory.

Two thoughts were echoing round her mind.

*If she had not approached him, he would still be alive.*

*If she had not put pressure on him, he would still be up in Oxford, looking out of the window at the quad and the flowers.*

She was sick again.

Ferguson appeared in the doorway, and handed her a towel off the rail.

She took it gratefully, too overwhelmed with the gruesome images of Drewitt to say anything.

*Another person dead.*

Her head reverberated with questions.

*How many more was Malchus going to kill?*

She needed desperately to understand what he was up to.

*What was important enough to kill Drewitt?*

*And how did the Ark fit into it all?*

What seemed sure was that wherever Malchus went, death invariably followed.

Emerging from the bathroom, she could smell fresh coffee coming from the sitting room. She wandered in, and saw Ferguson putting two cups down on the table.

He sat down on the sofa and looked again at the photograph of Drewitt. "Did you see what's cut into his chest," he asked as Ava walked over and sat down next to him.

She took the phone from him, and gazed again at the bloody mess where his chest had been.

As she tried to filter out the blood and gore, she thought she could make out individual letters. It looked like:

# APOC ZOZB

Ferguson squinted at it. "It looks like it was carved in a hurry. From the amount of blood, I'd guess he was still alive at the time."

For a moment, Ava thought she would be sick again. But it passed.

"It looks like APOC ZOZB," she answered, "whatever that means." She felt her voice trail off as her eyes moved up from the phone and into the middle distance, where they gazed unfocused.

*What kind of people did this?*

She had seen many things in her time, but the animalistic savagery of Malchus and his men ranked up there with the worst she could imagine.

As she struggled to understand, a fresh wave of guilt hit her.

*Drewitt would be alive if she hadn't interfered.*

"It's not your fault," Ferguson broke the silence. He was looking at her closely, concern on his face. "Drewitt made his own choices. He knew what he was getting into."

Ava did not answer.

"Just like you. You know who Malchus is, and what he does."

Ava shook her head. "I'm doing this because I need to. I want to. But I involved Drewitt. I forced him. This wasn't his fight, and I pushed him into it."

Ferguson shook his head. "He didn't get where he is—or rather … was," he corrected himself, "by being pushed around. He could've said no. But, just like you, he wanted the chance to go after Malchus. And you gave it to him."

"Look, I know you're trying to make me feel better … ," she shot him an appreciative glance, leaving the rest of the sentence unsaid.

Ferguson nodded in acknowledgement, leaving her to her thoughts.

He waited until she had finished her coffee before speaking again. "If it's any help. I know what you're going through."

"You had nothing to do with this," she answered. "There's no reason for you to blame yourself."

"Soldiers sometimes have guilt, too," he said quietly.

"Over what?" she answered. "Isn't it what you're trained to do?" She saw the flicker in his eyes, and regretted it the moment she said it. "I'm sorry. I didn't mean it that way."

He got up and refilled their mugs with coffee from the pot. "You're right. Doing the job has never bothered me."

"Then what?" she asked, her curiosity piqued

"You worked with the Increment?" he replied. "I saw it in your file."

She had. It had been an amazing and terrifying experience.

When Her Majesty's Government needed to put men onto the ground anywhere in the world for covert and deniable lethal violence, they turned to the Increment. It was a specially selected team of SAS and SBS troopers from Hereford and Poole who acted as MI6's private shock troops. She had heard its name had been changed since she left, but the unit was still the same. They did not do high-profile embassy sieges and aircraft hijackings, or even sabotage behind enemy lines. The regular SAS was there for that. The Increment was the elite within the elite—for the operations only a handful of people ever knew about.

She had worked with them on the ground on a number of occasions— the last one being a strike against a Yemeni-backed arms franchise based in Mogadishu's steamy Bakaara Market. The Increment had not arrived with the usual SAS fanfare of Agusta helicopters, black ops gear, respirators, and night vision goggles. They had merely sent in a small team with long hair and straggly beards, wearing grubby *ma'awis* and baggy shirts caked in a week's worth of grime. The men had appeared from nowhere in the crowded market and taken out the merchants' throats with overpowering ruthless force before merging back into the crowds.

Ferguson's voice pulled her back to the present. "So you know that military operations are rarely a clean business. Engagements are chaotic, and it's not only the bad guys who get hurt."

Ava was listening. "So what happened?"

"Have you ever been to Afghanistan?" he asked, sitting down in the armchair opposite her.

She shook her head.

He glanced at the floor before looking over at her again. "It's not like we didn't know it was going to be tough."

He leant forward, rubbing his hands slowly, his elbows resting on his knees. "It's always been the same. The list of invaders who underestimated Afghanistan goes back all the way. Alexander the Great's army got into serious trouble there. It was a graveyard for the Brits in the three Afghan wars of the 1800s. And the Soviets' heavy tanks failed after a decade of brutal combat in the '70s and '80s. For as long as anyone can remember, Afghan farmers have proved again and again they can beat state-of-the-art military technology. So despite the politicians telling us we'd be home again with no bullets fired, some of us knew it wasn't going to be that easy."

"Where in Afghanistan were you?" Ava asked, picturing in her mind's eye the silk roads that snaked crossed it, connecting Europe to Asia and the East Indies.

"Sangin." He spoke the name with the familiarity of someone who knew it all too well.

She looked blank.

Catching her expression, he explained. "If you follow the river Helmand upstream from the lakes on the Iranian-Afghan border, you head east towards its source, seven hundred miles away in the Hindu Kush."

He was staring into space thoughtfully. "On the way, you pass along mile after mile of fertile river valley—home to about half the world's annual opium crop. Beyond the irrigated fields there's nothing but dust and desolation. If you're really unlucky, you'll stop a quarter of the way along, about sixty miles from Lashkar Gah. That's Sangin."

Ava nodded. "I know where Lashkar Gah is."

Ferguson continued. "Last year, some genius put a Forward Operating Base there, in an old farmer's compound. And with a great sense of the absurd, he called it 'Malta'." He shook his head. "Even though the name made it sound like a sunny holiday destination, there definitely weren't any balmy marinas, nightclubs, or cocktails by the pool. It was a rat hole, surrounded by people who really didn't want us there."

He took a sip of his coffee. "You would not believe the stuff that went on. Laughing children leading us into machinegun ambushes. Semi-permanent engagement with an invisible enemy, half of them whacked out on chemical cocktails to keep them going round the clock."

"Our night vision meant we ruled the darkness, so we barely slept. Enemy snipers and dickers were everywhere. They may not have been very accurate with their AKs and old Enfields—but they only had to get lucky a few times."

"When we weren't dodging the snipers, we ran the gauntlet of the IEDs they planted along our patrol routes by night as quickly as we could mark or clear them by day. All the time, incessant 107 millimetre rocket attacks pulverized our flimsy base, while doped-up suicide bombers walked up to patrols and detonated themselves. We were being pinned down and butchered in a dozen ways. It was unrelenting."

He paused. "I don't know what the TV screens showed the world, but I can tell you—it was as close to Hell on earth as anything I've ever encountered."

"I had heard it was bad." Ava said softly.

"The pen-pushers in the Ministry of Defence have since admitted that losses at Malta were up there with casualty rates in the trenches of the First World War." He pursed his lips.

Ava was watching him as he was talking. There was a fatalism about the way he was remembering. She realized they could not be easy memories for him to carry around. He could not have found it straightforward being back in the civilian world again, where few people had any real idea what went on in far-flung military conflicts.

He swirled the coffee around the mug. "Every now and then we got kitted-up and went out into the cornfields to try to flush them out. The crop grew over twelve feet high. You couldn't see a thing."

"Towards the end, I was leading a patrol through a nearby housing compound out in the corn. I'd done it a hundred times before. It was a typical set-up—a small cluster of shacks made of mud, brick, and straw, surrounded by a mud wall, all abandoned years earlier."

"I had three men with me. They were experienced soldiers. Professionals. They'd all done it many times before, too. I don't know what happened, but as we were leaving the compound, I turned round, and the rear two weren't there. They were just gone."

"There are standard operating procedures, and there are times when you throw away the rulebook. This was one of them. The remaining two of us immediately went back in, unsupported."

"But we found the compound deserted. There was no sign of anyone. The locals were good at that—when they wanted to, they just melted into the corn and poppy fields, the sand, and the streams."

"What happened?" Ava asked quietly.

"The bodies were dumped in the compound that evening," he answered. "I'm not going to tell you what had been done to them." He looked away. "I struggled for a long time over what to tell their parents and girlfriends."

He took a deep breath. "Inevitably, the mood at the base turned. The company's blood was up. We wanted to find whoever had done this. If we'd known where the enemy position was, the men would have fixed bayonets and gone after them. There would've been nothing I could do to stop them."

"But we didn't know where they were. They were invisible."

"When some enemy were spotted coming and going from the derelict compound a few days later, the men asked to call in a B-52 and finish them off. As the commander, I agreed. It was a standard procedure."

"We immediately sent out a patrol to laser paint the compound and radio in air support. We didn't have to wait long before we heard the drone of the eight turbojets, and within minutes the mud compound and surrounding area was hidden by brown and black smoke, flattened by a pair of five hundred pounders."

He paused, and wiped a hand across his face. "We found out later that there had been five enemy combatants holed up in the abandoned compound, but there had also been two families—mothers and their seven children—all sheltering in a pit dug out as a basement. God knows what they were doing there. One of the children was still just alive. They brought him to Malta where the medical officer fought to patch him up, but he died on the medevac helicopter to Camp Bastion."

"Christ," muttered Ava, almost inaudibly.

"Lying out in my tent that night, I couldn't escape the recurring thought that it was all my fault. I should've kept my men safe—that was my job. And I should've ordered a proper observation on the housing compound to ensure there were no civilians before we bombed it back to the stone age. I should've insisted we spend the time to track who came and went. But I didn't."

"Something happened to me after that. No one in the unit blamed me—I'd just been doing my job. No one wept for the civilians either. These things happen in war. But I knew I'd let them all down. Whatever the army said, people were dead because of me, and they shouldn't have been."

"Over the coming days, the feeling did not fade away—it grew. Something inside me had changed. A leader with guilt and doubts is no kind of a leader in that environment. So I decommissioned, and left. All I knew was that my two men and those families were dead—all because of me. I had failed each of them."

He looked up at her. "So you see. We all have our Anselm Drewitts."

Ava was not sure how to respond. Hearing about more violent deaths was not making her feel any better.

"But what I've learned since then," he continued, "and I don't know if it'll mean anything to you tonight—is that feeling guilty won't change anything. But getting on with your life, doing something positive, will."

He got up to leave. "It's late. Thanks for the coffee. I'd better be going."

Ava looked up at him, suddenly aware that for some reason she did not want him to leave quite yet. "You can stay in the spare room, if you like," she offered. "We've got an early start tomorrow."

"We have?" he asked, taken by surprise.

"Sure we have," she got up, a new look of determination engraved into her face. "We need to solve the code on that medal, and then use it to find Malchus—before someone else ends up like Drewitt."

# DAY EIGHT

———— ◆ ————

## 57

*Dagenham*
*London RM10*
*England*
*The United Kingdom*

OTT HAD EXPLAINED to Uri that there was a bookshop run by an old man in Dagenham.

It was just off the high street, tucked away among the chain stores and bargain shops, opposite a run-down car park. But it was not a normal bookshop, as there were no novels, coffee-table books, children's stories, or travel guides for sale.

Instead, it was a long-standing left-wing mecca—open since the '60s, piled high with Marx, Engels, Trotsky, copies of *Socialist Worker* and *The Morning Star*, and other publications Otto lumped together as "degenerate".

It acted as something of a clearing house for the East End's left-wingers. They gathered in its few saggy armchairs around an old kettle, surrounded by notice boards advertising meetings, trips, trade unions, study groups, socials, and other liberal activities that clearly turned Otto's stomach.

There had been no ambiguity in Otto's meaning. If Uri wanted to meet the Skipper, he first needed to show what he could do.

The bookshop was his test.

Uri figured that Otto and the Skipper would probably be happy if he put a London brick through its window. Or sprayed the front with abusive graffiti. Or roughed up the owner, or perhaps even a customer or two.

But Uri knew he could do far better than that.

And he could do it well.

It was just the sort of thing he was good at.

He had needed to do some shopping first, though.

All the ingredients had been readily available—a square biscuit tin from a grocery shop, a dozen bottles of nail polish remover and hair bleach, some sulphuric acid, and finally a pot of nitrocellulose paint.

He had purchased the liquids at different pharmacies and hardware shops over the course of a day, not wanting to arouse suspicion. He had also bought a few other necessities, including a couple of pairs of chemical-resistant gloves and a cheap pager.

It had been a while since he had cooked up this particular recipe. But he had previously had plenty of training on it, and a quick refresher on the internet was all he needed.

When his instructors back in Israel had shown him how easy it was to buy the various ingredients, he had been amazed. But he had soon learned that assembling them safely was not such a simple task. Limbs and lives were regularly lost by those who were sloppy or cut corners.

As he had followed the instructions that first time, in the Institute's underground science and technology laboratory by the West Glilot junction just north of Tel Aviv, he had been pleased to discover he was a natural bomb maker.

It just required patience and a cool head.

And he had both.

One problem he had quickly discovered back in the lab was that the chemical reactions gave off strong fumes—corrosive enough to strip the paper off walls.

But in Maze Hill the smell was hardly going to be a problem. It was not as if he had to make the device in a five-star hotel room.

It had been child's play to break into a small unused building on a nearby industrial estate. The whole area stank with the all-pervasive smell of paint and chemical fumes—and no one had noticed a few more.

Now, approaching the bookshop with the volatile package safely in his rucksack, he checked his watch.

It was coming up to 3:00 a.m.

Alert, he looked about—scanning the area for anything out of the ordinary. But he need not have bothered. The streetlamp opposite the bookshop flickered on and off, illuminating empty pavements in front of a row of tatty shop fronts.

There was nobody about. Most pubs had kicked out their most loyal customers at 11:00 p.m., the late-night kebab shops were closed, and even the stragglers had finished weaving their drunken way home.

Uri did not pass another soul on the street.

That was good. Not only for security, but also because he did not want any innocent casualties. Sometimes they were unavoidable, but on this occasion he needed to avoid victims. He did not want the police turning their inevitable investigations into a murder hunt.

He had done a recce of the bookshop the day after meeting Otto in *The Lord Nelson*, and he had been pleased with what he found.

The shop was an old-fashioned design—a small two-storey Victorian building with a pair of large bay windows bulging out of a dark wooden frontage. The black gloss paintwork looked tired, but the bowed windows lent the shop an individual feel among the bland concrete shops on the street.

The entrance door was set back a little, in between the two windows, at the end of a short porchway decorated with attractive blue and white diagonal floor and wall tiles.

Uri had been less interested in the architectural features than the security. He had scanned the area carefully, gratified to see that neither the shop nor the street had any visible CCTV cameras.

*Perfect.*

He had not bothered with an elaborate disguise. In his experience they were more trouble than they were worth. A baggy shapeless anorak and a beanie hat were more than enough to make him unrecognizable on any blurry camera footage that might pick him up in the area.

Checking again there was no one about, he approached the bookshop swiftly, cutting across the car park to avoid the cameras on the roads at either end.

Arriving in front of it, he bent low by the half-height iron gate drawn across the front door, and quickly slipped the biscuit tin out of his rucksack.

It was wrapped in a padded brown envelope addressed to the bookshop. If anyone saw the package lying there, they would just figure it was a parcel of books.

Anyway, it would not be around for long.

Putting the package gently onto the ground, he pushed it up against the low iron gate so the blast would take down the door as well as the bay windows.

Standing up, he casually stepped away and back onto the street.

There was still nobody about.

Moving briskly, he made his way back into the car park and out over the low wall of *The Three Tuns* pub. As much as he would like to have stayed around to watch his handiwork, his priority now was to put as much distance between himself and the shop as possible.

As he walked quickly away, he passed a set of catering bins outside a Chinese restaurant. Pulling off his baggy beige coat, beanie, and rucksack, he dropped them into the bins and went on his way, now a different shape entirely thanks to the tight-fitting light-blue fleece he had been wearing underneath.

Heading past a closed garage, he found a night-bus stop, and hopped onto a half-empty bus. It did not matter where it was going. He was counting on changing buses several times anyway, to confuse any camera surveillance that might have picked him up.

As he looked out of the windows at the drizzle beginning to fleck the drab empty streets of the suburbs, he checked his watch periodically to see when ten minutes was up.

When the minute hand told him it was time, he pulled out his mobile phone, slipped in a pay-as-you-go SIM he had picked up from a charity shop, and called the pager. As he heard it connect, he hung up instantly.

Three miles away, the pager in the biscuit tin received the signal and lit up, sending an electrical impulse deep into its circuits.

It was enough.

The bomb exploded with a savage intensity.

As the ferocious blast wave rippled out, the front of the shop was vaporized. At the same time, a deep percussive boom tore through the night as neighbouring shop alarms and sprinkler systems began pointlessly to wail and sprinkle water.

In the comfort of the bus, Uri guessed the owner of the bookshop was going to have a serious shock when he received the inevitable phone call from the police. But it could not be helped. The building and stock were almost certainly insured, and anyway—the owner must have known the shop was a target. It was his choice.

Uri was home by 5:30 a.m. He got his head down immediately, and when he woke at 9:00, it was all over the local news, exactly as he had hoped.

That would give Otto and the Skipper something to think about over their breakfast.

It was by no means the first time his work had hit the headlines. He smiled as he recalled the sudden fatal outbreak of Legionnaires' disease at the health club in Marrakesh. His superiors had learned the site was being hired for a convention by people whose interests lay very counter to their own. Uri had been proud of the Legionnaires' disease idea. That had been one of his better ones.

He got up and took a shower, standing in the bath and spraying himself with lukewarm water from the cheap rubber hose attached to the bath's taps.

After towelling himself dry, he put on a clean pair of jeans and a casual shirt, before settling down to wait for Otto's call.

---

## 58

*10b St James's Gardens*
*Piccadilly*
*London SW1*
*England*
*The United Kingdom*

AVA AWOKE IN the night.

She had been dreaming of the strange letters slashed into Drewitt's chest.

Something about them was bothering her, but she could not put her finger on it.

They made her feel uneasy.

Unable to go back to sleep, she eventually got out of bed and pulled back one of the curtains.

It was still dark outside, and the street was eerily quiet.

Slipping on a shirt and jeans, she headed down into the study, where she flicked on a side-lamp and sat at the desk.

Unlocking her phone, she peered at the glowing screen and pulled up the gruesome photograph of Drewitt—focusing on the crude writing slashed hurriedly into his chest:

APOC ZOZB

As she stared at the strange letters, she could feel her uneasiness growing.

Something was not right about the phrase, but she could not tell what.

She had the strong sense there was an important feature she was overlooking.

*What had she missed?*

She looked closely at each letter, narrowing her eyes in an attempt to focus on every last detail.

*What was it that did not click?*

She gazed at the lines and angles of the cuts, and forced herself to start the process again—to think clearly, taking it one step at a time.

As she looked at the deep wounds, she felt a wave of revulsion on remembering Ferguson's suggestion that Drewitt may have been alive when they were carved into him.

She traced the incisions, imagining exactly how they had been cut, but stopped suddenly at the last letter—the germ of an idea forming.

Staring hard at it, letting the thought take shape, she felt a prickle of excitement as she realized she had been right to have doubts.

It was faint, but it was there.

She *had* made a mistake the night before.

And as she looked at it more closely, she could see it had been a big one.

It was not a letter B at all.

It was the number eight.

She peered at it hard.

*Definitely.*

Her subconscious mind had seen it, and had been trying to push it forward into her consciousness. The error had been nagging away in the part of her mind that never slept. But now she could see it clearly.

It was an easy mistake to make on such a small photograph, especially as the vicious gouges were obscured by the trickles and splashes of blood splattering Drewitt's chest. But as she looked at it more intently, she was now absolutely sure of it.

It was indisputably an eight.

Her mind whirring, it meant she had to go back to square one. If she had been mistaken about the final letter, she could equally easily have made an error over any or all of the others.

Printing the photograph out full size, she peered at the cuts more closely, running through in her mind the many options of what the other letters could be.

In no time at all, she realized her mistake had been far larger than just the last letter. She had completely misread the entire last word.

It was not ZOZB or ZOZ8 at all.

It was her basic assumption that it was a word which was wrong.

It was not only the last character that was a number and not a letter. They all were.

The second word was a string of numbers.

The first Z was not a Z at all—it was a two. And the second Z was not a Z either. It was trickier to see, but she could now make out quite clearly it was actually two characters—a seven followed by a dash. It had been done hurriedly, or maybe Drewitt had been moving. Either way, the dash started low and close to the bottom of the seven, pushing the two together, making them look like a Z.

She could feel her breathing coming more quickly as she looked at the whole phrase.

It now made total sense to her—conclusive confirmation she had been wrong first time.

APOC 20 7–8

With a growing sense of foreboding, she knew exactly where to look.

Reaching for the large hardback Bible on her reference shelf, she flicked quickly to the very end, to the dark and prophetic Book of the Apocalypse, also known by its more modern name—the Book of Revelation.

Thumbing her way to chapter 20, she ran her finger down the page until she got to verses 7–8.

As she read the text quietly in the half-light, she felt herself go cold:

> And when the thousand years are expired, Satan shall
> be loosed out of his prison, and shall go out to deceive
> the nations which are in the four quarters of the earth,
> Gog and Magog, to gather them together to battle.

It was not the words themselves that chilled her. She understood the text for what it was—an unusually vivid and dramatic example of first-century southern Aegean eschatology.

Its Satanic prophecy held no special fears for her.

But she was well aware that to men like Malchus it was biblical truth.

And she was beginning to see what lengths he would go to in its name.

She could quite believe Malchus thought he was doing preordained work to prepare for an age of darkness—that he saw apocalyptic times ahead, with himself at the centre of his own twisted Armageddon.

She knew enough about men like him to realize the message was also personal—a taunt, a challenge, maybe even an explicit warning, broadcasting his achievements and plans.

She had absolutely no doubt he meant the message for her. Why else would he have taken the picture on Drewitt's telephone and sent it directly to her?

She stared at the prophetic text.

*Was it a clue about what he was planning?*

*About why he wanted the Ark?*

She thought of Israel's Jezreel Valley, and of the hill of Megiddo, which had given its Greek name to the apocalyptic battle of Armageddon that would mark the end of time.

Although Megiddo was once an important city state, now it was an unremarkable deserted archaeological site overlooking a kibbutz and not a lot else.

It had always struck her as a most unlikely place to stage the final war for humanity.

*What was Malchus telling her?*

Turning again to the photographs of the medal on Malchus's desk, she stared at them, trying to find a connection that would help unlock the medal's meaning.

Deep in thought, she lost track of time, until the light began to show around the edges of the window.

Getting up, she pulled open the heavy curtains and let the weak grey dawn light in.

As she did so, she thought again of Drewitt.

Naturally, Ferguson would need to report the murder to Prince, who would decide what to do.

She was pretty sure Prince would keep the British police away for as long as possible. The Americans did not need the British constabulary getting interested in Malchus and unintentionally jeopardizing the ongoing operation.

Ava was still contemplating the photographs of the medal and the bloody message when she heard the gentle thunk of an e-mail arriving in her computer's inbox.

Waking the screen, she opened the e-mail programme and immediately saw it was from Saxby.

She had been wondering when he was going to be in touch. After all, he had told her to go to London and wait for him to contact her.

She clicked open the e-mail, and read it quickly.

It was short, and to the point:

> BE AT THE ROYAL SOCIETY TODAY AT 9:00 A.M.
>
> ASK FOR ME.
>
> YOURS, E.S.

Getting to the Royal Society would be no problem. It was less than ten minutes' walk from her house.

She closed the e-mail and returned to her thoughts.

As she gazed out of the glass at the dewy window boxes, she hoped very much that Saxby would be able to clear up one or two things for her.

She certainly had some questions for him.

---  ◆  ---

# 59

*10b St James's Gardens*
*Piccadilly*
*London SW1*
*England*
*The United Kingdom*


AVA WAS STILL in the study when Ferguson emerged from his room several hours later—dressed and ready for the day.

"Look at this," she said, calling him over to the desk to share her discovery about the message carved into Drewitt's chest.

"So he's preparing a biblical confrontation?" Ferguson replied when he had read the chilling lines from the Book of the Apocalypse.

"Whatever he's up to, it doesn't sound good." Ava had been turning the gory message over in her mind, but was still no closer to understanding why Malchus had sent it to her.

She swivelled the office chair around and looked across at him. "Anyway, while you've been taking time out, I've come up with a solution to the puzzle on the medal."

He looked amused. "How do you expect me to be any use if you don't leave me anything to do?" He dropped down into the comfortable leather chair opposite her.

She flicked off her computer screen. "There's no time to sit around now. We need breakfast, and then I have to meet Saxby."

She darted into her room and got dressed, before opening the front door and showing Ferguson out.

She headed for the French café where Ferguson had followed her two days previously, and made for a quiet table in the corner, away from the queue snaking back from the till.

"So," she announced once they were seated and had placed their order with the cheery waitress. "The puzzle says: 'THE HOLY CHURCH OF ROME. CLEMENT THE THIRD. HOME OF THE HOLY BLOODY BULL. UNDER THE PROTECTION OF THE STARS'. I think I may have made some progress with it."

Ferguson was listening attentively.

"The references in the first two lines to the Church, Rome, and Clement all seem to point strongly to Pope Clement III," she began. "He was a thoroughbred Roman, who became pope in his late fifties."

Ferguson nodded.

She continued. "Then we have: 'HOME OF THE HOLY BLOODY BULL' and 'UNDER THE PROTECTION OF THE STARS', which suggests we should be looking for a bull issued by Pope Clement."

"But presumably he wrote dozens?" Ferguson objected. "How can we know which one?"

"Fortunately, the medal gives us a strong clue." Ava took the phone out of her pocket and opened up the picture Drewitt had sent her, putting it on the table between them. "We're not after just any bull from Clement. It needs to be holy and bloody."

She watched as Ferguson lapsed into thought.

"The Inquisition?" he suggested. "They were known for their bloody tortures, weren't they? Maybe Clement condemned a specific group of heretics? Or gave written authority to use a particularly gory torture?"

Ava took a bite of the croissant the waitress had put down next to her. "The Inquisition only began a few years before Clement's reign, and it didn't really get going for another two hundred years after that. So it's possible, but not very likely."

Ferguson wrinkled his brow, thinking again. "Then what about the whole body and blood thing in the mass? Was that big in Clement's day? Did he publish any bulls about it?"

Ava's eyes widened for a moment.

It was a good idea.

"You could be onto something there," she answered thoughtfully.

"The idea that the bread and wine used at the mass becomes the actual flesh and blood of Jesus during the ceremony only really became locked down as the formal Church doctrine of 'transubstantiation' in the twelfth century, around the time of Clement. Most people think it started at the Last Supper, but in fact it took over a thousand years to really firm up as a solid Church doctrine. That's what all the allegorical Holy Grail stories that began to emerge in the twelfth century were all about." She paused. "We should definitely keep it in mind—Malchus is just the type to have a Grail obsession."

Ferguson took a sip of his coffee. "What else? Did you come up with any other solutions?"

"Not out of ideas already, are you?" Ava asked, feigning disapproval.

He shook his head in disbelief. "I'm doing pretty well for a man who's spent more of his life on a firing range than in a library."

"I'm not awarding prizes for another couple of days," she smiled. "You're doing fine so far."

They paused to order a refill of coffee from the waitress who had reappeared beside their table.

"Maybe we need to think more laterally," Ava continued. "There's one other obvious possibility for a holy and bloody bull—and it's the biggest thing to have happened during Clement's time as pope."

Ferguson looked up at her, inviting her to finish her thought.

"The crusades," she answered.

"Richard the Lionheart and Saladin fighting over Jerusalem?" Ferguson asked, clearly relieved Ava's answer was something he had heard of.

She nodded. "In fact, there were eight crusades to the Holy Land stretched over a period of two hundred years. But I'll bet the medal is referring to the most famous—the one you just mentioned, between Richard and Saladin."

"So Clement started the crusades?" Ferguson tucked into the hot toasted sandwich that had appeared in front of him. "I'm surprised he's not better known."

Ava shook her head. "They began much earlier. The first crusader army started walking from Europe in the summer of 1096, and finally arrived at the gates of Jerusalem to take the city back from the Muslims three long years later, in the summer of 1099."

"Take it back?" Ferguson looked uncertain. "When had Jerusalem ever been Christian before then?"

Ava sipped the scalding coffee. "The Jewish kings lost control of Jerusalem to the Babylonians in 597 BC. After that it changed hands many times—conquered successively by Persians, Greeks, and finally the Romans in 37 BC. So when the Roman Empire officially adopted Christianity in the late 300s, Jerusalem automatically became Christian—until the Muslims conquered it in the seventh century."

"So why no crusades until 1096?" Ferguson looked puzzled.

"The Muslim rulers were tolerant and allowed Christians to worship there and make pilgrimages to the biblical sites. But in 1073 the Seljuq Turks seized the city, and began violently and cruelly persecuting Christian residents and visitors. For people back in Europe, that changed everything."

"Anyway," she continued. "The first crusade was definitely bloody. It was an orgy of slaughter. The Christian crusaders butchered anything alive in Jerusalem: women, children, animals, everything. The reports of the time say it was a slaughtering frenzy. The knights were even apparently throwing women and children off rooftops. The blood and gore in the streets was running ankle-deep."

"Bloodlust," Ferguson muttered quietly. "Never pretty."

"The crusaders then ruled Jerusalem as a Christian city until 1187," Ava continued. "They crushed all attempts to topple them, and figured their success was a sign from God they were his true chosen people."

"What changed in 1187?" Ferguson asked, finishing the last bite of his sandwich.

"Salah ad-Din Yusuf ibn Ayyub," Ava replied. "Better known as Saladin—a Kurd from Iraq who decided enough was enough. He knew the regional Muslims were too busy squabbling amongst themselves to be a serious threat to the crusaders. So he first set about uniting them all in order to build a power base. Before long, he single-handedly controlled all the countries surrounding the crusaders' lands."

"Smart move," Ferguson acknowledged.

"As a result, Saladin was able to mobilize the first really coordinated Muslim force the crusaders had ever seen. It was a massive army, and finally faced the crusaders between Haifa and Tiberias at two hills nicknamed the Horns of Hattin. The crusaders were politically split into two feuding camps, and their battle order was in disarray. Saladin exploited their weaknesses, encircled them, cut off their access to water, and the result was a rout. The crusaders lost everything, even Christendom's most precious possession—the True Cross, which the crusaders had always carried into battle with them. With no crusader army left, Jerusalem fell quickly. All was lost."

"Not good for the pope," Ferguson muttered.

"The news was received back in Europe with horror," Ava confirmed. "People thought God was punishing them all for their many sins. And that's where Clement comes in. He became pope a few months later, and rapidly made it his number one mission to seize Jerusalem back. After all, losing Jerusalem weakened the papacy he had just inherited. It looked like the Christians weren't God's chosen people after all."

"So what did he do?" Ferguson asked. "How does a pope conquer a city over two thousand marching miles away?"

Ava took another bite of her croissant. "He pulled together Europe's three most battle-scarred warlords—Emperor Frederick Barbarossa of Germany, King Henry II of England, and King Philip Augustus of France. Although he had a bit of work to do first, as all three leaders had their own problems at home—especially King Henry of England."

"I thought England was quiet in Henry's reign?" Ferguson asked. "The civil war was well and truly over by then."

Ava shook her head. "Definitely not peaceful. Henry's sons spent years sending their armies against him to try and seize their inheritances early. They were all at it, although the very worst was Richard."

"Richard the Lionheart?" Ferguson looked incredulous. "Did you say he fought his own father, the king, in battle—just to get his inheritance early?"

"Many times," Ava nodded. "And so did Richard's brothers. They were a poisonous family. When Henry finally died, he said that of all his sons, it was the legitimate ones that were the real bastards."

Ferguson burst out laughing. "You're making this up."

"I'm afraid not," Ava shook her head. "Henry was a great king in many ways. But he finally died of weariness after Richard and his lover, the king of France, beat him in battle and took chunks of France from him—"

"His what?" Ferguson interrupted. "I misheard you." He looked at her in shock. "For a moment I thought you just said that Richard and the king of France were an item?"

Ava grinned. There was no point in knowing history if you could not have some fun telling people things that shocked them.

"You're inventing this," Ferguson objected.

Ava raised her eyebrows in amusement. "Historians hate admitting it—especially stuffy English ones. They come up with all sorts of explanations for the awkward chronicles. But the old texts are totally clear. One chronicler famously wrote that the two men were so inflamed with love for each other that they shared a bowl at mealtimes and, as he delicately put it, did not have separate beds."

"This is the most scandalous history lesson I've ever heard," Ferguson interrupted. "You're rewriting my education."

Ava dipped her croissant in her coffee, French-style. "Oh there's much more about our great King Richard the Lionheart that the schoolbooks don't tell you."

"There is?" He looked appalled. "Like what?"

"It's ironic the English worship him so much," Ava replied, "because he loathed England. He lived in France, and never bothered learning to speak English. He only wanted England for its royal title so he could join the exclusive club of kings. He spent around six months in England in his entire life—and that was only to sell off everything that wasn't nailed down to raise cash so he could crusade in style with his friend the French king. He's even on record saying England was a dreary rainy place, and he boasted he would've sold London if he could find a buyer."

"This is treason!" spluttered Ferguson. "Richard the Lionheart is a national hero. The main statue outside the Houses of Parliament is of him, for God's sake."

"Funny old world, isn't it?" Ava smiled. "Anyway, this is all relevant because Pope Clement III eventually put his trust in the combined mailed fists of Barbarossa, Richard, and Philip Augustus. Going on the number of battles they had each fought and won, Clement figured he had a crack team to recapture Jerusalem."

"Hence the bloody bull," Ferguson nodded. "Jerusalem was lost, so he sent the three of them off east to get it back?"

"Exactly," Ava confirmed. "Except it didn't turn out so well. Barbarossa was the most experienced warlord of them all. But he never made it there. While crossing Turkey, he rode into the river Göksu and got washed away. It seems his armour was too heavy for whatever he was doing. Anyway, that was the last anyone saw of the crusade's leader."

Ferguson burst out laughing again. "Europe's most hardened warrior? Drowned swimming in his armour?" He shook his head. "Someone needs to make a film of all this—it's unbelievable."

Ava continued. "So Richard and Philip Augustus went on alone. And when they got to the Middle East, it started to get seriously violent. Although they failed to recapture Jerusalem, they did plenty of slaughtering. Richard bulldozed anything he could find. When he ran out of villages and villagers in the Holy Land, he sailed across to Cyprus and razed that, too."

"That was pretty normal for the period, though." Ferguson objected. "Medieval war wasn't known for its gentleness."

Ava took the last bite of her croissant. "Richard proved himself to be a seriously vicious man by anyone's standards. Furious with Saladin for repeatedly stalling during negotiations for the return of the True Cross, Richard lined up three thousand captured Muslim men, women, and children at a place called Ayyadieh, in full sight of Saladin's army, and sent his men in to beat and hack them to death. There were no survivors."

"Christ," whispered Ferguson. "Along with the slaughter you mentioned when the crusaders took Jerusalem, no wonder the crusades still raise such passions in the Muslim world."

"Well, Saladin promptly had all the Christian prisoners executed in retaliation. So no one comes out of it well. But there's no doubt Richard was an extremely brutal man."

"Anyway," Ava concluded, "it would be fair to call Clement's crusade bull a holy bloody bull, and the medal Drewitt sent us might be in English and French to reflect the crusading armies of Richard and Philip Augustus."

Ferguson wiped his mouth with a napkin and digested what Ava had been saying,

"What about 'UNDER THE PROTECTION OF THE STARS', then?" he asked. "How does that fit into all this?"

Ava looked pensive. "I've been wondering about that. Maybe it's a reference to where we'll find a copy of the bull. And hopefully when we do, the purpose of the medal, and Malchus's interest in it, will also become clearer."

Ferguson took the last swig of his coffee. "So how do we go about finding it? Who keeps these bulls today?"

"The Vatican chancery would have made many copies," Ava replied. "Some were kept in the Vatican archives, others sent out all over Christendom to stir the preachers and armies. We have to find one that is somehow 'UNDER THE PROTECTION OF THE STARS'."

"But what does that mean," he asked.

"Almost anything," Ava acknowledged. "Maybe there's an archive controlled by a family whose name is Stelle, or Estrellas, or Etoiles, or Sterne, or some other word for stars. Or perhaps the archive is in an old decorated building that has stars over the doorway or on the ceiling. Or maybe it's kept in a place where it's bathed in starlight by night. I don't know. We're going to have to find out where surviving copies are held."

"And also where copies were kept when the medal was struck," Ferguson added.

Ava nodded.

Glancing at her watch, she drained the rest of her coffee and stood up. "Time to find out more about the mysterious Saxby."

------------- • ◆ • -------------

# 60

*Maze Hill Railway Station*
*Maze Hill*
*London SE10*
*England*
*The United Kingdom*

URI WAS ALREADY on his second cup of bitter coffee. He did not particularly like the taste—it lacked the complexity of the cardamom-laced *kafe shachor* from back home, but it did the job.

He picked up his mobile phone the instant it buzzed and looked at the number flashing on the small screen.

It was Otto.

Uri had been wondering when he was going to call. He must have seen the news by now.

Otto's tone was business-like. There were no niceties—just a simple instruction. "The railway station in thirty minutes. Be there." Then the line went dead.

Uri grabbed his new designer coat from the back of the chair and headed out.

He walked swiftly and purposefully through the cool morning air to Greenwich Park—one hundred and eighty acres of medieval royal hunting land cutting a swathe of green across south-east London.

Once inside the ancient enclosure, he strode past the unassuming strip of brass laid into the ground marking zero latitude—the official dividing line between the eastern and western hemispheres, and barely took in the striking view of the Millennium Dome, spread over the Greenwich Peninsula like a vast and helpless upturned beetle,

As he hurried on through, the park was already filling with joggers streaming past local residents taking a moment to relax on the wooden benches and catch a few rays of the elusive sun.

Heading to the historic park's north-east corner, he exited onto Maze Hill itself, and arrived at the ugly suburban railway station in good time.

He knew exactly where Otto would be.

Making for the long concrete expanse of Platform One, he immediately clocked Otto sitting on a bench at the far end, his sharp features looking pinched in the early morning light.

There was no one else around.

He had been wondering how Otto would react.

He suspected Otto may well think he had gone too far—attracting unwelcome police interest. But it had been a calculated risk. Uri had wanted to make a statement that Otto could not ignore, and he was confident he had left no traces. The police would draw a blank—as they always did with his work.

As Uri approached the end of the platform, Otto began clapping slowly. "Very nice, Danny. Very impressive." His tone was not friendly.

Uri did not respond.

Otto's narrow face exuded suspicion. "So where did you learn to do that?"

Uri shrugged, sitting down next to him on the bench, digging his hands into the pockets of his coat.

"Are you military, Danny?" There was a distinct wariness in his voice.

Uri shook his head slowly.

"What then?" Otto did not sound happy.

"I told you," Uri stared straight ahead. "I'm into the heavier stuff."

"I can see that," Otto's tone was curt. "I wasn't born yesterday. That's quite an unusual little skill you've got there." He paused, looking across at Uri with open hostility. "What do you take me for, Danny? People don't just learn to make acetone peroxide bombs from some article in a magazine." He glowered at him. "So go on, where did you learn to do that?"

Uri knew he needed to keep it vague—nothing traceable or verifiable. "I've done jobs before, if that's what you mean," he answered nonchalantly.

"No, it's not what I bloody mean, Danny," Otto snapped, letting his impatience show. "Stop fencing with me. Who've you worked for? I want details—places, names."

Uri kept his tone businesslike. He had no option except to bluff it out. "I'm not a red, if that's what's bothering you." He paused to inject a note of sincerity. "I wouldn't be here if I was, would I?"

"Well, at least that's a start," Otto replied, clearly still suspicious. "So what are you, then?"

Uri took his time in responding. "Flexible," he answered vaguely.

"Come on, Danny," Otto cut him off. "You need to do better than that. What were you doing in *The Lord Nelson*? Who are you with?" He looked at Uri with suspicion. "Are you even English, I wonder? You talk funny."

"I'm not the law, if that's what you mean," Uri replied.

"I figured that out all by myself," Otto snapped. "The old bill round here don't normally plant high street bombs in the middle of the night."

"Look," Uri replied. "What do you want me to say? I'm not like you. I'm not political."

It was true. He classed himself as a Zionist, but that was not a political belief as far as he was concerned—it was a tenet of his country's survival. Beyond that, he had never been interested in left-right politics. Anyway, he could not afford to be in his job. He had seen different governments come and go—from hard-line right wing to liberal and left. He had to be above it—serving the state and people, whoever they elected.

Otto continued to glare at him with suspicion. "So why are you here? What do you want?"

"I'm a craftsman," Uri replied carefully. "A journeyman. I go wherever my work is … ," he paused, "appreciated."

"Just another gun for hire?" Otto asked, a hint of disdain in his voice.

Uri nodded. "Something like that."

Otto glanced down at his shoes before looking back up at Uri. "Since I saw the news this morning, Danny, I've been wondering if I made a big mistake with you. Don't get me wrong—you've got a certain style. But I don't like surprises. I did some asking around, and no one knows you, Danny. You're a bit of a mystery, and that makes me nervous."

Uri gazed thoughtfully into the middle distance. Otto might not like the mystery, but he knew that one way or another Otto's group would not want to pass up the opportunity of employing Uri's particular skills. All he had to do was stick to his story. "I've told you. I've been around. I don't advertise."

Otto looked pensive, lapsing into silence.

Uri tapped his foot and set his jaw. It was time to back off. He needed to set this up so Otto wanted him, not the other way round. "Well," he concluded. "You've got my number." He got up to leave.

"Not so fast, Danny." Otto put out a hand to indicate he should sit back down. "The Skipper will decide."

Uri smiled to himself.

*Progress.*

"Where?" he asked.

"Tomorrow night. Be outside the *Khyber Pass Curry House* round the back of Belmarsh prison, nine o'clock sharp. I'll find you there."

"What's the occasion?" Uri kept his voice expressionless.

"A get-together. A few beers. Maybe a speech. Might even do you good to meet some of the crew. Learn something."

"I'm not interested in the others," Uri replied.

Otto's face darkened. "Don't get cocky, Danny. I've got my eye on you. There's no place for loners or show-boaters—they're unpredictable, and that's not how we work. We've got a chain of command and a structure, and we do things the right way. Authority's important for us, Danny. You need to understand that."

Uri nodded. "Sure."

"Do you work?" Otto asked, changing the subject.

"I'll find something." Uri put his hands deeper into his pockets. He had no intention of getting a job. The fifty thousand pounds he had hidden at the flat would see him through just fine.

"Good," Otto nodded. "You'll need to be able to pay your way. This isn't a free ride."

"So were you here?" Uri asked Otto, looking around the deserted grey railway station.

Otto looked blank.

"In 2002—the Battle of Maze Hill. It was on this platform, wasn't it?"

Otto allowed himself a half-smile. "So, you know your local history, Danny. Yes. I was here. So was the Skipper. Hell of a day. You would've loved it."

From what Uri had seen of the press reports when researching the extremist scene in Maze Hill, he doubted very much he would have enjoyed it at all. It had been a pre-arranged pitched battle between football firms running amok on the platform with sharp and blunt weapons, while bloodied members of the public ran screaming for their lives. It was free-for-all random chaotic brutality—a far cry from the clinical operations Uri got satisfaction from.

But then he knew he was not a team player.

"We did time for that, me and the Skipper," Uri confided. "A couple of years each—in Belmarsh, as it happens. That's where we met some of the lads from the London National Socialist crew. So when we got out, we built up the Maze Hill *Staffel*. And we haven't looked back." He paused and glanced at his watch. "Alright then," he got up to go, "see you tomorrow night, Danny."

Uri nodded. He sat and watched as Otto wandered down the platform and out of the station.

*So far so good.*

———— · ◆ · ————

# 61

*6–9 Carlton House Terrace*
*Piccadilly*
*London SW1Y*
*England*
*The United Kingdom*

IT WAS A short walk from Ava's house to St James's, then down past England's senior royal palace onto the grandeur of Pall Mall.

It was still early in the morning, and Ava could see in through the wide windows of a succession of exclusive gentlemen's clubs, where immaculately dressed waiters tended members with ironed newspapers and tureens of bacon, eggs, black pudding, kedgeree, and a host of other staples that make up the traditional English breakfast.

Turning right under the large gilded statue of Athena guarding Waterloo Place, she steered Ferguson past a manicured lawn enclosed by elegant iron railings, and into the white mansions of Carlton House Terrace.

"This is it," she said, stopping outside a grand porticoed building. "The Royal Society."

She could see Ferguson looking at the crest by the doorway. It was a plain silver shield with the three lions of England in the upper left quarter. Under it were the Latin words: 'NULLIUS IN VERBA'.

Heading up the main front steps, she presented herself to the liveried doorman, and announced she was there to see Saxby. With Ferguson in tow, the doorman showed her into the grand and ornate nineteenth-century building, and up to the first floor, where he knocked on an imposing set of gilded white double doors.

They opened to reveal Saxby, wearing a grey flannel suit and holding a small bone china saucer and cup of coffee.

"Ah! Dr Curzon," he smiled. "Thank you for coming at such short notice."

"Of course," Ava answered warmly, taking his outstretched hand and shaking it.

Ferguson sat down on an elaborately upholstered sofa nestling in an alcove to the left of the doors. "Don't worry about me," he said breezily. "I'll wait here." He picked up a leaflet from the marble rococo coffee table and began reading.

"Nonsense, Major Ferguson," answered Saxby, without a hint of theatricality at showing he knew who Ferguson was. "You're a valuable part of the team."

Ava was momentarily poleaxed.

*How on earth did he know Ferguson's name?*

She quickly recovered herself. After all, how did he know about her? Or Kimbaba? Or anything else?

One of the things about Saxby, she was beginning to realize, was that he seemed to know a great deal.

"Come in," he beckoned them. "Please. In fact, there's someone I'd like you to meet."

Saxby ushered her into the large square room. It was traditionally furnished in the period style of the grand building—with delicately painted gold and sky-blue roundels of plasterwork on the crisp white walls and ceiling. There was a set of leather sofas and armchairs around a large fireplace housing a rack of ornamental fire irons in its grate. A pair of black-figure classical vases stood on tall polished dark wood tables flanking the fireplace, and over the chimney breast there was a large oil painting of a seventeenth-century nobleman.

"My Lord—Dr Curzon," Saxby announced her to a tall man with an aquiline nose and dark goatee sitting in a high wing-backed armchair by the fireplace.

"Dr Curzon, the honour is mine," the man answered, rising to shake her hand. He spoke with a heavy French accent. "Allow me to introduce myself—Olivier De Molay."

Ava looked at him closely.

He was immaculately tailored. Everything was handmade, down to his shoes. The style was classic, as was his beard and hair. He could as easily have walked out of a photograph from the 1920s or 1970s as the 2010s. His dark eyes were quick and lively, and his easy movements suggested he was in better health than many men half his age.

Saxby interrupted her thoughts. "Dr Curzon, it is Lord De Molay's Foundation that is currently employing your services."

*So this was her patron.*

She looked at him again, assessing whether he appeared the kind of man who would collect artefacts like the Ark or the jasper amulet Saxby had given her.

He brushed Saxby's comment aside with a wave of his hand. "That sounds too grand, Edmund. I'm a mere steward. I look after the Foundation, until it's someone else's turn."

Despite his self-effacing words, or perhaps because of them, it was clear to Ava that behind the charm De Molay was a man used to exercising real power.

He was, in fact, exactly the sort of person she could imagine being a passionate collector of rare artefacts.

"I wanted to thank you personally for the wonderful Alexander-Abraxas amulet you so kindly donated to the museum," she smiled. "It will be one of our prize exhibits."

"I am delighted it's found such a good home," he nodded. "There are some things the public are meant to see."

*And some they're not?* Ava wondered.

"In any event, we're extremely grateful you wish to continue assisting us," he continued. "Do you have everything you require?"

Ava felt decidedly unprepared to answer the question. One of the things she had hoped to learn from this meeting with Saxby was exactly what *was* expected of her now.

"Things aren't completely clear at present," she admitted honestly, thinking of Drewitt and the medal. "But we have some leads."

His nodded slowly. "Excellent." He put down his coffee-cup on a low side-table and straightened his cufflinks as he stood tall again.

"I'm afraid I have another engagement I must attend," he concluded in a genial tone that clearly indicated the meeting was over. "Nevertheless, I'm sure Edmund has explained to you," he nodded towards Saxby, "that we have very considerable resources at our disposal. If you need any assistance—whether you are here or far from home, we have people who can come to your aid." He smiled at her. "But I'm sure you know that already."

It was news to Ava. But before she could reply, he had given a crisp nod of the head, and sailed passed her.

"If you need anything at all, Edmund is always there to help you." He turned at the door. "It has been a pleasure meeting you, Dr Curzon, and I look forward to doing so again soon."

With that, he nodded a farewell to Saxby, and was gone.

Saxby closed the doors behind him, and invited Ava and Ferguson to sit.

"So," he addressed Ava when they had each taken a leather armchair around the fireplace. "This is a little awkward, as we're in uncharted territory for the Foundation. As I mentioned previously, Lord De Molay is a man of peace, and recent events are not at all the type of scene in which we have any experience."

"But?" Ava asked, sensing there was more.

"You see," he continued, "the dilemma is that we are not talking about a Gutenberg Bible or a golden *aureus* minted by Julius Caesar. Both of those are very desirable for any serious collector, but there are a number of examples of each that could be pursued." He paused. "However, there's only one Ark, and it's quite unique. Therefore we have concluded, after much thought, that the Foundation cannot hope to stay in the game unless it has someone of your skills representing its interests."

"I'm glad that's settled," Ava replied, concealing her relief. "So do you know who took the Ark from Dubai, and who has it now?"

Saxby nodded. "Our sources tell us it was a man who goes by the name of Marius Malchus."

Ava took a slightly deeper breath as she felt her heart beat faster.

*So it was Malchus.*

"I see you know of him?" Saxby was watching her closely.

"I'm learning more about him all the time," Ava answered honestly.

"As are we," Saxby was sombre. "It seems he's a fanatic, an extremist—prone to grand visions and violence."

"Is he working alone?" she asked, eager for even the smallest scraps of information.

"We believe so." Saxby replied. "He does not seem to be in partnership with anyone beyond his organization. It looks like he was behind the original theft from Aksum, and now he has retaken the Ark after the thieves failed to deliver it to him."

Ava paused, gazing up at the oil painting over the fireplace.

*How did Saxby know all this? Was he in touch with Hunter? Or Prince? Or was he hearing it from somewhere else?*

"Before we go any further," she asked. "Can I ask where you get your information?"

Saxby eased himself forward in his chair a little. "I don't think it will come as a surprise to you to learn the Foundation is extremely well connected."

"So I understand." Ava could see Saxby did not want to go into details. "What did De Molay mean, saying you had people everywhere?" she pressed him.

"Exactly that, really," he smiled. "The Foundation is not without friends. We usually find there are people in most countries who can accommodate whatever requests we may have."

"I'm not sure I understand," Ava was still in the dark. "You mean, you have people who owe favours you can call in? Services for services?"

"No, no." Saxby looked appalled. "We are not the Mafia, Dr Curzon. Our work is directed towards making the world a better place. We are, if anything, a philanthropic organization."

"How can I be sure of that?" Ava was feeling a mounting concern that the more she found out about the Foundation, the less she seemed actually to know about it.

Saxby's expression was thoughtful. "Would you allow me a few days in which to address this for you?" He paused. "Meanwhile, let me reassure you—there's nothing you will find objectionable in the aims or activities of the Foundation."

Ava thought it over for a moment, then nodded. It was not unusual for trusts and wealthy foundations to be secretive. They rarely sought attention and publicity when carrying out their private aims and objectives. She had waited several days already. A few more would not hurt.

"So what do you want from me now?" Ava asked. "The Ark is in private hands and no longer for sale."

"We've been giving this much thought," Saxby replied. "For now, I'm afraid, we have no conclusion. We would therefore appreciate it if you could use your ... ," he paused delicately, "wider skills, in order to find out whatever you can about Malchus, and what he plans to do with the Ark."

This was exactly what Ava had been hoping to hear.

She nodded her assent. "But my involvement is based on two conditions. First. I'm doing this because I believe Malchus is the wrong sort of person to be holding the Ark."

"We couldn't agree with you more." Saxby looked sombre.

"And second," she continued, "if I recover the Ark for the Foundation, you will enter into an open dialogue with me on scientific access to it."

Saxby looked pensive. "I give you my word." He paused. "Now, you mentioned to Lord De Molay that you have some leads?"

"Actually," Ava replied, "on that topic, there's something I wanted to ask you." She glanced across at Ferguson, who was looking around the room, taking in all the details. "Do you know anything about the Third Crusade?"

Saxby leaned back in his chair. "How interesting you should ask. The answer is yes. I do. The Foundation has a considerable interest in the topic."

"This is a bit of a long shot," Ava began, "but have you heard of any surviving copies of the papal bull that launched the Third Crusade?"

"*Audita tremendi?*" he prompted.

A frown passed over Ferguson's face.

Noticing it, Saxby turned to him. "All papal bulls are known by their opening words, Major Ferguson. For example, the bull *De sepulturis* of 1299 prohibited crusaders from boiling dead bodies in order to be able to take the bones home for burial in Europe. The bull *Dudum siquidem* of 1493 by the Spanish Borgia pope Alexander VI gave the Americas to Spain. And Pope Gregory XIII's *Inter gravissimas* of 1582 dropped ten days from October that year to correct the drift of one day every hundred and twenty-eight years, thereby establishing the modern calendar we all use today. And so on."

Ferguson nodded.

"The bull that launched the Third Crusade was called *Audita tremendi*." He paused. "Surviving copies? Off the top of my head?" He was thinking aloud. "No. I don't think so. You see, Pope Gregory VIII wasn't pope for long. But I'll look into it for you. We have excellent records of such things—"

"No. Not Pope Gregory VIII," Ava interrupted, correcting him. "Clement III. He was pope when the Third Crusade started."

"Ah! A common mistake," Saxby shook his head. "The crusade was actually called by his predecessor, Gregory VIII—the fifty-seven-day pope."

Ava was not sure she had heard right. "Clement was pope at the time of the Third Crusade. Didn't he issue the bull that launched it?"

Saxby shook his head. "I'm afraid not. It was all rather dramatic. Gregory became pope in October 1187, and issued the bull four days after donning the Triple Crown. The crusade was a subject very dear to his heart. But he was dead by mid-December that year. So Clement took over the task of preparing the crusade, but the bull was already in circulation."

Ava's heart sank.

*Her theory was wrong—there was no 'bloody bull' from Clement.*

She felt a crashing wave of disappointment.

So what did the medal mean?

She was back at square one.

Maybe Ferguson was right? Perhaps it was linked to the Inquisition or the body and blood of the mass?

She turned to Saxby, deciding that she had little to lose by sharing her discovery with him. It was a long shot, but worth trying. "Do you know anything about a medieval Vatican medal with a picture of the Menorah on it?" she ventured. "Probably from the 1100s, but I could be out by a century either way."

To her surprise, Saxby's eyes lit up. "My God. You've seen it?"

She could feel her pulse quickening.

"Someone brought it to my attention," she admitted, trying to keep her excitement concealed. It was clear from Saxby's reaction that the medal was something special. "What can you tell me about it?"

He sat back in his chair, his tone earnest. "You've heard of the Knights Templar?"

"Of course," she answered. "The pope's crack troops of the crusades, later abolished in a blaze of scandal, and now the subject of many theories of hidden treasure and secret knowledge."

"Exactly." Saxby nodded. "Legends abound. But there's one specific story about the Knights Templar and the Menorah. It's alleged the knights undertook excavations deep into the Temple Mount, down to the ancient Temple of Solomon itself. Supposedly one of the objects they recovered was the great Temple Menorah—thought for centuries to have been lost. The legend says they shipped it back to Rome, and presented it to the pope."

Saxby paused. "But the pope was afraid of it, and increasingly feared revenge from God for having taken a sacred Hebrew object. Unable to look upon it, he hid it away where it would not be found. But, at the request of the Templars, he cast three identical medals with clues where to find it, in case one of his successors took a different view. One medal was given for safekeeping to each of the Orders of crusading knights—the Knights Templar, the Knights Hospitaller, and the Teutonic Knights."

Ava was listening breathlessly. "And?" she asked.

"That's it. No one knows if it's a true story or a fairy-tale."

"What do these medals look like?" Ava asked, quietly.

"Interestingly," Saxby continued, "although the pope did not want the Menorah on his conscience, he knew it was now an official possession of the Vatican. So he cast the clues onto lead medals, forged in his chancery, each carrying the official papal stamp of Peter and Paul. And, perhaps most unusually, in honour of their importance, he ordered them to be twice the size of his ordinary bulls."

Ava gripped the sides of her chair tightly. "In which century was this supposed to have happened?"

"Oh. Very definitely twelfth century. When the Templars still occupied the Temple. You see, they lost Jerusalem in 1187 to Saladin. So the medals are indisputably from the late 1100s."

Ava could feel the blood pounding through her ears. "Has there ever been any rumour of any of these medals surfacing?"

Saxby shook his head. "As with all things to do with the Templars, history and myth weave seamlessly together. Who knows whether it's truth or fiction?" He paused and smiled. "In fact, when it comes to the Templars, the truth often turns out to be far stranger than fiction."

As Ava looked around the room, it felt like time was slowing.

So now she knew what Malchus was after.

*The Menorah.*

It made complete sense. If Drewitt had been right and Malchus was trying to recreate the Temple of Solomon, then it was logical he would need the Menorah as much as the Ark.

And somehow he had found one of the medieval Vatican's medals.

*No wonder he killed Drewitt to protect it.*

As Ava let the new information sink in, she felt a chill pass through her.

If Malchus was collecting the sacred objects from the Temple of Solomon—the home of the Hebrew God—then the quotation from the Book of the Apocalypse took on a whole new meaning.

It was not yet clear what he was doing, and how it tied in with his neo-Nazi cult, but she suddenly had an icy feeling that Malchus's plan may indeed involve something biblical and apocalyptic.

———— ♦ ————

# 62

*Green Park*
*London SW1*
*England*
*The United Kingdom*

AVA AND FERGUSON emerged from the Royal Society in silence.

They headed down Pall Mall, and through the small side streets into the wide expanse of Green Park.

Ava chose an unoccupied wooden bench out of earshot of the other park-goers, and sat down, staring at a group of pigeons pecking avidly at a spray of seeds left on the ground by a well-wisher.

"So, what did you make of all that?" she asked Ferguson after a few moments. "What on earth is this bizarre Foundation?"

Ferguson looked at her, his eyes gleaming. "Did you see the portrait on the wall over the fireplace?"

Ava shook her head. "I didn't really take it in. Sir Robert something?"

"Moray," Ferguson nodded. "Sir Robert Moray."

The name meant nothing to Ava.

"*The* Sir Robert Moray?" Ferguson hinted.

Ava was still none the wiser. She had no idea who he was talking about.

"What did he do?" she asked.

"What didn't he do is more the question." Ferguson answered, sitting down next to her. "He's legendary."

"Well go on then," she encouraged. "I've a feeling this is going to be your moment of glory."

"The first of many," he beamed. "Moray is a famous Scot. He fought in the French army, in the elite *Garde Ecossaise* under King Louis xiii, and then in the Scots army that captured Newcastle in 1640. He was cosmopolitan and educated—a soldier, diplomat, and literary man. But his main claim to fame was as a spy for the great Cardinal Richelieu of France, then for King Charles i and King Charles ii of England."

"What was so special about him that everyone wanted him as their spy?" Ava asked, her curiosity piqued.

"That's just it," Ferguson replied. "Here's the juicy bit. He was the first man ever to be made a freemason in England."

"And how on earth do you know all this," Ava stared at him in amazement.

"You can't tell there's some Scots blood in me? The name Ferguson doesn't give you a clue?"

"Yes," Ava answered, "but—"

"When I say he's legendary, I mean that he's a legend in my grandfather's village of Craigie, in Perthshire. My grandfather used to go on and on about him. True, he was the only famous person ever to come from there, and it was a long time ago. But my grandfather used to talk about him so much that we figured my grandfather was a closet Jacobite or freemason or something."

"I had no idea freemasonry was so old," Ava frowned.

Ferguson nodded. "Apparently records of Scottish freemasonry are the oldest in the world, going back to the late 1500s. By Moray's time, most of the leading Scots revolutionaries were freemasons."

This was all news to Ava. "I thought freemasonry was a modern Protestant organization?"

Ferguson shook his head. "Not according to my grandfather. He was adamant it was a network for aristocratic Scots rebels—many of them Catholics. And it became even more so in the 1700s, when the Scottish rebellions loyal to the Stuarts tried to topple the new Protestant German kings of England. Much of the revolution was planned in secret by Catholic Scots freemasons apparently. It only became Protestant later, when the new Hanoverian kings of England took it over and purged it."

Ava looked at the top end of the park, watching the occasional red bus cruising down Piccadilly—stopping to let bag-laden shoppers and sightseers on and off. "So what's a painting of him doing in the Royal Society?"

Ferguson pulled a piece of paper out of his pocket. "I borrowed this leaflet from the table outside the room we were in." He looked pleased with himself. "It says the Royal Society is the oldest scientific academy in continuous existence. It's a fellowship of the world's most eminent scientists, elected for life based on their outstanding scientific achievement—people like Newton, Darwin, and Einstein." He paused. "I don't know about you, but I didn't get the impression either Saxby or De Molay know one end of a test tube from the other."

"Is that what you think we're dealing with?" Ava asked. "Freemasons? Is that what you reckon the Foundation is?"

"Give me a minute," Ferguson answered, pulling out his phone and tapping something on the screen.

He peered at it for a moment, then scrolled down a page. "Here we are," he replied. "It says the Royal Society was founded in 1660 by a group called the Invisible College, which included many prominent freemasons. And, surprise, guess who was the first chairman of the Royal Society, and got the society its royal status from his friend King Charles II?"

Ava could see where this was going. "Sir Robert Moray?"

"Exactly." Ferguson looked at her with satisfaction.

She watched as a crowd of tourists headed down towards Buckingham Palace, which stood a few hundred metres to her south. Fitting, she thought, that they should be discussing these ancient royal intrigues within sight of the palace.

"I'm just wondering," he continued, "what Saxby and De Molay were doing in there? What kind of a Foundation gets VIP treatment at the Royal Society in this day and age, and is allowed to hold private meetings in one of the main reception rooms under a portrait of Sir Robert Moray? I'd say they would have to be heavily connected."

"I don't know," he continued, answering his own question. "But I'm not convinced they represent some private trust fund or millionaire's institute. Their Foundation sounds old and historical from the way De Molay said he was just the current steward, and from Saxby's admission that it had a special interest in the crusades and possessed relevant records."

Ava lapsed into thought.

"By the way," Ferguson turned to her. "What did the Royal Society's motto mean? The one on the crest outside the door—'NULLIUS IN VERBA'?"

"Oddly enough," Ava answered, "it's really quite fitting if we're dealing with freemasons. It means 'Take nobody's word for it'."

———————— • ◆ • ————————

# 63

*Piccadilly*
*London SW1*
*England*
*The United Kingdom*

AVA'S HEAD WAS reeling as she headed north from the calm of Green Park onto the busy hum of Piccadilly.

Although she had at first been delighted when Saxby had confirmed she was still engaged on the case, her mood had changed when he had told her that Pope Clement III had never issued a crusading bull.

She felt bruised by having been so mistaken.

She had thought all the pieces fitted together so well—Pope Clement, Richard the Lionheart, King Philip Augustus of France. It had seemed such a neat solution.

All of that was now in the dustbin.

She was back at square one.

She retraced the deductive steps she had gone through, trying to isolate where she had gone wrong. But whichever way she viewed it, she was forced to the conclusion she had simply not done her homework. If she had looked it up, she would have known that Pope Clement III did not issue a crusading bull.

She had been too quick to draw conclusions.

On the plus side, though, the meeting with Saxby had brought a number of important breakthroughs.

If Saxby was right about the Templars and the Menorah, she now knew what the Vatican medal was for and, perhaps more importantly, what Malchus was now up to.

He was after the Menorah.

And if Ferguson was right, then the identity of the shadowy Foundation might be coming into clearer focus as well.

She looked up the bustling thoroughfare. The many restaurants and sandwich bars had started putting out their chairs and tables, which were beginning to fill with the lunchtime crowd of office and shop workers, as well as the permanent groups of multilingual shoppers and tourists.

Ferguson pointed towards a quiet-looking restaurant a few doors up one of the side streets. Ava nodded, still lost in thought.

It was relatively early, and they were the first lunch customers to enter the low-lit restaurant. A waiter appeared from the back and ushered them to a table by the window—no doubt hoping to entice other diners by putting a young couple on display.

Ava shook her head. Old habits died hard. She nodded to a small round table in the far corner, well away from prying eyes out on the street.

She sat down in the heavily stuffed chair and pulled the photographs of the medal out of her pocket, dropping them onto the crisply laundered white tablecloth between her and Ferguson.

"So, I was wrong about the medal," she said, failing to keep the disappointment from her voice.

Ferguson peered closely at the main image. "We need to keep thinking." He pointed to the large ring of writing around the edge:

✠ EL ✠ SAIN ✠ MUSTIER ✠ DE ✠ ROME ✠

"You mentioned that the crosses between the words 'The HOLY CHURCH OF ROME' are traditional decoration," he said. "You don't think they mean anything?"

She shook her head. "You often find them on religious inscriptions from the period. They usually don't have any special significance."

"I bet Malchus likes them," Ferguson observed. "They look like Nazi Iron Crosses. Right up his street."

Ava gazed down at them. "The shape is called a cross patty. You see them a lot on medieval objects—even in the Crown Jewels of England as the centrepiece of the great imperial state crown."

As her mind started to swing into gear, she looked at the photo with a new focus. "Actually," she conceded, an idea forming, "there could be a connection here."

Ferguson raised an eyebrow.

"It's also the cross the Templars used as their emblem," she said, "which could be linked to the fact the Templars found the Menorah."

A look of surprise crossed Ferguson's face. "I hadn't realized the German military used the Templar cross."

"Absolutely," Ava nodded. "The Germans started using it for their medals and military in the 1800s, I think."

"They still do," Ferguson added. "It's quite a shock when you first see it on a modern German tank rolling alongside you."

"But," Ava continued, "the interesting thing is that the Germans chose it because it was the emblem of the great medieval German knights of the crusades—the Teutonic Knights. Saxby specifically mentioned them when he said a copy of the Vatican medal was given to each of the Knights Templar, the Knights Hospitaller, and the Teutonic Knights."

"So the cross patty was the emblem of both the Templars and the Teutonic Knights?" Ferguson was frowning. "Wasn't that confusing?"

Ava nodded. "The medieval Germans were so impressed with the Templars that they created their own special version of them—the Teutonic Knights. They even adopted the Templars' cross patty, although they flipped it from red to black."

"So we've got a medal covered in crosses that could either be decorative, or related to the Knights Templar or Teutonic Knights." Ferguson drummed his fingers on the table in thought.

Ava could feel her spirits lifting. It felt good to be thinking it all through—opening up other avenues and possibilities.

"I had no idea the cross patty was so widely used," Ferguson mused. "Apart from the German military, I've only ever seen them used as consecration crosses."

Ava looked up with surprise. "Consecration crosses?"

"Yes—you know," he stopped drumming, "on the walls of traditional churches."

"That's what I thought you said." Ava paused. "Don't take this the wrong way," she framed the question carefully, "but how do you know about consecration crosses?"

"Twelve crosses on the walls of churches showing where the building was blessed with holy oil," he replied in a matter-of-fact tone, implying everyone knew such an obvious thing. "Come on, Dr Curzon, keep up— you of all people should know that." He looked at her with an expression of feigned disappointment.

"Either you were once a very geeky altar boy," she replied slowly, "or there's something major you're not telling me."

"Definitely never an altar boy," he confirmed.

Ava could see it was not something he wanted to talk about, and felt her curiosity rising even further. "Go on," she pressed. "You've got me interested now."

"It's not a very interesting story." He fiddled with a bread roll the waiter had placed beside him.

"Seriously," Ava replied, "If we're going to be spending time together, then I need to know all your secrets." She tried to keep her tone light, but failed to entirely mask her genuine curiosity.

Ferguson's expression folded into one of resignation. "Okay," he replied slowly, rubbing his hand over his face. "I did some studying a long time ago—to be an architect."

Ava's eyes widened.

"Is that so hard to believe?" he looked bemused. "When I was younger, I was fascinated by buildings. I used to spend hours trying to work out how they had been put together—the engineering, the physics, the behind-the-scenes bits that people weren't meant to see. Like most fans of buildings, I became intrigued by the amazing designs of old churches and cathedrals, where I often saw consecration crosses bolted, carved, or painted onto walls. At first I didn't know what they were, so I looked them up. There you are. It's no great mystery. That's how I know about consecration crosses."

"What happened?" Ava asked. "Why aren't you hovering over a plan table with a set-square and compasses as we speak? When did you decide guns were more fun?"

He pulled the bread roll apart, and began buttering it mechanically. "During my third year of study, my parents and elder sister were killed in a car crash … ."

"Oh God, I'm sorry," Ava instinctively put her hand onto his. He looked up at her, surprised.

Embarrassed, she pulled it away.

"It was a long time ago," he replied, recovering quickly. "I gave up studying and looked after my younger brother for a few years. When I eventually needed money for the pair of us, I had no real qualifications, so joined the army. As I said," he concluded, "it's not a particularly interesting story."

Ava recognized his difficulty in talking about it. She found herself equally tongue-tied in talking to strangers about her father's death.

"Anyway," he changed the subject. "What looks good on the menu?" He ran his eyes down the stiff cream card—it was covered in French cursive writing, designed to look like a sign in a Parisian vegetable market.

"Who eats this stuff for pleasure?" His voice was filled with incredulity. "Steak *tartare*? That's raw bloody beef, isn't it?"

As she heard his words, Ava felt a bolt of electricity shoot through her.

The colour rose in her cheeks.

"What did you just say?" she whispered hoarsely.

Ferguson looked lost. "I asked who would actually choose to eat raw beef? I mean, if it's a question of survival, I've definitely eaten worse, but to pay good folding money—"

Ava shook her head, interrupting him. "You asked if it was *bloody* beef."

Ferguson continued to look blankly at her.

Flushed with excitement, Ava pushed back her chair, and stood up. "We've got somewhere we need to be," she announced hurriedly.

Before Ferguson had time to stand up, Ava was at the door, leaving him to apologize to the waiter, and follow her out onto the street.

<blockquote>

---- ◆ ----

# 64

*Soho*
*London W1*
*England*
*The United Kingdom*

ONCE OUTSIDE THE restaurant, Ava made a quick call on her mobile phone to make sure Cyrus Azad was at his office.

He was, and readily agreed to look into what Ava hurriedly asked.

She was ninety-nine per cent sure she was right, but of everyone she knew, Cyrus would be able to confirm it the quickest.

And time was of the essence.

Her main fear was if she really had now cracked the puzzle on the medal, then it was possible Malchus might already have solved it, too—or he soon would.

If Cyrus confirmed her conclusion, they would have to act fast. She was keenly aware there was a clock ticking in the race with Malchus, and there would be no prizes for second place.

Hailing a black cab, she jumped in, giving the cabbie an address in Soho. Ferguson piled in after her, pulling the door closed on the already moving car.

As the taxi drew away into the traffic, she had no time to look about.

Usually as she passed through Piccadilly Circus she found herself dis-

<blockquote>

370

tracted by the immense neon and LED advertisements on the north-west corner, or by the iconic statue of the winged archer, Anteros, the world's first cast aluminium statue—misidentified by most Londoners and tourists as Eros, the Greek god of love, beauty, and sex.

But not today. Her head was spinning with thoughts about the medal—and the implications of her discovery.

"So where are we going?" Ferguson asked.

"Somewhere you're going to love, if you're still interested in buildings," she answered enigmatically.

Cyrus had been a former colleague from the British Museum—but his interests, as well as his heritage, had led him to leave the rarified world of the museum and start up his own consulting business. As far as Ava knew, the centre he now ran was unique in the world.

After a short journey beyond Piccadilly into the rabbit warren of small streets that made up Soho, the cab pulled up outside the address she had given the driver.

When Ava had first visited Cyrus's offices a few years earlier, she had expected to find him in a tatty basement under one of the hundreds of gaudy sex shops, adult cinemas, and prostitutes' walk-ups that filled Soho. But she had been surprised to discover that the area had been completely made over, and was instead jammed with trendy restaurants and new media offices—a world away from the infamous garish red light area it used to be.

She paid the cabbie, and pushed open a door next to a chalk white anodized plaque engraved with the words:

INSTITUTE FOR MITHRAIC STUDIES AND RESEARCH

As she entered the small but fashionably furnished reception area, Cyrus emerged from an open door to the back office.

He had not changed a bit. Still the same scruffy beard, tangled black hair, and Buddy Holly glasses, although the ill-fitting tie and overly pointed leather shoes were a clear concession to his new status as a businessman rather than the eternal researcher she had known.

"Ava, great to see you!" he smiled broadly as she stepped past the sofas towards him.

She gave him a hug, before introducing Ferguson. "So was I right?" she asked, keen to hear the answer to her question as soon as possible.

"Always business before pleasure," Cyrus replied, shaking his head. "Follow me," he instructed, leading them through a doorway and down a flight of stairs into a small darkened theatre-room filled with three short rows of velvet cinema chairs.

"We use this for our educational screenings," he explained. "Mainly to academics, but occasionally corporates—especially ones involved in digging, building, or drilling on Mithraic sites."

"And that," he continued, "is how we got this." He walked over to the far end, which featured a large rectangular plate of glass mounted about a foot in front of the wall. As he touched it, around five square yards lit up to show a range of computer icons.

Cyrus swiped both hands across the glass, dragging the icons off the screen, to be replaced with a picture of his institute's logo.

"Is that what I think it is?" Ferguson asked, stepping over to the screen and peering at it, a note of admiration in his voice.

"It sure is," grinned Cyrus, clearly delighted with the opportunity to show off his toy. "Multitouch screen—courtesy of an aerospace-defence company that shall remain nameless. We helped them build their office basement car-park in the Middle East around a mithraeum they discovered while sinking the foundations. The temple is now preserved and visitable, and they still got to develop their offices. Everyone's happy."

"A mithraeum?" Ferguson asked, gently touching the screen.

Ava nodded to Cyrus. "Go on, you tell him. You'll do a much better job than me. It's why we're here, anyway."

Cyrus wiped his hands across the screen again, dragging a small icon into the centre, which he then expanded into a full size picture of a classical statue of a man. He was young, fully clothed in a short belted tunic, and looking at the viewer with a hint of challenge in his eyes. His head was covered with a strange long cap, and he had a short cape billowing out behind him. In his right hand he held a vicious-looking dagger, which he was plunging into the meaty neck of a fallen bull which had vegetation sprouting from its tail.

"This ancient god," explained Cyrus, "is Mithras. He was the central figure in what was once ancient Rome's leading religion. There were over seven hundred temples to him in Rome alone. The imperial soldiers carried his mystery religion all over the empire, so there are archaeological remains of Mithraic temples spread far and wide over Europe and the Middle East. There's a very famous one right here in London. Specialists usually refer to a temple of Mithras as a mithraeum."

"What do you mean 'mystery religion'?" Ferguson asked. "What's that?"

"There were dozens of them in the ancient world," Cyrus answered without hesitating. "They were basically religions with temples like all the others, but there were some major differences, too. Most importantly, they claimed to reveal special secrets and powers, but only to people initiated into their mysteries. That's where we get the word 'mystery'—from the Greek *mystes*, meaning initiates."

"In one way or another, these mystery religions all focused on death and rebirth, invariably symbolized by the yearly cycle of the sun, or plants, or animal fertility—anything that dies and is reborn once a year, giving an annual pattern that can be celebrated."

Cyrus swiped at the screen, pulling up classical images of five ancient gods and goddesses.

"Don't tell me—Bacchus and Osiris," Ferguson said, nodding towards a heavy bearded face emerging from a vat of grapes, and a man carrying a candy striped sceptre and flail, and wearing the high crown of Upper Egypt with a single red ostrich feather either side of it.

"Correct," Cyrus nodded. "And Orpheus with his lyre, Cybele with her lion-chariot, and Demeter with her fruits and grains. All of these gods and goddesses were widely worshipped in secretive mystery religions. They all died and were reborn again every year, symbolizing the death of nature in winter and the return of life in spring."

The image on the screen changed to a Greek temple. "The site of the greatest mystery cult was at Eleusis, where the mysteries of Demeter and Persephone were celebrated. They involved a dramatic underground journey and culminated in a climactic ritual, possibly involving psychoactive drugs, in which the initiate was symbolically killed and brought back to life. Many famous people were initiated there. But like most mystery religions, almost no details survive, so we have only the scantest idea of what went on."

Cyrus pulled up another picture—this time of a Roman mosaic laid out like a ladder. It showed seven individual emblems, all enclosed in roundels. "Mystery religions usually had a system of grades. Mithraism had seven—Raven, Bridegroom, Soldier, Lion, Persian, Sun-Runner, and Father. This mosaic is taken from the floor of an actual mithraeum, and clearly shows the sequence of the grades. As initiates progressed in their commitment to the religion, they were welcomed into ever deeper secrets. They even had some kind of recognition handshake, and called each other *syndexoi*—meaning those joined by the right hand."

"Like freemasons?" asked Ferguson.

"Who knows?" answered Cyrus with a shrug. "The mysteries and freemasonry are both similarly shrouded in secrecy. So we can't really tell. But yes, many experts believe freemasonry is somehow connected to the mysteries as there are some ritualistic similarities."

"Freemasons seem to be cropping up everywhere these days," Ferguson mused, rubbing his chin.

"Anyway," Cyrus continued. "Initiation into successive grades of a mystery religion was a common system in the ancient world. In fact, there's one classic mystery religion still surviving today—a true Roman mystery religion, completely frozen in time in all its strange details, but alive and well in the modern world. If you want to get a feel for Roman mystery religions, you couldn't do better than to start there."

Ferguson looked blank. "Don't they have laws against those sorts of cults these days?"

Ava shook her head. "Far from it. Cyrus is talking about the largest religion on the planet."

"Exactly," Cyrus nodded. "Christianity. Although to get the full undiluted mystery religion you have to look at the traditional Roman Catholic Church, which has barely changed in the seventeen centuries since the emperors of Rome bowed before its incense-perfumed altars."

"Seriously?" Ferguson stared at Cyrus.

"Unquestionably," he answered with a smile. "I'm sure Ava will tell you all about it. The Catholic Church still talks about initiation into the mysteries of salvation and the sacraments. And even today its believers are specifically initiated into a series of grades—Catechumens, Baptized, and Confirmed for the lay people, then the ordained grades of Deacon, Priest, and Bishop. Each of these grades brings new powers, insights, and privileges."

Ava nodded. "Christianity is, though many people find it hard to accept, a text-book classical pagan mystery religion," she confirmed. "As you'll see if you flick through the Bible, there's no mention of any of these grades. The early Church simply created them in order to position itself as a mystery religion. The Graeco-Roman Empire already had mystery religions with Greek themes, Egyptian themes, and a load of different Middle-Eastern themes. Christianity was its attempt to make one with a

Judaic flavour. They could never have known at the time, but by bolting elements of existing mystery religions onto the Jewish texts, they created one of the most successful religions of all time. And the mystery religion that gave most elements to Christianity was Mithraism."

"But I've heard of Bacchus and Osiris and some of those other gods you mentioned," Ferguson noted. "How come I've never heard of Mithras?"

"Simple," Cyrus answered. "The same reason most people haven't heard of him."

"The Church erased him from history," Ava completed the thought.

"Why would they do that?" Ferguson asked. "It's a bit conspiratorial, isn't it?"

"Not at all," replied Cyrus, dragging another image onto the screen. This time it was a series of smaller pictures. One showed a man holding a sheep on his shoulders. Another had the face of a man with a sunburst behind his head. The next one depicted a man in a chariot, racing across the heavens. The final one was of a man wrapped in grape vines.

"Maybe this will help," Cyrus explained. "The first is a picture of Attis, the immensely popular shepherd god worshipped all over Asia Minor, the Middle East, and in Rome. It's from over a thousand years before Christ. He lived, castrated himself, died, and was then resurrected—a cycle of death and rebirth that was reenacted every year by his eunuch priests. Like the other mysteries, it's essentially a cycle of nature and fertility. As a matter of interest, did you know that in the Gospel of Matthew, Christ recommends men castrate themselves for the kingdom of heaven? At least that's what Origen, the early Alexandrian scholar, thought Christ meant, and he did it."

Ferguson looked at Cyrus, bewildered.

"Anyway," Cyrus continued, pointing back at the screen. "The second and third images are of Apollo, the sun god. The last is Bacchus, the wine god. All of them were very popular mystery gods in ancient Rome. Now watch this," he said. As he touched the screen, the pictures morphed into almost identical images—clearly from different buildings, but essentially exactly the same.

"These are all very early images of Christ from old churches, including the Vatican. As you can see, Christ is depicted identically to the pagan gods—as the shepherd, the sun god, and the vine. It's early copy-and-paste."

Ferguson looked stunned. "Are you saying Christianity just *copied* all these old religions?"

"Absolutely," Cyrus answered. "It's human nature. Think of the world of business. If your competitor has an idea the public likes and buys, you ride that train and incorporate similar ideas into your own product. Why wouldn't you? Why reinvent the wheel? Religion is no different."

"I'm not sure I follow," Ferguson looked at Ava. "Aren't religions set in stone, in holy books like the Bible?"

"Where in the Bible does it say Christ was born on the twenty-fifth of December?" Ava asked him with a smile.

Ferguson looked blank.

"Exactly. It doesn't. But the twenty-fifth of December was Mithras's birthday. So the Church borrowed the date to try and encourage converts from Mithraism to feel at home with Christianity. Late December was honoured by many mystery religions as it is falls soon after the winter solstice—the darkest and coldest time of year when the sun is weakest. Hence the days following the solstice were an appropriate date for religions to choose for the birth of their gods, who came to conquer and banish the darkness. Christ was simply slotted into this tried-and-tested matrix."

Ferguson looked shocked. "Seriously? They built religions with templates, like websites?"

"Deadly seriously," Ava answered. "And there's way more. As Cyrus says, there's actually very little original in Christianity. Lots of gods died and came back from the dead. Orpheus went down into the underworld, just like Christ. Mithras even died for three days, like Christ. And why do you think Christ rises from the dead every year at the time of the spring equinox—exactly the moment when winter is over and the sun begins to be dominant again, bathing the earth in warmth and life. It's the oldest religious celebration of all."

"The followers of Mithras even used to share a sacred meal of bread and wine, which the Christians copied," added Cyrus. "In fact, almost all the key elements of Christian belief are modelled on older religions." He pulled up an instantly recognizable sculpture of a woman with a baby on her lap. "Who's this?" he asked.

"Mary and Jesus," Ferguson answered with conviction. "That's obvious."

"Wrong," said Cyrus. "It's from Egypt, long before Christ, and shows Isis with her son, the sun-god Horus."

Ferguson shook his head in bewilderment,

"There are an infinite number of other examples," Cyrus continued. "For instance, where in the Bible does it say that priests should circle the altar at the beginning of the mass?" He paused. "Nowhere—it's an old ritual copied from the sun-worshipping religions, in which the priest acted out the annual circle of the sun. And where in the Bible does it say altars should face east? Nowhere. Again, it is taken from the sun-worshipping cults, which faced the rising sun."

"If I accept all this," Ferguson asked, "how did the Church wipe out all traces of Mithras?"

"Well," Cyrus pulled up a picture of the catacombs under Rome, showing early anti-Christian graffiti. "Basically, for three hundred years, Christianity and Mithraism were locked in a battle to the death, to see which would become the empire's official religion. Ultimately, Christianity won—largely because Mithraism was only open to men. Once Christianity was the official religion of the empire with the support of the emperor, it was untouchable. From that position of strength, it began obliterating all traces of the other mysteries to make sure they could never again be a threat. Like the great fire of Alexandria, for example, in which the local Christian bishop stirred up the crowds to destroy the vast pagan library attached to the Temple of the Muses. As Mithraism was Christianity's chief competitor, it set about destroying Mithraism with particular harshness—and left posterity with very few traces of what had once been a massive international religion."

Ava walked over to Cyrus. "So am I right? About there being a mithraeum in Rome, in the Basilica di San Clemente?"

Cyrus nodded. "Completely. In fact, I didn't even have to look it up. You're the second person to ask me the same question in two days."

Ava's blood ran cold. She looked across at Ferguson, who was staring at her grimly.

"Who was asking?" she said in a low voice.

"I'm not sure," Cyrus answered breezily. "He didn't give a name"

Ava felt a surge of apprehension as her pulse increased.

*Did Malchus already know?*

*Was he ahead of her?*

She shivered involuntarily.

"Was the caller German?" Ferguson asked.

"I was wondering about his accent," Cyrus mused. "I couldn't quite place it. But now you mention it, I think he probably was." He looked at

Ava and Ferguson. "What's the matter? I get enquiries all the time—I've got a great website, you know."

Ava walked over and grabbed Cyrus by the arm. She knew he liked nothing better than to share his expertise and enthusiasm with others. "Cyrus, you have to think hard. What exactly did you tell him?"

"I was busy. I asked him to call back later. He was very insistent. He's going to call again today." He turned to Ava, frowning. "Why? Is there a problem?"

Ava squeezed his arm harder. "You have to listen to me very carefully, Cyrus."

His eyes widened. "What is it, Ava? You're scaring me."

"Cyrus, promise me something," she continued, looking him full in the face. "When we leave here today, close the centre, and take a holiday for a few weeks. The man who called you is very dangerous indeed. People are already dead. Just leave town. Please. For me."

Cyrus turned pale. "What are you mixed up in, Ava?" He looked visibly shaken.

She released his arm. "It's going to be okay. We just need to get to the mithraeum before he does. Can you help us with that?"

"Sure," he replied in a subdued voice. "What do you need?"

"For now, just talk us through it," she answered. "Give us as much detail as you can."

Cyrus nodded. "Okay." He turned to the screen. "You were absolutely right. There's a mithraeum in the Basilica di San Clemente in central Rome." He pulled up another icon, expanding it into a three-dimensional architectural plan of a large church. As he swiped the screen, the picture rotated in three dimensions.

Ferguson's eyes never left the screen. "That's a seriously neat trick."

Cyrus smiled. "It was recently modelled by a Roman university archaeology project. I've got access to lots of this kind of stuff. Three-dimensional architectural reconstructions are all the rage these days."

Ferguson continued peering at the screen.

"This is the Basilica di San Clemente," Cyrus announced. "Built in the twelfth century, containing the tomb and relics of Saint Clement of Rome and Saint Ignatius of Antioch." He swiped the space on the screen underneath the image, and another layer of building appeared beneath it. "And here, under the basilica, is a fourth-century church which houses the tomb of Saint Cyril."

"So they built one church directly on top of another?" Ferguson asked, fascinated. "That takes a lot of skill."

"And a strong motive," Ava chipped in.

Cyrus nodded. "Not only that." He swiped underneath the image again, and a third layer appeared—much smaller this time. "And here, underneath both churches, is the second-century mithraeum."

Ferguson peered closely as Cyrus rotated the image so he could see it from all sides. "It looks like a small cave," he concluded.

"Yes," Ava confirmed. "Mithras was allegedly born out of a rock in a cave—so many of the Mithraic temples were cut out of the rock and made to resemble caves."

Ferguson gazed at the screen, then at Ava. "But I still don't get it," he said. "Why are we looking at this mithraeum?"

"It was you talking about consecration crosses that made me think of a physical building," Ava conceded.

"But why a mithraeum?" he continued. "What's the connection?"

"That was you, again," Ava acknowledged. "When you said *bloody* beef, it reminded me of the ritual ceremony at the heart of Mithras worship."

Cyrus's eyes lit up. "The *taurobolium*."

Ava nodded.

"Oh, you're going to love this," he said to Ferguson as he wiped the architectural plan off the screen, and pulled up a picture of the inside of a mithraeum. "I've just finished CGI modelling it for a satellite television programme. Do you want to see it?"

"Definitely!" Ava replied, dropping down in one of the cinema chairs. Ferguson did likewise.

"Just watch this," Cyrus announced, also sitting as the animated graphics began to unfold.

A young man wearing nothing but a dark loincloth walked apprehensively into a decorated mithraeum. A simply vested priest directed him to a pit dug into the ground, where he lay down, before the priest laid a grille over him and stepped away.

"Is that it?" asked Ferguson. "Some kind of ritual burial?"

"Just watch," Cyrus whispered, as the priest led in a muscular bull decked in gold jewelry and garlands of green shrubs. Other worshippers followed, and some sort of ritual began.

Ava was watching Ferguson's face, and could see his apprehension as the priest pulled a long glinting ceremonial knife from inside his robes.

As the members of the congregation restrained the bull, the priest stepped forward, raised the knife, and plunged the blade deep into the bull's neck, drawing it sharply across the animal's throat. As the bull crumpled to its knees, its dark blood gushed onto the bars of the grille, drenching the man in the pit below with the hot gore.

"And that," said Cyrus, "is the *taurobolium*. Not to be confused with the tauroctony." He swiped his hand across the screen, and brought up the first image he had shown them at the very beginning—with Mithras holding a knife to the throat of a bull with vegetation growing from its tail. "The tauroctony was a sacred scene—the commonest one to survive in carvings of Mithras, in which Mithras himself, representing the sun, slays the bull, which represents the moon. Again, it's another dying and rising image, showing the conquering power of the sun—hence the vegetation growing from the dying bull's tail. That's why Mithraism was also called the religion of *Sol Invictus*—the unconquered sun."

"So what was the point of the *taurobolium*?" Ferguson asked. "Why did they drench the believer in blood?"

"Purification," Ava replied. "Believers were washed clean and purified by the blood. The cult of *Magna Mater*, the Great Mother, also performed the same ritual. And other religions had a *criobolium*, which used a ram instead of a bull. And there are, quite plainly, parallels with Christian beliefs, which promise that Christ's followers are washed clean in the blood of the sacrificed lamb. Again, another idea Christianity borrowed from the older mysteries."

Ferguson turned to Ava, growing excitement in his expression. "So the mithraeum in Rome is the 'HOME OF THE HOLY BLOODY BULL'?"

"Exactly," Ava stood up and nodded for Cyrus to enlarge the architectural plans of the basilica again. "The whole puzzle fits perfectly. 'THE HOLY CHURCH OF ROME, CLEMENT THE THIRD' means the third level down in the Basilica di San Clemente in Rome. 'HOME OF THE HOLY BLOODY BULL' confirms it means the subterranean mithraeum. And so does 'UNDER THE PROTECTION OF THE STARS', which references the astrological themes of Mithraism."

Ferguson looked at Ava with a spreading grin. "That's brilliant."

Cyrus gazed at both of them, an expression of bewilderment on his face. "What on earth are you both on about?"

Ava had forgotten Cyrus has no idea about the medal. "It would take too long to tell you now," she said, heading for the stairs. "We need to go."

Reaching the door, she stopped. "Please, Cyrus, promise me you'll close up for a few weeks and take a holiday. You mustn't be around when he calls or comes visiting."

"Understood loud and clear," he answered, flicking off the multitouch screen. "Stay longer next time, Ava. Better still," he managed a smile, "commission me for an exhibit at your museum."

At the top of the stairs, Ava pulled open the front door and turned back. "I might just do that. Thanks again, Cyrus. Now go and start packing." She gave him a wave as he closed the door behind her.

Ferguson followed her onto the pavement. "So does that mean what I think it means?" he asked.

Ava looked at him, her eyes sparkling. "I'll bet money on it," she replied hurriedly. "Whichever pope it was who wanted to hide the Menorah, he put it in the Basilica di San Clemente, three levels down in the mithraeum."

Ava's expression turned grim. "But if Malchus is ahead of us and already has the Menorah, then God help us all. We have to beat him to it. Heaven only knows what personal apocalypse he's planning. We need to get to the Menorah before he does."

Ferguson nodded. "Count me in."

"So we're agreed." Ava replied, "Then it's time to see whether De Molay and Saxby can help organize a little Roman adventure."

Ava picked up her phone and scrolled through the address book, stopping when she got to Saxby's number to punch the dial button.

He answered after one ring, and listened carefully while Ava told him exactly what she needed.

---  ◆  ---

# 65

*The Burlington Arcade*
*Piccadilly*
*London SW1*
*England*
*The United Kingdom*

MALCHUS STRODE INTO the Burlington Arcade, flanked by two of his men.

For nearly two hundred years, the elegant boutiques lining either side of its red-carpeted passageway had discretely sold luxury goods to royalty, the aristocracy, and London's more affluent shoppers.

Malchus had no time for its history, cachet, or elaborate glassed roof— although he quickly noted the arcade's beadle in his gold-trimmed frock coat and top hat. The cheery guard looked paunchy and out of shape— more use in enforcing the arcade's ban on whistling and singing than providing any effective physical security.

That suited Malchus fine.

It was almost closing time, and there were relatively few people about.

He made his way down the exclusive alleyway of shiny wood and glass oriel-fronted shops, past old-fashioned jewellers, silversmiths, antiquarians, and clothes-makers.

He knew precisely which shop he was looking for, and halted abruptly outside it.

Glancing up at the hand-painted sign, *Courcy's Oriental*, he pushed open its dark polished door, and headed inside.

The small shop was crammed with glass cases of pottery, ceramics, and other artefacts. The main space was dominated by an oriental suit of armour, complete with silk and velvet undergarments, while the wall behind it was hung with icons of Arabic-looking saints from the Eastern Church.

The room was low-lit, with a simple warm glow coming from two Persian vase lamps at either end of a table running behind the main counter. The vases were acting as bookends, sheltering between them an impressive collection of leather-bound volumes in a variety of eastern languages.

At the sound of the door opening, a man appeared from the back of the shop. He was heavy-set, in his late fifties, with a grey beard to match his thinning hair.

On seeing Malchus and his companions, his welcoming smile faded quickly.

"I had hoped never to see you again." He growled at Malchus with naked hostility. His accent gave him away as the product of an expensive English education.

"I shan't be troubling you for long," Malchus said as he approached the counter. "And there's no point calling security," he was speaking quietly. "I know where you live."

The shopkeeper's face turned a shade paler.

Malchus placed a stiff-backed brown envelope onto the counter, and slid a sheaf of glossy photos out of it, fanning them onto the glass countertop.

Courcy dropped a pair of black tortoiseshell half-moon glasses from his forehead onto his nose, and peered closely at the images, leafing through them slowly.

When he had finished, he looked up at Malchus. "I presume you have the original manuscript?"

Malchus nodded.

*It was safely tucked away. Requiescat in pace, Alex Hibbit.*

"Hebrew and Aramaic," Courcy informed Malchus. "Judging by the handwriting, thirteenth-century—although the inclusion of Aramaic suggests the content is almost certainly very much older. Palestinian school, maybe?"

He pushed the glasses back up onto his forehead. "I'm not sure I can help with this. If it's hot, there aren't going to be many buyers. It's too identifiable."

"Shut up," Malchus glared at the shopkeeper. "It's not for sale. I want you to translate it precisely for me, word for word."

One of Malchus's men picked up a small terracotta figurine from a shelf. It was simply made—a crude blob with a head: only recognizable as a woman by the large breasts she was cradling in her arms.

"Please, put that down." Courcy's voice was strained.

"Ashtoreth?" the man smirked, reading the label. "Expensive is she?"

"More than you could afford." Courcy looked nervous. "So please, put it back."

"Who was she then? This expensive lady?" The man's tone was mocking.

"The mother goddess of the Middle East. Worshipped by almost everyone."

The man kept his eyes on the shopkeeper as he held the statuette out in front of him at arm's length, before slowly opening his hand wide, dropping it. The figurine landed hard on the tiled floor, instantly smashing into shards and dust.

Courcy's knuckles whitened as he pressed his hands onto the countertop.

"Come now, Mr Courcy." Malchus intervened. "Aren't all classical antiques made in Chinese sweat shops these days?" There was no humour in his voice.

"Not all of them," Courcy spoke through gritted teeth. "When do you need the translation?"

"I'll come by to collect it tomorrow evening." Malchus turned on his heel and made for the door. He paused at the shelf of figurines, and picked up another one, taller and more graceful. It was also terracotta—a slim naked woman wearing an elaborate headdress, bending slightly to remove a sandal. "Aphrodite," Malchus said, without reading the label. "Truly charming."

"Dear God, put it down, please." Courcy's voice was pleading. "That one really is genuine. I'll have the translation done by tomorrow. I give you my word."

Malchus paused, staring at the shopkeeper, challenging him. Slowly, he placed the Aphrodite figurine back onto the shelf. "Very well. Make sure you do. My friends here can be quite clumsy when they're upset." He indicated for the men to follow him, before turning back to Courcy. "I'm relying, as always, on your discretion." His look left no ambiguity.

With that, he pulled open the shop door, and disappeared into the arcade.

## 66

*The Bunker*
*Thamesmead*
*London SE2*
*England*
*The United Kingdom*

URI CHECKED HIS watch.

He had thrown away his Luminox and replaced it with a Prada—much more Danny Motson. The quartermaster back in Tel Aviv would give him grief over the additional paperwork. But no doubt the old soldier would eventually come to see the trendy accessory as a useful addition to his cavernous warehouse of operational props.

It was 8:40 p.m. He was twenty minutes early—exactly as he had planned.

Walking casually, blending in with the other pedestrians, he easily found the *Khyber Pass Curry House*. Peering through its net-curtained windows, the heavy chairs and deep damask fabrics looked like they came from the same catalogue as the furnishings in the dozens of similar restaurants he had noticed dotted around London's suburbs.

He still did not quite understand why English people insisted on calling Pakistani restaurants 'Indian' more than sixty years after Lord Mountbatten oversaw the partition of the country. But there was a lot he still did not get about the English. Including why they partitioned so many countries in the first place.

Weaving his way across the bus lanes and slow-moving traffic to the other side of the busy street, he wandered a further twenty yards down, before taking up an observation position inside a run-down off-licence. Feigning interest in a range of gaudily packaged discount beers, he kept his eye on the battered grey metal door next to the restaurant.

It was still light, enabling him to see clearly the succession of visitors who presented themselves at the door before pressing a small grey bell on the metal jamb beside it. A square grille at eye height slid back for them to identify themselves, then the door was opened just wide enough to let them through.

He could not see anything behind the door beyond a dark corridor.

Unsurprisingly, the visitors were all men. They looked on average a little older than the crowd who had been at *The Lord Nelson* the night he had met Otto.

*So this was a more senior gathering.*

Uri's watch now showed 9:05 p.m. He would not start to get concerned about Otto until 9:45 p.m. In his experience, transport was notoriously unpredictable in all the world's big cities.

The selection of budget beers lining the cramped shelves in the off-licence was quite impressive. He had not heard of most of them. He doubted many people had.

Catching sight of someone who looked a little like Otto a few hundred yards away on the other side of the street, he moved to the window and peered around a pyramid display of promotional cans.

"Are you buying?" The stubbly man behind the counter was plainly annoyed at Uri's lengthy indecision. Uri realized he had been the only customer in the shop for the last twenty minutes.

"Not today." Uri left the shop, now sure the man on the other side of the street was Otto. He headed back towards the restaurant, leaving the shop-owner grunting with frustration at the lost opportunity for an argument.

Uri timed it so he arrived in front of the metal door at the same time as Otto.

"Alright?" Otto nodded at Uri, as he pressed the bell.

The grille slid across, and was immediately followed by the sound of a heavy bolt being drawn back on the other side of the door. The bouncer had recognized Otto instantly, Uri noted. There had been no need for any form of identification.

Once inside, Otto appeared to know his way. He showed Uri into a dark corridor—dimly illuminated by three low-power bulbs hanging from a high ceiling, each shrouded by a cracked industrial lampshade.

At the end of the bare corridor, Otto led him through a fire-door into a hot dingy hallway which ended in a decrepit flight of stairs going up, and a dirty goods elevator going down.

Stepping towards the elevator, Otto dragged aside the diamond-latticed iron grille gates and motioned for Uri to enter the doorless elevator. Once inside with the gates closed, he punched the grubby green button on the control panel—a metal box hanging off the wall on a thick stalk of wires, and the elevator began to judder downwards.

As the cage hit the bottom and Otto again pulled the gates aside, they emerged into another gloomy hallway.

Otto led him past two scuffed grey doors, and made for an identical one at the far end. As he pushed it open and ushered Uri through, Uri was temporarily disorientated by the sight that greeted him.

He had been expecting a neon strip-lit basement converted into some kind of meeting room or clubhouse—perhaps with a small snooker table and maybe a fridge full of beer.

Instead, what he walked into took him totally by surprise.

It was a large room—three or four times bigger than he had been imagining. The walls were whitewashed brick, with no windows or doors. The sense of unexpected size was magnified by the double-height ceiling.

It was a cavernous space.

He took in all the relevant details in an instant.

*Only one way in and one way out.*

He tried hard to imagine what the room had once been. It was hard to tell—perhaps a workshop?

The plain walls were sparsely hung with cheap framed photographs from the 1920s and 1930s. They depicted scenes of glamorous women in double-breasted suits or silk dresses and furs drinking from champagne coupes; men with razor-sharp partings and black evening dress smoking unfiltered cigarettes; jazz musicians perspiring over small drum kits and upright basses; and policemen with surly expressions wielding wooden truncheons beside Black Mariahs with white-walled tyres.

It only took Uri a second to work out where he was.

It was a speakeasy—an illegal unlicensed drinking club.

He knew they were becoming ever more popular in Europe and the States as people were tiring of the usual pubs, clubs, and cafés, and were now seeking the thrill of illicit entertainment.

But it captured none of the yesteryear glamour and panache of America's prohibition-era night spots shown in the photographs on the walls.

The bar Uri was looking at was not decked out with exotic cocktail glasses or curvy bottles of tantalizingly coloured liquids. And there were no dimly lit velvet alcoves, tables draped in crisp linen, voluptuous hostesses, or jazzmen in spangled suits on the stage.

The owners of this London dive had made a clear choice. The focus here was on hard drinking, not aesthetic decadence.

The result was a bleak space with a dimly lit bar serving beers direct from the barrel, wine from uncooled bottles, and an array of cheap spirits stacked on a shelf in cardboard boxes.

Fittingly, the clientele were sitting around scruffy Formica tables on metal chairs. At the far end, Uri could see a small stage with a pair of anaemic lights shining on it—but there were no musicians tonight.

All in all, it was depressingly seedy.

"Don't know what its real name is—don't think it has one." Otto explained. "We call it *The Bunker*. One of the lads works behind the bar." He looked around proprietarily. "Punters keep themselves to themselves in here. Suits us fine."

Otto headed towards the bar. "As it's a bit of a private event tonight, it's only us allowed in. Management don't mind—we drink our share."

Otto led Uri to the bar, where he could see the Skipper was already half-way through a pint of beer, deep in conversation with a middle-aged man in steel-rimmed glasses, who was lighting a cigarette from the one he was just finishing.

The Skipper's black hair was slicked back for the evening, but he was still wearing the same leather jacket with the sleeves pushed up displaying his monumental forearms.

Uri could now see the tattoos clearly. They were interlocking runes and Germanic symbols. He made out the distinctive triple-triangle of the *Valknut,* and the sharp aggressive points of the *Wolfsangel.* There was nothing as blatant as the ss's two *Sig* runes side by side, but there may as well have been.

As the Skipper struck a match and cupped it around the end of an unlit cigarette in his mouth, Uri recognized the large smudgy dots just below each of the knuckles on his left hand, and a quincunx of five inky points on the web between the thumb and first finger of his right.

*Prison tattoos.*

That figured. The Skipper looked like a man who had earned his reputation.

Otto drew level with the Skipper, and indicated for Uri to stand beside him.

Catching sight of Otto and Uri, the Skipper slapped Otto on the back, before turning to look at Uri carefully, taking his time. When he spoke, his voice was flat and expressionless, with a strong south-London accent. "So you're the lad who makes things go bang?"

Uri figured it was not a question. He did not answer.

As he waited for the Skipper to say something else, he became aware of a mild stir over by the door. Someone was entering, surrounded by a small crowd. As Uri tried to see what was happening, the group moved into the room, heading down the centre towards the stage.

It did not take long before he caught a glimpse of the man striding purposefully in the centre of the group.

There was no mistaking him.

He recognised his face instantly from the photographs Moshe had shown him back in Tel Aviv. They had pored over them together after Uri had returned to base following the failed operation with the team from *Sayeret Mat'kal* against the warehouse in Astana.

Once Moshe had got wind the Ark was to be auctioned at the Burj al-Arab in Dubai, he had decided against the high-risk strategy of sending Uri into the UAE, opting instead to monitor the next move closely. Once the Ark had been helicoptered out of Dubai, he called in a few favours and spoke to some friendly people on the ground. Pulling the data together, he quickly reached the same conclusion as the Anglo-American team led by General Hunter, Prince, and DeVere.

Their man was Marius Malchus.

As soon as Moshe had the name, it did not take him long to fish out the file. They had data on him going back to his Stasi days, and the Collections Department had been keeping a very close eye on his increasing neo-Nazi activities. They did not want any surprises from his kind of group.

Stealing another glance at Malchus walking confidently down the bar, Uri felt quietly pleased with himself.

So far so good.

Now all he had to do was get close enough to kill him, and recover the Ark.

He told himself to keep it slow, and to stick to the plan.

*It would all come in good time.*

For now, he had to work on Otto and the Skipper. His priority was to establish relationships with people who could vouch for him when he began to get close to Malchus.

As Malchus drew level with their group, he nodded an acknowledgement to the Skipper, who responded to the greeting with a reciprocal nod.

Uri tried hard to suppress a small smile.

*He could not believe his luck.*

If the Skipper had a high enough profile to enjoy a personal relationship with Malchus, then his next moves just got a lot easier.

Uri was pulled back from his thoughts by the sound of the Skipper's voice. "Otto tells me you're a *ronin*."

Uri kept a blank expression. He had no idea what the Skipper had just said.

"In feudal Japan, *ronin* were *samurai* with no master. Soldiers of fortune. Is that what you are, Danny?"

Uri shook his head. "It's not about money. I like what I do."

The Skipper's expression did not change. "We're a tight crew, Danny. You need to understand that."

"Sure." Uri returned his look, unwavering.

"What I'm saying," the Skipper continued, leaning towards him a fraction, "is that you're not one of us. I'm sure there are ways we can help each other, but I'm telling you now, if you step out of line, I'll snap your neck myself." He paused, no hint of any expression on his face. "Is that clear enough for you?"

Uri nodded. "Crystal."

The Skipper drained his pint. "Now. Enough talk. Things are about to kick off. Stick around tonight as long as you want. Enjoy the bar. I'm sure Otto will be in touch."

Putting his empty pint glass down onto the counter, the Skipper moved off with Otto following close behind. They headed for the far corner by the stage, and sat at an empty table.

Uri ordered himself a beer and stayed by the bar. He was not going to leave just yet. Now he was inside, he might as well find out what these people got up to in the privacy of their lair.

## 67

*The Bunker*
*Thamesmead*
*London SE2*
*England*
*The United Kingdom*


URI LOOKED AROUND.

The room was filling up. There were no empty tables any more, and people were starting to stand around in groups.

After a few minutes, a middle-aged man wearing a football shirt took to the stage. Tapping the microphone to check it was working, he launched into an enthusiastic speech of welcome.

To the cheers of the crowd, he announced that later in the evening they would be screening a film one of them had put together of extremist demonstrations from around the world.

To whoops of approval, he assured the audience the footage was uncensored and depicted scenes of explicit violence against opposing demonstrators and the police. He was particularly pleased to announce that it featured several British demonstrations, along with numerous people present in the room.

However, before they got round to that, he wanted to make way for someone who needed no introduction. A man well known to all of them. Someone they were privileged to have address them with a few words. With that, he stepped aside and welcomed onto the stage, "the supreme leader of the Thelema in England."

Uri allowed himself a small smile.

This was getting better and better. The chance to hear Malchus speak was a truly unexpected bonus. It would give him an opportunity to get an idea of the kind of man he was. How he moved physically. How aware he was of his surroundings. What made him tick. And all of that from an anonymous distance—Uri would be just another member of the crowd.

There was a hushed silence as Malchus rose from his table and walked slowly over to the podium.

Dressed head to toe in black, he stood out starkly amid the checked and coloured designer casual clothes filling the room. But it was not the aesthetic black of an artist. Quite the opposite. There was something effortlessly malevolent about the boots, jeans, high-buttoned shirt, and floor-length soft leather coat. They combined with his pale face and dead green eyes to suck the colour out of anything near him.

Malchus stared at the audience for an uncomfortably long time, gazing left and right, inhaling the atmosphere. As he finished taking in the crowd, he began nodding slowly, as if satisfied with what he saw.

When at last he spoke, his voice was low, but amplified crisply and clearly by the microphone and PA system, adding an additional level of depth and richness to his words, which resonated commandingly around the basement.

"I want to speak to you this evening—to offer a few words, because we must at all times remember, or be reminded, exactly what we stand for." He looked around expectantly, making full eye contact with individual members of the audience.

"Many of you are already friends. But even if we have yet to meet, I know we have a great deal in common—so it's important we retain the will and courage to speak the absolute truth."

Uri felt a tap on his left shoulder. "Which firm are you with, then?" He turned to see a wiry rat-faced man looking at him inquisitively. He was in his early forties, with an accent that sounded like he was not originally from London.

Uri had no intention of taking his eyes off Malchus. He inclined his head towards the stage. "Sorry, mate. Not now."

"Oh, are you one of his, then?" The man continued, oblivious. "The Thelema?" He blew a cloud of cheap mini-cigar smoke in Uri's direction.

Uri focused back on what Malchus was saying. "So it's in this spirit that I tell you—the world is in chaos." He gazed around, his expression inviting intimacy, shrinking the space around him. "The political classes have betrayed us. Honest people have turned to the left and right but found no answers—just the same old corrupt solutions that only benefit capitalism and its masters: the fat bankers and warmongers."

He took in the room, confidently. "We propose a different way—National Socialism. National and socialist both mean looking after the interests of everyone. There aren't any classes or differences under National Socialism—only the will of the people."

Uri watched the audience sitting round the tables. They were listening attentively.

"But we don't stand for the will of the people manipulated and distorted through a corrupt democracy. In our National Socialism, the people speak and act directly."

"I'm more with the hard right, myself," the rat-faced man next to Uri cut in again. "You know, street stuff. No disrespect to the Nazis. *Blitzkrieg*—I always liked that. Throw everything at the enemy hard and fast so they don't know what's hit them." He was plainly excited, leaning towards Uri, speaking quickly.

"Mate," Uri gave him a hard stare. "I'm trying to listen." He turned back to Malchus.

The man seemed unable to take a hint. "And what they did in the East—wiped thousands of miles off the map. Total War. You've got to respect that."

Uri was not interested in the rat-faced man's barroom opinions, no doubt absorbed from some satellite TV channel the night before. He had to take the opportunity to listen to Malchus—to get a feel for the man. He turned to the rat-faced man. "Look, you're probably a great guy. But not now. Okay?"

Malchus had started moving, and was now pacing the stage theatrically, walking in and out of the subtle lighting, which was throwing deep shadows over his heavy-lidded eyes.

He had promised only a few words, but from the way he was developing his rapport with the audience, it was clear he was settling in for something of a speech. "We must be prepared to be brutally ruthless in how we implement the will of the people." He looked about assertively. "The world is sick, and extremes are needed to combat extremes."

It was subtle, Uri reflected. Malchus was undoubtedly preaching extremism and violence, but at the same time managing to sound calm and reasonable.

"Power comes from strength," Malchus continued, "so we shouldn't hesitate to develop the strength of the people behind us. They're with us, and for their country. They're bound by blood to the soil." He eyed the audience expectantly, seeking approval.

He was met with nods from the various tables.

He paused, heightening the drama. When he spoke next, he had changed tone—now sounding confidential, as if reminiscing by an intimate fireside. "Our struggle isn't a new one. It was born a long time ago. Many have already given their lives in its cause, but it was never in vain. Their blood is the baptismal water of the new era that's dawning."

Uri could feel the levels of emotion in the room rising. He had not been expecting Malchus to have charisma—but he clearly did when he wanted to.

It was chilling.

The man next to Uri blew out another cloud of smoke. "Baptismal water of a new era? Forward men! Thousand-year *Reich* and all that." He was smirking, clearly finding something highly amusing.

Uri tried to tune him out. But the monologue was incessant, and he was leaning too close. "If they wanted to last longer, they should've done more people. Do you know how many they slotted?" He looked at Uri, inviting him to answer. "Not soldiers. I mean civilians—you know, cleansing."

Uri did not answer. This was not a conversation he had any desire to join.

The man did not wait for a response. "I'll tell you. Nineteen million—nine million Russians, six million Jews, two million Poles, one-and-a-half million gypos, and then a bunch of masons, gays, and cripples."

The man was really beginning to annoy him now.

"But they just weren't big league," the rat-faced man continued. "You've got to be like Stalin or Mao if you want to be taken seriously. They each done seventy million."

Uri took a deep breath and focused back on Malchus, trying to ignore the man's pathetic attempt at impressing him.

Malchus was beginning to step up a gear. "We've had many successes, which is to be expected—nature is the ongoing triumph of the strong over the weak. But we must never be complacent. We cannot rest until we've finally accomplished what we set out to achieve."

The man next to Uri was nodding now. "He's good, isn't he? I'll give him that. He hasn't said anything he could be done for. But we all know what he's saying." He smirked. "He's a class act, that one."

Uri did not answer. But he had to agree with him. Malchus was good at what he did.

Uri recognized the populist style of the speech—eerily reminiscent of the 1930s newsreels he had been made to watch as a teenager back at school in Haifa. He even thought he recognized one or two of the phrases. The only thing missing was a backdrop of billowing swastika flags.

Usually he had no time for politicians and their manipulative speeches. In his experience, they were all the same—stoking up the emotion so they could peddle their own interests wrapped in some unattainable utopian vision. He had never bought it, preferring life on his terms—him, on his own, doing the job he was good at. He did not need any political justification or vision to legitimize what he did. It was enough that he was government-sponsored.

He had often wondered what he would be doing if he had been born in a different country, a different race—American, Russian, or Chinese. He figured it would probably be the same work. All governments needed his particular talents.

But he knew this assignment was not like other jobs he had done.

Making contact with Otto at *The Lord Nelson* had been a huge rush—one of those evenings when he had known for sure there was no other job in the world he would rather do. It had made him feel alive to be in the midst of his enemies, deceiving them—staying one step ahead.

He had been looking forward to the same again tonight—to be riding the danger and the adrenaline. But as he watched Malchus pump up the hardcore audience in this seedy drinking hole, he realized he was now taking it to another level.

He was in a fevered and extremist environment he could not hope to control. The people surrounding him lived in their own bubble of hatred, with no rules except a code of racist violence. He was getting ever deeper into their dark circles, and what had begun as an adventure at *The Lord Nelson* had now taken him into lethal waters.

He was under no illusions. If any single person in the room found out who he really was, the authorities would be fishing his pulped remains out of a skip on some wasteland tomorrow.

*This was a job he was going to remember for a long time.*

Malchus's voice was not only getting louder, it was increasing in pitch, too. "To those who say there are only a few of us, I say it's not our absolute numbers that matter—it's our conviction and determination. And to those who accuse us of being agitators, I say that our numbers are growing. We speak for many. But what have our critics got to offer? What faith do they have to give to the people?" Malchus looked accusingly at the audience, as if they were his critics.

He had them hanging off his every word.

"It's time to act. And what counts above all are deeds not words. Make no mistake, my brothers—we're in the vanguard of a new Enlightenment, and we must hold aloft our flaming ideals. But we will not allow ourselves to put 'Victory' on our banners until we have triumphed. Until then, we will only write the word 'Fight'."

"So go on, then." The man next to Uri seemed bent on irritating him. "Are you with the Thelema?"

Uri knew Danny Motson would have a snapping point. He spun to face the man. "Look, I've asked you politely, but you're not getting it. Do me a favour—get out of my face."

The man's genial expression changed in an instant to one of unmistakeable hostility. "Who do you think you are?" he rounded on Uri. "You might be some big shot where you come from. But you're a nobody here."

"Look—" Uri began, but was cut off.

"I know everyone, and I've never seen you before," the man snarled. "Who the hell are you, anyway?" He turned to face the bar, grinding his mini-cigar out in a large plastic ashtray.

Uri took a deep breath. This was rapidly getting out of hand. "No disrespect. I just want to listen to the man up there. That's all. Alright?"

"No it's not alright." The man had worked himself up into a quiet rage. "It's not alright at all. Someone needs to teach you some manners."

With no warning, the man slugged down the remaining amber spirit in the balloon glass he was drinking from, upended it, and drove it firmly into the top of the wooden bar. A number of shards broke off its lip, leaving a jagged edge where the rim had been a moment earlier.

He had done it quickly and quietly. No one else at the bar seemed to have noticed.

He turned to Uri, leering, brandishing the jagged weapon. "Come on then. Let's go." He jabbed the glass towards Uri a few times, as if sparring with an imaginary target. "I've got your attention now, haven't I?"

Uri reluctantly stopped listening to Malchus and focused fully on the man waving the broken glass at him.

He was more agile than he had imagined.

More hostile, too.

Uri quickly guessed this was not the first time the rat-faced man had wielded a broken glass in a bar brawl.

He cursed under his breath. This was all he needed.

As he turned to face the man full on, he caught sight of Otto and the Skipper over at their table. To his surprise, they were looking over in his direction with interest, but quickly turned back to their own discussion once they saw he had spotted them.

It struck Uri as odd that they seemed embarrassed to have been seen watching him.

As he continued to watch them out of the corner of his eye, he saw them look over to him again.

Suddenly the penny dropped.

He had thought there was something odd about the way the rat-faced man had been goading him, and then immediately picked a fight with minimal cause.

*It was a set up.*

The annoying rat-faced man had been primed to pick a fight so the Skipper could see how Uri handled himself.

*Not subtle. But thorough.*

Uri smiled to himself. The rat-faced man had done a pretty good job.

Rapidly assessing the new development, there seemed only one good choice.

If they wanted a show, he would give them one.

*No problem.*

The man was still taunting him. "Come on then, sunshine. You're going to learn some manners."

Uri relaxed himself, letting his shoulders drop, and bending his neck slowly to the left and then to the right.

His eyes never left the man.

"I'm gonna carve you," the man threatened, his eyes narrowing.

Uri looked at the jagged glass being pointed at him, aware of the damage it could do. Broken glass or bottles were like a fistful of scalpels—capable of slicing through flesh, muscles, and nerves, leaving a slashed mess of severed tissues that surgeons were unable to put together again.

It was a highly effective weapon.

"You're going to remember me," the man leered.

*Not as much as you'll remember me*, Uri thought.

The man was moving his weight from one foot to the other, trying to confuse Uri as to when the attack would come.

"I'm going to give you something you won't forget," he growled.

Uri ignored the adolescent monologue, and kept his eyes firmly locked on his adversary's face.

He saw it first in the man's small eyes, a split second before he lunged with the jagged glass, a hard punch at Uri's face with the improvised weapon.

But Uri knew what was coming, and was quicker. He parried the arm powering towards him, deflecting it off course so it sailed harmlessly past his ear.

Whipping round, he grabbed the man's extended arm with both hands and twisted it hard and viciously, forcing his assailant over, his chest parallel to the floor, his arm wrenched out at right angles behind him.

Keeping hold of the man's wrist with one hand, Uri aimed a savage flat-handed blow at the back of the exposed elbow.

There was a squelching and popping sound as the elbow flexed the wrong way and the ligaments sheared. The man shrieked in pain, his face contorting into a mask of agony. Turning to face Uri, he realised his mistake too late, as Uri's fist hammered hard into his Adam's apple.

The man staggered before dropping to the floor, his eyes bulging as he struggled for air—a look of incomprehension on his face at how in less than three seconds he had a snapped arm and a crushed larynx.

Uri stood over him, contemplating whether to stand on his broken elbow and force an apology.

"Alright, I've seen enough." The voice was familiar. Uri turned to see the Skipper approaching with a hand held up to stop him. "Come with me, Danny."

Uri gave the man on the floor a final glance. His throat would heal if he was lucky, but the arm would never be the same again.

That was fine by Uri. The man was a nasty piece of work. Anyway, he had been in the wrong place at the wrong time. Life was like that.

Uri followed the Skipper out through the door and back into the stuffy hallway.

The larger man pushed open one of the other two scuffed grey doors, and indicated for Uri to follow him in.

Once inside the small room, Uri quickly took in that it was empty apart from a bare table.

It was just the two of them.

The Skipper leaned up against the wall and looked at Uri, as if assessing a piece of livestock. "Take off everything except your underwear," he ordered simply, his voice as flat and expressionless as before.

Uri had thought he might be searched at some stage of the evening, although he had been expecting merely to be patted down.

*Clearly not.*

"I'm not the law, if that's what you're thinking," Uri answered.

The Skipper did not reply,

"There's no wire," Uri added. He patted his shirt theatrically to demonstrate there was nothing concealed underneath.

"Just do it." The Skipper's voice was cold.

Uri hesitated for a moment, wondering if there was any way to avoid the indignity of stripping off.

The Skipper looked over at him, unimpressed. "I warned you, Danny. Either you're a team player, or you're not."

With a sigh, Uri began unbuttoning his shirt. It's what Danny Motson would have done. He folded it loosely and put it on the floor, then unbuckled his belt and took his trousers off.

To Uri's surprise, the Skipper walked away. "Wait here." The larger man shot him a warning look before leaving the room.

The grey door swung shut, leaving Uri to wonder what on earth was happening. The Skipper could clearly see he was not wearing a wire. So what was the delay for? He had no desire to hang around half-undressed for any length of time.

In less than a minute, the door opened again.

Unsure who it was or what intentions they might have, he braced himself. The blood was still up, and he was quite happy to lay into anyone who wanted to have a go.

But it was the Skipper, accompanied by the man with the steel-framed glasses he had seen him talking to when he had first entered the bar with Otto.

The man was carrying a slim grey metal box.

"This is one of the team docs," the Skipper announced, leaning again against the wall opposite Uri. "He patches up the lads when they need a puncture repair."

The doctor had yellow stains on his uneven teeth, and smelled strongly of alcohol and stale nicotine. Looking at him, Uri doubted he had many female patients. Or even a current medical licence, for that matter.

The doctor placed the metal box on the table and stood in front of Uri, looking him up and down.

"Open your mouth," his speech was rasping.

Uri did as he was asked, and the doctor peered carefully at his teeth.

*Were they serious?* Uri wondered. Did they really think he might have a concealed transmitter in his fillings?

Clearly they did.

"Stick out your tongue."

The doctor looked at it critically, before indicating for Uri to turn his head. He peered closely into each of his ears.

"Hold out your hands, palms down."

Uri held them out, and the doctor examined his nails carefully before straightening up again.

"Now, drop your pants."

"Come on." Uri stared at the doctor. "Seriously?" But even as he said it, he knew he was wasting his time. They were being thorough. He could have something concealed there. If he had been in their shoes and had taken it this far, he would have insisted on the same.

Glancing up, he saw the Skipper scowling at him.

He knew he had no real option but to comply. He was working. This was his job. It was what he was paid to do. If he refused to go along, he risked torpedoing all his achievements so far, and he could not afford to do anything that jeopardized his chances of getting to Malchus.

Barely concealing his annoyance, he did as he was asked.

The doctor looked down. "Not Jewish, are you?"

*To Hell with them*, Uri thought. *All of them.* He wanted them to know who they were dealing with.

"Sure. Israeli. Born and bred. Can't you tell?" he stared defiantly at the doctor,

The doctor chuckled at the joke, before turning to the small metal box he had placed on the table.

Uri was not sure quite what was happening. The body search he understood. But why had the doctor looked at his nails? And his tongue?

The doctor turned around. He was holding a familiar object—a strip of canvas with a long rubber tube and bulb attachment.

Uri fought hard to keep the look of surprise off his face. "Are you serious?" he turned to the Skipper, looking for some clue to what was happening. "You're giving me a medical?"

The Skipper did not answer.

Uri watched with irritation bordering on hostility as the doctor wrapped the canvas strip around his upper arm, pumped the bulb so the inflatable tourniquet tightened round his lower bicep, checked his watch as he decreased the tension, and took Uri's blood pressure.

"Date of birth?" the doctor asked.

"Twenty-first November, 1978," Uri answered automatically. He had committed it to memory before leaving Israel.

Placing the equipment back in the metal box, the doctor turned to the Skipper. "He's fine. No problems."

"Like I said, I'm not wearing a wire." Uri did not wait to be asked, but began to put his clothes back.

The doctor continued. "Perfect Aryan type. Good health, fitness, and bearing. No imperfections."

Uri looked over at the Skipper incredulously. "All of this tonight—a fight, a medical. Do you do this for everyone you take on?"

The Skipper shook his head. "I needed to see how you handled yourself." He paused. "And for what I've got in mind for you, there's always been a medical, by order of *Reichsführer-ss* Heinrich Himmler himself. So, congratulations, Danny. If you want it, you're in. You just passed full ss selection. I'm putting you in the *Stosstrupp*, the elite Shock Troops."

# DAY NINE

———— • ◆ • ————

# 68

*Via Labicana*
*Rione Monti*
*Rome*
*The Republic of Italy*

THE HOT MEDITERRANEAN sun beat down from the cloudless blue sky onto the back of Ava's neck.

It had been a few years since she had been in Rome. It felt good to be back.

Rounding the south side of the mighty Colosseum, she looked up at the towering shards of the largest amphitheatre ever built by the ancient Romans, still casting its immense shadows over the city centre after nearly two thousand years.

She passed an animated tour leader, explaining in a loud voice to a group of bag- and camera-bedecked sightseers that in Roman times the great amphitheatre was built over a vast underground wonder world of tunnels, chambers, and cages. He described how they connected to the stadium floor via eighty shafts, some fitted with hydraulic lifts, so the stagehands could manoeuvre anyone or anything into the arena in seconds.

The tourists stood agog as the guide told them the arena had not only been used for blood-soaked gladiatorial bouts, but at times was covered in trees and bushes, then filled with rhinoceros, giraffes, elephants, and other exotic wildlife for live animal hunts. On several notable occasions, it had even been flooded to stage epic re-enactments of great Roman naval battles.

Walking around it, Ava gazed up at the seating area once specially reserved for the powerful Vestal Virgins, Rome's most privileged women. They lived their extraordinary lives free of ownership by husbands, and enjoyed the unique status among Roman women of possessing property, the right to vote, and even the power to grant condemned prisoners their freedom by a single touch.

Ava had always been amazed how they were volunteered for the prestige and privilege before they were ten years old. They began with a decade of study. Once trained, they spent a decade tending the sacred flame of Vesta and officiating at state ceremonies. Then they ended their careers with a decade sharing their knowledge with the neophytes. When the three decades were up, they were finally free to leave the House of the Vestals and marry—although few did, preferring instead the comfort and privileges of their status as the high-priestesses of Rome. Ava had even heard it suggested that the origin of the expression to be 'over the hill at forty' came from their freedom at that age to leave the House of the Vestals at the foot of the Palatine Hill and return, over the hill, to their family homes.

It was a sobering reminder, she mused, that 'pagan' did not always mean barbarous.

She looked over at Ferguson, and nodded at him to turn east, down the ancient Via Labicana.

Given the short notice, Ava had been thankful she did not need any special gear for this operation—just good old-fashioned deception. She had told Saxby the plan and what she required. It was pretty straightforward. As her instructors had drilled into her at every opportunity: complexity led to problems. The simpler the better.

In constructing the plan, she had been aware that the main challenge lay in the fact the basilica was a large building, open to the public. That meant there was zero opportunity for her to explore the underground mithraeum unobserved or undisturbed.

In addition, she was pretty sure there would be extensive internal camera surveillance. The equation was simple. Churches contained highly valuable artefacts, while cctv cameras and monitors were relatively cheap. One good pair of church candlesticks was worth more than the cost of installing an entire surveillance system. Therefore the basilica would be wired for visuals.

As she walked further down the Via Labicana, away from the Colosseum, she scanned the area for the van she had asked Saxby to park a few doors up from the basilica's entrance.

Expecting a nondescript vehicle, she failed to register the two faded blue *Gas di Roma* vans parked ahead of her at the junction of the Via Labicana and the Piazza di San Clemente. She did a double take as Saxby stepped out from the lead van, his silver hair glinting in the sunshine.

As she drew level with the van, she peered into the passenger window, noting the stained and tired-looking upholstery, the battered equipment, the dog-eared log books, and the other scattered paraphernalia.

There could be no doubt—it was a genuine working gas van.

"How on earth ... ," she looked questioningly at Saxby. "I thought you'd just get a plain van, maybe spray it a little?" She trailed off, wondering if Ferguson was right. Perhaps the Foundation was a network of freemasons after all?

Saxby smiled. "There's not much we can't do if we put our mind to it."

Registering the dubious look on her face, he continued. "You must be a little baffled by it all, Dr Curzon. And I don't blame you. Rest assured, I haven't forgotten my promise to explain to you more about the Foundation, and what we do. Maybe once we're finished here and have some time?"

Ava nodded.

That would be good.

She had decided to continue working with the Foundation in order to recover the Menorah. And she knew that the Foundation was ultimately her best chance of getting to Malchus. But she needed answers to some fundamental questions if she was going to continue the arrangement.

"You've shown faith in us, and put your life on the line in our service." Saxby's eyes softened. "In my opinion, exceptionally, I believe you're therefore entitled to know more of who we are, and what we do. And," he gestured to the vans, "how we come to have this small amount of influence."

*That was an understatement.*

She had been impressed by how quickly Saxby had provided her and Ferguson with aeroplane tickets to the Eternal City. But that was clearly the least of his abilities.

The Foundation evidently had more than a 'small amount' of influence. In fact, it seemed to be incomparably well-connected and resourced. Ava had asked Saxby for a van that could plausibly pass as a gas repair van. But he had effortlessly acquired two real vans belonging to one of Italy's major gas companies.

He was plainly playing in the major league. She was used to MI6 or the comparable agencies of other countries having access to networks of friends in industry who could provide equipment and employment at a moment's notice. But she had never heard of a private organization with the same reach or influence.

She was aware that Italy was a country where people still looked after friends and family. But she had the strong impression Saxby would have been able to pull off the same trick in Washington, Moscow, Bombay, Shanghai, or a dozen other global cities.

"And the men?" She had counted three in each van, all wearing remarkably authentic-looking and lived-in engineers' overalls.

"That's where the illusion ends, I'm afraid." He looked apologetic. "They're not real gas engineers. But don't worry—no one will know the difference."

Ava glanced at them again, noting that, without exception, they were alert-looking athletic men in their twenties and thirties. "Who are they?"

"Friends," he answered, "professional and discreet." He did not elaborate further.

That was fine by Ava. She needed physically able men more than gas engineers. "Have they been briefed?"

"Yes, exactly as you required." Saxby slid open the door of the second van and ushered Ava and Ferguson inside, handing them each a pair of overalls bearing the multicoloured logo of the gas company.

"What's the emergency services' response time?" Ava slipped the overalls over what she was wearing.

"Twenty minutes—maybe more, maybe less. It depends on traffic and their unknowable Roman sense of timing. It could be anything, so you'll need to be quick."

Ferguson pulled up his left sleeve and primed the countdown dial on his canvas-strapped steel watch. He set it for fifteen minutes. "To be safe," he explained to Ava.

She watched as the men got out of the second van and heaved a large metal flight case from the back. It was worn and dented, and the gas company logo stencilled onto it was chipped and battered. It would do nicely. It looked sturdy, and had a strong set of wheels underneath, exactly as she had requested. They put it onto the pavement.

Returning to the van, they took out an equally wide but much thinner case, just as worn, and placed it on top of the first one.

It all looked like standard emergency response kit.

"Okay. Let's go," Ava announced, zipping up the remaining few inches of her overalls and grabbing a safety helmet from the rack inside the van.

Turning to the drivers, she gave further instructions. "Follow us into the Piazza di San Clemente. Park just outside. Make sure the vans' back doors are open at all times, and keep the engines running. We could be out of the building any time."

"Good luck." Saxby lowered his voice and leant a little closer to her, almost conspiratorially. "So, do you really think it's still there?"

Ava seriously hoped it was, or she was going to look ridiculous. And she expected that if this turned out to be a false alarm, the Foundation would not be so keen to continue with her services either.

"We'll soon find out." She injected as much optimism into her voice as she could, hoping he had not registered her moment of anxiety.

As she and Ferguson moved off alongside the men wheeling the flight cases, the two drivers jumped out of their vehicles and followed them round into the Piazza di San Clemente, where they placed a large orange and black striped emergency barrier outside the basilica's entrance.

Its bold letters left passers-by in no doubt as to the serious problem:

ATTENZIONE!

FUGA DI GAS.

È ASSOLUTAMENTE VIETATO L'INGRESSO ALLE

PERSONE NON AUTORIZZATE.[12]

Ava was acutely aware of the noise the cases were making as the men rolled them along the pavement.

*This had better work.*

She reminded herself she had designed this to be a high-visibility operation. It was not a stealth exercise. She wanted people to look at them.

---

12 Warning! Gas leak. It is absolutely forbidden for unauthorized persons to enter.

They were at the squat doorway set into the ancient porchway in no time. Passing through it, they moved into a tranquil tree-shaded cloister of Ionic columns clustered around a small fountain in the centre of a cobbled quadrangle.

At the opposite side of the courtyard, behind a colonnade of five arches, lay the entrance to the basilica. It was flanked by a pair of thin palm trees, and had a simple white façade with just one airy round-topped window underneath a large triangular pediment.

Striding quickly across the courtyard and through the central archway, they were in.

———— · ◆ · ————

## 69

*Basilica di San Clemente*
*Via Labicana*
*Rione Monti*
*Rome*
*The Republic of Italy*

ALTHOUGH AVA HAD done her research on the basilica and knew pretty much what to expect, she was unprepared for the sheer scale of what greeted her as she edged inside the front door.

She had never seen anything quite like it in a twelfth-century building.

Churches of the period were usually mini-castles.

They had impregnable stone walls pierced by tiny windows, and were normally built around wide arched columns supporting low barrel-vaulted ceilings. She was particularly fond of them. It was easy to imagine medieval knights in dirty chainmail clanking around inside to the disapproving glares of women in silks and elaborate head-dresses.

But the Basilica di San Clemente, although it had clearly begun life as a large twelfth-century building, had been ever more richly rebuilt and decorated over the centuries.

The result was one of the most lavish churches she had ever seen.

It was like stepping into a Fabergé egg.

The ceiling soaring high above her was divided into diamond, oval,

410

and myriad other coffers with gilded stucco ridges creating dozens of separate sections. It resembled an elaborate chocolate box—each compartment filled with an intricate fresco.

As her eye moved down the cream-coloured building, it was unavoidably drawn to the east end, where the entire domed wall behind the high altar was spangled with a gleaming golden mosaic of glass and stone, completely filling the vast concave apse.

Glancing at it, she could see blue streams feeding a colossal tree of life with vines, flowers, peacocks, and deer all playing across it, above a row of thirteen dutiful-looking lambs. In its centre, growing out of the spreading tree of life, binding it all together, there was a cartoon-like crucifixion with white doves perching on the cross.

"Look there," Ava pointed to either side of the mosaic, whispering.

Ferguson squinted hard.

"The men depicted either side. Their names are written into the mosaic beside them." She leant closer to him, pointing out where she was looking.

He spelled them out hesitantly. "AGIOS PAVLVS' and 'AGIOS PETRVS?"

"Exactly. Just like on the medal. Saint Paul and Saint Peter."

Ferguson looked uncertain.

"*Agios* is the Greek for saint," she explained. "In the twelfth century, they often mixed up Greek and Latin in religious inscriptions. And there was no letter U—they used a V. So it just says Saint Paul and Saint Peter. I get the feeling it's not a coincidence that the two saints feature on the medal, and here they are, too."

Dropping her gaze downwards from the mosaic, she spotted the huge high altar housing the relics of Saint Clement, the third pope. She did not have much interest in him, save that his execution sounded particularly barbarous. The Romans had tied him to an anchor and thrown him off a ship into the Black Sea.

As her eyes moved to the foreground, they travelled along the mesmerizing decorations in the cream-coloured marble floor—inlaid with multicoloured stones, marble, and glass to create hypnotic swirling geometric patterns.

In the very centre of it all, her eyes rested on a small rectangular enclosure with low white carved marble walls. Inside it, two rows of ancient wooden pews faced each other across a central aisle. It was a choir. A very old one—sixth-century, according to the discrete sign.

The overall effect of the basilica was breathtaking.

Ava thought back to the Burj al-Arab in Dubai. Granted, a visitor to the seven-star hotel could be waited on hand and foot. But somewhere in the passage of time down the centuries, the subtlety of craftsmanship had been lost, even for patrons with the deepest wallets.

She glanced across at Ferguson, who was still looking stunned at the intricacy and skill of the decoration.

"Look there," he pointed to one of the pillars on the right side of the altar. "Consecration crosses."

She followed his finger, and sure enough, a cross marked where the building's wall had been blessed.

"This has to be a good sign," Ava whispered. "Saint Peter, Saint Paul, and consecration crosses."

He gave a low whistle. "It's unbelievable. Not like the churches back home."

"Amazing," she added. "It isn't even famous." She glanced. "As you can see—there are barely any tourists in here."

Spotting movement up ahead, she dropped her voice. "Here we go."

The two van drivers who had entered after them were now making purposefully for the choir, where a chubby white-haired priest was collecting leaflets from the ancient pews.

As he bent, his elderly movements were restricted by his bulky clothing—a long white tunic, belt, and dangling rosary, topped off with a full-length black cloak and a short black shoulder cape.

She instantly recognized the medieval habit of a Dominican friar.

She had known a group of Dominicans when she was working in Amman. She had regularly visited Jerusalem, where they ran the *École Biblique*—Jerusalem's most prestigious school of archaeology,

She had rapidly discovered they were an order of intellectuals with a rich past—as scientists, philosophers, and even as heretics.

At the *École Biblique*, as she pored through their treasures, she had been fascinated to learn of the order's famous members down the ages. There were scholastic titans like Albertus Magnus and Thomas Aquinas, whose razor-sharp logical minds lit up the emerging universities of Europe, sweeping away the intellectual gloom of the dark ages. There were also bold and progressive scientists like Giordano Bruno, who was burned at the stake long before Galileo for stating the sun was a star and for believing there was intelligent life on other planets. On the darker side, later, there was the restless inquisitor Bernardo Gui, who alone racked up nearly a thousand convictions of heretic Cathars around Toulouse. And then the obsessive Heinrich Kramer, whose twisted but thorough witch-hunters' manual, the *Malleus Maleficarum* or *Hammer of the Witches*, had caused the death of hundreds of innocent women.

Looking around the church, she thought on a lighter note of a more famous and certainly more cheerful member of the order, and figured he would probably have liked the building very much. In his own eyes, he had been a simple Dominican priest from Tuscany. But the world knew him as one of the most penetrating and sensitive painters of all time—Fra Angelico.

All in all, Ava had learnt from her Jerusalem experiences that the Dominicans were usually mentally sharp, frequently mavericks, and rarely to be underestimated.

They were certainly good at surprises.

As the van drivers approached the priest, they showed him their official gas company ID cards. She could not follow their fast Italian, but knew they were explaining that a gas leak had been detected underground, and the entire building needed to be evacuated immediately.

"Let's just hope he doesn't have a PhD in physics," Ava whispered to Ferguson.

"The priest?" He stared back at her blankly.

"Don't worry, I'll explain another time." She pointed towards the sacristy and book shop. "Let's move. The stairs are that way."

"And ... go!" Ferguson announced, pushing the button on his watch to start the fifteen-minute countdown.

The drivers rapidly cleared the ground floor of the few members of the public looking about, then disappeared into the bookshop and down the steps to the lower levels, where they began officiously expelling the remaining flustered-looking tourists from the building.

Moving fast, Ava and Ferguson followed them into the bookshop.

———————— • ◆ • ————————

# 70

*La Gioconda Café*
*Maze Hill*
*London SE10*
*England*
*The United Kingdom*

URI COULD NOT afford to relax.

Although he was making good progress with Otto and the Skipper, he knew he also had to build out the rest of his life as Danny Motson.

He needed to work on his cover—to do things in character, to develop observable patterns of behaviour.

In short, he needed to do what a normal person would do.

He had long ago found that the quickest and easiest way to achieve this was to get into a few routines that would make it look like he was settling in.

As tempting as it was to keep himself to himself, he needed a visible public life—however small and controlled. If he was going to pass as just another guy who had moved into the area looking for work, then he had to be seen doing exactly that. Attention to these details would be vital if Otto or the Skipper came asking questions about him. And after last night at *The Bunker*, that seemed increasingly likely.

He didn't want to get too friendly with anyone, of course—just enough to remove the natural suspicion of outsiders, to fix him as a member of the community.

So he quietly established a daily public routine.

Every morning, he purchased a copy of the local newspaper and *The Sun* from *The Ottoman Convenience Store*—a metal-grilled bazaar that smelled mildly of bleach, and sold everything from mousetraps to cheap wines, and flip-flops to cling-filmed trays of unidentified oriental sweets. As he paid, he was careful to exchange a few pleasantries with whichever extended family member happened to be behind the till that day.

Then he took his newspapers and sat in a nearby café, where he made a show of reading the jobs pages—circling interesting advertisements and telephoning the relevant numbers.

It had taken some effort to find the perfect café. But he had finally managed, and it was working well.

The fatty breakfast festival of fried pork on offer in the various English greasy spoons had been a nonstarter. And the branded coffee shop chains were too impersonal.

What he really needed was a small place that served breakfast like back home—vegetable salad, goat's cheese, bread, olives, some pastries, and a steaming spiced coffee. But that was not going to happen. And it would attract a lot of attention if he tried ordering anything even remotely similar.

So he settled for a compromise—a late breakfast at the homely Italian café, *La Gioconda*, in the next street.

It was intimate, and run by a family from Campania who had decorated the walls with the usual array of garish prints and plates painted with landscapes and prominent buildings from their native region.

As he was unemployed, there was no need to be one of the early crowd. So he waited until the cake-munching clusters of Italians had finished their traditional breakfasts, before he sat at his usual small round metal table and enjoyed a sweet coffee, fresh bread, cheese, olives and a few spoons of Mediterranean salad off the all-day menu.

It was cheap as dirt, and the family who ran it became increasingly friendly as they got to recognize him.

He stayed for forty-five minutes every day, reading his papers and glancing occasionally at the small silent television in the corner. He did not understand the Italian captioning on the rolling news programme, but the presenters were usually easy on the eye.

Once he had finished with the job advertisements, he browsed quickly through the classifieds in *The Sun*.

But he was not shopping or looking for lonely hearts.

It was where they had agreed Moshe would communicate with him in the unlikely event Tel Aviv triggered the contact channel.

Moshe had carefully chosen a paper that could be found all over England and, in case the mission took Uri abroad, in most other countries, too. As a failsafe, it could even be accessed globally via its online version.

There were, in fact, two messages Moshe could publish. One would be for Uri to make contact in case there had been any critical developments. The other would be to stand him down and bring him back home.

But Uri knew Moshe. The veteran did not do chitchat and idle talk. He had briefed Uri thoroughly on the background and operational objectives. In Moshe's world, that was enough. He now expected Uri to make of it what he could. That was the old-fashioned way. It was how Moshe liked it. And it was why he had chosen Uri.

Uri expected that if he ever saw a message from Moshe, it would be telling him to wrap it up and report back to base.

He was therefore genuinely surprised on turning to the classified section to see Moshe had activated the contact channel.

The pre-agreed advertisement was there in black and white:

FOUND. ONE OLD METALLIC TRUNK WITH EXTENDABLE HANDLES. LUGGAGE LABEL BELONGING TO MR MOSES.

Uri read it three times to make triple sure. But there was no doubt. And it was hardly likely to have been published by anyone else. Moshe had chuckled as he dictated the message to Uri for him to memorize. It was exactly Moshe's sense of humour.

There was a contact telephone number at the end of the advertisement. Uri quickly tapped it into his phone, and sent an SMS.

This was going to be interesting.

---

# 71

*The Mithraeum*
*Basilica di San Clemente*
*Via Labicana*
*Rione Monti*
*Rome*
*The Republic of Italy*

ONCE THROUGH THE bookshop, Ava turned into the wide staircase leading down to the fourth-century Roman church below.

The pale stone steps were shallow, with down-lighters under the banisters casting a dim glow onto the thin apricot-coloured bricks of the
ancient wall. Occasional wall lamps, neat glowing cylinders on poles,
added to the eerie lighting.

As she stepped off the last of the long flight of stairs, she found herself
in the old church's small narthex—the ancient antechamber where the
unbaptized catechumens stood to observe the Christian mysteries from
without.

Immediately to her left, she could make out two thin classical columns sunken into the crumbling brick wall. They stood one-and-a-half
yards apart, guarding what had once been the entrance to the church,
long-since bricked up. A large iron grille now sat firmly between them,
seeping cold musty air from the old church onto the stairs.

Ava shivered.

Following Ferguson into the dark nave, she paused for a moment to let her eyes adjust to the extraordinary sight around her.

It was a long low room, with rows of squat solid columns dividing it into four dark aisles stretching away into the gloom.

In stark contrast to the upper basilica, this much more ancient church was not covered in a rainbow of gold, stones, glass, and marble—but simply made of bare honey-coloured brick and tufa.

Ava gazed in awe at the faded frescos just visible between the low brick arches—all suffused with a dull orangey warmth thrown off by more of the glowing cylinder lights on poles.

Aware a clock was running, she barely had time to register the ancient paintings. But as she moved quickly through the aged vaulted church, she saw a Greek-looking Madonna in an ornate headdress, a scene of souls descending into limbo, a pope in immaculate ninth-century dress, and a host of other images she could barely take in.

The late Roman age was not her speciality, but she had a good working knowledge of Roman Christian archaeology, and could instantly tell that this was one of the most important buildings in existence from the period.

"Come on!" Ferguson grabbed her arm and pulled her away from the frescos. "You can do the tourist bit another time."

Following him, she hurried through the dimly lit vault, feeling a noticeable drop in temperature.

As she got closer to the far end, she was suddenly aware of a low rushing sound in her ears.

Telling herself to keep it together, she made for the far end of the left aisle, where she could see Ferguson disappearing down another staircase.

Moving quickly, she passed a plain stone altar table set over a rough granite sarcophagus, and realized it must be the tomb of Saint Cyril—the inventor of the first Slavic alphabet who gave his name to Cyrillic, and was now joint-patron saint of Europe. Without pausing, she ran past the ancient tomb and hurled herself down the crooked staircase behind it at full speed.

The stairs were older than the ones from the upper basilica. She figured they dated from the period of the first church, some time in the fourth century.

It was darker on these stairs, and as she followed them around an abrupt left-hand dogleg, she could hear the rushing sound in her ears more loudly.

Half worried she might be having some kind of seizure, she felt the noise became more distinct as she hit the bottom of the stairs and she realized to her relief that it was definitely not inside her head.

"Roman sewer system," Ferguson shouted back at her from up ahead.

She nodded, looking around to get her bearings.

This lowest level of the complex was dark, dank, and cold—exactly as she had expected. They were now three floors below street level, where no sunlight ever penetrated. There was occasional electric lighting, but the good Dominican friars who ran the basilica above clearly had no funds to heat the bowels of the building.

Looking around, she was staggered to realize she was on the remains of what had once been a first-century Roman street. Next to her she recognized the unmistakable arrangement of an *insula*—a typical Roman apartment complex that had shops on the ground level and residences on the higher floors.

Unable to believe her eyes, she registered that most of the area was cordoned off, still unexcavated.

It never ceased to amaze her how many archaeological sites around the world had been identified but then remained unexplored. She was in the middle of Rome, once one of the richest cities in the world, and here was a slice of it still waiting for someone to unearth its prizes.

Moving forward, the brick walls glowed an eerie dark orange in the half-light, reminding her of the great fire of Rome that had ravaged them in AD 64. Some people had blamed the emperor, Nero, saying he wanted to clear the area for his new palace. But he was having none of it, and placed the blame squarely on the city's Christians, whom he nailed to crosses, doused in pitch, and set alight—human torches to illuminate the night sky. She often wondered how many children enjoying Roman Candle fireworks knew of their gruesome origin.

Focusing back on the job at hand, she followed Ferguson down the musty dank corridors—first left and then right, until she suddenly found herself in the heart of the ancient Mithraic complex.

She briefly thought of Cyrus in his Soho office. She prayed he was already many miles away from London—on a hot beach somewhere, far from Malchus.

Looking about, she could see an antechamber to her right, complete with pilasters and a ceiling spangled with vegetative and geometric patterns.

But to her left was the reason they were there—the second-century temple of the Mithraic mysteries.

Her heart began to beat faster.

"One minute gone. Fourteen left," Ferguson announced as the men carrying the flight cases arrived behind them.

She ducked further along the corridor, leaving the temple behind for now. She quickly needed to check the rest of the complex for any further information. Even the smallest detail could make a difference.

The mildewy corridor ended abruptly at a doorway opening into a large room. Its broken dirty floor was made of black and white mosaic, and the walls featured seven niches of varying sizes along with the faded portrait of a bearded Roman in a scarlet cloak. It looked like some sort of Mithraic schoolroom—the niches no doubt for objects symbolizing the seven grades of its mysteries.

Heading back to the temple, she ducked into the low space just in time to see the gas men opening the smaller flight case to reveal an array of tools.

The temple itself was a small hollow, about ten yards by six, hacked directly out of the tufa. The walls and ceiling were covered in original rough Roman concrete, applied unevenly to recreate the atmosphere of Mithras's original cave.

There was a small stone altar at the far end. Above it, a low barrel vault spanned the space, marred by a hole where excavations from the church above had broken through. Along the two main walls, irregular short-backed stone benches provided the temple's only seating.

"Two minutes gone. Thirteen remaining." Ferguson's voice sounded crisp and controlled.

The main object in the room stood alone in the middle of the floor: a square pedestal supporting an engraved bas-relief of the tauroctony—the mandatory scene of Mithras slaying the lunar bull.

"Is this what you were expecting?" Ferguson asked, looking around the cramped temple.

Ava nodded. It was a textbook mithraeum. Exactly as she had imagined, its bare decoration gave modern visitors no real idea of the original experience. The same was true of the great temples of Greece and

Rome, and even the majestic castles, cathedrals, and churches of medieval Europe. Just like all of them, this small temple had originally been completely painted in a riot of blazing bold colours.

In stark contrast, the drab grotto around her was a forlorn husk of the vibrant multicoloured space it had originally been, with its rich Mithraic symbolism embedded into the long-vanished mosaics, paintings, and objects that formerly adorned it.

Right on cue, there was a loud click, and all the lights went out.

*Excellent.*

The van drivers had been tasked to find out from the lady in the bookshop where the principal electricity breakers were, and then explain to her that the possibility of gas build-up and naked light bulbs was not a good combination. They were also to insist that just flicking off the light switches was not sufficient—the whole power system needed to be shut down in case anything was sparking anywhere along the many miles of old cabling.

As Ava had anticipated, the lady had clearly been only too happy to cooperate.

So far so good. Now the cctv cameras were safely off the grid, she and the men could get to work.

She flicked on the headlamp mounted to her helmet, and the others quickly followed her lead. As each LED kicked five hundred lumens out into the gloom, the dark interior of the rock-temple was suddenly crisscrossed with piercing tunnels of bright white light.

"Spread out." She did not have to speak loudly. It was a small space. "Quickly. Test all the walls, and the fronts and seats of the stone benches. See if anything seems hollow."

The men silently fanned out across the room, and began tapping the stonework with the tools they had taken from the flight case.

With no electric light, the temple regained some of its former drama.

As Ava set to work on a section of stonework, she could imagine the ceremonies the temple had hosted, with costumed initiates moving through the mysterious grades of Raven, Bridegroom, Soldier, Lion, Persian, Sun-Runner, and Father.

There was something primal and energizing about the setting. It reminded her of the symbolic power of caves in the human subconscious, and the strong traditions in the early Church that Christ had been born in a cave, not a stable. She was endlessly surprised people did not realize that many of the traditional Bible stories, like the stable, were not universally accepted in the early centuries.

The sound of the tools striking the concrete and stone echoed around the small temple, but so far with no result.

"Five minutes gone. Ten remaining." Ferguson's countdown underlined how little time they had.

"It's in here somewhere," she announced, confident she was not mistaken. "Keep trying the walls."

She tapped the bench in front of her. The stone was completely smooth, worn by centuries of use.

*If only the stones could tell what they had seen.*

"Eight minutes gone. Seven remaining,"

Ava could feel the pressure mounting quickly.

*More than half the time was gone.*

They needed to hurry up.

The men were working methodically and purposefully with no discussion or duplication of effort. They operated like a thinking organism, each methodically alongside the other.

As she watched them, Ava could not help wondering who they were, these 'friends' of the Foundation.

Only one group of people she had ever come across worked this effectively and efficiently as a team.

The military.

But if that was right, she was struggling to identify their country of origin. They all understood her English, yet the drivers had spoken native Italian to the priest, and she had overheard French and even some Spanish when they had been ushering the tourists out.

She did not know of any multilingual armies in the world. It was possible they were mercenaries, she supposed, but that would not square with Saxby's insistence that the Foundation was a peaceful institute.

"What do you reckon?" Ferguson's voice came from the far wall behind her. "Has it gone?"

Ava shook her head emphatically. "It has to be here."

He tapped the wall in front of him with the heel of a hammer. "Eight hundred years is a long time."

She gritted her teeth as she stretched round the end of the bench. "An object like the Menorah leaves its footprint wherever it goes. If it'd been moved, it would've left some trace." She ran her fingers along the stone's smooth edges. "An artefact of that significance couldn't have been taken away without leaving some kind of a trail—accounts, rumours, myths, legends, anything. Some noise would have echoed down to us if it'd been discovered here."

He checked his watch again. "Nine minutes gone. Six remaining."

He was cool under pressure. She gave him that. Her own insides were beginning to knot.

"Try the floor," she ordered the men. "There'll be flagstones under the compacted dirt. Scrape around to find the edges. See if any of the flagstones are a different height, texture, or colour. Look for any anomalies."

She began to feel sweat prickling down her back. Even if they found it, it would take them a while to get it out.

The knot in her stomach tightened.

They were running out of time.

She got down on her knees by the doorway and began scraping away at the dirt floor to reveal the flags underneath, worn smooth by years of shuffling feet.

She ran her fingers along the edges of the stones, realizing with a wave of disappointment they were all bonded tightly with ancient Roman cement.

"How long?" The strain was audible in her voice.

"Ten minutes gone. Five left." Ferguson joined her, examining the ancient grouting between two large flags.

One of the gasmen approached her. He was short but powerfully built, and his deeply creased face indicated he had spent his life smoking professionally.

"We've checked the rest of the floor." He spoke with a sandpaper voice and thick French accent.

"And?" Ava looked up at him expectantly.

He shook his head.

She caught sight of the name label on his overalls, illuminated in the beam of her helmet torch. "Is that your real name, Max?"

He shook his head. "But it'll do."

"Okay, Max," she stood up. "We've got about four minutes left." She could feel the sweat now running freely down her back. "Search the antechamber." She did not think it was likely. But they had to be thorough.

Max and one of the men moved quickly out of the temple and into the opposite room. In no time, she could hear the sound of them banging the stonework.

Turning back to the temple, she looked around with increasing desperation.

*Where was it?*

It had to be here.

*Think!*

The space was small. There were not that many places it could be.

*Where would the Vatican hide it?*

She tried to focus on the clues again.

*Where would she hide it?*

It was definitely in the Basilica di San Clemente—she was sure of that. And there could be no doubt the mithraeum was the third level down, and the home of the bloody bull.

*So what was missing?*

Beads of perspiration began to appear on her face.

A little voice of doubt deep inside began to gnaw away at her.

*Had she made a terrible mistake?*

She reassured herself immediately. She was absolutely sure she had not made any errors this time.

*So where was it?*

"Twelve minutes gone," Ferguson announced grimly. "Three remaining."

She thought again of the clues. She had been over them a thousand times.

*Were there any weaknesses in her solution?*

She looked up again at the barrel ceiling. It was just bare stone now, but seventeen hundred years ago it was painted a deep midnight blue and spangled with gleaming stars.

So she knew she was right.

*It had to be here—'under the protection of the stars'.*

"Two minutes left," announced Ferguson, a sense of urgency creeping into his voice.

Ava stared around the room with increasing desperation.

*What had she overlooked?*

Looking upwards again, she suddenly froze.

*Of course!*

'UNDER THE PROTECTION OF THE STARS' depended which side of the stars you were. From where she was standing, 'under' could mean behind.

*In the roof.*

"Check the ceiling," she shouted breathlessly, staring up and flooding the space above her with the bright light from her head lamp. The Vatican could have concealed it in a roof chamber, hidden behind the stars, brick, and plaster.

The men began testing the small barrelled ceiling with their tools, probing it for signs of hollow cavities or irregular thickness.

It did not take them long. One by one they turned to Ava and shook their heads.

She pushed back the safety helmet and wiped the sweat from her forehead.

*This was not happening.*

She was running out of options fast.

Max had returned from the antechamber. His expression said it all.

"Check the schoolroom at the end of the corridor." She pointed him in the direction of the room with the seven niches, and he set off quickly with a team of two.

She watched as the beams of light from their helmets disappeared down the narrow corridor, before she turned back to focus on the temple itself.

The only object in the room she had not investigated was the square pedestal with the bas-relief of Mithras standing proudly in the centre of the room.

It was a nonstarter—much too small to hold the Menorah, or even part of it.

She had not given it much attention, but as she looked at it, she realized it was actually one of the best preserved tauroctony scenes she had ever seen—beautifully carved, its edges still sharp and defined, standing out in crisp relief against the shadows cast by the LED light from her head-lamp.

She would love to have taken a photo for Cyrus. Mithras was standing triumphantly, his Phrygian cap firmly wedged on his tousle-haired head, his cloak billowing dramatically behind him as he sliced the throat of the bull with his wide-bladed knife. The paint had come off centuries ago, but when the carving was new it would have been spangled in bright colours—the dun brown of the bull, the green of the leaves growing from its tail, the silver of the knife, the midnight blue and gold of the stars under his cloak ... .

*Oh God.*

Ava stopped dead. Poleaxed.

"Quick!" she shouted, her voice catching in her throat. "In here. Move this pedestal." She ran to the doorway and yelled down the corridor. Max reappeared quickly with the other gasman.

"What is it?" Ferguson asked, hurrying over to her. "What've you found?"

"The underside of his cloak," She half choked, her voice hoarse with excitement. "It would've been painted with stars. Dozens of them. But it rubbed off centuries ago." She paused, gulping in a breath. "The Menorah is under here. Under this pedestal. *Under the protection of the stars.*"

She leant her shoulder hard up against the cold stone and pushed with all her might, joining the four gasmen and Ferguson, shoving for all they were worth.

Ferguson's watch started beeping as the countdown hit zero. "Out of time," he announced through clenched teeth, the veins bulging on his neck.

"Come on!" Ava grunted, straining to move the slab of stone, perspiration breaking out on her face.

The men redoubled their efforts, and together they all gave a massive shove.

With a sudden lurch, the stone pedestal came free from the grit and grime that had glued it in place for so long.

Manoeuvring it carefully, they pushed it clear of the single large flagstone on which it was set.

Reaching for the toolbox, Ava grabbed a thick crowbar and a short-handled lump-hammer.

Placing the crowbar's sharp chisel-tip over a fine line of Roman cement binding the flag in place, she lifted the hammer high over her head.

She felt Ferguson's hand on her shoulder. "Are you sure you want to do that?" He sounded anxious. "This floor is a Roman antique."

"Not this bit, if I'm right," she answered, smashing the hammer down hard onto the head of the crowbar, splintering the cement with the force of the blow. "I'm willing to bet this is a medieval repair to the original floor—sealed after they hid the Menorah."

She prayed she was not wrong.

Moving the crowbar around the flagstone, she pounded it deep into the cement on all sides, smashing the bonding into tiny fragments.

"Sixteen minutes gone. One minute over," Ferguson announced, gazing anxiously at Ava.

"Nearly done." She was breathing hard from the exertion, wiping the sweat out of her eyes as she punched the crowbar deep into the near-side crack, forcing the tip several inches under the flagstone.

Leaning hard on the bar with all her weight, she tried to prise up the flagstone. Lacking sufficient leverage, she worked it further under the stone, and began rocking it.

As the flagstone slowly lifted, she jemmied it up off the ground, her muscles starting to tremble with the exertion. As she got it high enough for the men to help, Ferguson and Max moved in beside her. They grabbed hold of the flag's edge and, straining with the weight, swung it up and out of the way.

All eyes swivelled expectantly to what was underneath, bathing the area in the torchlight from six lamps.

*Nothing.*

It was just more dirt.

"Damn it!" Ferguson turned away, his voice wracked with disappointment.

He looked at his watch. "Seventeen minutes gone. Two over." He sounded flat with resignation. "We've got to go. The emergency services are probably already outside."

The gasmen moved towards the tool case to begin packing up.

Ava held up her hand. "Wait." Her voice rang clear around the room.

She could feel a stillness, as all eyes turned to her, spotlighting her in their head beams.

There was silence.

She placed both hands firmly on Ferguson's left shoulder. Leaning on him hard, she lifted her right knee high, then stamped the heel of her boot down hard with all her force onto the dusty square of earth.

There was a loud splintering sound as a thin layer of wood gave way, and her boot disappeared into a void, closely followed by the sound of dirt and chips of broken wood hitting a stone floor several yards below.

—————— · ◆ · ——————

# 72

*La Gioconda Café*
*Maze Hill*
*London SE10*
*England*
*The United Kingdom*

URI DID NOT have to wait long for a response. Whoever had placed the advertisement for Mr Moses's piece of old luggage was monitoring the telephone number closely.

When the reply came, it was just one word.

URIM

He breathed a sigh of relief.

*Good.*

At least he had not responded to some old person's personal travel tragedy.

He typed the reply quickly.

THUMMIM

It was one of Moshe's favourite identification pairs.

The old man had been appalled when Uri confessed he had no idea what the words actually meant. Moshe had told him firmly that his ignorance was shameful, and he should look them up.

Uri figured he would get round to it one of these days.

He looked around the café, listening to the rain's insistent hammering on the large windows.

A queue was beginning to form by the glass cabinets at the far end of the room—the early lunchtime takeaway crowd, hungry for generous sandwiches with a Mediterranean twist.

Turning back to his phone, he initiated a second pair of identifiers to double check the identity of the person at the other end. He punched the single word in quickly.

YAEL

The answer came back within seconds.

JUDITH

Uri smiled.

*So far so good.*

He liked that pair. Strong biblical names. Heroines. Both killers.

He nodded at the pretty dark-haired waitress approaching his table with a pot of steaming coffee. She looked good in her black skirt and clingy white top. She refilled his cup and smiled at him, her dark eyes crinkling around a proud Italian nose that had not changed for millennia.

He did not return the smile. He was in England for one purpose only— and it did not include distractions. Anyway, he wondered, who was she kidding? Any man she smiled at would have to go through an interview committee of her extended family before he even found out her name.

His phone buzzed again as the person on the other end now initiated the third and final pair of identifiers—a multi-word sequence indicating a heightened level of security required for the most sensitive communications.

IRGUN AND LEHI

Uri knew the responses by heart to all the current fifty-odd pairs of identifiers. He typed quickly.

ANONYMOUS SOLDIERS

Taking a bite of bread and olives, he reflected that he had no way of actually knowing who was on the other end of the phone. It may have been Moshe himself. But it could just as easily be someone Moshe wanted him to connect with. That person could be in Tel Aviv, or sitting at the table next to him in the café.

Still, it made no difference. Given the correct wording of the newspaper advertisement and the faultless progression through the three levels of identifiers, it was safe to conclude this was an official communication. There was no need to go into the complexities of one-time pads and other mathematically driven randomizing codes and ciphers. They had their place, of course, but for the purposes of identification in the field, the pairs were sufficient. The likelihood of anyone else guessing them accurately was infinitesimally small.

There was always the possibility the codes had been compromised, of course. But that was a permanent feature of life. Unless there was any reason to suspect they had been blown, Uri was to assume all was fine—standard operating procedure.

Finishing the bread and olives, he wiped his hands on the paper napkin and waited for whatever was coming.

In less than a minute, the cheap black phone buzzed again.

He picked it up and pressed a button to wake the screen.

Scrolling through the incoming message, it would have struck anyone else as meaningless gibberish—three unrelated sentences placed together randomly and incoherently.

OLD LONDON STATION
BETWEEN THE PILLARS
IS THERE NO PITY FOR THE WIDOW'S SON?

This time, he did allow himself a smile.

It was definitely an official message. It was an old joke in the Institute.

He knew exactly what it meant, and what he had to do.

He took a final mouthful of coffee and got up, tucking the newspapers under his arm.

Rifling through his pockets, he pulled out what he owed for the break-fast, and left it along with a tip on the chequered tablecloth.

Someone had left a present for him in London. All he had to do now was to go and get it.

## 73

*The Mithraeum*
*Basilica di San Clemente*
*Via Labicana*
*Rione Monti*
*Rome*
*The Republic of Italy*

AVA TURNED TO Ferguson. "What did I tell you?" Her eyes were shining wildly. "I knew it was here!"

But before she had finished the sentence, he was already on his knees with the lump hammer, smashing away the remainder of the thin wooden covering.

She knelt down beside him, her heart pounding fit to burst. As she gazed across at him, splintering away the remaining wood, she began to feel dizzy with nerves.

If she was wrong about the Menorah being down there, she strongly suspected her archaeological career was over. Breaking into a seventeen-hundred-year-old mithraeum and demolishing its floor without permission would not be well received by the Baghdad museum authorities. And when word of it got around her colleagues, it was unlikely to win her any future job offers.

But as she peered down into the inky blackness, she was equally overwhelmed by the thought that the real Menorah might actually be down there—waiting, just feet from where she was kneeling.

She grabbed the crowbar and joined Ferguson, chipping away at the jagged edges of the wooden opening, clearing a hole large enough to see what was below.

If the Menorah truly was there, it would be one of the greatest archaeological finds of all time.

Unearthing fabled artefacts had been what drew her to archaeology in the first place. But she had long since abandoned thoughts of discovering any of history's truly iconic objects. Instead, long hours in libraries and down sandy holes in the Middle East had replaced her early dreams with the wonders of discovering more day-to-day items—jewels and writings, weapons and ceremonial objects. These had become her all-consuming reality. And they had delivered all she wanted. And more.

But now, peering down into the dark musty chamber, she was acutely aware that part of her was reassessing that view.

In that moment, she knew that more than anything else she wanted the Menorah to be there. And she yearned to be the one to discover it.

Getting close to the Ark had whetted her appetite for the unthinkable.

A bitter feeling rose in her throat as she recalled her failure with the Ark. Not only had she not found or examined the Ark, she had not even seen it. And now Malchus had it.

She would not let that happen again.

Craning her neck to illuminate the chamber below, at first she could see nothing. The bright beam from her head lamp only picked up the thick lattices of centuries of cobwebs, shrouded in the waves of dust billowing in the disturbed air.

But as she circled the beam around the chamber, she thought she saw something in the far left corner.

"There!" She angled her head to illuminate the area. "Do you see it?"

Ferguson directed his head lamp to the same place as hers.

She peered through the gloom, straining to see more closely, but the cobwebs and dust were obscuring the view, preventing her seeing any more clearly.

Maybe it had just been her eyes playing tricks on her.

Dangling the crowbar into the hole, she let go of it.

The metal landed with a loud clunk—the noise cannoning around the underground chamber. "Good." She looked down at it resting on the flagstones beneath. "Solid floor."

"Are you coming, then?" she asked, swinging her lower body into the void.

Before Ferguson had time to answer, she had let go, and felt herself falling several feel to hit the hard floor below.

A moment later, Ferguson landed behind her. "Is this the room where they drenched the initiates in bull's blood, then?"

She barely heard him, as she picked up the crowbar and moved quickly towards the chamber's far corner. As she neared it, the dancing beams from their head torches began to pick out what she was now sure was a solid shape, veiled behind the sheets of cobwebs and caked in centuries of dust and grime.

It was about waist height, and spiky looking.

Approaching it, Ava's heart was in her mouth.

Stretching her arm forward, she pulled apart the last curtain of cobwebs with the crowbar.

As she did, she could hear the rushing sound in her ears again, but this time knew it was the blood and adrenaline hammering round her system and not the Roman plumbing.

Focusing on the object in front of her, she felt lightheaded.

There was no mistaking it.

Although blackened with dust and filth, it was unmistakeably a seven-branched candlestick.

She goggled at it, wide-eyed, taking in its shape and the reality of what she was looking at.

Reaching out a hand to touch it, an electrical charge of excitement pulsed through her at the sensation of the cold metal under her fingers.

There was no doubt in her mind.

*This was the Menorah from King Solomon's Temple.*

She tried to speak, but no words came out. Her mouth made several shapes, but her windpipe caught the escaping air, preventing it getting through to her vocal folds.

"So what do you think?" Ferguson was staring at it critically. "It doesn't look much like the Menorah."

Ava snapped out of it. "What?" she mumbled, her mind coming back into focus. "Doesn't look like the Menorah? Yes. Oh yes it does."

Her body was flooding with emotions. She was finding it hard to process the fact she was standing in front of the Menorah. All her suppressed fantasies of one day finding an object like this came bubbling up in a fountain of awestruck elation.

"Are you sure?" He sounded increasingly uncertain.

She was aware of a grin opening up across her face. One she was finding very hard to control. "No. I'm not sure. I'm *positive*." She answered breathlessly, steadying her voice. She was certain of it. "I'll bet my life on it."

"I know you're the archaeologist," he replied, "but it just doesn't, well—it doesn't … look like what I was expecting." He trailed off, sounding uncertain.

"You mean like in pictures?" she asked.

Ferguson nodded. "Or the carving on the Arch of Titus."

"You've been doing your homework," she smiled.

"Well, I've done a little research of my own," Ferguson gazed at it. "The Arch of Titus—which is only about six hundred and fifty yards from here, by the way—has a carving of Roman soldiers looting the Jerusalem Temple in AD 70. It shows them carrying off a load of booty, including the Menorah."

"And on that carving, the Menorah looks like this?" Ava scraped the tip of the crowbar through the deep dust on the floor, outlining a rough shape.

"That's it," agreed Ferguson. "Exactly."

"And you're correct," Ava could barely contain her excitement. "Which is why this one," she nodded towards the candlestick, "*is* the real one."

"But it looks nothing like it," objected Ferguson.

"The picture on the Arch of Titus is a red herring." She stepped closer to the candlestick. "It was carved over ten years after Titus sacked Jerusalem in AD 70. But records say the candlestick he looted was a replacement, made by the Maccabees after the Syrian-Greek warlord Antiochus Epiphanes plundered the Temple and took the real one in 168 BC."

Ferguson looked nonplussed.

"Although you're right," Ava continued. "All the world's thousands of Menorah images assume it has round arms, just like on the Arch of Titus."

"So how can this be the real one?" Taking the crowbar from Ava, he did his own drawing in the dust on the floor. "If I'm not mistaken," he nodded towards the candlestick, "our one here looks like this." He finished drawing it in the sand, and stood back.

Ava nodded. "Correct. For over a thousand years, pictures have shown it with round arms. But the oldest known carving of the Menorah was recently found in Israel, in the ancient synagogue of Magdala—a village now famous as the home of Mary Magdalene. The carving was done by someone who had probably seen the original, or who was following an early Jewish tradition. It's the most reliable evidence available."

"Go on." Ferguson was looking at her with interest. "What did it show?"

Ava pointed at Ferguson's drawing. "That." She pulled more of the cobwebs off the candlestick, revealing the shape of the grimy arms more clearly. "See? They're angled."

"You think that's the genuine shape?" Ferguson still sounded dubious. "You reckon everyone's got it wrong all these centuries?"

"Definitely." Ava lifted her helmet slightly to wipe the sweat off her brow. "Think about it. Everyone has always believed it had round arms. So why would a forger, if this is a medieval forgery, make a fake with anything other than round arms? Or look at it the other way. How would a medieval forger know to make angled arms if our knowledge of the angled Magdala Menorah carving only dates from a few years ago?"

Ferguson still looked uncertain. "But how come the image on the Vatican medal has round arms, if the Vatican had seen this original?"

Ava began to rub at the grime on one of the arms. "I'm willing to bet the Vatican didn't want to publicize what the Menorah really looked like, as people would ask questions. After all, according to the story, the Vatican wanted to hide it and pretend the Knights Templar had never given it to them. So they perpetuated the myth of the round arms."

As the black grime came away under Ava's finger, a patch of dull yellow metal appeared.

Ferguson let out a long low whistle. "So—this really is the Menorah, then." He sounded stunned, as the reality began to sink in.

"I truly believe it is," Ava answered in a low voice, gazing at the sacred candlestick.

As she peered at it, she could see the Magdala carving was exactly right. Even down to the base, which was not built up of square slabs to give the effect of a stepped plinth, as on the Arch of Titus. Instead, it was a plain pyramid, out of which the trunk of the candlestick grew directly.

But it was the arms that continued to fascinate her. She pictured in her mind's eye the drawing by Maimonides, the Jewish sage of medieval Córdoba in Spain, who had depicted the arms as sprouting straight up, like the branches on a wrapped-up Christmas tree. That image had always intrigued her. But now she could see that even he was clearly wrong, although closer than anyone else.

She could not wait to get it cleaned up to examine it properly.

It would answer so many questions about the early history of the Hebrews. Exactly how old was it? Were there any inscriptions on it? Was it an original Hebrew object, or had it been captured from another people and adopted? Was it all original, or a composite built over time? Where did the gold come from? Was it really melted-down possessions and jewellery as the Bible said, or did it originate from an identifiable mine? Did it show signs of foreign workmanship, like the Temple of Solomon itself, made with skill and labour from pagan Lebanon?

"So—angled arms, then? Who's going to tell the people who make the Israeli flag?" Ferguson joked.

*Not to mention everyone else.*

She had not even begun to think of the disputes this would cause. She had not had time to consider very much beyond keeping it safe—away from Malchus.

*And who would claim it?*

Ownership of so many of the world's great artefacts was disputed—often for centuries. She had learnt to her frustration that museums employed armies of lawyers to build complicated arguments that took decades to sort out.

No doubt ownership of the Menorah would be a major ongoing headache. Many groups would claim it—the Basilica di San Clemente, the Vatican, the city of Rome, Israel, one or more Templar orders—the possibilities were endless. There was potential for decades of litigation.

"Christ." She slapped Ferguson's shoulder as she snapped out of her reverie. "What's the time? We've got to get out of here."

He hurriedly looked at his watch. "You don't want to know. Twenty minutes. We're five minutes over."

"We have to move. *Now.*" She was already halfway across the room, standing underneath the hole in the roof up to the mithraeum above.

"Max, we need ropes," she yelled up at the creased face peering in.

Heading back to where Ferguson was standing, she grabbed hold of the Menorah. "Take the other side. We've got to move it to the hole so we can winch it out."

"It's not going anywhere if it's solid gold," Ferguson noted pragmatically. "Not without some help from the others."

Ava took a firm grip and indicated for Ferguson to do likewise. "It was supposedly carried about the desert by a nomadic people. Anyway, they weren't that rich. It's hollow."

On her nod, they gave it a shove.

It moved.

"Thank God for that." The relief in Ferguson's voice was palpable, as together they slowly slid it across the floor until it was directly under the hole punched into the roof.

Sweating profusely, they looked up. Max was already dangling three ropes down through the hole. Grabbing the swinging ends, they quickly tied them to the main shaft and the outer branches.

As they finished securing it, Ava gave the command, and the four men above took the strain on the ropes.

For a moment nothing happened. Then, agonizingly slowly, the Menorah began to rise into the air.

Ava watched with trepidation, praying the knots would hold fast. She had no desire to be on the front pages as the archaeologist who found the Menorah, then broke it.

As the sacred candlestick disappeared out of sight, up into the body of the mithraeum, there was a short pause before a rope came down again.

"Ladies first." Ferguson nodded towards the rope.

Ava grabbed hold of it, and climbed up it quickly, gripping the rope between her calves and shins, crimping it between her feet in fluid move-ments as her arms pulled her up.

Ferguson followed, arriving beside Ava back in the mithraeum a few moments later.

"Right—into the box," he ordered, as the gasmen untied the ropes from their prize.

Removing the lid of the large flight case, they placed the Menorah carefully into its padded interior, fitting loose foam blocks around the metal to wedge it into place.

Once the case's sturdy clasps were safely locked down, they swept all the dirt and shards of broken wood back down through the hole, before replacing the flagstone and manoeuvring the bas-relief of Mithras back into place.

Whoever next came down into the mithraeum would have no idea anything had been touched.

Heading for the stairs, Ava forced herself to slow her breathing.

She had to remind herself that the hardest part was over.

They were just gas engineers, exiting a building they had made safe. She had nothing to worry about. Nobody would search the cases.

The men's overalls were soaked with sweat patches. And so were hers. In addition, she and Ferguson looked filthy.

Still, it was summer, and gas engineers had to get into some grubby corners. She reminded herself that passers-by would not know what she knew. They would just see a group of hot and dirty engineers. It would be nothing unusual.

As they headed back along the narrow damp passage to the foot of the steps, Ferguson silently showed her his watch—twenty-three min-utes elapsed. They were on heavily borrowed time. It was a miracle the police were not there already.

With her heart in her mouth, she arrived at the foot of the staircase. The four gas engineers took the handles of the large flight case—two either side. She and Ferguson picked up the smaller one between them, and set off first.

It was still dark as she swung herself onto the stairs. The electricity had remained off, so she focused on climbing the steps carefully.

As she took the first step, she was suddenly aware something was not right.

In fact, it was very badly wrong.

Beams of white light were dancing over the stairs.

Looking up, she froze at the sight of at least six powerful white torches, all shining down into the stairwell.

*What the .. ?*

The blazing white lights were blinding, and for a split second it was difficult to make out what was happening. But she was suddenly aware of one very disturbing thing.

*The lights were moving rapidly towards her.*

As her brain whirled to work out what was going on, she simultaneously realized there were other lights mixed in with the white ones. They were different, smaller—tiny beams of searing bright green, scything through the space in front of her, ending in dots dancing on the walls around her.

Her mind was still processing this new information, when a millisecond later a voice deep inside screamed at her to move. At the same time, a sickening jolt of adrenaline ripped through her already strung-out system.

Survival instinct took over. Barely aware of what she was doing, in one fluid movement she dropped the flight case and dived back down the stairwell.

Ferguson had evidently reached the same conclusion and simultaneously done the same, landing beside her in a heap at the bottom of the steps just as several hot bursts of semi-automatic gunfire raked the walls of the stairwell, discharging a hail of supersonic rounds through the space where the laser sights had found her head a split-second before.

---

## 74

*The Roman Ruins*
*Basilica di San Clemente*
*Via Labicana*
*Rione Monti*
*Rome*
*The Republic of Italy*

"SOMETHING TELLS ME that's not the police," Ava yelled, diving behind the large flight case holding the Menorah.

Her mind was racing.

*Who on earth was shooting?*

"You think?" Ferguson panted, grabbing her by the overalls, pulling her to her feet and hauling her into the darkness.

She did a double take at the sight of the four gasmen running alongside her, now carrying handguns instead of the Menorah case. The unassuming gas engineers were gone—they now moved like a unit of soldiers, hustling her and Ferguson into the darkness.

"We'll be easy targets here." Ava gulped down air, trying to clear her head. "The corridor is a dead-end beyond the temple. It'll be like shooting fish in a barrel."

She turned back towards the stairs, pointing at the rusty locked iron gate leading into the Roman *insula* apartment complex beyond. "We need to get into there if we're going to stand any chance."

Max pointed to the two men in the lead. "Cover the stairs," he ordered briskly, effortlessly shifting from the quiet spokesman of the group to their authoritative military commander.

The men peeled off and moved swiftly to the base of the staircase. Crouching low either side of it, they took it in turns to fire short bursts up the stairs at the moving lights.

The noise of the gunfire was deafening in the small space, and the air quickly filled with the scent of cordite.

Max rapidly examined the locked gate, before pumping a round at point blank range into the chain holding it shut.

The rusty metal links burst open, and as the chain fell to the floor with its large padlock still intact, he shoulder-barged the gate open, ushering Ava and Ferguson through into the non-public part of the ruins.

Motioning for his men to follow, they abandoned their fire positions by the stairs and hurled themselves towards the dark alleyway,

"The Menorah!" Ava yelled, as the men ran straight past it, casting light beams wildly around the confined space.

They looked at her as if she was insane.

They were right, she realized. The flight case would never fit down the narrow ancient alleyway.

Before any of them could speak, she anticipated the objection. "Then we'll have to get it out." She turned and ran back down the alley towards the stairs.

"*Mais, elle est folle?*" Max looked after her incredulously.

"Yes and no." Ferguson sped past Max. "No time to discuss her mental state. The Menorah's what we came for."

Max nodded, and signalled his men to follow her.

Passing through the gate again, Ava could see the lights still sweeping the stairs from above.

Max moved quickly into position at the bottom of the steps. Taking cover behind the flank wall, he fired repeated bursts upwards, pinning the attackers down.

Arriving in front of the large flight case, Ava yanked open its catches and pulled off the heavy lid. Ferguson and the gasmen were already alongside her, heaving the Menorah out from the foam padding.

With Ava leading, they headed back into the alleyway with the Menorah slung between them.

From the stairway, she could hear their assailants still returning Max's fire.

Pushing deeper down the narrow passageway into the crumbling Roman ruins, Ava could suddenly hear the thudding of boots behind them. Her heart racing, she turned to look over her shoulder, and saw a cluster of lights moving dimly at the alleyway's entrance.

Their attackers were no longer on the stairs. They were down on the mithraeum's level.

And they were catching up.

Pounding further into the darkness, Ava reached a short flight of crumbling steps dropping down to the right—into another complex of ruined Roman buildings.

Without hesitating, she took the stairs two at a time.

Arriving breathlessly at the bottom, she scanned left and right.

Her helmet lamp revealed she was in a room with walls of terracotta brick and patches of decorative tiling. Through the gloom, she could make out that it interconnected left and right to similar rooms via a pair of identical low central archways.

In no time, the others arrived panting behind her.

"Got any spares?" Ferguson asked Max, indicating the handgun the Frenchman was carrying.

Max nodded to the two men nearest him, who reached into their overalls and unclipped auxiliary handguns from shoulder holsters. They handed them silently to Ava and Ferguson.

"Do you know what you're doing with those?" Max sounded dubious.

"Good old Browning HP," Ferguson answered, grasping the teak grips and settling the handgun comfortably in his hand. "You read my mind."

Ava did not reply. She was busy ejecting the magazine to check it had the full complement of thirteen rounds, before clicking it back into place and cocking the hammer.

Max nodded, satisfied. He handed them each two spare clips. "How many men?"

"Six, that I could see." Ava flicked the thumb safety off the Browning. "Maybe more."

At the sound of the pursuers' boots getting louder, Ferguson spoke rapidly. "We'll have to separate—take them individually."

As he spoke, two of the men carried the Menorah through the archway to the left and into the next room, placing it out of sight behind the arch.

Max was sweating heavily. Ava could see the concentration in his lined face as he worked out the optimum way to lure the enemy in.

Making a rapid decision, he indicated for two of his men to follow him through the right-hand arch, and for the other one to go with Ava and Ferguson to the left.

Three a side. It was the best they could do.

Stepping past the Menorah and through the archway, Ava could immediately see there was another archway to her right. She headed for it, and as she looked through it, saw that ahead of her lay at least four more rooms, all connected by identical low arches.

"One room each?" Ferguson suggested to the gasman with them.

He nodded an acknowledgement and tucked himself behind the first archway, ready to intercept anyone who came his way.

Ferguson and Ava moved swiftly to the next chamber.

"You take this one," Ava said, leaving Ferguson and heading through to the following room.

Once in place, she saw the beams on the helmet lamps go out in the rooms ahead of her. Following suit, she reached up and flicked hers off.

Now they were in position, all they could do was wait in the darkness to pick off anyone who tried to enter their side of the complex.

Alone, the black was absolute. She could see nothing, leaving her ears to overcompensate, amplifying the sound of the nearby rushing water until it filled her head.

Her heart was pounding.

*Who on earth was after them?*

It was definitely not the police. They did not take head shots with no warnings from the top of staircases in fourth-century churches.

There was only one person she knew who was likely to be in the Basilica di San Clemente, armed, and on the attack.

*Malchus.*

Even saying the name in her head revolted her. She still had not got the image of Drewitt's mutilated body out of her mind.

*Had he done something similar to her father's body? Had they simply not told her?*

She shuddered.

A flash of dim light interrupted her thoughts, followed a millisecond later by the crack of a shot. It came from the other side of the complex, where Max and the other two men were hiding.

It sounded like small arms fire, and was quickly answered by something heavier.

Malchus and his men had obviously turned right, and were now being engaged by Max and his team of two.

In no time the gunfight intensified. The acrid smoke began to drift across into her room, and the blackness around her was repeatedly pierced by flashes of light from the muzzle flares.

She strained to count the signature barks of individual weapons, but could tell little except the engagement seemed to be developing into a full-on contact between the two groups.

Up ahead, she could see Ferguson in the flashes of weak light, motioning for her to join him.

Moving rapidly and silently, she slipped through to where he was.

"I'm going to engage them from behind," he whispered at her. "You stay this side with our friend here." He pointed to the gasman in the room ahead, and moved off into the darkness.

She slipped quickly back to her room, feeling the dirt and rubble crunching under her feet.

There was a moment's lull in the gunfire before it started up again.

It was a game of cat and mouse in the dark.

As the dim flashes of light became more frequent, the gasman in the room ahead of her indicated that he was also going to follow Ferguson into the other side. He motioned for Ava to remain where she was.

Thinking fast, she realized that if both Ferguson and the gasman were gone, she would have to move forward two rooms to be beside the Menorah. There was no way she was going to leave it unprotected. It was the whole reason they were there. It was what they were fighting to defend.

The sound of gunfire from the other side continued, although it seemed a little more muffled now, more distant, and she could no longer see any flashes from the muzzle flares. She guessed they were all moving further away—deeper into the complex.

As the sound of gunfire continued, for a moment she thought it was coming from behind her.

The incessant discharges had numbed her ears, and the rapports sounded as if they were echoing sharply off the low-ceilinged brick walls in all directions.

She was becoming sonically disorientated.

But as another round of shots cracked through the darkness, she was increasingly sure they were coming from behind her.

*Was that even possible?*

She supposed it would mean both sides of the complex were somehow connected, and that the men were fighting their way round in a loop.

As she stared into the total blackness, any lingering doubts were finally dispelled by a series of dim muzzle flashes that temporarily illuminated the walls deep in the complex behind her.

Max and his men were drawing the attackers further in, bringing them round full circle. They probably did not know that the two sides of the ruins were connected.

No one did. The terrain was unmapped.

Unknown.

She needed to move. To protect the Menorah.

Grasping the Browning firmly in both hands, she tucked her elbows in, and ran forwards to the archway in front of her, swinging through the full arc of the opening. The flashes behind her provided just enough light for her to scan the chamber high and low, the gun following her eyes.

She passed through the archway quickly, immediately swinging wide left and right to check the blind corners behind her.

All clear.

Moving at speed across the rubble-strewn floor, gun at the ready, she tucked herself in beside the next archway, and prepared to clear it.

By the intermittent dim light, she could now see the Menorah in the room straight ahead of her.

Raising her gun again, she stepped forward.

But she never made it to the arch.

Without warning, she felt something cold and hard rammed into the back of her head from behind, as an iron grip encircled her, pinning her arms to her body.

---

## 75

*The Roman Ruins*
*Basilica di San Clemente*
*Via Labicana*
*Rione Monti*
*Rome*
*The Republic of Italy*

AVA INSTINCTIVELY STAMPED down hard behind her, aiming to catch the ankle of whoever had just grabbed her.

But her foot passed harmlessly into thin air.

In response, the metal object being pressed into the back of her head was rammed against it harder.

On autopilot, she threw her head backwards to hit her captor in the face with the back of her skull. But whoever it was behind her swerved neatly out of the way, and she was rewarded with a hard blow to the back of her head with the butt of what she was now certain was a gun.

For a moment she saw a shower of purple and silver stars, then the grip around her arms and chest tightened.

"Well, well. Are the good fathers of the basilica among your privileged money-laundering clients, then?" The deep resonant voice was close by her ear, mocking.

She had known who it was before he spoke. She had sensed him the moment he touched her.

A wave of visceral loathing washed over her, before it was rapidly replaced by a hot bolt of intense anger.

She could not believe she had been captured.

Not now.

*Not by him.*

"How's your bodyguard's leg?" she taunted, defiantly, gritting her teeth. She was not going to give him any satisfaction—no sense of the rage and cold fear she was feeling.

There was silence.

"I hope I didn't ruin his fun," she continued, forcing a breeziness into her voice. "I think he had something special in mind. But I doubt he would've been very good at it."

She figured she had nothing to lose. If he had wanted her dead, he would already have pulled the trigger. It was much more likely he needed something from her first.

And she could guess what that was.

"What makes you think I'm remotely interested?" His tone was dismissive. "You're all expendable."

She felt him step closer. "But what I do care about," his voice sounded suddenly more urgent, "is finding the Menorah."

"Too complicated for you?" she mocked. "Need a hand?"

She thought she heard a low chuckle.

"Actually, I already have an expert assisting me." There was a long pause. "You."

Ava snorted.

"I don't mind admitting, I was having difficulty with the medal," he continued. "But after you went sightseeing in Oxford with Lord Drewitt, I realized the answer was right in front of me. You had obviously tried to recruit him, and he had no doubt accepted. So I left the medal for him to find. And the rest you know. I commend your dedication and motivation—especially once he was dead and you redoubled your efforts in his memory. All I had to do was follow you." He paused. "So you see, I have a most expert helper. The very best. And she has led me right to the prize."

Ava could feel the anger rising in her throat.

But not with him.

With herself.

*How could she have been so naïve?*

He had set up the hoops, and she had dutifully jumped through them all, like some keen competition dog.

"So, Dr Curzon," his tone was no longer conversational, "give me what I came for."

The words hit Ava like a slap in the face.

She was momentarily stunned, and could feel her colour rising.

*He knew her name.*

Wracking her brain, she could only assume he had finally identified the CCTV photograph he had taken of her at Stockbridge House.

To her surprise, as the sense of shock passed, it subsided into a gritty feeling of grim satisfaction.

Her cards were on the table. "That's right," she snarled. "So now you know."

"How touching." Malchus answered. "The avenging daughter."

For a moment, time stood still.

Ava could not believe what she had just heard.

*He was as good as admitting it.*

She could feel her anger turning white hot.

*He had killed her father.*

He was still speaking, oblivious. "Yet her first act of filial vengeance is to lead me straight to the Menorah." His tone was jeering. "He would've been so proud of you."

Ava's mind was a blur. She was barely aware of her actions as she spun round, aiming her shoulder and raised arm directly at his face. But before she had made a quarter turn, he had pulled the gun away from the back of her head and rammed it hard up into the soft flesh under her jaw.

A firework show of exploding lights and searing pain erupted inside her head, stopping her dead in her tracks.

As her vision cleared a moment later, he flicked on her helmet lamp, and she found herself looking into the eerily lit fleshy-lipped hairless face she had come to despise.

"Just so there are no misunderstandings." He was enunciating his words slowly and precisely. "People like you and your father may have your occasional uses, but you're essentially irrelevant. Now. Where's the Menorah?"

Struggling through the pain, Ava tried her best to speak slowly and clearly. "Maybe you should have a closer look at that Vatican medal," she choked. "I understand there's a code on it."

Malchus's dead eyes widened a fraction. "I assure you that you will not be laughing for long." He twisted the muzzle of the gun into the bundles of nerve endings under her chin. "So, answer me."

The pain was excruciating.

"Do you really think," Ava grimaced through the tears of agony she could feel pricking the back of her eyeballs, "that I'd ever help you?"

"Of course," He leant in closer, but was distracted by a sudden noise behind him.

Turning to look over his shoulder, he saw Ferguson framed in the archway behind him, illuminated by the glow from Ava's helmet lamp.

With his gun aimed directly at Malchus's head, he stepped carefully into the room, never taking his eyes off Malchus.

Ava could see a thin film of sweat on Ferguson's face, but his eyes were clear and alert, and his voice rock solid. "I'm giving you three seconds to release her. I've got a clean shot to the top of your neck. You'll be dead before you see my finger move."

Malchus smirked smugly. "I don't think so."

"You want to try me?" The words may have been a question, but there was no doubt it was a threat.

As Ferguson finished speaking, three of Malchus's men entered the room behind him. They filed in slowly, their machine-pistols trained on him.

"It doesn't change anything." Ferguson kept his gun on Malchus.

"If you pull the trigger," Malchus sounded smug, "the very next thing to happen, before I hit the floor, is my men will execute Dr Curzon." He paused, turning Ava round so she faced Ferguson head on. "Who knows? Maybe they'll even let you live. Just so you can always remember your moment of glory."

Ferguson did not blink. "It may have worked that way back with your Stasi cronies. But not here. Nobody's going to obey your orders once you're gone."

Malchus laughed contemptuously. "These men don't follow *me*. They belong to a tradition. My death would change nothing. They'll go to the grave for the cause, as faithful as Jesuits. Blood, steel, honour, and a thousand year rule—these ideals transcend individuals or leaders." He looked at his men, then back at Ferguson. "So, put your gun down."

Ferguson did not move.

There was a blinding flash of light and a deafening discharge from behind Ferguson, and one of Malchus's men dropped to the floor with a gurgling sound, clutching the jet of crimson blood pumping from his neck.

"Stop!" Malchus shouted to his men, who had swivelled round and were preparing to return the fire.

Malchus called through to the gasmen in the next room. "If you attempt another stunt like that, Dr Curzon is dead."

Ava watched as Max and the three gasmen emerged slowly into the room, their weapons trained on Malchus's men.

Ava could feel the tension in the room rising.

It was a Mexican stand-off.

All it took was one jumpy finger, and a lot of people would get very badly hurt.

"Decision time." Malchus looked at Ferguson and the gasmen with a condescending smile. "Who wants to die first?"

Ava had heard enough. Ferguson's finger was rock steady on the trigger. She caught his eye. When she spoke, her voice came out strangled with pain, but still clear. "Kill him."

Malchus looked blankly at Ferguson. "Our fates are in your hands, Major Ferguson. Who lives and who dies? Today, you get to be God."

Ava could see Ferguson wrestling with the options. From his expression, it was clear he wanted nothing more than to take out Malchus, then try his luck with the remainder of his men. But she could also see a part of him was unsure. She figured it was that part which was still back in Afghanistan, with the mutilated soldiers and the dead families.

"Do it," she urged, choking as Malchus ground the gun deeper into the soft flesh under her chin.

She could see Ferguson's jaw tighten as he stared unblinking at Malchus. Then, agonizingly slowly, he bent down and laid the Browning onto the gritty floor. "This isn't over," he growled quietly as he came back up, his eyes never leaving Malchus's.

"Such loyalty!" Malchus gloated. "I'm touched." He turned to Max and his men. "I believe that's your cue."

With a face like thunder, Max signalled almost imperceptibly to his team. One by one, they bent down and laid their weapons on the ground, as Malchus's men moved to encircle them.

"Now," Malchus continued, as if nothing had happened, "in all esoteric traditions, there must be balance and order. The universe requires stasis—as above, so below. Therefore," he pointed to his dead man on the floor, "blood calls for blood." He looked around the room expectantly. "Volunteers?"

Without waiting for an answer, he pulled his gun from under Ava's chin and aimed it directly at the gasman nearest him.

Ava watched in horror as he squeezed the trigger.

She barely heard the explosion as she saw the gasman crumple. He dropped to the floor as if a puppeteer had cut his strings—a small entry wound on the front of his forehead, and a mushy mess where the back of his head had been a moment earlier.

She saw Max turn white, and Ferguson ball his hands into fists.

Drawing in deep breaths, she realized Malchus was now shouting at her. "I'll ask again, Dr Curzon, where is the Menorah?"

Ava clenched her teeth to block out the pain of the gun he had again jammed under her jaw. The muzzle was now searing hot from the summary execution.

She shook her head. "Go to Hell."

"Find it!" Malchus bellowed to his men.

Three of them peeled off, the beams of their gun-mounted tactical lights cutting through the gloom as they spread into the neighbouring ruins.

It took only an instant before the men searching the front room spotted it, and yelled back to Malchus that they had it.

Still pinning Ava's arms to her sides, and with the gun pressing hard up under her jaw, he walked her through into the next room.

As half a dozen torch beams hit the Menorah, Ava could sense Malchus's excitement. It radiated from him—a dark lustful exhilaration.

He stepped away from Ava towards the Menorah, but the respite was short lived—one of his acolytes immediately moved in behind her, holding his machine-pistol to her head.

She watched as Malchus approached the Menorah reverentially, holding out a hand, brushing it lightly.

With his arms outstretched, he began to speak in a low voice. She could not hear any full sentences, but it seemed to be some kind of incantation. As she strained to make out what he was saying, she caught only the words, *"Ein Sof."*

Nothing else.

She frowned, unsure if she had heard right.

The *Ein Sof* was the name of the all-powerful creator in the ancient occult Jewish mystical tradition of the Kabbalah. It was an intensely secretive discipline, passed down the centuries by rabbi masters to their worthy disciples. Bizarrely, in more recent times, diluted elements of it had been taken up by pop stars—who combined it with yoga and science-defying health drinks in some weird New Age feel-good cult.

"What I don't get," Ava's voice shattered the silence, interrupting his awed incantation, "is your obsession with the ancient Hebrews. Aren't they everything people like you despise?"

Malchus spun to face her, his eyes black and blazing. "Be silent!"

"Nazism and Hebrew rituals," she continued, unabashed. "What am I missing?"

Malchus stepped towards her, real anger in his face. "It's not their puny religion I seek." He nodded to the gunman nearest her, who kicked her hard in the back of the leg.

She fell to her knees with the savagery of the blow, as the guard rammed the machine-pistol into her head again.

Malchus returned to the Menorah, and continued reciting.

He was speaking quietly, and she could pick out a few occasional words. She heard *"Phosphoros"*, the Greek version of the Latin name Lucifer or 'light-bearer'. And *"Demiourgos"*—the Gnostics' evil creator god, who made the world and humans, trapping immortal 'light souls' into lives of pain and decay on this earthly Hell.

Watching him, she was struck by his single-mindedness and total focus.

When coupled with his absolute disregard for anything that got in his way, it was chilling. She had long ago come to the conclusion he was clinically insane. But what she was only coming to appreciate now, in his presence, was the malevolence that physically radiated from him.

It was terrifying.

When he was done, he turned back to the room. "Box it up." He pointed to Ava, Ferguson, and the gasmen. "Bring them."

He stalked out, leaving his men to put the Menorah back into the flight case and shepherd Ava and the other prisoners out at gunpoint.

As she tramped back down the alley, she felt a crushing wave of despair. She could not believe she had solved the medal's enigmatic clues, found the Menorah, and was now about to lose it.

*To Malchus.*

And she could not escape the feeling that it was all her fault.

*She had led him directly to it.*

As they arrived at the stairs back to the fourth-century church above, Malchus went up first. The rest followed.

At the top, Ava was again grateful for her head lamp. The floor was treacherously uneven, and the vast brick pillars seemed to rise out of the gloom in unexpected places.

She could hear the wheels of the flight case rolling on the ground behind her.

It was torture knowing she was about to lose what lay nestled inside it.

But she was also aware she had a more urgent concern. Now that Malchus had the Menorah, he had little further practical use for her. The likelihood he would now put a bullet into her head had increased exponentially.

She glanced at Ferguson. From his granite expression, she figured he was thinking the same.

There was suddenly a loud clunking sound, and with no warning the lights came on.

Even through the lighting in the lower church was dim and subtle, it was still far too bright for Ava's eyes, which were accustomed to the gloom downstairs.

She squinted and lifted a hand to her face, but as she did so, saw a figure standing up ahead, at the far end of the low-lit fourth-century church.

She immediately recognized the black and white habit of the Dominican priest from upstairs. His medieval costume fitted perfectly into the old church—like a painted image from an illuminated manuscript or one of the wall frescoes. The only thing that spoiled the picture was the large double-barrelled shotgun he was pointing at them.

He looked anything but pleased. "You can stop right there." He waved the weapon at them. His voice was loud, his accent broad Irish.

Malchus held up a hand, and the group drew to a halt in the left aisle beside the large excavation hole leading down into the mithraeum.

"Gas indeed," the priest chuckled. "There's no gas in this church. We can barely afford electricity." He shook his head in bewilderment. "I don't know what you fellas are up to, but the boys-in-blue will be here in a jiffy."

Malchus indicated for his men to make their guns less obtrusive.

The elderly priest moved forward, swinging the shotgun from side to side at them as if it was a thurible billowing incense.

He glowered at them. "I was thirty-five years in a slum parish off the Falls Road in Belfast. I've seen more guns and yobbos than you have, and I know how to deal with them all. I'm afraid you picked the wrong place for your little craic."

Ava smiled to herself. Maybe not a PhD in physics, but certainly full of surprises.

He eyed the flight case. "Thieves is it?" He looked unamused. "Well, I've dealt with a lot worse." He paused, looking around. "What's in the case then?" He kept his gun trained on the group as he approached it.

"Be my guest." Malchus smiled. "A man of your learning might find it interesting."

The priest moved over to the flight case, keeping his shotgun on the group all the while. As he got closer, she could see it was an antique, but she was under no illusions that it probably had just as much stopping power as anything Malchus's men were carrying.

The old priest flipped the flight case's catches, and pushed the lid back, a look of incomprehension crossing his face as he saw the large grimy candlestick inside.

"Now where did you get that, I wonder" he began. But before he had got any further Malchus lunged towards him.

The priest swivelled the shotgun, pointing it directly at Malchus.

But he was not quick enough.

Malchus emptied two rounds into the old man's chest and one into his skull, before pushing his white-haired head backward over the low rail guarding the hole down into the mithraeum. Malchus kept pushing, and suddenly it was over. The priest toppled backwards over the railings— the weight of his head and gravity carrying him sailing down into the mithraeum below.

With a sickening crunch, Ava heard his head hit the temple's flag-stones.

As the priest fell, Ferguson seized the opportunity to make a dive for a weapon. He launched himself at the stocky gunman nearest him, bringing a shoulder and bent upper arm hard into the man's face, splintering his nose into a bloody mess as he made a grab for the machine pistol he was loosely carrying.

But the bulky man was strong. Too strong. He kept hold of the gun, and Ferguson was left trying to wrench it from his grip.

"Enough!" Malchus commanded, as his man was poised to smash a fist into Ferguson's face. "We don't have time. Get the ropes." He pointed to the coils in the bottom of the Menorah's flight case. "Tie them."

The men retrieved the ropes and directed Ferguson, Max, and the others to move over to a dim arcade of columns, where they began tying them to the vast uprights.

Ava was left standing by the flight case.

She watched with contempt as Malchus approached her. "Are you going to cooperate for once? Or am I going to have to hurt you?"

Ava gave him a defiant stare, unable to conceal her loathing. "Tricky choice. I'll give you three guesses."

His nostrils flared momentarily with anger, before he pushed her roughly to the floor, forcing her arms back around the column behind her. Tying them tight so she was firmly lashed to the pier, he returned to face her, his nose only an inch from hers, his gun rammed into her temple.

She gazed at his revoltingly hairless head, into his lizard-like green eyes, her heart hammering. "That's it?" she spat. "A simple execution? No speech? No self-congratulation?"

Malchus did not flinch. When he spoke, his voice was honey soft. "Dr Curzon, your eventual death at my hands will be a thing of beauty, not a squalid shooting." He paused, allowing his eyes to run lustfully over her face and down to her chest, "I'm going to keep a close eye on you, and I look forward to a more thorough collaboration. Another time."

He was so close she could feel his hot breath on her lips. "So please, always remember that wherever you are—I'll never be far away."

She turned her head away in disgust, wanting nothing more than to wipe the loathsome expression off his face. She pulled hard at her arms, but the ropes had been bound tight, restricting all movement.

With that, Malchus and his men were gone.

And so was the Menorah.

Ava sat for a moment, breathing heavily—too overwhelmed by everything that had just happened to speak.

Three people were dead, and she could only imagine how many ancient bricks, tiles, frescos, and other irreplaceable artworks now had ammunition rounds lodged deep in them.

She thought of the sign she had seen in the courtyard on entering the basilica. It had been put up by an eighteenth-century pope, Clement XI, and read simply:

THIS ANCIENT CHURCH HAS WITHSTOOD
THE RAVAGES OF THE CENTURIES

She prayed it could take today's anarchy in its stride, too.

---

· ◆ · ────────

# 76

*Basilica di San Clemente*
*Via Labicana*
*Rione Monti*
*Rome*
*The Republic of Italy*

AVA CONCENTRATED ON slipping her hands out of the tight knots binding her to the vast stone column. At the same time, she tried to erase from her mind the grotesque image of Malchus leering over her.

Her arms were aching from their unnatural position, and every movement sent bolts of pain shooting through her stretched shoulders.

Looking around the dimly lit crypt, she could see that the second Malchus had left the ancient chamber and headed up the stairs to the grand basilica above, Ferguson and the gasmen had also begun trying to tear themselves free of the great piers.

She knew she had to get loose quickly. If Malchus was still close by, then there remained a chance the Menorah was not completely lost.

All she had to do was get free of the constricting ropes.

Gritting her teeth, she scrunched up her hands to make them narrow enough to slip through the knots. Pulling hard, she felt the bones and cartilage crunching together as she struggled to drag her hands free.

She closed her eyes, and focused on finding a quiet spot within herself where she could blank out the searing pain. She disconnected herself from the present, and shut out the feedback coming from her senses. So she was not at first quite sure whether the noise she heard was real or imaginary.

"Quiet!" ordered Ferguson, confirming it was real, cocking his head as the room fell silent.

Ava stopped pulling at her hands, and dragged herself back to reality, listening intently.

It was definitely there.

She could make it out more clearly now.

It was footsteps coming down the stairs.

A fresh burst of adrenaline coursed through her system.

There were limited possibilities who it could be. And few of them were welcome.

If it was Malchus returning to finish them off, there was little she or any of them could do. They were all immobilized, tightly lashed to the enormous columns—sitting ducks for any executioner.

On the other hand, if it was the police, alerted by the gas vans or the noise of the shooting, then they could expect an uncomfortable reception.

The *Polizia* would certainly want to know about the pockmarks and chunks of masonry taken out of the ancient walls, and the dozens of empty cartridge cases littering the floor—not to mention the three dead bodies down below.

It would all lead to many hours of dogged and unpleasant questioning at the gloomy *Questura Centrale* downtown—and all their different and hurriedly invented accounts would not hang together for a moment. They had not had time to prepare a common story, and the likelihood of them all spontaneously offering the same explanations was zero.

All in all, if it was the police, things would get serious very quickly, and Ava had no desire to languish in the Italian criminal justice system. It would almost certainly take an intervention from Prince and DeVere to resolve it, and that would raise a whole new line of unwelcome complications. She and Ferguson had not exactly kept Legoland in the loop about their trip to Rome, and she had no desire to sit through another self-righteous lecture from Prince.

As her eyes travelled down the gloomy nave, she barely noticed the world heritage frescoes this time. Her sole focus now was the hope that the visitor was not Malchus or the police.

Through the half-light, she saw a figure emerge into the low-ceilinged basilica.

He was moving quickly towards them, his head swivelling from side to side as he took in the chaotic scene.

Her heart in her mouth, it took her a few seconds to recognize the tall lanky frame and smooth head of full silver hair as the man moved out of the shadows into the light.

*Saxby.*

She breathed an audible sigh of relief, feeling the tension dissipate.

*Thank God.*

"There's a knife in the toolbox," she called over to him urgently, nodding towards the slim flight case. "Hurry!"

Saxby reached the flight case and glanced down through the hole in the floor to the mithraeum below, where the priest had fallen head first.

"Christ." He turned pale at the spectacle below, before quickly grabbing the knife and hurrying over towards Ava.

He had her free in no time, then turned to slice open Max's bonds.

"What in God's name happened here?" He was looking around in bewilderment, shell-shocked. He passed the knife to Max, who quickly set about freeing the others.

"Come on!" Ava jumped to her feet, rubbing her numbed wrists to get the blood circulating again. "We need to find him. He can't have got far."

"We're already on it." Saxby was close behind her. "The vans are following him."

In an instant, the despair and anger that had been building lifted a fraction. She felt a sudden surge of hope.

*Of course!*

She had forgotten about the vans—they had been waiting outside with their engines running.

She bolted for the stairs, desperate to be out of the church and in a car.

To be moving.

She *had* to be there when they caught up with Malchus.

She had unfinished business with him.

Sprinting up the stairs, she halted dead in her tracks on the top step, grunting with unexpected pain as she squeezed her eyes closed against the blinding brightness.

Her pupils were still dilated from the long period in the subterranean gloom, and entirely unprepared for the Roman morning sunlight bouncing off the millions of tiny golden and glass mosaic tiles studding the apse and coffered ceiling.

She opened her eyelids again more slowly, allowing her irises time to adjust.

Moving surprisingly fast for a man of his age, Saxby arrived at the top of the stairs beside her.

"Does he have it?" he was slightly breathless, uncertainty etched into his face. "Did you find it? Was it here?"

Ava opened her eyes in a narrow squint and looked at him bleakly. She could not bring herself to say the words in case they unleashed the volatile cocktail of disappointment, frustration, and anger she was feeling.

Ferguson arrived at the top of the stairs behind them, closely followed by Max. "If the vans are on him," he looked purposeful, "we still have a chance."

Heading for the basilica's central door, Max leant in towards Saxby and spoke quietly and hurriedly to him. Straining to listen, Ava heard him report that one of his men was dead. Saxby replied that he would make the necessary arrangements with the commandery at Aubagne.

Ferguson moved closer to Ava. "That's one mystery solved then. There's only one outfit I know headquartered at Aubagne." He had clearly also been eavesdropping.

He turned to Max. "You're *Légionnaires*?"

The short Frenchman hunched his shoulders and turned down the corners of his mouth in a classic Gallic shrug. "Depends who's asking."

It was not a resounding confirmation, but it was enough. "I did a job with your thirteenth in Djibouti a few years ago." Ferguson placed a hand on Max's shoulder for a second. "I'm sorry for your loss."

"*Merci.*" Max's lined face was set like granite. "He and I served together side-by-side for seven years. And today I watch him executed like a dog." He shook his head, a murderous expression darkening his eyes.

"Come on." Ava was nearing the door, spurred on by a determination that Malchus could not be allowed to add the Menorah to his collection, in which the Ark was already the centrepiece.

As she hit the door and burst out into the bright sunlit courtyard, she heard Saxby barking rapid orders into his phone for all airports to be watched, and for a clean-up team to come in and remove the bloodied bodies from the basilica's lowest level. He confirmed he would take care of the Italian police, then he hung up.

461

Ava froze in her tracks, not believing what she was hearing.

*Who gave orders like that?*

Did he really have the Italian police and border control in his pocket? Could he actually make corpses quietly disappear from a public place in a major European capital city?

*Who on earth was he?*

The questions that had been welling up for days now exploded in her head.

At first, she had been content to accept Saxby's assurances that the Foundation was a private institute interested in ancient artefacts. It had suited her to give him the benefit of the doubt.

But recent events had changed all that decisively.

It was absolutely clear that Saxby had not been straight with her at all.

Since meeting him, her life had become distinctly more dangerous. But that was not what was bothering her most. She had never had, or wanted, a quiet existence.

What was profoundly troubling her was the realization that she truly had no idea who Saxby was, what the Foundation did, or what she was getting herself mixed up in. She was offering her services to an organization she knew absolutely nothing about.

As the conflicting thoughts tumbled through her head, she spun around to face the old man, her eyes blazing. "Who on earth are you, Saxby? Now would be a good time for answers." She glared at him. "You owe me an explanation."

Saxby's eyes narrowed as he strode between the arches of the portico and across the cobbled courtyard.

Nearing the archway separating the tranquil quadrangle from the noisy street, he looked back over his shoulder, his expression set grimly. "Have it your way then, Dr Curzon. If you're truly ready for the answer, then come with me."

———————— ⋅ ◆ ⋅ ————————

# 77

*Rome*
*The Republic of Italy*

SAXBY POINTED TOWARDS an unmarked sleek black coach up ahead—its interior obscured behind a row of dark tinted windows.

It was parked immediately opposite the main entranceway to the Basilica di San Clemente, and Ava had spotted it as soon as she emerged through the ancient church's stone archway.

Oddly for such a large vehicle, its clean modern lines and shiny metal-work blended unobtrusively into the mix of ancient and hi-tech modern that was everywhere in Rome.

Saxby approached its single slim door, which hissed and popped open revealing a low-lit interior.

Perplexed, Ava followed his invitation to climb inside. Ferguson, Max, and the others were right behind her. Saxby entered last.

She had already come to the conclusion that nothing Saxby said or did could surprise her any more.

But what was inside the coach did.

The driver's compartment was fully sealed off, leaving the rest of the cabin a long open-plan space, divided into two.

The walls and ceiling were covered in a plush dark fabric and the muted light filtering through the tinted windows was augmented by a suffused glow coming from artfully recessed lighting.

Immediately in front of her was a large seating area with four coffee-brown armchairs facing each other in front of a matching sofa. In the corners between the seats were low wooden tables supporting old-fashioned lamps. And in the centre was an ornate butler's table, its highly polished brass hinges lending an air of elegance.

It was a timeless arrangement that would have been equally at home in a White House reception room or the apartments of a university dean.

Behind the sofa was a partition of lightly tinted glass, broken only against the right wall by a narrow door opening into an office built around an antique L-shaped desk. The main section of polished mahogany was bare save for a large elaborate telephone console, while the side sprig against the wall supported an assembly of six sleek black flat-panel monitors.

Ava instantly recognized the man who rose from behind the desk to greet her.

Despite the different setting, he was unchanged from when she had seen him at the Royal Society the previous day—the same dark eyes, patrician air, neatly clipped dark goatee, and effortless charm.

But in contrast to his geniality on that occasion, De Molay's expression now was grave.

"Dr Curzon," he began, as the coach pulled away from the curb and swung out into the traffic, "I wish these were better circumstances."

Ava was in no mood for small talk. She had a thousand burning questions.

She looked searchingly at him and then at Saxby. "I'd already come to the conclusion you didn't represent an obscure private Foundation with a side interest in antiquities before I saw … ," she gestured around at the coach, "this."

"You'd better take a seat," De Molay advanced through into the front area, and waited until Ava had sat down, before himself sinking into one of the armchairs.

He gestured for Ferguson and Saxby to sit with them, before turning to Max. "Keep an eye on the monitors," he instructed. "The vans are in pursuit."

The Frenchman nodded, disappearing quickly into the back office, followed by his men.

Ava peered through the glass into the rear section, and focused more closely on the screens, which were displaying a dynamic map of Rome with three green dots moving swiftly along its narrow roadways—the first slightly ahead of the others.

"Smart." Ferguson complimented Saxby, who was also craning to look through the partition at the flat-screens. "You fitted a transmitter into the case."

Saxby nodded. "Experience suggests it pays not to leave these things to chance."

"So, Dr Curzon," De Molay began. "You're correct in guessing the Foundation is not what it seems. Therefore it's only fair we reveal to you a little more about who we are—or else Edmund tells me we may lose you as an ally."

There was something of a challenge in the statement, but Ava returned his gaze without flinching.

Saxby lifted a copy of an English newspaper off the corner table beside him. He passed it to Ava, pointing at the main article. "You've seen that?"

She looked at the headline.

GENERAL DANQUAH CONFIRMS HIS TRIP

She was aware of the story. It had been in all the papers recently.

General Danquah, the de facto military ruler of a large central African country and international pariah, was planning to visit the Federal Republic of Somalia—one of the only countries still to maintain diplomatic relations with him. Danquah's office had been busy pumping out press releases announcing his visit was to celebrate an initiative in the glorious cause of Pan-African unity. But eager journalists had not been slow to ferret out that the real purpose of his trip to Mogadishu was to cement a multi-million dollar deal to supply him with an arsenal of up-to-date Iranian-made surface-to-air missiles.

"Remember that headline," Saxby looked at her gravely, "and watch the news this evening."

This was not the sort of revelation about the Foundation Ava had been expecting. "You're behind Danquah?"

"Not quite," Saxby took back the paper. "We believe we can make the world a safer place."

"With arms deals?" Ferguson made no effort to hide his scepticism.

"Maybe this will help," De Molay announced, picking up a battered wooden box from the table beside him, and opening the lid.

Ava watched with interest as he began to lift a long chain off the folds of the faded sky-blue silk lining its interior.

With mounting incredulity, she saw the chain was made of sturdy gold links, each as thick as a matchstick, alternating between solid and filigree work, with a break every five inches for a hammered gold cross-patty the size of a walnut, each with a blood-red ruby at its centre.

As he pulled the chain clear of the box, she realized there was something chunky suspended from it—an ornamented and gem-encrusted gold pendant the size and shape of an oversize chess pawn.

De Molay put the chain down between them onto the polished surface of the butler's table.

Even without examining it, Ava knew in an instant what it was.

The grand chain was unmistakably an elaborate piece of medieval jewellery. There could be no doubt. Nobody made gold chains in those proportions and with that degree of craftsmanship any more.

She could also immediately tell it had been made for a highly important person—a member of a royal or noble family, or a senior churchman. It exuded wealth and influence. Few could afford that quality, even among the privileged elite who filled the castles of medieval Europe.

"Go on," De Molay encouraged with a smile. "You can pick it up."

Ava reached out, lifting it gingerly off the table with both hands. She knew that if it was pure gold, which was rarely the case with jewellery, it would be nineteen times heavier than water. She could not tell its exact weight without scales, but even from just holding it, she was left in no doubt that it was solid gold.

She also knew without looking what the pendant dangling from it was for, and she suspected the reason De Molay had given it to her was engraved onto its base.

Taking hold of the pendant and turning it over, she was not disappointed.

Exactly as she had anticipated, the gold bore an image cut into the metal in counter-relief.

At its centre was a crude picture of an oriental building—a portico with four arches topped by a large striped dome with an outsize cross on top. None of the lines were straight. It was as if drawn by a child.

Around the edge of the image she could clearly read three words in mirror writing:

✠ DE ✠ TEMPLO ✠ XPISTI ✠

She gazed back at De Molay, open-mouthed.

"There's the other side, of course," he smiled. "The head twists over."

Looking more closely, she saw a hairline join running around the base of the pendant a match head's width from the bottom. Inserting her thumbnail and twisting gently, the end popped off into her hand, the size and shape of a thick coin.

Flipping it over, she caught her breath at what was looking up at her.

She already had a suspicion what the building on the front was, and what the writing around it meant. But now gazing at the image on the reverse, there could be no doubt.

She could feel her pulse quickening.

The metal intaglio showed two medieval knights sitting together on the back of the same galloping horse. They wore flowing surcoats, and each carried a long kite-shaped shield protecting his body from shoulder to calf. Their heads were covered by chain-mail coifs, and each knight was brandishing a vicious looking lance. Around the image were the words:

✠ SIGILLUM ✠ MILITUM ✠ XPISTI ✠

Ava stared at De Molay and Saxby in a partial daze.

She knew exactly what she was looking at. She could see the knights in her mind's eye—their billowing white surcoats emblazoned with bright red crosses.

At last she managed a reply. "You've got to be joking?" She spoke quietly, her eyes travelling slowly from one man to the other.

"What do you think?" De Molay asked gently.

Ava let the chain run through her fingers as she placed it back onto the table. She replied slowly. "I think I need you to tell me what you're doing with this."

De Molay nodded, settling back into his chair. "What I'm about to tell you is in the utmost confidence." He fixed her with an intensity she had not seen in his face before—the geniality gone, replaced by an earnest severity. "If I discover you've breathed a word of what I'm about to say, you'll never see or hear from us again." He shot a similarly firm glance at Ferguson. "The same goes for you, Major Ferguson. Do I make myself clear?"

467

Ferguson nodded. "But is someone going to tell me what that is?" He nodded towards the chain on the table.

"It's a seal die, or matrix," Ava replied. "You push it into wax, and it creates an image—a seal."

"I guessed that," Ferguson looked across at her. "But what's its significance?"

"It means," Ava began, pausing to take a deep breath. "It means these gentlemen," she indicated De Molay and Saxby, "want us to believe that they belong to an Order all experts say was eradicated seven hundred years ago."

De Molay looked at Ava and Ferguson in turn. "You may have expected threats to ensure you don't tell others what I'm about to tell you. But none are needed, because if you ever repeat what you're about to learn, no one will believe a single word of your story. You'll be labelled as deranged—like conspiracy theorists, obsessed with the Opus Dei, the Illuminati, the New World Order, the Rosicrucians, or whatever else is flavour of the month. But do please believe me—you'll never hear from us again, and that will mean you'll have lost your one and only realistic chance to track down and retrieve the artefacts we are now all so earnestly seeking."

Ava nodded.

"Understood." Ferguson stared at the seal matrix. "I guess 'SIGILLUM' means seal. What's the rest?"

"It means Seal of the Knighthood of Christ." Ava answered. "'MILITUM' comes from the Latin *miles*, meaning a knight—where we get the name Miles. And 'XPISTI' is a medieval spelling for *Christi*, using the Greek alphabet for the first two letters."

"The X and P together," De Molay added, "the first two letters of the word Christ in Greek, were often written over each other as a monogram to form one letter called the *Chi Rho*. It's one of the most ancient Christian symbols in existence."

"Say it then," Ava paused, turning to Saxby. "Tell him who you are. I don't think I'll quite believe it until I hear it."

Saxby took a deep breath. "Very well. The Foundation is an ancient brotherhood. But what you know of us is almost certainly a farrago of half-truths and speculation, fed by rumour-mongers over the centuries."

"So I was right," Ferguson cut in. "That portrait of Sir Robert Moray at the Royal Society gave it away—you're freemasons."

"Freemasons?" Saxby shook his head. He paused, allowing himself a half-smile. "Well, yes and no. That is—not entirely."

Ferguson raised an eyebrow. "That's cleared it up."

"Major Ferguson," De Molay leant forward in his chair, his expression sombre. "You must understand, we're not accustomed to speaking openly. It's something of a rarity for us to explain who we are to outsiders."

"Our Order has been hunted and persecuted down the centuries," Saxby continued, "for more reasons than I care to think of. So we live in the shadows, and are not very practised at emerging into the daylight."

De Molay stretched his arm over the table and picked up the chain and seal matrix again. He paused before continuing, touching them thoughtfully, his voice tinged with an air of nostalgia. "Once, a long time ago, we held our heads high across Christendom. We moved in the uppermost circles of influence, the right-hand of kings and popes. We wove the very fabric of power in a way that few have done before or since. With our monks' hoods and mailed fists, we ruled the land and sea, the royal courts and papal curia. Our citadels dominated every great Christian town—from Jerez to Jerusalem. The Order's blood red cross was a symbol of might that has rarely been rivalled."

He gazed distractedly into the middle distance. "But if there's one constant thing in life, it's change. So when our Order came to a sudden and brutal end, we retreated from the open light of day, and moved into the shadows."

He was running the heavy chain through his fingers as if it was an outsize rosary. "But the truth is—we never went away."

Ava felt a shiver shoot down her spine. She was struggling to take on board what she was hearing. She knew De Molay and Saxby could only be talking about one Order—the seal was unmistakeable, unique. And the historical description De Molay had just given fitted perfectly.

She glanced at both men. "Why should we believe you? You know as well as I do there are thousands of fantasists out there who claim to be that Order, and they are all certifiably mad."

"Is someone going to tell me what you're all talking about?" Ferguson interjected. "Which Order?"

"Tell him then." Ava gazed at Saxby, the gentle light glinting off his silver hair.

Saxby seemed at something of a loss. He glanced at De Molay.

"Well then I will." Ava continued, turning to Ferguson. "They're claiming to be the Knights Templar, for two centuries the heroes of Christendom, the medieval Church's elite military unit. The knights who won their bloody spurs in the crusades, then turned their victories into a business empire with riches to rival kings."

"The knights you said first found the Menorah in Jerusalem?" Ferguson asked Saxby.

The older man nodded.

"But after two centuries as Christendom's most skilled soldiers, bankers, and advisers to kings and popes," Saxby continued, "they were brought down by the king of France in a storm of scandalous accusations—black magic, idol worship, secret ceremonies, blasphemy, and homosexuality."

Ferguson's eyes widened. "Was there any truth in them?"

"The charges were politically motivated," De Molay countered. "King Philip of France was ambitious but bankrupt. He coveted the power of the pope and the wealth of the Templars. He calculated that if he destroyed the pope's most powerful Order, he would be seen as stronger than the pope. At the same time, he figured he would get his hands on the Templars' money, which he needed to fill his barren coffers and fund his wars. It was win-win for him."

"But," De Molay continued, "he also knew that if he wanted to bring the popular knights down, he first needed to turn public opinion against them. So he ordered his lawyers to fabricate the usual slew of medieval accusations—each guaranteed to appal the God-fearing public. He knew exactly which buttons of public opinion to press, as he had recently thrown the exact same slanders against his last enemy, Pope Boniface VIII. In fact, he was largely responsible for Pope Boniface's death, after which he arranged a posthumous trial to accuse the dead pope of heresy, idolatry, black magic, and sodomy. Having seen the power of the charges on that occasion, he then hurled the same ones confidently at the Templars. And he faced no resistance from the new pope, Clement V, who sat quietly on the sidelines."

"That doesn't make much sense." Ferguson frowned. "If the Templars were such a rich and influential Order within the Church, why would the pope hang them out to dry?"

"Corruption," De Molay answered simply and sadly. "Once King Philip had rid himself of Pope Boniface, he rigged the election of a weak

Frenchman to replace him as pope." De Molay shrugged. "The new pope, Clement V, owed King Philip everything. The king had given him the pope's Triple Crown, and he could take it away just as easily."

"Without any protection from the Vatican, the knights were brutally tortured for seven years in Philip's dungeons, forced to confess all sorts of terrible things. But eventually the Order's seventy-year-old Grand Master could no longer stand the public shame. Despite the terrible tortures, he began a passionate defence of the Order, definitively denying all charges, and giving his broken knights the strength to withdraw their blood-soaked confessions and assert their innocence."

De Molay turned to Ferguson. "As you may know, in medieval times, withdrawing a confession of heresy was effectively suicide. The knights knew they would no longer be treated as penitents undergoing spiritual rehabilitation. Instead, they would be classified as relapsed heretics, fallen back into their previous errors. Having spared their lives once, the Church would not do it again. Instead, it would send them to the pyre, to cleanse their corrupted souls with fire."

"Nevertheless, even knowing the terrible consequences, many of the knights followed their leader, withdrew their forced confessions, and willingly chose death to clear their names and consciences."

"But that's not the end of it." Ava continued. "Even though the pope shut down the Templars, and all its members were either burned at the stake, imprisoned for life, or pensioned off into other Orders, there have ever since been rumours the Templars secretly survived as one of the most powerful clandestine societies in history."

She turned to De Molay. "Something like that?"

The old man nodded his assent.

"You do know how absurd this all sounds?" Ava replied slowly. "The idea that the Order survived? Only the most ardent conspiracy theorists believe it. All the experts confirm the Templars ceased to exist in 1312, officially shut down for all time by the pope. It's pure fantasy to believe the knights still exist, perpetuating some secret mission."

"And yet," De Molay answered wistfully. "Here we are."

Saxby spread his hands in a gesture of openness. "Dr Curzon, you already have the most convincing piece of evidence."

That was news to Ava. She wracked her brains to see if there was something she had missed, but she was not aware she had yet heard or seen anything conclusive.

Saxby nodded in the direction of the head of the Foundation. "Does the name De Molay not mean anything to you?"

As Saxby spoke the words, it was as if she was hearing the name for the first time. She had not registered it properly back at the Royal Society—her mind had been on other things

But now, in the current context, her brain made the connection immediately. "But that's—" she began, before being interrupted by Ferguson.

"Does someone want to tell me what you're all talking about?"

"The last Grand Master of the Templars," she explained to Ferguson, "the one who was burned at the stake. His name was Jacques de Molay."

De Molay cut in. "Along with Hugh de Payns, who founded the Order two hundred years earlier, Jacques de Molay is the most famous of all our Grand Masters. He was a war hero, then later the man who led the knights to the pyre and into history's pages."

Ferguson raised his eyebrows. "A war hero? In the crusades? From what I hear, it was butchery. There's nothing heroic about that."

De Molay settled back into his chair, shaking his head. "The Templars were no butchers. They did not exist at the time of the carnage when Jerusalem was captured. And there are no records that they ever committed any atrocities. Quite to the contrary."

He paused. "Jacques de Molay was an old man when he was burned. The doomed last stand of the crusaders had been twenty-three years earlier, at Acre in Palestine. Jacques fought there—and was one of the few survivors."

"I've been there," Ava murmured. "You can still feel the drama among the ruins."

"The fall of Acre was the stuff of legend," De Molay continued. "And it tells you something very important about our Order's values."

De Molay stroked the chain, letting it run through his fingers as if he was in prayer. "It was 1291, nearly two hundred years after the Christians first took Jerusalem, and a hundred years after Saladin had seized it back again—a century in which the crusaders had been pushed further and further towards the sea. Now, of all the great Christian cities in the crusader states, only Acre remained. If it fell, the crusades would be over."

"The Muslim forces were ranged under Sultan al-Ashraf Khalil and his Mamluks—brutal hardened soldiers, quite unlike anything the crusaders had ever seen before, and a far cry from the genteel chivalry of Saladin a century earlier. The Mamluks had been crushing the crusaders in battle after battle, and the outcome of the siege of Acre was never in doubt. The Muslims had vastly overwhelming numbers, and it was merely a question of how and when the end would come."

"The Stalingrad of the crusades," Ferguson muttered.

"Something like that," De Molay acknowledged. "It didn't take the sultan's troops long to smash into Acre. Soon they had control of most of the city, and the inhabitants were massacred or taken into slavery. Only the Templars' compound held out, filled with the Order's knights and terrified civilians seeking protection and shelter. The sultan offered safe passage to all civilians if the Templars surrendered their tower. Grand Master William de Beaujeu had already died in the fighting, so a senior Templar named Peter de Severy went to the sultan's camp to negotiate the handover and save the civilians. He knew it would mean the almost certain execution of all Templars, but he did it to save the civilians."

"The deal was agreed. But once the Templars opened the gates of their tower, the incoming attackers immediately began violating the women and boys. Appalled, the Templars slammed the gates closed and killed the sultan's men who had so blatantly reneged on the agreement. Knowing the end was near, they heroically loaded the petrified civilians onto the Orders' boats and dispatched them to nearby Cyprus. Everyone else had already fled—even the King of Jerusalem and the cowardly Master of the Hospitallers."

"Now the Templars stood alone. The sultan sent a message to the Templars that he wanted to apologise in person to Peter de Severy for the barbarous behaviour of his men. So de Severy again went to the sultan's camp with a few trusted knights, only to be pushed to his knees and beheaded in full sight of his men watching from Acre's battlements."

"The end came fast. Alone and hopelessly outnumbered, the Templars turned to face the full force and anger of the sultan's crushing army. They fought valiantly, but it was over quickly. My ancestor, Jacques de Molay, was one of the very few to survive. When the bedraggled remnants of the Order regrouped in Cyprus, he was voted in as the new Grand Master."

"So that was the end of the crusades?" Ferguson shook his head, deep in thought. "Another disastrous Middle-Eastern adventure by Western powers."

De Molay nodded. "Yet the Templars had always been different. They were born in the East. Many spoke Arabic. When they lived in the Temple—the converted al-Aqsa mosque on the site of King Solomon's Temple—there are Arabic records proving they let Muslim friends in to pray there. The knights represented something very different from the average blood-soaked crusader."

He paused. "Nevertheless, after the massacre at Acre, the remaining Templars looked about, and realized the world had changed. No one was interested in Jerusalem or crusading any more. It was the dawn of the 1300s. The Church was evolving. Europe had other priorities. It was now time for the Renaissance and the Medici, for explorers like Marco Polo and writers like Dante and Chaucer—a world of fresh ideas and new dawns. It had no interest in crusaders with their outdated vision of a Christian Palestine guarded by knights and castles."

"What happened?" Ava could see Ferguson was fascinated. Echoes of his own experiences, she imagined.

"Grand Master Jacques de Molay set about finding a role for the Templars in this new world. It's clear he struggled, but then in 1307 the king of France launched his crushing attack on the Order, and everything changed. The rest you know."

"So where do all the stories of magic and treasure come from?" Ava asked.

De Molay smiled. "There had long been rumours the Templars discovered treasures in Jerusalem. Some said it was gold. Others claimed it was an explosive secret relating to Jesus or the Bible—something the Church could not afford to be made public, so the Vatican paid the Templars off in return for their silence. Yet others said it was secret esoteric knowledge learned from eastern mystics. Whatever it was, people whispered that the Order had secret riches and unnatural powers. And Jacques de Molay's death only proved it."

"What was magical about his death?" Ferguson looked bemused.

"De Molay's last words as the flames caught him," Saxby answered, "were to challenge the pope and the king to meet him in heaven so God could judge which of them was truly guilty."

"And," Ava continued, "both pope and king were dead within the year. So, the legend of Jacques de Molay became destined for immortality— the man who summoned a pope and a king to divine judgement beyond the grave."

There was silence as they all digested the story, before De Molay spoke again. "To some, my ancestor is an icon of resistance against tyrannical oppression." He smiled. "A high-profile victim of a political trial. To others he is one of Europe's great mystical figures—a sorcerer and magician who died fighting to protect arcane secrets."

Ava gathered her thoughts before changing the subject. "Forgive me," she challenged De Molay, "but none of this actually proves anything. Anyone could call themselves De Molay. And any serious collector could have picked up your Templar chain and seal on the black market for the right price. How does any of it prove the Templars still exist, or that you're truly connected to them?"

Saxby turned to face her directly. Gone was his enthusiasm for talking about the Order's past. His voice was now deadly earnest. "Dr Curzon, you have to ask yourself why we would make up such a story? I actually agree with you—it's a highly implausible tale. But if we were going to fabricate a cover story to protect the Foundation's identity, we'd hardly select a group like the Templars, about which you're rightly sceptical. Wouldn't it be easier for us to invent something about a front for a covert government agency? Or a cartel of influential industrialists and bankers? Or perhaps even an organized crime syndicate? Any of these would be more plausible, and more likely to silence your curiosity. By saying we're the Templars, we're only inviting a hundred more questions and doubts."

Ava could see the sense in what he was saying. If they were making this up to keep her onside, it was a risky strategy to pick a group as implausible and controversial as the Templars.

On the face of it, the idea they were the Knights Templar was an outrageous claim.

But, despite herself, a part of her was close to believing them. Deep down, as far-fetched as it all seemed, she had for some time been privately wondering if there was a Templar connection.

She had first thought of the Templars when she had noticed Saxby's e-mail address in Baghdad the day he first contacted her—es@trample. net. She had immediately seen the crude anagram of 'Templar'. But she had thought little more about it—anagrams were hardly an exact science. After all, eleven-plus-two was an anagram of twelve-plus-one. One could go on seeing unrelated connections and coincidences forever.

But she had thought much more seriously about it at the Royal Society in London, when Saxby had seemed so knowledgeable about Pope Clement III and the crusading bull for the Third Crusade. That depth of knowledge was, she knew, hardly something ordinary members of the public possessed in such detail.

At the time, when she had questioned Saxby, he had answered that the Foundation had "a considerable interest" in the Third Crusade. That reply had struck her as odd. She had immediately wondered how many organizations were interested in a series of battles that took place over eight hundred years ago and over three thousand miles away. She had instinctively thought of the Templars—one of the few groups prominent in both the catastrophe that led up to the Third Crusade, and the battles of the Third Crusade itself.

Then, later at the same meeting, her suspicions had been further aroused when Saxby related the detailed legend of the Templars finding the Menorah in Jerusalem and passing it to the Vatican. As she heard him relate the story, she had again wondered who would know the amount of detail Saxby clearly possessed. After all, she had specialized in biblical archaeology for over twenty years, immersing herself in the strange history of its artefacts, and she had never once come across the legend. When she had tried to research it afterwards, she had found no information on it anywhere. It was as if Saxby had simply made it up. Yet, the account had been accurate in all regards, as the Menorah had indeed been where the medal said it would be.

And finally, she had again thought of the enigmatic white-robed knights back at the basilica, when she had overheard Saxby telling Max to take their fallen comrade to "the commandery." She knew 'commandery' was the name medieval Templars used to describe their fortified monastery-castles. She remembered reading about them when visiting a Roman dig near the Templars' castle at Kolossi in southern Cyprus. She had, in fact, seen it on the back of a wine bottle, *Commanderia* wine, which claimed not only to be the world's oldest named wine, but also to bear the name of the area—the Templars' Grand Commandery in Cyprus.

So, as far-fetched and implausible as De Molay and Saxby's claims sounded, on some level they tied in with her own speculations and growing suspicions.

She breathed deeply, trying to see a way through the myriad possibilities of truth and fabrication.

*Was it really possible?*

She glanced across at Saxby. He still looked every inch the English aristocrat. There was not a silver hair out of place, and his face was a picture of calm and reason.

Looking over to De Molay, she could believe he was from a family that traced its line back to the crusades. She could readily imagine his ancestors riding into battle under the hot Middle-Eastern sun, and it was not such a stretch of the imagination to picture his face swathed in a chainmail coif and a great helm.

She felt the need to pinch herself.

Could the 'Foundation' really be Europe's most elusive and mysterious underground chivalric Order?

"You'll understand," she explained after a moment. "It's pretty hard to believe what you're telling me. I'm sure you know that. And if I'm totally honest, I'm not sure I want to be connected to an ultra-secret society inside the Catholic Church."

She was cut short by a short chuckle from Saxby. "Have no fears on that account," he grinned. "You see, we're hardly fans of the Church ourselves."

"But you're a Church Order." Ava countered. "It's what the Templars are—a-dyed-in-the-wool papal army. It's in your DNA."

"Were." De Molay corrected her. "We *were* a Catholic army. Once. But do you really think the Order would stay loyal to a Church that threw it under a bus to save the skin of one minor medieval pope whom history has long forgotten?"

"Anyway," De Molay smiled. "The picture is a little more involved. You see, there may be some truth in the idea the Templars had moved on in their religious thinking, even before the crusades came to an end."

"Are you saying the king of France was right?" Ferguson sounded incredulous. "That the Templars *did* have secret heretical beliefs?"

"Well," De Molay looked genially across at him. "Heresy is a strong and judgmental word. It depends on your perspective."

Ava shook her head. "Forgive me, but it doesn't work that way."

"Go on." De Molay raised an eyebrow.

"There was no such thing as religious freedom at the time—you were a Catholic or a heretic," Ava continued. "As monks, the Templars had even less choice than most."

"Monks?" Ferguson sat forward in his chair. "I thought you said the Templars were soldiers. Knights."

"Knight-monks," De Molay clarified.

"Knights and monks, at the same time?" Ferguson looked unconvinced. "That sounds pretty contradictory."

"You're right," De Molay answered. "It was a radical idea—forged in the heat, blood, and uncertainty of the fragile early crusader kingdom. Once the First Crusade had conquered Jerusalem, the barons took the prime land, and the rest of the knights went home, leaving the new Christian lands largely undefended, and highly vulnerable to attack. The settlers urgently needed crack troops to defend them from enemies all around. So the Templars were born—religious warriors: half-knight and half-monk, ideologically committed to a Christian Palestine. On one level they were no different to any other medieval monks. They took vows of chastity, poverty, and obedience. They had chapels in their commanderies in the crusader states and all over Europe, where they prayed the monastic hours eight times a day, just like all other monks. But, when they weren't praying, the Templar monks didn't spend their days illuminating manuscripts or making cheese and beer. They trained relentlessly for war. And when it came, they crushed everything in their path. They were lethal professional warriors in an age of amateurs."

"But they weren't free to just change their minds about what they believed," Ava objected. "They were monks—part of the Church's religious fabric."

"And yet, many earnest and holy people drifted into heresy in medieval times," De Molay countered. "Joan of Arc, Jan Hus, Savonarola. Giordano Bruno, the Beguines and Beghards, the Fraticelli. The list goes on and on. And many others, like Francis of Assisi, Hildegard of Bingen, and Roger Bacon, lived dangerously close to the edge, under permanent threat of being hauled in and condemned." He paused. "And you must see that the pope's betrayal changed everything." De Molay appealed to her. "The knights had been among the most famous and powerful people in Christendom for two centuries. Yet as they burned, they knew their two main reasons for existence, the Church and the crusades, now had no more use for monks of war."

"So what did they become?" Ava asked.

"Well," De Molay frowned. "That's the mystery that has inspired a million myths. There are legends of our appearing throughout history, usually to avenge De Molay. One story says some of us fled to Scotland, where the excommunicated King Robert the Bruce provided shelter against our common enemy, the pope. It is said we fought alongside the

Bruce at Bannockburn against King Edward II of England in revenge for Edward's allowing the pope's men into England to interrogate imprisoned Templars."

"Apparently we built the enigmatic and esoteric Rosslyn chapel in Scotland, encoding our secrets into its walls in riddles which remain unsolved to this day. And in Scotland we also apparently founded freemasonry, which we used as a spy network to coordinate the Jacobite rebellions under the Old Pretender and Bonnie Prince Charlie in 1715 and 1745."

"Some have also seen our hand in the great English Peasants' Revolt, in which much of London was damaged, although the Temple area was mysteriously spared."

"And our revenge on France was apparently the French revolution, in which the kings of France lost their throne forever."

"Others have suggested it was Templar red crosses that flew proudly from Columbus's three ships, the *Niña, Pinta,* and *Santa Maria,* as they set off to discover the Americas. Apparently we sponsored his voyage, and gave him access to our old naval maps. We then established the United States on Templar and freemasonic values, with full independence of the state from the Church, guaranteed by the fact a great number of signatories to the Constitution and the Declaration of Independence were, or soon became, freemasons."

"And then of course," he sat back in his chair, strangely animated at the chance to speak openly about the Order's hidden life, "people say some of the knights' confessions to their inquisitors were true, and that we really did have secret esoteric rites, like worshipping an idol called Baphomet which could make crops grow and flowers bloom."

Ava felt she may never get another opportunity to ask. "So are any of these stories true?"

De Molay put his hands on his knees and tapped his foot a few times in thought. He smiled ruefully. "My ancestor, Grand Master Jacques de Molay, may have been old—but he was no fool. He saw clearly the Order was doomed, and knew he would be sacrificed on the pyre of the king of France's ambition to make his country more powerful than the Vatican."

"So as the end approached, he secretly charged fifteen of his most faithful knights with a critical mission—to be carried on for all time, underground. Entrusted with their covert orders, the fifteen fled the Paris Temple under cover of darkness the night before the king's men arrested all Templars in the land. The fifteen galloped across country to the port of La Rochelle on the west coast. There, they boarded one of the Order's ocean-going ships, weighed anchor, and sailed off into the night, and history—never to be seen again. The king's men hunted for them at length, but no trace was ever found."

"Were they the knights that fled to Scotland?" Ava asked, "to seek sanctuary with Robert the Bruce?"

De Molay shook his head. "No. They went ... elsewhere. As you can imagine, the knights felt the pope's betrayal bitterly. Jacques suddenly saw the medieval Vatican for what it was—a powerful machine, whose inner heart beat to the rhythm of European politics and not the gospels their priests read in church for popular consumption. He realized everything he and his men had given their lives for was empty. So he gave orders for the fifteen knights to do exactly what both the king of France and the Vatican had done—to reinvent themselves in a role fit for a new world without crusading."

"But what was the mission given to them?" Ava looked openly at De Molay, hoping her candour would inspire a similarly frank answer from him. "Where did they go? What has the Order secretly stood for during the last seven hundred years?"

"*Flamma fumo est proxima,*" De Molay answered enigmatically. "There's rarely smoke without fire, Dr Curzon. Although the king of France was largely unaware of it, his accusations of secret rites and esoteric knowledge were not wholly untrue."

Ava's eyes widened.

De Molay's eyes twinkled. "Let's just say the Orient has always been a mosaic of religious philosophy and belief—the crucible of so many of the world's great religions. Through long years in the Middle East, something of its ways rubbed off on the Templars. They came to know that the world was not as black and white as the Church had led them to believe."

"They converted to another religion?" Ferguson asked, amazed.

De Molay looked uncomfortable for a moment. "No. They were finished with organized religion. But you'll forgive me if I do not elaborate. We've been very candid with you. But some things are best left unsaid. For all of us."

Noting Ava's disappointed expression, he added benignly. "You now know more about us than any living person who is not part of our Order. I said I'd tell you who we are. I did not say I would, and indeed I cannot, give you every detail. And it's best for you if I don't. It will be a burden for you to keep silent about these things. But I hope we have given you enough to answer your questions for now."

"Well, maybe if I could just ask one more thing," Ava began, but was cut short by Max's voice coming through from the adjoining office, where he was still watching the monitors.

"The tracker's not moving any more." Max's heavily accented voice was calm and factual. "Our vans will be there in about thirty seconds."

De Molay and Saxby jumped up and ran through to the office, immediately followed by Ava and Ferguson.

Max punched a button on the telephone. "Bravo One this is Zero. Report status. Over." He directed the order into a small microphone stalk jutting off the complex-looking telephone control panel.

The telephone's speaker kicked into life. "Bravo One. Target is in car park and stationery. Over."

Max pushed the button again "Zero. Investigate with caution. Over."

There was a pause. Ava could hear van doors sliding open, and the unmistakable sound of weapons being readied.

After a moment, the voice came again over the sound of running feet. It was breathless. "Bravo One. Approaching the target. Standby. Over."

There was a long pause, before the voice resumed. Its tone was flat, the urgency gone. "Bravo One. Target abandoned. No sign of occupants. Over."

Max thumped the desk hard and swore under his breath as he pushed the button again. "Zero. Where's the flight case? Over."

Ava looked at De Molay. His face was ashen.

There was a pause before the voice came again. "Bravo One. Affirm the flight case is here. It's empty. I repeat. The flight case is empty. Over."

The words hit Ava like a physical blow. "Tell them to keep searching." She could feel a mounting panic. "We can't let him get away."

"Zero. Search the area." Max barked into the phone. "They can't be far. Bravo Two as well. Over."

Ava peered at the screen. "Where's that car park? Assuming they switched vehicles, where could they be heading?"

Max held a finger to the monitor, showing a large neo-classical building of some kind, with a maze of streets radiating off it. "The Victor Emmanuel monument."

A wave of hopelessness crashed over her. It felt almost physical. She knew the Victor Emmanuel monument. It was a traffic nightmare—a massive white marble folly around a hundred and fifty yards long, cut into a labyrinthine old neighbourhood at the base of the crowded Capitoline Hill. Dozens of roads radiated around it, feeding back into the crowded surrounding area, offering a limitless rat-run of traffic pandemonium.

She pushed the hair back off her face. "They're gone." She spoke slowly, her voice flat and dejected. "We'll never find them round there."

She was fuming. Malchus had this all planned. Even down to the change of vehicle.

De Molay looked over at Saxby. "What's Plan B, Edmund?" There was no mistaking the authority in his voice.

"We wait," the older man replied. "If Malchus tries an airport or border crossing, we'll know about it."

"I wouldn't hold your breath." Max cut in grimly. "The north of Italy has a hundred and one ancient paths across the mountains, carved through the clouds by generations of smugglers. They're all off the grid. And the rest of Italy is one long coastline with an infinite number of places to get a boat away. If they want to get out, they will."

De Molay turned to Max. "But that's going to take organization and time?"

Max shrugged apologetically. "I could get us out of Italy under the radar in a hurry if I needed to. So we have to assume they can, too."

Despite wanting more than anything for Max to be wrong, Ava knew instinctively he was right. The chances of Malchus allowing himself or his men to be tagged or picked up as they took the Menorah out of the country were next to nil.

"What now?" Ava asked, deflated. The Menorah was doubtless on its way to join the Ark in whichever safe place Malchus used for storing his most precious objects.

Her frustration was rising to boiling point. For all the power of Prince, DeVere, and now De Molay, no one seemed to have any idea where Malchus was holding the looted artefacts.

Saxby turned to Ava, the anxiety showing on his face. "It's best you leave Italy immediately, in case there are any wrinkles in smoothing out the mess at the basilica. We'll get you on a flight back to London this afternoon. We'll rendezvous there when I'm done. I'll contact you. For now, the most useful thing you can do is try to work out why Malchus has gone to such lengths to get the Ark and the Menorah, and what he plans to do with them."

Ava nodded silently.

She could not think of any better plan.

For now the trail was dead.

—————— · ◆ · ——————

# 78

*Undisclosed location*

THE WALLS OF the north-west room of the isolated house by the lake were bare, except for a large oil painting of an Elizabethan nobleman.

His face looked elderly, but keenly intelligent eyes shone from the age-worn face. His long white beard was sharply pointed in the fashion of the day, but his close-fitting black skullcap lent an air of austerity and asceticism. The small gilded plaque fixed to the bottom of the frame read simply:

IOANNIS DEE

1527–1608

LONDINENSIS[13]

Beneath the old man's gaze, Malchus had lit three tall black candles on great bronze tripods at each of the room's cardinal points. Their flickering flames cast a dull sallow light around them and onto the painting.

He had also hung a large silver thurible over the mantelpiece, with a block of smouldering charcoal inside it covered by a light dusting of white-hot ash.

---

13 John Dee, 1527–1608, London.

It had taken him an age to find a censer quite like it—but he finally had, from a discrete dealer in Budapest.

Like the more typical church thuribles, it was heavy solid silver with three long chains allowing it to be hung or swung. But it was not the usual lidded pot with fine decorative holes through which the sweet incense smoke could escape. Instead, it was capped with a diminutive smoke-blackened goat's skull, whose curling twisted horns and pinched face forged a cruel frame around the gaping black eye and nostril sockets.

He checked that everything he would need was assembled in the room, before taking a purifying cold shower and anointing himself with the remainder of the sacred Exodus oil of myrrh, cinnamon, calamus, and cassia.

When he was ready, he wrapped a freshly laundered black sheet around his waist, and entered the room from the south.

Taking the thurible down from its hook, he sprinkled a pinch of the *qetoreth* Temple incense onto the hot ashes. Within seconds, the pungent spicy bitter-sweet smell of the stacte, onchya, galbanum, and frankincense began streaming out of the goat's nostrils and vacant eye sockets.

Swinging the thurible gently as he moved, he walked slowly anticlockwise around the dimly lit room, pausing to genuflect at the guttering candles marking each point of the compass. As he passed through the four stations, he offered invocations at the four quarters to the dark Guardians overseeing his work.

Satisfied the space was properly consecrated, he picked up the silver metal case from among the small pile of objects he had laid out.

He flipped open the catches and lifted the lid.

Nestled inside, wrapped in black velvet pouches, were the seals he had cast in the woods. He had trimmed down the sprues and cleaned the excess wax off the edges so they were now smooth and unblemished.

*They were perfection.*

He lifted out the four smaller ones first. Carefully unwrapping them one by one, he laid them on top of their velvet bags.

He gazed at them reverentially, drinking in the sight.

The seals of power had not been reunited for four hundred years.

*Until now.*

He ran his fingers slowly over their raised markings, as if he were reading braille—feeling the forces that coursed within them.

He shivered with anticipation.

Picking up a rolled red silk rug, he unfurled it, laying it out in the dead centre of the room. He had measured it meticulously. The instructions were precise. It was exactly two yards square.

Next he took the four small seals, and placed them onto the rug in a square formation, one yard by one yard.

When satisfied with their arrangement, he turned to the wooden table he had placed in the corner. He had felled the tree himself last Samhain, then sawed the timber when it was dry. He needed to feel connected to the tree—to its life force, and to its death. In cutting it down with his own hands, he had sealed the necessary etheric bond between them.

The table was light, and still smelled of fresh timber. He had not varnished or painted it. He needed it in its raw natural state.

He placed the table down in the centre of the room so that each leg lay on one of the four small seals, channelling their energy upwards to the tabletop.

*Good.*

He gazed at the arrangement with satisfaction. The table was a yard square, and the legs were each a yard long.

It was exactly how it should be—a perfect cube.

These things mattered.

*All was correct.*

He glanced up at the sombre portrait of Dr John Dee looking down on him. He knew the Elizabethan magus would approve. After all, had he not written down the instructions all those centuries ago so others could follow in the work?

Inhaling a deep lungful of the incense, relishing the ancient sacred taste in his nose and mouth, he took up a pot of yellow oils and a brush, and began painting a series of complex angelic and demonic sigils on the table's untreated surface. He did not need a picture to copy. He knew the patterns by heart.

Once the invocations had dried, he bent low and solemnly lifted up the great *Sigillum Dei.*

He looked again with satisfaction at the multiple layers of messages encoded on its embossed whorls. It was an interlaced geometric marvel: a pentagram over a circle within a septagon within a septagram within a septagon within a circle divided into forty quadrants, all intricately labelled with the glyphs and symbols of the adepts.

*It was sublime.*

He laid the great seal carefully onto the table's surface, making sure it was in the exact centre, then covered it with a red silk tablecloth, precisely one-and-a-half yards square, so the silk completely covered the seal and hung down over the sides of the table, its long tassels almost brushing the ground.

He stared at the arrangement long and hard, looking for anything out of alignment.

But it was perfect.

Satisfied, he bent to pick up the crowning touch—the object that would sit at the apex of the energies channelled by the table of power—Dr Dee's great dark mirror of Tezcatlipoca.

The dullards in the British Museum still had no idea it was missing. There were no doubt hundreds of tourists a day ogling the impotent substitute Malchus had switched it for.

*Idiots.*

*Couldn't they feel the difference?*

How could they not know that one of the mirrors had been bathed in the hot sacrificial blood of young Aztec men, screaming as their hearts were ripped bloody and beating from their smashed ribcages? While the other was merely a plain slab of obsidian from a stonemason's yard.

Holding the sacred mirror over the table, he placed it in the middle of the cloth so it rested directly over the centre of the great seal.

Offering a quiet prayer, he stood back to admire his handiwork, drinking in the sight.

*It would soon be time.*

Taking up the thurible again, he sprinkled fresh crystals of qetoreth over its hot ashes. Wafts of the biting smoke filled the room as he began to intone the opening of the liturgy, *"Introibo ad altare domini inferorum."*[14]

His heart singing, he walked slowly around the table anticlockwise, censing his unholy altar, focusing on the Great Work he would accomplish there.

---

14 "I enter unto the altar of the Lord of Hell."

# DAY TEN

—————— · ◆ · ——————

# 79

*10b St James's Gardens*
*Piccadilly*
*London SW1*
*England*
*The United Kingdom*

AVA WOKE SLOWLY.

She felt disorientated at first, struggling to remember where she was.

Although she was rarely fazed by time-zones or jetlag when travelling, the first few seconds after waking were often confused.

On the table beside her head, the glowing red digital readout above the radio's matt white speaker told her it was 6:00 a.m.

She blinked fuzzily, unsettled by the strong sunlight creeping around from behind the heavy creamy curtains.

Brushing the hair out of her eyes, she realized she was in London, where the sun rose well before 5:00 a.m. in summer. After so many years in Africa and the Middle East, her body seemed permanently programmed to be closer to the equator, where the sun was never an early riser.

Looking round, she took in the familiar honey-coloured bookshelves and the pair of upholstered chairs. Her clothes from last night lay on them in a pile—she had been too tired to put them away.

As her mind cleared, she recalled arriving back from Rome late the previous evening.

The hot and overcrowded commercial flight had stood on the tarmac at Rome's Leonardo da Vinci – Fiumicino airport for one-and-a-half hours before finally taking off. She had spent the time praying the delay had nothing to do with the authorities trying to find her and Ferguson. But eventually the aeroplane had started moving, after the captain had sheepishly explained that engineers had been replacing his damaged seat.

When the wheels were up at last, Ava breathed a sigh of relief to be finally out of Italy, and away from the mess Saxby was hopefully clearing up at the Basilica di San Clemente.

She got out of bed and threw on a set of clean clothes, recalling that Ferguson had come back from the airport the previous night straight to her house.

He had wanted to be ready and waiting when Saxby called.

She padded into the light-flooded kitchen, and flicked on the kettle. While the majority of the world woke to the bitter aroma of coffee, she still preferred to start the day with the more subtle smoky flavours of tea. It was a habit she had carried with her since childhood.

Glancing through into the sitting room, she saw Ferguson had not made it to his bed. He was asleep, fully clothed, on the long sofa.

She stared at his face for a moment, surprised by how familiar his features were becoming.

As she looked at him, she was suddenly aware it had been a long time since she had let anyone sleep on her sofa.

With a jolt, she realized it had also been three days since he asked her to give him the time to prove he could be useful.

She had assumed the three days would pass relatively swiftly, and then she would be free of him—and, more importantly, of Prince. That had been an offer she could not refuse.

But now, without even thinking about it, she knew that quietly, over the three days, she had come to reassess that view.

It was not just that he had been useful. He genuinely had. She had to give him full credit for thinking of consecration crosses, and for piecing together the Foundation's freemasonic connections—whatever they might turn out to be. He was also the one who had got her thinking of the Mithraic *taurobolium*, and who had kept her focused after Drewitt's murder. She was finding it very useful to have intelligent company around. He helped her think more clearly.

But beyond that, she had also become aware that he had his own personal reasons for wanting to remain involved, and she needed to take those into account, too. He had begun to talk animatedly about what was happening, and it was plain he was getting in as deep as she was. Although his official role was as Prince's eyes and ears, she could clearly see he was now motivated by something stronger—more personal.

No doubt he still wanted to recover the Ark, and perhaps also the Menorah for the political reasons he had expressed to her back on the airfield in Qatar on that first day. But he now seemed to have a deeper, more personal interest, too. Having seen what Malchus's thugs had done to Lord Drewett, and after being at the receiving end of Malchus's brutality in Rome, he now gave all the indications of also having a few scores he wanted to settle himself.

All in all, she concluded, if he wanted to stay around and see this through, she was not going to object.

The kettle shut off with a click, breaking her thoughts.

Heading back into the hallway, she saw a free London tabloid newspaper had been pushed through the letterbox, and now lay on the Turkish rug covering her dark wooden hall floor.

A photograph of General Danquah stared up from the bottom of its front page.

Curious, she picked up the paper and took it back into the kitchen, where she spread it out onto the dark granite counter.

The headline read simply:

Danquah Beset By Travel Difficulties

She scanned the article with mounting curiosity.

It appeared that around the time she had been sitting on the tarmac in Rome last night, the Somali authorities had been turning General Danquah's presidential flight away from Mogadishu's revamped Aden Adde airport, citing irregularities in the filing of his flight plan. It seemed he had been forced to turn around mid-air and fly home again without ever touching Somali soil.

Is that what Saxby had wanted her to see, she wondered, when he told her to keep an eye on the story?

Had the Templars somehow used their influence to foil Danquah's lethal shopping spree?

Perhaps it was, she mused. It would certainly be consistent with De Molay's cryptic assertion that the Templars existed to make the world a safer place.

So was that what they did, she wondered? Wield their influence to pull strings from behind the scenes?

If so, she was not sure it made them an organization she wanted to be associated with. Few people would mourn the end of an African dictator's arms-buying trip. But it left open many questions about what else they may be involved in. Politics? Diplomacy? Finance? The legal system?

If they were some sort of self-appointed vigilante force, then who was to say that everything they did was for the common good? And who stopped them if they got it wrong?

She thought of the gossipy Roman poet Juvenal, whose thorny question about those in power was still as relevant as it had been two thousand years ago—*sed quis custodiet ipsos custodes*? But who shall guard the guards?

Checking her watch, she calculated it was 7:15 a.m. in Rome—an hour ahead of London—so it would be fine to call Saxby. She picked up her phone off the counter, found his number, and dialled.

He answered almost immediately.

"So General Danquah didn't make it after all?" she noted.

"Ah, you saw that." Saxby sounded pleased. "It seems a busybody Somali airport official spotted one of the questions on the General's flight plan had been incorrectly filled in. Something to do with the wake turbulence category of the aircraft and whether it had a heavy, medium, or light maximum take-off weight." He paused. "I don't understand all the ins-and-outs myself. But it seems these details are vital, and the Somalis are very strict with their paperwork apparently."

"Don't tell me," Ava hazarded a guess, "the long arm of the Foundation even extends to air traffic control in Mogadishu?"

"Something like that," There was now a more serious tone in his voice. "What's the point of power if you don't use it for your aims?" He paused. "I should be back in London later today. I'll call."

With that, the line went dead.

Ava put the phone back down onto the counter, and took a sip of tea.

If what Saxby had said was true, then the Templars were clearly an Order with extraordinary reach.

Taking a bite of a shiny red apple from the polished wooden fruit bowl, she was suddenly distracted by a flurry of sharp clicking sounds.

She cocked her head to listen.

It was coming in bursts, and sounded weak and tinny, as if it was being made by a cheap mechanical toy.

It stopped for a moment. Then it started again.

As she listened, trying to focus in its source, she was surprised to realize it was coming from the phone she had just hung up and put onto the counter.

Intrigued, she stepped towards it, and could now clearly hear its small speaker relaying the clicking noises of what sounded like someone typing in short bursts.

Baffled, she picked it up, and was surprised to see the screen was not locked, but fully awake and moving, displaying a live feed of Prince's head and shoulders.

The tall American was sitting at her laptop, obviously unaware of the real-time video stream beaming direct from her web-camera to Ava's phone.

Ava looked closely at the image moving slowly on her phone's screen, aware something about it was not quite right.

She stared at it long and hard, before realizing it was not the image of Prince that was wrong, but what her screen was displaying. Or rather, what it was not displaying, because she could not see the normal inset box showing the corresponding image of her that was being simultaneously beamed to Prince. That was standard on her video app.

Disconcerted, she put down her cup of tea and tapped the screen to pull up some options, but nothing happened. It continued to stream the video of Prince.

Perplexed, she hit the round home button to close the app down.

It made no difference. The image of Prince remained firmly on the screen, with Prince seemingly wholly unaware Ava was watching her.

Confused at why she was seeing a picture of Prince at all, Ava stared at the screen, bewildered how her phone came to be connected to the camera on Prince's laptop.

She had never accepted any requests to add Prince as a contact, and she had never even called Prince from her phone, let alone set her up in the address book. Even if she had jogged the phone when putting it down after her call with Saxby, or even if it had malfunctioned and randomly dialled someone from its address book, there was no way it could have found Prince, because Prince's details were simply not in her phone, in any form.

At that moment Prince looked up into her laptop's camera.

Her hard blue eyes were staring directly at Ava.

Ava flinched involuntarily, embarrassed by the unexpected eye contact. She had no idea how she would explain this.

But it never happened. Prince did not bat an eyelid, but merely continued typing and peering at her own screen with a slightly irritated expression. She seemed puzzled by something.

"What the ... ?" the American muttered. "Can't they get anything right?" She tapped a key on her laptop, and the picture on Ava's phone flickered then disappeared, only to be replaced with a live image of Ava that appeared to be streaming from her phone's camera. A moment later, the screen blacked out, and the live feed of Prince returned.

"Christ," she heard Prince mutter in irritation, frowning at her laptop's screen. "What's wrong with this thing?" She furrowed her eyebrows, clearly still unaware Ava was watching her. "How hard can it be?" She sighed in exasperation. "I said I want to see *her*, not me."

Ava again heard the sound of a key being struck forcefully. Then the image and sound cut out, leaving her phone screen completely black.

She reeled.

*Had she heard right?*

She felt a flush of indignation.

*Prince was watching her?*

Her mind whirring with the new information, she looked on with incredulity as the phone's black screen was replaced by a scrolling list of file names—line after line of white text flashing across the background.

It looked like the phone was dumping some kind of activity log. She had seen her computer do it before. But never her phone.

The titles of the files in the data dump were composed of six-digit followed by four-digit sequences, which she immediately recognized were sequential date and time stamps. From the .mov extensions at the end of the file names, it was immediately apparent they were video files.

As the list finished scrolling, a confirmation message appeared:

> GV5.SYS – ADDRESS D48S8J59
> PHYSICAL TRANSMISSION DUMP COMPLETE

> END TRANSMISSION LOG

> TRANSMIT OKAY

Ava felt the familiar hot prickle of adrenaline.

*What on earth?*

Had these files been sent? From her phone?

She put her finger onto the screen and swiped downwards, scrolling back up to the top. As the list sped backwards to the beginning, she was amazed to see there were over a hundred files.

They were in accurate date and time order, and as she arrived at the top of the list, she was stunned to see the date of the earliest file.

She looked at it more closely, frowning.

*It couldn't be.*

But there was no doubting it. There it was, unmistakable, in black and white.

The first file was dated the night she had arrived back in England from Dubai after the auction fiasco at the Burj al-Arab.

*The night she had met DeVere and Prince at Legoland*

Incensed, she tapped one of the files.

The video panel opened, and began to play.

The picture on the screen showed an indistinct expanse of white. But she recognized the voice immediately. It was hers.

*"It's the obverse, or front, of a papal bull. In the olden days, the Vatican sent riders all over Christendom with written orders and letters from the pope. The most important documents were called 'bulls'."*

She recalled the conversation immediately. It had been in her house— the night Drewett sent her the photographs of the medal. She had been explaining the significance of the images to Ferguson.

As the video continued, she heard his voice reply.

*"Like the animal?"*

Thinking back, she realized her phone must have been on the table in front of them at the time, where she usually put it when she was indoors. The white image was her ceiling, which the phone's camera had been pointing at.

Then there was her voice again.

*"Except the word comes from the name of the seal attached to the docu-ment—the bulla, from the Latin word meaning to boil."*

Outrage rising, she tried another file.

Again, it was her voice.

*"And why do you think Christ rises from the dead every year at the time of the spring equinox—exactly the moment when winter is over and the sun begins to be dominant again, bathing the earth in warmth and life. It's the oldest religious celebration of all."*

Although the screen was blank, the conversation was unmistakably the one she had with Cyrus and Ferguson in Cyrus's projection room.

She kept opening files until it became apparent all of them were videos of her conversations over the last few days.

It was clear her phone had been recording her.

Some of the files just showed blank or dark screens. Occasionally there was an image—usually of a ceiling or the inside of a bag or pocket. She guessed her phone was rarely pointing at something interesting when she was having a conversation. But the audio was invariably of her discussing something.

Suddenly it made sense.

Prince was tapping into her phone to hear what was going on. If it was interesting, she was recording it, and then sending herself a copy of the file.

That explained why there were so many files, and also why her battery had been draining so fast, like the afternoon of her run-in with Malchus at Stockbridge House, when she had tried to call Ferguson from the pub afterwards, but her phone had been flat.

Furious, she strode through into the sitting room, and saw to her relief that Ferguson was now awake

His face was crumpled, and she could see the last few days had taken their toll on him. She felt a fleeting pang of guilt for having given him the slip at Stonehenge.

From the quizzical look on his face, he had clearly caught on that something was wrong.

"You're not going to believe this," she fumed, tossing the phone to him, "Prince bugged me."

"What?" He looked bewildered.

"My phone. She's been remotely activating the video."

Ferguson sat up, fully awake now. "How can she do that?" He looked at the list of files on her screen, and scrolled down through them. "Jesus," he muttered, "I didn't even know you could do this on an iPhone."

"Clearly you can." Ava was incensed.

*How dare she!*

"I don't get it." Ferguson was tapping individual files, bringing up the videos. "How do you hack an iPhone? Did she send you an executable file?"

Ava shook her head, angry with herself. "She got me to do it for her."

Ferguson looked perplexed. "You hacked your own phone?"

Ava sat down, and breathed a long sigh as she realized just how easily Prince had played her.

"Before we went down to Stonehenge, she gave me a flash drive with the photos of Malchus and a cx file. I attached the flash drive to my phone so I could read the files."

"And you uploaded a hidden suite of spyware at the same time." Ferguson shook his head. "I'm impressed. We always underestimate her people." He put the phone down on a table beside the sofa. "Have you got the flash drive?"

Ava shook her head. "It splintered into a thousand pieces under one of your front wheels." She felt livid. "I had to destroy the files she passed me."

"Clever," he nodded grudgingly. "So she even got you to clean the evidence, too."

Ava let out another long slow breath. "It would seem so."

She had been half wondering whether he may perhaps have been in on it with Prince. Or at least aware of it. But from his reactions and expression, it was clearly all news to him.

"There's no need to look so impressed." She stood up. "It means we have to assume Prince knows everything we know. About Malchus, the Menorah, and even the Foundation. About every discussion we've had since I got back from Dubai."

Ferguson shook his head grimly. "This is going to complicate things."

"Well there's only one thing for it." She had reached a decision.

She stood up, and threw him his jacket, which was lying over the back of one of the armchairs. "Our American friend is in London. She said she was going to coordinate the U.S. angle from here. It's time you played the dutiful employee and met up with her to give her an update of our progress—and more importantly, to find out exactly just how much she now knows."

---

◆

---

# 80

*Regent's Park*
*London NW1*
*England*
*The United Kingdom*

AT EXACTLY 7:00 A.M., Ava slipped through the wooded Avenue Gardens gateway into Regent's Park.

The sweet smell of the flowers was heady, and the vibrant colours filling the manicured horticultural beds around her shone in the clear sunlight.

It was one of those days when the park was looking at its best.

Even though the various gates had already been open for two hours, there was barely anyone about—just a few determined joggers taking the opportunity to stretch their muscles before spending the day anchored to one of London's millions of desks.

She remembered once reading that in medieval times the parkland had belonged to Barking Abbey. It had been part of the monastery's possessions at Tyburn—a name infamous for the royal gallows which had operated there for six centuries, barely a mile to the west of where she was standing.

She shuddered at the recollection that Queen Elizabeth i had swapped the simple gallows there for the 'Tyburn Tree'—a large triple-posted scaffold for efficiently executing batches of up to twenty-four people at a time.

*So much for 'Good Queen Bess'*, she thought, as she moved further into the still park. It was a dark period in England's history, and Elizabeth deserved the title 'Bloody' equally as much as her half-sister, Mary.

Turning left and rounding a small ornamental stone fountain spraying cool clear water into a lichen-coated basin, she spotted a sign declaring Regent's Park to be one of the Royal Parks—eight square miles of nature that breathed as London's lungs, bringing greenery and air into the heart of the congested metropolis.

Prince had readily agreed to Ferguson's suggestion of meeting in the park. It was located centrally, and offered hundreds of places where they could walk and talk in privacy among its anonymous lawns, formal flower gardens, dense woods, and sprawling lakes. They were all largely secluded, and free from the risk of electronic surveillance or observation from vehicles.

Prince and Ferguson had arranged to rendezvous at 7:15 a.m., so Ava had a quarter of an hour to find a hidden observation post and get herself into position.

She headed across the springy green lawn in the direction of the Inner Circle.

Prince and Ferguson were due to meet by the small gate in the hedge opposite Park Street West, so Ava wanted to place herself in the trees about two hundred yards north-west of them. She had calculated that from there she would get a clear view of their meeting, and whichever path they chose to take.

Heading quickly to the other side of the lawn, she arrived at an area of dense trees that led eventually to the sunken open-air theatre. She settled herself down on a tree stump in a clump of evergreen bushes, and took out the compact military binoculars Ferguson had lent her.

Training them on the small gap in the hedge agreed for the rendezvous, she saw Ferguson arrive first.

She and Ferguson had split up a few hundred yards before entering the park, so he had walked the remainder of the Outer Circle by himself, just in case Prince or any of her colleagues were watching.

Ava wanted to stay well out of the way. This was to be Ferguson's meeting.

Prince did not need to know how closely he and Ava were now working together.

"Maybe we should go to the zoo when we're finished here?" he suggested jovially, looking around to try and spot Ava.

She heard him clearly though the small flesh-coloured receiver inserted into her left ear. It was undetectable to any passer-by, as was the direct audio signal it was receiving from the sensitive mini-microphone embedded into the winding crown of Ferguson's otherwise unremarkable black metal sports watch.

He had snapped the watch onto his wrist and given her the earpiece and binoculars before they had left the house. "Welcome back to the Firm. I'll need you to sign for these." he had joked. She could not help but smile. There were some aspects of the job she still missed—like the camaraderie of these operations.

Watching him now from across the park, she thought perhaps if circumstances were different she might quite like to go to the zoo, which was in an adjoining section of the park, not far from where she was sitting.

Or, she wondered, questioning herself more closely, was it that she would quite like to go to the zoo *with him*?

She immediately pushed the thought out of her mind.

Her life was complicated enough already.

Besides, she lived in Iraq. It had been her decision to move there, away from family and friends. She had taken it gladly, and would do so again in an instant. But just now, sitting in a calm and sensuous English park on a bright summer morning, it was tempting to think of what life might be like if she lived in England again. There was always her family's house in Somerset. She had long thought one day she would return there permanently.

"I've got eyes on." It was Ferguson's voice in the earpiece again. He was speaking softly now.

Ava looked back to where he was standing, as a tall woman entered the small gateway into the park.

She checked her watch. It was 7:15 a.m. exactly.

She recognized Prince immediately. Her long auburn hair was, as usual, tied back into an austere bun, and she was wearing a crisp white cotton shirt under a sober grey jacket and calf-length skirt. She had an elegant navy blue rain mac slung over one arm.

"So what have you got for me?" she asked Ferguson, nodding a greeting at him and shading her eyes from the sun. Her tone was businesslike. She was clearly in no mood for pleasantries. "What has our friend Dr Curzon found out about the Ark?"

"She needs more information on Malchus," Ferguson replied matter-of-factly. "He's not an easy man to find."

Prince started walking west, along the narrow path hugging the inside of the park's outer border, giving Ava a clear view of their route, only obscured every now and then by a tree. If they headed beyond the Wildlife Gardens and towards York Bridge, she might have to move, but that would be fine. The trees and bushes provided her with plenty of cover.

"Not even in Rome?" There was a heavy note of sarcasm in Prince's voice. "Do you want to tell me what that little jolly was about?"

Ferguson set off alongside her so they were walking abreast. "She knows he's collecting biblical artefacts. But she's in the dark about where he's keeping them. Or even why he wants them."

There was a pause, in which Ava could only hear the sound of their shoes on the hard dirt. "So you're not going to share with me what you've been working on, then?" Prince was clearly not happy at being given the brush-off. "There's nothing you want to tell me, for instance, about a group calling itself the Foundation?"

Ava smiled to herself.

That was good news.

Prince must have heard them discuss the Foundation, but clearly lacked further details.

"She didn't find any leads to the Ark in Rome, if that's what you're asking." Ferguson was playing dumb, as they had agreed.

"Look," Prince stopped walking and turned to face Ferguson, the trees casting a dappled shadow onto the two of them. "There are an increasing number of organizations joining this particular party." She paused, her voice striking a more sombre tone. "Dr Curzon is going to need friends like us if she's going to navigate her way successfully through this mess."

What happened next was so quick that if Ava had blinked, she would have missed it.

Without warning, Prince's body lifted a few inches off the ground, spun ninety degrees in the air, then slammed to the ground in a spray of red mist. With a split second delay, Ava heard a high-pitched zipping sound through her earpiece, ending abruptly in a wet thudding noise

She gasped in horror as she heard Ferguson's voice coming over urgently. "She's down!"

Ava could see that.

Prince was lying on the grass, her face in the dirt, her torso twisted at a right angle to her legs. But more disturbing than the odd position of her body was the six-inch gaping hole in the middle of her back, along with the sprays of blood and shreds of soft tissue spattered over her neat grey jacket.

It looked as if a tank shell had passed straight through her.

The American's expression was glassy and still. She had not had time to register any shock or pain before her entire system had comprehensively shut down.

Ava had never seen anyone killed by a sniper before, but she knew that only a round from a high-powered sniper's rifle made that sound and inflicted that kind of damage. One well-aimed shot was all it took, leaving behind the massive telltale injuries of a supersonic high velocity round that had torn and tumbled its way through soft body tissue.

As Ferguson's shout faded in her ears, Ava instinctively dived for cover, hitting the mossy ground as hard and fast as she could.

Until she knew what the situation was, she had to assume the sniper was still out there, and potentially taking aim again. For now she had no information on whether it was a targeted hit on Prince or a disgruntled Londoner taking out his rage on the public. In a big city, all options were open.

But whoever the sniper was, he clearly knew what he was doing. This was no Hollywood attempt to hit Prince between the eyes. It was just one well-aimed shot to the centre of the body mass. It was as professional as it got—and the results were visibly devastating.

Ferguson clearly had similar thoughts. Ava saw him reach down with lightning speed, then zigzag the five yards to the nearby fence separating the park from the Outer Circle. He was over it in an instant, and gone.

Ava glanced around, praying no one had seen him beside Prince when she had dropped. Although the park was virtually empty, he absolutely did not want to be connected to the murder of a senior U.S. intelligence officer.

Still on her belly, she rapidly scanned the south-east corner of the park where the shot must have come from, peering through the binoculars for any clue to where the sniper was hiding.

As she swivelled the binoculars around the park's periphery, she suddenly saw it—a tiny glint reflecting in the early morning sun.

Zeroing in the binoculars, she could see a grey ice cream hut in an empty children's playground. It was not yet open and serving refreshments, but she had definitely spotted something flash in its window.

Focusing her eyes back on where Prince was sprawled, she could make out a clear line of sight from the hut to the body.

She pulled out her phone, and punched Ferguson's number.

He answered immediately.

"Something moved in the ice cream hut, children's playground by the Avenue Gardens," she panted.

"I'm on it. You stay put." Ferguson hung up.

His watch was still transmitting, and she could hear the sound of him running. She could not see him yet, so figured he was approaching the hut from the back.

In under a minute, she heard his breathing quieten, then the slamming sound of a door being shoved open hard.

There was a moment's pause before his voice came over her earpiece.

"He was here. It reeks of cordite. But he's gone now."

Ava picked herself up off the ground and began jogging around the perimeter to Ferguson. It would have been quicker to go straight across the open lawn, but she had no way of knowing if the danger had fully passed.

She sped up, running faster, trying to work out who would want to kill Prince.

*Malchus?*

Unlikely, she reasoned. She was not even sure if Malchus had ever heard of Prince.

*The Foundation?*

They certainly had the skill and resources to pull it off. It would have been child's play for Max and his *Légionnaires*. And the Danquah affair showed the Foundation seemed unafraid to intervene in international affairs when it suited them.

But she could not think of a single good reason why the Foundation would want to kill Prince, still less in such a public, high-profile, and risky way.

Arriving at the ice cream hut, she found it was, in fact, a solid flat-roofed metal caravan on wheels, although it looked as if it had not been moved for many years.

The door was usually locked, but the dull chrome hasp was hanging open, and the padlock was gone. Whoever removed it had probably sheared it with bolt-croppers, then had the sense to take the evidence away.

Pushing the door open, she doubted very much anyone who was that careful would have left any traces or fingerprints.

This had been a professional job.

The hut would almost certainly be forensically clean.

It was warm inside, and stuffy from the hot air being expelled by the three chest freezers lining the back wall. From the tattered and faded stickers on their lids, it was clear they housed the stock of multicoloured ice creams and lollies dished out on sunny and rainy days to the capital's children and their long-suffering parents.

The rest of the hut was cramped, making it difficult to move. The wooden shelves on the walls overflowed with cardboard boxes of crisps. And most of the floor space was piled high with shrink-wrapped palettes of fizzy drinks.

She breathed in deeply. Ferguson was right. A gun had undoubtedly been fired inside the hut within the last few minutes. The smell was unmistakable.

He was looking at the small window, which was open a few inches, giving a clear line of fire to where Prince's mangled body lay about three hundred yards away. "I've already notified HQ she's been hit. They're sending a clean-up team, which will hopefully get here before the par-kies find the body."

Ava pulled the miniature receiver from her ear and put it into her pocket.

"What did you pick up from the ground beside Prince?" She had been baffled to see him waste precious seconds reaching down, when all instinct and training would have told him to get as far from Prince's body as fast as he could.

"This," he answered, holding out a slim silver mobile phone. "It fell out of her pocket as she went down." He already had it flipped open, where he had been scrolling through it while waiting for Ava. "I thought it might tell us something about why she was monitoring you."

He handed it to Ava, pointing at the screen. "What do you make of this?"

Ava looked at the small blocks of black writing on the screen. They appeared to be a series of text messages Prince had recently exchanged with someone whose name she had saved in her contacts simply as 'K'.

Ava read the exchange of messages slowly.

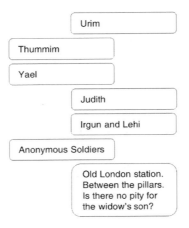

"Does any of it mean anything to you?" Ferguson looked at her hopefully.

She stared at the messages for a few moments, scrolling up and down, going over each line to try to make any connections.

"My God," she murmured slowly, as the light began to dawn.

*It couldn't be.*

But the more she read and re-read the texts, the more it seemed to make sense. "I don't believe it," she whispered.

"What?" Ferguson moved in behind her to look at the messages.

Ava breathed out heavily. "This explains why she was so hostile to my suggestions the Bible may not be a hundred per cent historically accurate. And why she dismissed any claims the Ethiopians may have to the Ark."

"Why?" Ferguson was peering at the screen.

Ava looked up at him. "The 'URIM' and 'THUMMIM' were two objects the high priest of Israel carried in his sacred breastplate—jewels, or wood, or bone, no one is quite sure. He used them for cleromancy—like 'yes' and 'no' dice, to tell the will of God."

She scrolled down. "And the next pair, 'YAEL' and 'JUDITH', are two women from the Bible. Yael saved Israel from military defeat by feeding the enemy general with milk, then once he had fallen asleep, she hammered a tent peg through his temple. Judith performed a similar feat by ingratiating herself with the enemy general, Holofernes, whom she then decapitated while he was in a drunken stupor."

Ava looked up at Ferguson. "Are you beginning to see a pattern yet? You know the next pair, right? The 'IRGUN AND LEHI'?"

Ferguson nodded. "Zionist paramilitary terror groups in Palestine in the 1930s and 1940s, fighting for a Jewish state."

"Right," Ava nodded. "And 'ANONYMOUS SOLDIERS' was their marching anthem."

"So how does that explain Prince's attitude to the Bible and the Ark?"

Ava looked pensive. "I'd say the senders of these messages have a strong interest in the history of Israel—and especially in its military successes. And that raises the likelihood of them belonging to one organization in particular."

"What, like AIPAC?" Ferguson suggested. "American friends of Israel?"

Ava shook her head. "I think it's more serious than that." She paused. "If her contact, K, is short for *katsa*, then our friend Prince has been leading a double life—with the Mossad."

"Christ." Ferguson muttered under his breath. "That's all we need."

Ava turned for the door. "We need to get out of here." She was through it in an instant, and jogging towards the gateway back to the Outer Circle.

Once out of the park and onto the noisy pavement, she took the SIM out of Prince's phone and handed it to Ferguson along with the phone unit. "Wipe our prints and lose these, separately—far away from here." Ferguson nodded as she hailed a black cab, incongruously spray-painted all-over with an advertisement for a beach paradise somewhere. She let Ferguson into the cabin, before climbing in herself.

"Drop me at the nearest tube station, please," she asked the driver, before giving Ferguson back the binoculars. "I haven't got time to get stuck in traffic. You can take the cab home, where you could start looking further into De Molay and Saxby and their story about the Foundation. See if the Templar angle really could add up."

"What about you?" he asked, winding down the window to let in some fresh air. "Where are you going?"

Ava smiled. "I'm going to follow up on the last SMS Prince sent to the *katsa*: 'OLD LONDON STATION, BETWEEN THE PILLARS, IS THERE NO PITY FOR THE WIDOW'S SON?'"

Ferguson rubbed a hand over his face as the cab pulled up outside a narrow flight of steps down into a tube station. "Don't tell me that means something to you?"

"Not to me," she smiled, getting out of the cab. "I'm going to ask the widow's sons themselves."

---

·◆·

---

# 81

*London Underground*
*London*
*England*
*The United Kingdom*

AVA HAD LEARNED long ago that some things had not changed in the century and a half since London's irrepressible Victorian engineers had put in the world's first underground railway.

It was still the quickest way to get around town.

The network's builders had taken a boundless pride in all aspects of their gleaming new project, ensuring it was the envy of the world—state of the art in functionality and style.

But as Ava looked around the starkly bare concrete platform, which had long since lost its bespoke glazed tiles and polished wooden finishings, she could not help but wonder what the Victorian pioneers would have thought of it now.

When the train arrived and she got on, she was greeted by an overcrowded worn and grotty interior. The saggy seats were covered in a drab threadbare orangey fabric, and the windows opposite her were graffitied with thin angular black writing, preserved for posterity under layers of grey dust.

It was clear the underground no longer needed to look attractive in order to guarantee the unending flow of customers that crammed into its four thousand ageing carriages every day.

She gazed into the middle distance, ignoring the distractions of the garish advertising posters plastered above the seats directly opposite her.

She was going over in her mind the thought processes that had brought her here, making sure she had not made any errors.

Time was critical, and she could not afford to take a wrong turn.

Not now Malchus had the Ark and the Menorah.

Back in the ice cream hut, she had reached some conclusions about Prince's furtive phone messages to K.

Most importantly, she had immediately recognized what the first six SMS messages were.

From the hours she had spent learning similar sequences, she was certain they were pre-agreed pairs of identification words—simple exchanges designed to enable agents in the field to single out their friends.

If her assumption was correct, it made decoding the sequence of SMS messages significantly less daunting, because the identification word-pairs had no meaning—just a purpose. There was no hidden message. They were purely functional.

They almost certainly meant nothing more than that whoever chose the words back in Tel Aviv wanted to reinforce the idea of a strong and combative Israel.

But what had struck her more than the symbolism of the word-pairs was the fact Prince and K had used three sequences. It suggested there was something unusually secure and confidential about their exchange. She could not tell whether it was the fact they were communicating or the content of the message, but either way, the two agents were displaying an unusually high level of caution.

Taken together with the militaristic tone of the word-pairs, it had reinforced her suspicion she was dealing with the Mossad. She could think of few other agencies which combined that level of thoroughness, paranoia, and aggression.

But as she had stood in the ice cream hut and looked down at the messages, the one that stood out the most was the last.

It was of a completely different character to the others.

OLD LONDON STATION

BETWEEN THE PILLARS

IS THERE NO PITY FOR THE WIDOW'S SON?

For a start, it was made up of full phrases.

And second, it had not elicited any response from K.

If she was right about the first three exchanges being identification pairs, then the last three lines were almost certainly the main message—the real reason for the entire communication.

At first she had been able to make no sense of the three lines at all.

She knew for certain there was no underground or railway station in London called 'OLD LONDON STATION'. She was sure of that.

She was also positive there was no old or disused station simply called 'LONDON STATION'. The abandoned ones were well known—like British Museum, Lords, and Trafalgar Square. She had never heard of one called 'LONDON STATION'.

But if the first line was baffling, the second and third were even more elusive.

Based on the strongly biblical themes of the identification pairs, she had pondered whether the phrases 'BETWEEN THE PILLARS' and 'IS THERE NO PITY FOR THE WIDOW'S SON?' might also be drawn from the Bible.

Perhaps 'BETWEEN THE PILLARS' was a reference to the Hebrew Nazirite, Samson—famous for his suicide attack on Gaza's great temple to Dagon?

According to the book of Judges, he had been standing between the temple's pillars when he unexpectedly pushed them over, bringing down the roof and the three thousand people on it, raining fatal chunks of masonry onto himself and the crowd of his enemies in the temple around him.

Like most of the heroic stories of the Old Testament, modern scholars viewed it as a symbolic tale rather than eye-witness history. Nevertheless, Ava had recently been fascinated to learn that excavations in the region had uncovered the fact that Philistine temples of the period did indeed have two central columns supporting the roof. Although she had also been interested to read that from their size, it would have taken an earthquake measuring high on the Richter scale to move them an inch.

Still, she was only guessing, and by no means certain that 'BETWEEN THE PILLARS' was a reference to Samson. It was a possibility. A guess. Nothing more.

Prince's third line—'IS THERE NO PITY FOR THE WIDOW'S SON?'—was equally enigmatic.

All she had been able to think of was the Bible story in which Jesus stumbled across a Galilean funeral procession outside the village of Nain. On learning that the dead body was the only son of a widow, he had brought the corpse back to life. It was the first of his three raisings of the dead, and was often described as the miracle of the widow's son.

But, as she had turned the idea over in her head, she instinctively knew she was on the wrong track.

The biblical references Prince and K had used in the identification pairs—the 'URIM' and 'THUMMIM', and 'YAEL'and 'JUDITH'—were drawn from the *Tanakh*, the Hebrew sacred scriptures better known in the West as the Old Testament.

So the story of the widow of Nain did not fit alongside them at all. It was from a different source altogether—the New Testament, which was a collection of unrelated Christian writings stapled onto the Hebrew scriptures by the Church many centuries later. Ava found it hard to believe Prince and the *katsa* would suddenly switch to Christian texts. It would make no sense if they were both working for the government of Israel.

She shifted in her train seat, trying to block out the noise of the scuffling school party of French teenagers that had just got into the carriage.

She had reached these conclusions quickly back in the ice cream hut. But as she had forced herself to think of all the possible angles, it had occurred to her there may actually be no biblical link at all to the three lines of Prince's actual message.

After all, why should there be?

The identification pairs were one thing.

Prince's message was quite separate.

Wracking her brain for other possibilities, she had at first drawn a blank, until something had begun to stir at the back of her mind.

It was a more radical thought, and not something she knew much about.

But as she had continued to puzzle over the message, it had begun to seem more and more worth considering.

*Freemasonry.*

It was not a connection she would normally have made. But it had popped into her mind as a result of Ferguson's revelations about Sir Robert Moray and the Invisible College and Royal Society, and Saxby and De Molay's hint that the Templars were somehow responsible for the secretive fraternity.

Knowing next to nothing about the freemasons, Ava had been intrigued enough to do some research while waiting at home for the car Saxby had sent to take her and Ferguson to the airport en route to Rome.

She shifted in her seat again. It was hot in the carriage, and the French teenagers were getting increasingly rowdy. Looking up at the tube map on the opposite wall, she was pleased to see she only had one stop to go.

Once she had started surfing freemasonry, she had initially been delighted by the amount of information she had been able to dig up on the shadowy brotherhood. But her pleasure had rapidly turned to frustration as she discovered the vast majority of the information was maddeningly cryptic and impenetrable—much of it raising far thornier questions than it answered.

She had rapidly understood that the information made little sense without certain keys, which she soon discovered were not available to the general public. In no time, she felt as if she was trying to watch a scrambled satellite television channel without the all-important decoding chip.

After several hours of research, she had come away wrestling with a baffling world of veiled allegories, symbols, and secrets surrounding the building of King Solomon's Temple three millennia ago.

But she felt none the wiser.

However, as she had looked at Prince's sms messages in the ice cream hut, she had been surprised to recognize that the three lines of message could easily be connected to the shadowy fraternity.

From what she had read, 'BETWEEN THE PILLARS' could have been a phrase lifted straight from a freemasonic text. Although she had not understood the reasons why, she had seen in her reading that freemasons attached great significance to the architecture of pillars and columns.

Taken by itself, this connection to freemasonry was tenuous.

But it was the third line—'IS THERE NO PITY FOR THE WIDOW'S SON?'— that had stopped her dead in her tracks and made her think of them.

Although the freemasonic website she had seen it on had been unclear, she was sure she had seen a reference to providing 'help for the widow's son'.

The words Prince had typed were a little different—'IS THERE NO PITY FOR THE WIDOW'S SON?' But she was nevertheless struck by the distinct similarity.

Overall, she had realized, a freemasonic explanation for the enigmatic combination of pillars and the widow's son seemed more promising than her first thoughts about Samson and the widow of Nain.

As she had hailed the cab with Ferguson, she also realized that following up on the freemasonic angle presented the perfect opportunity to find answers to something else that had been bothering her.

On De Molay's coach in Rome, Ferguson had asked if the Foundation was a front for freemasonry. Saxby had replied cryptically, "Well, yes and no. That is—not entirely."

Ava had been struck by his evasiveness, and wanted to ask more. But the conversation had quickly moved on, and she had forgotten about it until later that evening, when she had again been struck by quite how odd an answer it had been.

*What was he hiding?*

Was there some connection between the Templars and the freemasons that he was not prepared to talk about?

She was not at all sure.

But it was something she now urgently needed to find out.

Her thoughts were interrupted by the train slowing down as it pulled into Covent Garden tube station.

She hurried out of the carriage and headed for the elevators back up to ground level—and to the worldwide headquarters of the ultra-secretive fraternity of the freemasons.

---

$\cdot \blacklozenge \cdot$

---

# 82

*Freemasons' Hall*
*Covent Garden*
*London WC2*
*England*
*The United Kingdom*

EMERGING FROM THE dark red tiled exterior of Covent Garden's well-preserved Victorian tube station, Ava squinted against the bright morning sunshine.

She stepped through the automated barriers and onto the bustling pavement, and was immediately swept into the ever-present throng of tourists heading for the colourful street theatre and zany entertainers that had long ago replaced the calm of the medieval vegetable garden tended by the monks of nearby Westminster Abbey.

Walking quickly down Long Acre, she could already see Freemasons' Hall at the next junction, dominating the surrounding streets. It was a monumental pentagonal building, whose hulking nose nestled within the junction of Great Queen Street and Wild Street.

Crossing onto the small traffic island in front of its tip, she gazed up at its colossal Portland stone façade.

The main entranceway featured a large square-panelled door flanked by two vast columns, each rising to twice the door's height, before giving way to a deep entablature of three stepped cornices, all supporting what looked like an immense open bell tower.

It loomed inscrutably over Covent Garden like some outlandish ziggurat.

Despite the building's oddity, Ava could not help eyeing it appreciatively. The days were long past when people spent money on buildings of its quality. It was among the last of its breed—an art deco masterpiece, personalized by the freemasons with their own special lexicon of arcane architectural symbolism. She picked out multiple sets of columns and numerous groups of tripled features.

Tearing her eyes away, she hurried towards the entrance. Fascinated as she was by what archaeologists of the future would make of the curious building, she had work to do. She was not there to sightsee.

Now Prince was dead, time was ticking more urgently. The American's murder changed everything. The Pentagon would be all over the operation—as would Mossad, if Ava was right about K being one of its *katsa* agents. Files would be hitting senior desks already, and men in grey suits in corner offices would want answers and results.

It was going to hot up quickly.

Someone somewhere would know Prince had been monitoring Ava, so it was inevitable she would be picked up and hauled in for questioning sooner or later. The only real unknown was when and where.

But before she got dragged into an interview room in Legoland, there were things she first needed to find out. Like what Prince's final text message meant. And whether her assassination was connected to the Ark.

Reaching the tip of the formidable building, she climbed the shallow steps up to the great front door, flanked either side by large triple torches.

As she got closer, she was surprised to note that the doorway had no handle or bell. Peering more closely, she could now see that it was not meant as an entranceway. The large double doors looked as if they were permanently locked.

She shook her head, smiling to herself.

It was a good joke. She realized she would have been slightly disappointed if the world's oldest secret society had a front door.

Turning, she headed down the south-east side of the building, along Wild Street. But as she followed the wall around, she was surprised to find there was no way in here either—merely high windows and another set of smaller locked doors.

With increasing concern, she skirted the building's nose again, and this time tried the north-east, down Great Queen Street.

To her growing alarm, this side was also unwelcoming, with no obvious public entrance.

It was a long building, so she kept going, increasingly perplexed by how anyone got in or out. But as she caught sight of the Grand Connaught Rooms further down, she saw to her relief a set of sliding glass doors set into an ornamental stone doorway at the far end of the building.

Taking a deep breath, she headed for the discreet entrance. Crossing the large pentagram inlaid into the pavement, she entered.

She had never been to a freemasonic building before, and had no idea if she would even be allowed inside.

She half expected an alarm to go off, signalling that a woman had breached the outer perimeter. At the very least, she imagined walking straight into a surly guard who would turn her around and frogmarch her straight back out onto the street again.

In fact, as the glass doors slid shut behind her, she found herself in a vast and sumptuously decorated marble atrium with a grand and ornate double-switchback staircase at the far end. The decoration was breathtaking—an unspoiled gem of art deco interior design.

To her right, two uniformed men sat behind a highly polished antique wooden enquiry desk.

Looking confident, she walked over to the desk and addressed the man nearest her. She had no idea if he would be helpful or not, but she was at least going to try—it was why she had come.

"Is there someone I can talk to?" She glanced hopefully at the athletic-looking man—ex-police, she assumed.

Above his head, she could see an elegant old wooden board, hung with what looked like the timetable for the day—lists of lodges and what she imagined were the names and numbers of the rooms in which they were scheduled to meet.

The man looked up from his newspaper.

"What sort of enquiry, madam?" He was relaxed but alert.

She had been going over the story in her mind, and had no real idea if it would work. As there was only one way to find out, she took a steadying breath, and began.

"I'm from Rorschach and Partners—an old firm of notaries in Zug,

Switzerland. We've recently been engaged by a new client, and have come across an old document in the papers we don't fully understand. Strange as it may sound, we think we need help from someone who knows about freemasonry." She smiled a little awkwardly. "Is it possible to talk to anyone here who can help? Discretely, of course."

The guard nodded understandingly. He stood up, and passed her a form pinned to a shiny old Bakelite clipboard. "Fill this out, please."

She quickly wrote out her assumed name—'Kate Adams'—a contact telephone number, and a fake signature, before handing the clipboard back.

"Please wait here for a moment." The guard took the clipboard and form and disappeared into a back room.

Her training had drummed into her that the best cover stories were the ones closest to the truth. They were the easiest to remember, and there was no need for elaborate details that could be forgotten under pressure, or faked documents that risked discovery.

But to be convincing, even a simple cover story needed thought to flesh it out as credible and strong, and she had not had the time.

She had opted instead for second best—a cover that was plausible but hard to verify. One she could be tight-lipped about without arousing suspicion. She figured no one would expect to find details about a firm of notaries in green and sleepy Zug, where for the last fifty years the world's rich had been increasingly managing their affairs away from the public eye. It was not the type of business that had a website or glossy brochures.

She looked about the vast atrium, tapping her foot. The guard seemed to be taking a long time. She checked her watch. He had been gone six minutes.

She was about to ask the other guard if everything was okay, when the first guard reappeared from the backroom, nodding. "Sorry to keep you, madam. You're in luck—Mr Cordingly will see you."

Ava followed the guard's directions, and headed off down a grand corridor of shiny inlaid marble floors and glossy dark wood-panelled walls.

The air was still and heavy with the smell of floor polish. Geometric chandeliers hung discretely from the ornate creamy ceilings, casting a low light into the endless lengths of corridor. It was a very male atmosphere, and she could not help wondering how long it had been since a woman's shoes had walked down its dark hallways.

Stopping in front of the door the guard had described, she read the brass nameplate screwed neatly onto it:

MR L CORDINGLY
DEPUTY GRAND SECRETARY
UNITED GRAND LODGE OF ENGLAND

She knocked twice, the sound resonating deeply in the heavy wooden door.

It was opened almost immediately, just a crack.

"I need to be somewhere else, Miss Adams." The voice was polished, warm, and smooth—a man used to talking. "If you don't mind accompanying me as I walk, please tell me how I can help."

The door opened wider, partly revealing a tall alert man in a dark pinstripe suit.

He stepped through the doorway into the corridor, and as he did so, she got a full look at him, bathed in the gentle light from the small chandelier above.

As her eyes focused, her heart missed a beat at what she saw.

*His tie.*

While the rest of the world was awash with a kaleidoscope of patterned ties bought everywhere from railway stations to glitzy designer boutiques, a certain type of English gentleman could still be relied upon to wear a traditional striped or crested tie announcing his school, university, or regimental affiliations.

She continued to stare in disbelief at the neat strip of material around Cordingly's neck.

It was like nothing she had ever seen before.

It was plain black, ornamented in the centre with a large coat of arms.

The Latin motto emblazoned in a blue banner across the bottom was troubling enough:

AVDI VIDE TACE

which she quickly translated as 'Hear. See. Be Silent'.

She was unsure whether it was an observation, a command, or a threat.

But it was not the words that stopped her dead—it was the image itself.

The full achievement of arms, as her colleagues specializing in heraldry would call it, was a shield in the centre bearing the actual coat of arms, supporting figures left and right, and an object resting on top of the shield.

Her eyes skirted over the shield, which was unexceptional. It was charged with the usual array of stylized castles, chevrons, and lions that most old English organizations seemed to favour. It was more tasteful than many she had seen, enlivened with striking reds, yellows, and blues—or, using the quaint medieval vocabulary of heraldry: gules, or, and azure.

But what caught her eye and her breath were the two supporting figures standing either side of the shield—and the very recognizable object they were sheltering.

She peered intently, double checking she had seen it correctly.

She had.

From what she knew, heraldic supporters were typically lions, unicorns, bears, or other impressive beasts. Occasionally, they were people, or even plants.

But what she was looking at fitted into none of these categories.

They were angels—but not the chubby infant *putti* that decorators of chocolate boxes loved so much.

Their nude adult torsos were male, but the voluptuous faces, oval eyes, long eyelashes, pouting mouths, and flowing black hair rendered them unmistakably androgynous.

Each had a long wing raised high over the top of the shield, almost joining to create a feathered canopy protecting the object they sheltered.

"It's the crest of the United Grand Lodge of England," Cordingly informed her.

She looked up at his face, embarrassed to have been caught staring at the tie.

"The crest gives us a lot of trouble," he smiled, setting off down the corridor. Ava fell into step beside him. "If you look at it closely, you'll see the angels have cloven hoofs."

*Of course they had.*

It was one of things that had first caught her eye.

"Conspiracy theorists see it as proof we're devil-worshippers." He chuckled. "And they don't stop there. They say our eccentric American Brother Albert Pike's infamous writings confirm our Satanism, as do our links with the Illuminati. That's before we get into our supposed crimes, like murdering our Brother freemason Wolfgang Amadeus Mozart for spilling our secrets in his mysterious opera *The Magic Flute*."

He did not seem overly troubled by what people thought of him and his fellow freemasons.

"They're not just any angels." She looked at them again, trying to make sense of what they were doing on the heraldic arms of the freemasons. "They're cherubs, which the Bible tells us had cloven hoofs." She paused. "The most famous and beautiful cherub was, of course, the devil."

"Indeed." He threw her a sideways glance. There was a hint of interest in his eyes.

"But that doesn't make every cherub the devil," she continued, wondering why he had raised the subject.

*Was he testing her?*

"Just Lucifer," he nodded, continuing to walk purposefully down the corridor.

*Was he trying to tell her something?*

"Of course, to be technically accurate," she continued. "Lucifer was never a devil, or even evil."

"Oh?" He raised an interested eyebrow.

"How could he be?" She smiled. "He's a planet."

Cordingly turned to look at her with an expression of curiosity.

"In ancient Rome," she explained, "Lucifer was another name for the Morning Star, the planet Venus. The word Lucifer just means Light-Bringer—it's a direct translation of the Greek name *Phosphoros*."

"Centuries later," she continued, "early Christians found the mystical Hebrew book of Isaiah, which recounted opaquely how the Morning Star fell from heaven. The early Church artfully blended it with another Hebrew story, not in the Bible, which told how angels had rebelled and been cast down from heaven. So the Church wove these two tales together and spiced up the result by mixing in the attributes of other gods and demons like Satan, Baalzebub, Pan, and Mephistopheles. From all these different forces of darkness, they moulded the one 'true' devil—a worthy adversary for Christ and his new Church. In this syncretic melting pot, Lucifer went from being a Roman planet to the infernal Lord—even though the original Hebrew texts never mention Lucifer at all, and specifically state that the leader of the rebel fallen angels was called Samyaza."

Cordingly said nothing. He was looking at her keenly, unblinking.

She decided to press the point, anxious to see if he would be more forthcoming about the tie. "Don't people ever wonder how the devil can be a burningly beautiful angel, a cunning snake, an infernal monster, a lustful goat, a beast from the abyss with seven blasphemous heads, and a red demon with a pointed tail, all at the same time?"

Cordingly's eyes narrowed. "You seem to know an awful lot about it." His voice was more cautious now.

"Not really," she shrugged. "It just interests me."

Cordingly lapsed into silence.

If he had wanted to tell her anything, he had clearly changed his mind, and the moment had passed.

She wondered if she had gone too far. But she figured she had no option but to play it boldly. She had no idea how long he was going to continue talking to her, and she needed to make sure she got as much information as she could—from what he said, and from what he did not say.

She glanced back at his tie again, and at the other object on it that had so startled her when she had first seen it.

It was resting on top of the shield, where normally there would be a helmet showing the bearer's social rank under a crest of plumed feathers.

It was the last object she had ever expected to see on an English coat of arms—all of which were officially approved by letters patent from one of the four ancient Kings of Arms at the Royal College of Arms. Nothing got onto a coat of arms without justification. She could only imagine the conversations that must have been had in order to grant the object to the freemasons on their crest.

She gazed at it again, not quite believing her eyes,

*The Ark of the Covenant, glowing with an inner radiance.*

A shiver ran down her spine.

She had come to Freemasons' Hall hoping for a clue to help her decipher the strange text message Prince had sent to her Mossad *katsa*. But instead, within minutes of arrival, she found herself staring at an image of the Ark—the object that had been propelling her across continents for the last ten days.

She fumbled for a moment, trying to make the mental connections.

Had Prince been telling the *katsa* something about the Ark? Who had it? Where to find it? Why it had been taken? Was there an underlying freemasonic connection? Was that why Saxby had been so hesitant in answering Ferguson's question about the Foundation and freemasonry?

Looking towards the end of the dark corridor, she felt a sudden pang of vulnerability.

She was in an unfamiliar building with a man she did not know, inside the cavernous headquarters of a group known for its implacable secrecy—and, she now knew, with a major interest in the Ark.

She could not help wondering if she had just walked into some kind of trap.

As she followed Cordingly deeper into the building, she could feel her pulse quickening.

She did not mind the adrenaline. It was good—it kept her sharp. But she needed a cool head if she was going to find answers to the meaning of Prince's text message. And her best hope was the man walking beside her.

She could not afford to bungle this.

With the metal tips of his shoes ringing out on the marble floor, Cordingly turned into another virtually identical corridor.

They passed an open set of double doors with a small brass knocker in the shape of a square and compasses. As she glanced through the doorway, she found herself looking into one of the most peculiar rooms she had ever seen.

It was square, with walls of lightly striped soft pink and green stone rising to an ornate domed ceiling looking down over a large black and white chequerboard carpet. Around the four edges of the carpet, comfortable red-cushioned antique chairs were arranged in rows, separated by three grand wooden thrones. One had a sun carved into its intricate high back, while another had a moon. She could not make out what was on the third.

Cordingly saw where she was looking, and quickly pulled the doors closed.

Under any other circumstances, she would have had a dozen questions about such an intriguing room. It did not look Satanic, she had to admit, although it was plainly for something unusual.

But she was not there to get distracted.

Focusing back on the reason she was in the building, she turned to Cordingly. "Why do you have the Ark of the Covenant on your crest?" She tried to keep the question casual sounding.

He paused, choosing his words carefully. "Freemasonry places a great emphasis on King Solomon's Temple—the building, and the people who created it." He touched his tie, as if to reinforce the point. "The Temple was, of course, built to house the Ark—so the Ark has always been an important," he hesitated, trying to find the right words, "symbol for us."

It sounded like a weak explanation, and from the expression on his face, he knew it. "According to a leaflet I saw at your front desk," she countered, "freemasonry was only founded in AD 1717. So how can there be any connection with King Solomon's Temple, which dates from around 957 BC, if it ever existed?"

Cordingly smiled briefly. "You are discounting the possibility that freemasonry is older than it looks—or than we openly acknowledge."

She shot him a quizzical glance.

"Take this coat of arms that fascinates you so much." He indicated the crest on his tie. "It's medieval—traceable to at least the 1400s, to the London Company of Stonemasons. If you'd looked at the leaflet closely, you'd have seen the wording is very precise. It says freemasonry 'announced itself' to the public in 1717. As I'm sure you will appreciate, that leaves wide open the possibility of a secret existence for many centuries before that. After all, there are clues."

"Like what?" Ava asked, her curiosity piqued.

"You may not witness a pebble being thrown into a pond," he replied, "but you may come across the ripples that tell you it happened."

Ava had spent most of her professional life interpreting just such ripples. "So what allows me to connect the medieval London Company of Stonemasons to King Solomon's Temple?"

Cordingly smiled. "I'd start with the gothic arch if I were you."

"In architecture?" Ava wanted to hear this.

He nodded. "European stone masons flocked to the Holy Land during the crusades, and they learned the techniques of pointed arches from the Muslims. When the stonemasons returned to Europe, they bought the new technology back with them."

Ava was unimpressed. "If that's true, it's only a link to the medieval crusades. You've still got another two thousand years to get back to King Solomon's Temple."

Cordingly closed another partly open door as they walked past it. She thought she saw another black and white chequerboard carpet inside.

"Well, what if some of the crusaders lived on the site of King Solomon's Temple in Jerusalem? And what if they used armies of European stonemasons to build their castles and palaces? What if those stonemasons dug down into Temple Mount for stone, right into the remains of King Solomon's Temple itself?"

Ava could feel her mouth growing dry.

*Another connection.*

"When you say crusaders," she asked slowly, "you're talking about the Knights Templar, aren't you?"

Cordingly flushed. His demeanor changed immediately. He hesitated, then answered hurriedly. "I'm not sure of the details. Anyway, this small talk is not why you came here today."

It was obvious she had hit a sensitive area. She could see he looked uncomfortable. The polite move for her now would be to back off. But she needed answers, and this meeting with Cordingly was possibly her only chance.

She tried another angle. "Wasn't the Templars' battle flag black and white, like the chequerboard carpets in the rooms we've been passing?"

"I don't know," he brushed the question away. "I'm really not an expert on these things."

Ava was becoming increasingly unnerved by his growing reticence.

She not sure how any of what Cordingly was telling her fitted in with Saxby, the Foundation, Malchus, Prince, or the Ark—but she had the strong sense a number of currents were beginning to converge.

She also could not help feeling she was nearing the far edge of the shallows, and any minute now the coastal shelf was about to drop away to very deep dark waters.

———————————————— • ◆ • ————————————————

# 83

*Freemasons' Hall*
*Covent Garden*
*London WC2*
*England*
*The United Kingdom*

THE DEPUTY GRAND Secretary of the United Grand Lodge of England led Ava into a wide and elegant two-storey room. It was built in the same lustrous marble and polished wood as the long corridors they had just passed through, but was laid out as a library and museum.

As they hurried through, she tried to look into the enticing mahogany display cases set at regular intervals. But she barely had time to take in any of the exhibits, and only caught a fleeting glimpse of Sir Winston Churchill's aging apron, and a collection of miniature wooden squares, compasses, and other freemasonic objects carved from bed bunks by Allied prisoners of war.

"So, Miss Adams," Cordingly's tone was more formal now. "I understand your visit is a professional one, on behalf of your firm."

Frustrated that he had been so tight-lipped about the Templars, Ava hoped he would be more forthcoming about Prince's message.

She pulled a square of paper from her pocket, and unfolded it to reveal a set of geometric symbols.

She held it out for him to see.

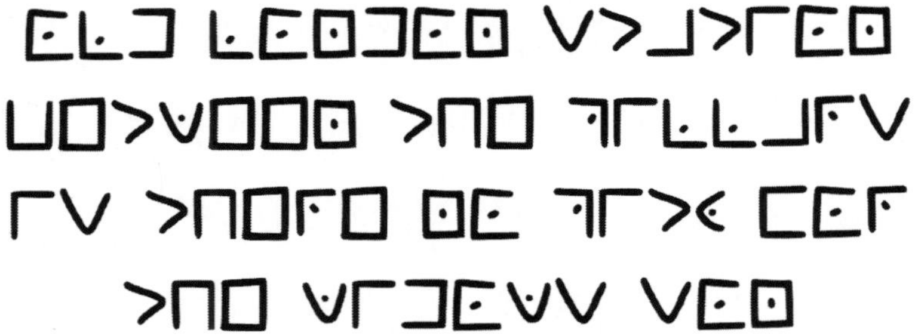

"One of our clients recently lost a patriarch who had led the family for thirty years," she began. When we opened the strongbox of deeds and legal records entrusted to his executor, we found this document filed away with the other papers."

Cordingly took the sheet from her, pulling a pair of slim silver glasses from his jacket's top pocket. He scanned the page briefly, before taking the glasses off again.

"It's the Freemasonic Cipher." He looked unimpressed. "It hasn't been a secret for several centuries. You can find it in most elementary code-books. You really don't need me or anyone else in this building to tell you about it."

Ava thought she heard a note of bitterness in his voice. Or was it disappointment?

"So we were right," she continued. "It's definitely freemasonic?"

He nodded. "Freemasons used it centuries ago, and so did our good friends the Rosicrucians. The seventeen-hundreds were dangerous times, and brotherhoods like ours required secure ways to communicate."

He looked at the paper again. "It was a good code back then. But the world is more sophisticated now. I rather suspect a twelve-year-old today would have few problems solving it."

Ava was perfectly aware of what it was—an extremely primitive substitution cipher. She had scribbled the symbols onto the paper herself while in the underground carriage in the hope of giving a plausible excuse for visiting Freemasons' Hall.

"All you have to do," he continued brusquely, "is draw two noughts and crosses grids then two X-shaped grids. Together they give you twenty-six segments in which to write out the letters of the alphabet in sequential order. To distinguish the second of each pair of grids, you put a dot in each of their segments. That's it. You now have twenty-six distinct and identifiable shapes to use instead of the twenty-six letters of the alphabet."

"Yes, we got that far," Ava confirmed. "We were able to decipher it pretty quickly. It reads: 'OLD LONDON STATION. BETWEEN THE PILLARS, IS THERE NO PITY FOR THE WIDOW'S SON?'"

She paused for a reaction, even a flicker—hoping the references to 'THE PILLARS' and 'THE WIDOW'S SON' would mean something to him.

His stern expression remained unchanged. "If you were able to decipher the message by yourself," his tone was testy, "then what do you need us for?"

"We wanted to be sure it was freemasonic," she explained. "So I'm very grateful for your confirmation. But more importantly," she glanced down at the paper in his hands, "we hoped you might help us with the meaning, which our research suggested could also be freemasonic. We can't make any sense of it." She looked at him hopefully.

As they were talking, they drew near to a tall display cabinet, its glossy wooden frame glowing under the light of the delicate chandeliers. Inside, she could see a collection of pictures and photographs of famous freemasons. She was surprised to recognize so many—Isaac Newton, Christopher Wren, Voltaire, Mozart, Goethe, Conan Doyle, Oscar Wilde, Bakunin, Mark Twain, Robert Burns, Walter Scott, Houdini, Edmund Burke, Kipling. Hogarth, and a wealth of U.S., British, and other statesmen and soldiers. There were dozens of familiar faces.

Cordingly stopped suddenly and wheeled around, frustration and anger clouding his face. "Let's not waste any more of our time, shall we, Miss Adams? Or should I say, Dr Curzon? So let's stop pretending. Why are you really here?"

Ava heard her name like a slap. It caught her off guard, and she struggled to keep her face expressionless, barely registering his question.

He waved an arm over his head, indicating the scale of the vast building around them. "Don't be so surprised, Dr Curzon. And, if you'll permit me, don't be so naïve, either. Our brotherhood has survived in various guises for many centuries." His voice dropped lower. "I should've thought it was obvious we are careful."

Ava was still reeling from having her identity exposed so starkly. *How could he have known?*

There had been no security—no request for her identity. And the name she had given the guard downstairs had been false. It was simply not possible that Cordingly could know who she was.

She replayed a mental film of her arrival at the building, reliving how she walked down both its sides before entering the glass doors and speaking to the security guard.

As she focused on remembering, her eyes settled on the tall display case of pictures and photographs behind Cordingly. There was a small dog-eared card attached to it. Only half reading it, she saw it requested viewers not to touch the glass.

With a sudden surge of realization, she understood. "The guard." She looked accusingly at Cordingly. "He checked me at security."

Cordingly nodded almost imperceptibly.

"The Bakelite clipboard," she continued. "He took a set of my prints from it."

Cordingly blinked slowly.

She took it as a 'yes'.

"Dr Curzon, we have friends who help us. We have no choice, you understand, because we also have enemies who would hurt us. Our survival does, at times, require certain measures."

She was not sure what he meant by that.

*Was he threatening her?*

She could feel the alarm bells beginning to go off in her head.

She was deep inside a building belonging to one of the world's most shadowy organizations. Her identity had been compromised, and she had been caught lying to them. For all she knew, they had murdered Prince, and laid a trail for her to walk right into their lair.

She was confident she could take care of Cordingly if things turned ugly. But she had no idea who else was in the building—or how to exit quickly if she needed to.

He fixed her with a hard stare. "However, Dr Curzon, I don't believe you're one of our enemies." He handed the piece of paper back to her. "But you have lied your way in here, and I'd appreciate an explanation."

Glancing out of the window to clear her head, Ava was acutely aware her options were now very limited.

If she made up another story and continued trying to bluff it out, she would be moving forward blind, risking a wrong move which could land her in even more trouble.

Without needing to think it through any further, she knew her best chance in the circumstances lay in total honesty.

Now was no time to start improvising.

She nodded slowly. "Okay."

Cordingly raised his eyebrows in an expectant gesture, clearly keen to hear what she had to say.

"You'll appreciate that for security reasons I can't share all the details with you," she began. "But the coded message is linked to something of great historical and political importance, which is currently attracting the interest of a growing group of international intelligence agencies." She paused, noting his granite expression. "I'm sorry for misleading you. But a number of people have already been killed in connection with this affair, and the message could be an important piece of the jigsaw."

He pursed his lips, weighing up what she had said. "You do know how far-fetched that sounds, don't you?"

"More far-fetched than the Deputy Grand Secretary of the freemasons pretending not to know anything about the Knights Templar?" She returned the rebuff.

Two could play at that game.

He ignored her. "I don't suppose you have any proof of your story?"

"Look," Ava countered. "You asked for the truth. I've given it to you." She held out the piece of paper again. "Can you help me or not?"

He sighed and took it from her. "I don't know what you want from me, but the second and third lines of the message do mean something. Quite a lot, in fact."

Ava felt a wave of relief.

He handed her back the piece of paper. "But I'm afraid that's as much as I can tell you. You see, freemasonry may not be a secret society any more—if it was, you wouldn't know we even exist. But we do definitely have things we do not discuss openly. And I'm sorry to say that these are among them."

Having come this far, Ava was in no mood to be brushed off. "I assure you this is something you would want to help with." She looked again at the Ark on his tie.

"I'm truly sorry," his expression was sombre. "I'll tell you this much—it's not an X-marks-the-spot map, if that's what you were hoping."

Ava could feel her chances of discovering anything useful slipping away. "People are dying, Mr Cordingly."

He started walking again, his shoes echoing on the glassy floor. "Come with me," he called over his shoulder, leading her into a wide ornately decorated atrium.

Following him into the grand atrium, she did a double take at the extraordinary sight that greeted her.

At the far end was a vast rectangular art deco casket of burnished brass and bronze, set on its front and sides with bold figures. An ethereal glow from a spectacular stained glass window immediately behind it illuminated the lustrous metal, bathing it in mellow dappled reds, blues, and yellows. Framing it all perfectly, the altar was flanked by two monumental marble pillars, each supporting a dramatic cluster of lamps.

It was a shrine.

Ava paused, overwhelmed—incredulous that such a grandiose and unspoiled 1930s chapel could be hidden away in this secret building, unknown to tourists and guidebooks.

"It's a memorial." Cordingly dropped his voice. "In fact, this whole building is a shrine, dedicated to the generation of freemasons cut down in the First World War. The casket is the spiritual nerve-centre of this whole building—peace through sacrifice: a lesson we've learned many times in our long history."

It was one of the most extraordinary memorials she had ever seen.

His voice softened. "I'm sorry people are dying. But it happens every day. If I tell you what those last two lines mean, I'll be betraying the oaths and values that we have kept for centuries, which brothers have died for."

"That's a bit dramatic, isn't it?" Ava did not follow his train of thought. She indicated the memorial. "These men didn't die for freemasonry. They fell in the First World War, like millions of others."

"Yes and no," Cordingly replied. "Freemasonry is a philosophy—standing for equality and tolerance, and the things that unite all people. When freemasons fight for freedom, they are also fighting for their most profound beliefs."

He contemplated the altar thoughtfully. "You may think our secrets are silly and pointless. Or perhaps you think we are occult and dangerous. But we treasure our values. Many freemasons have made the ultimate sacrifice for them."

He gestured at the room around them. "This shrine is only a memorial to those cut down in the First World War. It says nothing of the many killed in other conflicts—like the thousands of freemasons put into Hitler's death camps for their membership of the Craft. Here, in this place, we remember them all."

Ava's eyebrows shot up. "Hitler persecuted freemasons?"

Cordingly nodded grimly. "They were targeted along with all those the *Reich* deemed dangerous or deviant. The Jewish tragedy was shared by a great number of others. Many people forget that the majority of those executed by Hitler were not Jewish. We often overlook the millions of other innocent civilians liquidated on ideological grounds for their race or beliefs—Poles, Slavs, Soviets, gypsies, Catholics, freemasons, homosexuals, the handicapped. It's a long and tragic list."

"Why freemasons?" Ava asked with incredulity. "What did Hitler have against them?"

"It's obvious really," Cordingly replied. "The Nazi state rested on the idea that certain races are biologically and culturally superior to others. Our freemasonic teaching is the polar opposite. We believe in the fundamental equality of all people. The Nazis therefore saw our beliefs as a dangerous and deviant heresy. As a result, many brothers were imprisoned and killed for their 'degenerate' beliefs. But our Order stood firm. We did not bend or buckle."

"I had no idea," she answered quietly.

"So, Dr Curzon, I'd help if I could. Truly. But I will not betray my promises. I'm duty bound to keep them—to the living, and to the dead."

This was not at all what Ava had wanted to hear.

"For what it's worth," he continued. "I don't think the message would mean much to you anyway. For a start, the first line is not freemasonic. And the last two lines, even though they have a freemasonic meaning, are not coherent when put next to each other in this way. I'm not at all sure myself what the whole message means."

The words hit Ava like a blow.

For all his reticence, Cordingly no doubt understood the message as well as anyone could. So either he was not being honest with her, or she had to face the possibility she may have made a mistake. Maybe it was not freemasonic? Perhaps there was another angle she was missing?

As they passed through the Memorial Hall and into another glossy marbled corridor, he stopped outside a numbered committee room door.

"I'm sorry I can't help further." He reached into his pocket and pulled out a leaflet. "There's a floor-plan of the building on the back." He handed it to her. "Follow this corridor all the way down and then left, and the map will show you how to get to the exit."

She nodded her thanks.

*A brick wall again.*

"Just one more thing," she asked, deflated. "If you knew I tricked my way in here, why did you agree to see me?"

He placed a hand on the door handle, before answering slowly. "Actually, it was your work in Baghdad."

She was no longer surprised at what he knew about her. His database was clearly plugged in where it mattered.

"Are you aware there are no freemasonic lodges in the Middle East?" He pursed his lips thoughtfully.

She shook her head. It was not the sort of thing she had ever thought about.

"There were once." He looked back down the corridor at the dappled and colourful light coming from the shrine. "We used to be a global brotherhood. After we unveiled ourselves here in Covent Garden in 1717, Britain spread our beliefs throughout the empire, and all over the world. There were thriving lodges across Europe, the Americas, the Middle East, Africa, and Asia. You could find us from Chicago to Cairo, and Karachi to Kuala Lumpur."

He looked solemn. "I had hoped maybe your visit here today might directly or indirectly reveal there was again freemasonic activity in the Middle East." He shrugged. "So we're both disappointed."

He held out his hand to shake hers.

"The secret handshake?" she smiled ruefully, as she felt his hand wrap around hers.

His eyes twinkled, but there was nothing out of the ordinary in the warm handshake he gave her. "I'm sure you think us foolish, with our handshakes and secrecy. But one day the world will recognize our contribution to the tolerance and civilized liberal values at the heart of what is best in Western thought. We've been around in one form or another for centuries, and our loyalty is our strength. Enemies of our beliefs have tried to bring us down many times. But none have ever succeeded. The Church's Inquisition failed to break us, and so did the twentieth century's dictators. Whether we are kings or paupers, and we are both and more—we stay silent and true. Even the ruthless agents of the KGB learned nothing when they tried to penetrate our ranks during the Cold War."

He nodded to indicate the interview was over. "Good luck, Dr Curzon. I hope you find your answers. You can keep the map."

But Ava was no longer listening. A panel of floodlights had just flashed on in her head.

*The map.*

*The KGB.*

*Of course!*

She kicked herself.

She could not believe she had not seen it before.

She turned on her heels and run back down the echoing marble corridor, shouting a hurried goodbye to the startled man watching her disappear into the palatial depths of one of London's least-known buildings.

—————————————— • ◆ • ——————————————

# 84

*Brompton Road*
*South Kensington*
*London SW7*
*England*
*The United Kingdom*

AVA WENT OVER the message again in her mind:

OLD LONDON STATION

BETWEEN THE PILLARS

IS THERE NO PITY FOR THE WIDOW'S SON?

*How could she have been so blind?*

She continued to kick herself as she headed away from Freemasons' Hall and towards the underground station.

The answer was so obvious, and had been staring her in the face all along.

It was pure espionage history—just the sort of thing Prince and the *katsa* would have used.

*And she should have recognized it.*

'LONDON STATION' was not a railway or tube station. It was another kind of station altogether.

*A spy station.*

And not just any spy station. 'LONDON STATION' was the infamous name the KGB used for their elaborate London operations during the Cold War.

It was 'old' because the KGB no longer existed. In the new modern post-*Glasnost* Russia, it was now the Federal Security Service, the *Federal'naya Sluzhba Bezopasnosti*. The Kremlin apparatchiks said the old days were gone and it was now a fresh organization for a new era. But all watchers of the Former Soviet Union knew nothing had changed. It was still the same people in the grim Lubyanka building, plying their grisly trade.

Despite Cordingly's assertion that he immediately recognized parts of Prince's phrase, she had begun to have doubts when he said it was not an "X-marks-the-spot map." It had made her seriously consider the possibility the message did not have any connection with the freemasons.

Because if Ava was now right, that was precisely what it was: a map giving the *katsa* directions—almost certainly to a dead letter box, where she suspected Prince had left something valuable.

She should have twigged straight away, because Prince was not referring to just any dead letter box.

It was the most famous one of all.

Ava remembered being taught about dead letter boxes during her training back at MI6's centre at Fort Monckton. At first she had thought it all sounded amateurish and melodramatically cloak-and-dagger—largely irrelevant in the modern world of hi-tech gadgetry. She imagined there must be a hundred and one cleverer and more efficient ways to pass data covertly in the computer age.

But that was before her instructors had split the students into teams to set and uncover their own dead letter boxes. It was only then she learned how difficult they were to identify.

She and her fellow students quickly became expert in how to take multiple forms of transport to 'clean' off any pursuers before visiting their dead letter boxes. And they were shown how to set pre-agreed signs to indicate when the box was full and needed clearing—anything from the number of plant pots on a balcony to the way a newspaper in a public rubbish bin was folded.

On joining her first desk, she had rapidly seen how effectively dead letter boxes really worked in hostile territory. She quickly understood why they had stood the test of time so well. Their simplicity, anonymity, lack of reliance on gadgetry that could malfunction or be discovered, and their ultimate deniability, were unbeatable.

She raced out of South Kensington's confusing underground station, and rushed northwards.

The KGB's main dead letter box in London was legendary. She and her fellow students had all smiled when they were told about it. But they soon realized it was an inspired idea.

It was in a large building with an infinite number of dusty corners. People of all nationalities came and went at all hours, seven days a week, and they moved about it at their own speed, kneeling and standing as they pleased. And none of this behaviour ever raised any eyebrows.

It was a perfect place for hiding information.

She emerged onto Cromwell Road by the leafy twelve-and-a-half-acre site of the Victoria and Albert Museum—the heart of London's Albertopolis. With around a hundred and fifty galleries filled with decorative arts and thronging crowds, it was a supremely anonymous place.

But she hurried past it, to the smaller building next door.

Built around twenty years later, its pollution-encrusted Portland stone façade meant it could easily have passed for an extension of the museum. But the towering statue of the Virgin Mary high over the porchway gave it away instantly as something else.

It was a Catholic church—a rather grand one.

Ava ran through the iron gate fencing it off from the busy street, and pounded up the six shallow stone steps to its portico.

There were three sets of heavy doors into the building, and she made straight for the nearest one. As she approached, she caught sight of the wooden board screwed to the wall to its right. It displayed the times of mass, and she was surprised to see the fathers of the Oratory still offered a number of daily services in Latin.

She knew it was the first Catholic church to have been built in London after Catholicism became legal again in the mid-1800s, but she had no idea it was so old-fashioned. Even the pope rarely said mass in Latin any more.

It was clearly a very traditional place.

As she pushed open the heavy door and entered the cool of the dark building, she paused to take in the sight.

When she and Cyrus had explained to Ferguson that Christianity was an ancient Roman mystery religion, still largely unchanged after two thousand years, she realized she should just have brought him here.

The church was cavernous, larger than most cathedrals, heavy with neo-classical art and statues. So much so, it looked as if it had been carried stone by stone from ancient Rome. With a little imagination, she could have been in the Roman Pantheon, where the old rites to the pagan gods had eventually given way to the new state religion of Christianity.

As she entered, diagonal tunnels of bright light from the circular windows in the roof pierced the immense gloom, increasing the drama of the ancient scene inside.

The first thing to hit her was the smell. It did not seem to come from anywhere in particular, but to have been impregnated into every inch of the decorated ancient walls, the big-eyed statues, and the gilded portraits of heroic saints hanging in agony and ecstasy.

It was a rich sweet and spicy scent—a heady mix of incense, candle smoke, and polish, recently topped up by the cloud of frankincense and myrrh lingering thickly over the high altar from the mass that had just ended.

The handful of people who had attended were now shuffling towards the doors—some stopping in side chapels to light candles or rub the toes of saints in whom they trusted.

She knew what she was looking for.

The 'pity' of the widow.

It was a common statue in Catholic churches—usually known by its Italian name, the *pietà*. She knew exactly what it would look like. They were always the same—a distraught young mother cradling the mutilated corpse of her executed son.

She thought back to Prince's message.

The clue she had missed was the word 'pity'. She could not believe she had not spotted it sooner. Prince's message read 'IS THERE NO PITY FOR THE WIDOW'S SON?' She had remembered that the freemasonic phrase was 'is there no *help* for the widow's son', but assumed the difference had not been important.

It had.

Prince's message had not been freemasonic at all.

The widow, Ava was now sure, was the Virgin Mary. According to ancient Church traditions, Mary lost her husband young. Although the Bible did not explicitly say Joseph died, it never mentioned him again after Jesus' childhood, and the theologians of the early Church quickly concluded Mary had been widowed.

Ava scanned the church for the *pietà*.

The amount of art ornamenting the building was overwhelming, but as she moved down the south side of the nave, she finally saw it—a wide marble statue behind an iron railing. It was about ten paces in front of her, obvious to anyone walking towards the high altar, just as it had been throughout the Cold War.

It was larger and grander than she had expected—a dramatic and poignant interpretation of a parent's desolation at the violent death of a child.

As she drew closer, she could see the side chapel it was tucked into was dedicated in gothic letters to Saint Patrick.

The dark recess was dominated by a high ornate altar bristling with oversize candlesticks. Above it hung an overbearing triptych featuring a golden painting of the grey-bearded patron saint of Ireland, dressed as a bishop. To the right was a bank of guttering candles, lit by the faithful hoping for intercession.

She remembered how Professor Duffy, one of her palaeography tutors at Harvard, always enjoyed telling incredulous Irish-American freshmen that Saint Patrick was not remotely Irish, but actually from England. They listened in horror as he explained Saint Patrick's connection to Ireland only came when he had the misfortune to be kidnapped by Irish raiders and carried off as a slave to their green wet and windy island.

It had opened her eyes to the myths surrounding the thousands of saints—many of which she discovered were shockingly inaccurate. Like when, years later, working in Jordan, she had discovered that Saint George, the bombastic patron saint of England, had never even set foot in the continent of Europe, let alone England. Born and brought up in Palestine, he never travelled further west then Turkey, where he was decapitated.

Looking around, she could see that people were still milling about after the mass. To avoid drawing attention to herself, she dropped some coins into the rusty metal box bolted loosely under the rickety candle rack, and stood in line to light a candle.

When the side chapel had cleared, she was finally able to approach the *pietà*.

It was a luxurious statue, carved from a block of creamy-grey marble. As she had expected, it was a classic arrangement. Mary sat, grief-stricken, cradling Jesus' broken body—her face hidden, her neck bent in sorrow.

By contrast, Jesus' face was rendered in fine detail. Gazing at it, she questioned, as she often did, why artists insisted on depicting him as a lanky well-muscled long-haired and bearded northern European. She wondered how western history might have been different if religious art had been more ethnically accurate. It would have shown him as a small olive-skinned short-haired and clean-shaven man—more identifiable with the faces on the streets of the Middle East than Scandinavia.

As she neared the *pietà*, she could see a long list of names inscribed on the wall behind the statue. Across the top it read: 'DULCE ET DECORUM EST PRO PATRIA MORI', which she immediately recognized as the famous line, 'It is sweet and noble to die for your country'.

On the black-and-white-checked marble floor were inlaid the words 'CONSUMMATUM EST', Jesus' traditional dying words, 'It is done'. Beside the lettering, she spotted the years '1914' and '1919' marbled into the floor, and realized that for the second time that morning she was looking at a memorial to the fallen of the First World War.

She had long ago realized that England was a country where the war dead were everywhere. The losses England had suffered in the conflicts of the twentieth century were still a defining part of the country's national identity.

Focusing back on the *pietà*, she knew the KGB's infamous dead letter box had been somewhere around the statue, but as she examined it critically, taking in the folds of carved fabric and the angles of the bodies, she could not see any obvious places to hide or retrieve anything. There were no cavities on the front or sides, and it was physically impossible to reach behind the statue, as it was set too far back from the protective iron railing.

Nevertheless, she was sure she had not made a mistake. This *had* to be where Prince had left the information for the *katsa*.

Stumped, she took a step back, and looked at it afresh.

*What was she missing?*

That's when she saw them—a pair of monumental pillars standing to the left of the *pietà*.

Looking around the church, she could see each of the many side chapels had a similar pair of pillars, flanking its entrance off the main nave. They were colossal structural columns, hewn and polished out of dark-veined marble, supporting the vast ceiling arches that covered each side chapel.

*Was that it?*

*Was that what Prince meant?*

She had been assuming that 'BETWEEN THE PILLARS' had been referring to the church's architecture in general. But perhaps Prince had meant exactly what she had written. Maybe the drop she had arranged with the *katsa* was not behind the *pietà* itself, but was quite literally 'BETWEEN THE PILLARS' next to the statue.

As far as Ava could see, it was the only place that anything could be hidden.

She moved closer, her eyes fixed on the pair of columns.

As she neared them, she could make out to her relief that they were spaced far enough apart for someone to reach an arm into the gloom between them.

Even though their square stone bases almost touched, there was a narrow gap running between them, and another to the rear between their bases and the wall. Either space was easily large enough to hide something small.

She needed to move quickly—to find whatever was hidden there, and get back to Ferguson. Whoever had murdered Prince was still on the loose. Until she knew who it was, and why they had targeted Prince, she had to assume she and Ferguson were also on the list.

But as she took the last few steps to the pillars, she could see a major problem developping.

A twenty-something man in a fawn corduroy jacket was talking to a stocky black-cassocked priest with an incongruous shock of scruffy blond hair. The man had pulled a small book from his pocket, and was pointing out a passage to the priest. The two were deep in discussion. And they had moved to stand directly in front of the pillars.

There was nothing she could do. They were blocking any chance she had of searching around the base of the pillars.

Whatever conversation the two men were having was too hushed for Ava to hear, but as the visitor in the corduroy jacket flicked to a different page and pointed to another section of text, it was clear he was asking the priest for an explanation about something.

She watched for a few moments, hoping they would finish or move on, but it soon became clear the two men were settling in for a long discussion.

She was going to have to do something.

Glancing directly across the nave to the north side of the building, she could see another priest standing in one of the side chapels opposite her.

With the germ of an idea forming, she made straight for him, briskly crossing the forty paces of the nave and heading into the candle-cluttered chapel prominently dedicated to the Sacred Heart of Jesus.

The waxy-skinned priest there was now placing a scarf-like stole around his neck, leaving it to hang down in front of him. It was an intense violet, slightly dulled with age, and heavily embroidered in gold threads with crosses and *Chi Rho* motifs.

As she approached, he moved towards the doors of an ornate mahogany confessional box set against the chapel's dark west wall. The cubicle was covered with intricate carvings, and topped with a large wooden dome that reminded her of illuminated medieval manuscript images of Jerusalem's churches.

There was a small carved doorway in its front for the priest to enter. But unlike in many films, where the earnest heroine sat in the darkened box, separated from the priest by a thin wooden lattice, pouring out her guilt into the shadows, here there was no second door.

Instead, the box was flanked either side by lumpy faded floral floor cushions—so parishioners could kneel on the ground and speak to the priest through the dark wooden grilles cut into the box's sides.

Confession here was clearly very public.

Ava shuddered. Despite the beauty of the woodwork, it looked like an instrument of humiliation.

Arriving in front of the priest, she was still thinking quickly.

"Excuse me, Father," she started, guessing that was how to address a priest here. "Are you hearing confessions now?" She had no idea whether priests heard confession in the middle of the afternoon. But it was worth a try.

He nodded. "For the next thirty minutes." He indicated for her to kneel on one of the floor cushions.

She pointed to the priest with the scruffy blond hair over by the *pietà* statue. "Can I have him?"

"Father Xavier?" he asked, glancing across at his colleague.

He was the only other priest in the building, so she nodded.

"I'm afraid that won't be possible." He sounded put out. "I'm on duty." He pointed to the name stenciled in gold letters above the cubicle's doorway: 'F. BLOUNT'. "I assure you, I know how to hear a confession." He indicated again for her to kneel. "I've done it once or twice before, you know."

She carried on, aware she needed to be quick. "Father Xavier knows my situation. I spoke to him last time … ." Her voice trailed off. She had no idea if she was allowed to pick a priest for confession.

"It doesn't work that way." He was sounding irritated. "Any priest can hear confession. It's all the same to God."

"I'd feel more comfortable speaking with him," she continued. "It'll save going over things again."

He was clearly not used to being questioned. "If you want to say confession, I'm the duty priest."

She could see she would have to force the issue. "Then I'm sorry for having troubled you," she did her best to sound sincere. "I'll just see Father David at Saint Rose's this evening. He knows me."

The priest looked exasperated. "Do you have the faintest idea how many confessions we hear in a week?" He glared at her. "I'm sure your situation is very interesting, but with no offence intended, I doubt very much Father Xavier remembers you." His expression left her in no doubt just how much this conversation was annoying him. "Please." He indicated the cushion again.

As she began to walk away, she could sense his indignation following her.

She had not gone more than a few paces when she heard the sigh of exasperation.

"Very well," he called after her. "There's no need to go anywhere else." He sounded as if all was far from well. He plainly did not like changes to routine. But she assumed it did not look good turning people away. "Please wait here."

She watched as he headed across the near-empty nave towards the twin pillars by the *pietà*. She could see him interrupt Father Xavier, and explain the situation to him, pointing across to her.

Aware time was short, she darted quickly under the arch leading east into the next side chapel, and walked swiftly down through the remaining chapels to the far end of the church.

Moving as fast as she could without attracting attention, she crossed the hard marble floor in front of the high altar to get back to the south side.

Glancing to her left as she passed the elaborate sanctuary, she noticed two oversize gold seven-branched Menorah candleholders flanking the high altar—each glittering from the guttering candle burning on its central spike.

Seeing them there, she felt a hot flush of anger at the reminder of her failure.

As she arrived back at the south aisle of the church again, she ducked into the row of side chapels and archways that would lead her back up to the *pieta* from the other side.

Hurrying along the interconnecting corridor, she noted that this section of the church was distinctly more feminine.

She first entered a luxurious chapel to the Blessed Virgin, complete with a regal statue of Mary atop a towering altar, her body swathed in a cape of real woven gold. Striding through without stopping, she passed into a chapel dominated by a painting of Saint Mary Magdalene.

Having the two chapels side by side struck her as presenting a neatly simplistic view of women—the faithful mother and the sensual courtesan. But she knew that the archetypes they represented—maternal and erotic love, life, and death—ran deep in the human psyche, and featured prominently in many religions. As a curious teenager, she had been amazed to learn that in ancient Greece and Rome, sacred prostitution was an ordinary part of religious life.

Sex and religion were no strangers. Even the Bible mentioned male and female prostitutes serving in King Solomon's Temple in Jerusalem.

She hurried on.

Arriving back in front of the twin pillars, she could see that the young man in the fawn jacket had moved off, and the two priests were now over by the confessional box. Father Xavier was kissing the heavy violet scarf that had been around the other priest's neck, and putting it on.

Aware this was now her chance, she dropped to her knees on the hard floor, and thrust her hand deep into the gap between the square stone bases of the two shiny pillars,

It felt gritty, as if it had not been cleaned in a long time.

Reaching the end, she had to stretch right around the pillar in order to brush her fingers along a similar void running behind the columns. She tried her left arm first, sweeping her fingers along the dusty space behind the right-hand pillar.

She was crouching low, relying on the array of heavy pews filling the nave to keep her hidden from the two priests on the other side of the church. But she knew they would quickly spot her if they looked closely.

She continued to grope for whatever it was Prince had left.

*An envelope?*

*A package?*

But she could not feel anything.

It was empty. There was nothing there.

She felt along the dusty gap again.

Still nothing.

Turning, she pulled her left arm out and tried with her right, this time behind the left pillar.

She could see the two priests looking about with an air of bewilderment—wondering where she had gone.

It would not be long before they noticed her.

She focused all her efforts in concentrating on what she could feel in the darkness behind the pillar. Extending her index finger, she ran it carefully along the tight space between the pillar's base and the wall.

Again, there was nothing except more grit and grime.

She began to wonder if she had made an error, but quickly dismissed the idea. She could not have made a mistake a second time. The dead letter box interpretation of Prince's message made complete sense.

*It must be here.*

She pushed out of her mind the idea the Mossad agent may already have cleared the box, or that a cleaner had moved whatever had been there. Or even the possibility that some espionage obsessive had found it while visiting the church on a Cold War pilgrimage.

She felt around again, willing something to be there. She desperately needed whatever Prince had left.

She had no other leads.

She glanced over at the confessional again. The priests had seen her, and were now heading back across the church towards the *pietà*. Father Xavier looked pleasantly bemused beneath his mop of blond hair. The other was scowling deeply.

Desperately, she leant in further, jamming her shoulder harder into the narrow gap between the pillars. Prince had been tall, with long limbs, so her reach would have been long,

She stretched her arm as far as she could, stabbing in the dark with her fingertips.

Finally, she felt her middle finger brush against something smooth. It was not cold like the stone of the pillar base, and felt more regular.

The priests were now in the middle of the nave, only ten yards away.

She tried to pull the object towards her, but it was just too far out of reach.

Wincing with pain, she rammed her shoulder harder into the space between the pillars, and straightened her arm to extend her reach another few fractions of an inch.

She raked at the object with her nail, feeling beads of perspiration beginning to break out with the strain.

Hooking it with her middle finger, she tried to slide it toward her. But she could not get a grip on it.

Glancing up anxiously, she could see the priests getting closer. It would only be moments before they were upon her.

Just as it seemed as if the object would never move, she suddenly felt it slide a fraction closer to her.

Concentrating for all she was worth, she got a nail under it, and managed to sandwich it between her index and middle fingers.

Pinching it tightly, and blocking out the pain in her shoulder, she quickly pulled her arm back and looked with elation at what was in her hand.

She recognized the small rectangle of millimetre-thick black plastic immediately. It had no maker's name on it, but the nine tiny silver teeth on its underside were unmistakable, as was its one diagonally clipped edge.

*An SD memory card.*

The storage device was so small and thin she could easily have missed it.

Shoving it deep into her coat pocket, she stood up and ran quickly to the exit, just as the priests arrived back at the *pietà*.

As she pushed through the double doors and out into the noisy world of London cars and taxis, she threw a glance back into the calm candle-lit church one last time to see the bewildered priests staring after her with incomprehension.

---

## 85

*10b St James's Gardens*
*Piccadilly*
*London SW1*
*England*
*The United Kingdom*

ARRIVING HOME CLUTCHING the slim plastic SD card as if it was one of the Crown Jewels, Ava found Ferguson at the dining table, hunched over his laptop.

She waved the data card at him in triumph. "Special delivery for Mossad."

He smiled with amazement as he stood up, "How on earth did you find that?"

"You wouldn't believe me, even if I told you," she beamed back, heading into the study.

He followed her through into the book-lined room, where she inserted the small plastic card into a slot on her computer, before flopping down into the chair.

"Now, what was so important it had to be passed on to Tel Aviv?" she muttered, as the screen came to life revealing the contents of the flimsy plastic card to be a single unnamed folder.

Ferguson moved in behind her, peering at the small icon that had appeared on the large flat-panel monitor.

Remembering the Trojan that Prince had planted on her phone, she scanned the card thoroughly for concealed code.

It was clean.

As she clicked on the folder, it opened to reveal six bulky files of images.

The first file began with an image of the buff outer cover of a manila folder. It was unlabelled, save for a large alphanumeric catalogue number stencilled above the distinctive flaming torch and deep blue atom-ringed globe crest of the U.S. Defense Intelligence Agency. It was the same crest Ava had seen in Qatar on the files Hunter, Prince, and Ferguson had been reading when they first summoned her.

Scrolling through the images, it was instantly apparent they were all concerned with one particular subject.

"Is this the DIA file on Malchus? The one Prince showed you?" she asked Ferguson, without taking her eyes off the screen.

He nodded. "But she only gave me extracts. There's way more material here."

Ava continued scrolling through the images. There was no way of knowing if the SD card held the full U.S. records, but as she opened all six files, she calculated it was at least six hundred pages long—a thick dossier by any standards.

The reports were filed chronologically, starting with the details Ferguson had recounted to her. Just as he had said, the ageing close-typed pages charted Malchus's rise through the ranks of the black market crime gangs in Dresden, before he came to the attention of the ever-vigilant Stasi, who then launched him on his new career.

She tore her eyes away.

As much as she wanted to find out everything there was to know about Malchus, to gain any insights into what made him tick and what he could be planning, she could read the history later.

For now, she needed information on his current activities.

"Prince was a dark horse." Ferguson was still gazing over her shoulder at the screen. "If she was Mossad, it seriously widens the field of who might have wanted her dead."

"Including the Americans, if they knew," Ava offered the unpalatable thought. "Another high-profile trial of a U.S. intelligence officer passing secrets to the Israelis might have been an embarrassment too far for the suits in Washington and Virginia."

"Probably better than life as a traitor in a U.S. federal facility," Ferguson added grimly.

Flicking directly to the end of the file, Ava was pleased to see that it included more recent entries.

She hit a button on the keyboard, and the high-speed printer beside the desk began to hum, churning the file out into its tray.

As she scanned through the more recent documents, she was relieved to see there was nothing identifying her or referencing the encounter in the Basilica di San Clemente. It was possible Prince had removed certain documents from it, but with any luck it simply meant that Prince's people were still some way behind piecing together what was actually happening.

As the images flashed across the screen, she recognized the cx report on the Stonehenge rally that Prince had slipped her after their frosty meeting at Legoland.

Arriving at the most recent material, it became clear Malchus had no intention of letting his life be minutely catalogued by surveillance teams. He had been playing the game a lot longer than they had, and it showed. The U.S. agents had been able to piece together little more than a hazy portrait of an elusive man who was meticulous in avoiding routines or patterns.

As she flipped through the pages, she was astonished to see the Americans were even unaware Malchus had been visiting Stockbridge House. There was no mention of the country mansion at all.

Most disappointingly, there seemed to be no clues to where Malchus was currently based. All the U.S. watchers had uncovered were a series of discreet hotels and guesthouses he used in the outer reaches of London.

Quite evidently, none of them looked like somewhere he would hide objects the size and value of the Ark and the Menorah.

Ava could feel the disappointment beginning to mount.

As she neared the end of the file, her eye was suddenly caught by one of the few grainy photographs they had managed to snap.

She paused, surprised, unsure what to make of the long-distance rain-lashed shot of Malchus meeting Lord Drewitt at Beaconsfield Services—a drab roadside rest area on the uninspiring stretch of motorway between London and Oxford.

She paused, startled to see the two men sitting together.

She had assumed Malchus was only using Drewitt for the safety of his country house—a parasitic relationship ensuring him a secluded base in the country away from prying eyes.

But the photograph showed the two men poring over a clutch of papers spread out on the half-empty motorway restaurant's plastic table.

They were plainly working on something.

Together.

She wracked her brains for what Malchus could need from the Master of All Hallows College, Oxford. The prickly old don was an economist, not an expert in biblical artefacts. He was definitely not a political sympathizer. And she doubted very much he shared any of Malchus's darker occult interests.

She saw again in her mind's eye the image of Drewitt's mutilated body, and felt a renewed wave of guilt and anger towards Malchus.

Reaching the last page, she leant back in her chair, lost in thought, contemplating the two main questions posed by the sp card.

*Why had Prince wanted to pass the information to Mossad?*

*And what had Malchus and Drewitt been working on together?*

She had no answer to either question. She would read the full file later, and maybe the answers would become apparent. But it would have to wait. For now, Prince had unknowingly given her the lead she needed.

Standing up, she looked over to the printer, where the last section of the file was dropping into the tray.

"Some light reading for the journey," she announced, scooping up the pages. "Pack a bag. We're paying a house visit."

Ferguson raised an eyebrow.

"Judging by this," Ava flicked through the still-warm printed pages, stopping when she got to the photo at the service station, "Malchus was working on something with Drewitt. We need to find out what it was."

Fifteen minutes later, they were in Ferguson's car heading west out of London, back down the road to Wiltshire—to Stockbridge House.

---

⸱ ◆ ⸱

# 86

*Stockbridge House*
*Nr Newton Tony*
*Wiltshire SP4*
*England*
The *United Kingdom*

IT WAS JUST after lunchtime when Ferguson pulled the metallic grey four-by-four off the tree-shrouded country road.

Manoeuvring it skillfully, he tucked it into a dense copse of trees to shield it from the view of any passing traffic.

Now, heading into the shady woods on foot, Ava led him swiftly north-wards towards the country home of the late Lord Drewitt.

In other circumstances, she would have made her way more slowly—enjoying the sinuous and leafy greens of the ageing oaks, chestnuts, and beeches enveloping them.

But she knew time was critical. Prince was dead, and she had no idea who had ordered the hit.

Or, equally worryingly, who might be next.

Looking about, she was acutely aware that the last time she had seen the secluded building she had been running away from it as fast as she could, leaving Malchus's bodyguard with two nine-millimetre holes in his thigh.

The patchy layer of dried twigs nestling on the green carpet of moss and wild grass snapped underfoot as she and Ferguson moved forward. There was nothing they could do about the noise, but it did not matter much. There was no one nearby, and stealth was not the priority. The trees merely provided cover so they could approach the house unobserved.

After a hard ten-minute walk, the forest of gnarled trunks started to thin, and she could see the pale stone of Stockbridge House showing through the widening gaps in the trees.

The grand house was exactly as she remembered it—a secluded Elizabethan manor surrounded by a gravelled drive, flowerbeds, and ornamental lawns.

To get inside the building, they would eventually need to break cover from the protection of the trees, and cross the final distance in the open. But first, she needed to know if anyone was home.

Loosening the straps on her rucksack, she slipped it off her back and reached inside for the small black rubberized field telescope she had packed before leaving.

Training it on the nearest window, she slowly rotated the slim polarizing filter mounted over the lens. As it turned, the myriad reflections on the window melted away, leaving the glass entirely transparent— offering an unobstructed and clear line of sight straight into the room behind it.

If she had still been with the Firm, she would have had the benefit of one of the portable x-ray or radar devices they issued for these operations. But now she was on her own, she had to make do with what she could improvise.

Nodding at Ferguson to stay where he was, she slowly moved clockwise around the building, always staying behind the tree-line, training the telescope on each window in turn to check for signs of occupation inside the house.

It only took a three-quarter circuit round the building to scan all its windows, before she retraced her steps to where Ferguson was waiting.

"There's no sign of anyone," she reported, slipping the telescope back into the rucksack and hoisting it onto her back again. "Let's go."

Breaking from the cover of the trees, she hurried across the crunchy gravel towards the house's imposing stone porchway. It was a shady flag-stoned area under an archway, that would have looked as natural on the front of an Elizabethan church as on a manor house of the period.

Arriving in front of the ancient heavy door, she tried pushing it. Sometimes people in the countryside got careless and left things open.

But not this time.

It did not budge.

She could immediately see there was going to be no easy way of getting in. The wood was old and hardened, and the hinges were concealed.

With no alternative, she dropped one knee onto the age-smoothed flagstones, and peered at the door's only lock.

The polished brass-faced keyhole was shiny but worn, softened by decades of use and exposure to the elements. It looked like it had been on the door since the early days of Queen Victoria's reign.

Delving into her jacket pocket, she took out a small brown leather pouch, and removed two slim metal tools.

"Going old school?" Ferguson nodded at the picks.

Ava squinted into the old keyhole, trying to make out any details of the antique mechanism inside. But there was nothing to see. The strong sunlight obscured the view completely, leaving just a dark void behind the keyhole.

"Here goes," she muttered, inserting the tension wrench into the hole, running its L-shaped tip delicately along the bottom until she felt it bite. Turning it, she twisted the barrel a fraction to the right, and was pleased to find it moved freely, indicating the lock was well maintained.

*So far so good.*

Ferguson was behind her, keeping an eye on the driveway and the woods. "It's clear," he reassured her. "No sign of anyone."

Keeping the barrel rotated with the tension wrench, she inserted the second pick. Unlike the first, this one had a short bent end.

It was a delicate task, and she needed to use only the lightest touch.

Steadying her breathing, she focused all her concentration on the small metal tools.

Gently feeling the lock's smooth inside contours, she analyzed the information her hands were relaying, recreating in her mind's eye a three-dimensional map of its moving inner parts.

She knew broadly what to expect, but experience had taught her that old locks were quite unlike the modern mass-made ones off an assembly line. When things were old and hand-built, nothing was standard or predictable.

Pushing the pick to the far end, she stroked the lock's roof, feeling for the outline of the farthest pin.

As the pick skated lightly over the invisible parts, she finally felt it. Pushing gently upwards, she heard the quiet but welcome click of the sprung pin above moving clear of the cylinder.

With the first pin done, she allowed herself to relax and breathe normally for a few moments. Then she drew the pick fractionally towards her, and felt for the next one.

Finding it more quickly than the last, she nudged it upwards until she again heard the telltale click of its upper pin sliding harmlessly out of the way.

Her confidence growing, she deftly repeated the procedure until all the pins were clear of the barrel plug.

"The moment of truth," she announced with a grimace, giving the tension wrench a decisive anticlockwise twist.

To her relief, it moved easily, accompanied by the satisfying heavy clunk of the large deadbolt sliding out of the doorjamb and back into the lock's casing.

"A woman of many talents," Ferguson whistled quietly but appreciatively. "I'd probably just have drilled it myself. Much more fun." He pushed lightly on the brass knob in the centre of the door, easing it open a fraction.

"I can believe that." Ava stood up, and dusted herself down, enjoying a moment of satisfaction at how smoothly she had picked it. "But we don't want to leave any traces."

She pushed the door wider, and pointed at the small white cupboard she had seen Malchus's bodyguard open when they had brought her in as their prisoner.

Arriving in front of it together, she pulled its thin door open to reveal a spray of multicoloured wires bunched around the predictable cluster of dusty hallway fuse-boxes and junctions.

But she was not looking for those, and her eyes immediately travelled to the centre, where there was a brushed metal numeric keypad, whose orange LED display was rapidly flashing the number twenty-seven in large luminous characters. As her eyes locked onto the blinking number, it dropped to twenty-six, then twenty-five.

"Your turn," she indicated to Ferguson, noting the grey telephone line snaking out of the alarm box. "And it looks like it's hooked into the local police station."

Ferguson already had an inch-thick cream-coloured plastic box the size of a small postcard in his hand. Slipping it firmly over the keypad, he pushed a rocker-switch on its side, and stood back.

"You're sure it'll work?" She eyed it with uncertainty. "It looks a bit amateur."

"It's a lifesaver," he reassured her, tapping the box confidently. "Very few people change their codes regularly. So it easily detects the four buttons with the most wear and tear and finger grease. Then it's child's play. Instead of trying the full ten thousand combinations of a zero-to-nine keypad, it just cycles through the only twenty-four possibilities." He looked up at Ava confidently. "It's sound. Honestly."

The LED clock was still counting down. It was now showing zero-eight. She shot Ferguson a concerned glance.

"Have some faith." He paused, staring at the readout as it clicked down to zero-four. "Although obviously," he conceded, "it needs enough time to work."

She looked again at the numeric display. "Is this the best the technical lab can do?" she asked, hearing the anxiety in her voice.

"I doubt it." He looked amused. "But it's all they'll trust me with."

"I don't think it's—" Ava began, but was cut short by the howling sound of an alarm going off by the front door.

"Christ," Ferguson yelled. "Change of plan."

Reaching inside the rucksack, he pulled out a pair of wire-cutters.

"Don't!" Ava shouted above the deafening noise. "If we're lucky, the police will assume it's a malfunction or a false alarm tripped by an animal. It happens all the time. But if you cut anything and trigger a secondary system, they'll prioritize the incident."

Ferguson threw the wire-cutters back into the bag and ran towards the front door, pulling off his thin fleece jacket.

"What are you doing?" she yelled, struggling to be heard.

"Just start looking for whatever we came for," he shouted back.

Without waiting, she ran across the high hallway, darting in and out of the shafts of bright light streaming in from the diamond-leaded windows.

She headed straight for the main reception room where Malchus had first brought her. It was exactly as she remembered it—three sofas at the near end, and a large desk at the other.

The sun was pouring through the windows—a soft afternoon light infusing the room with the gentle brightness of an English summer's day. It was a peaceful room, and she found it hard to reconcile its current calm with memories of the violence on her last visit.

She pushed the thoughts out of her mind as she brushed past a row of dark wooden bookcases displaying a collection of leather-bound books nestling alongside the obligatory modern economics texts of Drewitt's trade.

She headed for the far end of the room, beyond the French windows leading onto the patio and fountain where she had escaped Malchus's thug.

Reaching the desk, she heard the alarm at the front of the house become muffled for a few seconds—then stop completely. An alarm was still sounding somewhere at the rear of the house, but at least she could now hear herself think.

She had to assume they did not have long. The nearest town where there was likely to be a police station was about twenty minutes away according to the map she had looked at earlier. But there could easily be a patrol car closer by.

She needed to be fast.

Drewitt's desk was a graceful antique hardwood table, polished to a lustrous deep sheen. It stood on an unassuming but elegant pale blue oriental rug of the sort that litter English country houses. She noted approvingly that the desk did not have the usual ostentatious lamp or leather blotter.

It was a working academic desk—piled with Drewitt's books, journals, and papers. There was no computer in sight. Instead, from the copious sheets filled with neat handwriting, she figured Drewitt was of the generation that still preferred a pen to a keyboard.

She ran her eyes inquisitively over the books' spines. They were exactly what she expected from an academic specializing in economics, with titles on politics, markets, and economic theory.

Slipping on a pair of tight milky-white latex gloves from her pocket, she began leafing through the papers on the desk. She needed some clue, anything, to what he had been working on with Malchus.

But as she rifled through the pile, it proved to be no more than administrative correspondence—a mail-shot for an upcoming conference, a request to attend an anniversary dinner at another Oxford college, proofs from an editor of an article for a *Festschrift* in honour of a recently deceased colleague, and a stack of mundane mail on college life.

There was nothing out of the ordinary that she could see—no indication what he and Malchus may have been collaborating on.

As she finished with the papers, she heard the alarm at the back of the house fall silent. She was not sure what Ferguson had done, but the calm was welcome, although it did not change the fact there was a good chance the police were already on their way.

Looking about, she noticed with a pang of remorse that a jacket still hung on the back of the desk's chair. It was a golden-brown tweed with a large check, topped off with a burgundy silk handkerchief poking from the outside breast pocket.

She could just imagine Drewitt wearing it.

Slipping her hands into its pockets, she was unsurprised to find them empty. Drewitt had struck her as fastidious—not at all the kind of man to ruin the line of his clothing with bulky objects stuffed into the pockets.

As she patted the jacket down to make sure she had missed nothing, she unexpectedly felt something slim in the inside breast pocket.

At that moment, Ferguson entered the room. Without speaking, he joined the search, checking behind the large pictures hanging on the long wall between the tall bookcases.

Pulling the slim object from Drewitt's jacket pocket, she could now see it was a stiff white envelope addressed in a dark emerald-green ink to Drewitt. It was postmarked 'Foyers', and the stamp was from Scotland.

"You said you're part Scots?" she called over to Ferguson.

"The name still doesn't give it away? Not even a bit?" He walked over to her. "Why, what have you got?"

"Do you know a place called Foyers?" she showed him the envelope.

He nodded. "It's small, though. Just a village. On the shores of Loch Ness."

Ava examined the envelope. The top had been slit neatly open with a razor-sharp knife. She pulled the edges apart, revealing a single sheet of folded paper nestling inside.

She took the page out carefully, and spread it out on the desk.

Like the envelope, it had been handwritten with a broad-nibbed fountain pen. The first line was in a deep vermillion red, with the rest in the same dark emerald-green ink as the envelope.

It was immediately obvious the writing was different from the hand that filled the pages of notes on Drewitt's desk. He had therefore clearly received the letter from someone else.

She looked hard at the paper. Her first impression was that it contained five lines of eccentrically looped writing, followed by a final line in a plainer script. But as her eyes focused on it, she realized to her surprise that she could only read the last line.

Peering more closely, she suddenly saw why.

What had looked like ordinary curly writing filling the first five lines was, in fact, nothing of the sort.

She stared in disbelief at the page.

"What on earth is that?" Ferguson had walked up behind her, and was peering down at the paper.

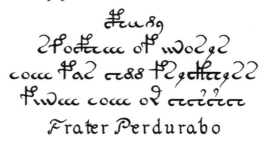

"What is it?" she heard herself repeating, dazed. "Actually, that's the easy part."

"Not from where I'm standing." He shook his head, staring at the odd writing.

Ava gazed at it, her mind flooding.

"Ava, what is it?" Ferguson touched her arm, pulling her out of her reverie.

"This," she answered slowly, focusing back on the page, "is almost certainly what we came for."

He furrowed his brow, peering down at the bizarre glyphs. "But what does it say? Does it mean anything to you?"

She shook her head slowly. "If it did, I'd be famous."

"But you know what it is?" She could hear the frustration in his voice.

"Oh yes," she replied, staring at it bleakly. "It's one of the most infamous codes ever devised."

"So what's the problem?" There was a note of enthusiasm in his voice. "Let's get it home, look it up, and decipher it. It shouldn't be a problem, right?"

She paused, before turning to look at him with a growing sense of helplessness. "The problem, as you put it," she spoke softly, reluctant to say the words. "is that in the six hundred years since the code was first used, no one has ever been able to crack even one single letter of it."

---

## 87

*Stockbridge House*
*Nr Newton Tony*
*Wiltshire SP4*
*England*
The *United Kingdom*

AVA SLIPPED THE enigmatic letter back into its crisp envelope, and tucked it away into her pocket.

"We need to find Malchus's lair," she announced, crossing the room and heading back to the airy hallway.

"Haven't we got what we came for?" Ferguson was following behind her.

"You cover the ground floor," she pointed down the hallway towards the west wing of the house, where there were more large day rooms. "I'll take upstairs."

Ferguson glanced at his watch.

"I'll be quick," she reassured him over her shoulder, climbing the wide staircase, taking the loosely carpeted steps two at a time.

Striding along the upper hallway, she did not have time to take in the paintings, vases, and other country house paraphernalia.

She knew what she was looking for.

As she headed down a step into what seemed to be an older part of the house, she felt it before she even knew it was there—an uneasy feeling, an inexplicable sense of something not right. She struggled to put a name to it.

The closest she could get was malice.

Reaching a pair of fluted columns flanking a small but elegant lobby, she could see a suite of rooms leading off the parquet-floored vestibule.

The feeling was stronger here.

Pushing open the suite's main door, she found herself in a dark room.

She had no doubt the deep blue cloth wallpaper had been considered elegant in its day, but now it seemed only to suck out what little brightness managed to penetrate the narrow leaded windows.

She had never been an expert on Nazi memorabilia, but the decoration left her in no doubt these were Malchus's rooms.

On the far wall was an antique marching banner—its bold ornamented swastika and 'THULE GESELLSCHAFT 1919' lettering leaving her in no doubt about the *völkisch*-racist politics of the men who had once carried it. Under it, she recognized the faded interwar photographs of stony-faced Nazi henchmen posing in Munich under similar standards.

The shrine-like atmosphere made her skin crawl.

She struggled to understand how anyone could want such images around them.

Opposite, on the facing wall, she recognized the large picture of the breasted and horned Baphomet ram—an ugly pentagram blazing on its forehead.

There was nothing subtle about the room. She had little difficulty believing it served Malchus well as a private retreat.

She tried to imagine just how intimidated Drewitt must have been by Malchus's threats. There was no other explanation for how he could have tolerated this room—in his home. No one with a sane mind could have chosen these images as decoration.

Looking around, she recognized the desk by the window. It had been the one in Drewitt's photographs of the medal.

*So this is where he was caught.*

She felt a flash of anger, remembering how Malchus had set Drewitt up, then killed him to motivate her.

*Well, she was definitely motivated now.*

There was nothing on the desk apart from two tall brass lamps, one at either end. Its surface was otherwise clear. There was no sign of any laptop, phone, papers, or anything that might give her a clue what Malchus was up to.

The atmosphere in the room sent a chill down her spine. The feeling of malice she had sensed in the hallway was stronger and all-pervasive here—a palpable malevolence.

Hearing a noise, she spun round, her nerves already on edge, her muscles tensed.

*Was someone there?*

She stared at the door, listening acutely.

*Was this what Drewitt had heard before Malchus found him?*

She told herself to stay calm. There was no one in the house. She had checked it carefully, and the burglar alarm had been on when they entered.

She had seen nothing to suggest they were not completely alone.

On the other hand, if there was someone there, even if it was Malchus—*especially* if it was Malchus, she would be ready this time.

She strained to listen, but could hear no further sound.

Walking quickly but quietly out and across the lobby, she looked up and down the hallway.

It was deserted.

She relaxed. It must have been her imagination—or one of the many noises an old house can make.

Stepping back into the room, she bent down to pick up a book lying on a small wooden table beside a sturdy armchair.

The title page said it was a private edition of Aleister Crowley's *Liber XV Missa Gnostica*.

It meant nothing to her. But as she flicked through it, she could see it was some type of occult equivalent of the Catholic mass. But in place of a priest, bread, wine, and the usual prayers, there were cakes, a lance, invocations to strange ancient deities, and a naked priestess on the altar.

She noted with interest that Malchus had signed his name in the *Ex Libris* box on the book's flyleaf, and had added meticulous handwritten notes and amendments to some of the pages.

She pulled out the envelope she had found in Drewitt's jacket.

The handwriting was identical.

*So, the letter was from Malchus.*

She put the book of ritual down, and looked around for anything else Malchus had left lying about.

Hearing another noise, she froze again.

This time there was no doubting it.

It was a footstep.

Wheeling round, she saw a figure in the doorway silhouetted against the bright light from the hall.

She recognized the intruder's outline, but for a fleeting second could not place it.

His shape was familiar yet unexpected, and her brain took a moment to identify the profile.

It was not Malchus. She was sure of that.

Suddenly it clicked into place. He was not someone she had ever contemplated might be at the house.

*DeVere.*

As he stepped into the room, the cheery greeting she was about to give him died in her throat on seeing the grim expression on his face— and the small Kahr nine-millimetre he was pointing directly at her.

There was no airy greeting from him either.

"I warned you, Ava." He was speaking slowly and deliberately. "I specifically warned you."

"Peter, what on earth—" she began, bewildered.

"I told you," he cut her off. "In London, by the river that night. I specifically warned you to leave it alone and go back to Baghdad."

He stepped further into the room, allowing the light to fall onto his grey chalk-striped suit and heavy-rimmed glasses.

His tone was threatening, and there was no ambiguity about the way in which he was pointing the diminutive silver and black weapon at her.

"But you didn't listen, did you?" The reprimand was unmistakable. "I take no responsibility for this situation, Ava. I couldn't have been clearer. I even specifically told you to trust no one. How much more could I have done? I imagined any person of your intelligence would get the hint. But," he stared at her accusingly, "just like your father, you don't know when to leave something alone."

Ava's mind was spinning as the horrific realization of what she was hearing began to dawn on her.

"On the floor," DeVere ordered, motioning with the pistol's muzzle towards the rug. "Face down, hands behind your head."

She stared at him, a rage rising inside her at the implications of what he was saying. "What if I don't?" She glared at him. "What are you going to do?"

DeVere's eyes were cold and clinical. She was chilled by the change from their usual jovial expression.

"If I could silence your father, I'll have no problem doing the same to you." There was no mistaking the steel in his voice. "Now do as I say."

Ava barely heard him. The blood was hammering though her ears as the words sank in.

She fought to process the information.

*DeVere? Killed her father? Not Malchus?*

She sank to her knees in a daze.

"I said face down." The voice was harsh. As she leant forward, she felt his foot in the small of her back, pushing her onto the floor.

"I warned him to steer clear of Malchus, too. I told him to stay away. But just like you, he thought he knew better."

Pinned onto the floor, her chest crushed by the weight of his foot, she twisted her head to get a better look at him

He was standing beside her—the black hole of the handgun's barrel pointing straight at her head. There was no emotion behind the heavy-rimmed glasses—just cold resolve.

A wave of revulsion rushed through her.

*All these years.*

*The lies he had told.*

*The crocodile tears he had shed.*

"Malchus is mine, you see." He was speaking slowly. "Always was. He's my asset, and I wasn't going to have your father blunder in and ruin everything." He stared at her impassively. "And neither will you."

She was barely listening. Her eyes were searching the room for anything she could use against him. But it was sparsely furnished, and there was little in the way of furniture or anything else that could serve as a weapon.

With a mounting sickening feeling, she realized that if he wanted to pull the trigger, there was absolutely nothing she could do.

Her only chance was to delay the moment. If she could buy more time, an idea might come to her.

Or he might make a mistake.

She had to play for time.

"What do you mean, your asset?" she asked, unable to keep the scorn from her voice, "You mean you are on his payroll?"

DeVere eyed her carefully. He seemed to be weighing up whether or not to respond. Making up his mind, he continued. "When the wall came down in '89, western Europe was rapidly flooded with ex-soviet-bloc intelligence officers on the lookout for a deal to give them a new life. Malchus wasn't the only one to try his luck in England. Boatloads of them came across the channel. But unsurprisingly, most turned out to be mediocre low-level apparatchiks of minimal interest. It took years of debriefing them to discover we knew more than they did."

"But Malchus was different, right?" Ava prompted.

He ignored the contemptuous tone in her voice. "I knew nothing of Malchus. But when the Thelema hit our radar screens, I made it my goal to penetrate the organization—to get close to their inner core, which I soon found orbited around Malchus. The beauty of it was that I didn't have to act very hard in my new role. You see, Malchus and I have a lot in common, in the way we see things."

She could feel the weight on her back diminishing slightly as he became absorbed in talking and ceased treading down so hard. But she was under no illusions. The gun was still pointing directly at her head.

"How did the Firm's vetting never catch you?" she asked. "You're delusional."

"Why?" There was a flash of anger in his eyes. "Because I love my country and refuse to stand by while it obsessively self-harms?" He glared at her. "I've served all my life. I've never asked for riches or recognition. The only reward I ever wanted was to see my country stand tall. But instead I've witnessed it sicken and wither—its identity eaten away by an aggressive cancer. I will not apologize to anyone that I care for our heritage. The real insanity is how the rancid politicians have sold us, turning a strong proud nation into a putrid sore-ridden cripple, its infected lifeblood slipping away. Our land has a pervasive sickness, and it needs strong medicine."

"And you seriously think Malchus has the cure?" Ava could not keep the incredulity from her voice.

"Don't treat me like an idiot," he snapped. "I'm not some star-struck adolescent."

Behind his head she could see the dark eyes of the hellish Baphomet ram on the far wall gazing out over them, casting its malign aura into the room.

She felt trapped in a scene of surreal madness.

"So Malchus runs his neo-Nazi operation in England, and you protect him?" Ava shook her head. "You'll never get away with it."

"But I already have," he smiled nastily. "For longer than you can imagine. It's so easy, you know. People only see what they want to see."

Ava did not reply. She stared at him, trying to reconcile the man she knew with the ranting stranger pointing the gun at her.

"No one suspects a thing," he sounded smug. "I'm very good at covering my tracks. It's one of the skills the job has taught me."

"The letter from C," she asked, "the one whitewashing my father's death and blocking any prosecution of Malchus—that was your doing, wasn't it?" She stared up at him, only managing to control her anger in order to get the answers she needed to hear.

"You know about that?" He looked confused for a moment. "Never mind. The secret will stay in this room with you."

"So it was you?" she insisted.

"You see, Ava, it's all very simple. I've always wanted Malchus to succeed. So I can't allow anyone to check up on him. Fortunately, as he's my asset, I get to tell the story. As it happens, C was happy to sign the letter because he had read the file."

"Which you had falsified."

He gazed at her blankly. "Only the naïve believe what they read, Ava—especially in government files." He sneered. "I wrote his file the way I wanted it, then had it classified for the most senior eyes only to keep snoopers away. As far as C knows, Malchus is a key asset in the fight to discover what happened to a significant quantity of Former Soviet Union weapons-grade uranium. That makes him a vital asset to be protected."

"According to the file, your father had the bad luck to be in the wrong place at the wrong time—one of those accidents that happens despite the best planning. Soon after that, Malchus fell foul of the Turkish authorities and did a spell in an Istanbul prison, but after a suitable delay I managed to get him out quietly. And so here we are."

The pressure on her back increased as he trod down harder on her again, only reminding her that she still had no plan for how to get out of the situation.

She needed an idea fast. She had to stall him.

"So did you kill my father?"

He looked down at her coldly. "It doesn't make any difference now."

"It does to me," she spat back through gritted teeth, wishing more than anything there was a poker or anything metal and heavy in the firegrate beside her. But it was empty.

"I wasn't there when it happened." DeVere continued. "But I won't lie to you. He was getting in the way—becoming too interested in the Thelema. I didn't actually pull the trigger, if that's what you're asking. But then in our line, we don't always have to do the work ourselves, do we? Although," he looked at his pistol then at Ava, "we do occasionally have to get our hands a little dirty."

Ava glared at him with undisguised hatred. "You're not going to get away with this."

"Somehow, I don't think you're in a position to make any threats." He eyed her coldly.

As much as it pained her to admit it, he was right.

*She had to keep him talking.*

"Why does Malchus want the Ark and the Menorah?"

DeVere looked blankly at her. "I don't know. And to be honest, that's his business." He paused. "But one thing I do know is that your involvement stops here."

He pointed the gun at her back, directly behind her heart. "Time to pray, Ava. And say hello to your father from me."

She stared angrily at him, refusing to let the conversation end. "We're not done, yet."

"Oh, I think we are." He straightened his arm to take the shot.

"What about Prince?" she asked, trying to focus on the question and keep the fear from her voice. "That was a clever hit. It was you, wasn't it?" From everything she had just learned, she was now sure it had been. She prayed his pride would not be able to resist crowing about it. She needed more time.

"You catch on quick." An arrogant smirk spread across his face. "She was getting too close. But actually it was you who signed her death warrant."

Ava stared at him straight in the eye, defying him to pass the blame onto anyone else.

"Oh yes," he nodded. "When you told me on the bridge that the Americans had a file saying Malchus was involved in your father's death, you as good as wrote the order. You see, I had religiously cleaned all the MI6 files and filled them with history the way I wanted it to be read. It hadn't occurred to me the Americans also had a file. But thanks to you, I was able to find the file in Prince's office and destroy it. And then? Well, you know how we all hate loose ends. So," he paused, "now things are back to normal."

"Not quite," Ava retorted, an idea forming in her mind.

It was something of a long shot, but she had very few options left. "There's a copy," she said slowly. "She passed the information on."

"To you?" DeVere snorted. "Well that's hardly a threat, is it? Your adventure is over." The expression in his eyes was flinty.

"Not just to me." Ava paused, relishing the chance to see his reaction. "To her Israeli handlers from the Institute." Of course, she knew Prince's SD card and the information never got near Tel Aviv, but DeVere did not need to know that. She could afford to be a little creative with the truth.

For the first time since DeVere had entered the room, she saw a hint of uncertainty in his eye. "Mossad? Prince? How can you know that?" he challenged her. "You're lying."

"Let me show you something." Ava arched her back upwards, dislodging his foot. She rolled onto her left hip, and with her right hand reached for her jacket's inside pocket.

In one fast fluid motion DeVere pulled back the silver slide on top of the handgun and released it, drawing a round from the magazine into the chamber with a loud click. "I wouldn't do that if I were you."

Ava froze, the adrenaline pumping hard.

He kept the weapon trained on her. "How stupid do you think I am?" He moved around to face her. At the same time, she moved onto her knees.

She could feel the cold of the metal as he pressed the pistol's hard muzzle into her forehead before he bent down and reached to get whatever was inside her pocket. "Keep your hands where I can see them," he ordered bluntly.

He had done it beautifully. Exactly as she had hoped. She had got him where she wanted him, and in less than a second the opportunity would be gone. It was the only chance she was going to get, and she had no intention of missing it.

He was watching her hands, so was completely unprepared for what happened next.

In a lightning-fast movement, she whipped her head round, and sank her teeth deeply into the soft flesh of his wrist, biting down as fast and hard as she could until she could taste blood and feel bone.

Roaring with pain at the unexpected wound, he staggered back towards the doorway. Seizing the moment, Ava launched herself at him, smashing her shoulder into his upper legs with all her force.

It was second nature to her that an attack requires maximum aggression and maximum speed. That was the mantra of all combat training she had ever done, and she was having no difficulties summoning both. Her blood was up, and she channelled the full force of her anger into the assault.

The power of the impact sent him careering off balance.

Now on her feet, she made a grab with both hands for the gun still pointing at her, wrenching it violently sideways, hoping to dislodge his grip as he staggered backwards. He howled again in pain, but this time it was as his index finger, trapped inside the trigger guard, was neatly dislocated.

To her surprise, despite the force of her onslaught, he recovered quickly. Steadying himself, he moved backwards, away from her rising knee.

With panic swelling, she saw him place his middle finger over the injured one lying on the trigger, and begin to squeeze.

Time seemed to slow completely as she calculated there was no time to do anything except hurl herself towards him in an urgent attempt to be on the other side of the gun's barrel by the time his finger finished squeezing the trigger.

Flinging herself forward, she heard the deafening bang of the round detonating, as the room simultaneously filled with the biting smell of igniting gunpowder.

But to her surprise, as her ears stopped ringing, she realized nothing had changed.

She and DeVere were still both standing.

Confused, she twisted round over her shoulder to look at her left hand—still holding the gun.

She shook her head, trying to focus clearly.

Something did not make sense.

She still had her hand on the gun, and could not understand why she had not felt the top slide recoil as he had fired. She could not see the spent cartridge shell anywhere on the floor either.

She wondered for a moment if her confusion was a symptom of a severe injury. Perhaps she was going into shock from a massive close-range gun trauma?

As she blinked a couple of time to clear her head, DeVere's grip on the handgun loosened, and he crumpled before her, dropping like a stone to the floor—revealing Ferguson in the doorway behind him holding his small steel-blue Sig Sauer.

"I had a clear shot." His tone was matter of fact. "So I took it." He entered the room, tucking the pistol back into the waistband of his jeans.

"Nice work, by the way," he added, noticing the livid fresh bite marks on DeVere's wrist. "Remind me not to get too close to you."

Ava stepped back, still dazed.

She looked down at DeVere's body. His head and shoulders lay in a patch of sunlight on the floor—the criss-cross pattern of the window's leading casting a matrix of diamonds over his frozen features. Trickles of blood and fluid dribbled out over a clump of brain matter poking from a ragged hole where a small piece of his skull had sheared off. His dead eyes looked back up at her with a glassy emptiness.

Her eyes were locked on him—the full horror of the last fifteen minutes only now beginning truly to sink in.

*DeVere and Malchus? In it together?*

She still could not believe it. She felt paralyzed with incredulity looking at the corpse of the man she had thought for so many years was a family friend.

Ferguson touched her arm, breaking the moment. "There are no cellars. The house is clean. We need to get out of here."

Snapping back to reality, Ava tore her eyes away. She felt a cold purpose seeping through her as she bent down and pulled the gun from DeVere's fingers, placing it carefully into her pocket. It would be clean, unregistered—untraceable by the regular police.

From the way things were going, she figured it may come in handy.

She headed for the door. "There are no guards or security here," she concluded. "It's clear the Ark and Menorah are somewhere else. Right now, we need to get back to Freemasons' Hall."

Ferguson shook his head. "It's not safe going back to London. We can't risk it. There are going to be too many people looking for us. We need to lie low."

But Ava was no longer listening. She was walking briskly back down the hall towards the stairs.

———————— • ◆ • ————————

# 88

*Freemasons' Hall*
*Covent Garden*
*London WC2*
*England*
*The United Kingdom*

THE SECURITY GUARD behind the front desk in the vast art deco foyer of Freemasons' Hall was the same one Ava had spoken to earlier.

She announced herself to him, and asked to see the Deputy Grand Secretary again.

The guard did not seem bothered by Ferguson's presence. He nodded a polite acknowledgement to them both, before making a phone call. After a discussion she could not hear, he put the receiver down and pointed her down the lustrously polished corridor to Cordingly's office.

"It's open," Cordingly called out as she knocked on the heavy wooden door.

Pushing it wide, she saw Cordingly rising from behind the large desk dominating the well-proportioned office—its cream walls and polished dark wood decorations entirely in keeping with the singular and striking style of the building.

He was wearing the same black tie as before, and Ava found herself again distracted by the blatant central image of the Ark and the cloven-hoofed cherubs guarding it.

"Dr Curzon? Back again so soon?" He looked surprised, but was smiling warmly. "I did think you had left rather quickly this morning."

Cordingly stepped around the desk as she introduced Ferguson. "I do hope your trip hasn't been wasted," he sounded slightly apologetic. "But I'm sorry to say my position remains unchanged. I've made promises I deem inviolable, and I'm afraid I simply can't assist with the text you showed me earlier."

"You helped more than you know," Ava reassured him. "It turned out not to be a freemasonic code—just designed to look like one."

He failed to keep a flash of relief from his face, indicating for her and Ferguson to take a seat in the suite of comfortably upholstered chairs grouped around a low walnut coffee table. "So, to what do I owe the pleasure this time?"

"Your library," Ava smiled, walking over to the armchair he had indicated and sitting down. "As we passed through it this morning, I glimpsed a section on cryptology."

"A discipline in which we have a long history," he confirmed. "As I mentioned, there have been dark times in our past when circumstances required us to operate in the shadows." He steepled his fingers, leaning his elbows on the worn arms of the deep chair. "But forgive me. You said the code you brought me was not freemasonic—so how can our library help you?"

"This is something else entirely," Ava explained. "Another matter—a locked door to which, I think, you may this time genuinely hold the key."

Leaning forward in his chair, his voice became more serious. "Forgive me, Dr Curzon, but is your enquiry connected to the matter you came to me about earlier? An issue of 'historical and political importance' I think you said, which has attracted the interest of several international intelligence agencies?"

"The answer to the previous clue has brought us to another one," she explained.

He looked pensive. "Treasure hunts are something we are familiar with in this building. However, as I clearly told you, our organization promotes the interests of the brotherhood of mankind—those things upon which all civilized humans can agree. In a word, we don't do politics. We're not here to help individual governments with their partisan opinions and rivalries. We have brothers and sisters in hundreds of countries, and their continued safe existence is only guaranteed by our reputation for unwavering non-participation in these things."

Ava leant towards him. "I can assure you, the forces at work here are not national political ones. To the contrary. They are an unwelcome danger to us all."

"From whose point of view?" Cordingly asked shrewdly. "It's often a matter of opinion, I find."

"Not in this case," Ava countered. "A truly dangerous group is pursuing an objective we have yet to understand fully. But if, as you said, the Nazis were your chief twentieth-century persecutors, then you have more reason to be afraid than most."

Ferguson reached into his back pocket and took out his wallet. Removing a hard plastic card, he handed it to Cordingly.

Ava could see on it the distinctive blue and white logo of London's Metropolitan Police force, with Ferguson's photograph in the top left corner and the designation 'CO19' in the top right above the words 'FIREARMS COMMAND, SFO'.

Cordingly raised an eyebrow. "Will this check out?"

"Feel free to make whatever calls you need to," Ferguson reassured him.

Cordingly stared at the card, tapping it against his thumbnail. "Very well," he replied after a pause, handing the card back to Ferguson and staring at them both keenly. "You have whatever help I can give you. But understand this, if things are not as you say, you'll have a lot of explaining to do—and not just to me."

The threat hung in the air for a few seconds, before Ava nodded solemnly. "Perfectly understood," she confirmed, changing tone. "I was wondering, do you have anything in your library's cryptology section on Voynich?"

Cordingly looked blank. "I've absolutely no idea. How do you spell it?"

Ava wrote the word on the small pad he passed her, before handing it back to him.

"I'll see what we have," he stood up. "Please excuse me."

As soon as Cordingly had left the room, Ferguson pulled out his mobile phone and glanced at it. Ava could see from the screen that he had five missed calls.

"HQ," he confirmed her unspoken suspicion. "I guess they want to have a little chat with us."

Ava pointed to the photocard he was sliding back into his wallet. "Since when were you a special firearms officer?"

"You don't think I'd pass selection?" he feigned a look of disbelief. "The Firm issued it to me when I started doing odd jobs for them. It's my get-out-of-jail card if anyone gets too curious about what I'm up to. It works wonders when I'm pulled for speeding."

"You think you're still approved?"

He nodded. "It should check out just fine. The HR desk-jockeys at Vauxhall Cross haven't fired me yet—although it won't take long once they find out that I'm the reason DeVere doesn't need his corner office anymore." He slipped the wallet back into his pocket. "It's a good job our friend here didn't call the number. I'm afraid our masters are not going to be very friendly when they find us."

That was an understatement, and Ava knew it. Now DeVere was dead, they were prime suspects for his murder, and did not have a single shred of evidence to support the story DeVere had confessed to her, or the fact he had been about to gun Ava down in cold blood.

She was all too aware the situation had become intensely dangerous for her and Ferguson.

She would be able to show them Prince's file on Malchus, and they could compare it with theirs, which had been tampered with by DeVere. They would see the discrepancies. But on its own, the file only showed that someone had been interfering with the records. To prove the full extent of DeVere's treachery, she would need to find Malchus and bring him in.

Malchus was the only person who could corroborate DeVere's involvement. His testimony about DeVere's loyalties would be the only evidence that would give her a chance of explaining their innocence.

And it was not just DeVere's death that threatened her. There was Prince's assassination, too. DeVere's confession of pulling the trigger had gone with him to the grave. The authorities would soon find out Ferguson had arranged to meet Prince that morning, and the records would quickly reveal that he had been first on the scene to report the assassination. That would make them number one suspect for that murder, too.

The only thing that would help explain both deaths was if Malchus could be persuaded to give a frank account of DeVere's double life.

But it was a long shot. He could easily choose simply to blame her for both deaths. It would be child's play for him to implicate her, and get her out of his way permanently. Perhaps he would even blame her for Drewitt's murder and that of the priest and Max's man in the Basilica di San Clemente as well? She had no alibi for any of them, and had clearly been involved with all the dead individuals.

She could only hope that Malchus's vanity would rise to the challenge, and he would enjoy telling the service how one of their own senior officers had duped them for so long.

Failing that, she would have to hope the Firm's purpose-built 'interview rooms' with their trolleys of chemicals in the basement at Legoland would be enough. They were not the squalid torture chambers Malchus had presided over back in Berlin. The British interrogation teams knew how to get what they wanted from people like Malchus in more sophisticated ways. With a prize like him, there would soon be a host of officers lining up after his confessions to forgive his crimes, turn him, and become his new handler. He was too useful to be locked up.

But she knew they would be wrong to try to run him. He was too skilled at dissembling, and would be back to his usual habits in no time. DeVere's death would be an inconvenience for him, no doubt, but he would soon convince someone else in the establishment to extend a shield around him. She doubted he would have too much difficulty finding a sympathizer, or someone who could be paid, threatened, or blackmailed to protect him.

How to deal with him more permanently would be her problem— but one she would have to wait to solve until after she had found his museum of biblical artefacts, and after he had cleared her name.

*All in good time.*

First she had to find him.

And she had to do it before the authorities found her and Ferguson.

She now knew for certain his main base was not at Stockbridge House. Drewitt's home was a convenient secluded spot an hour and a half from London, but there was no evidence he had the Ark and the Menorah there.

He was plainly keeping them somewhere else.

The postmark 'Foyers' on the letter to Drewitt was more intriguing. But somehow she could not quite see Malchus in Scotland. He was an urban creature—more at home in Dresden, Berlin, or London. She could not imagine what could attract him to the rugged Highlands, miles from his supporters and the action.

"Are these what you're looking for?" Cordingly re-entered the room, closing the door behind him. "What's this all about, anyway? The librarian got quite excited when I said Voynich."

He was carrying a pile of books—the largest of which was a glossy hardback, its cover decorated in the same loopy writing as on the letter from Malchus to Drewitt.

He put them down in front of Ava and pointed to the largest one. "He told me this is a full-size facsimile of the entire manuscript—quite rare, apparently."

Ava opened the book and flicked through a few of the two hundred shiny photographs of light brown vellum folios covered in the same strange characters. Most of them also had fantastical illustrations in muted blue, brown, green, red, and yellow inks.

Ferguson exhaled loudly. "There's a whole book of that writing?"

"Do explain," Cordingly sounded as mystified as Ferguson.

"It's the Voynich manuscript," Ava leafed through the bizarre pages, "and is as unfathomable to today's cryptologists as prehistoric stone circles are to modern archaeologists."

"Don't governments have departments that can do this sort of thing?" Cordingly looked sceptical. "Surely they could crack it in a jiffy?"

Ava shook her head. "The world's top cryptologists have wrestled with it ceaselessly. Everyone has tried, from the best-resourced spy agencies like Bletchley Park, GCHQ, and the NSA all the way to leading professors of mathematics and linguistics using the latest supercomputers. But every single person and team has drawn a blank. No one has ever deciphered a single letter of it."

Cordingly looked at her with incredulity. "So what on earth is it? What could be that securely enciphered?"

Ava shrugged. "No one knows. Its drawings are of plants, herbs, constellations, and miniature people. None of them seem to make any sense. They're as much of a mystery as the strange alphabet itself."

She slid the book across the table to Ferguson, who began turning the pages, gazing at the astonishing folios as they changed from images of phantasmagoric plants to circular groups of naked women wearing crowns and holding stars. As he kept flicking, the theme of the images changed again, with the nude women now pictured standing amid harebrained laboratory equipment and what looked like engineering pipe-work.

"Listen to this," he announced, reading aloud from the accompanying introductory notes.

> For years, the enigmatic manuscript's author was assumed to be the medieval English Franciscan friar Roger Bacon (c.1220–92), the undisputed intellectual colossus of the high middle ages, who made gunpowder and described motorized vehicles and flying machines two hundred years before Leonardo da Vinci. His fascination with experimental science was often seen as heretical, and he spent a period in prison for his 'novelties'. He taught at Oxford and Paris, and was a fierce advocate of knowledge, whether or not it agreed with Christian teaching. He is known to have worked on advanced cryptography, used codes for his research, and specifically referred to using characters not known to anyone.
>
> Recent scientific analysis, however, has dated the vellum and inks in the Voynich manuscript to the first three decades of the 1400s, and traced its most likely origin to southern Germany or northern Italy.

"Very interesting," Cordingly mused. "The early fifteenth century was a relatively peaceful period for free-thinkers. The medieval Inquisition was effectively dead, and no one had yet dreamed of the terrors of the Spanish Inquisition, or the later rigid Roman Inquisition that burned Galileo." He turned to Ava. "So is the Voynich manuscript Christian or heretical?"

"I believe on one page there's a nude female figure holding a cross," she answered. "But that's the only Christian imagery in the whole text."

"Well, well. A genuinely heretical medieval text. Fascinating," Cordingly looked delighted.

Ferguson continued:

> Its first known owner is believed to be Dr John Dee, Elizabethan scientist and notorious magician. He

added page numbering to its folios, before selling it to the Holy Roman Emperor, Rudolf II (1552–1612).

Emperor Rudolf then gave it to his pharmacist, who had cured him of an illness. Fifty years later, it appeared in the hands of an undistinguished alchemist in Prague, before passing via the rector of the city's Charles University to Athanasius Kircher—the most curious and brilliant mind of the age. Kircher spoke twelve languages, including Aramaic, Persian and Coptic, and was the leading authority on hieroglyphs, as well as author of an encyclopedia on China. He was fascinated by everything from music to botany and geography to engineering. He has been described as 'the last man who knew everything'.

Yet even Kircher failed to make any progress with the inscrutable manuscript, and on his death it was handed around a number of Church libraries, until in 1912 the Jesuit college at the Villa Mondragone near Frascati sold it to an ex-Russian-revolutionary turned antiquarian book dealer named Wilfrid Voynich, after whom the tantalizing manuscript has ever since been named.

"I still find it hard to believe a text from the 1400s can really be so complicated that modern experts and computers can't crack it." Cordingly sounded doubtful.

"Maybe if it seems like nonsense, perhaps it is?" Ferguson suggested. "Who's to say it isn't just an elaborate hoax?"

"Most experts believe it's real," Ava countered. "Sophisticated analysis of the patterns and frequency of the characters, syllables, and words shows that the text has all the characteristics of a genuine language. It's highly unlikely a fifteenth-century forger would want to, or be able to, create a hoax of this technical linguistic skill and complexity."

"So people have tried absolutely everything?" Ferguson was shaking his head, mystified.

Ava nodded. "Pretty much every known theory—from a new language or alphabet to simple and complex substitution ciphers, one-time pads, and steganographic codes. But despite the hundreds of thousands of hours of effort, it has never yielded up a single recognizable word."

"I've never heard of anything like it," Cordingly looked bemused. "Why would someone go to all this effort?"

"In medieval times, knowledge could be dangerous," Ava explained. "Sometimes people had to hide away their learning. So perhaps it relates to a forbidden subject like alchemy. Or maybe even one of the more occult branches of medicine—some of which were linked to forbidden subjects such as astrology, like when to harvest pharmaceutical plants, or the best time to administer particular remedies."

Ferguson caught Ava's eye, interrupting her thoughts. He nodded towards a flat square briefcase on the table by the window. In it, she could just make out what looked like a white robe, emblazoned with a large red cross patty. Rolled up beside it was a leather belt with a looped frog to hang a sword.

Cordingly glanced up from the manuscript and noticed where she was looking. He stood up immediately, and walked across to the case, shutting it hastily.

"I thought it was all aprons and badges, not crusader knights' uniforms?" Ferguson pointed to the rows of framed photographs on the walls displaying groups of men in dark suits sporting a seemingly infinite variety of elaborate aprons and medals.

Cordingly shook his head. "As we're all friends, I can tell you that this building," he nodded towards the photographs, "is the headquarters of traditional freemasonry. But let's just say that a lot of things happen beyond these walls. You could say this building is a gateway."

"That was the cross of the Knights Templar in your briefcase," Ava pressed him. "If you'll forgive me for raising it again, you seemed a little reluctant to talk about them earlier."

He gazed solemnly at her. "Some things are better left unsaid, Dr Curzon."

*The Templars again, and another brick wall.*

Ava turned back to the pile of books he had brought from the library. Aside from the colour facsimile, the others were an assortment of studies and theories about the mysterious manuscript.

"Do you mind if I keep these for a few days?" she asked, scooping up the pile.

"Of course not," Cordingly smiled. "I'm glad to be able to do something for you."

Ferguson stood up, and as he did so, Ava saw him slip something into his pocket from a pile of stationery on a side table.

Cordingly ushered her and Ferguson to the door. "And maybe," he added with a twinkle, "one day you'll be able to do something for us." He paused as he turned the brass handle and showed them back into the elegant shiny corridor. "Who knows," he smiled enigmatically, "perhaps you already are."

# 89

*The University of Oxford Botanic Gardens*
*Rose Lane*
*Oxford OX1*
*England*
*The United Kingdom*

MALCHUS HEADED PURPOSEFULLY down the ancient university city's High Street.

It was a warm evening, and young people were beginning to fill the pubs along the narrow side alleys radiating off the medieval thoroughfare.

He had nothing but disdain for them. At their age, he had already set out on his chosen path.

Walking briskly, he passed the high-windowed Victorian Examination Schools, and continued on to where he knew the elderly man would be.

The old professor's routine was as regular as clockwork.

As the jumbled architecture became more uniform and the crowds of tourists calmed and thinned out, he drew level with the austere Tudor frontage of Magdalen College.

Turning right, he passed through a small gate and down a short flight of steps into a tree-covered area. Ahead of him loomed an imposing triumphal stone archway, its bays housing the figures of King Charles I and II implausibly draped in togas.

He ducked under a doorway in the high wall, and said nothing as he quickly paid his entrance fee.

Once into the lush green Botanic Gardens, one of the oldest and most varied in the world, he headed down its central path, past the fountains and wooden box-wheelbarrows parked up beside the acres of flower-beds. He made straight for the end of the ancient ornamental Walled Garden, where he knew the elderly man would be.

He assumed the ageing professor came here for the tranquil atmosphere—to be surrounded by the wonders of nature's calming beauty.

*Today would be different*, Malchus mused.

Nature had its dark side, too.

He carried on to the garden's far end, passing a vast stone urn set on a pedestal in the middle of the path. It was decorated with large malevolent rams carved on either side, their diabolical horns folding back to serve as handles.

He smiled to himself.

It seemed oddly fitting.

Beyond it, he spotted the professor gazing thoughtfully into the distance, sitting alone on one of a pair of wooden benches in the shade of the spreading trees.

Malchus could see he had once been a powerfully built man. But now age had rounded his shoulders, and his face had sagged.

He was wearing a cream linen jacket over a black shirt and trousers. An overly-wide white circular collar announced he was one of Oxford's many priests of the high tradition in the Church of England.

Malchus sat down next to him and looked around. Directly ahead was a small pond sheltering an island overtaken by a vast plant with unfurled leaves several yards across. Behind him, the river flowed past lazily.

Ahead in the distance he could see a tall square bell-tower with delicate octagonal turrets dominating the other side of the river. But he had no interest in what it was. The only thing he wanted in this city was locked inside a different tower.

"Professor Stone?" he asked, breaking the silence.

"Do I know you?" The man was softly spoken. There was no suspicion in his voice—just a warm curiosity.

"I've been watching you," Malchus answered.

The elderly man was still gazing into the middle distance. "If you're selling something, I'm afraid you're wasting your time." His voice was gentle. There was no reproach.

"You've caused me a lot of trouble," Malchus continued.

"Oh?" The elderly man's voice betrayed only the faintest hint of his childhood Polish.

"You don't drink, gamble, whore, or have any vices to blackmail you with. And you don't have any children to threaten. All of which leaves me with limited options."

He had the priest's attention now. The white-haired man was looking at him in confusion.

"But what you do have," Malchus spoke slowly, dropping his voice, "is a sister—whom you visit every Tuesday afternoon at the St Aldate's nursing home."

The old professor was gazing at him in bewilderment.

"Let me make it simple." Malchus pulled a photograph out of his pocket, and handed it across.

The priest's elderly eyes crinkled as he looked at the image, attempting to make sense of it.

Malchus glanced around impatiently. He could hear the birds singing, but doubted the old man was listening to them any more. His watery eyes were staring at the photograph, the skin on his face now pale and tight.

Malchus looked down at the photograph.

It was rather good, even if he said so himself.

It showed an elderly woman lying in what appeared to be a raised hospital bed. It was plainly after lights-out in the facility, as the woman was asleep and the room was in shadow.

The photograph was normal in every way, except for the rough noose of rope looped around the old woman's neck, with its bulky hangman's knot lying over her frail chest.

"I was a little amazed," Malchus confided, "at the lack of security. But these private care homes watch their profit margins, and I imagine it would be a luxury to have staff supervising each room all night."

Malchus took the photograph back, watching as the old man placed his hands on his knees to steady the visible trembling.

"What do you want?" His soft voice was choked. "Please God, don't hurt her." He looked about wildly—fear evident behind his eyes. When he spoke again, his voice was a whisper. "I've no money. I'm nobody."

Malchus sneered. "There's no need for such modesty, professor. Not with me. Others may not share our interests, but your work on the *Dead Sea Scrolls*, especially the final battle in the *War Scroll*, is unparalleled."

"She's a good person." His voice was hoarse.

"Then this is exactly what you will do." Malchus handed him an envelope.

The priest opened it slowly, his hands shaking as he removed the word-processed piece of paper inside.

Taking a pair of large tortoiseshell reading glasses from his jacket's outside breast pocket, he read the note slowly.

When he spoke, his voice was frail. "What makes you think the deity would favour a man like you?"

Anger exploded inside Malchus with a searing ferocity.

He thrust his face into the priest's, and spat out an answer. "You think you're chosen? Do you suppose the God who led armies in triumphant conquests of bloodletting and skull-crushing cares anything for lace-wearing sycophants like you? Do you imagine the God who slashed and ripped his way through his enemies' jugulars with a flaming sword of vengeance and retribution is in any way interested in eunuchs bleating hymns?"

"You're an obscenity." The old man's body shook.

"Read your Bible," Malchus snapped. "Didn't the God of Israel punish those who failed to follow as he commanded? Didn't he instruct armed men to slaughter the unfaithful, to go throughout Jerusalem and 'Kill, without showing pity or compassion. Slaughter the old men, the young men and women, the mothers and children. Defile the temple and fill the courts with the slain.' Ezekiel, chapter nine."

The priest shook his head. "That's the Old Testament. God is love and our redemption. His gift of Christ and the new covenant changed everything."

Malchus sneered. "And God said, 'The people of Samaria must bear their guilt, because they have rebelled against their God. They will fall by the sword; their little ones will be dashed to the ground, their pregnant women ripped open.' Hosea, chapter thirteen. You are ignorant of your own God, priest. You have made your religion as you want it, not how it is."

"You're an abomination," the priest whispered.

"*You're* the abomination," Malchus spat back, his eyes blazing. "You were made in God's image, yet you suppress the strength and power he gave you, and twist his hard creed into the shrill whining of stricken women. You and your kind disgust me."

Malchus held out the photograph showing the sinister image of the old woman. "If you fail me, you will fail her."

Removing a lighter from his pocket, he took back the envelope. Holding it together with the photograph, he lit the corners. The curling yellow flames took quickly, lapping up the paper hungrily. As the images of his sister began to char and disintegrate, the old man turned a shade paler.

Malchus stood up. "I'll be back for it tomorrow."

He turned the burning paper the other way up and watched as the flames consumed the last of the picture and envelope.

Dropping the charred remains, he ground them into the grass with his heel.

The bells from two nearby steeples began to chime loudly, one after the other.

"*Finis, cinis, vermes, lapis oblivio,*"[15] Malchus quoted, standing and brushing himself down as he turned to leave. "I'm sure a man of your learning understands well."

---

15 "End, ashes, worms, stone, oblivion."

• ◆ •

# 90

*The Freemasons Arms*
*Covent Garden*
*London WC2*
*England*
*The United Kingdom*

BACK ON THE pavement outside Freemasons' Hall, Ava looked about. "We need somewhere quiet to think."

She crossed the street and ducked into the porchway of a high-fronted pub.

"Seriously? In here?" Ferguson was looking at the large lettering above the hanging flowerpots over the doorway. It read simply, *The Freemasons Arms*. "Aren't we trying to avoid the police? It's probably full of them."

"I doubt it," Ava pushed open the left-hand door, noticing the same Ark and cherub crest on the swinging pub sign. "They like to keep their membership under the radar."

The interior was a typical Victorian London pub, complete with large wooden tables and long leather-backed benches. Etched mirrors advertised the pub's brewery, leaving the remainder of the walls free for a range of football memorabilia and the mandatory widescreen plasma televisions. The bar itself stretched the length of the room, adorned by the obligatory polished brass foot rail.

583

The room was largely empty. They were served quickly, and took their drinks to a nearby table.

Ava spread Malchus's cryptic letter out onto the battered but highly polished wooden tabletop between them, and contemplated it quietly.

It clearly had three distinct sections, all in Malchus's hand—the first line in vermillion red Voynich, the next three in emerald green Voynich, and the last in emerald green ordinary letters.

"What does that mean?" Ferguson asked, putting his finger on the fifth line. "'FRATER PERDURABO'. I can only remember that *frater* is Latin for brother."

Ava had been turning it over in her mind since she first saw the words. She knew their literal translation—that was straightforward. But the phrase was vaguely familiar, and she had a frustrating feeling she had come across it somewhere before. Still, the plain meaning of the words was simple enough. "*Perduro* means to go on forever," she explained, "or to endure. So it simply means 'Brother, I will go on forever'."

Ferguson looked grim. "Another madman dreaming of a thousand-year *Reich*."

She took a sip of her cider, enjoying the punchy aroma of apples. "Did you find anything on De Molay?" She was conscious they had not had a chance to discuss what he had been researching while she had been chasing after Prince's sD memory card. "Did you get anything to confirm whether the Templars still exist, or if he's their leader? Any leaks or rumours?"

He sighed with resignation. "Unfortunately, Olivier De Molay turns out to be as much of an enigma as the Order he claims to lead."

He leant forward across the table so as not to be overheard. "I couldn't find any public records on him anywhere. And I'm not at all clear how he could even be descended from the last Templar Grand Master, Jacques de Molay."

"Because the Templars took vows of chastity?" Ava asked. "I had been wondering about that."

Ferguson nodded. "But who knows. It's possible Jacques may have had a child before joining the Order. It happened. No less a person than the founder and first Grand Master, Hugh de Payns, was married and had a son before he felt the call to create the Templars."

Ava turned the idea over in her mind. It was an intriguing possibility. "In those days, a married man could only join a monastic order if his wife had left this world—either through a grave or the gateway of a nunnery." She paused, aware the answer to her next question could kill off any claim Olivier De Molay had to be legitimately directly descended from the last Grand Master. "Did you find any evidence Jacques married young, before giving it all up for the Templars?"

Ferguson rubbed a hand across his face in consternation. "It's bizarre. No one knows anything about Jacques' early life. Nothing at all. It's a complete blank until he was elected Grand Master in his fifties. In fact," he shrugged, "there's so little material available, it's almost as if someone didn't *want* the world to know about his early life. It's like it's been systematically erased."

Ava sat back against the buttoned leather cushion of the bench.

*Another dead end.*

They seemed to be everywhere when it came to the Templars.

She had been hoping Ferguson's research would have uncovered something—anything—that would help throw some perspective onto the story Saxby and De Molay had told them on the coach in Rome.

She was increasingly aware that she still had no real idea who Saxby and De Molay were. They plainly had significant influence of the sort usually reserved to clandestine government departments—but she had no real sense whether the Templar claim was true or a cover for something more sinister.

It made the urgency of solving Malchus's letter even more acute.

With every passing hour she was drifting further from her chance of recovering the Ark and the Menorah. And although they were making progress, at times it felt as if they were taking two steps back for every one forward.

She looked down at the strange letter lying on the table, and then up at Ferguson, who was flicking through the small pile of books on the Voynich manuscript she had borrowed from Cordingly.

"There seem to be a lot of theories about what the Voynich manuscript is—all by eminent experts in their different fields." He read off the back covers. "Alchemy. Pharmacy. Botany. Cosmology. Astrology. Medicine. Magic. They can't all be right."

Ava could see where he was going. "You still think it's a hoax?"

He tapped his beer glass gently on the table, preoccupied. "A couple of things are bothering me. For a start, the text doesn't have any punctuation. Doesn't that seem odd to you, if it really is a genuine language?"

"In the beginning God created the heaven and the earth," Ava answered with a smile, "and the earth was without form and void and darkness was upon the face of the deep and the spirit of God moved upon the face of the waters."

"I didn't take you for the type who got religious at moments of tension?" He looked at her uneasily.

She tried to keep the amusement off her face. "The Hebrew scriptures, which they call the *Tanakh,* make up most of the Bible. They include the well-loved tales of the creation, the garden of Eden, Noah's ark, the tower of Babel, Jacob's multicoloured coat, and a hundred other familiar stories. We call it the Old Testament. But, just like the Voynich manuscript, none of it has any punctuation."

"You mean someone added it later?" Ferguson looked incredulous.

She nodded. "Standardized punctuation is a relatively recent thing. None of the original ancient biblical texts had it. People have refined it in the last five hundred years. Basically, they had to make it up."

He put his glass down, staring at her. "You enjoy doing this, don't you?"

"In fact," Ava continued, "if you want to get technical, the lack of punctuation is the least of the Old Testament's problems. A much more challenging difficulty is the fact that it was written in biblical Hebrew and Aramaic—two dead languages that did not even have alphabets."

Ferguson raised an eyebrow. "I don't know how you sleep at night."

She smiled. "Dead languages have words whose subtleties or meanings we often don't know. And both languages are written with abjads—a uniquely Semitic system in which you only write consonants, with no vowels. So if I write 'bnd', you have to put in the vowels. You need to decide whether I meant 'band', 'bind', 'bond', 'boned', 'u-bend', or anything else you think of that fits. As you can imagine, it's easy to guess incorrectly and create totally different words and meanings. In the case of the Old Testament, you have to do it for six hundred thousand unvowelled and unpunctuated words which frequently don't have any spaces between the words either, as they often wrote texts in one continuous stream of letters. There are similar problems with the Greek of the New Testament, too. Although it does have vowels, it was also usually written without any spaces or punctuation."

Ferguson looked horrified. "So how on earth do people know what the real Bible says? Who decides? How does anyone choose which version is reliable?"

Ava looked over at a sign on the wall proclaiming: 'THE FOOTBALL ASSOCIATION WAS FOUNDED HERE IN 1863'. "I suspect most people are largely unaware there are different versions of the Bible's core texts. They probably imagine there's one original old Bible locked away in a vault somewhere, like the official French metal metre ruler from which all others in the world were once measured. But the truth is the opposite. There's no template copy of the Bible, just many hundreds of differing manuscripts and fragments for theologians to argue over. There's the Alexandrian Septuagint, the Masoretic from Babylon or Tiberias, the Dead Sea Scrolls, and a load of others. But it's not something people talk about a lot. For instance, in the English-speaking world, most people only really know the 1611 King James Bible, frozen in the language and limited textual scholarship of Shakespeare's time. It's an amazing work, a milestone in western thought, but no one could seriously say that reading it gives anything like the same experiences or meanings as the various ancient Hebrew and Aramaic texts."

Ferguson took another sip of his drink, shaking his head. "You're a very dangerous lady to know. I'm not sure the world is ready for you."

Not dangerous, she reflected. She had just always had a fascination for the questions other people did not ask. It was one of the things that had driven her to archaeology in the first place. She had never been satisfied with the explanation that an object was 'old' or 'historical'. She wanted to take things out of the numbing fog that blurred the centuries into a misty 'olden times', and find the details that connected them to real people who made, needed, or used them.

Of course, she knew the Bible was a collection of treasured and sacred texts for billions of people, revered for over two thousand years. But she could also see it with professional eyes as an unruly family of physical manuscripts—copied and translated thousands of times over the millennia, in and out of a variety of languages, with all the errors involved in those delicate processes.

The thought of scribes scratching away at their vellum and parchment brought her back to the Voynich manuscript, and something she had noticed in Cordingly's office.

She opened the large Voynich facsimile book again at a random page and turned it round so Ferguson could see it. "Another remarkable thing about the manuscript is the handwriting itself—the *ductus*, or flow of the author's pen. Do you see it's not broken or blotchy at all?"

Ferguson nodded.

"That means the scribe was happy writing the alphabet. It suggests he had done it many times before. Because normally if someone writes unfamiliar characters, the writing is hesitant and choppy as they stop regularly to check its accuracy."

"So whether he was writing or copying, he knew the letters intimately." Ferguson finished the thought for her.

"Exactly," Ava took another sip of her cider and sat back, feeling her energy coming back, "which makes a one-off fraud seem less likely."

"There's another thing bothering me," Ferguson flicked through the pages of the large facsimile book deep in thought. "People write to communicate. So unless the Voynich manuscript is a private journal, the readers would've needed a key. What if that key was once part of the manuscript?"

"Here," he pointed to a descriptive table in the book he had open in front of him. "It says the manuscript has lost a number of individual pages and two whole quires, whatever they are."

Ava sat forward—more alert now.

*She had missed that.*

She quickly took two napkins out of the small chrome box in the middle of the table. "If you want eight sides to write on, you take two large sheets of paper." She laid the napkins on top of each other, and folded them down the middle, creating a small booklet of four pages with eight sides. "Each section like this is a quire. Newspapers are still made this way, but with more pages. To build an old book, you simply stitch a group of quires together." Peering at the descriptive table he had found, she could see that the Voynich quires were mainly made of four sheets. "So if Voynich is missing two whole quires, that's potentially thirty-two sides of writing."

"And here," Ferguson pointed at the table again, "it says the manuscript contains a stub where one page has been hacked out."

"If you're right, and it came with a key," Ava tucked Drewitt's letter back into her pocket, "then we have to find Malchus or Drewitt's copy of that key. We may've missed it at Stockbridge House. Or maybe in Drewitt's rooms up at All Hallows College."

"What I don't get," Ferguson looked pensive, "is if it's not a hoax, why would anyone still need the original key? Why can't they just crack it? It simply doesn't make sense to me that modern computers can't break it.

They can perform ten thousand trillion operations a second. It's not like Bletchley Park any more—you don't have to put everything onto binary punch-cards and feed them into a wheezing computer the size of two rooms."

The words hit Ava like a blow in the solar plexus.

She stared at him.

"What?" He looked unsure what he had said.

"That's it!" she answered breathlessly.

Ferguson looked at her in confusion.

"Don't you see?" She could feel the fog lifting. "We don't need to crack Voynich, *because Malchus hasn't either*. He may be shrewd, but he's not cleverer than a supercomputer. And I don't believe he found an ancient key either—it would be in a medieval language, and I don't imagine that's his strong point."

"Then what?" Ferguson looked uncertain. "How did he send a letter to Drewitt in Voynich?"

"He didn't." She struggled to keep the elation from her voice. "All he's doing is using its characters. Blindly. You just said it. At Bletchley Park they turned unreadable codes into readable punch-cards—an 'alphabet' that made codes intelligible to computers."

Ferguson looked blank.

"Computers can't read real Voynich any more than we can. So people studying Voynich over the years must've turned it into alphabets that can be understood and read by humans and computers. That's the only way they can work on it."

"So there's a modern key?"

"Yes," Ava could feel the excitement rising, "It's not a translation into intelligible words. It won't tell you what the Voynich manuscript means. But it will let you swap the Voynich text in and out of an alphabet we can actually read. That's how computers can count and analyze its letter and word distribution patterns."

With a mounting feeling of exhilaration, she pulled out her phone and searched the internet for Voynich alphabet transliterations.

It only took a few moments before she found one. "I knew it!" She handed the phone to Ferguson. "It's called FSG, and was drawn up by military code-crackers in the 1940s." She took the phone back and searched again. "And here's another, called CURRIER, from the 1970s."

Excited, she kept searching.

Within a few more minutes, she had found five different alphabets—all used at different times by code-breakers to turn Voynich's tortuous glyphs into ordinary readable letters.

"Now what?" Ferguson asked. "It's going to take forever to apply those to the text in Malchus's letter."

Ava finished her pint and stood up. "We don't have the time or expertise to do this." She put the empty glasses back on the bar. "We need Socrates."

"Isn't he dead?" Ferguson collected the pile of books and tucked them under his arm. "I thought an eagle dropped a tortoise on his head two-and-a-half thousand years ago."

"That was Aeschylus," Ava pulled open the front door and headed out onto the noisy street. "And no—he's very much alive."

She made a quick phone call, before turning back to Ferguson. "We need a cab to the British Museum."

Ferguson looked up and down the street. "You'd best give me your phone first. When they realize we've gone AWOL, they'll use the phones' GPS to pinpoint us."

She pulled it out of her jacket with resignation and handed it to him, watching as he slipped it along with his own into the envelope he had removed from Cordingly's office. He walked across to a bright red cast iron pillar box sunk into the pavement nearby, and pushed the envelope through the narrow slit at the top.

He headed back over to Ava. "There's a mail collection in fifteen minutes. It'll buy us a bit of time—but not much."

———————— · ◆ · ————————

# 91

*British Museum*
*Bloomsbury*
*London WC1*
*England*
*The United Kingdom*

THE TAXI DROPPED Ava and Ferguson in Montagu Street, at the rear of the great museum.

Hurrying through an unassuming back door, Ava knew exactly where she was going. She had been a member of the museum's staff since 2004, starting in London, then on secondment to Jordan, and finally Baghdad. She came back regularly, and could have navigated her way down its endless corridors in the dark.

A lot had changed since the grand but unfashionable old Montagu House had become the first British Museum in 1759. Successive building projects had created a world-class facility built around eight million artefacts and Europe's largest covered square.

It had been her home from home for years—from long before she had become a member of staff. Throughout her life, she had spent innumerable hours in its long galleries—at times surrounded by hordes of other visitors, at others with just the sound of her own footsteps as company. She knew many of the collections intimately: Africa, Egypt, Greece and

Rome, the Middle East—everything from the exuberantly painted Egyptian mummies' sarcophagi to the grand austerity of Greece's great Pergamon altar.

She also knew exactly where she would put the Ark and the Menorah, if she ever got hold of them.

They would be the museum's star exhibits.

Housing the treasures in London would not please everyone. Yet at least the huge city had the experts to look after them, along with the vast number of scholars and visitors to study and enjoy them.

They arrived at a sign marked 'DEPARTMENT OF THE MIDDLE EAST'. The security guard greeted her like an old friend, opening the door and waving them through.

Ava arrived in front of the first office door, and knocked. A slim middle-aged Indian woman rose to great her. The identity tag round her neck read 'PATRICIA DAVIES'.

"Baghdad too hot for you?" the woman beamed.

Ava smiled back at the longest-serving member of the department. "We're recovering some amazing exhibits. And we're not lending them to you or anyone else," she replied. "So if you want to see the real glories of Mesopotamia, you'll have to come and visit."

"I'm sure," Patricia nodded. "Although we could do with you back here now, given all the footage of the Middle East on television. The department's never been so popular." She paused. "Anyway, I've booked Socrates for you. He's all yours. Just let me know when you're done."

"We'll be quick," Ava thanked her. "I owe you."

"You usually do," Patricia replied, sitting back down behind her desk.

"By the way," she called after Ava. "There was a man here asking after you earlier. He wanted to know if you still worked here. He wouldn't say who he was."

Ava felt her blood run cold.

She stared at Ferguson.

His grim expression said it all.

"English?" Ava asked.

She nodded. "Not memorable looking. Cut glass accent. Expensive shoes."

Not Malchus then. But it described most of her former MI6 colleagues perfectly.

*The net was tightening.*

Ferguson headed for the door. "We need to be quick. They'll have the place under surveillance already."

Ava nodded, and led Ferguson through a long series of sterile corridors to a back staircase signed, 'DEPARTMENT OF CONSERVATION AND SCIENTIFIC RESEARCH'.

Reaching the bottom of the stairwell, she opened the double doors and could immediately feel the drop in temperature and smell the clean recycled air.

As they hurried down the corridor, they passed a series of large windows revealing a row of laboratories packed with cabinets of drawers and shelves piled high with boxes.

Towards the end, they came to a set of thick slightly tinted glass doors.

Ava punched a code into the wall-mounted keypad, and the doors slid apart with a quiet hiss, revealing a sleek lab fitted with wall-to-wall clinical white surfaces and a number of workstations. It was low-lit by controlled lighting, and there were blinds pulled over two small windows close to the ceiling.

"Welcome to Socrates," she announced proudly to Ferguson, "the museum's mainframe for everything from x-radiography to electron microscopy and radio carbon dating."

Stepping over to the middle terminal, she dropped down into the yellow padded swivel chair in front of it and clicked the keyboard, bringing the screen to life. "But in addition, he's no slouch with languages."

"Here," she handed Drewitt's letter to Ferguson. "Put it face down on that scanner." She pointed towards an A2-size glass panel set into the worktop against the right wall.

Ferguson placed the paper carefully onto the glass and covered it with the black rubber mat lying rolled beside it.

Ava was meanwhile on the internet, finding the character sets of the five Voynich transcription alphabets she had identified earlier.

She uploaded them one by one into Socrates.

Sitting back and hitting ENTER, the scanner started to hum. A moment later, the computer's black screen dissolved, to be replaced with a pale grey grid of squares, nineteen across by five down. One by one, they filled with blue images of the strange characters spelling out Malchus's message.

"This programme is the gateway to the electronic inscriptions catalogue," she explained. "We take detailed photographs of every inscribed object, whether it's stone, pottery, coin, wax, textile, bone, or anything else. We scan the images in, and create a permanent electronic record which we can share with other museums."

"So Socrates is all-knowing," Ferguson nodded.

"As well as that," Ava continued, "for damaged, faded, or partial inscriptions, Socrates can match them off against the existing database or user-defined data sets."

"Do you get a lot of inscriptions the curators can't read?" Ferguson sounded surprised. "If the experts here can't make something out," he waved his arms to indicate the people in the building, "then who can?"

Ava continued staring at the screen, examining the letters closely. "You'd be surprised. There are a vast number of variants of each ancient alphabet depending on period and region. Just think how much hand-writing has changed in the last two hundred years. The same is true of ancient writing and inscriptions. Being able to match fragments of let-ters through Socrates is invaluable."

"Here, it's ready." She clicked the mouse. "Watch this."

The large grid shrank and moved up to the top of the screen, while five identical smaller grey grids appeared in a band across the bottom. There were empty, with a label above each one:

BENNET CURRIER EVA FROGGUY FSG

The white departmental telephone beside Ava rang.

It was Patricia. "Ava, that man, he's here again, and there's another one with him, too." She sounded anxious.

Ava took a deep breath, then replied quickly. "It's okay. Just tell them you haven't seen us."

"I did." Ava could hear the tension in Patricia's voice. "But I don't think they believed me. Ava, who are these people? Are you in some kind of trouble?"

Ava was thinking fast. "I'll be gone in a few minutes. Just deny every-thing." She put the phone down and turned to Ferguson. "They're here. They must've seen us come in."

She turned back to the terminal and struck another key. "Here goes. We need to pray this works."

The letters in the larger grid began to flash one by one, and identical copies of each letter dropped quickly down into the same respective posi-tion in each of the five smaller grids below, morphing on their descent into recognizable letters and numbers from the modern Roman alphabet.

In a few seconds it was done, and all five of the smaller grids across the bottom flashed simultaneously to indicate the task was complete.

Socrates had transliterated the Voynich characters in Drewitt's letter into readable text.

But as Ava looked at the five grids, she felt a flood of disappointment crashing over her.

There was nothing even remotely resembling an intelligible text. The writing in each box was gibberish—just garbled letters and numbers.

"It didn't work." The frustration in Ferguson's voice was evident. "We need to go."

Ava peered hard at the five grids. She was sure she had not made a mistake.

She did not believe for a moment that Malchus had actually cracked Voynich. He had to be using it as an alphabet. And she doubted he had the expertise to create his own transliteration. He must be using one of the standard ones.

Ferguson moved quickly to the glass door and opened it, peering out into the corridor. "If these guys are who I think they are, they can walk through walls. We could have company any minute. We'll be sitting ducks in here."

"Give me two seconds." Ava tried to block out all thoughts. The answer had to be there, hiding in the five baffling grids.

She rubbed her eyes and looked at each one carefully in turn, willing herself to see a pattern.

Ferguson pulled out his Sig Sauer and flipped the safety off. "You need to hurry," he urged her. "This could get noisy quickly."

"Just a minute." She stared at the screen intently. The answer was there somewhere. She was sure of it.

"We're overstaying our welcome." Ferguson's voice was sounding increasingly tense.

She continued to stare at the screen, unable to hold back a growing anxiety that she had somehow got it wrong.

Then in the blink of an eye, she saw it.

*There!*

"It's that one," she stabbed the screen excitedly, pointing to the EVA alphabet.

"What?" Ferguson was still at the door.

"Look." She blew the third grid up to full screen size.

```
        J C   6 9
     V Z R U G   R I   P R V H V
  F R G   J D V   4 0 A   X V H O H V V
     I L O G   F R G   R 1   4 8 6 4
     F R A T E R   P E R D U R A B O
```

"I don't get it." Ferguson was frowning at the screen, shaking his head.

"The other four are completely random jumbles of letters and numbers," Ava replied with mounting excitement. "But in this one," she tapped it, "each word sequence and number sequence is whole." She counted the characters quickly. "Leaving aside the 'FRATER PERDURABO', there are eight whole words and two complete numbers. If we were using the wrong alphabet key, then the letters, numbers, punctuation and other symbols would all be randomly jumbled up within the same words—like in the other four. But this has whole uncorrupted words and numbers. The only two exceptions, '40A' and 'RI', could be house numbers, postcodes, or something similar."

Ava flicked onto the internet and quickly searched for the EVA alphabet. She was well aware precious time was passing, but if the museum was under surveillance, this was going to be her only chance. They would not be coming back.

Ferguson moved swiftly into the room and picked up the letter from the scanner, stuffing it into his pocket. He returned to the door, and raised the handgun in readiness.

Ava was reading out loud to Ferguson from the screen in front of her:

> "EVA is the European Voynich Alphabet, the most widely used of all the Voynich transcription alphabets. It strives to use Roman letters that resemble their allocated Voynich characters. When used in computer fonts, numbers are based on the handwritten page numbers added onto the manuscript by Dr John Dee."

She swivelled the chair to face Ferguson, her eyes gleaming. "This is it. It's the only one that makes sense. And the Dr Dee reference would be right up Malchus's street. It's exactly what he would choose. All we have to do now is work out what it means"

She heard the footsteps running down the corridor a second before Ferguson's voice. "Ava—move!" He punched the button by the door and it slid shut with another hiss. "Two of them." He was rushing towards her. "And they're not wearing lab coats."

She hit print, and waited the agonizing few seconds as a hard copy of all five grids appeared in the printer under the workstation. Grabbing them, she flicked the power button, crashing the terminal immediately.

"This way," Ferguson urged, standing on the desk and ripping aside one of the blinds, yanking open the small high window behind it.

Ava climbed up onto the desk and hooked her fingers over the wooden frame. Hoisting herself through the small open window, she landed hard in the narrow concrete light well.

Seconds later, Ferguson arrived beside her, pulling the window shut behind him. As she scrambled to her feet, she caught a glimpse of the doors of the lab sliding open and a pair of feet entering.

Her heart hammering hard, she did not stop to see any more, but sprinted down the light well to the short flight of concrete stairs at the far end.

She had only one thought—to put as much distance between them and their pursuers as fast as possible.

Ferguson was beside her, running hard. "They'll be watching everything. We can't use public transport, hotels, or any of the regular safe houses. We need to completely disappear."

Arriving at the stairs up to the main esplanade level, they climbed them two at a time.

"Do you like Chinese food?" he asked breathlessly as they headed across the courtyard, losing themselves in the heaving throng of anonymous tourists sweeping out of the museum's main gates and into Great Russell Street.

---

## 92

*Chinatown*
*Soho*
*London WC1*
*England*
The *United Kingdom*

STRIDING BRISKLY, AVA and Ferguson mingled with the crowds spilling out of Bloomsbury and onto the top of Charing Cross Road.

Whoever was after them would not be far behind.

She glanced over her shoulder anxiously.

Ferguson checked his watch. "What do you know? They should be serving food by now."

"You know a safe house with a restaurant?" She crossed over onto the west side of the road, joining the international throng heading from Oxford Street down to Leicester Square.

"Something like that." Ferguson ushered her off the busy road into a narrower side street.

It was quieter here. They were moving away from the main tourist areas, and in no time she could no longer hear the laughing and jostling of the crowds.

Spotting a man in a denim jacket turn into the road seventy-five yards behind them, she stopped and looked at a shop window until he had passed.

"Was he following us?" Ferguson asked.

Ava shook her head. "I don't think so. But let's make sure."

Ferguson turned left into the next street, and after twenty yards ducked into a recessed doorway. Ava followed.

Shaded by the doorway, they were invisible to anyone turning the corner.

They waited for ten minutes, but there was no sign of anyone.

Carrying on down the street, they turned right, right, and then left, until they were walking quickly in their original direction, but one road parallel.

The atmosphere in the narrow streets was a world away from the busy West End thoroughfare they had left behind. The bustling coffee-shops, fast food chains, and ticket kiosks for London's shows had evaporated, replaced by a variety of Chinese supermarkets, businesses, and restaurants.

"Very close now." Ferguson announced, indicating for her to turn into a dark covered alleyway.

It smelled of rubbish bins and urine.

Ava was not aware that this part of Soho was off limits to surveillance teams, but she kept quiet—intrigued to see where Ferguson was taking her.

Emerging from the end of the alley, she noticed that the street signs had changed. In place of the traditional bold English lettering, the signs were now bilingual, with Chinese logograms occupying the lower half of the iconic white plaques.

Turning into an even quieter street, Ferguson led her quickly past a pet shop and what looked like a building contractor's office, before stopping outside a narrow but inviting restaurant. He pushed the door open, and ushered Ava inside.

The ceiling was hung with tasselled red square lanterns, and delicate wooden screens of slim geometric batons adorned the walls. The furniture was lacquered a shiny black, and an invisible sound system played the faint but unmistakable strains of mellow oriental strings and flutes.

It was still relatively early, and there were only a few other diners. Ava suspected it was rarely full. It was not exactly well positioned for passing trade.

Ferguson closed the door behind them, and a solemn-looking waiter approached.

As he drew closer, Ava saw his expression change. There was a flicker of uncertainty, followed by a look of surprise. Then his mask of fixed professional courtesy crumpled into a smile of recognition.

He advanced on Ferguson warmly. "You came back."

Ferguson smiled, dropping his voice. "I was wondering whether you could do me a small favour."

Ava was surprised to see the waiter answer without hesitation. "Anything." He had not batted an eyelid.

"I need two beds for the night." Ferguson was speaking quietly.

The waiter glanced over at Ava, then back to Ferguson. "For you and your friend? Somewhere discrete?"

Ferguson shook his head. "Not like that. As I said—two beds. We need to disappear. And a laptop, too, if you can get me one."

Ferguson pointed to a quiet table away from the windows with a view of all the doors. The waiter nodded, and seated them there. "Leave it with me." He disappeared into the back of the restaurant.

Ava looked across the table at Ferguson. "Do you have that effect on all waiters?"

A waitress in a shimmering silk cheongsam quickly laid the table with an orange and red floating lily in a glass, and black chopsticks decorated with blue cranes. She placed a small bowl of pickled vegetables in front of each of them.

"I used to live near here," Ferguson confided when the waitress had gone. "I came in a bit when I was home on leave."

"That's it?" Ava was unconvinced.

Ferguson looked down at his plate. "They once offered to do me a favour. Now seemed like a good time to ask, that's all."

She shook her head. "The waiter acted like nothing would've been too much trouble. You could've asked to marry his sister and he'd have said yes."

Ferguson pincered a piece of pickled cucumber between his chopsticks and ate it thoughtfully.

Ava raised her hand slightly to call over the waitress. "If you don't tell me," she threatened, "I'll ask one of the staff."

"Okay," Ferguson looked resigned. "Just put your hand down."

Ava wanted to hear this. It was not often she saw Ferguson being reticent.

"About a year and a half ago, I was the last person here one night. I finished and went to wash my hands. When I came back, I heard a table being knocked over and crockery hitting the floor."

"I edged open the door," he pointed to the washroom door at the back of the room, "and could see there were three men in hoodies. One was going through the till. The other two were working on the waitress. The larger one was holding her, while the smaller one was opening her cheek with a Stanley knife. They were all laughing and jeering, egging him on. They were sky high on something, and the last thing they expected was a bloke running out of the washrooms at them."

"You soldiers are all the same. It's always about you." Ava shook her head in mock disapproval.

"And you wonder why I didn't want to tell you." He paused. "The lad with his fingers in the till got introduced to the base unit of that old-fashioned telephone over there. The bloke with the knife found himself talking to a fire extinguisher at close range. And the one who had been holding the girl was still on the floor whimpering over his shattered kneecap when the kitchen staff and other waiters came through to see what the noise was."

"What happened to the waitress?" Ava asked.

Ferguson paused. "Not good. She was badly shaken and needed stitches."

"And our waiter?" Ava glanced in the direction of the swing doors he had departed through.

"The girl's uncle—first on the scene from the kitchen, where he'd been cleaning up."

"What happened to the attackers?"

Ferguson took a sip of the beer that had appeared. "A passer-by coming out of the restaurant opposite called the police. But when they arrived, no one here wanted to say anything. The police carted the men away. I guess they had a night in the cells and were then released."

Ava was appalled. "So they got away with it?"

"I doubt it very much," Ferguson lowered his voice. "Our friends here belong to a very private community. They don't talk to the police, and they don't go to court. But that doesn't mean crimes go unpunished. They have a strong traditional code."

He took another mouthful of pickled vegetables. "I never asked what happened to them. And I don't want to know. But I doubt they'll be thinking of causing trouble in Chinatown again any time soon."

The waiter returned and spoke softly to Ferguson. "It's arranged. But first, the food is on me." He took Ferguson's menu. "You won't need this."

Ava handed him her menu, too. "I should hang around you more often," she confided once the waiter had gone. "I could get used to this."

Ferguson sat back looking contented. "One thing's for sure. We're going to be undisturbed this evening. Our colleagues from Vauxhall Cross and Millbank may have this town sewn up with microphones, cameras, cars, watchers, and snitches in every conceivable place. But we just fell off the radar. We're in London's very own Bermuda Triangle."

# DAY ELEVEN

———— • ◆ • ————

## 93

*Maze Hill*
*London SE10*
*London*
*The United Kingdom*

URI WOKE WITH a start.

But too late.

The men in balaclavas were already on top of him.

He slept with a sidelight on, so he could always see what was happening. But they had been quiet and quick. He had no time to reach for the handgun he always kept under his pillow.

His arms were yanked hard behind his back and rapidly secured tightly with what felt like rope. At the same time, a wide strip of masking tape was stuck roughly over his mouth, and a thick hood was pulled down over his head.

As the world went dark, he tried lashing out with his legs—but they did not move. Men were already sitting on his lower body, and he could feel his ankles being bound tightly.

There was nothing he could do except force himself to override the reflex to panic.

Most of all, he had to stay alert—to not miss any details. Any one of them could save his life.

The men were clearly professional. It was obviously not the first time they had done this. They moved swiftly and in silence, as a team.

He had already worked out they did not want to kill him—at any rate, not yet. If they had, he would be dead already.

He tried to slow his breathing, but his body was surging with adrenaline as he tried to protect himself from whatever assault was about to begin.

But it was all guesswork. He could see nothing, and would have no warning of an attack. One could come from any direction.

He felt himself being rolled roughly onto his side, then onto his back again, while something was wrapped around him. He could not work out what it was until he heard a long zip being done up from his feet to his head.

He knew what that sound was all too well.

*He was being sealed inside a body bag.*

He could feel the sweat pouring off him, as he braced for whatever was going to happen next.

There was the unmistakable sound of the slide on an automatic handgun being drawn back, cocking the weapon. Then he felt something hard being rammed into the base of his skull.

After a few seconds, the gun was withdrawn.

It was a warning.

The threat was severe. He knew that. He had seen four men in his room the moment before they hooded him, and he had to assume there would be more—at least one at the door, and perhaps one or more going through his possessions.

With no warning, he felt himself being lifted roughly off the bed.

He was totally at their mercy. He wanted to protect his head, but his hands were bound behind his back. If they planned to kick him about or throw him out of the window, there was nothing he would be able to do to protect himself.

But he was being held firmly, and could feel himself bumping against the men carrying him. He had no idea where they were taking him, but from the unmistakable foetid smell, he could tell they had left his flat and were now in the corridor.

As they reached the stairs and he sensed his body being angled downwards head first, he began to struggle. It was a reflex action, but he stopped when he felt a hard blow to his head, and the men's grip on him tightened as they began descending.

It took all his willpower to stop himself from shouting out. His logical mind told him they were holding him firmly, and were not about to throw him down the concrete stairwell. But his natural instinct was to struggle and get as far away from the danger as possible.

*Who were these people? What did they want?*

If he was honest, the list of people who might like to take him on a little trip was not exactly short.

He and his colleagues from the Institute lived under the permanent threat of being uncovered by their country's enemies—which they all knew included a long roll-call of hostile governments and paramilitary groups.

The fact he was in the *Metsada* department and carried out political assassinations for a living was probably not even the issue. It would be enough for most of their enemies to know he was active Mossad. He could work in the car pool for all the difference it would make.

If it was not one of his country's enemies, it could just as easily be the British authorities. Nobody had kept the MI5 liaison at Thames House in the loop, and they would not take kindly to a covert operation being run on UK soil without their knowledge. If they found out what he was up to, he could expect an unfriendly reception and a seat on the next plane back to Tel Aviv.

Or maybe it was his own side? It was always a possibility. The local Mossad team had not been alerted to his presence, and there was no guarantee any of them knew his face. They could even be using outside contractors. Or perhaps they had been monitoring Malchus's organization, and wanted to ask a few questions of the latest ss recruit?

Finally, there was always the chance he had been betrayed. Not by Moshe, he was sure of that. But something had definitely gone wrong. The secure sms message he had received to clear the old KGB dead letter box at the Brompton Oratory had turned out to be a wild goose chase. There had been nothing there to recover, and he had no response from the contact's phone number, which he had been texting at intervals ever since.

Maybe his contact had been captured and was singing like a canary?

It was all speculation. But he needed to work through the possibilities. Knowing who had him could save his life.

There were no doors at the bottom of the grimy stairwell, which opened directly onto the pavement. He could hear a car engine idling close by—but quickly realized there were two. There was no other traffic or street noise.

It must be the very small hours of the morning—between 2:30 and 4:00 a.m., he guessed.

A moment later, he registered multiple bolts of pain to his head, back, and knees, as he felt himself being stuffed into a car boot.

To confirm it, the lid slammed shut above him with an unmistakably ominous thud.

It was soon followed by the noise of car doors being pulled closed, before there was nothing but darkness and the sound of the rapidly accelerating engine.

## 94

*Maze Hill*
*London SE10*
*England*
*The United Kingdom*

THE CAR STOPPED without warning, and Uri was bundled out of it.

He had no idea where he was.

He could be anywhere.

He estimated he had been in the boot for at least twenty minutes. But it was impossible to be sure.

He was hauled into a building, and dropped onto a hard floor.

He felt the body bag being unzipped, and hands lifting him out, standing him on his feet.

He was leant up against something cold and hard, and belts were tightened around him, lashing him upright.

With no warning, the hood was ripped off, and he could see again.

Blinking, he saw he was in an industrial space—an old factory, he guessed. The concrete floor was cracked, with holes marking where machinery had once stood.

The walls were London brick—an indeterminate red-brown colour he had seen in old industrial buildings everywhere around. Years of neglect had covered them in a grimy patina that now seemed part of their design.

The only light was from a clip-on bulb in a wire cage clamped to one of the pillars and wired onto an old car battery.

The building looked as if it had been thoroughly gutted years ago. The few high windows were covered with warped metal sheeting. All that remained at floor level were rows of rusty iron pillars supporting the high ceiling.

He was tied to one of them.

It smelled damp. There was a faint tang of salt in the air, which meant they were somewhere near the river—presumably in one of the many derelict buildings that silently witnessed the Thames' heavy mercantile and industrial past.

The floor immediately around him was noticeably more dirty and stained than the rest. He suspected it was not the first time someone had been brought here and tied to this pillar to be worked over.

One of the balaclavad men approached him.

He could only watch as the punch came—a savage blow to his solar plexus, intensified by the matt black knuckleduster wrapped around his attacker's fist.

There was nothing he could do except brace himself for the impact, which sent an explosion of pain tearing through his torso and directly up to his brain.

The man pulled off his balaclava and looked at Uri.

Uri stared back at him without blinking.

*It was Otto.*

But he was no longer the Skipper's deferential number two. The man in front of him now was very definitely in charge.

The others had melted away around the room.

This was plainly Otto's show.

"Did you know, Danny," Otto's tone was purposefully breezy, "SS men were required to administer punishment beatings to their fellow soldiers, sometimes to the death, to teach them the discipline of absolute obedience. To turn them into a purifying storm of steel."

Uri saw the fist coming again, and braced himself against the hard metal ridges that smashed into his stomach a split-second later.

He could feel the pain rip through him, but stifled the urge to show it. As he lifted his head up again, Otto tore the strip of masking tape off his mouth.

"But in your case, Danny, this exercise has a purpose. You see," he paused to punch him viciously in the gut again, "I know the Skipper likes you, but I must say," he unleashed another hard blow at his solar plexus, grunting as he did so, "personally I have my doubts."

Uri was clenching his teeth to stifle the pain. He wanted to lash out, but it was pointless.

"The thing is, Danny," Otto moved away, and slipped off the knuckle-duster, "I've been doing a bit of research on you. And do you know what I've found?"

Uri gazed back at him, his face set like stone.

"Well, you see, that's just the problem. I can't find anything. You're a ghost, Danny."

*So that was what this was about.*

"There's no Danny Motson born on the twenty-first of November 1978 in Liverpool." Otto leant in, putting his face a few inches from Uri's. "So my question, Danny, is who are you, and why are you interested in us?"

Otto bent down and uncoiled a long double hose. As he picked it up, Uri could see it ended in a slim metal pipe with an angled nozzle.

His heart began hammering against his ribcage as he recognized what it was.

Looking behind Otto, he saw the pair of small battered and chained cylinders of pressurized gas, confirming the worst.

"Do you know how hot this gets, Danny?" He looked at Uri, but did not wait for an answer. "No? I'll tell you. Six thousand three hundred degrees Fahrenheit."

Otto held the nozzle a few inches from Uri's face. "So let's start with some answers, shall we?"

"I told you," Uri answered through gritted teeth, "I was in Australia. I just got back."

Otto smiled nastily. "I'm not interested in where you've been, Danny. I want to know who you are."

"I've told you my real name," Uri challenged him. "Which is more than I know about you, 'Otto'."

"You catch on quick, Danny." Otto let out a low chuckle, but there was no humour in it.

Uri had prepared the cover meticulously with Moshe before leaving Israel.

He did not want anything that involved false papers or a complicated web of alibis.

He had quickly come up with the idea of Danny Motson—a loner with no past except a shadowy history in the world of organized crime.

It was a perfect cover for the assignment. In the world he was entering, there were dozens of guys like Danny.

Moshe had wanted to set up one or two people who would vouch for him if any questions were asked, but Uri had refused point blank. He did not want to have anything riding on the credibility of anyone else.

Danny was a loner. And that suited Uri just fine.

"I said my family's from Liverpool," Uri slipped quickly into the story. The key was to deliver it with absolute confidence. The consequences of being unconvincing were stark. "You never asked where I was born. It was Rhodesia—when some of us still thought it was British. The '64 to '79 war destroyed most records and paperwork. And I haven't exactly registered for a social security number since."

Otto shook his head, opening the regulators and valves on the cylinders. He pulled out a metal cigarette lighter and touched it to the tip of the nozzle. With a loud popping sound, a long ragged yellow acetylene flame shot out of the pipe, roaring loudly.

"You see, Danny. That all just sounds too convenient for me." He moved a step closer towards Uri. "And I don't like coincidences."

Uri watched as Otto turned a small screw on the handle, blending in the pure pressurized oxygen, increasing the temperature of the flame by over a thousand degrees. As the oxygen rushed in, the jagged billowing yellow flame narrowed into a vicious-looking tube, and turned a loud hissing blue.

Apart from the noise of the torch, the warehouse was silent. Uri thought he heard an engine pass by outside, but then it was gone.

Otto held the flame closer to Uri's face. The heat was searing. At its core it was hot enough to turn solid steel cherry red in seconds. He would be incinerated in less—the flame was three-and-a-half times hotter than a crematorium.

"I think it's time we showed you who's boss, Danny. You're a bit big for your boots, for a new boy. Maybe you need to learn a little bit about who runs things around here."

The heat was becoming unbearable. Uri could feel the sweat pouring off his face and torso. Behind the flame, Otto's eyes were gleaming with a savage intensity.

With a sickening burst of clarity, Uri realized this was never to have been an interrogation.

*It was an execution.*

He stared Otto in the eye.

Death was not something he thought about much. But he knew one thing. When it was his turn, he would go down fighting like the warriors of old—Samson, Saul, Ahab, Judas Maccabeus. The list was long. When he went, he would join his country's roll of honour.

"You think you're ss, Otto? An elite political soldier?" Uri spat out the challenge. "You're a joke."

Otto shook his head. "Have it your way, Danny." He took a step closer, bringing the end of the nozzle up towards Uri's eye.

With no warning, Uri became aware of footsteps on the hard concrete floor. They were approaching quickly behind Otto.

"Alright, that's enough." The voice came from the shadows, but Uri knew it from the evening at *The Bunker*.

It was the Skipper.

Uri was suddenly aware of the huge man striding across the room. His face was calm, but it was clear from the tone of his voice he was not happy with the scene he had walked in on.

"Untie him." He glared at Otto. "Now."

Otto stared at Uri for a few seconds, before slowly shutting off the acetylene screw on the handle and letting the flame die. He kept his eye contact with Uri all the while, defiantly.

Uri was under no illusions. It was not over as far as Otto was concerned.

Otto put the hose down, and moved behind Uri, untying the belts and cutting the ropes with a butterfly knife he pulled from his pocket.

Uri stayed where he was by the column, gently stretching his hands and legs, allowing the blood to start circulating again.

As the Skipper drew level with Otto, he tossed Uri a set of car keys. "Get lost, Danny," he ordered. "Keep your phone on. Wait for orders."

Uri resisted the urge to look back at Otto. This was a job. He had priorities. He would not let it get personal.

He nodded at the Skipper, and headed for the door.

Once outside, he inhaled the night air deeply, trying to calm the storm of endorphins his system was pumping out in elation at having made it out alive.

It was not the first time someone had tried to kill him. And it would not be the last.

But it had certainly been the closest.

As he headed for the car, he realized he should be thanking Otto. That degree of jealousy could only mean Otto felt Uri was a threat to his position in the organization.

Uri smiled.

He was obviously making an impact within the group's inner circle of power. It meant he was getting closer to the centre.

To Malchus.

---

## 95

*Chinatown*
*Soho*
*London WC1*
*England*
The *United Kingdom*


AVA WOKE EARLY.

The waiter had been as good as his word.

After supper, he had led her and Ferguson through a series of poorly lit back alleys in the heart of Chinatown, before finally arriving at the rear of a shop. It was long past closing time, and the tatty metal shutters had been pulled down so Ava could not tell what it sold.

A middle-aged woman had answered the security door, ushering them wordlessly into a room in which four men were smoking and playing mah-jong with small bone tiles. The woman had pulled aside a black silk curtain to reveal a concealed door and staircase leading up to a hallway, bedroom, and bathroom.

The waiter accompanied them into the bedroom. A threadbare golden dragon strode across a faded watery red silk cloth pinned to the wall, and a stubby grey plastic Buddha water fountain bubbled on top of a pile of video recorder boxes. There were two mattresses with blankets on the floor, a metal table with an old laptop on it, and two chairs.

Otherwise the room was bare.

The waiter had given Ferguson a set of keys. "Nobody will bother you," he had reassured them.

And he had been right.

She and Ferguson had collapsed onto the mattresses almost immediately, and fallen asleep exhausted.

Awake now, she looked at her watch. It was 5:30 a.m. Ferguson was still sleeping on the mattress on the other side of the room.

She had slept fitfully, woken repeatedly by a recurring dream of DeVere's lifeless eyes.

As she had lain awake in the dark, her mind kept wandering back to Malchus's enigmatic letter.

The text clearly divided into three sections. There was the phrase 'JC 69' in red at the top. Then the three green lines of message. Finally, the ending in Latin: 'Brother, I will endure forever'.

She had been going over and over the possibilities of what it could all mean.

The 'JC 69' was almost certainly separate from the message itself. The fact that it was in a different colour from the rest of the text had to be significant.

Was it personalizing the message for Drewitt, she wondered? His codename? A greeting of some sort? But she quickly ruled the idea out. Malchus had specifically addressed the envelope to Drewitt, so there was no need to repeat his name again in the first line of the message.

The only plausible explanation she could think of for the different colour was that it was a line of plaintext, or *en clair*, as her former colleagues at GCHQ called it. That meant it was not enciphered text, but an important piece of information in plain English giving instructions, like how to set the wheels on the decoding machine, or which cipher key to use.

If it was an *en clair* instruction, then it was vital. It was the key to the whole message—a puzzle within a puzzle that would unlock the rest.

As Ava lay on the mattress staring at the ceiling, she tried to think it through.

'JC' could be almost anything. And the '69' was equally enigmatic—it could refer to a year, an age, a distance, a grid reference, the astrological symbol for Cancer, or almost anything else.

Cycling through the possibilities in her head, trying to narrow them down, she found it was instead having the opposite effect—generating an endless variety of additional avenues.

As she wrestled with the baffling phrase, the early morning light began to seep through the blinds.

Unable to sleep, she pushed aside the blanket and got up.

Padding quietly through to the bathroom, she found two travel tooth-brush kits from an international hotel chain, and an old blue rubber shower hose attachment. Pushing its cups over the taps, she climbed into the bathtub and sprayed herself with the water. It was not exactly hot and relaxing—but the sudden chill did the job of fully waking her up.

By the time she was dressed and had made a cup of tea from the kettle in the corridor, she felt clear and ready to start properly.

She sat down at the small silver laptop, and opened up the letter from Malchus and the EVA printout from Socrates.

She started with the enigmatic first section—'JC 69'.

Although the most famous 'JC' was Jesus Christ, it seemed a long shot. Jesus had lived from around 4 BC to AD 30—so the '69' could not be a reference to his age or any calendar year during his lifetime.

As she considered the options, she heard Ferguson stirring behind her. "Hard at it?" he asked, running a hand through his hair and climbing off the mattress. "Have you made any progress?"

She shook her head. "I'm wondering if 'JC 69' is a line of *en clair*, point-ing Drewitt to a particular key. The most obvious 'JC' is Jesus Christ, but that seems pretty unlikely, given Malchus's interests."

Ferguson headed through into the bathroom, and in no time she could hear the sound of the shower.

Turning back to 'JC 69' and Jesus, it also seemed unlikely to be any kind of date associated with his followers, as the modern Christian cal-endar of BC and AD was unknown in Jesus' day. The Roman military who occupied his country with an iron fist based their calendar on the regnal year of the current Caesar, none of whom ever survived as long as six-ty-nine years. The Jewish calendar of Jesus' day was no use either, as it was not remotely standardized.

The more she considered it, the more a solution based around Jesus seemed fundamentally implausible. Malchus was definitely not a Chris-tian, and it was far-fetched that he would use anything to do with the life of Jesus as a key for his message.

"I was wondering, what about *The Jewish Chronicle*?" Ferguson suggested, re-entering the room, dressed and ready. "It's widely available, and Malchus clearly has an interest in certain aspects of Jewish history."

"Let's give it a go," Ava nodded. "It has acres of text that change every day. It would be a perfect key."

Flicking on the laptop, she navigated to *The Jewish Chronicle*'s home page. "Look," she pointed to the screen. "It's been published every Friday for around a hundred and seventy years. That means the sixty-ninth edition came out sometime in the early 1840s."

Ferguson sat down beside her, peering intently at the screen. "So there *is* a '69' edition they could have used?" The excitement was mounting in his voice.

Ava hunted around the website until she found the section with the past editions.

"Damn!" she muttered under her breath, leaning back in her chair, pointing to the relevant part of the screen. "Access to old editions is not freely available. You have to buy it."

"And Malchus and Drewitt would not want to leave payment trails," Ferguson concluded flatly.

He looked at the EVA printout intensely, tapping on the table. "What about Julius Caesar?" he suggested. "He was alive in 69 BC wasn't he?"

Ava could feel a smile breaking out on her face.

*That was much more like it.*

"Now he's someone Malchus may well have chosen," she agreed, opening up a fresh browser window. "A brutal and ruthless dictator— probably something of a role model for him."

Ava navigated to an image of Caesar to help her think. It was the only known bust of him dating from his lifetime, and she had been struck by it ever since she had seen the original in Turin.

He seemed strangely ordinary-looking for the most successful military conqueror of his time—as well as writer, dictator, philanderer, pagan priest, and finally god. She suspected she would not have looked twice if he had passed her in the street. Unlike Malchus—with his hairless head and soulless dead green eyes.

She scrolled through Caesar's list of writings, hoping one would catch her eye—something that might appeal to Malchus.

But despite Caesar's fame as an author, she was surprised to find that the list of his writings was unexpectedly short—mainly accounts of his wars.

Just as she was about to rule him out, she felt a flutter of excitement as she saw the last entry on the page. She rested the cursor on a single line. "It says that Caesar's aunt Julia died in 69 BC, and he gave a famous speech at her funeral."

*Was that it?*

Typing quickly, she searched for the actual text of the speech.

Maybe all she would have to do was write out the first twenty-six letters of the text, omitting repeats, until she had all the letters of the alphabet in the order they appeared in the text. To make allowances for the shorter Latin alphabet, she would use the same letters for I and J and also for U, V, and W, but that would not be a problem. Then she would map the first to A, the second to B, the third to C, and so on. The result would be a perfect new alphabet based uniquely on the text of Caesar's speech.

It was basic cryptography. Virtually uncrackable without the key.

But clicking open the Latin text of Caesar's oration at Julia's funeral, she felt an instant jolt of disappointment. "It's only a couple of lines long. No more than sixty words." She scrolled a little further. "And look, this text wasn't even written by Caesar. It was reported by a Roman historian born over a hundred years after Caesar's death."

She sat back with a sigh.

*Another dead end.*

She took another mouthful of the hot tea, and walked over to the window. Opening two slats of the blinds with her fingers, she peered out.

The view from the back of the building looked out over the varied rooftops of Chinatown. It was indistinguishable from anywhere else in central London—just a jumble of air-conditioning units, extractor fans, and chimneys.

She could not see the street, so had no idea if anyone was there who might have followed them the night before.

If anyone was waiting, she would find out soon enough.

She sat back down at the table—for now, her only priority was to get to the bottom of Malchus's letter.

She wondered if perhaps she was approaching it wrong.

She retraced her steps. Malchus's original message in the Voynich alphabet had been a cipher—the substitution of one letter of the English alphabet for a corresponding one in the Voynich alphabet.

Looking at the text Socrates had produced from the European Voynich Alphabet, she was willing to bet the jumbled English was also a cipher. It would be the most obvious choice.

Ciphers were more sophisticated and flexible than codes, as they did not require long books of precise pre-agreed code phrases with different meanings. Ciphers were much more flexible. Any message could be simply enciphered and sent, so long as the reader knew which key was being used.

She stared down at the page.

*So which cipher was Malchus using?*

She was sure the answer lay in the *en clair* line at the beginning. It would hold the answer to which key he had chosen.

She gazed at it for the hundredth time.

Ferguson was staring at the floor. "Caesar was a great general though, wasn't he, with armies all over the Mediterranean?" He looked up at her. "So how did he send messages to his troops?"

"Let's have a look," Ava nodded, sitting down and pulling up a browser page before typing in a query.

As the answers filled the screen, she could feel her pulse start racing.

"My God!" she gasped.

"What is it?" Ferguson asked, craning to see the list of search results that had appeared.

"That's it!" she turned to him excitedly, and then pointed back at the screen. "Look. The Caesar Cipher. It says he sent hundreds of confidential military messages to his troops all over France, Spain, and North Africa. Apparently he ensured their security by using the Caesar Cipher, a form of encryption he invented, which was named after him along with the month of July, the Julian calendar, and Caesarian births.

"Well how does it work?" Ferguson urged her, leaning forward in his chair intently.

"It shifts the letters of the alphabet a fixed number of places," Ava explained, reading off the screen. "A one-shift Caesar Cipher turns 'ABC' into 'BCD'. A two-shift Caesar Cipher turns 'ABC' into 'CDE', and so on."

"Simple but effective," Ferguson nodded. "The cipher text will be completely meaningless to anyone who doesn't know how it was created."

Ava was typing excitedly. They were onto something. She was sure of it.

*This had to be the answer! It would appeal to Malchus on every level.*

She opened a new spreadsheet on the laptop and wrote out the alphabet sequentially five times in bold capitals along the top row—one character per cell. When it was done, she locked them in as her reference line.

Underneath it, she typed in the alphabet again, then shifted it sixty-nine places to the right.

"What's the first line of the EVA printout?" she asked Ferguson, getting ready to enter it into the spreadsheet.

"V Z R U G," Ferguson read off, as she typed it in.

She looked at the result, first using the original as the base, then the shifted text.

To her disappointment, both results were nonsense.

She repeated the exercise, but this time shifting the text sixty-nine places to the left.

Still nonsense.

Next she tried shifting the alphabet six places, then a further nine, working both left and right.

The results were still gibberish.

Ava could feel the frustration building. "This has to be right," she muttered, staring at the two rows of alphabet on her screen. She thought with a smile that she needed whatever computer Cordingly had been envisaging when he suggested governments had machines that could crack any enciphered text.

But she did not have one, so was going to have to do it the old-fashioned way—by trial and error.

She hunched over the computer and tried to think of other permutations—six times nine was fifty-four. She tried a shift of fifty-four from the beginning of the alphabet. Then from the other end.

The results were all still meaningless.

"What other letter shift could it be?" she asked Ferguson, looking up in frustration. "It has to be a Caesar Cipher. But what are they using as a key? And why 'JC 69'?"

Ferguson stood up and walked over the window. "Well, we're definitely making progress. I'm just grateful it's not still in Voynich."

Ava froze.

"What?" he asked. "What did I say?"

She could feel a flush of excitement as the significance of his throwaway remark sank in.

*Could it be?*

She sprang up, and reached for the pile of books Cordingly had lent her.

*Was it really that simple?*

"Why would they use another text," she asked breathlessly, "when they already had Voynich, open right in front of them!" She could feel her excitement mounting. "It makes perfect sense."

Dropping the large facsimile book onto the table, she turned to the first page and found the sixth line, then the ninth letter along. Bringing up the EVA alphabet, she read it off.

It was a 'Y'. The twenty-fifth letter of the alphabet.

She cleared the spreadsheet of all her work so far, leaving only the reference alphabet in bold across the top. Under it, she wrote out another alphabet, this time with a twenty-four-shift, so the 'A' of the second row lined up with the 'Y' in the original alphabet.

Reading them off and writing them down, she looked at the result, feeling a wave of disappointment.

It was another senseless jumble of letters.

Frustrated, she turned to the sixth page, and ran her finger down to the first letter of the ninth line.

It translated as a 'D'.

Quickly deleting the previous alphabet, she wrote out another one— this time with a three-shift, mapping the 'A' in her reference line to the 'D' in her code line.

Looking at the text she was tapping out, she gasped as a word appeared:

SWORD

"Oh my God, look at this." She stabbed the screen breathlessly.

Ferguson leant over her, peering at the screen. "Well, keep going!" The excitement in his voice was unmistakable.

Steadying the trembling in her hand, she continued to read off the characters from Malchus's letter and type the deciphered words out:

SWORD OF MOSES

With the colour rising to her cheeks, she quickly read off the rest and wrote out the remaining two lines:

COD GAS 178 USELESS

FIND COD OX 1531

She could feel her heart pumping hard.

*It couldn't be.*

She stared at the whole message:

SWORD OF MOSES

COD GAS 178 USELESS

FIND COD OX 1531

FRATER PERDURABO

"What on earth is that?" Ferguson sounded bemused. "Does it mean anything?"

"It does to me," Ava whispered, finding it impossible to tear her eyes from the screen.

"What?" Ferguson urged her. "What does it mean?"

She turned to look up at him. "It means," she answered slowly, "that Malchus is undoubtedly quite insane."

She felt dazed.

"Give me a moment." She turned back to the laptop and began searching again.

She knew exactly where to look.

Once she had finished, it finally all made sense—the Ark, the Menorah, King Solomon's Temple, Drewitt, the apocalyptic references. Everything.

"Are you going to fill me in?" Ferguson was staring at her.

Ava got up and walked over to the window. "There's sinister magic in the Bible," she answered slowly. "And we seem to have walked right into it."

"In the Bible?" Ferguson looked at her sceptically.

Ava nodded. "People just don't think of it that way, because it's the Bible. But it's there. Miracles are magic. We just don't use the word. And at times it's very dark. For example, King Saul banned all sorcery in his lands, and then disguised himself to visit the witch of Endor, before ordering her to raise the dead prophet Samuel from the grave so Saul could consult him. Witches raising dead bodies is dark magic in anyone's book."

Ferguson looked pensive.

"Or, in King Solomon's Temple, there were a series of ritual curses that the Temple priests would write on scrolls. They would then wash them off in water that a woman suspected of adultery was forced to drink. If she was guilty, their curses would make her stomach swell up, she would miscarry, and her thigh would wither. Again, cursing people with physical deformities is usually thought of as pretty sinister magic."

"Unbelievable." Ferguson shook his head in amazement.

"*The Sword of Moses* is an ancient manuscript that comes directly from this magical Hebrew tradition. It's very old dark magic, for summoning and conjuring."

"Demons?" Ferguson asked.

Ava shook her head. "Yahweh."

Ferguson looked dubious. "Don't millions of Jews and Christians call upon Yahweh every day?"

"Not like this." Ava dropped her voice. "*The Sword of Moses* contains conjurations for summoning Yahweh, and commanding him to do the conjuror's bidding."

Ferguson stared at her. "Like black magic?"

Ava nodded slowly. "As you can imagine, it's something the rabbis have kept quiet about over the centuries. It's not anything they want to publicize. And they definitely don't want it falling into the wrong hands. But, over the years, copies of many strange things have wound up in far-flung libraries as old secret collections are moved around and forgotten. From Malchus's message, it looks like he's got hold of a manuscript of *The Sword of Moses* from the British Library, but found it's corrupted—perhaps by scribes making errors when copying it centuries ago. So he's heard of a version in Oxford, and now he wants that, and was using Drewitt as master of All Hallows College to find it for him. Now Drewitt is dead, he's presumably found someone else to help him."

Ferguson dropped down into the chair beside her. "So what's he up to? Why does he want this manuscript so badly?"

Ava had been asking herself the same question, but she was struggling to accept the answer she had come to.

"We know he has the Ark and the Menorah—the two main objects from the Holy of Holies in King Solomon's great Temple in Jerusalem. And Drewitt told us he thought Malchus was trying to reconstruct the Holy of Holies. So that all connects."

"We also know from the Bible that Yahweh used to dwell in the Holy of Holies, and before that in the Tabernacle tent—using the Mercy Seat on the lid of the Ark as his throne." She paused. "If Malchus is now seriously trying to acquire *The Sword of Moses*, which is a conjuration to summon Yahweh, then we have to face the possibility that he believes he can somehow create a portal in his reconstructed Holy of Holies and summon Yahweh there to do his bidding."

"That's ridiculous." Ferguson pulled a face. "Who believes in that stuff these days? He'll be a laughing stock."

"It doesn't matter what any of us believes," Ava felt cold. "His occult-obsessed neo-Nazis will lap it up, and so will armies of other zealots and racists. They'll be lining up to follow him. If they believe he truly has the power, then it comes to the same thing. He will have loyal legions marching to do his work."

"Any divine power he will claim may be completely illusory," she continued, "but he will be leading his henchman behind the Ark, one of the single most powerful religious icons in history—one, many believe, the Israelites carried before them into the great battles which shaped the course of their civilization. Belief in the Ark's power and sanctity has been at the heart of Judeo-Christian culture for thousands of years. The political and cultural fallout of a neo-Nazi group parading behind it will shake the world as we know it. Given the extreme tensions and fragility of the Middle East at present, it could trigger a war of religious and cultural identity that would risk sucking in the old and new global superpowers. Malchus's delusions could unleash the start of a very long dark night of conflict."

She paused, speaking more quietly. "No wonder he's quoting lines about the final battle of Armageddon."

Ferguson wiped Ava's searches from the laptop's internet cache and deleted the spreadsheet, before picking the laptop up and snapping its screen off at the hinge. "Then we'd better find that manuscript before he does."

Ava was already on her feet. "We need to get to a payphone."

Ferguson headed into the bathroom and filled the basin with water and soap before dropping in the two halves of the laptop. "I'll make it up to our waiter," he reassured Ava, nodding at the electronics sinking to the bottom of the basin in a flurry of bubbles.

Downstairs, he left the keys on the table among the ashtrays and mahjong tiles, before closing the main door firmly behind them.

Out on the pavement, Ava looked about. There were no cars around, or any sign they were being watched.

They found a payphone in the next street.

Ava dialled a number in Oxford.

After a few minutes of being passed around, a man's voice answered.

"Duke Humfrey's Library. Dr Hendey speaking."

"I'm with the British Museum," Ava began, "currently retrieving objects looted during the Iraq war."

"I see. How can I help?" The voice did not sound as if it was used to being helpful.

"You have a manuscript, I believe, *The Sword of Moses*, shelfmark Cod Ox 1531."

"Yes. Cod Ox classifications are ours. It's *Codex Oxoniensis*, which means Oxford Codex, but I'm sure you know that. I think that the series you want is part of the ancient Hebrew collection." His speech was precise and pedantic.

Ava cut to the chase. "Has anybody taken it out recently?"

"Our reader records are private." The man sounded piqued. "That's not information we give out."

Ava was in no mood for games. "Please listen very carefully. If anyone requests that manuscript, you mustn't give it to them."

"This is ridiculous," the voice at the other end of the line spluttered. "You can't tell me how to run my library."

"Even if it's a reader you know well," Ava continued, "you mustn't let anyone have access to that text."

The voice on the other end of line was openly hostile now. "I'm sorry, what was your name again?"

"Let me ask it another way," Ava continued, with a new authority in her voice. "How many pages of priceless illuminations and text have been razored out of manuscripts in your collection over the last five years?"

There was silence at the other end of the line.

"It's one of your biggest problems," Ava continued, "and you know it. Our current work has made us aware of a large market for stolen-to-order manuscript pages. I'm working closely with the international authorities—and we know that a serious international buyer has recently placed an order for pages from your copy of *The Sword of Moses*. So, please—do us all a favour, and protect the text. Otherwise, if something happens to it, I'll have to inform the university authorities that I warned you clearly of the threat."

There was silence at the other end of the line. When the voice spoke again, the tone had changed. "What do you want me to do?"

"Get on the phone immediately and speak to your colleagues at the British Library. Ask them to e-mail you their microfiche photocopy of Cod Gas 178, which is another, slightly different version of *The Sword of Moses* that they hold."

"Once they've sent it to you, disguise the fact it's the British Library version. If anyone comes in asking for your manuscript, tell them the original is away for conservation, and they are welcome to work from the microfiche version instead. Give them the British Museum copy, not the Oxford version. That's very important. They must think it's a microfiche copy of the Oxford manuscript and not suspect it's the British Library one. It should delay them for the time being."

"I understand," the voice replied.

"Good," Ava breathed a sigh of relief. "We're on our way, and will explain more when we get to you. Meanwhile, keep a record of anyone who tries to consult the manuscript. But don't try to stop them. Just give them the microfiche copy. We don't want to alert them to our suspicions."

"Very well," the voice replied. "I'll have passes waiting for you at the front desk."

———— · ◆ · ————

# 96

*Bethnal Green*
*London E2*
*England*
*The United Kingdom*

THE SKIPPER HAD told Uri to meet him at a group of lock-up garages behind one of the large council estates in the East End borough of Bethnal Green.

Uri had arrived early.

Looking about, he found it hard to believe such places still existed.

The area was run down and neglected in a way he had rarely seen anywhere in the world. It had more in common with a Johannesburg slum than the gleaming skyscrapers of London's financial district, which were so close he could almost hear the traders shouting to each other across the banks' floors.

The old shops that had once served the locals had closed down long ago. They now lay boarded up and graffiti-covered. He could not tell whether they had been abandoned because of financial hardship or the soaring levels of violent street crime. Either way, it spoke volumes about the neighbourhood.

There were no tramps or dossers in the doorways. He guessed the streets were too dangerous.

There was a smashed car on the corner. The bonnet was stoved in and its insides gutted—no doubt the conclusion and highlight of a night's joyriding.

Across the road was a dilapidated Irish pub. It had no external decoration or swinging sign—just the badly painted word 'O'Dwyers' on the wall, and more steel and bars on its door and single window than on a border checkpoint back home.

The estates had been built when the Victorian slums had been knocked down, he guessed. This had once been Jack the Ripper territory—mile after mile of England's most deprived communities, wrecked by poverty, drugs, and crime.

If he was honest, he could not see that things had changed a lot in a hundred and twenty-five years.

He had parked up by the entrance to the dead-end road of garage lock-ups, so he had a clear view of everyone coming and going. He liked to see who else turned up to meetings he was attending. He was not a fan of surprise visitors—especially after the stunt Otto had pulled.

He did not want to wait too long. The car would attract attention on the street, and it made him vulnerable. Even though it was broad daylight, he was well aware no one would bat an eyelid if he was carjacked.

He fingered the miniature Beretta 950 Jetfire in his pocket.

It had been child's play to get hold of a weapon in south London. All it had taken was a whispered word in a martial arts shop, and he had it the next day. High-street catalogue shopping would not have been easier. He doubted very much he would use it seriously on any would-be carjacker. The last thing he needed was attention. But it would certainly help him make anyone chancing their luck think twice.

There was almost no one on the streets, and little traffic.

He assumed the area was controlled by local gangs, as he doubted the police got this deep into the borough very often.

A car came down the road, interrupting his thoughts.

He watched in his mirror as it approached.

It was the Skipper.

Uri had left his engine running, and immediately pulled out after the Skipper, following him into the narrow road. There were no houses on it—just scruffy lock-up garages down either side.

Parking three-quarters of the way down, the Skipper got out of his car.

"Apologies for Otto's sideshow last night, Danny," the Skipper began as Uri approached. "Don't sweat it. He won't be pulling anything like that again for a while. I had to teach him a little lesson after you left."

Uri had thought as much when the Skipper ordered him out.

"Anyway," the Skipper looked penetratingly at him. "I wanted to know whether you're still with us." There was nothing friendly about his tone. It was more a challenge than a question.

Uri met his gaze. He shrugged. "It depends what you've got." He knew he was slowly winning the Skipper's confidence, but time was not on his side. He needed to up the ante if he was going to make significant progress. "I haven't seen any action yet. Just talk. I liked that bloke at *The Bunker*. The one making the speech. He said we need to be brutally ruthless—that the world was sick, and extreme measures were needed. That sounded good."

"Malchus," the Skipper replied. "Our *Staffel* is ultimately under his command. There are a lot of independent groups like ours, but we give all our allegiance to the national federation. Malchus is the *Reichskommissar* for these islands."

Uri looked unimpressed. "But what's actually going down? Like I said, I'm not in it for the politics."

"I was hoping you'd say that," the Skipper looked pleased. "As it turns out, with Otto out of action, I'm a man short for a little job. That's why we're having this chat. How do you fancy a bit of travel? As it happens, it's for something Malchus is putting together."

"Count me in," Uri answered unhesitatingly, not taking his eyes off the Skipper.

The Skipper nodded. He walked several doors down and crossed the road to the lock-ups on the other side, before stopping at one with a van parked in front of it. Bending down, he took the large padlock and chain off the sliding metal doors.

"Inside," he ordered Uri, pulling aside one of the doors and making room for Uri to enter. He followed behind and slid the door closed behind them, before snapping on a switch that brought a single ceiling-mounted fluorescent tubelight on with a flicker.

Uri had not been sure what to expect. But it had not been this.

The lock-up was filled with metal racks and shelves, all piled high with kit. He could see combat knives, empty glass bottles, boxes of nails, a door ram, batteries, acid, bleach, heavy tools, rope, mobile telephones, police scanners, radio jammers, and even a few night vision headsets.

It was a quartermaster's store. But not a traditional military one with tents and mess-tins.

This was a cache for urban guerillas.

And a well-stocked one.

"We'll need to get you tooled up, Danny. Do you know what the *Leibstandarte* is?"

Uri shook his head almost imperceptibly.

"The *Leibstandarte Adolf Hitler* was the *Führer's* personal bodyguard. They were the best men in the ss, the elite of the elite. Like a Praetorian Guard."

The Skipper opened a metal cupboard, and took out a leather waistcoat. He threw it across to Uri.

It looked to Uri like something worn by a back-patch motorcycle club member. It was made of a single piece of black leather, with no sleeves, pockets, or buttons.

On the back was the outline of a white circle, and inside it, also in white, were the two large jagged *Sig* runes of the infamous ss lightning bolts.

On one side of the front was a badge, again outlined in white, with the three lions of England under the words 'BRITISCHES FREIKORPS'. And on the other was a monogram of the letters 'L.A.H.' in gothic script, suspended in the claws of a large Nazi eagle.

He closed the cupboard. "Wear it for the job. You've earned it. In fact, try it on," the Skipper prompted. "It's your size."

Uri stared numbly at the waistcoat.

Something deep inside him was ordering him not to comply. He knew it was not just a piece of clothing to be taken on and off like a jumper. It meant much more than that.

Back at *The Bunker*, when the Skipper had told him he had been selected for the ss, he had almost laughed out loud, it sounded so absurd.

But now he was faced with the uniform and symbols, he was finding nothing funny about it at all.

He knew that the people who wore these clothes in the twenty-first century were not playing games. They were every bit as serious as their World War Two predecessors. Given the opportunity, they would just as readily knife their victims in quiet alleys, shoot them by the roadside, or slaughter them in extermination camps.

This was not a game.

He looked at the waistcoat again. These were the symbols of a crack regiment of the ss—the political military elite of the Nazi machinery. Their Death's Head division ran the camps, and their frontline soldiers led most of the atrocities against those the Third *Reich* deemed unfit to live. Putting on the waistcoat would be a betrayal of the memory of all those whose last sight on earth had been a leering face under an ss skull cap-badge.

He stared at the waistcoat, wrestling with the implications.

The simplest solution would be to drop the Skipper on the spot. He had the Beretta in his pocket. The Skipper would be dead before he hit the ground.

But at the same time, he thought of Moshe and the fear in the old man's eyes—of his parting words that their enemies could get hold of the Ark and humiliate them with it. They would tell the world that Israel's God had abandoned his chosen people. Moshe had been clear about the stakes, and the total absence of any room for failure.

Uri turned the waistcoat over in his hands while he wrestled with the contradictory thoughts flashing through his head.

Instinctively, but reluctantly, he knew what he had to do. He could not change the past. But if he was to stand any chance of recovering the Ark and restoring it to his country, then the Skipper was for the moment his only route to Malchus.

Tightening his jaw, he slowly unfolded the waistcoat.

It felt like he was moving in slow motion as he slipped it on.

The Skipper had been right. It fitted perfectly.

The huge man nodded and opened another two cupboards. They were filled with racks of weapons.

"You'll need a short and a long," he ordered, picking out a handgun and a submachine gun.

Uri took the pistol from him.

He had recognized it the moment the Skipper had opened the cupboard door. It was legendary—the Luger P08, issued to German troops in both world wars. The heavily angled grip and pencil barrel were iconic, unmistakable. He pulled back the toggle to cock it before squeezing the trigger. It clicked loudly as the mechanism fired, echoing around the lock-up.

Even after over a century, it was still a superb weapon, as effective now as when it had been patented in 1898. Looking closely at the chassis, he saw the famous '42' Mauser stamp.

It was the real article.

He put it down on the workbench and took the submachine gun the Skipper was holding out for him. It had a right-hand grip like a pistol, and a long box magazine for the left hand protruding under the barrel.

"M40 Schmeisser nine-mil," the Skipper nodded. "Autofire only. Lethally accurate. The mag takes thirty-two rounds." The Skipper threw him a black canvas holdall, and opened a drawer stacked with assorted magazine clips. "Take a load. We're done here."

Uri put the weapons into the bag, and dropped in ten spare magazines for each.

"You've got a serious set-up here," Uri glanced around.

"It's like peeling an onion, Danny—layers within layers. There's lots of groups like us. You'll see soon enough."

The Skipper closed the cupboards and flicked off the light. He showed Uri out of the lock-up, and put the padlock and chain back onto the doors again.

"Meet me outside Maze Hill station at five o'clock this afternoon. Bring all the gear." He thumped Uri on the shoulder, and climbed into his car. Uri wandered back to his. He put the bag into the boot, and inserted his key into the ignition.

The whole ss fetish made him sick. If the Skipper and his crew had been playing at ordinary soldiers, that would have been fine. But there was nothing ordinary about the ss. Their *Einsatzgruppen* had drunkenly machine-gunned thousands upon thousands of innocent people into pits. They were not soldiers. They were politicized butchers.

If he was honest, the ss's role as propaganda-fuelled political soldiers was not what nauseated him. They were not the only soldiers in history to have fought for a political ideology. Such soldiers were commonplace in every age, killing for a political vision. He probably classified himself as one.

What made him nauseous was the nature of their particular ideology, the core mantra of their world view—their pathological hatred of his race.

That made this personal.

He took a deep breath, forcing himself to de-emotionalize.

He was on a job. An important one.

He had to go along with the Skipper, to see if it would get him closer to Malchus and the Ark. He needed to keep zeroed in on the objective.

He fired up the engine and drove off. He could do it. He was good at staying focused.

But he also knew that when the time came, he would like nothing better than to put a bullet in the Skipper's head.

———— · ◆ · ————

# 97

*Duke Humfrey's Library*
*Bodleian Library*
*Broad Street*
*Oxford OX1*
*England*
*The United Kingdom*

AVA'S SHOES ECHOED on the stone floor of the ancient university's medieval proscholium.

Its high gothic ceiling looked down over a bare corridor that would not have been out of place in one of the great medieval monasteries.

The grand antechamber was empty, except for a central reception point and, at each end, a small oval wooden desk guarding access to the library's two main staircase towers.

Ava picked up the passes left for her at reception, swiped them at the glass swing barrier by the southern staircase, and ran up the medieval tower with Ferguson close behind her.

Passing the low doorway to the first floor reading rooms, she carried on up the narrow stairs with their small medieval windows and gothic wall tracery. Arriving at the second floor, she peeled off through a set of blue and gold metal doors under an impressive Tudor stone doorway, and into Duke Humfrey's Library.

She had always thought it was one of the most striking rooms in England.

It was H-shaped, and they entered at the long eastern wing's southern tip. At the same time, a student in a dark green hoodie disappeared into the stairway at the wing's far northern end.

Light streamed in from a large mullioned gothic window, casting a mellow glow all around the warm dark polished wood covering the floors, walls, and ceiling. Centuries-old bookcases filled every inch of wall space, and arched wooden colonnades supported elegant first-floor galleries with ornamental balustrades.

Directly ahead, the bookcases were filled with ancient leather-bound books in a variety of shades, from ochre to oxblood. Most had no titles, save for occasional Latin or Greek abbreviations inked onto the spines in an ancient spidery hand.

In an area left unchanged since medieval times, one section of antique books had small metal plates bolted into their covers, with heavy hand-made chains linking them to bars running the length of the shelves.

The silence was total.

Looking about, her priority now was to find the librarian she had spoken to on the phone.

She passed another security desk and walked quickly into the middle section of the library—a wide corridor linking the two end wings.

The atmosphere was different here. The ceiling's wood-panelled coffers were filled with painted crests of the university's arms, and the whole roof structure was supported by beams decorated in pale swirling floral patterns.

She walked between the rows of freestanding antique bookcases— each sheltering gnarled desks where scholars had sat for centuries, poring over dusty volumes under the watchful eyes of austere figures looking down from old paintings.

This was the oldest section of the great library.

To her right, behind an aged wooden grille, was the reserve area—a screened-off section of cubicles hidden behind the panelling, from where the librarians issued materials ordered from the vast underground book stacks.

A lady in a baggy grey jumper and glasses picked up a sheaf of loose folios from the reserve desk, and headed back into the library, leaving Ava a clear view of a thin-faced man in a blue-checked lumberjack shirt, who was doing up the brass and leather buckles on a large wooden-backed book.

"Dr Hendey?" she asked, introducing herself. "Dr Curzon. We spoke earlier this morning."

He nodded an acknowledgement, putting down the book and walking towards her. "I'd appreciate it if you'd tell me what's going on. How did you know someone would come this morning to consult—"

But what he was saying was lost, as a piercing shriek from the west wing of the library shattered the scholarly hush.

Irritation crossed his face for a split second, before giving way to alarm as he realized something serious had happened.

Ferguson moved first, followed by Ava and the librarian. They ran down the corridor to the west end of the library, and were greeted by the sight of the middle-aged woman in the baggy grey jumper standing up behind the nearest of the long readers' tables. Her hands were clasped over her mouth in horror.

Ava looked in the direction the woman was staring, her face frozen.

*Oh God!*

She felt a wave of nausea rise in her throat.

*Not again.*

At the far end of the wing, in the dimly lit north-eastern corner, between the columns of the arcade, an elderly man in a cream linen jacket was hanging by the neck from the upper gallery.

A rope had been secured around one of the sturdy balusters supporting the first-floor railing, and he hung from it by a noose, which only partially obscured his white clerical collar. A pile of large books lay undisturbed a few inches under where his feet were gently swinging.

From the angle of his neck and the unnatural position of his body, it was clear he was very dead.

There was no one else in the west wing of the library except for the woman, and Ava could immediately see from the curling ancient music folios in front of her that she had not been the one consulting *The Sword of Moses*.

Ava looked back at the dead priest, and then to the librarian. "Was it him, reading the manuscript?"

The librarian nodded dumbly, his face a mask of horrified incomprehension at what had happened in his library

She could feel an intense anger rising in her throat.

*Everywhere Malchus went, he left a trail of death.*

"Where had he been sitting?"

The stunned librarian nodded numbly towards an empty seat at one of the long wide tables with the library's traditional oak book rests and tall brass lamps.

Ava strode over to it, and looked down at the desk where the priest had been working.

The printout of the British Library's microfiched codex of *The Sword of Moses* was open, resting on a pile of large green triangular foam wedges. The papers were weighted down with a long string of small cylindrical lead weights sewn into a cream-coloured snake of cotton.

She looked at the ancient Hebrew and Aramaic text, and began translating it to herself:

> If anyone wishes to use this Sword, which fulfills every wish and reveals every secret, and performs every miracle, marvel, and amazing thing, then speak to Me in the following manner, read this to Me, and conjure in the following way, and I will instantly be called upon and be well disposed towards you, and I will give you authority over this Sword, by which to fulfil all your desires.

She shuddered, before moving her gaze to the old priest's papers.

He had been taking notes in a large unruled notebook with a black cloth binding. No ink was allowed in the old library, so he had been writing with a sharp pencil in a small, clear, and precise hand.

On the first page he had written:

The Sword of Moses
Cod Ox 1531

But whatever he had written on the next few pages was now gone—torn out of the notebook, leaving only the telltale ragged stubs of ripped paper.

*So Malchus had what he came for.*

Whatever the old priest had noted down from the manuscript, Malchus had pulled it out and taken it with him.

Ava's heart sank.

She dropped down into the chair next to the priest's, fighting off a wave of dejection.

Malchus had gone, and he would not be back.

The librarian walked over to her. His face was deathly pale. "Shouldn't we take him down?" His voice was weak and hesitant. "It's not decent, leaving him there ... like that."

She shook her head. "Forensics will want the area undisturbed."

"Forensics?" He looked confused. "I just can't believe it. Professor Stone? Stealing manuscripts? Suicide?" He shook his head, bewildered.

"Not suicide." Ava informed him gently.

The librarian's eyes widened. "Murder?" he whispered, horrified.

"I expect they'll find he met the killer up there." She pointed to the first floor gallery above where he was hanging, accessed by a narrow staircase recessed into the bookcases. "I imagine he was knocked out, perhaps by inhalation to make no sound, then the noose was put around his neck, and he was lowered over the railing—I would guess with another rope looped under his arms so he could be gently put in place without any noise. That pile of books on the ground is merely to make it look like suicide."

"How can you possibly know all this?" the librarian asked, aghast,

"You won't find any obvious signs of foul play," she replied. "The murderer is exceptionally talented at this. He used to do it for his government. Unless we find him, the coroner will almost certainly record suicide or an open verdict."

"Shouldn't we seal the building, or something?" The librarian pulled a mobile phone from his pocket. "I'm calling the police."

"How many exits are there here?" Ferguson asked, striding towards him, "off this floor?"

"Just the two," the librarian pointed over to the other end of the room, "where you came in, north and south."

Ferguson spun round, as if stung. "That wasn't a student in the hoodie," he shouted, running back towards the door they had seen the figure exiting through as they had entered.

The moment Ferguson said it, Ava knew he was right.

There had been something odd about the figure.

*Why had she not seen it?*

His walk had been more solid—heavier than a young person's.

*Damn!*

She sprinted after Ferguson. He was already at the north staircase, so she peeled right to take the south. She hammered down the steps as fast as she could, passing no one on the way.

*He could still be here!*

She could not let him get away.

Again.

At the bottom of the steps, she arrived at the oval desk guarding the tower stairway.

"Did a man wearing a green hoodie just leave?" she demanded breathlessly.

The attendant looked back at her blankly.

"Where's your CCTV?" She peered over the counter, looking for any screens that might show a live-feed from cameras around the building.

There were none.

He shook his head. "That's University Security up at the Old Observatory. Nothing to do with us."

She could hear Ferguson on the far side of the proscholium, asking similar questions.

"Please—it's important," she urged the guard, who continued to look blank, until his face lit up a little. "Oh, mature student, was it? Broad bloke. Yes. A few minutes ago. Didn't have a bag or anything."

"Which way?" Ava was running for the front door.

"Can't really say," the guard was looking after her. "Is it important?"

"Call security," Ferguson shouted over as he headed for the door after Ava. "And tell your manager. The library's going to be closed for the day."

Outside the main door, Ava looked about the stone-flagged medieval Schools Quadrangle, shielding her eyes from the sunshine bouncing off the honey-coloured high stone walls.

*Malchus could be anywhere.*

She was going to have to make a guess.

There were ten doors off the quad, each labelled in Latin with the name of one of the old schools. She took in Music, Law, Grammar and History, Astronomy and Rhetoric, but had no time to read them all—he could have gone into any one of them, then back into the labyrinth of the library complex.

Alternatively, there were three main exits out of the quad. One to the left, one to the right, and the main gate straight ahead through the Tower of the Five Orders.

As she sprinted for the main gate, she could see Ferguson heading out of the left exit.

Once through the medieval archway, she looked up and down the street. To her right was the unmistakable dome of the Radcliffe Camera library, and beyond that the spire of the medieval university church. To her left, there were buildings leading up to a crossroads, and beyond it a tree-lined avenue.

There was no sign of anyone wearing a dark green hoodie.

He could be anywhere by now, wearing anything.

There were college and faculty buildings all around. All were open, and he could have ducked into any of them. It would have only taken seconds to rip off the hoodie and lose it.

She ran down to the square surrounding the Radcliffe Camera, but there was only a party of tourists clustered around a guide holding up a large blue and white golf umbrella.

Returning the other way, she peered into the front quadrangle of a small college opposite the library's main gate.

It was empty.

Sprinting up to the crossroads, she looked around the busy junction, but there was no one resembling Malchus among the various groups on the pavements or entering the innumerable bookshops and teashops.

With increasing desperation, she headed into a pub on the corner, and hurried through the warren of sofas and chairs filling its low-ceilinged rooms and snug bars.

*Nothing.*

She ran out onto the pavement and down the narrow old street.

But he was nowhere in sight.

She stopped dead and looked up and down one last time, but there was little point.

*She had lost him.*

Dejectedly, she walked slowly back towards the crossroads. A few doors down she passed a shop selling music and books. She peered through the door, but there were no customers inside.

As she turned away, her eye was caught by the window display, showcasing a retrospective of 1960s and 1970s psychedelia.

In the centre was a hyper-colourful Led Zeppelin box-set, which proudly announced the inclusion of their concept film, *The Song Remains the Same.*

Next to it was the bizarre cover of the Beatles' *Sgt Pepper's Lonely Hearts Club Band*, prominently featuring the band dressed as military musicians surrounded by the faces of dozens of counterculture icons. Glancing at the cover, she could not help but notice, in the top left hand corner, the unmistakable fleshy bald head of Aleister Crowley.

As she quickly scanned the window display, she could see a range of related books as well. Their jackets largely featured the bright swirly contrasting patterns and bubble typefaces of the time. But among them were a few more traditional covers—including one titled *The Avatar of Aiwass*, decorated with the same fleshy photograph of Aleister Crowley as on the Beatles' album. It was a recent biography of the man the subtitle claimed was 'the Beast 666'.

She could only imagine how much it would have appealed to Malchus.

She pushed open the shop's door, and picked up the book on Crowley.

She had been thinking on and off about Crowley's *Gnostic Mass*, which Malchus had been reading at Stockbridge House. It seemed to hold echoes of the ancient world whose artefacts she handled every day—one in which priestesses and priests celebrated the mysteries together, in the days before the Abrahamic religions pushed women to the margins.

She paid at the counter and returned to the street. Retracing her steps to the library's sober gothic quadrangle, she found Ferguson entering from the opposite side. He had clearly done a circuit, but from his frustrated expression she could see he had not found anything either.

She leaned up against the railings of the imposing bronze statue in front of the entranceway to the proscholium.

A wave of despondency broke over her.

*Malchus was gone.*

Worse—he had left no leads.

The letter Drewitt had been carrying had brought them this far—to the library's manuscript of *The Sword of Moses*, where she had been hoping to intercept Malchus trying to access it.

But he had been and gone.

Once again, he had been one step ahead.

After the adrenaline of the last few days, the disappointment was overwhelming. Even though she had successfully duped him by switching the manuscripts so the old priest's notes would prove useless, the fact remained that the trail had gone stone cold.

With the priest's death, Malchus had disappeared, taking all clues with him.

Dejected, she glanced at the Latin sign over the main doorway.

ACADEMICIANS OF OXFORD—THOMAS BODLEY BUILT THIS
LIBRARY FOR YOU AND THE REPUBLIC OF THE LEARNED. MAY
IT TURN OUT WELL!

She felt exhausted with frustration and anger.

For all Thomas Bodley's good intentions, her day in the library had decidedly not turned out well.

———— • ◆ • ————

# 98

NEITHER AVA NOR Ferguson spoke as they got into the car.

There seemed to be a tacit understanding between them that there was nothing useful to be said.

They had lost Malchus at the ancient medieval library, and with him all chance of finding out where he was headed with the dead professor's translation of *The Sword of Moses*.

After all the progress they had made. After they had come so tantalizingly close. For the first time since General Hunter had airlifted her to Qatar, Ava felt as if she had hit a brick wall.

She had no idea where to turn next. Malchus was gone, and she had no meaningful leads on where to begin the hunt for him and the Ark again.

She stared blindly out of the lightly tinted window as the four-by-four pulled away from the built-up area of the city and nosed into the gently undulating and hedgerowed countryside.

To fill the silence, Ferguson flicked on the radio, leaving it pulsing away quietly in time with the purple spiking lights of the graphic display.

Ava was lost in her thoughts.

The frustration and disappointment were overwhelming. She could not bear to think they had come so close for it to end like this. It had so nearly all been in reach—the Ark, the Menorah, exposing her father's killer, and clearing her and Ferguson's names.

But with Malchus's escape from the bookish hush of Duke Humfrey's library, she could not help but feel she had lost all chance of getting closure on any of it.

It was almost too much to bear.

She opened the glossy book she had purchased on Aleister Crowley, and began to flick distractedly through the text and plates.

It seemed a standard type of biography. It started with Crowley's childhood, being brought up by strict Christian parents active in the ultra-puritanical Plymouth Brethren. It then chronicled his time at Cambridge University, as a mountaineer and star chess player. But the majority of the text focused on his increasing exploration of the darker sides of life, his rebirth as 'the Great Beast 666', and the infamy that increasingly followed him as he revelled in an ever more unconventional lifestyle.

As she turned the pages, her eye was caught by a stylized diagram of a striking star-shaped motif. Its aggressive spiky shape was immediately familiar, but for the moment she could not recall where she had seen it.

Grateful for the distraction from brooding over her failure, she tried hard to think where she knew it from. An Egyptian temple carving? A Mesopotamians stele? She cycled through the image library in her head, trying to remember exactly where she had encountered the unusual shape.

Without warning, Ferguson braked dramatically, forcing the stream of cars immediately behind them to swerve and overtake unexpectedly.

She shot him a concerned look.

"We're being followed." He sounded tense. "I wasn't sure at first. But I am now. They're hanging back deliberately, two cars behind."

Ava twisted in her seat to look out of the large rear window.

She did not need him to tell her which car it was. The red BMW 5 stuck out like a sore thumb to anyone who knew what to look for.

It was the standard issue car for the intelligence services and the police's armed response and diplomatic protection units. If any of the more shadowy echelons within Her Majesty's government ordered a tail, then she was looking at their vehicle of choice.

Predictably, its cabin was filled with three alert-looking men in a classic configuration—driver and navigator in the front, and observer-radio operator in the back.

She knew the set-up well.

The car would have been completely worked over by the Firm's engine shop. They would have reinforced the chassis and retrofitted the hardware under the bonnet with a wealth of performance-enhancing parts. Additionally, there would be several packs of spare number plates in the boot, helpfully supplied by the Driver and Vehicle Licensing Agency in Swansea.

It was all textbook.

As she took it in, she realized some things never changed. Despite decades of evidence demonstrating the need for new procedures, surveillance crews seemed incapable of including women in the teams to make themselves look less obvious.

"We're sitting ducks here. We need to lose them," she confirmed to Ferguson, peering closely at the large satnav screen embedded into the dashboard. "We'll never manage it on the motorway. But there's a turn off ahead." She could not make out the place name. "It looks like it leads to a small town."

"Got it," Ferguson noted, turning sharply off into the slip road without indicating.

Looking back at the men pursuing them, Ava felt a wave of despondency building from the pit of her stomach.

However much she tried to think of different outcomes, it seemed ultimately inevitable that the Firm was going to catch up with them sooner or later. And when they did, she knew that without Malchus they had little prospect of proving their innocence.

She did not fancy her chances. Or Ferguson's.

They had no hard evidence to implicate DeVere, and by far the easiest option for the grey men in the top floor suites would be to hurl the pair of them to the dogs. It would save the bureaucrats a great deal of embarrassment and difficult conversations around DeVere's rogue activities.

But her thoughts were cut violently short as Ferguson abruptly yanked the wheel to the left, swerving across towards the side barrier.

"Trouble!" he yelled, as the car in pursuit, now speeding aggressively, pulled alongside them. The driver was motioning unambiguously for Ferguson to pull over and park up.

Ferguson glanced at Ava, the unspoken question hanging in the air between them.

She shook her head firmly.

"I didn't think so," he grimaced, slamming his foot down hard on the accelerator, pulling the car sharply off the slip lane into a smaller road leading to a residential street.

The houses here were uniform—squat two-storey blocks of pebble-dashed concrete with a few square yards of grass at the front. To give a degree of privacy from the road, the windows and door glass were draped on the inside with a variety of net curtains.

"Hold on!" Ferguson warned, accelerating hard, trying to put more distance between himself and the pursuing BMW, which had turned into the narrow street seventy yards behind them, and was gaining fast.

Ava watched with mounting alarm as the high-performance car put on a burst of speed and began to catch up. But this time the driver was not indicating for Ferguson to pull over. He was going too fast.

And getting too close.

Before she could shout a warning to Ferguson, the reinforced government car slammed hard into their rear right side.

The impact shook the four-by-four, shunting it sideways with a sickening lurch. But it was the heavier and more powerful vehicle, and responded quickly as Ferguson pulled it back into the middle of the road, narrowly avoiding a row of parked cars and accelerating out of harm's way.

As the street of houses came to an abrupt end, Ferguson squealed the car right onto a section of link road.

But Ava could immediately see it was not over.

Before she could catch her breath, the BMW's engine howled, and it drew level with them, then swerved viciously, hammering into their side.

Harder this time.

Ava was flung against the walnut panel lining the inside of the passenger door. At the same time, she was aware of Ferguson battling to keep the vehicle on the road. It was careering dangerously off course, set to plough into the neighbouring ditch.

But Ferguson's reactions were quicker. Wrenching the wheel, he dragged the car back into the middle of the lane, ahead of the BMW.

She could see a sheen of sweat on his forehead, and could feel her heart hammering against her ribcage.

It was clear the men in the BMW were not messing around. She had at first assumed they simply intended to arrest her and Ferguson, and take them back to whoever in Vauxhall Cross was running this operation.

But now she was not so sure. The BMW was not observing any degree of 'reasonable force' that she could see.

Quite the opposite.

She could hear its engine screaming, and even without looking, knew it was about to slam into them again.

Powerless to do anything, she watched out of the corner of her eye as the BMW closed on them hard and fast.

She could feel the bulk of DeVere's pistol in her pocket. If she and Ferguson survived the impact of the next attack, she might have no option but to use it—although firing on serving MI6 officers acting in the course of their duty was not going to win her any friends when the inevitable reckoning came.

"Hold on tight!" Ferguson shouted, flipping a black rocker switch at the base of the steering column and jabbing the accelerator harder, pulling ahead of the BMW.

"What does that do?" Ava yelled over the noise of the engines, indicating the switch he had pushed.

"This," he grunted, stamping hard on the brakes as they drew level with a set of amber traffic lights guarding a crossroads.

The four-by-four screeched to a brutal and abrupt halt.

With no time to react, the BMW smashed into their rear at high speed, catapulting Ava forward in her padded seat with a vicious jolt. For a second, she could feel the straps of her seatbelt cutting into her savagely. A moment later, she was thrown violently back into her chair as the lights turned red and Ferguson floored the accelerator for all he was worth, shooting over the crossroads with a roar of speed.

Ava craned round just in time to see the crumpled BMW skid sideways into the crossroads behind them—the occupants blinded by six puffy white airbags filling the passenger cabin.

A fraction of a second later she heard the high-pitched screech of locked wheels, followed by the deep wrenching crunch of twisting metal and shattering glass as a van steaming across the junction piled into the side of the already crippled BMW.

Ferguson did not slow down or stop to look back at the carnage he had caused. "We need to get out of here fast." He leant forward and flicked the airbag switch back on. "We won't have held them up for long."

As he rejoined the motorway, Ava's heart was still racing. Whoever was now calling the shots at Legoland had clearly given orders that it did not matter if she and Ferguson were dead or alive.

She knew from experience that if removing them permanently ever became a formal order, they would have to fall off the radar completely, and quickly. If she had learned anything from her stint with the Increment, it was that the government could find and deal with anyone. Anywhere.

It was not a comforting thought.

Ferguson flipped radio station, and Ava's mind drifted back to the disaster at the library.

She felt overwhelmingly dejected at the idea that the tide was turning against them.

The excitement of leaving London that morning as they had raced up to the medieval city of Oxford had evaporated—replaced with a leaden feeling of despondency.

Next to her, Ferguson began tapping on the leather steering wheel, beating out the time of the song playing quietly on the radio.

If she was honest, she was not in the mood for music, but it was better than admitting to Ferguson she was out of ideas for where to look next to find Malchus and the Ark.

He nudged the radio louder. It was playing a spacey, haunting tune, almost eastern—a tense hypnotic spiral of ascending thumping guitar chords.

She absent-mindedly opened the book on Crowley again at the page with the strange star, but quickly turned to stare out of the window, trying to clear her mind.

Ferguson sang along quietly under his breath, tapping out the relentless metronomic rhythm on the steering wheel:

> *"Oh let the sun beat down upon my face, stars to fill my dreams.*
> *I am a traveller of both time and space, to be where I have been."*

Ava's eyes were unfocused as she gazed out of the window at the varied greens of the landscape. But as the lyrics of the song filtered through into her subconscious, she felt an icy chill start at the base of her spine and crawl slowly up her back.

Ferguson continued singing along softly.

> *"To sit with elders of the gentle race, this world has seldom seen.*
> *They talk of days for which they sit and wait, and all will be revealed."*

As the melody changed and a chorus of strings began a dramatic rhythmic descending run, she sat bolt upright in her seat, feeling a knot tightening at the centre of her stomach.

"My God," she whispered.

"What?" Ferguson turned, clearly alarmed by the tone of her voice.

"That's where I saw it," she whispered slowly.

"Saw what?" he sounded mystified.

"The star." She twisted in her seat to face him. "That's where I saw the star." She jabbed a finger at the picture in the book. "At Stockbridge House, first time I met Malchus. He was playing with a rosary. But it wasn't a normal one. It didn't have a crucifix at the end—but a star, like this one. He stabbed it into my face."

She sat back in her chair. "That song reminded me." She nodded at the radio, feeling herself breathing heavily with excitement. "It all makes sense."

"The song?" He looked confused. "*Kashmir*. Always a favourite of mine on the headphones when flying back to the 'Stan. Made me feel optimistic somehow."

"I just can't believe it's taken me so long to see it," she interrupted him.

"See what?" Ferguson was still tapping the rhythm out on the wheel.

The fields around her had ended, and they were now passing through the endless miles of London's gloomy suburbia.

"Malchus," she replied. "Malchus and Aleister Crowley. It's so obvious. I should've realized ages ago. '*I am a traveler of both time and space, to be where I have been*'." She paused. "Don't you see? Malchus thinks he's Aleister Crowley, come back to life."

"That's a bit of a long shot, isn't it?" Ferguson sounded dubious.

She sat forward, focused now, pushing a stray lock of hair off her face. "I'll bet there's more." She flicked through the book, then turned to the Table of Contents.

As her eyes travelled down the list, she suddenly saw it.

"There! Look I was right!" She pointed to a section headed 'The Holy Books of Thelema'. "It all fits. Malchus chose the name for his group because of its association with Crowley. Hence his obsession with the 'will'."

She thumbed through the book to the section. And began to read it aloud:

"Crowley's creed of Thelema had a simple dogma at its core: 'Do what thou wilt shall be the whole of the law. Love is the law. Love under will'. It was an adaptation of the more ancient witches' philosophy: 'An if it harm none, do what ye will', while also drawing on one of the ancient world's most enigmatic and gifted mystics, Saint Augustine, who wrote in the fourth century, 'Love, and do what you will'."

"I still don't see it," Ferguson sounded uncertain. "There must be thousands of followers of Crowley out there. That doesn't mean they all think they're his reincarnation."

"But Malchus does," she insisted. She was sure she was right. "This six-pointed star," she pointed at the picture again, "Apparently it's called a unicursal hexagram—a continuous line, not like the superimposed triangles of the Star of David. It's centuries old. It says Crowley adopted it as his personal symbol. And I'll bet that's why Malchus carries it—because he thinks he's the new Crowley."

Ferguson glanced down at the page. "Isn't it on tarot cards?"

Ava blinked in astonishment. "I honestly wouldn't have thought you were the type."

He smiled back at her. "You'd be amazed what soldiers will smuggle into a barracks to while away the boredom. On the scale of possibilities, tarot is pretty tame."

Ava figured he was probably right.

She continued. "I think Malchus has more than a simple Crowley fixation. At Stockbridge House, in his room, I found a book by Crowley. It was a copy of the *Missa Gnostica*, or *Gnostic Mass*. I looked it up. It was the culmination of his life's work—his personal contribution to magical ceremony. It's a whole occult sacrament, his ultimate challenge to the Church's core practices."

She looked across at Ferguson. "But the important thing is that in Malchus's copy of the *Gnostic Mass* he had written notes all over it, rewriting entire sections. That's not what a star-struck fan would do. It's what the author would do."

"So he's obsessed with Crowley, and maybe fantasizes that he's somehow been specially chosen to continue his work." Ferguson sounded sceptical. "That still doesn't mean he thinks he's his reincarnation."

Ava nodded. The more she explained it, the more certain she was. "I think he's even trying to look like him. They have the same bald head and staring eyes."

She had at first assumed Malchus had never had any hair—a singular and startling accident of birth. But now she was not so sure. Given what she now knew, it seemed more likely it was a purposeful statement. She could easily believe he had undergone a freakish cosmetic procedure in order to emulate his guru.

She turned in her seat to face Ferguson. "I'm also willing to bet there's a Crowley connection with the words 'FRATER PERDURABO' in the last line of Malchus's letter. I don't think it means 'Brother, I will endure forever'. I have a feeling it's a name. And I suspect if we hunt it out, we'll find it's linked to Crowley—probably one of his magical names, designed to suggest that his ideas were immortal."

Ferguson looked thoughtful. "Even if you're right and Malchus thinks he's Crowley's reincarnation, it still doesn't tell us where he is—or where he's keeping the Ark and the Menorah."

Ava slammed the book shut, and put in on the back seat.

She could feel a smile of triumph breaking across her face. "Oh, but it does!" She was having trouble keeping her voice measured. "'I am a traveller of both time and space, to be where I have been'."

"I know *exactly* where he is."

She pointed at the radio. "It's not just about him believing he's Crowley's reincarnation. That song, *Kashmir*, is by Led Zeppelin, who once made a film, *The Song Remains the Same*. I just saw a reissue of it in the shop where I bought the book. I watched it years ago. It's mainly concert footage, but also some trippy '70s fantasy sequences of the band members. And here's the thing." She paused. "Part of it is filmed in the Scottish Highlands, at Loch Ness."

Ferguson glanced across at her, bemused. "Acid-dazed rock musicians taking time off to pay homage to the monster?"

"Exactly." Ava nodded. "But not the monster you're thinking of."

She strained to remember the details. "One of the band members had a house on the shores of the loch. Apparently he bought it because of his interest in the building's history—it's a grade one shrine for followers of the occult."

She pushed the button to lower the window beside her, letting in the cool air. "So go on, guess who the house once belonged to?"

"I wasn't aware Scotland had any famous occult figures. I thought we left all that to the English—Merlin, Mother Shipton, the Hellfire Club—"

"This one was very English," Ava cut him short. "And a bit more recent. In fact, the most notorious of them all. He wanted somewhere secluded to concentrate on his dark rituals, so he bought a house and land there, away from prying eyes."

She could see by Ferguson's expression that the penny had finally dropped. "Crowley?" He sounded genuinely surprised. "At Loch Ness?"

Ava nodded. "And that's where we'll find Malchus—and the Ark, and the Menorah. I'm *sure* of it."

She was still kicking herself for not having seen it sooner. "We'll need to get there fast. I just hope we're not too late."

She stared out of the window again, as the miles of run-down take-away restaurants and minicab offices sped past.

"We could do with some backup." Ferguson replied after a pause. "If Malchus is keeping the Ark and Menorah there, he's not going to let us just walk in and take them."

Arriving at a roundabout, he followed the sign for central London. "Can we get Max and his men?"

"I tried getting hold of Saxby this morning to find out how things were going in Italy," she replied. "I sent him an e-mail and tried calling. But I got an immediate bounce-back and a dead line. He must've been using a temporary e-mail address and phone number."

"We could try the Royal Society?" Ferguson suggested. "He and De Molay seemed well known there. Maybe they'd help?"

Ava shook her head. "Who knows how long it'd take to get anyone there to talk to us. And we can't afford to waste even one minute."

"So what do you recommend?" Ferguson was moving into planning mode. "We've no idea what we'll be walking into up at Loch Ness. It's his ground, not ours."

"We've got one shot," Ava replied. "And we should take it."

"Go on." Ferguson was weaving expertly in and out of the thickening traffic.

"Cordingly—our friendly Deputy Grand Secretary at Freemasons' Hall," she replied. "He knows more than he's saying. The robe in his briefcase was pure white with a large embroidered blood red cross patty. It was definitely a Templar's robe."

Ferguson accelerated, shooting through a light as it was changing.

"Then let's go and shake him up."

"There's no time," Ava replied. "Drop me at Euston station. I need to get to Loch Ness. I'm not losing Malchus again." She turned to the open window, breathing in deeply, savouring the cool fresh air. "You find Cordingly, and get him to alert Saxby and Max. Then join me there."

Ferguson shook his head. "I don't think that's a very—"

She cut him off abruptly. She was in no mood to debate. She had lost Malchus one time too many, and was not going to let anything jeopardize finding him this time. "He's got the Ark, the Menorah, and may soon have the real version of *The Sword of Moses*. We're out of time." Her voice left no doubt the topic was closed for discussion. "It may not be long before he makes his move. I'm not letting him out of my sight again."

As they drew into central London, they were soon hurtling down the west end of the Euston Road.

When the vast station came into sight, Ferguson avoided the signs for its car park, and made straight for the front entrance. Parking up directly outside, they sprinted into the building together.

It was a dreary 1960s concrete bunker. She had once seen a small old creased honeymoon photograph of her father and mother, arm-in-arm under a seventy-foot-high classical archway inscribed with the word 'Euston' in vast gold lettering. Beside the photograph had been another, showing them inside the majestic old Victorian station hall, complete with classical columns, elaborate ceiling, a grand and ornate split sweeping staircase, and high decorated windows. It had been more a palace than a public building.

But it had all gone—demolished and replaced by a cavernous grim concrete box she was sure could effortlessly win the award for London's most bleak and soulless building.

Running across the crowded concourse, she headed towards the ticket office, and soon saw what she was looking for.

An internet kiosk.

She handed Ferguson a bundle of twenty pound notes. "We can't use credit cards. They'll be monitoring our withdrawals. Get me a ticket for the next train to Inverness."

He made for a bank of nearby ticket machines, and began to punch in the travel selection.

Arriving at the internet kiosk, she loaded it up with pound coins, and typed in a search for Aleister Crowley's house in the Highlands.

She had no time to read the resulting screens in any detail, but printed off a handful of the top results.

Clicking through from one of the sites, she pulled up a map of Loch Ness.

It was a long narrow lake near the top of Scotland. Rarely more than a mile wide, it ran twenty-three miles like a thin blue snake, connecting the towns of Inverness to its north and Fort Augustus at its southern tip.

As Ferguson approached and passed her the ticket, she stabbed at the screen. "Look. There it is—Boleskine House, former home of Aleister Crowley and more recently the guitarist from Led Zeppelin." She looked at him in triumph. "The guitarist sold it in 1992 to an anonymous buyer, and it's been in unknown hands ever since."

She could feel her voice rising with excitement. "And there, only a mile away," she moved her finger directly south. "Foyers, the village where Malchus's letter was posted."

"Boleskine House." She ran for the platform, clutching the ticket and the sheaf of pages she had printed off. "That's where the Ark is."

---

## 99

*Maze Hill Railway Station*
*Maze Hill*
*London SE10*
*England*
*The United Kingdom*

AT 5:00 P.M. EXACTLY, a shabby white transit van pulled up outside the small grey-panelled railway station at Maze Hill.

The Skipper leant out of the driver's window, scanning the station area.

Uri stood up off the low beige wall where he had been waiting for him and walked towards the van.

The Skipper motioned for him to put his holdall in the back, and then to get in the front.

Uri had no trouble seeing why the large man usually got his way.

His size dwarfed the van's hot black plastic cabin, his hulking presence filling the space, dominating it.

Uri climbed in, ignoring the pungent smell of stale cigarette smoke. "So what's the job?" he asked, as they headed off down the tree-lined road.

"Import export," the Skipper replied, clearly not wanting to be drawn on the topic. "You'll find out soon enough."

They lapsed into silence until they reached a large Victorian gateway signalling the entrance to the Blackwall Tunnel under the Thames.

As they entered the tunnel, the underground road bent sharply in several places. Uri had read in a free newspaper a few days earlier that this was an attempt not to disturb some of London's remaining plague burial pits.

When they emerged from the tunnel, the Skipper turned to him.

"I hope you understand, Danny, that Otto's problem is not just jealousy. You see, he also has a limited imagination. On the other hand, you could never say that about me. I've been doing this a lot longer than he has, so trust me when I tell you that if you cross me, I'll mess you up in ways that'll have you begging to let Otto finish you off with his gas axe. Are we clear?"

Uri did not answer. He got the point.

As they began to leave London behind, they passed through a succession of small market towns. They had plainly once been a world away from the smoke of London, but now provided accommodation for the hordes of commuters who shuttled in and out each day on the bulging trains Uri had seen speeding through East London morning and evening.

"Let me tell you the rules, Danny," the Skipper continued. "I run my lads the old-fashioned way, and I'm accountable for our successes and failures. I've got no problem with people showing initiative—you're clearly resourceful and experienced. But if you cross the line, I'll carve you into small pieces and ship you back to Rhodesia or Liverpool or wherever the hell it is you came from, and I won't think twice about it."

*Not if I get you first,* Uri thought to himself.

Assuming the welcome speech was over, Uri changed the subject. "At the lock-up, you said Malchus was *Reichskommissar* for England?"

"It's a historic post." The Skipper took his hands off the wheel, pushing up his leather jacket sleeves once more, revealing the Nordic and smudgy prison tattoos.

Uri was not sure he had heard right. "Historic?"

"We didn't just start operating in England yesterday, Danny. We've been around a long time."

Uri wanted to get the Skipper talking. Maybe he would let slip something useful.

"The *Führer* had detailed plans for England," the Skipper continued. "England's cultural heritage is basically German and Viking, so the *Führer* always saw us as a key part of the *Reich*. He had all the details worked out."

Uri nodded.

"The *Reichskommissar* for Great Britain was going to have his HQ at Blenheim, where Churchill was born. The puppet government would be led by Mosley's Black Shirts. And the royal family would stay on, as they're Germans anyway."

"Many friends of the *Führer* this side of the Channel were preparing the way, Danny. If it wasn't for Comrade Stalin, the *Führer* would've taken England in a *Blitzkrieg*. We wouldn't have known what hit us. It's now a standard military strategy. The Americans do it routinely. But the modern world learnt it from the *Führer*, who was its master. Think about the trenches of the first war. Years and years bogged down in the same slippery fields while millions were cut down in the machine gun fire. For nothing. The *Führer* wasn't going to make that mistake. He did Poland in just five days. Then France, Belgium, and Holland all fell like nine-pins. England would've been next, if dealing with Ivan in the east hadn't become more urgent."

Uri was more than familiar with Hitler's *Blitzkrieg* tactic of over-whelming crushing military force. Israel had used it successfully against its neighbours in the Six Day War of '67 and the Yom Kippur War of '73.

They were on smaller country roads now, and the dormitory market towns had given way to picturesque villages miles from the railways, where the residents visibly still enjoyed quieter lives.

"What about resistance?" Uri asked. "I can't see people here giving Hitler a very warm welcome."

The Skipper nodded. "After the *Blitzkrieg* into England, there was to be a clean-up. An SS general, Dr Franz Six, was appointed to head up the specially formed *Einsatzgruppen*—SS liquidation squads which fol-lowed the armies into conquered territory. The UK-based *Einsatzgruppen* were to be centred in London, Birmingham, Liverpool, Manchester, and Edinburgh. Any non-cooperators were to be rounded up and eliminated. There was a black book of nearly three thousand high-profile names for immediate disposal—liberals, authors, intellectuals. And, to make sure any resistance was stamped out before it started, able-bodied men between seventeen and forty-five were to be transported to Europe as slave labour. Know your history, Danny—it's all there."

The Skipper paused, then pointed out of the window at a signboard roped onto a piece of scaffolding outside a garage undergoing repairs.

The name of the contractor was eastern European—Polish, Uri guessed.

"You say you're not political, Danny, but just look around you. Look at the mess. Are you telling me England made the right choice to fight Hitler? So we could drop off the world map within ten years, our Empire in ruins, a second-rate country whose only story is its lost glory days of war?"

As they left another village behind, the Skipper turned off the main road onto a bumpy unmetalled track whose gravel and dirt crunched under the tyres as the car bounced along. Uri could not see what lay beyond the screen of evergreen trees lining the road, but guessed they were on a back way into a farm.

After a few minutes of uncomfortable driving, the Skipper turned onto a tarmacked apron in front of a dilapidated open barn. It had plainly been disused for years and was missing large sections of its grey corrugated iron roof. The tarmac in front of it was faded and patchy, with weeds growing out of the many cracks and gaps. The whole area felt abandoned. Uri could not see any other farm buildings for miles. There was nothing but fields in all directions.

But the reason the Skipper had driven them there was right in front of him.

Uri had no difficulty recognizing the unique profile of the white Sikorsky s-70 helicopter on the tarmac. It was the civilian version of the U.S. military's Black Hawk, but without the heavy payload of weaponry.

As Uri and the Skipper stepped out of the van, the helicopter's top and tail rotors started up with a deafening whine.

On the Skipper's nod, Uri collected his holdall from the back of the van and climbed through the Sikorsky's wide rear door into the main cabin.

The layout of the interior had been modified for the flight. The usually comfortable VIP seats had been unbolted and replaced with ten moulded bucket seats, leaving a space in the centre for a number of industrial-looking riveted and wheeled flight cases.

Entering the hefty chopper, Uri immediately saw he was not alone. There were four men already seated. He recognized two of them from *The Bunker*.

With all his senses firing, it only took a split-second to size them up. He saw the alert expressions of experienced street-fighters—men with a disregard for any limits.

It was like looking into a mirror.

He did not need a second glance to know they would have no hesitation in cutting bits off him piece by piece if they ever found out who he really was.

Beside the men, he could also see a number of dark bags on the floor. From their size and shape, he assumed they contained similar hardware to the one he was carrying.

He nodded an acknowledgement, and sat down on an empty seat opposite them.

It was hot inside the cabin, and there was a strong smell of fuel. But he did not mind, and was grateful for the noise of the engines—he had no desire to join in any discussion with his fellow passengers.

He could feel his adrenaline levels rising. After all the planning and waiting, his undercover strategy was finally paying off.

This mission was a far cry from his usual operations, which he planned meticulously, staying in control of every variable, leaving nothing to chance. He choreographed his hits with the precision of a ballet, where even the smallest elements moved smoothly, like the cogs of a watch.

But here, in the helicopter, this was something completely different.

He was accustomed to being on his own, deep in enemy territory. But it was entirely new for him to have no idea where he was headed, or what he was expected to do when he got there.

Whatever it was, they were a heavily armed crew.

Something interesting was going down.

The Skipper appeared in the doorway, nodded at the others, then climbed in, followed by another man Uri had not seen before. The two strapped themselves into their seats, and stared into the middle distance in preparation for takeoff.

At the same time, Uri noticed another man climb into the cramped instrument-lined cockpit next to the pilot.

As the pitch of the two massive turboshaft engines increased, Uri sat back into the small seat and buckled himself into the harness, bracing himself.

Although he was heading into the unknown, he knew the only important detail of the operation.

Wherever they were going—it was taking him closer to Malchus.

————————————— ◆ —————————————

## 100

*Inverness to Foyers*
*Loch Ness*
*Scotland*
*The United Kingdom*

IT HAD BEEN a breathtaking journey.

As Ava left London behind, the train had quickly shuttled through the midlands and up the west coast of England, where it was soon lost in the romantic wilds of the rolling Yorkshire dales, followed by the striking peaks and waterways of Cumbria and the edge of the Lakes.

Cutting sharply across to the east, they had then entered the lowlands of Scotland, stopping briefly at the capital, Edinburgh, before embarking on the final dramatic section of the journey into the rugged untamed beauty of the Highlands.

Arriving finally at Inverness, the northernmost city in Scotland, she had quickly located the inevitable row of taxis outside the hangar-like railway station.

She jumped into the scruffy-looking one at the head of the line, and asked the driver to take her the eighteen miles south to Foyers.

He was an elderly man, wrapped in a puffy anorak and a tweed cap. He was sitting on a seat cover made of wooden beads, and gave every indication that he would first have preferred to finish the milky-looking tea he was drinking from a scuffed thermos flask.

As soon as he realized she was a "bonglie" from England, he had wanted to take her via Culloden—a moor four miles out of town where, he explained with rancour, English redcoat butchers had bayoneted a thousand of the Highlands' finest clansmen some two hundred and fifty years earlier.

Ava was well aware of the history of animosity between the Highlands and anywhere south of the border, and had no desire to be drawn into it.

But the driver was not giving up.

"When the English were done murdering on the moor," he spoke with the soft accent of the Highlands, "they scoured the lochs and glens for anyone they thought sympathized with Bonnie Prince Charlie—executing men, women, and children, and torching whole villages." She could see his face in the rear view mirror. There was real anger there. "They called it 'pacifying' the Highlands. Today we'd call it ethnic cleansing."

Ava knew the story—how the victor of Culloden, the king's son, had plants named after him in both countries. In England it was the pretty red and white wild flower, the Sweet William—while in Scotland the smelly common ragwort had become the Stinking Billy.

When Ava did not respond to his effort to educate her on local history, he lapsed into silence, leaving her free to gaze out of the windows at a landscape unlike any other.

It was early evening, but at this latitude on the fifty-seventh parallel, level with the Alaska Peninsula, the sun would not set for a while yet.

As they approached the great loch, the sight of the low grass and tree-covered hills surrounding the lapping water was breathtaking—made even more dramatic by the almost total absence of people. Save for the occasional small hamlet or lone house, the natural landscape remained unbroken as far as she could see in all directions.

Rarely had she been anywhere so ruggedly isolated.

Speeding down the loch's east coast, she could make out a promontory on the far side dominated by Urquhart Castle—a vast imposing hulk of a medieval ruin jutting out into the water like the stage set of a Wagner opera. She had heard of it—a Highland stronghold since at least the twelve hundreds. Looking at the monumental husk of what it once had been, she could almost feel the power of life and death its chain-mailed lords once wielded.

Contemplating the landscape, she could not help feel that although the scenery was dramatic and majestic, it was not peaceful or inviting. There was a palpable restlessness about it bordering on the sinister. The water was eerily dark, and there was something foreboding about its immense depth—over eight hundred feet, deeper than most of the North Sea.

She could see why Malchus had chosen to come here. There was an undercurrent of tangible menace.

"Nearly there now," the driver announced, shaking her out of her reverie.

She had asked him to drop her at Foyers, a mile beyond Boleskine House, as she did not want him or anyone else knowing where she was going.

More importantly, she had to be on foot and silent when she approached Boleskine House. She was alone, and needed stealth and the invisibility of the woods to cloak her.

"So, what takes you to Foyers?" the driver asked, "The falls?"

The Falls of Foyers had been described on one of the webpages she had printed off. It was a famous local natural beauty spot formed where the river Foyers entered the great loch—a picturesque tumbling waterfall a hundred and fifty feet in height.

"Business, not pleasure," she replied. "The power station." She had spotted on the map that there was a small hydro-electric facility powered by the falls.

It seemed as good a cover story as any.

"Then you'll not be one of the weirdos come to gape at Crowley's house?"

Ava's ears pricked up. "Whose house?" She feigned ignorance.

"You must've heard of him. The English fella. You know, the Satanist, the one the papers called 'the most evil man in Britain'."

"Did he live round here?" Ava asked, eager to draw out whatever information the driver knew. Local intelligence was invaluable.

"We'll pass it soon enough. We get black magic types come on pilgrimages here. It's not healthy, if you ask me."

"Who lives there now?" She assumed Malchus and the Thelema kept themselves to themselves, but locals everywhere always had a way of knowing their neighbours' business.

He shook his head slowly. "It's not a place for decent folk, if you get my meaning. Strange things happen there."

"Like what?" she asked, keeping her voice casual.

"They say Crowley chose the house specially so he could do an ancient black magic ritual—Abramelin or something it's called. You can read all about it in books, I'm sure. They say it takes six months and summons the spirits of Hell. The house was so full of evil shadows that Crowley had to use candles to light the rooms even on bright sunny days."

The driver wiped a hand over his face. "But he left unexpectedly, with the ritual unfinished. He was called away to Paris, or somewhere." He paused. "They say he never undid what he had done."

"What do you mean?" Ava asked.

"I'm no expert," he answered. "But I hear folks talking. They say if you summon something, then you have to banish it back again when you're finished. But Crowley never did. So the spirits he called up are still there. You'll not find a local going near the place."

"Has anything ever actually happened there?" Ava asked sceptically, aware these types of stories were usually no more than local folklore—tall tales to scare wide-eyed children.

The driver nodded. "There's a cemetery there. Used to be a medieval church beside it, before Crowley's house was built on the site. But the church burned down, killing everyone inside. Like I say, it's a bad place."

"But what about Crowley?" Ava persisted. "Has anything happened since he moved in?"

He nodded again. "Crowley's lodge keeper went mad, and tried to murder his wife and children. Then a local butcher cut off his own hand while reading a note from Crowley."

He angled the rearview mirror so he could see Ava's face more clearly. "After Crowley left, a retired army major living there shot himself in the head, right in Crowley's bedroom. And when that guitarist fella owned the house, his lodge keeper's young children both died suddenly—the daughter at her school desk, and the son on his mother's knee. And there was the man who lived there, looking after it for the guitarist. He heard and saw things."

The driver stared hard at Ava. "I'll say it again. It's not a place for decent folk. Bad things happen there. Always have. Always will."

He sped up as they approached a cemetery on their right.

*This must be it,* Ava realized.

It was an open area of wild grassland surrounded by a picturesque low stone wall. There were several hundred old upright tombstones dotted around it in no particular order, and she could also see a mort-house. Judging by the age of the various trees, the shape of the stones, and the heavy lichen and moss covering them, she guessed it was all several centuries old at least.

She knew from the map that the road they were on cut between the cemetery on one side and the house on the other.

Turning her head around to look up the hill, she caught her first sight of Boleskine House—a long low one-storey building, partially hidden behind a screen of trees.

There was a light on inside.

The driver said nothing. When the cemetery and house were out of sight, he spoke again.

"Here we are," he announced, drawing into a tiny hamlet. "Foyers." He pulled up at a small building no larger than an ordinary house. "This is the power station."

Ava paid, thanked him, and stepped out of the car.

As she was walking towards the small power station, the driver called after her through his open window. "Are you sure you don't want me to drop you at one of the guesthouses? It's getting late. There's one just a hundred yards further on."

Ava assured him it was fine, and made for the door of the power station.

He nodded and turned the car around, before winding up his window and heading off into the evening.

From the speed of his exit, he left no doubt he could not wait to be out of the area and back in the safety of Inverness.

———— • ◆ • ————

# IOI

*Boleskine House*
*Foyers*
*Loch Ness IV2*
*Scotland*
*The United Kingdom*

As THE TAXI sped off into the dwindling light, Ava turned to walk back along the side of the loch the way she had come.

There was no one else on the deserted country road, and she was lost in thought. Around her, the shadows began to fall, bleeding the colours and contours from the hills and lake until they became monochrome shapes, devoid of textures or details.

It did not take her long to cover the mile back to Boleskine.

She saw the secluded old cemetery first, on her left.

Earlier it had seemed an almost cheerful place—a pleasant corner of mellow stone and rustling trees. But now, in the half-light, it was distinctly more sinister, with the headstones throwing lengthening shadows out under the still branches.

The squat thick-walled mort-house dominating it was a gruesome reminder of the days when fresh corpses needed protection from the 'resurrection men'. Scotland's unique solution to the problem of body snatchers was in front of her—an impregnable stone vault where the cadavers could lie until so much flesh had rotted off there was nothing worth stealing and selling. Only then would the sexton put the decomposed corpse into the ground.

Ava turned away and looked in the other direction, up the hill, towards the screen of trees shielding Crowley's infamous house.

Despite the failing light, she could see it more clearly now than when she had sped past earlier in the car.

It was a long low pale building, one storey high. From the shape and style, she guessed it had been built in the late 1700s.

She counted eleven windows running along the main elevation, with the centre marked by a pointed gable sheltering a larger window. The symmetry was completed by rounded bays to the left and right, each lit by three windows.

The roof itself was local grey slate, and there were a number of visible low chimneys. Despite the chill of the summer evening, there was no smoke.

Although she had no proof yet, she instinctively knew it was Malchus's retreat.

As she looked more closely at the isolated house, she saw there was no main entranceway—just a small door cut into the northern side of the right-hand bay. From what she had read on the train, she assumed it was the entrance Crowley had built for his Abramelin ritual, which required a north-facing doorway from the 'oratory' onto a terrace, which was to be covered in fine river sand in order to see the footsteps of the infernal beings he conjured.

Although the long wall of the house faced the loch, the lack of any main doorway suggested to her it was actually the back of the building.

Thinking quickly, her first priority was to get a fuller sense of the surroundings before deciding how best to get into the house unobserved.

Leaving the road, she began to scramble up the steep hillside in order to skirt around behind the wide building.

As she climbed higher, she realized the grounds were more extensive than she had at first thought, and she was perspiring by the time she had got far enough through the rhododendrons, birch, pine, larch, and fir trees to be able to look back down on her target.

The first thing she noted was that her assumption was correct. The side of the house facing up the hill was the front. She could now clearly see a large sandstone entrance porch with double storm doors. It was at the end of a long sweeping gravel drive leading up from a small lodge house and an imposing set of tall wrought iron gates.

The drive was plainly the official way onto the estate, but she had no intention of drawing attention to herself by approaching that way. The gates were widely visible to any observer and might well be hooked up to a security system. In addition, it was a still night, and there was no traffic or other noise. Her footsteps on the gravel would ring out like gunshots, as well as leaving telltale tracks.

Retracing her steps, she scrambled back down the hillside until she was again level with the isolated house.

It was dark now, and she was struck by the beautiful but eerie moonlit view over the graveyard and loch.

Feeling her heart pounding hard, she climbed over a low four-bar fence and moved quickly and silently across the lawns between the flowerbeds and box hedges towards the side of the house.

Looking around, she could not see any cameras, and there was no sign of an alarm system.

She guessed that if the taxi driver was right and people avoided the house, there was probably no need for an electronic surveillance system. People's fear was the best security device of all.

Moving quietly along the back wall, she found all the windows dark and curtained.

As she approached the north-west bay where Crowley had cut his oratory door, she found what she needed. Although it had not been visible from the road, there was a faint chink of light coming through a small crack in the drawn curtains.

The gap was narrow, but it was enough for her to see a thin slice of the room beyond it.

On the far wall, hanging over the stone fireplace, she could see the right side of what appeared to be a painted portrait of a man in Elizabethan dress. She could only make out a sliver of his face, and could tell nothing more than he was an old man with white hair.

Closer to her, she could also see the lower section of a large floor-standing red-gold copper tripod, which she guessed from the room's mellow flickering light was a standing candelabrum.

Her restricted view did not allow her to see anything else apart from aged dark wooden floorboards and a segment of stone walls.

Listening intently, she strained to hear if there was any sound of activity inside—any indication there was anyone in the house.

But there was nothing—just silence, and the sound of the wind in the trees.

She slipped a hand into her pocket and quietly pulled out the Kahr nine-millimetre she had taken off DeVere. She flipped the safety to the off position, and pulled back the slide to cock it.

After glancing through the gap in the curtain one more time, she tried the door's handle, turning and pulling it gently.

The door did not move.

It was firmly locked.

She considered picking the lock, but quickly decided against it. She had no idea who or what lay on the other side, and there was no sense in putting herself in a vulnerable position—either when picking it or relocking it once inside.

Heading back towards the side of the house, she made for the dim light she had first seen from the road. As she rounded the corner, she immediately saw it was coming from one of the side windows.

She approached the window stealthily, and stopped outside it to peer into a dark room, whose open doorway allowed some of the light from the hallway chandelier to filter into it.

Unlike the old-fashioned room she had just seen at the back of the house, she was surprised to see this one was a study decorated as if for a 1930s German intellectual.

Its walls were a clean white, hung with Bauhaus-era circular graphic art, and the space was sparsely filled with minimalist furniture from the same period.

There was a plain desk of metal tubes covered with a taut white leather top supporting a curved chrome reading lamp. On the other side of the room was a tubular chaise longue, again made of chrome and white leather, but with a matching side table on which a number of books were neatly stacked.

The irony of the room was not lost on Ava. Malchus probably thought the style lent him an air of intellectual respectability, but it was in fact a style of design the Nazis had suppressed for its 'degeneracy'.

Focusing back on the window, she noted it was a standard sash, with no bolts or locks on the inside.

She inched it up a fraction then held her breath, waiting—listening for even the smallest sound.

But she was met only with silence from within.

Pushing the window's lower section up higher, she raised the wooden frame until it was half open, then paused again, listening for any indication she had been overheard.

*Still nothing.*

Moving as stealthily as she could, she climbed through the open window and landed on the study floor in a crouching position. As part of the same fluid movement, she raised the gun in both hands, covering the room with a sweeping arc, ready to unload rounds into anything that moved.

But she was met with nothing but stillness and silence.

*She was alone.*

Stepping quickly across the darkened study, she paused at its doorway, listening for the sound of anyone moving deeper in the building.

*Nothing.*

Nosing the pistol ahead of her, she stepped out into the hallway.

It was long and narrow, with a pillared opening on the left leading to the main front doors, as well as two large display alcoves, each filled with a bronze sculpture. Both were male nudes—one holding a flaming torch, the other a sword. They looked like 1930s fascist imitations of classical Greek art.

Moving further down the hallway, she tried the white-panelled doors leading off it, but found them locked.

The only open door was at the far end of the corridor, and as she looked through it into the room beyond, her breathing quickened.

The room's walls were covered in thin white rectangular tiles, each slightly bevelled, giving an almost three-dimensional effect. The only objects in the room were a long plain stone table and a deep ceramic sink fixed onto the wall next to it.

The room's clinical cleanness reminded her of a Victorian dissecting room or mortuary.

She did not want to imagine what Malchus used it for.

But what had caught her eye was a doorway in the room's far corner. It was exactly like the others in the hallway, except in place of the ornamental handles it had a large brass-faced keyhole with a long iron key protruding from it. Immediately above the keyhole was an oversize barrel bolt with a heavy padlock, hanging open.

She could feel her pulse quickening.

It was exactly what she had been looking for.

*A cellar door.*

And it was slightly ajar, letting a pungent smell of incense rise up from below.

She could hear nothing except for her own racing heartbeat, and there were butterflies in her stomach as she took in the enormity of where she was.

*This was it.*

*This had to be where he was keeping the Ark and the Menorah.*

She could feel the excitement she had been trying to suppress ever since she had seen the packing crate on the rusty tug boat in Astana. She had sensed then that she had been in the presence of the Ark.

And she could feel it again now.

All the frustrations of the past days ebbed away, as she knew with a surge of almost uncontrollable elation that she was about to come face to face with the Ark.

Pulling the wooden cellar door wider, she was surprised to find a three-inch-thick steel one just behind it. There was no handle on it, just a small hexagonal keyhole, a tumbler lock, and a large steel wheel.

But it, too, was open.

She raised the handgun in her right hand, pointing it into the cellar.

Her palms were wet with anticipation as she looked down the stone steps, which she could see clearly, illuminated by a warm flickering glow.

She could guess exactly what it meant.

In accordance with ancient tradition, Malchus was keeping the sacred objects in his own secluded holy of holies, lighting them gently by candlelight, and bathing them permanently with incense in an unending tribute of praise.

With the doors fully ajar, the odour was even more pungent. It was like no incense she had ever smelled. It was darker, heavier—like something from a street souk in sub-Saharan Africa.

She took a deep breath to steady herself, then stepped through the door onto the top step.

As she did, she felt a piece of cold hard metal being pressed into the back of her skull behind her ear. At the same time, she heard the unmistakable double click of a pistol's firing mechanism being cocked.

Before she could react, a familiar deep resonant voice spoke behind her.

"Dr Curzon, I have been expecting you."

For the first second, Ava was too stunned to react. But as she realized that Malchus was yet again coming between her and her prize, a bolt of white-hot anger shot through her.

*Where on earth had he come from?*

She had been sure the corridor and room had been empty.

*Had he been watching her all along?*

A volcano of rage erupted inside her.

*Was this some kind of game for him?*

"Put the gun down," Malchus ordered, "slowly."

"Or what?" Ava exploded, wheeling around, the challenge burning in her eyes. She was damned if she was going to let him come between her and the Ark again. It was her turn to have the Ark. She was angry enough to fight him with her bare hands if that was what it took.

"Don't tempt me, Dr Curzon," he replied, a cruel smile playing across his fleshy lips. "There's no one for miles around to hear what goes on in my little house. I beg you not to be difficult. For your sake."

He ground the barrel harder into her head. "Now I shan't ask again. Please put the gun down."

Seething, Ava's mind cleared enough to realize he was not making idle threats.

She knew the results of his handiwork—her father, Yevchenko, Drewitt, the priest in the lower church of the Basilica di San Clemente, and Professor Stone in the Bodleian. All of them slain in cold blood. But most of all, she remembered Max's man in the dark underground Roman complex outside the mithraeum—shot like a dog in revenge for the death of Malchus's henchman.

Malchus had not batted an eyelid as he executed him.

Flushed with rage, she knew Malchus was not only capable of killing—she had come to realize that he actively enjoyed it.

She could feel him pressing the end of the barrel harder into her skull.

Fuming, she knew she had no realistic alternative but to comply. This was not the time for heroics. If she wanted to see the Ark, if she wanted to see Malchus get what he deserved, and if she wanted to clear her and Ferguson's names, then she would have to stay alive.

Fighting the burning torrent inside her, she slowly bent down and put the Kahr on the floor.

---

## 102

*Boleskine House*
*Foyers*
*Loch Ness IV2*
*Scotland*
*The United Kingdom*


"WALK," MALCHUS ORDERED, pointing Ava towards the room's doorway.

One thing immediately clear to her was that with a gun trained on her at this pointblank distance, she had no realistic choice except to comply with his orders. He was experienced, armed, fit, and alert. She would have to be in a desperate position to risk attacking him without a weapon.

And she was not in one yet.

As she stepped away from the cellar door, Malchus picked up her gun and slipped it into his pocket.

Keeping his pistol trained at her head, he indicated for her to move out into the hallway.

He followed right behind her and stopped at the first door on the left, which he unlocked with a key from his pocket.

"Inside," he ordered curtly, keeping the gun on her at all times.

She stepped past him into the room and paused for a moment, stunned at the bizarre sight.

*So this was where Crowley had made his oratory.*

Hanging above the large stone fireplace, dominating the room, was the framed Elizabethan portrait she had spied through the window.

Now she could see the whole face, with its black skullcap and sharply pointed white goatee beard, she immediately recognized the figure. She did not need to read the nameplate fixed to the bottom of the frame to know it was the most notorious English magician of the troubled Elizabethan age—Dr John Dee.

She could also now see that the glow illuminating the room was coming from four great copper candelabra—each supporting three large guttering black candles. They were positioned along each of the room's four walls, slightly off-centre. Thinking back to the aerial map of the house and area she had printed off at Euston, she realized they marked out the four cardinal points—north, east, south, and west in an imaginary circle.

But in front of her stood something she had never expected to see.

It was a bizarre but perfectly square table—a cube, as high as it was wide, draped in a lustrous red silk cloth.

She recognized it immediately from its uniquely odd features and the drawings of it she had seen in the Enlightenment Gallery at the British Museum. But she was having difficulty believing it.

Because it was not supposed to exist.

But here it was.

Right in front of her.

She was looking at Dr John Dee's four-hundred-year-old Table of Practice—the occult altar he had designed for communicating with the angel and spirit worlds.

The floor beneath it was also covered in a matching red silk cloth, and on it, under each leg, were four grey wax seals, each lightly shot through with pink streaks and covered in intricate sigils and glyphs.

Eyeing the surface of the Table, she recognized what looked like Dr Dee's black Mirror of Tezcatlipoca, along with several piles of papers.

The most intriguing was an old manuscript—its quarto-sized vellum sheets buckled and rigid with age, their brown surface covered with medieval Hebrew and Aramaic writing.

Reading it upside down, she realized with a jolt that it was the original London manuscript of *The Sword of Moses*. She could not imagine how it came to be in Northern Scotland and not in an acid-free box on a shelf in the underground stacks at the British Library.

Beside it was a sheaf of computer-typed pages. The top one was titled:

THE SWORD OF MOSES
COD GAS 178

The writing underneath was in English, and evidently a translation of the London manuscript.

Next to the translation was a smaller sheaf of papers with a torn and ragged left margin—the leaves covered with small but meticulous writing in fine pencil.

With a flash of sadness, she recognized the handwriting from the pages she had seen earlier that day in the Bodleian. It was the last piece of research Professor Stone had ever undertaken—copying and translating what he thought was the Oxford version of *The Sword of Moses* for Malchus.

Faced once again with the lacerated lives Malchus left in the monomaniacal pursuit of his goals, she felt a fresh flush of rage at the human wreckage that invariably trailed in his wake.

Brushing aside the unpleasant thoughts, she turned her attention to the other side of the room, where there was a large square of oiled black canvas on the floor.

On top of it was one of the oddest chairs she had ever seen. It was L-shaped, with a short narrow seat and a high back. From the blackened wood, pitting, scores, and scratches, it was clearly several centuries old.

She had never seen anything quite like it.

Taking in its detail, her heart beat faster as she spotted three pairs of bulky black handcuffs on the floor beside it. They also looked antique—forged iron, she assumed.

Whatever the chair was, it had an unpleasantly sinister air.

She shivered slightly. The temperature in the room was the same as in the hall, but for some reason it felt distinctly colder.

"Sit," he ordered, motioning her towards the age-worn chair.

With a sense of foreboding, but aware she had no other realistic options, she moved across to the chair and sat down on the hard narrow seat.

"Cuff your ankles to the chair legs," he commanded, indicating the chunky black handcuffs on the floor.

She could sense the situation going from bad to worse, and every fibre in her screamed to get off the chair and out of the room.

But she had no choice. Malchus was out of range for her to attack him, and she did not fancy her chances without a weapon.

If she did what he asked, she may well end up getting hurt. But she definitely would if she made a break for it.

So it was simple maths. For so long as she was alive, there was hope of finding a way out. But if she gave him cause to pull the trigger, then it would all be over.

With every atom of her being screaming at her that it was a bad idea, she reached down and picked up the cold metal fetters.

She comforted herself with the thought that maybe the chair was not too heavy, and she could move it. Perhaps if she got the opportunity to stand up and lift it, the ankle cuffs might slide off its legs onto the floor, leaving her free to move.

Slowly, as if in a daze, she cuffed each of her ankles to the chair. To her surprise, the locks closed effortlessly despite their age and crude design. Malchus had plainly maintained them well.

"Now put the other cuff on your right wrist," he ordered, walking towards her.

She did as he asked and watched as he approached her from across the room, before moving behind the chair where she could no longer see him.

Without warning, she felt an indescribable wrenching pain as he pulled her arms behind the high back of the chair, and snapped the open handcuff shut around her left wrist.

It had been a lightning fast movement, and she had no time to react.

She was now pinned to the heavy piece of furniture by her legs and arms, leaving her no ability to move any of her limbs.

Her throat went dry.

"You were looking at my table," he observed, moving back around to where she could see him. "You know what it is, don't you?"

"A toy," she replied contemptuously. "A pitiful feeble-minded delusion. Dee's original objects are in London."

Malchus shook his head solemnly. "You are gravely mistaken. The seals are faultlessly faithful to the originals, and the British Museum's cherished cabinet now only holds a worthless piece of obsidian in place of the great Mirror of Tezcatlipoca."

Ava stared at him with loathing. "What makes you think the mirror in the museum's cabinet was Dee's original? It could've been switched many times over the centuries. And sometimes we display replicas—

especially of valuable artefacts."

Malchus's eyes narrowed. "*Non es digna ut intres sub tectum meum,*"[16] he spat at her, parodying the words of the mass. "The mirror speaks to those with a true heart. I have spent many nights with it, and I can vouch for its authenticity better than any museum curator."

Ava glared at him, pleased to have put him on the defensive.

"But you should be much more concerned about my chair," he changed the subject, smiling nastily. "You are honoured to sit on it."

"If you say so," Ava stared at him, not sure what he was implying.

"You see," he continued, "there aren't many garrotting chairs left, now it's no longer an official method of state execution."

Before she had processed the words, something in her subconscious that had been urging her to get off the chair finally broke through, sending an impulse to her legs.

Driving upwards, she held on to the seat firmly with her thighs and upper arms, lifting it and twisting it so the cuffs would slide off the legs to the floor.

But to her horror, the seat did not move an inch. She had barely registered that it was bolted to the ground before her head exploded with a searing pain as Malchus brought the metal butt of the pistol down hard onto the side of her skull.

Collapsing back onto the chair, a torrent of pain cascaded down through her head and shoulders.

As her focus slowly returned, she saw that Malchus was stepping over her. An instant later, she felt him sitting down onto her thighs, astride her. His hairless head was only inches from hers, and she could feel his breath on her face.

The expression in his cold eyes had changed, and was now one of uncontrolled animal lust.

Overwhelmed by panic, and fuelled by a cocktail of adrenaline and fight-or-flight chemicals, she bellowed with a mixture of terror and rage as she fought to stand up, to throw Malchus off her. At the same time, she hurled her upper body forwards, smashing him in the chest with her shoulder in the hope of toppling him.

As she twisted, the cuffs on her wrists behind the chair bit into her flesh viciously. But despite her superhuman effort, he remained on top of her.

---

16 "You are not worthy to enter into my house."

With a gasp of rage, she realized she was completely at his mercy.

To her revulsion, he raised his hands and began to caress her face, staring all the while into her eyes, his excitement mounting.

Her insides were writhing at his repellent touch. She turned her face away, staring at the wall.

"In medieval times," he spoke softly, "the Inquisition popularized the garrotting chair, especially for whores and adulteresses. The Spanish and South Americans inherited their affection for it. The last public execution on a garrotting chair was in Spain, in 1974—so you should consider your imminent and beautiful death part of a noble tradition."

He took one of his hands off her face, and slowly pulled from his pocket a length of red silk, exactly matching the material under and on the Table of Practice.

Instinctively, she threw her head forward to smash him in the nose with the crown of her skull. But he moved out of the way with ease, and her head thumped ineffectually into his hard chest.

He grunted, and the next thing she felt was a searing blow across the side of her face, delivered with such force her head snapped viciously to the side.

She did not stop to register the pain.

She began to buck and struggle for all she was worth. But however much she tried, he remained astride her, smiling smugly at her attempts to dislodge him.

She stared with mounting terror as he raised the piece of silk and began wrapping it slowly in a loop round her throat and the back of the chair.

Still straddling her lap, he began stroking her face again with his left hand, while he pulled the smooth silk tight about her neck with his right, twisting it around the back of the chair.

As he pulled the material, she could feel it begin to bite into the soft flesh of her neck

Panicking now, she knew that if he kept pulling the garrotte, she probably had no more than thirty seconds before the pressure on her carotid arteries would block the blood flowing to her brain and she would slip into oxygen-starved unconsciousness. After that, if he continued, brain death and total system shutdown would follow. If he squeezed hard enough in the right place, he would also crush her windpipe and larynx, although she would feel nothing by then.

She thrashed more wildly. But he was heavy, and may as well have her pinned down onto the chair with an iron girder. However hard she tried, he was still there, his sadistic reptilian eyes drinking in the sight of her desperate struggle for life.

She could not tell if they were tears of pain or desperation beginning to prick the back of her eyes, but she could feel her vision beginning to blur.

As the pressure around her neck increased, she tried to shout out. But no sound came from her throat, just a hoarse rasp.

She was gasping deeply for breath, trying to hyper-oxygenate her blood, struggling to get as much of the life-giving element to her brain as she could.

She had no idea how long it had been. Five seconds? Fifteen seconds? It was impossible to tell.

As her carotid arteries were compressed still further, her vision began to swim, and she felt overcome with light-headedness.

Despite her panic, she still refused to look Malchus in the eye. He may have control of her physical body, but that was all. There would be no other satisfaction for him.

Choking, she stopped struggling. It was pointless. She knew now that she not going to be able to get him off her, so her priority was to preserve what little strength she had, to stay conscious for as long as possible. To live for every second she could.

She had heard that dying people saw their lives flash before their eyes. She was having no such vision, and wondered if perhaps that meant she was not dying. On the other hand, she speculated groggily, how could anyone know what happened in the moments before actual brain death?

As the dizziness increased, she felt her physical strength ebbing away fast.

To her surprise, the weight on her thighs suddenly lifted, and Malchus moved round to stand behind her.

*Was it over?*

She tried to suck in air, but Malchus was still holding the garrotte tightly. Summoning the small reserve of strength she had left, she twisted her head slightly so she could see him out of the corner of her eye. The movement caused an explosion of white light in her head, but she was beyond caring.

Malchus had picked up a short dark wooden pole about a foot long.

As he inserted it into the loop of silk behind the chair, she could feel the pressure round her neck tighten unbearably as he started to turn the pole, mechanically twisting the garrotte tighter and tighter.

She could now hear choking and gagging noises, but was not sure where they were coming from.

She felt disconnected from what was happening.

A rainbow of searing bright stars floated in front of her eyes in a swirling mist of black and purple whorls.

Somewhere in the distance she thought she could hear chanting in Latin. But it did not sound right. The words were wrong. And it was not the usual harmonious tones of plainchant. It had a rough quality to it, discordant and violent.

Sagging, she was suddenly overcome with an overwhelming tiredness. She could no longer feel any of her body, and was aware only of a hot rushing sensation.

She felt hopelessly drunk. The room was spinning, and she was overcome with an unbearable urge to pass out.

Her hearing was going. She could still make out the malevolent chanting, but it sounded ever more indistinct, as if underwater.

Trying to focus her eyes on the wall one last time to stave off the slide into unconsciousness, she knew her sight was now failing terminally, too. Dark patches began to cloud the room.

She could feel the end coming.

As the rushing sound in her ears became deafeningly loud, her eyes rolled up into her head, and she felt herself keel over into an all-enveloping darkness.

—— • ◆ • ——

# 103

*Boleskine House*
*Foyers*
*Loch Ness IV2*
*Scotland*
*The United Kingdom*

IN THE HEAVY blackness surrounding her, Ava could hear someone gasping painfully, sucking in deep rattling lungfuls of air.

Mystified, she listened to the disturbing sound as the darkness in front of her eyes began to break apart, allowing kaleidoscopic patches of light and colour to appear.

She was being suffocated by a thick blanket of grogginess, and had no memory of where she was.

Confused, she tried to move, but her body was paralyzed—her arms and legs pinned down by unseen weights.

With rising anxiety, she tried to open her eyes, but the intense throbbing in her skull was too painful, and she could not break through it to move any of her facial muscles.

Listening more closely to the rasping breathing, she realized with alarm it was coming from her own throat.

It was her mouth, wildly gulping in air.

The knowledge seemed to trigger a reconnection with her body, and she was suddenly aware of an intense burning in her lungs as the air rushed in. She sucked it down hungrily.

As her heart and lungs filled her body with freshly aerated blood, her memory returned with a sickening jolt. She panicked at the image in her mind's eye of Malchus sitting astride her, his eyes filled with a perverted excitement as he revelled in the sight of her dying throes.

Breathing more freely now, she realized he was no longer on top of her, and her neck was not being constricted.

But she was acutely aware the danger might not have passed. It could just have changed into something else. Maybe he was going to keep asphyxiating and reviving her, again and again.

Forcing her eyes open, she blinked several times as she looked around the room.

To her relief, she could immediately see Malchus was no longer behind her. Instead, he was sprawled in an ungainly heap on the wooden floor—his nose newly crooked, and two trickles of scarlet blood flowing out from his nostrils onto his fleshy lips and chin.

He seemed oblivious to the injury, and was lying where he had fallen, glaring up with pure hatred at Ferguson, who was standing over him, the blue Sig Sauer aimed directly at his hairless head.

She felt an overpowering wave of gratitude towards Ferguson, who was looking at her with concern. She mustered a smile with what little strength she had. Her head exploded with a slicing pain as she moved her lips, but she did not mind. She had to be alive to feel pain.

Behind Ferguson, she could see the tall patrician figure of Saxby. She owed him a debt of gratitude, too. This was the second time he had arrived to pick up the pieces after Malchus had got the better of her.

He seemed as unruffled as ever. His charcoal-grey suit was immaculately pressed, and his full head of silver hair lent him its usual air of distinction.

As her breathing became more regular, she shot him a look of thanks. But when his eyes met hers, she was startled to see no warm greeting or acknowledgement—only a fixed expression of icy purpose.

With mounting disbelief, she watched as he turned towards Ferguson, aiming the pistol he was holding at waist height directly at Ferguson's chest.

"Drop it, Major Ferguson," he ordered him coldly.

Ava was not sure she had heard right.

*Was she hallucinating?*

She knew the mind played tricks when oxygen-starved,

*Was she still unconscious? Was it even possible to dream when unconscious?*

She bit her lip hard enough to draw blood in an effort to try to wake herself up. But the sight in front of her remained unchanged.

Ferguson had turned to stare over his shoulder at Saxby with incredulity, his gun still trained ahead of him on Malchus.

"Don't test me." The older man's tone was abrupt. "You were never part of the plan, and I'll gladly remove you from it."

Her mind was spinning.

*What plan?*

She was struggling to make sense of what she was seeing.

*This was all part of some plan?*

Ferguson kept his gun on Malchus, continuing to stare over his shoulder at Saxby, seemingly evaluating the likelihood of the older man carrying out the threat.

Needing no further cue, Malchus quickly stood up and stepped towards Ferguson. Swinging his whole upper body in a lightning-fast jab, he punched Ferguson viciously, a hammering downwards blow to the nape of his neck.

Saxby watched impassively as Ferguson dropped like a stone. The moment he hit the floor, Malchus stamped down hard on his wrist, grinding his shoe's heel into the soft flesh of Ferguson's inside lower arm. With a grunt of pain, Ferguson released the gun.

Malchus took a handkerchief from his pocket and wiped the blood off his face. At the same time, he kicked Ferguson's gun sharply away, sending it spinning to the wall, harmlessly out of reach.

Ava's mind was still reeling.

*Saxby? In it with Malchus?*

It did not make sense.

She struggled to see why Saxby would want to collaborate with Malchus.

*What possible interest could Saxby have in Malchus's neo-Nazi movement?*

It simply did not add up.

*Had they been cooperating?*

*For how long?*

The residual fog was making it hard for her to think clearly, but her thoughts were cut short as the door opened and a group of men entered.

They were heavily armed, and wheeling a number of large flight-cases.

She counted six gunmen in total, including the one who was evidently their leader—a tall hulking man with the forearms of his leather jacket pushed up to reveal a selection of tattoos.

It was immediately obvious to her that this group was not related to Max and his team of *Légionnaires*. There was nothing of the French team's quiet camaraderie or professionalism about them—just a sense of raw aggression and menace.

Saxby turned with authority to the large man. "Pack the artefacts in the cellar and then this table. We need to be out of here in five minutes." He nodded towards Ava and Ferguson. "Take these two to the helicopter, and put a guard on them."

The large man instructed four of the team to go below. They peeled off without a word, taking the biggest two flight cases with them. He then gave a quiet order to the tall dark-blond man beside him. She thought she heard the name "Danny", before the blond man stepped over towards her and Ferguson.

Malchus threw him a set of small black keys, and he swiftly removed the handcuffs shackling Ava's ankles, reusing one of the pairs to lock Ferguson's hands behind his back.

"Move." He ordered Ava and Ferguson, guiding her hands over the back of the chair's high back so she was free. He jabbed Ferguson with his submachine gun, pushing them both quickly out into the front hall.

Passing the white-tiled room leading to the cellar, she could see the four men had already disappeared down the steps, leaving the two large flight cases open in the upper room.

Slowing her pace as her heart rate increased, she wondered if she might catch a sight of the Ark as the men brought it upstairs.

She sensed the dark-blond man leading them was also walking a little more slowly as they passed the open doorway, but he ushered her on, and in no time they were out of the grand front doors and on the sweeping gravel path.

The outside air temperature had dropped significantly, and there was a cold wind whipping her hands and face. She breathed deeply, and felt the cloud of fog lifting further, enabling her to think more clearly again. Her neck was sore, and would remain so for days. But nothing was broken, and the bruising would heal.

Up ahead in the moonlight, she could discern the outline of a medium-sized helicopter on the lawn. She had not heard it land, although wondered perhaps if that was what the deafening rushing sound in her ears had been as she had blacked out.

The rotors were not turning. But there was a pilot in the front cabin, and he had his headset on, ready.

As they reached the helicopter, the guard slid open the main cabin's metal side door and ushered them inside, following behind.

There was no heating, and the grey ribbed walls of the helicopter were stripped down and uninviting, but she was grateful to be out of the wind. The moulded bucket seats were uncomfortable, but anything was a relief after the unyielding hard wood of Malchus's garrotting chair.

She looked at the guard, who had taken a seat opposite her and Ferguson. His submachine gun was cradled in his lap, pointed directly at them, his finger never leaving the trigger. She could see from the way he was watching them that he was not an amateur. He was alert. Trained.

"So who are you people?" she asked.

"No talking," he replied curtly.

From just those two words, she could hear there was something non-native in his accent. Eastern European? Afrikaans? She could not quite put her finger on it.

"Where are you taking us?" she persisted.

"I don't want to hurt you," he replied, his face expressionless. "Just be quiet."

There it was again. But this time he had said enough for her to recognize it.

She frowned, trying to make sense of what she was hearing. The group of men who had entered with Saxby were clearly with Malchus. They were thugs, just like the men he had brought to the Basilica di San Clemente with him—neo-Nazi paramilitaries.

But that made little sense if she had heard right.

Although it had only been the faintest hint, she would know it anywhere. She had visited the Dominicans' *École Biblique* archaeology school in Jerusalem many times in her years stationed with the National Archaeological Museum in Amman, and the accent was unmistakeable.

True, it was very subtle in his case—barely noticeable. It could easily have passed for a slight vestige of one of the many hundreds of regional accents in England, or possibly from one of the world's other English-speaking countries.

But she was in no doubt.

*The man opposite her was an Israeli.*

She sat back, lost in thought.

She had heard that some extremist modern British right-wing groups now had Jewish members, united in a newly discovered virulent anti-Islamism.

But that seemed unlikely—Malchus was a neo-Nazi, not a white supremacist.

On the other hand, and more worryingly, it could also mean the Israeli authorities were as interested in what was in Malchus's cellar as she was.

That would mean competition and complications.

Before she could explore her thoughts any further, the cabin door slid open, letting in a rush of cold air.

Silently, one of the armed men climbed in and pushed a button. A metal ramp began to descend with a low hum. When it was fully extended, he signalled to the men outside to begin loading up.

One by one, they wheeled the shiny flight cases up the ramp, moving them to the middle of the cabin. Working silently, they secured them to the floor with buckled canvas load straps.

Surveying the metal cases, Ava could feel her breathing quicken. She ignored the three boxes she knew contained the Table of Practice and seals, and concentrated on the two larger ones.

She wanted nothing more than to rush over, unfasten them, and rip off the lids. But she was still handcuffed.

The thought of being so close to the Ark was almost too much to bear. There, two feet away from her, was the object she had been thinking about day and night for the past eleven days, and on and off for most of her life.

But there was nothing she could do.

She was a prisoner, on possibly the most heavily armed helicopter in the British Isles.

Tearing her eyes away, she heard the rotor engines start as Saxby climbed into the cockpit beside the pilot, and Malchus and the remaining men buckled themselves into the seats in the rear cabin.

Although she had no idea where they were going, or what Saxby's plan for her was, her one consolation was that the Ark was going with her. That meant her chances of recovering it were not yet over.

That had to be enough for now.

She stared out of the window opposite her at the nearby trees and bushes. As the pilot opened the throttle, she watched the trees being whipped backwards, bending at impossible angles in the gale force rotor wash.

She breathed out, readying herself, as Saxby's voice came over the cabin speakers.

"This is a momentous night. The apocalypse that annihilates the present and ushers in a new world order appears in the mythos of all cultures. The ancient Akkadians, Babylonians, Hebrews, and Sumerians have it in their flood stories. The Christians prophesy Armageddon. And in our own northern European tradition it is the Twilight of the Gods— the Nordic *Ragnarök* or Germanic *Götterdämmerung.*"

He paused, letting his message sink in before continuing. "Brothers, tonight we take a decisive step towards that apocalypse. We begin the establishment of the Fourth *Reich* and the new Aryan Imperium."

———————————— • ◆ • ————————————

# 104

*Wewelsburg Castle*
*Büren*
*Paderborn*
*North-Rhine Westphalia*
*Federal Republic of Germany*

AVA HAD NO idea how long they had been in the air.

It had not been a good flight.

She had been trying to think through the possible connections between Saxby and Malchus, and none of the scenarios was positive.

In addition, the presence of the dark-blond man sitting opposite her was a complication she did not need. If he was just one of the hired thugs, then she had nothing especially to worry about from him.

But if he was Israeli government, that added a whole new complexity. Not only would she have to get the Ark and Menorah away from Malchus, she would also need to make sure the *katsa* did not interfere with her plans.

As the helicopter started descending, she got a view of their destination out of the window.

It was a castle—one of the most striking she had ever seen.

The fortification was perched on top of a high rock, whose tree-covered sides fell away sharply. It occupied a strategically commanding position, dominating everything around. Far below it, a river snaked along in the valley, silver in the moonlight.

The imposing castle's shape and grey outer stonework looked renaissance—early 1600s, she guessed. But from its strongly defensive position, she was sure there would have been previous castles on the site for well over a thousand years.

It had three high round towers connected to each other by long straight ranges, leaving a large central isosceles courtyard in the middle. By far the biggest tower, dwarfing the other two, was at the apex of the triangle, giving the building a perfect symmetry.

As she stared at it, the helicopter dropped towards the courtyard, aiming for the centre of the fortified buildings.

Once they had touched down, the men in the cabin around Ava reached into their holdalls and took out leather waistcoats. As they pulled them on, Ava could clearly see the fronts and backs were emblazoned with Nazi insignia.

On the front faces of the jackets were a variety of emblems, but all had the three lions of England under the words 'BRITISCHES FREIKORPS'.

She recognized the badge from the photos of the Thelema Prince had shown her at Legoland.

Saxby and the guard, Danny, ushered her and Ferguson off the helicopter at gunpoint. They crossed the cobbled courtyard and passed through an arched doorway into the largest tower. Ascending a dark stone stairwell, they stopped at the third floor, where they entered a low corridor.

There was minimal lighting, lending the castle a menacing air.

"Where are we?" Ferguson asked, as their footsteps echoed on the hard stone floor

"Wewelsburg," Saxby replied with an air of reverence. "The Vatican of the SS—Himmler's spiritual headquarters. But a renowned castle for centuries before. In its heyday under the bishop-princes, it was infamous as a prison for torturing and trying witches."

Saxby stopped outside a thick low door. It was almost square, and the ancient wood, toughened and darkened by the years, was reinforced with strips of bolted iron.

"Inside," he ordered, pulling the door open for Ava and Ferguson.

Ava had been expecting to enter a prison cell, imagining the hopeless state of the thousands of inmates whose lives had wasted away over the centuries in airless castle chambers.

But instead they stepped into a large circular solar, with windows spaced evenly around the bare stone walls. It was pitch dark outside, so the only light came from three flaming torches mounted into wall sconces. The shadows cast by the dancing flames gave the room a sinister feel, as did the oily smell and occasional wisps of black smoke they threw off.

Malchus was already there, sitting on a low wooden bench by the wide carved stone fireplace, leafing through a sheaf of papers. Ava could not clearly see what they were, but the writing looked like the translation of *The Sword of Moses* she had spotted on the Table of Practice at Boleskine House.

"Chain them up," Saxby instructed the guard, nodding towards a square-sectioned iron bar several feet long set into the stone between two of the windows. It was well above head height, and had probably originally been used for hanging weapons and armour.

The guard approached Ava and undid her left handcuff.

She would have loved to use the opportunity to make a break for it, but Ferguson was in no position to join her, and she could see that neither of them would make it even as far as the door. The guard had a submachine gun, and Saxby was still pointing his pistol at them. From what she could remember, Malchus still had his own gun and Ferguson's Sig Sauer in his pocket, too.

As the cuff came off, she stretched out her arms, grateful for the opportunity to get the circulation flowing into the numbed muscles again. They had been pinned together since Malchus had first put her on his garrotting chair. Although the guard had switched the cuffs to her front during the flight, she had still lost almost all feeling in her arms.

Before she had time to savour the freedom of being able to move her arms freely, the guard indicated for her to raise them above her head. She did, and he swiftly hooked the handcuffs through the bar, before snapping them tight around her left wrist again.

The wall was hard and uneven, and the stone was cold. But worse than that, the bar was high, and she had to stand on her toes to prevent the metal of the handcuffs digging deeply into her wrists and hands. It meant her calf muscles were forced to take her entire weight. Modern interrogation manuals would have described it as a 'stress position'—a technique forcing an individual group of muscles to take unaccustomed strain for long periods of time.

The guard shackled Ferguson immediately next to her, but his height meant he had both feet firmly on the ground. His arms would become painful after a time, just like hers, but he would be able to stay against the wall for much longer.

She gritted her teeth, resolving to shut off the pain when it started.

Her priority now was to get Saxby talking, to find out what he had planned for them. So much had happened so fast that she was still struggling to put the pieces together.

"So there are no Knights Templars, after all?" she looked at Saxby accusingly.

"Of course there are," he answered contemptuously. "They're very real."

"Then everything you told us about their mission was lies?"

"On the contrary," Saxby replied. "The Order is as De Molay and I described it. But I outgrew them many years ago, when I realized my true destiny lay elsewhere—to lead rather than to serve. As I explained to you very clearly, I see no purpose in power if one cannot use it for one's true aims.'"

"Destiny?" There was a note of scorn in Ferguson's voice.

Saxby spun round and glared at him. "I inherited my role in the Templars when I was young, Major Ferguson, direct from my grandfather. My father had died in the war and was, in any event, the black sheep of the family. The Templar Order was not for him. But I took my role as Seneschal deathly seriously. I studied the Order's history and traditions minutely and indefatigably. I became invaluable to them—their walking encyclopaedia, a repository of all their ways: the most Templar of the Templars, a pillar of their establishment."

Ferguson snorted. "I find that hard to believe."

"But there was something of my father in me," Saxby continued, "and it's become stronger as I've grown older. You see, the Saxbys are not an old English family. We did not come over with William the Conqueror. It was my grandfather who Anglicized the name when he settled in London in the 1920s, sensing England had more to offer a cosmopolitan European than the wrecked shell of post-war Germany. Our real name is von Saxburg, an ancient knightly family of the Uradel, Seneschals to the Templars for over seven hundred years."

Ferguson looked unimpressed.

Saxby continued. "My father had strong views about his natural heritage, and the duties it brought. He was not interested in aristocratic life in England, or in the Templars. He believed our rightful place was in Germany. So he returned home before the outbreak of war, and gained what he really wanted, what he believed best represented his contribution to society—the black tunic of the ss officer."

"So you had no choice? Nazism's in your blood?" Ava was not sure if Saxby had caught the note or sarcasm in Ferguson's voice. "Is that what you're saying?"

Saxby sneered. "Do you know what the *Lebensborn* children's programme was?"

Ava stared blankly back at him. She had never heard of it. Ferguson looked equally unsure.

"It means 'fountain of life'," Saxby explained.

"Don't tell me," Ferguson sounded contemptuous. "Experimenting on child prisoners?"

Saxby ignored him. "The *Lebensborn* was a revolutionary programme designed by the *Reichsführer-ss* Heinrich Himmler himself. Its mission was to breed perfect Aryans—to replace war losses and to repopulate the Slavic lands captured in the East with strong racial stock."

"A breeding programme?" Ava was appalled.

"The science of eugenics, Dr Curzon, racial selection, was very popular a hundred years ago. Even the endlessly admired Winston Churchill was a supporter. He wrote to the prime minister of Great Britain in 1910 that he was 'convinced that the multiplication of the feeble-minded is a terrible danger to the race', and he firmly advocated their sterilization. So don't tell me it's a fetish of the Third *Reich*. And Germany was not the only country to practise it either. Sweden was active in sterilizations until forty years ago, along with dozens of other enlightened democratic countries. And let's not forget the United States of America, which had the world's most widespread twentieth-century eugenics programme of all. It was law in thirty states until the 1970s, requiring the sterilization of the mentally incapacitated. So while the USA was criticizing the *Reich* for racial selection, they were busy doing the same thing, and they kept on doing it long after the war was over."

"And that makes it okay?" Ava's eyes were blazing with anger. She was not going to listen to his repellent justifications.

"All aspiring ss men had to pass rigorous physical and racial purity tests before joining. The *Lebensborn* programme then brought them together with specially selected young women who had undergone equally stringent tests. The children of these elite couples were born and raised at *Lebensborn* facilities, then educated in dedicated ss nurseries and schools."

He looked at them both expectantly, pausing for effect. "My parents had the honour of being selected for the programme, and I was born into it."

Ava was repulsed.

He was actually proud of it.

"Several months later, my father was killed in the Russians' final assault on Berlin, and my mother was reported missing-presumed-dead in the bombed out wreckage of the city. As the war was over, I was packed off to be brought up by my grandfather in England. And when I reached adulthood, he initiated me into my shadowy life in the Templars."

"You don't see any contradiction in belonging to the two organizations?" Ava was struggling to hide her incredulity. "The one standing for tolerance and peace, at least as you and De Molay explained it, the other for racism and conquest?"

Saxby turned on Ava, passion flaring in his eyes. "The Templars were once racial warriors, too. The fiercest. They fought to uphold the pure European way of life. But that was long ago. They renounced their heritage in 1312 and now pursue other aims. I long ago came to despise their spineless vision."

Ava shook her head in disbelief. His description of the medieval Knights Templars was a fantasy, rewritten to suit his poisonous politics.

He stepped over, closer to her, dropping his voice. "Anyone can join the Templars if they make it their mission. I was born to it, but I have an even more unique genetic birthright because of the *Lebensborn*—a singularly precious gift of the most sophisticated racial breeding programme the world has ever known. To be the first and only member of my family to have such an honour is something I value more highly than anything else. I'm the only *Lebensborn* survivor in our organization. And I therefore lead the international struggle back to our true Nordic European roots with pride."

"Leading men like Malchus?" Ava looked over towards him, hunched over the papers on the bench against the far wall. "And what do you suppose they'll bring you?"

"Together, we'll give birth to The Fourth *Reich*," he replied simply.

"So, what did you need me for," Ava asked, changing the subject, keen to learn the answer to something that had been bothering her. "Why did you recruit me when you already had Malchus?"

Saxby walked towards her, eyeing her pensively. "You're mistaken, Dr Curzon, if you think you haven't helped greatly. You've been quite invaluable, I can assure you. The Templars are very knowledgeable about objects like the Ark. That's how I knew where it was, at Aksum. When De Molay discovered it had gone missing, he instructed me to oversee the vital operation to retrieve it, little knowing that I was the one who had arranged for its removal from Ethiopia. So you see, your very involvement has kept the heavy finger of suspicion from ever pointing at me. You've helped me play the role of the concerned Templar beautifully. And I'm sincerely grateful to you."

*So there it was.*

*He had been using her.*

She felt ill, and her calves were beginning to ache from the strain of standing on her toes.

"But you turned out to be so much more than I ever bargained for," he continued. "I chose you because of the troubled history between Malchus and your father, and you have not disappointed. Your anger and desire to see him brought to justice have led you to help us very much. Without you, we might never have found the Menorah. For so long as you and Malchus were locked together in battle over the artefacts, all I had to do was sit back and let your collective expertise do the work for me. And you have both excelled. Where one of you had gaps in knowledge or abilities, the other filled in. I smuggled Malchus into our Templar archives where he found the Vatican's ancient medal giving details of the Menorah's hiding place, but it was your tireless ingenuity that solved the puzzle. Leaving the medal for Drewitt to pass to you was a master stroke on his part."

Ava could feel her blood rising. She saw again the image of Drewitt's mutilated body in her mind's eye.

"Malchus knew nothing of my arrangement with you, of course. I didn't want any nasty little jealousies developing. And, I confess, I was curious to see how you'd get along. I supposed that one of you might eventually kill the other. But we could not have that happening until the job was done. So, I even had to intervene to protect you once. When he took you to Stockbridge House after the rally at Stonehenge, he checked a photo of you in our database. I was alerted, and had to act quickly. I did not want him finding out you were former MI6. He might have decided to eliminate you there and then, before you'd been any use to me. So I blanked out the information he received back. I'm sorry if it caused you any trouble."

"This is not a game," she retorted, "for you to control like some puppet master."

"Quite so," Saxby replied calmly, nodding. "And for you it will therefore all end tonight."

Ava's stomach knotted.

*Was that part of the plan, too?*

"You've brought me a long way here just to kill me," she noted drily.

"Oh. I'm not 'just' going to kill you, Dr Curzon," he replied slowly. "Your death is going to be witnessed by hundreds, and will prove to be one of the highlights of the evening."

*I don't think so,* Ava thought to herself. Having survived the ordeal at Boleskine House on Malchus's chair, there was no way she was going through a torture-death experience again. If she was going to die tonight, it would be fighting, not as the victim in some sick spectacle.

"I'm rather pleased we got to you today before Malchus finished having his way with you," Saxby continued. "You see, the plan for you tonight is an idea I've been developing. And, I'm now convinced it's going to be perfect."

The strain on her calves was becoming agonizing. She concentrated on what Saxby was saying, trying to block out the searing pain.

"I've been watching you," he continued, "to see how appropriate you might be. And now I have no doubts, seeing as you have so many," he paused, looking her up and down, "talents." There was no ambiguity as to his meaning.

"I have a special role for you in tonight's ceremony," he continued. "Our colleague, Malchus, has agreed that he doesn't mind sharing the limelight with you, for the greater good."

"If you so much as lay a finger on her." Ferguson growled, leaving the threat hanging.

Ava looked across at Ferguson. She did not need him or anyone to fight her battles for her. But she felt touched by his support nonetheless.

"Major Ferguson, how very gallant you are," Saxby turned to him. "But it's utterly pointless you making threats to protect her. I have other plans for you."

"Bring them on," Ferguson urged him. "I can't wait. Is it going to hurt?" He was smiling at Saxby, taunting him.

Saxby ignored him, and looked back to Ava. "As you have no doubt noted by now, we have a special regard for the occult side of the Third *Reich*. Historians don't talk about it much, but it was a core tenet of the ss, who were the finest embodiment of its ideals. Pagan Nordic solar celebrations were instituted for them, and ss men even had special pagan wedding ceremonies. Their rings, daggers, and uniforms all bore magical Nordic runes, and here at Wewelsburg, the spiritual nerve-centre of the ss, Himmler was building an ss city steeped in the occult. More buildings were to be attached to this castle, and the northern tower, where we stand, was to be the tip of a vast building complex shaped like the Spear of Longinus."

"How do you reconcile all this half-baked religious mumbo-jumbo?" Ava interrupted again. "One minute you're speaking of Yahweh and *The Sword of Moses*. Then it's the Christian saint, Longinus. Then there are Nordic pagan solar ceremonies and *Götterdämmerung*. That's without mentioning Dr Dee's occult beliefs and Aleister Crowley's Thelema. How on earth can you follow all these creeds and traditions at the same time?"

Saxby smiled. "The Templars introduced me to freemasonry. Although I have nothing but contempt for their dramatics and charities, they have got at least one thing right. They teach that there are many paths, but that all are travelling on the same journey. Whether it's religion, philosophy, or magic—all traditions are merely aspects of the *Magnum Opus*, the Great Work."

"So you're an alchemist, too?" Ava shook her head. "Another one of your beliefs?"

Saxby's face darkened. "Be careful what you mock. Alchemy is the most complete expression of the processes underpinning all religions and philosophies." He turned to stare at Ava. "And that is why you fit so neatly into the plan, Dr Curzon. You see, since we first met, you have been walking down the oldest path in history."

"Enlighten me," Ava stared back at him, her jaw tightening.

"Ever since you began this quest, you have been spiritually purifying yourself for the ceremony tonight."

It was news to Ava.

"It always starts with *nigredo*, the blackening or putrefaction, when all the shadows circle and fill the vessel of the mind with conflicts and confusion. In your case, it was when you discovered the truth about your father's death, when you began to hunt Malchus, and when you found out about the Ark and desired it so much you were prepared to do anything for it, including sacrificing helpers like Drewitt. That was your *nigredo*, reducing you to the core passions that bubble within you."

"I did not sacrifice Drewitt." She was finding it difficult to control her anger. "Malchus murdered him for his own pleasure."

Saxby ignored her. "Then comes *albedo*, the whitening. It's the beginning of the stage of purification. For you, it occurred when you sensed a higher aim—a need to keep the Ark, the Menorah, and *The Sword of Moses* away from us for the good of mankind, at least as you see it. Your thinking had evolved, and you were no longer just acting for your own base instincts. You had developed a purpose—one you thought was noble. That is the process of purification."

"And you've been on this path, too?" Ava's tone was mocking. "How does what you do constitute anything noble?"

"It has taken me many decades to explore my own path, and I have found what it is I must do," he replied simply. "The Fourth *Reich* is for the benefit of all mankind."

"You're insane," Ava shook her head in disbelief. "No-one could ever call mass murder noble."

"Next to last comes *citrinitas*," he continued, ignoring her jibe, "the yellowing, in which the luminousness of the sun replaces that of the moon, and all is turned to burnished gold in the light of realization. That is what is happening to you now, as you begin to appreciate what this has all been for."

"And the last?" Ava recognized the stages of classical alchemy, but not the deranged interpretation he was putting on them.

"What the alchemists called *rubedo*, the reddening. It has many names, and is also known as the *coniunctio oppositorum*, the chemical wedding and the *hieros gamos* or sacred marriage. It is the final act of spiritual union, when the opposites within us and outside us are brought together and reconciled to form the perfect whole. It has many manifestations— gold, the philosopher's stone, the hermaphrodite born of Hermes and Aphrodite, mystical sex, and even the Jungian inner union of the self." He gazed at her. "But for you, it will be very special."

Ava had heard enough. "You're not going to get that lucky."

He continued as if he had not heard her. "You've heard of the goddess Anat?" His tone was now bordering on the reverential.

She nodded. "In early Hebrew traditions, when they were still poly-theists before the Babylonian captivity, Anat was widely recorded as one of Yahweh's wives."

Saxby voice dropped. "She was the ultimate warrior goddess for the ultimate warrior god. She is described as wading knee-deep in battlefield gore, tying severed heads to her breastplate and hacked-off hands to her sash. She was the sublime destroyer."

"This is all very interesting," Ferguson growled. "What's your point?"

"As you ask so bluntly," he turned to face Ferguson, "I shall tell you equally plainly. From the moment we met, I've been watching Dr Cur-zon's every move with interest. I wondered to myself if we could use her in our movement. And I'm now convinced we can."

Ava glared at him with contempt as he turned to look her up and down again.

"You're the perfect Anat. It's one thing for us to summon Yahweh. But wouldn't it be so much better if we offered him an earthly incarnation of Anat, sacrificing her life to him in a blood offering, knowing how sweet the smell of burning flesh is to his nostrils."

Ava went cold.

*Was he serious?*

It sounded so implausible she did not know whether to laugh or cry. But with an icy chill twisting in the base of her stomach, she realized that Saxby undoubtedly meant what he said.

Unless she thought of something, he was going to slaughter her like a sacrificial animal, then burn her flesh on an altar.

She could feel herself beginning to lose her grip. She recalled once hearing that people on death row regularly went mad, as the human mind was not able to cope with knowing the time of its own death.

Malchus's attempt to kill her that afternoon had come as a complete surprise. But here was Saxby, calmly telling her she was to die tonight.

Her heart was beating so fast she thought for a moment she would pass out. But she was brought back to reality by the sound of Ferguson's voice. "So you and all your followers are here tonight. You have the Ark, the Menorah, Dr Dee's paraphernalia, and *The Sword of Moses*. What exactly are you going to do with it all? How will it begin the establish-ment of the Fourth *Reich* and the new Aryan Imperium?"

Saxby gazed into the middle distance.

"Major Ferguson, tonight we will perform the Great Ceremony in this unique and powerful setting, in front of a packed audience of national socialists from all over the world—all of whom have come to see something special, but they do not yet know what. We will, of course, record it for release so the world will know who we are, and what we have achieved."

"And what exactly will you have achieved?" Ava asked.

Saxby's eyes were gleaming. "We will summon Yahweh, one of the greatest battle gods the world has ever known. I like to call it Project Emmanuel, which I do not have to translate for Dr Curzon, I am sure. It means 'God is with us'."

Ferguson snorted. "You don't seriously believe you can summon a god, do you?" His tone was incredulous. "What are you going to do when he doesn't appear?"

Saxby smiled slowly. "Traditional Christians believe, and have done for centuries, that every time a priest makes a sacrifice at his altar, their God physically comes down and enters bread and wine for them to eat and drink. Their priests do this conjuring every day of the week all over the world, and billions of people have no trouble accepting it. We are doing no different."

He paused. "We do not expect Yahweh to appear—please, we are not imbeciles. But Yahweh is clearly with us. What other conclusion can anyone draw from the fact he has let us have his Ark, his throne, where he used to sit, along with the Menorah lamp that was made to burn to his eternal glory. I don't expect everyone to believe in Yahweh or other gods. But, tell me this—how will Christians or Jews, who both believe they have been specially chosen by Yahweh, how will they explain that for over two thousand years he has kept his Ark from them, but now he has chosen to give it to us? It will mean their total humiliation. And that, Major Ferguson, will be the unbreakable corner stone on which we will raise the Fourth *Reich*."

On the other side of the room, Malchus let out a bellow of frustration. He jumped up from the bench and stalked over to Ava. "Where is it?" he hissed at her malevolently.

"What do you mean?" Ava asked.

Without warning, Malchus punched her hard in the gut. A sickening pain erupted in her abdomen as her muscles went into spasm.

He waved Professor Stone's notes at her. "This is merely another copy of the London manuscript."

"I don't know what you're talking about." Ava gasped, still reeling from the pain.

"I saw you both enter Duke Humfrey's Library this morning," he snarled. You had official passes. Don't play innocent. It doesn't suit you."

This time she saw the punch coming. She braced the muscles in her stomach as he unleashed another savage blow at the soft flesh of her abdomen. Stifling the urge to scream with the pain, she bent her torso in an attempt to protect it, lifting her feet off the ground. But it only served to transfer the pain directly to her wrists and shoulders, which felt like they would dislocate.

Saxby's eyes narrowed on her. "For your sake, I hope you're not lying."

Malchus pulled Ferguson's Sig Sauer out of his pocket, and jammed it into the crook of Ava's leg, behind her knee. "Gunshot injuries to the knees are among the nastiest. They're some of the most painful, and there's nothing surgeons can do to mend the splintered bone and cartilage fragments, nerves, and arteries. You'll never walk again. So one more time," his voice was rising in a crescendo, "where's the real manuscript?"

Ava could feel a cold sweat breaking out. But she knew she had to conquer the fear. From what Saxby had said, *The Sword of Moses* was crucial to the ceremony. It followed that if they did not have the manuscript, then they would not be able to go ahead with their plans.

By way of reply, she stared at Malchus defiantly, unblinking.

*She could do this.*

She braced herself for the gun's explosion and the unbearable pain that would follow. If she was lucky, she would pass out.

Malchus returned her gaze, watching her carefully.

"So, what are you waiting for?" she hissed.

With no warning, he spun round, and rammed the gun into the back of Ferguson's knee instead. "We can start with his knees," he suggested to Ava softly, "then move on to his ankles, elbows, and wrists—until you're ready to tell me."

Ava felt sick.

*This could not be happening.*

She looked across at Ferguson. He was flushed, and she could see a light sheen of sweat breaking out on his face. He caught her eye, and nodded his head, almost imperceptibly.

*So he was ready to take the fall.*

Her mind was racing.

"You have three seconds to make up your mind." Malchus cocked the gun. He began to count. "One ... ."

She knew that above all she had to stop Malchus and Saxby from holding the ceremony. And keeping the manuscript from them was the best chance she was going to get.

But even without looking again at Ferguson, she knew she could not do it.

He had been there for her since the beginning, had put his neck on the line in getting her information about her father, and had saved her life from both DeVere and Malchus. Without him, she would have died in Stockbridge House and on Malchus's chair.

At least if they both stayed alive for now they might be able to find another way of sabotaging Saxby's plans.

She breathed out heavily, signalling defeat. "I'll get it."

"Good," Malchus crowed. "That's better."

"Call the operator, and get me a connection to the Oxford University Security Department," she instructed him. "Then pass me the phone."

Malchus pulled a slim mobile out of his pocket, and did as she asked. After a moment, he held the phone up to her ear.

"I need to speak to Dr Hendey, the librarian at Duke Humfrey's Library."

"Do you know what time it is?" the voice replied lazily. "The library closed hours ago."

"I'm quite aware. Please put me through," she replied.

"It's closed," the voice informed her. "You'll have to call back in the morning."

Ava had to struggle to keep her voice calm. "Instead of arguing with me, which we can do all night, please just connect me to his home address. Tell him it's Dr Curzon from the looted artefacts project in Baghdad. He'll want to speak to me, I assure you, and will be very unhappy in the morning if he finds out you hung up on me. I wouldn't count on still having a job by this time tomorrow if I were you."

There was a pause at the other end of the line as she was put on hold. There was no jaunty music. After a few moments, she heard the librarian's sleepy voice. "Dr Curzon? Is there any news? The police aren't telling us anything."

"No. Nothing," she answered. "But tell me, do you have remote access to the library's archival database?"

"Yes." he sounded hesitant. "Why? Is there another problem?"

"I need you to send me a digital file of your manuscript, the Oxford copy, of the work we were discussing this morning, *The Sword of Moses.*"

There was an intake of breath. "I'm afraid that's not going to be possible," he replied. "The manuscript is only to be consulted in the reading room. I'm afraid I have no authority to send anyone a copy."

"Look." Ava had no time for this. "Unless you want two more people to end up like your friend Professor Stone in the next five minutes, I'm asking you please to send the copy of the manuscript."

There was a pause.

"I haven't lied to you, have I?" Ava coaxed. "I know it's a lot to ask, but you're the only person who can help. I'm not requesting the original manuscript—just a digital copy."

There was another pause, before the voice came back again, resigned. "Okay. Give me the e-mail address. It'll be with you in two minutes."

Ava gave him an internet e-mail address, and indicated for Malchus to hang up.

Her calves were now on fire. It was as if someone had taken out the tibia in each leg and replaced it with a red-hot poker.

Malchus walked back to the bench and put the phone down beside his battered leather bag. Opening it, he pulled out a slim black laptop.

"Give me your e-mail logon and password," he ordered Ava.

"No," she answered bluntly, the word ringing out clearly around the room.

Malchus and Saxby both stared at her in astonishment.

"Let me down off here. I'll do it," she added.

Malchus shot her a blazing look. "Let's not play games. Just give me the—"

Ava interrupted him. "Unless you've suddenly learned to read ancient Hebrew and Aramaic, you're going to need someone to go through the files to check they're genuine copies. Or do you have someone else in mind?"

Malchus glanced over to Saxby, who was leaning against the far wall. The older man nodded to the guard, who walked over to Ava and unlocked her hands, taking the cuffs off, and dropping them into his pocket.

Her calves were agony as she crossed the room, but she had no intention of letting it show.

Sitting on the bench between Malchus and his bag, she took his laptop from him and found an unlocked internet network. Clicking open a browser window, she quickly logged into her internet e-mail.

Malchus and Saxby were standing beside her, eyeing her every keystroke.

She had half hoped they would leave her the opportunity to send an emergency e-mail calling for backup.

*No chance.*

They were watching her like hawks.

As the e-mail pane opened, the message from Dr Hendey was already there.

Clicking on the file, she enlarged it on the screen so they could all see it.

The manuscript itself was physically small. Five inches high by four wide according to the first image, which showed the aged brown leather cover sitting between two white plastic rulers placed at right angles.

Although there were other manuscripts bound into the ancient volume, Dr Hendey had sent her just the pages of *The Sword of Moses*.

She clicked onto the first page of text and the screen filled with a sheet of brown vellum. It had some minor water damage, but the small medieval writing was firm and clear, running in perfectly straight lines right to left with no smudges.

She began to read out loud, translating it as she went.

> "In the name of the mighty and holy God, four angels
> are appointed to the Sword given by the Lord ... ."

"But does it have the names?" Malchus hissed, interrupting her excitedly. "The magical names of Yahweh that were missing from the London version—the core of the conjuration. Are they there?"

Ava skimmed through the files.

As she got towards the end, she found them—a list of dozens of magical names: a standard feature of ancient magical rituals.

She nodded, pointing to the image. "Here they are."

Malchus and Saxby peered closely at the screen, staring at the minute Hebrew characters.

She doubted they meant anything to them, but keeping her eyes fixed firmly on the writing, she took the opportunity to stretch her right hand out behind her. Feeling her way over Malchus's bag, her fingers at last brushed the cold metal of his mobile phone.

Pulling it slowly towards her, she slipped it into the back pocket of her jeans.

Seeing her move, Malchus stood up and walked round to where his bag was.

*Oh God.*

Ava's heart was hammering.

*That was stupid. What had she been thinking?*

She braced herself for whatever blow was coming.

But none came. Malchus opened his bag and pulled out a small black USB stick. "Save the file to this," he instructed her, handing over the stick.

She did it quickly, her pulse racing. It was now or never.

Malchus took the stick and walked across the room. "I'll be back," he informed Saxby, pushing open the heavy wooden door and striding out.

"Well, Dr Curzon," Saxby looked down at Ava. "As you are the only Hebrew and Aramaic reader among us, it seems we have another use for you tonight. The earthly representative of Anat will conjure Yahweh, then immolate herself on his altar."

Ava was barely listening. "I need to go to the washroom."

Saxby looked at her suspiciously, his eyes boring into her.

She kept her voice low and calm. She could not blow this. "What am I going to do? Jump out of a third floor window?" She started walking towards the door.

"Stay with her," Saxby ordered the guard. "It's down the corridor, on the right."

Ava strode confidently out of the room. She did not dare put her hand in her pocket to check if the phone was still there. But she could feel it against her hip—that was reassurance enough.

At the end of the dark corridor was a simple door marked: 'TOILETTE'.

She pushed it open, and stepped inside.

It was not a medieval hole in a bench hanging out of a window, but it was not far off—a damp, cramped stone room with most of the space taken up by an unstable-looking seatless lavatory and a tiny stained corner sink.

Sliding the bolt on the door, she pulled out Malchus's phone.

Flicking it on, she was greeted by a locked screen:

ENTER PASSWORD

She had to try hard not to shout with frustration.

She did not have time for this.

Staring at the small screen, she was surprised to see it wanted only three characters.

She tried what she had once heard were the two most common passwords in the world, each of which only had three characters—'GOD' and 'SEX'.

*Nothing.*

Slamming her fist hard against the cold stone wall, she wracked her brain for three-letter words that Malchus might have chosen.

She entered 'DEE'.

Again nothing.

If she did not get this cracked fast, she was going to lose her opportunity.

*Come on.* She ordered herself. *Think!*

It was corny, but she typed in '666', at the same time aware it was hardly the type of secure code she would expect from a former Stasi agent.

To her amazement, the password prompt melted away to reveal the phone's home screen.

*Yes.*

She breathed a loud and rapid sigh of relief.

*She was in.*

Flicking to the browser, she pulled up the homepage of the United Grand Lodge of England.

Clicking the CONTACT US tab, she found a pane where she could leave a message.

She typed in short bursts:

TO MR L CORDINGLY — AT WEWELSBURG CASTLE — FRIENDS
ARE FALSE — PARTY TO END ALL PARTIES — TONIGHT —
SOME OF US WILL NOT MAKE IT TO SURVIVORS' BREAKFAST —
MAX NEEDS TO BRING FRIENDS AND FIREWORKS URGENTLY
— KATE ADAMS

She signed herself using the name she had first given at Freemasons' Hall, hoping he would remember.

She was taking a big gamble.

Saxby might not be the only rotten Templar. It was possible Cordingly was in it with him, too. Maybe that was why Ferguson had arrived with Saxby and Malchus's paramilitaries instead of Max and his men.

But she had no choice.

There was no one else she could contact who would believe her story and react in time. It was Cordingly or no one. Besides, if Cordingly passed the message back to Saxby, she doubted her position was going to be any worse than it was at the moment.

She was interrupted by the guard hammering on the door. "What are you doing in there? Hurry up."

There it was again. The unmistakable hint of an Israeli accent.

"Just a minute," Ava called, trying to keep the tension from her voice.

She hit SUBMIT, and watched the screen disappear, replaced immediately by the United Grand Lodge of England's homepage.

She frowned.

*Had it sent?*

The guard pounded on the door again. "Don't make me break it down."

She had to pray the message was now winging its way to Freemasons' Hall.

She quickly opened up the phone's control panel and found the internet settings. She cleared the browser's history, cookies, and cache. When Malchus found it all wiped, he would probably assume there was a fault with his phone. At worst, he would suspect someone had tampered with it. But at least he would not know that it had been her—or what message she had sent.

She prayed the phone had not kept a record of her activity anywhere else. She did not know the model well enough to be sure.

"Okay. Have it your way," the guard announced. Hearing a massive crash as he slammed into the flimsy wood, she flushed the loo and opened the door, glaring at him.

"Come on," he ordered gruffly, shoving her at gunpoint back towards the room.

She entered at a fast pace, heading straight for the bench where she had been sitting.

There were two other guards in the front room now, and Ferguson was no longer pinned to the far wall. They had unshackled him, and were holding him between them. Saxby and Malchus were sitting on the bench.

Before anyone could stop her, she sat down quickly between Malchus and his bag and computer, knocking them both sideways.

She tutted as she reached out to stop the bag and computer falling to the floor. At the same time, she dropped the mobile phone softly onto the bench beside the bag, her body obscuring Saxby and Malchus's view of what she was doing.

She glanced across at Ferguson. The two guards either side of him had not noticed what she had done. But he had. He blinked slowly in acknowledgement.

*Good.*

She only prayed that someone would pick up the message and get it to Cordingly—and also that he was not in league with Saxby and Malchus.

He was her one and only hope.

"It's nearly time," Saxby announced. "We all need to prepare. Dr Curzon, the guard will take you downstairs, where you will ready yourself."

Saxby turned to Ferguson. "And you'll be pleased to know, Major Ferguson, that I have found a use for you." He wandered over to the metal-framed window behind which he had been standing, and opened it. "You'll assist Dr Curzon in keeping up her motivation." He nodded at the two guards. "Take him."

Malchus pushed Ava towards the window. After a few minutes, she saw Ferguson emerge into the castle's moonlit courtyard below, frog-marched by the two guards either side of him.

As the three approached the castle's well, Ava gasped in horror as the guards lifted Ferguson up, holding his feet over the stone-rimmed edge of the hole. Although his arms were free of the handcuffs, he had no time to land any punches. He tried kicking, but his legs were already disappearing down the deep shaft.

Before she had time to shout her objection, they had dropped him in.

Ava turned furiously on Saxby, her eyes blazing. "Get him out now, or I will not help you."

Saxby smiled coldly. "I don't think so, Dr Curzon. The only way to save him now is to go through with your part in the ceremony. Once you have read the conjuration and the sacrifice is complete, then we will retrieve him."

"Why on earth would I trust you?" she fired back at him.

"Because if you don't cooperate, we'll shoot him, and then come up with other ways of incentivizing you to play your part. You, I'm afraid, will not see the night out. He, on other hand, has the chance to live. The gift is in your hands."

Saxby pulled the window shut and twisted the large metal thumb screw, locking it. "Now, go and prepare yourself." He looked at her long and hard. "Tonight you will die like a goddess."

Feeling a sharp jab in the back of her neck, she spun round to see Malchus holding a miniature syringe.

With a hot nauseous feeling, she felt the ground rush up to meet her.

—— • ◆ • ——

# 105

*The 'Gruft' Vault*
*Wewelsburg Castle*
*Büren*
*Paderborn*
*North-Rhine Westphalia*
*Federal Republic of Germany*

AVA CAME AROUND slowly.

She felt groggy and confused, disconnected from her senses.

It was as if she was being smothered.

As she fought through the fog, she found a memory—the pain of a needle as Malchus injected something into her neck.

*She had been drugged.*

With a sickening rush, the scene in the castle's upper room came flooding back, along with Saxby's announcement that she would be ritually slain during a ceremony that night.

Forcing her eyes open a fraction, she saw she was not alone, but in a gloomy room together with a large group of people. It was hard to tell exactly how many—her brain was only half functioning, and the lighting was so low as to be almost non-existent.

Although she never had anxieties about enclosed spaces or crowds, she had a nagging feeling there was something very wrong about this particular group of people.

Something unnatural.

Staring blearily out at the faces, the fog lifted a little more, and she instantly understood what it was.

There were no women in the crowd—just men.

*And most of them were staring hard at her.*

With a rising panic, she shook her head to clear the haze and tried to turn, to see if the threatening scene was the same behind her as well.

But, for some inexplicable reason, her body was not responding.

Sensing real danger now, her brain finally kicked into gear, expelling the last vestiges of chemical confusion, and pulling her back to alertness.

Looking around, she could see she was in the middle of a dark circular underground room, on a raised stage.

As her brain reconnected itself to her body and she regained full use of all her senses, she understood why she could not move.

She had been tied to a tall wooden stake.

There were ropes around her chest, hips, and ankles—lashing her firmly in place. Her wrists were similarly bound, pinned to the front of the post above her head.

*Clever.*

Someone had thought this through.

It meant that if by some miracle she managed to free her hands, everyone watching would see immediately. She would have no chance of slipping them loose with no one noticing.

She was not going anywhere.

Judging by the leers on some of the onlookers' faces, it was also apparent that her being a woman, tied up, seemed to be the cause of much of their interest.

With a sickening jolt, she recalled that she was not the only one in danger. Ferguson was now struggling for his life, deep in the castle's well.

*And his survival would all be down to her.*

Saxby's words rang in her ears.

*"You're the perfect Anat. It's one thing for us to summon Yahweh. But wouldn't it be so much better if we offered him an earthly incarnation of Anat, sacrificing herself to him in a blood offering, knowing how sweet the smell of burning flesh is to his nostrils."*

She felt a hot mix of fear and outrage.

*Who did Saxby think he was?*

*Who gave him the power to decide who lives and dies?*

As her eyes became increasingly accustomed to the gloom, she was able to make out more of the room's details around her

What little light illuminated the scene was coming from a dozen incense braziers—small perforated lanterns arranged in a circle around the edge of the stage. They threw out a weak light from the burning flames and charcoal within, bathing the space in long shadows which moved with the restless crowd.

The room itself was an underground chamber, and had clearly been designed for elaborate rituals. If the ceremony was to be some sort of bloody neo-Nazi pagan sacrament, then Saxby had chosen the venue impeccably.

The vault had been built to resemble a cave, and was similar in size to the solar she had just been in. That was on the third floor of the large north tower, so she suspected she must now be in its basement.

High up in the domed roof, she noticed long angled stone tunnels ending in small windows, shining a glassy black. From their height, they looked like they just reached ground level.

As her eyes adjusted further, she could see that the walls were not hewn out of rough rock, but faced with 1930s neo-medieval brickwork—which explained the elaborate grey swastika motif moulded into the centre of the ceiling, its arms splayed out into extended geometric shapes.

She counted twelve small plinths around the curved wall. Above each was a matching niche.

*Was that where the urns of the twelve leading ss knights were supposed to have been buried?*

There was clearly a numerological significance woven into the room's fabric.

*Is that how Himmler thought of himself? Like some latter-day Christ, Charlemagne, or King Arthur, with his twelve loyal paladins?*

The whole effect of the low lighting and rough monumental architecture was primal.

If the building had genuinely been the spiritual headquarters of the ss, as Saxby claimed, then this looked like their purpose-built ritual room.

The low circular stage had been built up in the chamber's centre. It was black, and on it had been painted a large white unicursal hexagram like the one on the end of Malchus's rosary. The star was contained within a circle, and at each of the six points, where its sharp angles intersected with the curve, there was what looked like an occult sigil.

Malchus's team from Boleskine House was the closest group of men to her, forming an inner cordon round the dais's edge. From the sleek submachine guns cradled in their arms, it was clear they were the evening's security.

Beyond them, filling the rest of the darkened room, the other men were equally menacing.

They were exactly what she would expect of fascist gang members. Many bore the scars of street fights and bar brawls cut into their arrogant and aggressive features.

They were wearing random pieces of Nazi militaria along with their ordinary clothes—army jackets, leather trench-coats, stahlhelms, and black death's head caps, all with a variety of national flags stitched or painted on.

Judging by the telltale bulges in pockets, under arms, in waistbands, and around ankles, most of them were armed with handguns, knives, and an assortment of other concealed weapons.

She calculated there was probably more hardware surrounding her than if she had been abducted by the crime cartels of San Pedro Sula.

Seeing the expression of violent desire on many of the faces staring at her, it was all she could do to stop herself from imagining what horrors the evening held in store for her.

Glancing down at her body, she realized with a hot flush of indignation that the leering onlookers were not the only ones specially dressed for the occasion.

While drugged and unconscious from whatever Malchus had injected into her, someone had undressed her and changed her clothes.

She was now wearing a knee- and elbow-length hauberk of chainmail, partially covered by a similarly shaped plain black tunic, narrowly fringed in gold around the neck, elbows, and knees. It was pulled in hard at the waist with a purple-flecked black sash, and another identical sash dropped lower, hugging her hips. Tucked into it was a sword, gleaming in the dull light from the braziers.

It was a perfect period weapon, accurate in every regard—with its straight hard bronze blade extending around ten inches before bending into a lethal sickle-shaped arc.

Her period military clothing was completed by greaves on her shins and vambraces on her forearms, all made from boiled leather with bronze reinforcement bands.

When asked about ancient weaponry, she often enjoyed explaining that hardened bronze was actually stronger than wrought iron, even though the Iron Age came after the Bronze Age. The only historical reason for the military success of iron was the scarcity and cost of the copper and tin needed to forge bronze, compared with the relative ease and cheapness of iron production. As a result, long into the Iron Age, hardened bronze remained the metal of choice for high-status warriors—like in the Roman army, where the ordinary soldiers wielded iron swords, but wealthier officers still preferred bronze.

However, now was not the time to analyze antique weaponry. She had much more pressing dangers to think about.

As she swallowed drily and moistened her lips, she realized her face had been caked with a harsh white makeup, and her lips smeared coal-black with what tasted like ashes. She could not be sure, but she also thought her eyes had been painted with heavy black circles around them.

Glancing up at the backs of her hands, she saw someone had covered them with crude swirling patterns of dark orangey-red henna.

Becoming increasingly aware of her body, she realized that her hair was no longer in a ponytail either. It had been oiled, coiled into a rope, and piled onto her head. Tendrils escaped and hung down the side of her face and neck, smelling overpoweringly of perfumed oil—thick, spicy, and sweet: unmistakably exotic and eastern. As she moved her head fractionally, she could also feel and partially see a pair of heavy beaten metal discs hanging from her ears, and a thick torque around her neck. To top it all, there was something on her head. She sensed by the weight it was some sort of metal headband.

Saxby had clearly spared no expense on her costume.

If she was supposed to be a Bronze Age Middle-Eastern war goddess, she could not fault his historical accuracy. Had she been ten feet taller and made of painted wood, she would have been convincing in any cult temple.

But she was not, and nor was she at a weekend reenactment society meeting.

She was in real physical danger, and she could feel it palpably.

The atmosphere was aggressive and intimidating, and it seemed Saxby had meant what he said about her role in whatever macabre rite was to follow.

From where she was standing, she was on the left-hand edge of the stage, facing forwards. In front of her, built into the centre of the stage, was a large flame-blackened iron grate, beneath which red coals were smouldering under a dusting of white ash. It did not take her long to recognize it as a fire for burnt offerings.

*Including her.*

Trying to banish the horrific thought from her mind, she could feel the perspiration starting to run down her back.

On the far right of the stage were two objects draped in heavy black velvet coverings. Her heart began to beat faster as she realized one was probably the Menorah, and the other must be the Ark.

Despite the terror of her predicament, there was a part of her that even now felt an excitement at being in the same room as the Ark.

It was clearly to be an integral part of the ceremony.

She had waited so long to see it. And that wait would soon be over.

Behind her, at the rear centre of the stage, was Dr Dee's Table of Practice. It was flanked by two grand 1930s art deco wooden thrones, each with period ss lightning runes and stylized skull emblems carved prominently into their backs.

Without warning, the noise of the crowd suddenly dropped, and the wall of people at the front parted, allowing two figures to emerge and step forward.

Ava's breath caught in her throat as she saw their black robes and tall conical hoods, rising to a point a foot and a half above the top of their heads. Their arms were crossed in front of them, with their hands folded into the sleeves. They were completely swathed in black cloth from head to floor. She could see nothing of them save through the two small eye-slits in the sinister hoods.

It was a chilling sight—instinctively associated in her mind with pain and suffering.

Medieval brotherhoods of fanatical Spanish penitents and flagellants had worn identical *capirote* hoods as they tore their own flesh with whips, hooks, and chains. Victims of the most holy Catholic Inquisition had them jammed onto their heads before suffering unspeakable tortures and death. And on the other side of the world, in a gruesome throwback, the white supremacist Protestant knights of the Ku Klux Klan donned them in the deep south of the United States before mutilating and lynching their black neighbours.

A cold ball of fear tightened in the pit of her stomach as she stared at the two figures making for the stage, their hooded disguises promising nothing but degradation and pain.

---

## 106

*Wewelsburg Castle*
*Büren*
*Paderborn*
*North-Rhine Westphalia*
*Federal Republic of Germany*

IN THE TORCH-LIT third-floor room, Uri had watched through the window over the woman's shoulder as Saxby's men had dropped her partner into the castle's courtyard well.

"Major Ferguson", they had called him. British army, Uri assumed. He looked the part.

Uri was no fan of the British armed forces.

The animosity between their two countries went back to the 1940s, to the violent birth of the modern State of Israel, when Jewish terrorist groups and the British army had locked horns in a bloody insurgency as the terrorists tried to seize the country.

But the conflict had been over long before Uri's time, and at the moment he could not afford the luxury of continuing the wars of a different generation. Right now, he needed support. And Ferguson seemed to be the only person he had come across all day who might be able to give it.

It was the kind of gamble he usually meticulously avoided. But this was turning into a fully improvised mission. And, to Uri's surprise, he was thriving on it—relishing the need to stay one step ahead in an ever-changing landscape. He had not felt this kind of excitement before. It introduced an edge he had never imagined he would savour.

Anyway, if it came to the worst and Ferguson turned out to be a bad choice, he could always put him back where he found him.

He saw his chance after Malchus had drugged the woman and Saxby had ordered him to take her to the antechamber downstairs so she could be "prepared".

Once he had carried her unconscious body down and delivered her as instructed, he had found himself on his own. As far as the Skipper knew, he was with Malchus. As far as Malchus knew, he had gone back to find the Skipper. So no one would miss him.

He was free to make his move.

Looking out into the darkened courtyard, he could see groups of men in varying items of Nazi regalia heading for the north tower. He had not passed any of them on the stairs on his way down—so he assumed they were making for the tower's basement.

Ducking left, he entered the east wing—a long two-storey range leading down to a smaller tower at the castle's south-eastern corner.

The ancient hallway was low-lit, and he moved stealthily to silence any noise made by his shoes on the hard floor.

Most of the doors along the corridor looked as if they led to offices or other administrative rooms. He could see no lights shining from under any of them, and all appeared empty.

But they were not what he was looking for.

About three-quarters of the way down, he spotted a smaller less important-looking door.

It seemed much more promising.

Trying the handle gently, he found it was not locked, and opened into a modest-sized handyman's storeroom.

*It was ideal.*

He slipped inside and locked the door behind him, taking up an observation position at its darkened narrow windows, giving him a clear and unobstructed view out into the length of the courtyard.

He watched intently as streams of men continued to tramp across the irregular cobbles towards the north tower.

Observing them, he reflected that since he had begun researching his legend as Danny Motson back at HQ in Tel Aviv, he had spent countless hours familiarizing himself with the English extreme right-wing scene— lurking in their chat-rooms and poring through their propaganda-filled e-zines.

He reckoned he now knew more about their complex history, ideology, and operations than many of their own members.

The night Otto had taken him to *The Bunker* had been an eye-opener. In all his time with the Institute, he had never imagined he would have ringside seats at a neo-Nazi rally. Still less become one of their front-line soldiers.

For all its novelty, what he saw at *The Bunker* had not ultimately surprised him. England was a naturally liberal country filled with obsessives, of whom it was painstakingly tolerant. It had a long history of extreme left- and right-wing fringe politics, all of which it allowed to flourish so long as no mainstream laws were broken. But it was a philosophy that acted as a magnet for all sorts of concealed extremism, and if Uri had been an investigative journalist researching neo-Nazism, he would instinctively have started in England.

But here at Wewelsburg, looking at the improvised uniforms moving across the courtyard, he was shocked by the range of countries they came from—the Netherlands, Belgium, France, Austria, Switzerland, Sweden, Greece, the former Soviet bloc, the United States, South America, and white Africa. Almost the only flag he could not see was the Israeli one— although he had been as dumbfounded as everyone a few years ago when the newspapers had been filled with a story of the arrest of a violent anti-Semitic neo-Nazi organization of Jewish citizens in Israel.

He felt genuine physical anger towards these people, and knew he was getting emotionally involved. As a salary-earning member of the Mossad's *Metsada* division, no one was ever going to mistake him for a political liberal. He had no problem squeezing the trigger. But the men in front of him stood for the annihilation of his people. In his mind, that gave him the right to take it personally.

As the men continued to stream across the darkened courtyard, he began to feel impatient. There were many more men arriving than he had imagined, and he wanted to get on with the job in hand before the sheer number of people derailed his plans.

Rituals and ceremonies were not his area of expertise. He had never had much time for ouija boards and séances, and nor had he ever been particularly interested in religion. He had no idea who Anat was, or what *The Sword of Moses* was supposed to do. But he had smiled when he heard the name, *The Sword of Moses*. It described him perfectly. Moses was the English form of the Hebrew name Moshe, and that is exactly what he was—the old man's sharp unsheathed weapon.

Rubbing his hand across his face, he focused on how the situation had become more complicated.

On the helicopter over from Scotland he had heard the men next to him cursing how awkward it had been handling the seven-branched candlestick up the stairs.

Although he was pretty hazy on most of the Jewish Scriptures, he knew there had only ever been one important seven-branched candlestick in the history of Israel—the ancient Temple Menorah. He had no idea whether it still existed or had been destroyed thousands of years ago. However, if Malchus had a seven-branched candlestick as well as the Ark, then he had better take that as well. He would leave it to the experts back in Israel to sort out whether either of them were real.

But he had realized his biggest problem the moment the helicopter had dropped low over Wewelsburg. He had immediately seen that he would have no chance of just leaving with the Ark and the Menorah. It was a castle, and there was no easy way out of the building and off the mountain.

And that was where Ferguson came in.

The artefacts were too heavy for him to move alone. But, if he had help, he could hide them somewhere in the building, and then call in an ops team to come and pick them up when the coast was clear.

It was not a perfect plan, but it would achieve his objective. And he was all too aware of the consequences of failure. If he did not manage to hide the Ark and Menorah tonight, then Malchus would undoubtedly move them on somewhere else after the ceremony, and there was no guarantee Uri would ever find them again.

So he would locate them tonight, and then, together with Ferguson, secrete them somewhere in the castle.

That just left the question of how many people he was going to have to hurt as he implemented the plan

He had made up his mind back in London that he would put a bullet into the Skipper's head. He could not pretend it was a strategic priority. It was simple revenge for making him wear the ss *Leibstandarte* jacket. That was a humiliation the large man would pay for with his life.

Strictly speaking, executing the Skipper was not within operational parameters—not unless the Skipper defended the Ark with his blood, which seemed highly unlikely. But Uri would make him pay anyway. He was on a deniable mission, which meant he had a licence to handle the field operation any way he wanted. He would have to fill out the usual forms and explain his actions back at HQ afterwards, of course. But he doubted anyone at the Institute was going to lose sleep over the Skipper. He might in fact just be saving the local team another wet job down the line.

Anyway, he might not even admit to the killing.

However, the Skipper was no longer his only problem.

He had learned a lot more about Malchus since he had arrived at Boleskine House, and he had also discovered a great deal of troubling information about the group's leader, Saxby.

He had been thinking hard about what to do with the pair of them.

Saxby was easy. He would hand the old Nazi's details over to Moshe, and let the official channels take over. Saxby was someone HQ would definitely want to know about.

What they did with him was up to them. They might simply decide to keep him under observation, or perhaps infiltrate a suitable agent permanently into his organization. Or maybe one day he would suddenly disappear—lifted off the streets and put on a black flight to an unofficial facility, where they would pump him full of enough drugs to learn what he had eaten for breakfast every day of his life.

Uri did not need to think any more about it. The decision would not be his.

But Malchus—he was a different story entirely.

Uri knew that most people would never understand why he had chosen to do what he did for the Mossad. But to him it was a job. It always had been. He did it because his government asked him to, and he was good at it. He neither liked nor disliked the act of political killing. It was a necessary function, and it was his profession.

But from what he had seen and heard, Malchus had a very different approach. He did not work for any government, nor did anyone sanction his activities. He did what he did because he was a savage sadist who got visible pleasure and gratification from torturing, maiming, and murdering. It was a deviant pathology—an acute mental sickness. He was the face of the fanatical crusading knights who slaughtered in Europe and the East. He was Stalin's torturers from the gulags in Siberia and the soundproofed basements behind the Iron Curtain. And he was Hitler's camp commandants, snuffing out life on an industrial scale for a perverse bestial gratification.

Uri needed to think more about what he was going to do with him.

Focusing out of the window, he again noticed how well-armed the men streaming past were. He strongly doubted they were particularly skilled with their weapons, but it was a reminder that he was deep in hostile territory.

Eventually, the last of the men crossed the courtyard towards the north tower, and the area fell silent.

He checked his watch, and waited to make absolutely sure there were no more coming. When ten minutes was up, he slipped swiftly out of the room and back down the corridor, out into the quiet courtyard.

It was a cloudy night, and there was minimal light from the moon or the stars.

*Good.*

He did not want to be seen.

Striding over to the well, he peered over the edge.

It was a simple hole in the ground. There was no wall around it, roof on top of it, or winding mechanism over it. It was a plain circular hole with a four-inch stone lip running around its rim.

He could immediately see Ferguson at the bottom of the dark tunnel, treading water about six feet below ground level. He must have heard Uri's footsteps coming, because he was staring up at him, his face a mask of anger and determination.

The surface of the well's interior wall was slimy and smooth, and there was clearly no way he could climb out by himself. He had no option except to tread water and pray for rescue. Uri figured he must have been down there for almost an hour already, and after that amount of time he would, at the very least, be exhausted and perhaps in shock. At the worst, he may be developing hypothermia.

"Odd time for a swim?" Uri spoke softly. He could not afford to be overheard. Dozens of dark windows overlooked the courtyard, and he had no idea who could be looking out, unseen.

Ferguson glared back at him, clearly not taking any chances on whether it was a friendly visit.

Uri slipped off his ss waistcoat, and squatted beside the well's stone lip, wedging his feet against it.

Leaning over the dark hole, he dangled the waistcoat down towards Ferguson. It was not as good as a rope, but it was a solid piece of leather with no stitching or seams.

It should be strong enough.

"Grab it," Uri ordered, holding it as deep into the well as he could—a couple of feet above Ferguson's head.

Ferguson's eyes radiated mistrust.

"Or has someone made you a better offer?" Uri waggled the waistcoat.

Ferguson swung with his hand to reach it—but it was too far above him to catch hold of.

Uri leaned over a few inches more. Any further and he risked losing his footing and being pulled into the well. "Don't screw it up," had been Moshe's parting words. He had no desire for the old man to get a report on his desk saying Uri had blown the operation by drowning with a British soldier in a well.

He stretched his arm out as far as it would go. Ferguson made another grab for the waistcoat—but the lifeline was still out of reach.

Uri peered down. "Jump for it. On the count of three."

Ferguson nodded, and dropped his hands back down under the water, circling them by his sides.

Uri counted out loud. As he got to three, he gave an extra stretch of his back, lowering the waistcoat another inch. At the same time, Ferguson propelled himself up out of the water, making a grab for the leather with both hands.

It had not been a very spectacular jump—but it was enough. Uri could suddenly feel Ferguson's weight on the end of the waistcoat.

Taking a deep breath, he made sure his feet were firmly wedged against the well's stone lip, and began to lean backwards, levering Ferguson upwards.

In no time, he was panting with the strain. It was not a good angle for lifting a hundred-and-seventy-pound man with waterlogged clothing.

Uri had originally thought he would reel the waistcoat in, like pulling a rope in a tug-o'-war match. But now that Ferguson was on the other end, he immediately realized that would not work. If he let go with one hand, even for a fraction of a second, the leather would be ripped out of the other by Ferguson's weight, and they would be back at square one.

As if sensing the problem, Ferguson pulled himself up so he was holding the leather in both hands at chest height. Then, agonizingly slowly, he placed one hand higher than the other, and then again.

Uri nodded a grudging respect. He had assumed the man would have no strength left. But he watched as Ferguson doggedly inched his way up the leather lifeline, hand over hand, as if climbing a rope.

He could see Ferguson grimacing with the immense effort—the veins on his neck and temple bulging with the exertion as he hauled up not only his own weight, but also that of his sodden clothing and shoes.

Before Uri knew it, he felt a wet hand grab his wrist, and then the other one. He responded immediately, locking his hands around Ferguson's wrists as tightly as he could.

Grunting with the effort, he rocked backwards on his heels, drawing Ferguson slowly upwards.

Uri was strong, but his build was more slender than Ferguson's. The pain in his shoulders and arms was excruciating.

He could feel his vision starting to blur from the intense effort, when suddenly the weight on the other end of his arms fell away, as first one then another hand appeared on the well's stone lip.

He leant forward and grabbed Ferguson under the arms, hauling him out.

Ferguson collapsed onto the cobbles, gulping in air. He rolled over onto his back in a wet heap, his sodden clothes making a slapping sound as they hit the stones.

"I owe you one," he croaked to Uri.

"*Mazel tov*," Uri thumped his shoulder. "We can't stay here." He grabbed Ferguson by the upper arm and helped him stand.

"Your waistcoat," Ferguson whispered, nodding towards the well.

Uri shook his head. "Not my colour." He was glad to be rid of it. "This way." He pointed towards the tower he had come from. They could not risk entering the building through the north doorway. Ferguson would leave wet footprints, or they might run into someone leaving the ceremony.

They moved swiftly into the shadows beside the building, and made for the south-east tower.

"In here." Uri opened the door and led Ferguson back down the corridor to the storeroom.

Ushering him inside, he sat him on a chair and looked around. Beside the door was a set of hooks on which some gardening and decorating clothes were hanging.

"I take it you're not with them, then?" Ferguson asked.

Uri did not answer. He pulled a checked shirt, some tatty jeans, and a jumper off the pegs. "Put these on," he threw them to Ferguson. "You're no use to me with hypothermia."

As Ferguson began peeling off his soggy clothes, Uri turned to the small kettle on the windowsill and flicked it on, spooning a hefty mound of coffee into a mug.

"While you drink this," Uri explained, adding two equally large teaspoons of sugar, "I'm going to tell you what I need you to do."

---  · ◆ ·  ---

# 107

*The 'Gruft' Vault*
*Wewelsburg Castle*
*Büren*
*Paderborn*
*North-Rhine Westphalia*
*Federal Republic of Germany*

As Malchus stepped onto the stage, his mind and body were exulting.
*This was the night!*

The one he had been waiting for all these years.

Tonight it would all come together. After all the training, all the priva-
tions, the arduous path—tonight would be a night like no other.

He had performed the three days' preparation exactly as the manuscript instructed—washing his hands in salt, only eating and drinking
water once a day, bathing and praying as instructed, and carrying around
a piece of leather with the ancient inscription.

Frater Perdurabo, his guiding light for all these years, had never
achieved anything this great. He had unlocked the door for Malchus and
shown him the way—but he had never been able to cross the threshold
himself. The Englishman's life had been a preparation, like John the Bap-
tist—a lone voice readying the world for what would come.

And tonight was going to be that night, when it would all come to pass.

The work the Englishman had done at Boleskine House had been invaluable, as had the many discoveries of the great magus Dr Dee centuries before.

But Malchus knew that tonight there would be only one adept who would bring it all to fruition.

*Him.*

His heart sang. Tonight he would join the ranks of history's greatest.

And what more fitting place in which to achieve such an accomplishment than in the inner sanctum of Himmler's twelve select ss grail knights, where he and they were all to have been buried.

Crossing the stage, he glanced over at the woman who had become such a menace to him—a constant thorn in his side.

*Not for much longer,* he smiled to himself.

It incensed him that Saxby could have thought her worth anything. It had been *he* who retrieved the Ark, who had lovingly reassembled Dr Dee's Table of Practice with its sacred components, who had acquired the Vatican's Menorah medal, and who had located the manuscripts of *The Sword of Moses.* It had taken years of his life to acquire the skills necessary for the success of the plan.

And now Saxby was giving her credit for having "filled in the gaps." Malchus could feel his anger rising. He had given her the Menorah medal to save time—that was all. Surely Saxby could see that?

He sneered. Well, tonight would be his night. He would set all wrongs right. After tonight, she would not be able to trouble him any more.

And what a night it would be for her.

At first he had been livid when Saxby had interrupted his long-anticipated pleasures with her at Boleskine House. He had been revelling in having her all to himself, of enjoying her exquisite death in a private moment of ecstasy. He had wanted to treasure the memory. It would be one he would relish replaying in his mind many times.

But as he heard the older man's plan for the ceremony, he realized he liked it even better. He had so much enjoyed watching the final terror in her eyes as her panicked brain understood she was dying. And now, thanks to Saxby, he would have the pleasure all over again. Even better, her death tonight would not only be dazzling, it would add a whole new power to the ritual—one that he had not dared to consider.

*A human sacrifice. A burnt offering—just like Jephthah's daughter.*
He smiled broadly under his hood.

*It was perfect.*

The ignorant hypocrites never read their own holy book.

Well, tonight, on this most auspicious of nights, there would again be the offering of a young woman.

Reaching the Table of Practice at the same time as Saxby, he surveyed it closely, verifying that the objects were all properly laid out.

*Good. All was in place.*

In addition to the Mirror of Tezcatlipoca, everything he would need was there.

He took a deep breath, and readied himself.

There was a strict order to what had to be done.

Side by side with Saxby, together they began.

Saxby first leant over the table and picked up a deep silver bowl filled with a pungent minty infusion of hyssop. He passed it to Malchus, who took hold of it with his right hand, lifting out the silver handled asperges brush with his left.

He flicked the scented water first onto himself, and then onto Saxby, who bowed his head to receive the blessing.

"*Asperges me hyssopo. Exaudi orationem meam, et clamor meus ad te veniat.*"[17] Malchus intoned the words clearly and slowly, his deep voice resonating across the stage. He did not need to read them—he knew them by heart.

Carrying the bowl, he stepped towards Ava. She had been unconscious when he had tied her to the stake earlier. But now her eyes were open, and staring widely at him.

Dipping the brush in the bowl, he flicked water onto her three times. He knew she understood Latin. "*Ego te linio ut habeas vitam aeternam.*"[18] He was sure she would see the irony.

Returning to the table, he handed the bowl back to Saxby, who had meanwhile lit the charcoal in the goat's head thurible.

Malchus gazed at it again. The dealer in Budapest had excelled himself. He could not have asked for better. It was sublime—the Goat of Mendes itself.

Saxby reached into a small basalt bowl on the Table of Practice and took out several dark crystals of incense resin. It was Malchus's Exodus

---

17 "Sprinkle me with hyssop. Hear my prayer, and let my cry come unto you."
18 "I anoint you that you may have eternal life."

recipe, the Temple *qetoreth* incense—stacte, onchya, galbanum, and frankincense.

It would be perfect for tonight

He lifted the macabre lid off the thurible, and dropped the crystals onto the white-hot charcoal. Almost immediately, the bitter-sweet smoke began to belch out from the skull's charred eye sockets and nostrils.

Replacing the lid, he handed the smoking censer to Malchus, who held the silver chain high in the air with his right hand, pinching it lower down with his left, and swinging it in the direction of each of the Guardians of the four quarters, censing them in respectful greeting.

He inhaled the smoke deeply, satisfaction spreading throughout his body. *"Dirigatur oratio mea sicut incensum in conspectu tuo."*[19]

He had always been moved by the power of incense. It was one of the oldest practices of the adepts in existence—known from Greece, Rome, Egypt, and all over the Middle East, symbolizing invocations rising mystically to the Powers.

It was also for blessing and consecrating sacrificial offerings.

Stepping across to Ava, he slowly circled her three times anticlockwise, bathing her in the pungent spicy smoke.

He could see her blinking away the thick stinging clouds as he intoned the necessary words. *"Suscipe hanc immaculatam hostiam, quam ego indignus famulus tuus offero tibi."*[20]

Arriving in front of her again, he saw a look of panic as she registered the words.

*Good.*

Now she knew it was real. She was going to die.

Tonight.

He genuflected in front of her, locking his eyes onto her face. *"Ab illo benedicaris in cuius honore cremaberis."*[21]

Now he could again see the terror deep in her eyes as she began to struggle, trying to pull her hands clear from the ropes and writhe her body free from those strapping her to the post.

He turned away.

She could struggle as much as she wanted. If she was worked up, it would only make the ultimate pleasure more exquisite.

---

19 "Let my prayer be like incense in your sight."
20 "Accept this unblemished sacrifice, which I, your unworthy servant, offer to you."
21 "May you be blessed by him in whose honour you will be burned."

---

## 108

*The 'Gruft' Vault*
*Wewelsburg Castle*
*Büren*
*Paderborn*
*North-Rhine Westphalia*
*Federal Republic of Germany*

EVERY CELL IN Ava's body was screaming to get away from the mounting danger—a panic further stoked by the memory of that afternoon at Boleskine House, when she had left it too late.

Pulling wildly against the ropes for all she was worth, she tried to drag her hands through the loops binding them firmly to the post.

She did not care who saw. She just needed to be free.

But however hard she scrunched up her knuckles, the ropes remained welded to her wrists. The knots had been pulled tight, leaving no slack in them at all.

Time was now running out. Malchus and Saxby's obscene ritual was under way, and it would not be long before they turned their attentions to her.

As the ropes started to cut deeply into her flesh, the logical part of her brain told her she was getting nowhere. But she was not paying it any attention. Instead, she was listening to a wild and desperate voice, deep inside, telling her that if she could get free of the ropes, then she would have a chance. If she could get the element of surprise on her side, perhaps she could get past Malchus and Saxby. Dealing with the rest of the men in the room would not be straightforward, but maybe she could take Malchus or Saxby hostage. Perhaps that would buy her an exit from the castle.

As her mind raced through the myriad possibilities, she pulled herself up, stopping the uncontrolled trains of thought.

*All in time.*

She could work the details out later.

First, she had to get her hands free.

Summoning up a reserve of stamina from somewhere deep down, she tugged at her wrists again, harder this time—grimacing as she crushed the bones in her hand and felt the rope scything deeper into the raw flesh around her wrists.

But nothing moved.

Her lower arms remained securely bound to the stake.

Overcome with frustration, she resentfully bowed to her body's signals, and stopped. It was pointless. She was hurting herself needlessly.

Looking up, she could see Malchus had handed the smoking incense thurible back to Saxby, and was now walking over to the far side of the stage.

It was difficult to see in the dim light, but he appeared to bend over and open a trapdoor in the stage floor, before leaning over and lifting something out.

At first she thought it was a dark holdall bag, but as he stepped away, cradling it in his arms, she saw to her horror it was a young black goat, with immature short growths of bone in place of the horns that would grow in adulthood.

But from the way Malchus was walking purposefully with it towards the grate, she had a sickening feeling it would not see the night out, let alone another season.

Arriving at the front of the stage, Malchus reached up and took hold of a slim black chain hanging in the air. She had not noticed it before, but could now see it clearly, suspended from an iron bolt set into the stone ceiling.

Pulling the chain towards him, he deftly looped it around the goat's quivering left hind leg, leaving the bleating animal suspended upside down, barely a foot above the smoking coals.

He raised his hands in the air. *"Offero hanc hostiam viventem ut sit placens in conspectu tuo."*[22]

She watched with mounting revulsion as he knelt down and took up a ceremonial knife from behind the grate—the burnished steel glinting as it caught the light from the coals.

It was a vicious looking weapon—long, angular, and asymmetrical, with deeply curved edges and a series of holes in the flat metal decreasing in size as they ran the length of the blade towards its tip.

*"Haec dicit dominus, maledictus qui prohibet gladium suum a sanguine."*[23] He touched the lethal blade to his lips, before reaching forward and holding it against the young animal's slim throat. Ava could see the goat had been somehow stunned or sedated, but from its wide-eyed stare it was plainly still conscious, in accordance with the requirements of ancient rabbinic law.

She turned away in disgust. This was not something she wanted to watch.

She knew exactly what would happen. Malchus would draw the blade across the goat's throat, severing the carotid arteries and jugular veins, leaving the animal to bleed out—slowly. If he was skilled, he would also slice open the windpipe to stop the screaming.

She could hear his voice. *"Hic est sanguis foederis,"*[24] as the goat fell suddenly silent, and he stood again. She heard a hissing sound, and at the same time a salty metallic smell filled the air as two scarlet fountains pumped out of the glassy-eyed animal's neck and spurted onto the hot coals.

*"Et effundetur sanguis eorum sicut humus et corpus eorum sicut stercora,"*[25] he recited, as some of the blood landed in a shallow silver bowl he had placed onto the grate, while the remainder splashed straight into the spitting coals.

The sharp coppery odour of the blood was overpowering, making Ava's stomach heave.

She looked at the hooded figure, repelled by what she saw, feeling a chill pass through her as she tried to blank out the increasing thoughts of what he intended to do to her.

---

22 "I offer this living sacrifice that it might be pleasing in your sight."
23 "Thus says the Lord: a curse on anyone who keeps their sword from bloodshed."
24 "This is the blood of the covenant."
25 "Their blood will be poured out like dust and their carcasses like dung."

Within a few minutes, the goat's blood stopped flowing, and the animal hung motionless. He undid it from the chain, and laid its limp body onto the floor.

She looked with pity at the lifeless exsanguinated animal.

*Was that what he intended to do to her?*

*Drain her of all blood from her neck like an ancient Temple sacrifice?*

Turning back to watch Malchus, she saw he had deftly sliced open the goat's abdomen, and was following the biblical rules exactly. He had already exposed the steaming entrails, carved off the surrounding fatty sheath, and was now dexterously cutting out the long lobe of the liver and the kidneys.

The pungent smell of the animal's guts made her gag.

When he had finished disemboweling the carcass, he placed the fat and offal directly onto the hot bars of the grate, where they immediately began to give off a hot greasy bloody smell.

Raising his gore-smeared hands skywards, he gazed upwards, dedicating the meat. *"Offero holocaustum in odorem suavissimum domino."*[26]

His voice was pregnant with excitement.

Ava thought she was going to be sick.

Leaving the entrails charring, Malchus returned to the Table of Practice and took a seat behind it, hunching low over the Mirror of Tezcatlipoca, gazing into the smoky black volcanic glass.

Saxby meanwhile added more dark incense crystals to the thurible and moved over to the grate, where he began to process anticlockwise around it, blending the spicy-sweet fumes with the acrid smoke of the goat's burning innards.

At the Table, Malchus had begun chanting quietly, reciting a list of names.

"... Bael, Agares, Vassago, Samigina, Marbas, Valefor, Amon, Barbatos, Paimon, Buer, Gusion, Sitri, Beleth, Leraje, Eligos, Zepar, Botis ... ."

Sitting completely still, his voice dropped lower, and Ava struggled to hear clearly.

" ... Berith, Astaroth, Forneus, Foras, Asmoday ... ."

His voice eventually trailed off, muffled by the all-encompassing hood, until all she could see was an occasional flutter of the material as his jaw moved, softly mouthing the names.

---

26 "I offer this burnt offering as a pleasing aroma to the Lord."

The room was deathly silent—mesmerized by what was happening on the stage.

Eventually Malchus was still. Then he stood again, raising his hands and gazing ahead. *"Vastata est sancta domus tua, et ceciderunt portae sanctuarii tui."*[27] He rang a small hand bell solemnly three times—the high-pitched tinkling echoing eerily around the room.

Side by side with Saxby, he moved silently across the stage to the objects covered by the heavy black cloths.

Ava's pulse quickened. The ceremony was progressing, and if she was right, this is what she had been waiting for—the unveiling of the Menorah and the Ark.

Standing either side of the taller of the two objects, Malchus and Saxby each took hold of an edge of the thick cloth, and slowly slipped it off.

There was an intake of breath around the room as the material fell away, revealing what was beneath, leaving the lights from the braziers and the coals under the grate to reflect off the hand-hammered gold surface of the seven-branched Menorah, turning its shiny metal a deep lustrous orangey-red.

Ava gasped.

It was beyond magnificent.

She had never seen anything like it.

It was unrecognizable from the grime-covered object she had discovered at the Basilica di San Clemente.

There, in the airless cobwebbed chamber below the mithraeum, she had merely seen a dust- and filth-caked candlestick. It had been so encased in centuries of dirt that it could have been made of iron, wood, or plaster for all she knew. She had rubbed a small section to expose the metal underneath—but the rest of it might have been made of anything.

But the candelabrum she was looking at now had been lovingly cleaned up and was unquestionably all gold. It gleamed and glowed with an inner radiance, shimmering in the half-light with all the splendour of one of the greatest treasures of the ancient world.

It was overwhelming—a vast symbolic tree of life. Gold artworks of its size simply did not survive from the Hebrew Bronze Age. All that usually made it into museum collections were a few small remnants of personal jewellery.

---

27 "Destroyed is thy holy house, and fallen the gates of thy sanctuary."

Ava gaped at it.

The craftsmanship was flawless.

The main stem was exquisite. Each of its seven lamps was beaten into the shape of an almond flower—its five petals folding around to hold the oil basin. Beneath each flower was a supporting bed of buds and blossoms, and under each arm were three more almond-shaped cups for storing additional oil.

Shaking her head in wonder, she was still thrilled to see she had been right about the angled arms and triangular base.

Its shape alone would rewrite history.

It was more beautiful than she had ever imagined.

According to the Bible, the Hebrews had originally carried it with them on their wanderings in the desert. Wherever they stopped, they set it up in the special Tabernacle tent along with the Table of Showbread and the Altar of Incense, leaving the Ark screened off in the Holy of Holies at the far end of the tent. Then, later, when Solomon built the Temple in Jerusalem, they moved the items there permanently, and the Menorah's flame burned brightly night and day.

She could picture it in her mind, in the dark Temple, burning pure consecrated olive oil in all seven lamps from evening until morning, when only the central flame would be left to burn again until the evening.

It was an exceptional object, and she could easily understand that it had been one of the early kingdom of Israel's most treasured possessions.

But even though the Menorah was breathtaking—it was the item next to it that would dominate the international front pages.

It would be the find of the century.

After censing the Menorah with clouds of the pungent Temple incense, Saxby and Malchus moved towards the other shrouded object.

Ava could feel her breathing becoming so shallow it almost stopped

*This was it.*

This was the moment she had anticipated for so long.

Finally, she was going to come face to face with the Ark of the Covenant. She would have the historical Ark physically in front of her—not a dull grainy photograph like the one Prince had beamed onto the screen at Camp as-Sayliyah. It would be as tangible as the breathtaking Menorah beside it.

There was total stillness in the room as Malchus and Saxby arrived in front of it. All eyes were on them.

Ava held her breath, and felt her heart racing.

As the two men took hold of the cloth, the expectant silence was shattered by the harsh explosive sound of loud automatic gunfire—right outside.

Pandemonium erupted in the room, snapping Ava back to reality with a rude jolt.

Malchus's security team rushed for the door. Around them, weapons appeared from under clothing as the spectating paramilitaries scrabbled to arm themselves and pour out of the door towards the source of the shots.

Within seconds, Ava could hear fire being returned in multiple bursts, and in no time there was the familiar staccato chatter of a pitched gun battle.

Her mind was spinning.

*Who on earth was shooting?*

Possibilities raced through her mind.

Had some of the guests been outside? Had they fallen out? Given the kind of people attending, she doubted it would have taken more than a few raised words before weapons were drawn and the camaraderie shattered.

As the gunfire intensified, she could not help but hope Max and his men had arrived. She had no idea if they would have had time to get there, as she had no watch and no indication how long she had been knocked out. It had been long enough for someone to have dressed her, made her up, and tied her to the stake—but she had no sense whether it had taken ten minutes or three hours.

"Continue," Saxby ordered Malchus. "Tonight we—" but what he said next was drowned out by another deafening volley of gunfire.

*Closer this time.*

Ava prayed the battle did not move into the room. If rounds began flying inside, she would be in a highly vulnerable position. She had no way of taking cover and was defenceless—totally exposed to a stray bullet or anyone who wanted her dead.

Undeterred by the sound of fighting, Malchus and Saxby approached the black-covered mound next to the Menorah.

Ava was perspiring, unable to take her eyes off the dark cloth. She strained in the dim light to see their every move.

She did not want to miss anything.

Her heart was in her mouth as they gently pulled the cloth sideways, exposing the object underneath.

With her nervous system at breaking point, she stared at what the cloth had slid away to reveal—not believing what she saw.

She blinked several times to make sure her eyes were not playing tricks on her.

It seemed they were not.

She had been so certain it would be the Ark that she had not even considered the possibility it might not be.

But unless she was hallucinating, what she was looking at was definitely *not* the Ark of the Covenant.

She could feel the shock passing through her like a physical pressure wave.

With disbelief, she stared at the object lying on a red cushion on a table.

Disappointment and frustration crashed over her.

She sagged as the grim realization hit her.

*It had all been for nothing.*

She had come all this way to find they did not have the Ark.

She had got it dreadfully wrong.

Her capture had been pointless.

And now so would her death be.

She could feel herself choking with frustration as the sounds of the gunfire outside intensified.

She stared numbly at Saxby as he stepped aside, giving her a clear view of the object on the table.

It was a vicious-looking black iron spear tip, about a foot long. There were six sections of thin silver wire bound tightly around it, and a gold sleeve covering its centre. The lighting was dim, but she could also make out a Roman-era iron nail embedded into it.

She recognized it immediately, having seen it in the Imperial Treasury at Vienna's Hofburg Palace, when she had been in the Austrian capital giving a guest lecture on Babylonian cylinder seals at the *Kunsthistorisches Museum*.

It was the Lance of Longinus, or Spear of Destiny—the Roman weapon used to slit open Christ's side as he hung dying on the cross. The Allies had found it among Hitler's treasures in Nuremburg and given it back to Austria.

So what was it doing here?

*Had Malchus stolen it?*

She struggled to understand, and also to work out why she was looking at a small artefact from around AD 30 when it should have been a much larger one from 1290 BC.

Malchus had returned to the centre of the stage, and was now holding the silver dish filled with goat's blood high above his head, his eyes raised upwards in supplication. *"Et dabo prodigia in caelo et in terra sanguinem et ignem et vaporem fumi. Sol vertetur in tenebras et luna in sanguinem antequam veniat dies domini magnus et horribilis."*[28]

Whatever he was going to say next was drowned out as a hail of gunfire strafed across the cellar's far wall, kicking up clouds of dust as the bullets gouged deep holes in the stones.

Groups of the men were now running back into the crypt again, taking up defensive positions around the stage, training their weapons on the door.

The large guard with the tattoos made straight for Malchus. "Some German crew," he shouted up to Malchus above the noise of the gunfire. "And they're heavily tooled up."

---

28 "I will show wonders in the heavens and on the earth, blood and fire and billows of smoke. The sun will be turned to darkness and the moon to blood before the coming of the great and dreadful day of the Lord."

---

## 109

The 'Gruft' Vault
*Wewelsburg Castle*
*Büren*
*Paderborn*
*North-Rhine Westphalia*
*Federal Republic of Germany*

THE EXCHANGES OF gunfire outside the chamber were intensifying—
becoming louder and more sustained.

The hulking tattooed leader of Malchus's security team was close to
Ava, shouting orders at the other paramilitaries who had followed him
back into the room. He indicated for them to take positions on either
side of the cellar, leaving the centre clear. He pointed at the entranceway.
"Door funnel. Kill zone."

Ava's heart was hammering.

*This was not good.*

If the plan was to bring the fight into the cellar so the intruders could
be picked off as they came through the door, then Malchus and his ceremony were the least of her immediate worries.

Her chances of surviving a firefight in the enclosed space were not good.

Meanwhile, Saxby had finished censing the Spear of Destiny, and he
and Malchus were now crossing the stage towards her.

The smoke from the charring meat was mingling with the incense Saxby had been using to bless the various objects, creating a thick heady mix that was making Ava lightheaded.

As the two robed men approached her, she could feel her mouth going dry.

*Was this it?*

She stared into the eye-slits of their tall pointed hoods and thought with regret of Ferguson.

*How long had he been in the well?*

She had no way of knowing. She felt a pang of guilt. He would not be in this mess if it had not been for her. But at least while Saxby and Malchus were on the stage, focused on the ceremony, they would not be carrying out their revenge on him.

That would come later.

*Unless she could think of something.*

There were now more weapons joining in the exchanges outside— small arms and automatic fire.

The two sides were digging in.

To her surprise, as the two hooded figures drew level with her on the stage, they did not say anything or slow down, but carried on purpose-fully, walking straight past her.

Confused, she twisted her torso half around to see what they were doing, but the position of her body, lashed to the front of the post, severely restricted her ability to move.

Undeterred, she craned her neck around as far as she could, and looked out of the corner of her eyes into the darkened section of the stage directly behind her, where Saxby and Malchus were now walking.

Her heart missed a beat as she saw the area for the first time.

At the far rear left of the stage, beyond where Saxby and Malchus were standing, was a large object. And just like the Menorah and the Spear of Destiny, it was draped in a thick black cloth.

However, unlike the other two ancient artefacts, the heavy cloth over it was not able to conceal the unusual shape lying beneath it.

Ava could feel a prickle of electricity running up the back of her neck as all the hairs stood on end.

It was rectangular—like a packing chest, with what looked like two long poles sticking outwards from either side, a high peak above the centre of the top, and two lesser peaks at the top left and right.

In the split second it took her to realize what it was, the cellar began to feel unbearably hot, and she was suddenly finding it difficult to breathe. It was partly the angle at which she was twisting her neck, reducing the blood flow to her head. But it was largely the sheer shock of what she was looking at—seeing it there. Finally. In the same room as her.

*The Ark.*

She inhaled deeply, not quite believing her eyes.

*It had been there all along.*

She was perspiring.

*Right behind her.*

She watched in a daze as Saxby and Malchus stopped in front of it, one at either end.

She held her breath as they slowly took hold of the black cloth.

Time seemed to stand still and then move in slow motion as they gently slid the material off, revealing the object underneath.

If it had not been for the physical pain from twisting her neck round so far, she would have been sure she was dreaming.

When Saxby and Malchus had unveiled the Menorah, she had wondered if any antique artefact would ever be able to impress her as much again.

But now, looking at the Ark, she immediately knew the answer.

Stunned, she could only stare at it as an avalanche of intense emotions broke over her.

It was nothing like she had imagined, and like no drawing or model of it she had ever seen.

The sheer quantity of gold was spellbinding. It glowed and gleamed in the light from the braziers every bit as radiantly as the Menorah, bathing the air around it in a shimmering aura.

The Bible said it was made of acacia wood, then covered with gold inside and out, with four gold rings for the gold-covered carrying poles and a lid with hammered gold cherubim at either end.

But the Bible mentioned nothing about the sublime decoration.

She could not discern the details clearly, but she could see enough to tell her that the Ark and the lid were divided into panels of beaten gold. That was not so unusual. What was mesmerizing her was that every square inch of gold was covered in a riot of imagery.

Nothing had ever prepared her for this moment.

The Ark was indescribably beautiful—more intricate and skillfully made than she had ever imagined.

She did not doubt its age, but found it impossible to believe that these two objects—the Ark and the Menorah—had been created by Bezalel of Judah and Aholiab of Dan, two amateurs chosen in the Sinai desert as the Hebrews crossed from Egypt to Israel. From what she could see in front of her, the Ark and Menorah had undoubtedly been made in one or more workshops by whole teams of highly skilled and experienced artisans.

Dizzy with excitement, she tried to take it all in, to feast upon it. Others in the room were doing likewise. Despite the dangerously close gunfire, a large number of the men in the room were now crowding around the Ark.

They were partially obscuring her view, so she could see little more of the Mercy Seat than that the cherubim's wings stretched up at a dramatic angle to create a triangular space above the lid. According to the Bible, that was where Yahweh said he would meet with the Hebrews.

She had once put together a three-dimensional computer graphic recreation of King Solomon's Temple for the British Museum, and had included a replica Ark to scale. Looking at the real one now, she was pleased to see she had been correct in concluding it used the shorter cubit, which made it around three-and-a-half feet long by two feet wide.

It was still an immense size—a huge weight for the men who had to carry it around.

She stared, captivated by the extraordinary relic—a gleaming window into the long-lost roots of western history.

As she was drinking it in, Saxby had begun censing it, and Malchus had returned to the front of the stage, where he was crouching low by the grate. He had the bowl of hyssop in his hand, and was emptying the remaining drops onto the coals with a loud hiss. He dipped the now-empty bowl into the silver dish in which the goat's blood was still bubbling, then handed it to Saxby, before picking up a large old leather tome from the Table of Practice.

Ava watched closely as he headed towards her, the volume open in his hands.

*This was surely it?*

*The start of the section of the ceremony which would climax with her murder?*

She could not quite believe that they were continuing with the ritual.

*Surely the gunfight meant they would have to stop?*

But as Malchus continued to approach her, he showed no sign of calling a halt to the proceedings.

Breathing deeply to quell her rising panic, she noted that the curved knife he had used to slit the goat's throat was still on the floor by the animal's carcass. He had not picked it up yet, which was reassuring. But she knew it would not be long now.

As he drew level with her, she could smell the goat's dried gore on his hands. She tensed, unable to keep images of its slashed throat from her mind.

Malchus turned so he was standing beside her, and held out the book in front of him so they could both read from its aged pages. Ava did not recognize the title—the *Lemegeton*, but from the deep ochre cover, hard boards, leather thong binding, and typography, she guessed it was from the 1700s.

However, Malchus was only using it as a prop. On its large leaves lay the smaller loose typed sheets of his translation of the London version of *The Sword of Moses*, along with printouts of the small pages of tiny original Hebrew and Aramaic writing from the genuine Oxford manuscript.

He began reading from the translation in a loud clear voice:

> "Ye sacred angels, princes of the hosts who stand upon the thrones prepared for them before him to watch over and to minister to the Sword, to fulfil by it all the wants by the name of the master over all; you chiefs of all the angels in the world, I pray of you to do everything that I am asking of you, as you have the power to do everything in heaven and upon earth as it is written in the law."

Ava read along, following the text, wondering what part she was supposed to play.

> "I conjure you, Azliel, Arel, Ta'aniel, Tafel, Yofiel Mittron. With these your names, and with the powers you possess to which there's nowhere anything like, I conjure you to show me, and to search for me, and to do all my bidding."

She was listening carefully for any clues to how the ceremony would unfold.

From the ending of almost every name in '-el', it was clear the spell first called upon a cohort of angels to assist with the summoning.

On the far side of the stage, Saxby approached the Menorah and dipped the asperges brush into the silver bowl, covering it in the goat's blood.

Just as Malchus had done with the hyssop, he used the brush to flick splashes of it onto the Menorah. The globules of red sat immobile on the metal for an instant, before running down the glowing gold in thick viscous streams.

Ava assumed most of the neo-Nazis in the room would imagine it was just a piece of grotesque black magic theatre. But she knew all too well that the Bible was clear about the sacred properties of the blood of sacrificed animals. The Bible gave explicit and repeated instructions about daubing the altars of King Solomon's Temple in blood. It was also precise about anointing priests with it, as Moses had anointed Aaron and his children with the blood of a sacrificed ram, and likewise had sprinkled the blood from young bulls onto the people at the foot of Mount Sinai to confirm their dedication to God.

As she watched Saxby, she could hear the gunfire outside getting louder and closer. She could almost feel the air shaking with the discharges.

Malchus was still reading the conjuration as Saxby turned to the Lance of Longinus, and began blessing it with the blood.

Next to her, Malchus was now reading from the second sheet of his translation.

> "With the permission of my king, I conjure Yadiel, Ra'asiel, Haniel, Asrael, Yisriel, A'shael, Amuhael, that you attach yourselves to me and surrender the Sword to me, so that I may use it according to my desire."

Glancing further down the page, she could see that the conjuration culminated with the core of the spell—the list of Yahweh's mystical names to summon and bind him.

As her eyes flicked to the very bottom, she could see that where the list of mystical names should have been, the translator had written:

The original London manuscript only has an 'X' in place of each mystical name. It seems the medieval scribe of this redaction did not wish to make the spell widely available.

Saxby was now moving behind her, to the Ark. She twisted round as far as she could, in time to see him flick a brush of blood at it.

Once again, Ava could not help reflecting that, in their own warped and twisted way, Saxby and Malchus had done their homework. The biblical ritual in the book of Leviticus was clear that every year, on the Day of Atonement, the Hebrew high priest was to enter the Holy of Holies and sprinkle the Ark with the sacrificial blood of a goat and a bullock.

When Saxby had finished daubing the outside of the Ark with the blood, he indicated to the men around it to remove the lid.

He clearly meant to sprinkle blood inside it, too.

Beside her, Malchus was still reading from the spell.

"Fulfil for me everything that I have been conjuring you for. Deliver unto me with this Sword the secrets from above and below, the mysteries from above and below, and my wish be fulfilled and my word hearkened unto."

Without warning, she felt as if all the air in the room was suddenly on fire. It was so hot she could feel it burning inside her nose and mouth.

At the same time, there was a searing light and a deafening thunderclap that seemed to blow out her eardrums.

Before she had registered what was happening, shards of razor-sharp twisted metal hurtled past her head, and it felt as if someone had punched her viciously in the shoulder.

Disorientated and with her ears ringing, she stared around numbly.

The chamber was filling with black smoke, and beside her she could see Malchus lying on the floor. His hood had come off, and his face was bloodied. But he was conscious, gazing about in confusion.

Dazed, she saw a shard of gold sticking out of her shoulder. The chainmail had protected her from a more serious injury, but a long spike of gleaming metal had nevertheless punctured her skin and embedded itself deep into her muscle.

As she twisted round further to look behind her, she could no longer see any sign of the gold-covered Ark, lid, or carrying poles.

Instead, there was now a charred burning heap of smouldering wood fragments strewn across the floor, along with splinters and shards of tangled metal.

Her mind refused to accept what she was seeing.

*This could not be happening.*

Her eyes scoured the room for the Ark.

*It had gone.*

She stared in disbelief, first at the smoking remains, then at the scene of destruction in the vault around her.

The men who had been crowding around, helping Saxby lift the Ark's lid, were lying on the floor—a pile of bodies, many with whole limbs missing. Judging by the way they had fallen, it was clear they had taken the full force of the blast, shielding Ava from the brunt of it.

None were moving.

Saxby lay next to them. From the missing section of skull through which she could see a mess of mangled brain matter, it was immediately obvious he was also very dead.

Her head was spinning, and she still could not hear anything through the ringing in her ears. But she was thinking clearly enough to know something explosive had just detonated very close to the Ark.

As she replayed the scene in her mind, she realized that the explosion had been triggered the moment they had lifted its lid.

*Was that even possible?*

Suddenly, the realization hit her.

It was something that had bothered her in the days after she had left Dubai. And now it made sense.

*Arkady Sergeyevitch Yevchenko.*

As he had lain strapped to the table in his suite's kitchen at the Burj al-Arab hotel, his last word had baffled her.

"Insurance," he had whispered.

It had seemed a strange thing to say as a dying word, and she had been struggling to make sense of it ever since.

*Had this been his insurance?*

She shook her head in disbelief.

*He booby-trapped the Ark?*

It was unthinkable.

The Ark had survived for over three thousand years. And now it was gone, right under her nose—the handiwork of a paranoid Russian lawyer.

Distraught, she closed her eyes, fighting the urge to start screaming at someone.

Anyone.

Taking a deep breath, she opened her eyes again and looked down at Malchus, who was picking himself up off the floor.

But he never made it.

Two searing white lights ripped either side of the darkened room apart, followed a millisecond later by a pair of deafening deep percussive booms.

The effect on Ava's body was dramatic and instantaneous.

Her vision was bleached out as the intense flashes tore through her eyes, leaving her unable to see anything beyond a burning bright-white magnesium light stamped onto the back of her retinas.

Her ears, already deadened from whatever had detonated in the Ark, shut down completely so she could hear nothing except a high-pitched whistling. And as the fluid in her inner ear was bludgeoned by the heavy pressure waves, she lost her sense of balance, and the room turned upside down.

At first she thought she may have been shot in the head or had a stroke. But as her vision slowly returned, she was aware of armed men swarming the stage around her, and others fast-roping down at break-neck speed from the shattered high windows above.

Their balaclavas and unmarked all-black tactical ops kit gave away nothing about their identity.

They quickly formed a ring around the stage, their weapons levelled at the neo-Nazi paramilitaries standing and lying on the floor, equally as stunned as she was.

The intruders were shouting something, but Ava could hear only an eerie silence overlaid by the whistling in her ears.

Over by the main door, another armed group burst in. They came in hard, weapons raised at shoulder-height, with mounted flashlights sweeping the room, cutting the gloom into tunnels of fast-moving bright white light.

They were fully armoured in helmets and hard-plated ballistic counter-terrorism jackets. Their sleeves bore small rectangular German flags above eagles and the word 'POLIZEI'. Several of them also wore badges displaying parachute wings in oak leaves.

Still unable to hear, she was suddenly aware of one of the balaclavad men on the stage making straight for her, pulling a short-bladed dagger from his ops waistcoat. The glow from the braziers reflected on the brushed steel blade as he appeared to shout something at her.

With no hearing, she was wholly at his mercy—with no way of telling if he was friend or foe.

He arrived in front of her, still shouting something, but his lips were covered by his balaclava so she could not even lip-read what he was saying.

Beyond him, over on the other side of the stage, she saw two more figures rapidly fast-roping in. They were not wearing the same all-black kit as the others, and with a flash of amazement followed by overwhelming relief she recognized them immediately—Ferguson and the guard, Danny.

Ferguson was wearing different clothes to the ones she had last seen him in, but his expression was infinitely happier. Both were armed, and took up positions on the stage alongside the others.

She looked at the man with the knife, peering at his eyes through the holes in the balaclava. Finally, she recognized the deep shadows and crinkled lines of the Frenchman's lived-in face.

"Max?" she shouted, as the intense relief washed over her.

The man nodded, raising the knife to cut her hands free.

Breathing more easily now, she looked around intently, and saw that Max and his men were carrying FAMAS assault rifles. Reproaching herself for her lack of observation, that was the only clue she should have needed.

Frenchmen were patriotic to the end,

Quickly slicing through the ropes, Max helped her off the stake. She put her arms on him to steady herself, and with no warning he took hold of the shard of gold protruding from her shoulder and expertly pulled it out cleanly.

She was overwhelmed by a sudden stabbing agony from the metal slicing across the raw nerve endings in the wound. But the sensation quickly subsided into a more manageable aching pain as her body released a slew of natural opioids.

She stamped her feet and shook her arms to get the blood circulating again, before noticing that Max was saying something to her.

She pointed to her ears and shrugged to indicate she was deaf.

He lifted his balaclava so she could read his lips. "There's someone outside who wants to see you."

She nodded, moving closer to the edge of the stage, away from the stake. As she did, she spotted a hollow metal canister on the floor, the shape of an elongated drinks can with a dozen circular perforations drilled into the casing.

She was reassured to see she had not had a stroke.

*Stun grenades.*

Still reeling, she could see the German police shouting and gesticulating for the neo-Nazi paramilitaries to put their firearms down and lie on the ground.

None of them complied. They kept their weapons pointed at the killing funnel the policemen had just walked into, and at Max's men on the stage.

Their leader—the large tattooed guard—was a few yards away from her, still aiming his submachine gun at the policemen. It looked like a toy in his massive arms, but the expression on his face was anything but playful.

Slowly, in the gloom, he began to turn.

She could see one of the German policemen yelling at him, but she still could not hear anything. Before she knew it, the large man's gun was pointing directly at her chest.

His lips were moving.

As the whistling in her ears began to subside, she started to hear what he was saying. It sounded heavily muffled, as if her head was under a blanket, but at least she could dimly make out the words.

"Let us out, or she dies, and so do a lot of you." He spoke clearly and deliberately, slowly covering the last few yards to where she was, a thin sheen of sweat breaking out on his granite face. "I'll slot her right here. You've got ten seconds to decide."

All eyes were suddenly on him.

There was silence as everyone calculated the likely consequences if shooting started, although it was obvious that the wrong decision would turn the room into a bloodbath very quickly.

The tattooed guard was staring at Ava over the barrel of his gun. His nostrils were flared, and he was breathing hard.

She had seen the look often enough to know he was a man preparing to kill.

Instead of fear or panic, Ava felt a surge of elation.

The police may or may not make the right call. But she had absolutely had enough for one night of people making decisions that resulted in her getting seriously hurt.

Having been tied up under the threat of death for so long, her pent-up anger and fear exploded inside her in a rush of adrenaline.

Now she was free of the ropes, she no longer had to be a spectator.

*Not any more.*

Her destiny was in her own hands again.

In a lightning-fast movement, she lunged towards the big guard, drawing the lethal bronze sickle-sword from the sash around her hips, and swinging it up with both hands to a fighting guard.

It was an amazingly well-balanced weapon, and it felt good to no longer be the only unarmed person in the room.

She planted her feet two yards in front of the large man. "Let's do this," she hissed at him, feeling her muscles flood with blood.

She was angry, and had every intention of letting it show. "You don't need the gun," she taunted. "Or do you?" Her eyes flashed darkly.

She had been watching him since Boleskine House, and was keenly aware that he was very dangerous. He was alert and moved well, and could not have reached his position in the organization without being able to handle himself against people who knew how to fight much dirtier than she did.

But one advantage she did have was the element of surprise.

There was no way he would have anticipated this development.

It was a gamble. She was betting he needed her alive to use as a bargaining chip. But if she was wrong, she was happy to take her chances. At least it was a fairer fight then being tied to a chair or a stake and strangled or bled out.

"What's the matter?" Ava injected a note of mockery into her voice. "Never touched a woman before?"

She could feel the tension in the room like a charge of electricity, but was beyond fear. After all she had been through, it was exhilarating to be in charge of her own fate again.

There was a look of incredulity in his eyes, but it rapidly turned into a snarl of rage. He took a step forward, and she could see his finger starting to squeeze the trigger.

But he never got to finish the movement, as with a deafening bang, the back of his head vapourized into a fine red mist, and he dropped heavily to the floor.

Off to the side, through the dim light, she could see Ferguson's arm outstretched, and a small cloud of smoke dissipating into the air above the pistol in his hand.

Ava was breathing hard, trying to calm herself down.

"Put your weapons on the floor!" the brawny leader of the German police screamed at the neo-Nazi paramilitaries again. "Now!"

With Saxby dead on the stage and the Skipper down, one by one they complied.

"On the floor!" the policeman shouted. "Face down. All of you. Hands behind you heads."

As the men began sliding to the floor, the police moved swiftly among them, rolling them onto their fronts and securing their hands with zip ties.

Ava felt someone touch her arm. She swung round, the sword still raised.

It was Ferguson.

"Well, you look beautiful," he nodded appreciatively. "There was no need to dress specially for me."

Ava had been in the costume so long she had forgotten she was wearing it. She blushed under the heavy white make-up. "You like it?" She lowered the sword, recovering quickly. "Maybe I'll keep it then."

"You should seriously think about it," he nodded approvingly. "And the perfume, too. Very nice."

She smiled back at him—it was the first time she had anything to smile about all day. It was truly good to see him. "So you and Danny couldn't stay away?" she asked.

"His name's Uri. He's Israeli. I'd say Mossad, but he's keeping quiet about that."

"I thought as much," Ava nodded. This was an added obstacle. "What's he doing here?"

"Same as us," Ferguson answered, tucking his gun back into his waistband. "He fished me out of the well to help him. But when our German friends turned up, we decided to give them a hand. Then when Max arrived, it seemed rude not to accept his invitation to join in his rope games."

He looked at the wound in her shoulder. There was blood seeping onto her clothing. "You want to get that seen to."

Ava nodded. She would do it later. "So who called the German police?"

"Police?" He shook his head. "Don't let them hear you say that. They're GSG-9, the German version of the SAS. They can't be army by law, so they all leave and get a police uniform instead." He smiled. "Apparently once our MI6 tail had picked up our location at Boleskine House, the ever-diligent team at Legoland tracked the chopper to here. They couldn't get over the Channel in time to follow us, so they called in GSG-9 to pick us up. But as it happens, our German colleagues turn out to be much more interested in Malchus and his friends than whatever we may have done." He indicated the neo-Nazis being frog-marched out of the door. "They've done a good job. They got all the guys outside rounded up, too."

At the mention of Malchus's name, Ava suddenly realized she had not seen him for a while. The last time she had spotted him, Uri had been near him.

"Damn it!" she yelled, jumping off the stage, and running for the door. Passing Max, she shoved the bronze sword into his hand, and pulled a handgun off his belt kit. "I'll bring it back," she shouted, tearing past him and out of the cellar.

---  • ◆ •  ---

# IIO

*The SS Generals' Hall*
*Wewelsburg Castle*
*Büren*
*Paderborn*
*North-Rhine Westphalia*
*Federal Republic of Germany*

AVA SPRINTED UP the steep castle steps leading out of the cellar.

She *had* to find Malchus.

Losing him now, after everything that had happened, was simply unthinkable. She would never be able to forgive herself.

She ran out into the cobbled courtyard.

The pale moonlight was largely obscured by clouds, and she could only make out the armoured outlines and swinging tactical gun-lights of the GSG-9 team, who were roughly shepherding Saxby's followers into waiting vans, their engines throbbing in the cold night air.

Looking about properly for the first time since arriving, she could see that the ancient castle was a labyrinth of interconnecting rooms and hiding places.

*He could be anywhere.*

She had little idea where to start. Any choice seemed as random as any other.

The three sombre towers were high, and the imposing connecting ranges had three or four storeys each. There were easily over a hundred windows in the castle, and probably half as many rooms.

She stared at the glass, looking for a clue. But she could tell nothing. The windows shone black—the rooms behind them shrouded in darkness.

As she gazed around with increasing desperation, something told her that wherever Malchus was, the Israeli would not be far away.

Running back into the imposing north tower, she sprinted up the dark steps to the third-floor solar, where Saxby and Malchus had held her and Ferguson before the ceremony.

Pushing open the old iron-reinforced door, she found the torches had been extinguished and the large room was empty.

Taking the steps back down two at a time, she realized that on her way up she had failed to register an arched wooden door on the ground floor. Above it, she read the aged inscription incised into the old stone:

DOMUS MEA DOMUS ORATIONIS VOCABITUR

which she quickly translated, 'My house shall be called a house of prayer'.

The biblical quotation referring to the Temple of Solomon seemed starkly incongruous given everything she had experienced that evening. She assumed it was from the days when the castle had belonged to the local bishop-princes. It perhaps even indicated the room had once been their chapel.

Leaning her shoulder hard against the door, she found to her frustration that it was locked. But with her ear now only inches from the wood, she could make out muffled voices behind it.

Keenly aware that every passing second could mean Malchus was slipping further out of her reach, there was no time for luxuries like picking the lock.

Pointing her gun into the small ancient brass-faced keyhole, she took a deep breath, and squeezed the trigger. There was a chance it could blow her hand off, but she figured she was owed some good luck by now.

The noise of the discharge in the small stone corridor was deafening.

As the echo died, she smashed the pistol's butt hard into the lock, and to her relief she heard the mechanism clatter onto the floor inside the room.

Without pausing, she rammed the solid door with her shoulder and, after a moment's resistance, it yielded.

As she burst through into the room, she took a moment to take in the extraordinary sight.

It was dimly lit—illuminated by a single pool of flickering light thrown off by a sole flaming torch set in a wall sconce by the door.

The space was circular, just like the solar above and the cellar below—but distinctly grander than either. The ceiling rested on twelve solid pillars arranged in a circle of squat arches, creating a grandiose arcade around the edge of room. The overall effect was like some 1930s fascist take on a Graeco-Roman temple.

Malchus was on his back, spread-eagled on the blue-grey marble floor. He was lying directly over what looked like a large inlaid circle of over-lapping swastika crosses—their twelve long double-bent crooked arms spiralling out in an occult sun-wheel.

His black robe had been torn off down to the waist exposing his upper body, and Uri was kneeling on top of him, his back to the door, pinning Malchus's upper arms to the floor with his knees.

As Ava entered and Uri turned, she noticed the lethal outline of the Spear of Destiny in his hands, and dozens of livid deep bleeding incisions and gouges on Malchus's sweating body, arms, and face.

"Get off him," she ordered, pointing the handgun directly at Uri's chest.

"Just walk away," Uri snapped in reply. He turned to stare at her, his expression unwelcoming. "Leave."

Ava kept the gun trained on him, unwavering. "You heard me."

Uri glared back at her. "Your friend Ferguson killed the Skipper and lost me valuable intelligence. Now I have to get it from other sources." He glowered down at Malchus, then looked back at her. "Leave me to do what I have to do."

"Now!" Ava ordered him again, moving closer with the weapon.

"So the British can sit on whatever information he yields up and only trade it with us when it serves them?" Uri cocked his eyebrows at her. "My country's need of what he knows is greater than yours, I think you'll agree?"

Ava shook her head. "This has nothing to do with politics. It's now a police matter. There are things he needs to answer for, and I'm going to see he does."

"How very moving," Malchus sneered from under Uri, his voice a deep rasp. "Daddy's grieving girl turns out to be my saviour. I'm touched." He broke off, loudly sucking in a mouthful of air as Uri jabbed the spear tip deep into one of the cuts and twisted it.

"Be polite to the lady," Uri growled.

Through the mask of pain, Malchus glared at Ava, narrowing his eyes. "And precisely how long do you think it'll take me to convince the police to hand me over to MI6?" His eyes radiated conceit.

"I'll be on the streets again in days with the slate wiped clean. Thanks to DeVere, they know nothing about me or the wider organization. After tonight, they'll jump at the chance to run me as an asset." He smiled insincerely. "Maybe I'll even tell them something interesting every now and then."

He paused to let his words sink in. "And what will you tell them?" His tone was scornful. "You're a discredited former junior employee. An amateur. A disappointment. I've been doing this since before you were born." His eyes were mocking. "You're out of your league." Grunting with pain as Uri again jabbed the spear into one of the wounds, he nevertheless managed to finish his monologue with a note of triumph. "No one is going to touch me."

Ava looked down at his lacerated and blood-streaked face. "You overestimate your significance." She struggled to keep her voice calm. "After five minutes listening to your rabid delusions, they'll put you in a secure hospital and throw away the key. There's no jury trial for people like you. They'll lock you away in a mental hospital and the world will soon forget you ever existed."

"On the strength of your word?" Malchus jeered. "The woman who murdered Prince and DeVere and was the last person seen with Lord Drewitt?" He shook his head. "I don't think so. Without DeVere, you have nothing. I'll soon be one of the British authorities' best assets, and how long do you really think it'll take me to find another DeVere?" His eyes were gleaming. "Face it. I am, and always will be, more valuable to them than you."

Ava was buying none of it. She had heard enough. The sooner she could hand him over to the police and get the sound of his deranged gloating out of her ears, the better.

She turned back to Uri, her voice leaving no doubt of her intent. "Move away. I'm not going to ask you again."

Uri shot her a long resentful look. He raised his hands slowly into the air. "Okay. Your decision." He stood up off Malchus. "I'm done here, anyway."

Malchus smirked as Uri climbed off him—a smug mocking smile.

Ava pointed the gun at Malchus. "Now. Your turn," she ordered him. "Get up."

Malchus looked about conceitedly, putting his hands on the floor and pushed himself into an upright sitting position.

Without warning, Uri spun round with lightning speed. In one fluid motion, he extended his right hand with the spear blade still in it, and swung towards Malchus.

Before Ava could react, he drove the sharpened edges of the antique weapon's point deep into Malchus's throat, scything through the windpipe, oesophagus, and major blood vessels.

Malchus crumpled back to the floor with a strangled sound, clutching his throat with his left hand, a look of stunned disbelief on his face.

Uri barged past Ava, shoving the bloodied Spear of Destiny into her hands. "You know he's right. They'd have put him back on the streets in days."

With that, he was gone through the door.

"What are you even doing here?" Ava shouted after him, rage welling up inside her. "You didn't come for Saxby or Malchus. You're here for the Ark, aren't you?"

Uri stopped and turned slowly to face her. "So did you see it?" he asked quietly. "Was it the genuine Ark?"

The question sliced through Ava.

The pain of remembering its fate was physical. She could feel her stomach knot and her chest tighten.

She struggled to keep her voice under control, afraid the frustration of finally finding the Ark then losing it was all too much.

But try as she might to contain her feelings, they bubbled over. "If it wasn't for people like you, it might still be here." She could feel her pulse rising as the anger started to flood out. "You all treat it like it's some trophy—a symbol of power and favour, a talisman to bless your actions. You measure everything in political points." Her voice dropped. "You value nothing."

Uri shrugged. "It wasn't built to be put in a museum, I can tell you that. It's the ultimate statement of superiority and power. It always was. *Emmanuel.* God is with us. That's why the tribes carried it in the desert, demonstrating their favoured status. Whether you like it or not, it's a political totem. That's its function. What other purpose could it ever have had?"

The question hung in the air between them.

"Then we've both lost something today," Ava answered slowly.

"I'm not a romantic," Uri replied. "It's best where it is—beyond danger, where it can no longer be a threat to us."

Ava shook her head. She had no desire to hear any more. It was like being back at MI6—in a world where everything had a price and was ultimately expendable.

"The Ark may be gone, but it's not over," Uri added, walking away. "It never is."

That was not how it felt from where Ava was standing.

She had lost the Ark, the chance of seeing Malchus answer for her father's death, and the only person who could exonerate her with the British authorities.

With that, Uri was gone.

She watched him disappear down the corridor, before she turned back into the room, lost in thought.

She gazed down at Malchus, and at the spurting crimson fluid seeping through his fingers.

The sight of him lying in a pool of his own blood whipped up a storm of conflicting feelings inside her.

She had never wanted his death. That was not what this had been about. She had planned to see him answer for her father's murder.

But as she looked down at him, with his life pumping rapidly out of his neck, some primal force inside her could not help but feel satisfaction. She had seen his savagery at first hand. The world would be a better place without him. No one could argue with that.

As she looked at the bloodied hairless body, her mind filled with one sole thought. It was repeating again and again, bringing with it a strange sense of calm.

*It was over.*

The nightmare that had begun the day her father had failed to come home from Vauxhall Cross was finally at an end. Whatever twisted motives had been driving Malchus all these years were now as dead as he was, seeping out onto the floor along with his lifeblood.

Exhaling slowly and deeply, she tucked the gun into the sash wrapped around her lower back, and could feel the tension in her taut body begin to dissipate. Her shoulders dropped, and an overwhelming tiredness began to flood through her.

Stretching her neck from side to side to relieve the tightness, she suddenly just wanted to get out of the sordid castle.

Admittedly, she had not visited under the best circumstances, but there was something unwholesome about it, as if the walls had soaked up the dark deeds they had witnessed—from the ancient witch trials to whatever sinister solar or Irminist rites the ss had held there.

The abiding sense of malevolence was made all the more tangible by the broken body now lying splayed on the central sun-wheel, like some gruesome re-enactment of a medieval heretic broken on the wheel.

Turning and heading for the door, she suddenly caught sight of an unexpected movement out of the corner of her eye.

Whirling around in disbelief, she was in time to see Malchus had used his last ebbing strength to unclip a small black handgun from an ankle holster, and was now raising it in a blood-soaked hand, pointing it directly at her.

She had no time to pull her gun, or even to think.

Using the momentum from spinning round, she continued the arc of her arm, whipping it out as hard as she could—hurling the Spear of Destiny directly at him with all her strength.

She watched, mesmerized, as the crude Roman weapon flew through the air as if in slow motion. After what seemed an age, its ancient sharpened tip struck him in the middle of the forehead, instantly piercing the skin and shattering the bone, driving itself deep into his brain.

Without a word, he slumped back onto the floor, an obscene gurgling sound escaping from his bubbling lacerated throat.

When the gruesome noise stopped, he lay deathly still.

Ava walked over to the mangled body and looked down, breathing hard.

His lifeless green eyes stared glassily up at her—as cold and reptilian in death as they had been in life. The bulk of the spear was protruding from his forehead, but at least two inches of it were buried deep in his brain. She watched as a clear fluid trickled from his nose, and blood began to ooze out from around the spear tip onto his pale forehead.

He was as still as marble.

As she stared at him, she was aware her heart was hammering.

But there could be no doubt.

*This time he was truly dead.*

As the blood pooled on the floor around his neck, she felt a sudden and unexpected relief that the world was finally rid of a small slice of pure evil.

*It really was over.*

When she had arrived at Boleskine House that afternoon, she had not imagined for a moment that the day would end in a historic Nazi cult temple with her looking down at Malchus's mutilated corpse.

It was a gruesome sight.

In addition to the fatal head injury, Uri had punctured him dozens of times with the spear tip during the course of his interrogation, and the gaping cut to his neck was wet and ragged, leaving his upper body drenched in blood.

She turned her eyes away.

She had seen enough.

Trying to erase the gory image from her mind, she headed for the door, keen to be as far from his corpse as possible.

Making her way slowly out into the courtyard, she was suddenly grateful for the cool night air. She breathed it in deeply, taking a moment to clear her head.

The great triangular space was empty. The GSG-9 men had finished clearing the cellar and were now outside the main gate with their remaining prisoners. The fleet of vans had gone. She guessed they were waiting for more vehicles to come and ferry Saxby's supporters to the cells that awaited them.

There was no sign of Max and his team. They must still be downstairs.

Then she remembered the Frenchman had told her someone wanted to meet her outside afterwards.

Looking about, at first she could not see anyone. But as her eyes grew accustomed to the gloom, she eventually spotted him—a tall suited figure in the shadow of the doorway to the south-west tower.

She moved a little closer to see more clearly, pulling the gun from her waist.

The figure stepped forward from the darkness, allowing a sliver of moonlight to illuminate his quick dark eyes, aquiline nose, and black goatee beard.

She instantly recognized Olivier De Molay, Grand Master of the Knights Templar.

With no greeting, she raised the weapon and aimed it directly at him. "Don't move."

"I understand." His tone was sombre, made somehow more grave by his heavy French accent. "And I take personal responsibility for having put you in this position."

Ava kept the gun trained on him.

"It pains me very much to discover Edmund Saxby was mixed up in this horror. I am mortified. I've known him all my adult life." He looked at her wistfully. "And it's only now I discover what an abomination he truly was. We owe you a great debt, Dr Curzon—both my organization, and me personally." His eyes betrayed a mixture of sadness and anger.

She looked at him guardedly.

Maybe he was telling the truth. On the other hand, it was equally possible he was in it up to his neck along with Saxby and Malchus. After all, in one sense the crusades had championed violent white supremacy. Perhaps De Molay's Templars were the perfect sponsors of Saxby's vision for the new Nazi Imperium.

"So Cordingly got my message?" Ava asked, her voice giving nothing away.

De Molay nodded. "When Major Ferguson went to see him to explain you had gone to Loch Ness, he alerted Saxby, suspecting nothing. But when he received your internet message, he realized something was badly wrong, and immediately alerted me. As you requested, I brought our friends from the *Légion* in case of any trouble. And I'm glad I did. I'm truly relieved to see you are unharmed. Max and his men are also very grateful to you. They were hoping Malchus would be here. They took the slaying of their companion in Rome rather personally."

Ava suspected that Malchus and Max were unlikely to be in it together, given the hostilities in Rome. And Max and his team would hardly have stopped the ceremony and freed her if they were all complicit in the plan. But she was still not prepared to take anything at face value.

Not after Saxby.

"I'm sure you'll understand," she countered, "I need some convincing that Saxby was not following your orders." She paused. "Maybe you found out MI6 had alerted the German authorities and aborted your plans for this evening?"

De Molay's expression changed for a moment. There was a brief flicker of pain, then it was gone. "Dr Curzon. The Order I'm so honoured to lead was born in a different age, when ethnic and religious bigotry were second nature to all. Despite the famous crusader name my family bequeathed me, in my view the crusades were fruitless wars that achieved very little. When the crusades started, the Holy Land was Islamic, and so it was when the knights left in defeat after two hundred years of pointless bloodshed. Ironically, they arrived home in Europe to face the greatest battle of their history, against the king of France and the pope, who massacred them more comprehensively than any Saracen army ever did. It was a fiasco from start to finish."

She could see the sadness in his eyes. "But the medieval Templars were in a position to learn more quickly than most. When not under orders from the pope to fight, the Templars made many friends in the East. Some learned Arabic, avidly sucking up new knowledge—medicine, astronomy, mathematics, philosophy. Did you know some of the Templar knights used to let Muslims in to pray in their military headquarters, the Temple of Solomon, which for the centuries before the knights arrived had been the sacred al-Aqsa mosque?"

Ava did not answer.

She looked at him, unblinking.

"The medieval Templars were brave and noble and hungry for new experiences in a world that was not," he continued. "And that will always be their tragedy. It was a brutal age. Knights were vicious thugs who would sooner have raped and killed a lady than rescued her. The Templars changed that. They strove to be different—vowing themselves to protect women, children, and the vulnerable. They invented chivalry. But, like so many who are ahead of their time, they were sacrificed on the pyres of jealousy and ambition."

He paused, inhaling the cold air. "So you ask what we stand for? We long ago rejected our original calling and severed all ties with the Church that betrayed us to the hot irons and flames. But do not mistake me— we are still combatants. We remain soldiers of the spirit—but we fight now for a world where there can be no more crusades. We stand for everything that Saxby despised. We still take our ancient vow to protect Jerusalem, but we understand it very differently now. For us, Jerusalem is a state of mind—an ideal of harmony worth dying for, not an earthly place."

As his eyes met hers, she could see in them a deep iron resolve, but also a fleeting sadness, a wounded dignity.

*Was it another ruse?*

She continued to watch him carefully.

*Was he playing a role? Like Saxby?*

She had learned many years ago that people could mask their expressions, but she had heard a genuine and sincere sadness and weariness in his voice—and that was altogether harder to fake.

She slowly lowered the gun. "So what now?" She tucked it back into the sash. "You heard what happened to the Ark?"

He nodded. "Max will look after Major Ferguson. Meanwhile, I cannot change the past, but there's something I should like to do for you, if you'll permit me."

He picked up a small canvas bag on the floor beside him, and passed it to her. "I believe these are your clothes. One of my men found them. You may like to make yourself more comfortable, and then we can go. I have a helicopter ready outside."

"Where are we going?" Ava asked. "I've had enough surprises for one night."

De Molay smiled. "If you'll allow an old man a small indulgence," his eyes twinkled for the first time, "I shall leave you to find out when we get there. But I have a particularly strong feeling you're going to like it very much."

# DAY TWELVE

———— • ◆ • ————

## III

*Saint-Christophe de Montsaunès*
*Saint-Gaudens*
*Comminges*
*Haute-Garonne*
*The Republic of France*

DESPITE THE ENGINE noise, Ava slept soundly in the helicopter.

She had stayed awake long enough for De Molay to take off, but had fallen asleep as soon as the triangular outline of Wewelsburg Castle had receded into the distance beneath them.

When she awoke, De Molay had already brought them down in a grassy field on a sunny hillside, and was now standing outside the chopper holding small thick square china cups of espresso coffee and a plate with several hot croissants.

"I take it we're in France, then?" Ava smiled, picking up a croissant gratefully and enjoying it with the restorative bitter coffee

"There's a very obliging café owner just over there." He pointed to a small village visible beyond the field.

She looked at the laminated map beside De Molay's chair in the cockpit, and saw that it was showing an area just north of the Pyrenees mountain range, where France joined Spain. A circle and coordinates were marked in black china pencil almost exactly halfway between the

Atlantic and Mediterranean coasts.

As she finished the croissant and swallowed the last of the fortifying coffee, De Molay indicated a way across the field.

"It may not look it," he informed her as they started walking, "but in medieval times, this area was one of the main highways into Spain for merchants and pilgrims." He paused. "And one of the main routes into France for attacking armies."

Ava could feel the soft grass under her shoes. After the last twenty-four hours, it was a welcome reminder of the pleasanter things in life.

"In the 700s," he continued, "a Muslim army from Islamic Spain fought its way through here as far into France as Poitiers, where Charles the Hammer defeated it, and sent the attackers back over the Pyrenees. For the next seven hundred years, the people of southern Europe feared another Islamic invasion from Spain. Periodically, their worst nightmares came true. In the 900s, Europe's most powerful abbot was abducted by Muslims while crossing the Alps. And in the late 1100s, the great French coastal city of Toulon was sacked and razed to the ground by Muslim raiders from Mallorca. They were unsettled times."

He looked around the calm quiet countryside. "It's hard to imagine, but this area was on the very front line of defence against what everyone believed to be a permanent existential Islamic threat."

Ava looked around. It did seem hard to believe. It was just a sleepy slice of rural France.

Up ahead, the village started at the edge of the field with a picturesque mix of old stone farm buildings and residential houses in varying states of repair.

It looked completely normal—typical of rural southern Europe.

Except for one thing.

Dominating the view was the unmistakable rounded end of a twelfth-century Romanesque church.

The medieval building was tall and solidly built out of light stone and pale thin red brick. It was an unremarkable size for a church in a medieval town or city. But for a rural hamlet, it was colossal.

Ava followed De Molay down the tree-lined north side of the church and round to its front.

"You'll be pleased to know we've recovered the Lance of St Longinus," De Molay noted, as he led the way. "We'll make the necessary arrangements to return it to the Hofburg museum in Vienna. They'll compare it with their version. If it is indeed the real one, I'm sure they'll quietly make the switch. Publicity around such an object is in no one's interest."

Ava nodded. She had not had time to even think about the lance.

As she rounded the front of the church, she could instantly see from the distinctive architecture that it dated from the late 1100s—a period when the crusades in the Holy Land and the religious battles of the *reconquista* in Spain presented two of the most active fronts in the war between Christianity and Islam.

From the unusual thickness of the walls and the small size of the few windows, it had clearly been built by military engineers—more a castle than a church.

The west front was dominated by a wide flat pointed tower with space for a peal of five bells—only four of which were hung. It loomed over the bare front's only feature—a small central rose window. Otherwise, the west wall was stark and plain, evoking the cold impregnability of a castle's keep rather than the heavenly vision of saints and angels usually adorning churches of the period.

The only concession to decoration was around the narrow doorway, which was flanked by a pair of delicately carved stone columns and capitals—now smoothed by nine hundred years of sun, rain, and snow.

To Ava's surprise, the first of the carvings on the capitals to catch her eye was a grisly scene of a man being crucified in agony upside down.

Momentarily stunned, she could not conceive why a medieval church would feature such blatant Satanic imagery. Nor why De Molay would have brought her there.

But as she looked at two other scenes beside it—a man being decapitated with a sword and another being stoned, she realized it was just a series showing the deaths of the early martyrs. She had forgotten that Saint Peter, the first pope, had been crucified by the Emperor Nero on an upside-down cross.

"Built by the Templars?" she asked De Molay, who was standing behind her. But she already knew the answer.

He nodded, "This church is all that remains of the once-powerful Templar commandery of Montsaunès. The other buildings—the castle, living quarters, prison, ovens, stables, and the rest have all been lost over the years."

Pulling a large iron key out of his pocket, he turned the ancient lock with a loud click, and swung the heavy wooden doors open.

Passing under the entranceway's three arches, she was amused to see a carnival of fifty-two tiny medieval heads running around the underside of the outer arch, welcoming her in. They started on the left as normal human faces, then comically turned increasingly grotesque towards the right—their features transformed into pigs, monsters, and demons with bulging eyes and protruding tongues.

Ava had concluded a long time ago that no one could say medieval sculptors did not have a rich sense of humour.

Entering the church's cool interior, she could not help but notice the immense thickness of the walls. Unlike more delicate churches, this one was built as an uncompromising stone cocoon for the knights to shelter in when they took off their mail and pieces of plate body armour, swapping one defensive shell for another.

As she walked slowly down the ancient stone steps to floor level, the first thing to hit her was the typical smell of a French country church— incense, flowers, and a base note of mustiness.

Her eyes were at first unaccustomed to the internal gloom, and it took them a moment to recover from the bright light outside.

Behind her, she could hear De Molay pulling the wooden doors shut, locking them from the inside.

As her eyes adjusted to the light, she gasped.

Almost every inch of the pale stone walls was covered in medieval frescos. But they were very far from the usual holy scenes drawn from the lives of Christ, the Virgin, the apostles, and the saints.

She turned to De Molay, her eyes wide with amazement. "Why have I never heard of this place? It's extraordinary."

He shook his head. "It's a bit off the beaten track these days."

Ava simply could not believe her eyes.

She had seen some strangely decorated buildings before, but nothing that could remotely compare with this. "Well, it finally lays to rest the question of whether the Templars were into esoteric practices," she murmured, unable to take her eyes off the mesmerizing frescoes.

It was not the colours. They were simple enough—white, black, and red-ochre.

It was the designs.

The whole barrel of the entire white ceiling vault was spangled with small black eight-pointed stars—hundreds of them, laid out in neat offset rows, creating a photographic negative of an ordered night sky.

That was odd enough—not exactly normal church decoration. But not nearly as strange as what was mixed in with the stars in seemingly random and irregular places—large circles filled with an infinite variety of geometric patterns, as if drawn with the plastic gears of an oversize spirograph stencil set.

Ava had never seen anything like it. She had no idea whether the circles represented some planetary alignment wheeling around the night sky, a coded celestial map, a mystical exercise in the Kabbalah, or one of a thousand other possibilities.

On the main walls there were a few ordinary scenes—arcades with figures, and even a vision of Hell with a demon and cauldron. But other than those, they were completely covered in an array of bizarre square and diamond chequerboards.

And surrounding it all, in bands, borders, and random places, were hundreds more of the strange spirograph circles, rolling around the church, placed by some indefinable logic.

Some were filled with petals, others with crosses. Some were black, others white. They covered the interior of the church, seemingly haphazardly, although as she gazed more closely, she noticed that some motifs were very subtly repeated, suggesting there was an unseen thread somehow connecting it all.

Wherever she looked, she was confronted by the odd and inexplicable.

Immediately above her, the ceiling had two stylized Templar battle banners—the black and white *Bauçeant*—but they were wrapped into geometric patterns following some unknown numerological sequence.

Turning, she could see beside the rose window a centaur and a number of strange cross-hatched grids.

*Were they some kind of calendar system?*

She simply could not tell.

*Was the centaur supposed to be Sagittarius?*

*If so, where were the other zodiac symbols?*

She stared around numbly.

She was not used to being so utterly confounded. If someone at the museum brought her a collection of Egyptian hieroglyphs or a fragment of a cuneiform stele, she could decipher them more quickly than most people. But as she looked around the Templar church, she could not make sense of a single one of the strange outlandish symbols.

She shook her head in astonishment. She was inside a painted code-book every bit as baffling as the Voynich manuscript.

"What does it all mean?" she turned to De Molay breathlessly. "It's a code, isn't it?"

He smiled. "Believe it or not, the church frescoes are not what I brought you here to see."

Ava could feel her pulse start to quicken.

*There was more?*

But she was too intrigued by the incomprehensible symbols to let it go. "These are original twelfth-century frescoes. And I have never seen anything so blatantly cryptic. I wouldn't have believed it if I hadn't seen it with my own eyes." She was unable to keep the excitement off her face. "What do they mean?"

De Molay exhaled slowly. "It has baffled all experts over the centuries," he shrugged. "They say they have no clue. They classify it as 'unknown' esoteric decoration."

"But *you* know, don't you?" she pushed him. "You know exactly what it means. For a hundred and fifty years Templar knights in their white robes, and sergeants in their black ones, came in here and prayed and chanted eight monastic offices a day. This was the most important build-ing in their universe. They gazed upon these decorations hour after hour, day after day. But instead of deciding to be surrounded by paintings of biblical scenes and saints, they choose all this." She waved an arm to indicate the inexplicable paintings. "You can't tell me these designs don't have a crucially important meaning."

A rueful smile played around the corner of his lips. "Dr Curzon, I have been uncommonly open with you, and you therefore already know a great deal about the Templars that others do not. And I'm about to show you even more." He paused. "But some things, and these decorations are among them, will have to remain a mystery to you." He started walking down the nave "Please, this way."

She followed him down the stone-floored aisle, through the carved rail separating off the sanctuary, and up to the medieval high altar filling the inside of the large round apse she had seen from the field.

The altar itself was an imposing slab of ancient grey stone. It was carved to resemble a Roman sarcophagus, with a row of seven austere saints and bishops in rounded archways adorning the front.

"Jerusalem was lost to Saladin in the year 1187," he said, gazing up at the seven candles arranged up the stepped sides of the high altar top.

"Around the time this church was built," she nodded.

"When Jerusalem fell, the Templars lost their headquarters—the al-Aqsa mosque, or Temple of Solomon, as they called it, because it lay on the site of Solomon's ancient temple. They managed to save their treasures, but needed somewhere to keep them. They knew the Holy Land was no longer secure, and they did not want to put everything into the large London or Paris Temples, where there were far too many watchful and greedy eyes around."

"So they used places like this?" Ava asked. "Fortified commanderies in out-of-the-way locations?"

He did not reply, but instead reached down and took hold of the stony face of the carved bishop in the arcade on the far left of the altar.

He pulled it upwards.

With a loud click, the whole head lifted a few inches, temporarily decapitating the carved clergyman.

A panel in the altar, the width of the three end figures, swung open.

Ava was prepared for many things, but not what she saw in the large hollow cavity dug out underneath the altar.

She felt lightheaded.

*It couldn't be.*

She blinked to see if the image in front of her eyes would change.

But it did not.

She stared at De Molay in disbelief, bewildered.

"I saw it destroyed," she whispered in a daze, staring into the space under the altar, where the Ark of the Covenant was resting—gleaming and glowing in the mellow morning sunlight.

De Molay shook his head. "One of the Order of the Temple's solemn tasks is to protect the Ark—to prevent it from falling into the wrong hands, and to keep it safe."

"I don't understand," Ava was shaking her head in confusion. "I heard the explosion and saw the wreckage." Her shoulder was still throbbing as a physical reminder. "There was nothing left. It was decimated."

De Molay looked at her gravely. "You are mistaken, Dr Curzon. The Templars found the Ark in Jerusalem while excavating under King Solomon's Temple. They also found the Menorah. Realizing the enormity of their discoveries, they gave the Menorah to the Vatican in the hope of distracting attention from the Ark. As you know, it worked. The Vatican was terrified, and hid the Menorah, which was lost for centuries—until you found it."

He gazed at the Ark. "At first the knights hid the Ark in their Jerusalem headquarters. But when the city fell to Saladin in 1187, they brought it back to Europe on one of their many ships. They could not risk anyone seeing it, so they had to keep it away from the large cities where it might be discovered. When they came fresh off the boat from Jerusalem at Marseille, they learned that this impregnable new commandery had recently been completed. They quickly decided there was no better place for the Ark."

"So it's been here ever since?" she asked, incredulous, staring at its gleaming and exquisitely decorated surface.

He shook his head. "When the Order was officially suppressed in 1312, we lost our European commanderies, so had to start moving the Ark around. It was many centuries before we could bring the Ark back here to Montsaunès again. This is now only one of the many hiding places we use. As you can imagine, we have plenty of others at our disposal."

"But if you have the Ark here," she asked, unable to distinguish the Ark under the altar from the one she had seen at Wewelsburg, "then what did I see last night?"

He pulled the altar's concealed door wider, revealing more of the Ark. "You assuredly did see the Ark last night. But it was not this one."

"I don't understand," Ava frowned. "Is this a replica? Did the Templars make an exact copy?"

He shook his head. "Not us. Azariah, son of Zadok the high priest."

Ava put a hand onto the top of the altar to steady herself. "For Menelik," she whispered. "King Solomon's son by the Queen of Sheba? Are you saying the legend is true?"

De Molay nodded solemnly. "Most assuredly. When Menelik was grown and visited Jerusalem, he spent a long period with his father, King Solomon. When he desired to return home to Ethiopia, Solomon wanted him to set up a Hebrew state in Ethiopia, so he gave him the leading sons of the Hebrew nobility and priests. One of them, Azariah, the son of Zadok the high priest, stole the Ark and put it in Menelik's baggage train, leaving an exact replica in its place."

A thousand thoughts were racing through Ava's mind.

So there were two Arks!

The Queen of Sheba story really was true. Azariah really did make a replica Ark for Solomon's son by her, and he switched them.

De Molay shrugged, as if answering her thoughts. "Maybe he switched them, or maybe he didn't. Legends get twisted over the centuries. History has never been certain whether the real Ark went to Aksum or remained in Jerusalem."

Ava stared at the radiant ancient gold chest, struggling with the enormity of what De Molay was saying.

He raised his eyebrows to accompany a Gallic shrug. "So we have ours, and Aksum has theirs. Or rather," he corrected himself, "they *had* theirs—until last night, when it was destroyed." He looked down at the Ark nestling under the altar. "For the first time in three thousand years, Dr Curzon, the Ark you are looking at is the world's sole Ark."

"Did your Order ever compare them?" Ava asked, unable to take her eyes off the gleaming burnished metal covering every inch of the Ark. "Do you know which is the original Ark?"

"Maybe you can tell me?" De Molay answered simply. "To my knowledge, you are the only person alive, perhaps even since the time of King Solomon, who has seen both, as no one ever sees the Aksum Ark except the monk who guards it. But if the Menelik story is true, then one dates from the time of Moses, the other from the time of Solomon. There's not such a great difference between them—about three hundred years. So I always liked to think they are both genuine."

"May I?" Ava asked breathlessly, kneeling down to touch the Ark.

"But of course," De Molay answered. "That's why you are here. After all you have done for us, it's the least I can do for you." He moved to one side, and sat down on an ornamental wooden chair by the altar rail.

She put her hands out to touch the Ark, not quite believing she was not dreaming.

The metal felt reassuringly cold to her touch.

She was not hallucinating.

It was real.

Gazing at the scenes detailed in bas relief all over its golden surface, she had to keep a hand on it to steady herself, afraid she might keel over at the enormity of what she was seeing.

She could instantly see it overturned all the conventional wisdom.

Most experts believed the Hebrews had no visual art because their God forbade them from idolatry, false images, and making representations of anything in the heavens or on the earth.

But from what she could see in front of her, they were going to have to rewrite their textbooks.

She had never quite believed their theories anyway.

When she had made the three-dimensional computer graphic film simulation of King Solomon's Temple for the British Museum, she had done a vast amount of research, and discovered to her amazement that the Temple had been bursting with images of angels, animals, and plants.

The film had proved popular. People liked to be challenged, and most of them, it turned out, had no real idea what the historical King Solomon's Temple really looked like.

Her film showed that it had not been some vast palatial building like the Parthenon on the Acropolis in Athens, with its forest of monumental columns, unrivalled sculptures and friezes, and forty-foot-high gold and ivory statue of the Virgin Athena. Instead, King Solomon's Temple had been infinitely smaller and more intimate—as befitted a relatively minor tribal kingdom.

Basing her reconstruction faithfully on the Bible texts, the Temple turned out to be thirty-four yards long, eleven wide, and seventeen high. To help people imagine the scale, she had done a mock-up to show that a football pitch could comfortably contain eighteen King Solomon's Temples, with enough left-over patches to make another three-and-a-half.

It had been aligned east-west, the opposite of churches, and the priests entered via a porch in the east housing two vast bronze pillars, each over ten yards high, decorated with pomegranates, lilies, and chains.

The priests then passed through the Temple's main doorway of gold-covered juniper wood, and into the body of the Temple itself, which was entirely faced in wood so no stone was visible. The floor was gold-covered juniper, and the walls were panelled in cedar.

The space was dominated by the Menorah in the south, the Table of Showbread in the north with its twelve loaves, fresh every week, and the Altar of Incense in the middle up at the far west end.

Beyond the Altar of Incense, behind gold chains, a flight of steps led up to a veil of blue, crimson, and purple, lavishly embroidered with cherubim. Behind it lay double doors of gold-covered olive wood leading to the *Qodesh Haqadashim*, the Holy of Holies—a windowless eleven-yard cube floored and panelled in gold-covered Lebanese cedar.

No one ever entered the Holy of Holies, except the high priest, once a year on the Day of Atonement. In its mystical space, two gilded cherubim of olive wood spread their wings so they touched both walls and each other in the centre. In the middle, in the shade of their protective wings, nestled the Ark, which the high priest would sprinkle with sacrificial blood once a year.

The layout was not uncommon for a Middle-Eastern temple of the period. But it was the decoration which had delighted Ava the most.

The Bible explicitly stated that the walls and doors in the main Temple and the Holy of Holies were set with gilded carvings of cherubim, palm trees, and open flowers. And there were even sculptures of animals—like the twelve cast bronze bulls supporting the vast Sea of Bronze washing bowl, or the lions, bulls, and cherubim adorning the the ten movable bronze lavers.

As Ava contemplated the Ark in front of her, nestling under the ancient stone altar, she could see it was covered in exactly the same decorative motifs.

It was alive with cherubim, trees, and flowers—all beaten into the gold panels.

It was beyond exquisite.

She smiled with recognition as she looked more closely at the cherubim on the lid of the Ark, gleaming in the sunshine.

*Of course!*

She had recognized something Egyptian about them on the photo she had been shown back at Camp as-Sayliyah.

And now it made perfect sense.

They were not angels with wings as on Christmas cards. They were like Babylonian *lamassu* or the Egyptian sphinx, all from the same family of ancient Middle-Eastern protective creatures—endlessly creative mixtures of eagle-winged humans, lions, and bulls.

In all her dreams of discovering the Ark, she had never imagined it would be as sublime as this. The workmanship was flawless, and the design was bursting with animal and plant exuberance and fertility.

"What are you going to do with this Ark?" she asked, looking over at De Molay. "It would be the most visited exhibit in the world if you put it in a museum. Scholars would learn an immense amount about the ancient Hebrews from it, and people of every culture would be amazed by its vibrancy. I can say with complete certainty that it would be the greatest find in archaeology, ever."

De Molay inhaled deeply, looking pensive. "One day, perhaps. But I don't believe the world is ready for it yet. Strife between the three great Abrahamic religions is endemic in our generation—worse than it has been for centuries. The Ark would be too big a prize for those bent on chaos." He lowered his voice, as if to soften the blow. "It's better if we keep it safe until calmer times prevail."

Ava nodded mutely. The idea of leaving the Ark and returning to her day job left her feeling numbed. The sense of loss was almost physical. But after what she had seen at Wewelsburg, she realized she was being unrealistic if she really believed people would just let it sit in a museum.

"What about the Menorah?" she suggested quietly, tearing her eyes away from the Ark, trying to salvage at least one artefact for scholarship and the public. "I know somewhere we could give it a very good home."

De Molay shook his head again. "When Titus seized it from the Jerusalem Temple in AD 70, he was so aware of its propaganda value that he carved an image of its capture onto his triumphal Arch in Rome. And when Saladin seized the crusaders' True Cross at the Horns of Hattin in AD 1187, he dealt the Christians a blow from which they never recovered." He paused. "There would inevitably be someone waiting to use violence to take the Menorah for religious or political propaganda purposes. We must keep it safely for now, away from the limelight."

Ava stared wistfully at the two great cherubim on the Ark's lid—their proud lions' heads sheltered by vast shimmering outstretched eagles' wings.

She knew she should not be feeling disappointed by his answers. She had no reason to feel anything other than lucky.

Although she had dreamed of unveiling the Ark and the Menorah to the public, she had seen from Saxby and Malchus why that could never be. Perhaps on one level she had known it all along.

She sighed deeply, gazing at the burnished plants and animals adorning its panels, breathing vitality and energy into the gleaming metal.

She could not really complain.

From the first moment she had been told of the Ark back in Qatar, she had wanted to find out if it was real or a hoax.

And she had—and then some.

She had not only seen and touched it, she had been overwhelmed with ancient artefacts—two Arks and the Menorah: all of them genuine, priceless, and luminous ancient biblical relics.

As she glanced over at De Molay sitting pensively in the chair, gazing at the extraordinary symbols on the church's walls, she suspected the Ark was in good hands.

Aside from Saxby, the Templars had all shown deep integrity. Both Cordingly and his freemasons and Max and his *Légionnaires* had intervened decisively when they needed to, and had demonstrated an unswerving commitment to the ideals of their Order.

She looked at a cluster of pomegranates on the Ark—an ancient symbol of fertility—and thought of the clinical eugenic breeding that had produced Saxby. At least the events at Wewelsburg had dealt his organization a heavy blow. He and a number of his key henchmen were dead, and the remaining ringleaders were by now deep in the German criminal justice system, where they would be shown little lenience. Although she doubted their organization had been destroyed, it had definitely been severely damaged, setting it back many years.

And finally, as she looked at the Mercy Seat, where Yahweh was supposed to sit to give his orders to the ancient Hebrews, she thought of Malchus.

She had hoped his capture would help clear both her and Ferguson's names, and that he would spend the rest of his days in a secure mental hospital.

But, in some strange way she did not yet quite understand, Malchus's death had brought peace to the memory of her father. She had never been a fan of the doctrine of an eye for an eye and a life for a life. But it was a code Malchus lived by, and he had received justice on his own terms.

It seemed fitting.

De Molay got up from the chair and walked back to where Ava was kneeling by the Ark.

"We should be going now," he suggested gently. "It never pays to spend too long thinking about what might have been."

"I don't suppose you have a camera on your phone I could—" Ava began, but De Molay shook his head, pulling the altar closed again, and clicking the panel back into place, shutting the Ark back into darkness, concealing it from view.

"If you come back later today, I'm afraid it will be gone," he said gently. "It may come back here to Montsaunès again during your lifetime. Or it may not. Who can say?"

Ava nodded, unable to put into words the overwhelming emotions streaming through her.

"If I were you," he ushered her towards the narrow front door. "I would not spend your time thinking about the Ark. That is a burden I carry, and in many ways I envy those who do not have it."

Arriving at the top of the steps, he turned the key in the lock and opened the ancient wooden door.

Sunlight streamed into the cool church as Ava stepped out onto the pavement.

De Molay touched her arm lightly. "My honest recommendation is to forget all about the Ark and its guardians. We have kept it safe for many centuries, and we will continue to do so. One day we will give it to the world—when the world is ready."

He stepped up onto the pavement beside her. "I remain profoundly grateful to you for your willingness to help us. I'll have everything cleared with the English authorities, and they'll leave you and Major Ferguson alone regarding this whole painful episode. I give you my word you can go back to your life."

He put a hand on the church's door. "I must leave you now, Dr Curzon. I can recommend the café in the village. They have been instructed to give you a hot meal, and you will find they have a plane ticket home for you."

He re-entered the church, and turned to face her through the doorway. "As my brothers in the Order learned to say many centuries ago, may peace be with you."

She looked at his face one last time as he pulled the church doors closed, leaving her staring at its ancient gnarled wood.

The road was silent apart from the sound of the key turning and the heavy lock clicking shut.

"And with you also, peace," she replied softly, returning the ancient Middle-Eastern salutation, before turning away from the church and heading slowly in the direction of the café.

# EPILOGUE

———— ◆ ————

## 112

*National Museum of Iraq*
*Baghdad*
*The Republic of Iraq*

AVA HAD FORGOTTEN quite how hot Baghdad could get in the summer.

The air-conditioning in the museum's large low-lit medieval gallery was not working especially well, although the climate control inside the major cabinets was fine.

She would have to get it mended properly before the museum opened again to the public.

She straightened the long sword she was placing in the cabinet, balancing it on two clear glass pegs set onto the black-velvet-covered board.

The sword had arrived that morning by special delivery.

She had been back in her office, where it had felt good to be surrounded again by the mass of papers and maps giving clues to the whereabouts of all the thousands of looted artefacts.

She was looking forward to getting stuck in again—to finding pieces she would actually be able to put on display.

As she had been reading a report on the potential discovery of one of the museum's first-century BC alabaster heads from Yemen, now in an art-dealer's showroom in Lagos, a man from the mailroom had knocked and entered with a long package.

Intrigued, she had first slit open the accompanying note, which simply read:

London

My dear Dr Curzon,

Please accept this gift as a small token of the Foundation's deep gratitude to you, and of my personal friendship.

Islamic swords from the crusader period are rare indeed, so perhaps your museum will be able to find room for this one.

As you can see from the engraving on the blade, it belonged to an eminent Muslim knight. I am told he was from Baghdad. So it is fitting that it should go home again and not languish with us.

With warmest greetings,
ODM

Excited, she had removed the wrapping and padding from around the package. De Molay was right—Islamic crusader swords were extremely rare. She could not remember the last time she had seen one.

As she flipped the clasps on the case, her jaw dropped open at the sight of the sword resting on the foam inside.

It was unusually long, slim, and gracefully curved, with the blade fattening slightly before ending in a pointed tip. There was no pommel, and the ivory and wooden hilt bent gently in the opposite direction to the blade. All surfaces apart from the blade—the grip, bands, and quillons— were exquisitely decorated with delicate geometric patterns.

But what caught her eye most was the blade, which was covered with thin watery lines sweeping across in great flowing patterns.

Even just from a glance, she could tell that the medieval metalwork was undoubtedly genuine Damascus steel—a legendary technique of ancient steelmaking, now lost.

The sword had clearly belonged to an immensely wealthy Muslim knight.

The weapon was flawless, and quite the most valuable sword she had ever held.

As she read the name of the owner inlaid into the blade, she could not stop herself from laughing out loud.

*What were the chances?*

*De Molay had style. She had to give him that.*

Once she had the sword mounted correctly in the display case, she added the descriptive label she had printed, clipping it into the glass sleeve under the sword. It read:

---

## ISLAMIC SWORD
### Scimitar. Baghdad. 12th century.
### Damascus steel. Ivory and wood. Blade 40 inches.

ORIGINAL INSCRIPTION ON BLADE:

سيف موسى عبد الرحمن

*Saif Musa 'Abd al-Rahman*

(translation: The Sword of Moses, the Servant of the Merciful One)

---

Standing back to admire the exhibit, she bumped hard into someone behind her.

Unaware there was anyone else in the room, she spun around, instantly on her guard—but found herself looking straight into a very familiar face.

Ferguson.

He beamed, as if it was the most natural thing in the world for him to be in her museum.

"I found a job over here," he said, looking calm and relaxed. "I figured if this region has kept you interested for so many years, then I ought to give it a try."

Ava raised her eyebrows.

"I've left soldiering and odd-jobbing for the Firm. I'm strictly a civilian now. Back to architecture, in fact. I heard they needed people to help redesign parts of the city that were destroyed. I start on Sunday."

Ava could feel a smile breaking out across her face.

"If you've finished for the day," he announced breezily. I've been recommended a quiet little fish restaurant on the banks of the Tigris. Apparently the white wine is well chilled and the red snapper in pomegranate sauce with limes is excellent."

Ava linked her arm in his, a little surprised at quite how happy she felt to see him. "Then what are you waiting for?"

They headed out of the museum's front door, and into the baking courtyard with its pockmarked and shell-damaged walls.

As they strode out under the Ishtar gate, Ava pictured the original, as she always did—the glazed blue tiles alive with their army of winged lions. She thought again of the nearly identical cherubim on the Ark, and smiled wistfully.

Emerging from the gate and out onto the busy street, Ferguson turned to face her. "Actually, there was a little something I wanted to ask you."

"Go on," she asked. "I thought a simple meal was too good to be true."

"Well ... ," he began hesitantly. "An old army friend who went free-lance a few years back was telling me about a little in-and-out job not far from here. Achaemenid period antiquities on a sunken boat at the bottom of the Karan river. I thought I should let you know."

Ava stopped walking, not quite believing what she was hearing. "You know that's in Iran, right? They'll flay us alive if we're caught."

Ferguson grinned. "I know. Sounds right up your street, doesn't it?"

## THE END

---- · ◆ · ----

# POST SCRIPT

*The Sword of Moses* exists. It is a genuine ancient Hebrew magical manuscript for summoning Yahweh to do the conjuror's bidding. There are very few surviving manuscripts. London and Oxford each have copies.

The Ethiopian Orthodox Church claims the Ark of the Covenant was brought to Aksum from Jerusalem by Menelik, son of King Solomon and Queen Makeda of Aksum (the Queen of Sheba). It is kept today in the Chapel of the Tablet attached to the complex of Our Lady Mary of Zion. It is guarded by a solitary monk, who is the only living person ever to see it.

There are an estimated six million freemasons in the world. Written records go back to the early 1400s. Despite several centuries of intense research, the origins of the fraternity are entirely unknown.

The Voynich manuscript is held in Yale University's Beinecke Rare Book & Manuscript Library. It is arguably the greatest unsolved European cryptographic mystery of the last thousand years.

Boleskine House was owned by Aleister Crowley from 1899 to 1913. The guitarist of Led Zeppelin, Jimmy Page, bought it in 1971 and sold it in 1992. Its current owners are unknown.

Wewelsburg Castle in Paderborn, Germany, was acquired by Heinrich Himmler in 1934. Using slave labour from the nearby Wewelsburg/Niederhagen concentration camp, he undertook extensive works to build the ss General's Hall and the crypt for his twelve ss knights. He made Wewelsburg the cult centre of Irminism, his elite occult ss religion. When the war was lost in 1945, his order for it to be destroyed was not fully carried out. Fire ravaged the building, but only minor outlying parts were irreparably damaged. The details of the ss rituals conducted there are still shrouded in secrecy.

The medieval chapel of the Knights Templar at Montsaunès in the Haute-Garonne area of France was built in the mid- to late-1100s. The enigmatic occult frescoes are from the same period. No one has ever decoded them. They remain a supreme enigma.

---

# SOURCES CITED

1. Biblical quotations are from:

   — King James Bible: Opening quotation (Exodus 15:3); Chapter 58 (Revelation 20:7-8); Chapter 90 (Genesis 1:1-2).

   — New International Version: Chapter 28 (Exodus 25:10-22; 32:2-4); Chapter 31 (Mark 5:9); Chapter 53 (Exodus 29:20, 25); Chapter 89 (Ezekiel 9: 5-7; Hosea 13:16).

2. Malchus's rituals are largely drawn (and adapted) from:

   — the Latin edition of the Bible (*Bibla Sacra Vulgata*).

   — the various Latin rites of the Roman Catholic Church as found in the *Pontificale Romanum*, the *Rituale Romanum*, the *Missale Romanum*, the *Breviarum Romanum*, etc.

   — the black mass as published by A Melech, *Missa Niger: La Messe Noire*, Sut Anubis Books, Northampton, 1986.

3. The quotation in Chapter 17 ('He that walketh fraudulently') is taken from the translation of Proverbs 11:13 in *Arbatel de Magia Verum*, R Turner (tr), London, 1655.

4.  The quotations on Israeli archaeology in Chapter 28 are from Prof. Z Hertzog, *Ha'aretz Magazine*, Friday 29 October 1999 and Prof. I Finkelstein in R Draper, 'Kings of Controversy,' *National Geographic*, December 2010.

5.  The quotation from the Gospel of Thomas in Chapter 44 is from J Robinson (ed.) and T Lambdin (tr), Saying 108, *The Gospel of Thomas*, in *The Nag Hammadi Library in English*, Leiden, 1996.

6.  The lyrics in Chapter 98 are from Led Zeppelin, *Kashmir,* (Page, Plant, Bonham), *Physical Graffitti*, Swan Song, 1975.

Printed in Great Britain
by Amazon